THE CAIN SERIES

THE CAIN SERIES

BOOKS 1-4

MIKE RYAN

WWW.MIKERYANBOOKS.COM

THE CAIN CONSPIRACY

1

Syria—Two U.S. citizens were captured and being held hostage in the basement of a Syrian house in the city of Al Qutayfa. They were part of a 23-member United Nations peacekeeping force who were monitoring events in the Golan Heights area between Israel and Syria. The other hostages had already been released and negotiations with the U.S. for the safe return of the Americans had broken down. The U.S. government decided the best course of action was to send in a small, elite team of soldiers to find the hostages and bring them back home. The U.S. Ambassador set up a meeting with Syrian officials for the following week to talk about freeing the hostages knowing that it would never take place. With luck, the team of soldiers would bring the prisoners back before then. The plan was set into action for the following night.

A ten-man force of Team Delta soldiers slipped into Syrian territory using the Lebanon border to enter. Lebanese officials were appraised of the action and were completely cooperating with the mission. The Lebanese government was happy to help as they had their own issues with Syria. All entries between the two countries had been closed due to feuding and policy differences. Lebanon agreed to also let the U.S. use its airspace for the mission's conclusion. Black Hawk helicopters from the 160th SOAR would bring the team and its evacuees to safety into Lebanese territory before heading to their base in Israel. The Night Stalkers, as they're frequently called, are often used on missions conducted at night and at high speeds. Al Qutayfa was less than 50 miles from the Lebanese border, so a small band of soldiers could still reach the city on foot in a relatively quick period of time. It would also be close enough for them to evacuate on the Black Hawk and be out of Syria within minutes. The team had to be on guard for not only Syrian forces, but also rebels. It was possible for Syrian forces to be on one street and rebels on the next street over. Both were equally dangerous to the squad.

The Delta team was led by Captain Terry. He had led several rescue missions before and had been on the ground in Syria previously. An informant had given the tip about the location of the U.S. prisoners, and a picture taken with a cell phone was used as proof that they were still alive. They appeared to have some cuts on their faces so it was assumed they'd been beaten. There was no telling how much more time they had until they met their end, so the mission needed to take place now. They were being held in the basement of a four-story residence on the edge of the city. If there was a positive, it was that they wouldn't have to fight their way out of the entire city.

The squad reached the outskirts of the city by nightfall. They took cover amongst a clump of trees that were on the other side of the road that led into the city. There wasn't much activity on the roads, but enough for the team to stay under-cover as they waited a little while longer. They identified their target location as the informant marked the side of the building with black chalk. It was a rather plain looking building. Tan in color, there were four stories, with lots of windows and balconies. As soon as traffic slowed down a little more, they'd make their move on the residence. While they waited, Terry went over the plan with his men one more time. Once they breached the building seven of the men would go inside to rescue the hostages while three would remain outside. Two would protect each corner of the building and the other would watch the door to make sure the backs of the other two soldiers were protected. As he finished up, Terry's radio started.

"Romeo Two-Four to Echo One-Two, come in."

"This is Echo One-Two, over," Terry responded.

"What is your status, over?"

"We are just outside the target location. Waiting for activity to die down a little, over."

"Roger that. Let us know when you begin your approach so we can get Super Six-Two en route."

"Roger that."

Captain Terry continued talking to his men to make sure there was no confusion about anything. "Everyone remember the rules of engagement; nobody fires unless fired upon. We don't know how many people are in that building, so be alert."

The mission required precise planning and timing. Once Black Hawk Super Six-Two entered Syrian airspace, it could possibly be subject to air defense missiles. Israel became involved in the mission at the request of the U.S. government. Israel had previously been successful at confusing Syria's air defense system by using an array of intense electronic warfare operations to confuse and deceive Syrian communications. They were able to successfully block Syrian radar units to where they could not detect an enemy presence in their skies. Israel would attempt to do the same to protect their U.S. counterparts but could not guarantee the same results. Therefore, the ground team needed to radio Super Six-Two when they were ready to be picked up so they could arrive at the exact time needed. Any delay by the ground team or the Black Hawk would compromise everyone involved. A couple of hours passed and Captain Terry waited until midnight before beginning their approach. The road was virtually deserted and hadn't had any traffic on it for over an hour. He contacted JSOC in Israel to inform them.

"Romeo Two-Four, this is Echo One-Two. We're beginning our approach now, over," Terry said.

"Roger, Echo One-Two."

The Delta team emerged from the cover of the trees and quickly ran across the highway. They encountered no resistance and reached their target location without incident. There was a small fence surrounding the development, but it had numerous holes in it so the team had no problem getting through. It looked like the complex was going through some renovations as there was a small ditch in back of the property that ran the length of the building with some construction material along the fence. The soldiers took up residence in the ditch for a minute as they sized up the situation. Three men stayed in their positions in the ditch to cover their respective areas as the rest of the team approached the door. Captain Terry quietly turned the handle to see if it was open. He shook his head to the rest of the group to indicate it wasn't. It was a plain wooden door which wouldn't take much to break down. Terry stepped aside as another man stepped up with his size eleven boots and kicked the door open on the first try. The group quickly entered with their M4A1 carbines raised, ready to fire. They hoped it would be a mission where they could quickly identify the prisoners and get them out before anyone knew they were there, without an eruption of gunfire. This, however, would not be one of those missions. As soon as the Delta team breached the door, four men seated at a square wooden table jumped up with their weapons drawn. They were immediately taken down with a barrage of bullets. There were two more in the corner of the room that were dispersed of before they had a chance to reach their assault rifles.

"Nails, stairs," Terry yelled at one of the soldiers.

"Got it," he replied.

Nails was probably the most respected man of the unit. He was a ten-year soldier and was often picked for the toughest assignments. He was nicknamed Nails by his fellow soldiers for being as "tough as nails." He never complained about anything and just did his job as well as he could. Everyone respected him for it. Nails had his eyes, and his M4 locked on the stairs to the side of the room in case any of the insurgents came rushing down the steps. A few seconds later he had a couple targets in his crosshairs as two men came running down, only to be cut in half as they fell down the steps. The rest of the team carefully reached the basement steps and began descending them. It was pitch dark in the basement, though the Delta members could see with their night vision goggles on. As soon as they reached halfway down the steps, gunfire screamed out, and three soldiers jumped down the steps, diving onto the floor, ready to fire. The other three halted, and retreated up the steps. There were some barrels on the far side of the basement. It seemed to be the only spot for someone to take cover. Didn't take long to find out as a couple heads peeked over the barrels seconds later. The prisoners were tied together along the side of one of the walls so they were sure it wasn't them peeking over. The soldiers waited for the insurgents to fire so they could be sure of what they were hitting. There was a small piece of wood by Terry's hand that he picked up and tossed across the room, away from the prisoners. The noise drew the fire of the insurgents, which immediately caused the soldiers to fire in their direction. The two men fell into the barrels, knocking them over, as the men lay on the floor, bleeding out.

"Shit," Terry stated, as he heard gunfire erupting outside the building. He grabbed his radio to bring in the Black Hawk. "Echo One-Two to Super Six-Two, over."

"This is Super Six-Two, over."

"Prisoners secured, Six-Two. We're coming out now."

"Roger One-Two, we're on route. ETA ten minutes."

"Roger that."

The prisoners were quickly untied and asked a couple questions to make sure they were who they were supposed to be. Although their faces had taken a little pounding, they weren't in such bad shape that they couldn't walk, which would make the escape much easier. The group rushed up the steps where Nails was still holding down the steps.

"Sounds like trouble outside," Nails said.

The men outside found their own problems as a group of rebels heard the gunfire and rushed over to see what it was. The two soldiers on the corners were holding down their spots without much problem.

"Coming out," Terry yelled.

"You're clear," the soldier watching the door shouted.

The group came out, Nails guarding behind them.

"We've got ten minutes," Terry informed the group. "Let's move out."

As soon as they began to move, Nails started firing back into the building as insurgents came running down the steps. They got to the fence while still guarding their backs and one by one went through the hole. They were met with gunfire on the other side, though, as a group of rebels took position down the road. The team waited a minute as they figured out the best option. They had to move soon as more rebels were starting to flank them.

"Sir, we need to move," Nails yelled. "Starting to get hot back here."

Terry and two other soldiers started firing at the rebels on the road to provide a little cover for the rest of the team to cross the road as Nails kept firing towards the complex. Nails started to cross when he suddenly dropped to the ground. Terry looked behind him and noticed that Nails wasn't moving. He ran toward him and knelt down at his side. Nails was still breathing though it was heavy, and he appeared to be unconscious. Terry moved Nails' head and noticed the hole in his forehead. Terry and another man dragged him the rest of the way as the rest of the group unleashed a barrage of gunfire toward the insurgents.

"Super Six-Two this is Echo One-Two, we got a hornet's nest behind us, over," Terry quickly yelled.

"Roger Echo One-Two, we're comin' in hot and heavy," the pilot said.

"Roger that. We're putting smoke down just along the trees. Fire whatever you got north of that and it should give us a little more time."

"Roger One-Two. We got you covered."

Terry put down some green smoke to mark their positions so the Night Stalker could fire its machine guns on the enemy. Terry and his men continued through the trees as one of them carried Nails over his shoulder. Just as they reached the edge of the trees the Black Hawk came in as promised, firing its M240 machine gun just north of the green smoke rising through the air. A few rocket propelled grenades went scorching through the air, trying to take down the helicopter, though none hit their intended target. The rebels had no choice but to retreat or else they risked being cut to shreds by the Black Hawk. The Night Stalker then set itself down just beyond the trees as the Delta team rushed toward it. Once they all safely boarded, the helicopter was up in the air. The Israelis had successfully blocked the air missiles of the Syrian army so the helicopter was never in danger and didn't even appear on their radar. As the Black Hawk flew back to base, Terry took a few deep breaths and made sure the rest of his men were OK. A couple had minor bumps and bruises, but none sustained any major injuries, except for Nails.

"Romeo Two-Four to Echo One-Two, come in," the radio bellowed.

"This is Echo One-Two, over," Terry replied.

"Roger One-Two, what's your status?"

"We have one man critical and have both prisoners in tow. Will need immediate medical attention as soon as we touch down."

"Roger that."

2

New York—Director Ed Sanders was concluding a meeting with his deputy directors when a call came in on the intercom.

"Director Sanders, sir?"

"Yes, go ahead."

"We've just learned of a situation in Syria. The possibility exists for a new recruit."

"Excellent. We're done here. Bring the information in," Sanders said.

A man came in, file folder in hand, and walked around the oval table where the seven men were seated. He handed the folder to Sanders, who immediately began looking over its contents.

"So, what do we have here?" Sanders asked.

"A soldier with Team Delta is in critical condition in a combat support hospital in Israel. He was shot in the head while on a mission in Syria."

"And what are his prospects?"

"Actually, pretty good. He just came out of surgery about 30 minutes ago and is in stable condition. The bullet's been removed and they think he's gonna make it," the officer informed the staff. "His military record makes him an ideal candidate."

"Excellent. Get the jet ready for Israel," Sanders told his subordinate as he stood up. "Gentlemen, we'll convene next week as usual."

Sanders gathered a few things and called for his car to be ready. He summoned for a few operators to meet him. He made his way down to the basement where his car was waiting for him. He got in the back seat and began reading the background of the soldier he was about to meet. His military records, as well as his personal transcripts, went as far back as elementary school.

"What's the verdict, sir?" his lieutenant asked.

"There are some issues which we'll have to overcome. But nothing's ever perfect. I think he should do nicely," Sanders responded.

Israel Combat Support Hospital—The four government officials stepped into the hospital and were immediately taken to the commander, Colonel Jefferson.

"Can I help you, gentlemen?" Jefferson asked.

"We'd like to know all you can tell us about this man," Sanders said, handing the colonel a paper with the soldier's name on it.

"I'm not at liberty to discuss anything with you."

"I believe you will," Sanders said, pulling out his top-secret clearance. "Unless you wanna take this matter to the very top and I don't think you do."

"He had surgery early this morning to remove a bullet in his head. The surgery was successful, and he's currently recovering."

"What are the chances that he actually makes it?"

"I'd say he's already done it. Gunshot wounds to the head are fatal about 90% of the time. The biggest issue is the loss of blood. Most die before they even reach a hospital. For those lucky enough to get to a hospital alive, 50% will die during the surgery. So, considering he's made it through the biggest two hurdles, I'd say his outlook is good," Jefferson said.

"Is he currently awake?"

"Not yet. He'll be kept under sedation for the next couple of days so we can monitor him for any swelling in the brain."

"What will his prognosis be?"

"Impossible to say at this point. If you want to say a man who's shot in the head is lucky, you can say he is. The brain has two hemispheres, each with four lobes, and in his case the bullet was only lodged in one hemisphere in a single lobe. It appears that a limited amount of tissue was damaged."

"How long will it take for him to recover?"

"It depends on his condition. If he wakes up and the damage is as minimal as we think it is, he could be up and about within a couple weeks. If there's further damage, it could take months or years. The major issues would be motor, sensory, cognition, memory, speech, and vision. Any combination of damage in these areas could set him back in his recovery. I should also note that 50% of people who survive will suffer from seizures and require anti-epilepsy medication."

"I thank you for all the information, Colonel. I'm going to leave two of my men here for a few days in case anything arises that needs my attention. They will stay out of your way and will stay with our subject to observe the entire time."

"I don't suppose I can say no," the Colonel noted.

"You could. Wouldn't do you any good though."

"I thought not."

"I expect your cooperation with anything my men need."

"They'll get it."

"I'll be back in a few days."

Sanders left instructions with the officers he was leaving behind to stay by the soldier's bed until he was awake. They left the hospital to go back to New York for a couple days, eager for the soldier's awakening. On the flight back, Sanders worked out some of the details for the inclusion of a new recruit to the organization.

Once back in New York, Sanders asked his secretary to get Michelle Lawson on the phone for him. Lawson was one of the organization's top handlers. She had previously worked with the FBI as a data information specialist. She quickly gained a reputation for being extremely smart and acquiring mounds of information almost instantly. That was one of the principal reasons why Sanders wanted her in his employment. Lawson had been able to garner the trust of every agent she ever worked with, for being able to get anything they needed and helped them out of tough predicaments when necessary. Though she didn't have movie star looks, more of the pretty girl next door, she was an attractive woman that never used her looks to her advantage. She was on the smaller side, about 5'3" and thin, with short, dirty blonde hair. Within minutes, Lawson was on the line.

"Shelly, how are you?" Sanders asked.

"I'm good, sir. Your secretary sounded like she was in a hurry so I figured something important was going on."

"It is. We may have a new recruit in a few days."

"That's great."

"I'm still working out the logistics of everything, but I was thinking of adding him to your team. Are you able to handle one more? How many agents are you handling right now?"

"Right now, I have seven agents. One more shouldn't be a problem," she said.

"Fantastic. Where are you right now?"

"I'm in Madrid. I was going over a mission with Agent Samson."

"How soon can you wrap things up there? When can you get back to New York?" Sanders wondered.

"I can wrap everything up here tomorrow and be there the day after."

"That's fine. I would like you to be here when we introduce him to everything and to get you acquainted."

"I look forward to it, sir."

"Great. I'll see you in a few days then."

"One more thing. What's his name?"

"I guess that might be useful, huh? His name... is Matthew Cain."

Two days later Sanders got the call from one of his liaison officers in Israel to update the injured soldier's condition. The doctors were no longer giving him sedatives and expected him to be alert the next day. Sanders immediately booked a flight for his private jet to leave for Ben Gurion International Airport near Tel Aviv near midnight so he'd arrive the following morning. Once he and his staff landed, they promptly made their way to the hospital. They were greeted by his officers once they reached the hospital and went to Cain's bed.

"Has he been awake yet?"

"Not yet, sir, but they expect him to be pretty soon," an officer responded.

"OK. Except for Shelly, the rest of you clear out of here," Sanders told the bunch. "I don't wanna smother him with people the moment he wakes up."

Sanders and Lawson grabbed a couple of chairs and waited near the bed, pulling out their iPads to do some work while they marked time. They wouldn't have to wait long as the soldier woke up about an hour later. The government officials stayed out of the way as the doctors checked on him and made sure there were no complications. They were eager to finally talk to him and see the effects of the surgery. As the doctors were finishing up, Sanders stood at the end of the bed. He nodded at Lawson to follow the doctors out to speak with them.

"How are you feeling, soldier?" Sanders asked.

"Other than feeling like someone's using a sledgehammer on my head, I guess OK."

"Remember anything about what happened?"

The soldier lifted his head, slightly sitting up, and gazed down at the floor. A terrifying realization came over him as his mind was a complete blank. Sanders could tell by the concerned look that swept over his face that he was having trouble coming up with anything. The soldier ran his hand over his head, letting his fingers feel the stitches that permeated his skull.

"What's your name?" Sanders asked.

The soldier opened his mouth as if he was about to spit it out, but closed it a moment later, shaking his head in disgust.

"How long do I have to be in here?" the soldier asked.

"Doctors say a couple weeks, depending on how you do with everything," Sanders replied.

"You're not a doctor?"

"Don't really have the uniform for it," Sanders said, looking down at his black suit.

"Who are you?"

"Director Ed Sanders."

"Director of what?"

"Well, we'll get into that another time. The most important thing right now is you."

"I can't remember anything," the soldier said, frustration clearly evident in his voice.

"That might be the least of your worries. They'll be coming in here soon to test your other faculties."

Sanders started walking away toward Lawson, then stopped to look back at the soldier.

"By the way, your name is Thomas Nelson. You were a member of Delta Force on a special mission when you were shot in the head."

The doctors came back in and started talking to Nelson in more detail. Sanders took Lawson aside to make sure her discussion with the doctors was productive.

"Are they going to cooperate?" Sanders asked.

"They were a little hesitant at first, but I convinced them it was the best move they could make in the interest of national security. There'll be no problems," she replied.

"Excellent," Sanders said as his phone rang. "Stay in there with them to make sure there are no hiccups."

Sanders took his conversation outside to avoid any prying

ears. Lawson went back to Nelson as the doctors were checking him out.

"How's he looking?" Lawson asked.

"Vitals are looking good," a doctor noted. "Just saw the MRI results. There's no bleeding, clots, or swelling. Some minor tissue damage but, all in all, everything's looking fantastic."

"That's great."

The doctor left the room and Nelson lay still, staring up at the ceiling, wondering when he was going to start remembering things.

"I take it you're not a doctor either?" Nelson asked, not bothering to look at his visitor.

"No, I'm not."

"You with the other guy?"

"If you're referring to Director Sanders, then yes, I am," she replied.

"What do you want?"

"In a few minutes, a specialist is going to come in here and give you a series of tests."

"What kind?"

"Just to see what kind of additional rehab, if any, you're going to need. I've already heard about your memory. We're going to need to see if you're having any other difficulties with your vision, motor skills, things like that."

"If you're not a doctor, then why are you here?" Nelson asked.

"We work for the government in a top-secret capacity. I can't tell you more than that at the moment. What I can tell you is that we're interested in you working for us when you get out of here."

"Why would you want someone who's been shot in the head and can't even remember his name?"

"We've had our eye on you for a while. As long as the doctors think you're gonna make a full recovery, there's no reason for you not to work for us. As far as your memory, in our line of work, sometimes it's better that way."

"What kind of work is that?"

"Let's get you healthy before we discuss that."

The specialist came into the room and Lawson disappeared from sight. The specialist was a doctor who worked for the organization that flew in with Sanders and Lawson, so they trusted that Nelson could be left alone with him.

Lawson caught up to Sanders outside the hospital as he was finishing up his phone call.

"What's the word?" Lawson asked.

"As soon as he's ready to be moved… he's ours," he responded proudly. "The death certificate is being prepared as we speak. So, you need to get to work right away on preparing the necessary documents and making the notifications."

"I'll get on it."

"I want everything ready to go by the time he's able to leave here."

"What if he's not interested in joining?" she asked.

"What other options does a soldier with a particular set of skills and no memory have? He'll play ball."

After a couple hours of testing, the specialist emerged from Nelson's room.

"What's the word, Doc?" Sanders asked.

"Well, it's one of the most unusual cases I've ever seen."

"In what way?"

"He seems to be fine in every aspect. Now, I've heard of

cases where people shot in the head resume their normal lives immediately, so it's not unprecedented, but it is rare."

"So, there's no aftereffects?"

"Well, I didn't say that," the doctor continued. "I asked about his past and he couldn't tell me a thing about it. As far as his motor skills, vision, speech, everything like that seems to check out OK."

"Did you administer the Epideptriol?"

"I did."

"Give you any problems?"

"Nope. Not a bit. Told him it would help stimulate the tissues in his brain and maybe jog his memory."

"Great. Thanks, Doc."

"What's the Epideptriol?" Lawson asked.

"It's an experimental drug. It's designed to attack the part of the brain that controls your memory and kill the tissue," Sanders explained.

"He'll never regain his memory, will he?"

"Not if we can help it. It's in his best interest that he doesn't."

"Why? Why wouldn't you want him to get his memory back?"

"Without going into too many details, there are things in his past that would be better for him if he doesn't remember."

"I see."

"So, you must not ever tell him, even if he asks. That's a direct order," Sanders said.

"How often will the drug be administered?"

"Once a week to start with when possible. Hopefully down the road we won't need it as much, if at all."

Sanders noticed a solemn expression on Lawson's face.

"Don't go getting soft on me now," Sanders said.

"It just seems a shame for a person to go through life without remembering a thing about your past, who you are."

"Maybe it is. But it's what helps keep us in business," Sanders continued. "Let's get back in there and see what he has to say."

It was hard for the government officials to not see the dejection on Nelson's face as they approached his bed. They pulled up a couple of chairs and sat by his side. Nelson was fiddling with his fingernails, trying hard not to look at his visitors. It was embarrassing to not remember a thing about who he was. Sanders and Lawson quietly waited for the fallen soldier to acknowledge their presence. They could see how tough it was for him and didn't want to press him needlessly. A grimace rolled over Nelson's face as he stared down at the covers on his bed. He finally looked up at the pair sitting next to him, water filling up his eyes as he struggled to contain his emotions.

"I've been trying to remember anything... a name, a face, just something that might trigger the rest of my memory," Nelson began, wiping his eyes. "But I just can't."

"Sometimes it takes time for a person's memory to come back to them," Lawson explained. "Even the simplest thing could bring it back. It could happen right out of the blue."

"She's right," Sanders jumped in. "The key thing to remember is you don't have to fight this battle alone. We're here to help you. We can help get your life back together."

"Why? What's in it for you?" Nelson asked.

"The chance to add an experienced soldier to our staff. There's no question in our minds that your fighting skills could be a great weapon in our arsenal. We think you'd be a valuable piece of our organization," Sanders said.

"What part of the government are you with?"

"Well, that's something we really can't divulge to anyone who's not actively involved with us."

"What if I say no?"

"You're within your right to do so, though we don't see any valid reason why you would want to."

"Maybe I just wanna go home and be with my family."

"Home? Where is that? Can you tell us?" Sanders asked with a sarcastic edge.

Nelson looked away from the pair, angry that he couldn't answer the question.

"I'm sure my family could help get me through it," Nelson said.

"I'm sure they could if you had any," Sanders replied.

"What?"

"Your family could help you if you had any," Sanders repeated, looking at Lawson. "Unfortunately, you don't have any."

"I don't have any family?" Nelson responded dejectedly.

"See for yourself," Sanders said, handing Nelson his file. "From Seattle, Washington, you were the only child born to your parents who died in a car accident two weeks after you graduated high school. It was their deaths that led you to join the military. Alone and nowhere else to go, ten years ago you enlisted."

"No aunts or uncles?"

"One aunt who died from cancer when you were a child, and one uncle, who became a drunk and a petty thief who moved out to California never to be heard from again."

Nelson eagerly read the file, his eyes not moving fast enough for his brain to process the information contained in it. He reread the same passages over and over again, hoping some of it would change by the next time he read it. Sanders and Lawson gave Nelson all the time he needed to read and digest the file, watching his facial expressions as he ate it up. They knew it was something he needed to see to be able to move on from his situation. After half an hour of trying to unfold everything in his mind he finally put the folder down. He looked as confused and aggravated as before.

"Nothing seems familiar," Nelson stated. "Everything is as blank as it was."

"It's something to start with," Lawson replied.

"About our job offer," Sanders said. "What do you say?"

"You haven't told me anything about it yet. For all I know I'd be tending sheep."

"Not likely. Slaughtering them maybe."

"I'm not agreeing to anything until you tell me specifics," Nelson said. "You say everything's top secret? I understand that means you avoid saying too much. But unless you get specific I'm not doing anything."

Sanders looked at Lawson, wondering how much he should tell. She nodded as if to spur him on. Within a minute, he started to explain the details of the job offer.

"Without giving away our cover, we work for an ultra-secret agency that targets people who are a threat to the United States," Sanders said.

"You mean terrorists."

"Not necessarily. Could be terrorists, world leaders, dictators, people in a position of power, rebels, perpetrators of major crime, criminal organizations, or anyone that poses a threat or could do so in the near future. It casts a wide net. We're not pigeonholed into any one area. If we believe you're a threat to the United States, either financially, politically, or physically, then we're coming after you."

"And you neutralize the threat?" Nelson asked.

"We eliminate the threat," Sanders succinctly replied.

"You're a kill squad?"

"That's a very narrow way of looking at it, Mr. Nelson. We're not just a kill squad as you put it. Much like the CIA, we assemble mountains of information that may prove valuable to protecting our country."

"You're basically a black ops organization?"

"If that helps you to understand it in its most basic form... yes."

Sanders could see Nelson was thinking about the offer but didn't appear to be fully convinced yet.

"We do not pay people to kill. I can get anybody to do that. I can train a monkey to do that if I wanted to. Any target that's eliminated must be done in a way that completely exonerates the United States. The government does not officially condone or approve of these actions and cannot be implicated in any manner. If it's discovered we're behind some of these missions, it'd be one of the worst scandals in this country's history. Even bigger than Watergate."

"Watergate? What's that?" Nelson asked.

"Google it sometime. To get back on point, you don't get paid to kill. You get paid to be invisible. You get paid to scope out a target, infiltrate that target's territory, eliminate said target, do it without your presence being noticed or compromised, and without any involvement suspected of the United States. To take it even further, your life as it stands right now will be gone. You cannot be arrested, put in jail, appear in traffic court, criminal court, divorce court, or any court. Your picture cannot appear in any newspaper. Your name won't return any information in a computer, and your fingerprint won't come up in any database. To put it bluntly, you... do not exist."

"Why are you hung up on getting me? I'm sure you could get a thousand other guys to do the same work."

"You're a highly trained soldier, part of Team Delta. In addition, you've sustained an injury that we can easily pass off into your implied death. You also have nobody back home who would miss you or poke around into your disappearance," Sanders continued.

"My implied death?"

"As I said, once you begin working for us, you do not exist. You're officially dead. That means after you leave this room Thomas Nelson ceases to exist. He died on the operating table."

"How much time do I have to think about it?" Nelson asked.

"Oh, about ten minutes," Sanders replied, looking down at his watch.

Nelson looked up at the man standing next to his bed, wondering how he could expect him to make a life altering decision so quickly. He sat in silence, his face showing no expression, staring at Sanders. A numb feeling overtook his body. He slowly shifted his gaze over to Lawson, his face still void of life, taking it all in. He sat there digesting the information he'd just been given. Was it the life he wanted? To be a soulless, ruthless killer who had no past and didn't even exist? He thought about how changing his name would affect him, but considering he couldn't remember anything anyway, it really was of no consequence what anyone called him. After a few minutes of thought he shook his head in acknowledgment, reluctantly accepting the offer, knowing he didn't have many other options. At least with them he'd be a part of something. A group he could rely on and help him fill in any missing pieces, or questions he'd have. If he declined and went on his own, he had no family, and no one to turn to. That was an even scarier proposition for someone who couldn't remember anything.

"Well, I can't even express how happy I am right now," Sanders said. "Welcome to the team."

"Thanks."

"Sorry about changing the name but it has to be done."

"It's OK. I can't remember anything so it's not doing me much good anyway," Nelson stated.

"I can understand."

"So, what's my new name?"

"Matthew Cain."

3

Two weeks later—Sanders and his entourage of officials boarded the jet, bound for New York. Cain slipped into a seat against the window, staring at the landscape below as the ground became a blip on the radar.

"So, how'd you come up with Matthew Cain?" Cain asked.

"We give new agents new identities once they start working with us. We name them after people in the biggest organization ever created," Sanders replied.

"What's that?"

"The Bible."

"So, who do you name them after?"

"Killers. Seemed more fitting."

"Who am I named after?"

"Cain. He murdered his brother Abel and was the world's first murderer," Sanders said.

"That's comforting. So where am I gonna live when we get there?" Cain asked.

"Everything's been taken care of," Sanders replied. "You've got a nice apartment in the heart of New York City."

"Once we get back, you'll be given a package of everything you'll need," Lawson interjected. "Bank account, credit cards, car, passports, driver's license, everything."

"You'll notice that $250,000 has been deposited into your bank account to start with. Once we see that you're going to stay with us for a while you will get $500,000 deposited into your account every six months, the first of January and July."

"Nice."

"Money will be the least of your worries. Make no mistake, though, you will earn every penny of it.," Sanders added.

"What if I don't like living in New York?"

"You only have to stay there for a brief period. We want to make sure you're completely comfortable with the operation. After that, you're free to live wherever you like. More times than not you'll be off on an assignment, anyway. One of the trade-offs of that money is that you will be on call 24/7. You will make yourself available at any time of the day no matter where you are. If you are needed on an assignment immediately, you are to drop what you're doing and respond at a moment's notice," Lawson explained. "It is rare when that happens as we like to plan missions out a few days in advance, but it does happen and you will be available."

"That's not a problem. I obviously have nothing or no one to tie me down."

"That's the other thing I wanted to talk to you about. At one point this agency frowned upon agents having exterior relationships as they felt it would interfere in plans and at some point cause friction. What we found was some agents began to snap. Loneliness set in, there was nobody waiting for them, nothing to keep them going, and the stress of the missions wore them down. Now the policy is that we encourage you to make friendships and relationships outside of this agency. We want you to be happy and content and in return hopefully agents won't go off the deep end. The conditions are that you cannot tell them what you do. If you want to tell them you work in insurance, or sales, or even for the government, that is up to you. But your work here is top secret."

"And I'll even take it a step further," Sanders chimed in. "You're paid handsomely for your work here and in return for that we expect to be your number one priority. I don't really care what you do or say when you're at home as long as this agency is not involved. We are an ultra top-secret department and we must remain that way. Any slips by you about our work here to a friend, girlfriend, wife, reporter, anybody, will result in their immediate death... and probably yours. There are no reprieves and it's non-conditional. Is that clear?"

"I understand. How long will I be needed to do this?" Cain asked.

"There's no set timetable. We ask for ten or fifteen years. Anything after that will be evaluated on a case-by-case basis," Lawson said. "If you choose to walk away at that point you'll have fifteen million dollars in your bank account and free to live the rest of your life however you choose, though you'll forever be bound by the rules of disclosure about this agency."

"What about guns?"

"You'll be given your choice of weapons at the Center. Though you won't always travel with them. Due to airport security and customs, sometimes you'll need to acquire your weapon once you arrive at your target location. Typically, it's not a problem as we have operators and safety deposit boxes all over the world. Obtaining a weapon will be the least of your problems."

"What Center?"

"It's where our headquarters are."

"It'd probably be best to get some sleep if you can," Sanders said. "You'll need it once we get back."

Cain took Sanders up on the suggestion and dozed off for a while. They arrived in New York late that night, company cars waiting for them once they touched down. Sanders, Lawson, and Cain were driven away in the lead car with the other officers in the trailing car. Cain stared out the window intently, looking at the scenery.

"Have I ever been here before?" Cain asked. He could see the confusion in the faces of his companions once the words left his lips. "In New York, I mean."

"Not to my knowledge," Sanders replied.

A short time later they arrived at the Center, going into the underground parking garage. As they got out of the car, Cain took note of his surroundings. It was a natural instinct for him, something that he still remembered from his military days. He always had to be aware of what was around him, noting any possible trouble spots, no matter how peaceful or innocent something looked. This was one of those times when something just didn't feel right. He looked at the faces of Sanders and Lawson, who didn't seem troubled by anything, but still felt like something was off. They went inside the elevator, where Sanders pushed the button to go up to the lobby. Once the doors opened and they stepped off the elevator, they were surprised to find three armed men waiting for them, guns pointed at each of their faces.

"Anyone moves and you're all dead," one of the men yelled.

All three of the intruding men were wearing black masks and two were armed with AK-47s while the other just had a pistol. They forced Sanders, Lawson, and Cain onto the ground, lying on their stomachs.

"What do you want with us? Money?" Sanders asked.

"We don't want money. We want him," one of the men replied, pointing at Cain.

"He's new to our company. He doesn't know anything."

"We'll see about that."

One of the men pulled out another black mask, though this one didn't have any holes for the mouth or eyes. They sat Cain up and put the hood over his head. They stood him up as one of the men took the butt end of his rifle and smashed it into Cain's face. Cain immediately dropped to the floor as the blunt force temporarily knocked him out. Two of the assailants each grabbed one of Cain's arms and dragged him back into the elevator. The leader of the group kept Sanders and Lawson on the ground at gunpoint before joining the other two in the elevator.

About an hour later Cain started coming out of it. He emitted a low moan while moving his head. He opened his eyes but only saw darkness with the hood still over his head. A few seconds later the hood was pulled off. He tried to move his arms, but they were restrained, tied behind his back as he sat on an old wooden chair. Cain squinted, trying to adjust to the bright lights. He looked around the room but he was alone. There was nothing else even in the room other than the chair he was sitting on. There was a small mirror on the opposite side of the room. After sitting there for five minutes, wondering what his abductors had planned for him, someone finally entered the room. He was a middle-aged man, graying hair around his temples, and dressed in an expensive suit. He circled Cain a couple of times before speaking up.

"I'll start this out by explaining a few things to you," the man said. "I'm gonna get the information I want out of you one way or another. I'd prefer to do it the easy way. I'll ask you a question and you simply answer it honestly. If you'd rather do it the hard way, then I'm not opposed to that either. In that instance, we'll simply beat the information out of you using whatever kinds of torture amuses us at the moment. Understand?"

"Sure," Cain replied.

"First off, let's start with your name."

"Peter."

"Peter what?"

"Peter Pan," Cain said seriously.

"Peter Pan," his interrogator repeated with a laugh. "Somehow I don't think so."

"OK. My name really is Peter."

"Peter what?"

"Peter Rabbit."

The well-dressed man wasn't as amused with this answer as he was the one before it. He motioned toward the mirror for someone to come in. Seconds later two more men entered the room. Both were younger men, in their mid-twenties probably, and as well dressed as their superior.

"See if you can make him a little more willing," the elder man told them.

Cain knew what that meant and his face tensed up as he tried to prepare for what was about to happen. He closed his eyes just as a clenched right fist made contact with his jaw, knocking him and his chair on the ground. The other man pulled him up in time for a left hand to put him back onto the ground, the man's knuckles hitting Cain across the bridge of his nose. One of the men pulled him back up and immediately took the wind out of Cain by punching him in the stomach several times.

"I'll ask you one more time. Your name?" the leader asked.

Cain took a deep breath before answering. "It's Michael."

"Michael what?"

"Michael Jordan."

"You're a funny man," he said after letting out a laugh. He seemed rather amused by Cain's sense of humor.

"Not as funny as your face is gonna look after I'm done rear-ranging it," Cain threatened.

"Well, we'll see about that. Take Mr. Cain away for a bit and see how he likes the dark."

Cain looked at the man before him curiously, wondering how he knew his name and why he was trying to beat it out of him if he already knew it.

"Yes, Mr. Cain, I'm already aware of who you are," he said.

"Then why the muscle?"

"I told you I was prepared to do things either way you chose. I wanted to see which way you preferred. Apparently, you like to make things hard on yourself. So, we'll do it your way."

The younger men untied Cain, lifting him up from the chair. As they began walking, Cain tripped one of them then punched the other one, catching him off guard. Cain kicked both men as they lay on the ground. Once they were incapacitated he turned his attention to the leader who was just standing against the wall watching the activities. Cain put his hands around his neck but was soon met with resistance as several more men rushed into the room to stop him. They pulled Cain off the man and restrained him.

"What do you want with me?" Cain yelled.

"In due time, Mr. Cain. In due time," the leader replied.

The men put the hood back over Cain's head and led him out of the room. They walked him down a long, cold hallway that had bare white walls with a few doors on each side. They bypassed these doors until they reached the end of the hallway, a single door remaining. Once they reached their destination, they opened the door and shoved Cain in, quickly closing the door behind him. Cain's hands weren't tied together, so he pulled the hood off. The room was pitch black. Cain used his hands to feel around the edge of the room. He walked around the entire room, not feeling anything that would indicate a window or opening of any kind. He felt the door but there didn't seem to be a handle on it so he assumed it could only be opened from the outside.

The captors could see into the room through a piece of glass along part of the wall. Once they saw Cain sit down on the floor, they left to convene in the meeting room. They went into the room, where the man who ordered it all was already waiting for them.

"What did you think?" the well-dressed leader asked his superior.

"Nicely done," Director Sanders responded, smiling.

"Sir, do you really think this is necessary?" Shelly Lawson asked, concerned about Cain's condition.

"Unless you can think of another way in which case I'm all ears. We don't have time to subject him to six to eight months of intensive training to see what he can do. The best way to see him in action and see how he responds to situations is to throw him into a situation where he thinks his life is at risk."

"I just hope we don't lose him after this."

"We won't."

"How long should we keep him in solitary?" the well-dressed man asked.

"Leave him there for a week. We'll see how that changes him," Sanders replied. "Any objections, Shelly?"

"No," Lawson replied after a long pause.

Sanders ordered Cain to be kept locked up for a week, with no outside contact, except for one meal a day. He wanted to see how he'd act after being in a weakened state from not eating and being in constant darkness. Sanders stopped by to check on him every day to see if his demeanor started changing. Though it was tough on Cain not knowing what time of day it was or what was happening to him, he tried to use the time to his advantage. Though they were trying to starve him and make him weak, he tried to combat it and stay strong by doing pushups and sit-ups. He slept a lot and tried to not let his mind wander and think positively. He figured that they wanted him alive for some reason or they would've killed him already.

After a week had passed the same two men who worked him over before came in to get him.

"Smells like piss in here," one of them stated.

"I wanted it to smell like you were at home," Cain remarked, earning him a kick in the stomach.

"C'mon, it's time for another chat."

They dragged Cain up to his feet, helping him stand. He was a little weak but was able to stand on his own and walk by himself. There was another guard standing outside the room as they walked into the hallway and led him down the hallway into another room. It was the same room they interrogated him in before. This time he wasn't tied to a chair. All three men guarded the room before the well-dressed leader walked in.

"Looks like solitary confinement wasn't too harsh for you."

"Was a little too bright for my liking," Cain said sarcastically.

"Your humor serves you well."

"What do you want?"

"Who do you work for?"

"I don't know."

"Why are you in New York?"

"I don't know."

"Why were you with Sanders?"

"I don't know who that is."

"C'mon now, you don't know who you were with or where you are? You expect me to believe that?"

"I don't care what you believe."

"You should. Because the only way you're getting out of here is if you start making me believe what you're saying."

"Look, I've got a bullet in my head and I have memory issues. Doctors say I have something called sporadic amnesia. Sometimes I can't remember what happened an hour ago. As far as this Sanders guy, maybe I know him, but I just can't remember right now."

"Maybe you just need your memory jogged a little."

The leader motioned to one of the guards who stepped in front of Cain and belted him with a right hand, knocking Cain to the ground. As they helped Cain back to his chair, he noticed a gun inside the left jacket of one of the guards.

"The next time someone hits me it'll be the last mistake

they make," Cain said, hoping it'd provoke them into doing it again.

It worked as the same man stepped in front of him. He rose his arm up, ready to pounce, when Cain sprung up from the chair. He reached inside the man's jacket and pulled out his gun, quickly firing into his midsection. He fell to the ground and Cain turned around and fired at the other two guards, hitting them in the chest before they had a chance to remove their weapons. Cain then turned his sights on the leader of the group who looked shocked at what just happened. He wasn't armed and started backpedaling toward the wall. Cain circled around him as the man kept walking backwards until he found himself in the middle of the room. Cain made him sit in the chair as he started his own line of questions.

"Where am I?" Cain asked.

"New York."

"Who are you?"

"The Easter Bunny."

Cain wasn't amused and backhanded the man with the butt of the gun, smacking him across the side of his face.

"Who put you up to this?"

"Santa Claus."

Cain smacked him again with the gun, knocking him to the ground, and causing a deep cut on the man's forehead.

"Last chance to tell me what you know," Cain said.

The man stayed silent and Cain thought about putting a bullet in him but ultimately decided against it and instead kicked him across the face as he broke for the exit. Cain peeked out the door and didn't see anyone else out there and started down the hallway when lights and sirens started going off. He raced down the hallway and tried to open any doors he came across but they were all locked. Suddenly, he heard a commotion behind him as he turned around and saw a few men running toward him. He fired a couple shots in their direction and kept moving. He came across another door that was also locked but tried kicking it open. He knew he had to get the door open somehow or else he'd get captured again. He wasn't going to be able to fend them off forever in that hallway. Cain desperately tried to open the door without any success. As the men moved closer, he fired a few more shots. He ran out of bullets when the door suddenly opened behind him. He turned around and was shocked to see Sanders standing there. Since he wasn't restrained in any way, Cain assumed Sanders was somehow involved in his kidnapping.

"Hello, Cain," Sanders said.

"What the hell are you doing to me?" Cain yelled.

Cain put his hands on the collar of Sanders' suit, ready to shake some answers out of him. Instead, Cain got knocked out cold, hit from behind as one of the guards slammed a gun into the back of his head.

"Take him to my office," Sanders told them.

"What do you think?" the lead training officer asked.

"I think he'll do nicely," Sanders replied.

"I'm not sure it's the best test for him."

"He's a former member of Delta Force. We already know he's received great training. He doesn't need more of that. I think we saw exactly what we needed to see."

"Which was?"

"He's willing and able to kill at a moment's notice, without hesitation. He'll do what it takes to survive. Those are the most important characteristics that an agent needs. Everything else is gravy. Those are the attributes that some men don't possess. He does. He has them and he'll use them."

They took Cain to Sanders' office, laying him on a couch, where he lay motionless for a couple of hours. Once he started coming out of it he looked up at the ceiling for a few seconds. He quickly remembered what transpired and jumped off the couch ready for a fight with someone. He scanned the room and after seeing no one, stood at ease. Cain looked at the pictures on the walls and walked over to the desk. He began rummaging through the drawers, not sure what he was looking for, but hoping to find anything that might explain what was going on. He took some papers out of the bottom drawer and saw a revolver sitting there. He heard the handle of the door jiggle and grabbed the gun. He pointed it toward the door and was ready to fire as soon as it opened. Cain was surprised to see Sanders and Lawson walk through the door. The pair stopped in their tracks once they saw the gun pointed at them.

"Put that thing away," Sanders said.

"Give me one good reason why I shouldn't blow your head off right now," Cain replied. "You set me up."

"The first good reason is that you can't. There's no bullets in that gun."

Cain briefly looked at the gun while it was still pointed at Sanders and pulled the trigger.

"Lucky for me I wasn't bluffing," Sanders noted.

Cain sighed and felt defeated already as he tossed the gun on the desk.

"Sit down so we can talk," Sanders said.

Cain ignored his wishes and continued to stand in a somewhat adversarial manner.

"Please," Sanders said, trying to de-escalate the situation. "Sit down."

Cain looked at Lawson who nodded in agreement. After a few seconds of deliberating, he decided to comply, realizing he didn't really have any other options but to comply with their wishes. He sat back down on the couch as Sanders sat on the edge of his desk.

"Everything you just went through was a test," Sanders said calmly.

"A test?" Cain snapped.

"Typically, a new agent requires intensive field training that lasts anywhere from six months to a year. With your military background, I thought waiting might not be in our best interest. I wanted to get you out in the field as soon as possible but I needed to see how good you were to bypass the training. So, we devised this plan so nobody would get hurt but we'd find out about your abilities."

"I shot three men for a test."

"Wax bullets. I made sure all weapons were fitted with them for safety purposes. The men you shot are all fine."

"You intentionally left me in a dark room, trying to starve me to death."

"We had to see if you'd start to break. And we weren't trying to starve you, we gave you a sandwich every day."

"On stale bread."

"I'll have a word with our chef."

"So, how'd I do?"

"You did exceptional. I have no concerns. If we put you out in the field tomorrow, I'd expect outstanding results. If anything doesn't go according to plan, I can see you have the necessary attributes to..." Sanders explained before his voice trailed off.

"To what?" Cain asked.

"To survive."

Cain sat there digesting the information, not sure what he should be feeling. Sanders could see Cain still had some doubts.

"Look, I can understand you're a little agitated right now and I don't blame you for it at all," Sanders began. "But this is a tough business we're in. It's not for the weak minded or weak-hearted. We need to make sure who we're sending out there is up to the task. If you wanna go home and be pissed off for a while that's OK. But we think you'll be an asset to this agency and we think we can be an asset to you if you want help in trying to get your memory back."

As Cain pondered Sanders words his initial anger slowly started to subside. He still wasn't sure what they did was necessary to see what he could do, but he knew he would need some help in regaining his memory. He didn't know who else he would be able to turn to.

"I tell you what, why don't you go home and just think about things for a while. If you decide this isn't right for you, we won't stand in your way. You're free to go," Sanders told him. "But I think you'll come to the proper decision that this is where you belong. The right decision."

"Go home? Where's that?" Cain asked.

"We set you up with an apartment a few blocks from here. I'll have someone take you there. Relax for a little bit."

Cain knew he didn't need to relax for a while, or think about it for a few hours. He was in. He figured if anyone had the resources to help him get his memory back it'd be the government. He'd overlook this little stunt they created and do what was asked of him as long as the tricks ended there.

"I don't need time to think," Cain said, standing up. "I'll do it. But if anyone pulls something like this on me again, I will make them wish they hadn't."

"Understood," Sanders responded, smirking.

"I'll take you to your place," Lawson said.

"Before you leave, as a show of good faith, go over to the gun room," Sanders said. "Pick out something you like."

As Cain and Lawson left the room, Sanders pulled out his cell phone to make a call.

"Hey, it's me," Sanders said. "Are you free right now?"

"Yeah," the voice on the other line replied.

"Good. I have a job for you right now. He's on his way to his place in a few minutes. Could you be there waiting for him as a surprise?"

"Sure."

"Good. I'll pay you the usual fee."

Lawson led Cain to the gun room, where it looked like they had several hundred guns lined up. It was a small room that had a few tables locked together, not to mention shelves on the wall that were fully stocked with guns and ammunition. If the building was ever stormed by enemies they certainly had enough weapons and ammo to make the fight last a while. There were cameras at the door and inside the room to make sure nobody was taking guns out that was unauthorized. Cain walked around the room, carefully analyzing some of the pieces, picking a few up to get a feel for them. A couple felt really comfortable to him, perhaps because they were active military weapons, which he probably had used previously even if he didn't remember it. His eyes caught sight of a Sig Sauer M11 on the table. He picked it up and pointed it at the wall, instantly knowing he wanted it. He put it inside the back of his belt as he picked up a Glock 19, analyzing it thoroughly. He also shoved that inside his belt as he grabbed some ammunition boxes off the shelf.

"I'm taking these two," Cain stated.

"Planning on starting your own little war?" Lawson replied.

"I like to be prepared."

"That's fine."

Once they left, they went down to the garage, finding Lawson's car. As they drove away, Lawson wanted to get to know her new agent better.

"I just want to let you know I wasn't in favor of what they did to you this past week," she said.

"You weren't?"

"No. I didn't think it was necessary, but I was overruled."

"It's fine. Thanks for the concern though," Cain said. "So how long have you been working here?"

"Seven years."

"You like it?"

"For the most part. Like any other job, you have good days and bad. Some days are more stressful than others. But yeah, I do."

"How'd you get mixed up in this?"

"I worked for the FBI as an analyst. One day, out of the blue, I was approached about a new agency that was starting. It was top secret, completely off the books, that nobody knew about. It seemed exciting, so I joined up," Lawson said.

"I don't even know what it's called."

"We have no official name. Unofficially we're known as The Specter Project, or Project Specter."

"Is there a meaning behind that?"

"Specter means ghost, or a source of terror."

"I guess that does fit, huh? So, you're telling me nobody knows this agency exists? How's that possible?" Cain asked.

"I don't have all the answers either. I only know what they want me to know. He wasn't lying when he said this is an ultra-secret agency. As far as I can tell Sanders only reports to three or four people. Who those people are I don't know."

"I thought the CIA did this type of stuff."

"The CIA has become too well known to do many of the tasks we're now doing. Plus, there's too much red tape. Due to political pressures, they'd simply be unable to do some of the things we do. We're a completely unknown Black Ops division."

They continued talking about the organization for a few minutes until they wound up at Cain's apartment building.

"Well, here we are," Lawson said, handing Cain the keys to his apartment. "Eighth floor."

"Thanks. What happens tomorrow?"

"Nothing. Now you wait for us to contact you about an assignment. Just take it easy."

4

Cain went into the building and took the elevator up to his apartment. He stood in front of the door, trying to shake the feeling that something wasn't right, and stared at the door for a few moments. He unlocked it, and pushed it open without stepping inside. He took a few steps in, carefully surveying his surroundings, trying to notice if anything seemed strange. Suddenly, music started blaring from the bedroom, the door flying open. Cain immediately withdrew the Glock pistol from his belt, waiting for a figure to emerge in the doorway. A few seconds later the outline of his visitor became visible, causing Cain to relax the finger he had pressed on the trigger. He let his arm fall to the side, the pistol bouncing off his leg. The scantily clad woman dancing in his bedroom eased any fears he previously had. Cain put the pistol back in his belt before barging past the tight skirted blonde, whose ample cleavage was barely contained in her dress. He didn't pay much mind to her as he found the booming stereo and turned it off.

"Wrong kind of music?" she innocently asked.

Cain walked past her, once again not looking at her, on his way to the kitchen. He grabbed a bottle of water from the refrigerator and sat down on a bar stool at the counter, finally looking at his visitor.

"Who are you? What do you want? And how'd you get in here?" Cain finally asked.

"I have a special key," she teased. "And I'm your birthday present."

"It's not my birthday."

"Well, then I guess it's just your lucky day."

Cain continued to just sit there drinking his water. The woman was starting to get confused, unsure of Cain's uninterested behavior. She hadn't encountered that kind of resistance before.

"So, if you don't want me to dance what would you like me to do?" she asked. "Should I wait in bed for you?"

"Actually, I'd kind of like you to leave," Cain replied.

"What?"

"I don't know who put you up to this but I'm not interested."

"You're not interested? How can you not be interested? What's wrong with you? Are you some kind of weirdo or something?"

"I guess you could say that," Cain said as he got up to open the door.

The woman sighed and walked over to him. She closed the door and slowly caressed his chest with her fingers. Cain closed his eyes and grabbed her wrists, moving them off his body. He went back over to the counter to grab his water. The woman followed him.

"Is there something wrong with me? Not your type? What?"

"You're a beautiful woman. But I'm just not interested right now," Cain said.

"Wow. You're really a challenge, aren't you?"

Cain rolled his eyes, unsure of what else he could say to get the woman to leave, and walked over to the couch.

"Look, I'm tired, I've had a long day, and I really just want to relax for a little bit," Cain said.

"That's what I'm here for. To help you relax. Listen, if we don't do anything here then I don't get paid," she said in frustration.

"Who's paying you?"

"Sanders."

"Why?"

"He uses me every now and then for his employees."

"Do you know what we do?" Cain asked.

"I just know that you work for the government. Sanders says you guys are in frequent high-stress situations and need to get the tension out."

Cain grinned and let out a slight laugh.

"So, does that mean you're ready?" the woman asked hopefully.

"What's your name, anyway?"

"Destiny."

Cain looked at her, tilted his head and raised his eyebrows in amusement.

"Destiny? Really? What's your real name?" Cain asked.

"That is my real name."

"You gotta do better than that."

The woman looked up, biting her lip, and reluctantly replied. "Heather. Listen, I'd really like to get paid for this, so if you're still not interested, just sit back and I'll do all the work."

"You're persistent."

"I get paid a lot of money for this."

"How's Sanders gonna know nothing happened if you just walked out of here right now?" Cain asked.

"I don't know, it's Sanders, he knows everything. Wouldn't surprise me if he had this place bugged or cameras somewhere."

"Well, if it makes you feel better, you can stay awhile," Cain said as he lay on the couch.

"That's more like it," she replied as she walked toward him.

"Oh, no, no, you can sit on that one," he said, pointing to the sofa across from them.

"I can't believe this," she whispered to herself as she walked to the sofa, sitting down.

"If it helps, if anyone asks, I'll tell them you were great," Cain said.

"Thanks. Are we gonna do anything at all tonight?"

"Yeah. We can talk if you want."

"Talk? That's it? Just talk?"

"Well, I guess if you're hungry you can help yourself to the fridge."

"Are you always this difficult?"

"Mostly."

Cain grabbed the remote off the coffee table and turned the TV on. He flipped channels until he came across a documentary on black ops on The History Channel. He intently watched the program for the next half hour as Heather tended to her nails in boredom. Once the show ended Cain sat up and looked at Heather.

"Oh, is it over now?" she asked sarcastically.

"Oh, you still here?" he replied as he took a sip of water. "So why do you do this?"

"Why not? I like to have sex and I get paid a lot of money."

"Seems like you could be doing something more..."

"Dignified, maybe? More important? Like solving the world's hunger problem or finding a cure for cancer or something?"

"Maybe. You're an attractive girl. I'm sure there's a lot of other opportunities out there for you."

"Oh, there is. I also work at a strip club."

"You seem pretty proud of it."

"Hey, it pays the bills."

"So, what're you gonna do when the looks fade, and the dance moves are gone?" Cain asked.

"By that time, hopefully I'll have enough money saved where I won't have to worry about it."

"Is that what you're doing with all your money, saving it?"

"Is it really any of your business?" she asked.

"You're in my apartment, sitting on my couch, and watching my TV. If you don't like the questions, you can leave anytime you want."

"Fine. My goal is to save up a couple hundred thousand and then leave this city. Move to the country somewhere, buy a nice little house, and start my own business," she revealed.

"That's a lot of money."

"It is. I've still got a few years to go."

"What kind of business?"

"I don't know. Maybe something that involves the marketing degree I have."

"How does a girl with a marketing degree wind up here?"

"A lot of debt."

"Your parents approve of what you're doing?" Cain asked.

"My mother died when I was five. My father, if you can call him that, raised me until I was about seventeen. Then I left on my own."

"Didn't get along?"

"I was tired of the verbal assaults and physical beatings," Heather said.

"Sorry to hear that."

"Yeah. Met a guy who wanted me to get into that kind of life, and like a sucker I wanted to please him. Then a few months later he ran off with another dancer. There I was, stuck."

"Still could've left," Cain said.

"Guess I didn't know what else to do. Should've went with my sister."

"You have a sister?"

"Four years younger than me. She went to school to become a teacher. Haven't talked to her in a few years. She disapproved of my lifestyle," she said.

"Where's she at now?"

"I don't even know."

Cain sat there looking at Heather, nodding, with an approving look on his face. He liked that there seemed to be some substance to her, and that she wasn't just a pretty face with no ambition.

"How about a drink?" Cain offered.

"Sure."

Heather watched Cain head to the kitchen, actually

admiring him now that he didn't just jump all over her the moment he laid eyes on her. She put up the front with most men she came in contact with and pretended to love everything about what she did. She found most men offered extra tips when they thought she was really into them and all about the sex.

"Sorry, don't have anything stronger," Cain said with a wide grin, handing her a bottle of water.

Heather smiled. "That'll be fine."

Cain walked back around the coffee table, sitting on the couch across from Heather. He sat up at attention, eager to learn more about his companion.

"So, what about you? How'd you end up working for Sanders?"

"I was in the military. I was on the verge of leaving and he offered me a job," Cain said.

"You like it?"

"Well, I just started."

Cain sat back and stared at the ceiling, suddenly not feeling well. He wiped sweat off his forehead with his arm.

"Are you OK? You don't look so good," Heather said.

Cain put his right hand up to his ear, hearing a loud ringing sound. He squinted as he couldn't see with the bright lights shining in his eyes. A few seconds later his eyes closed entirely to block out the color streaks. Heather rushed over to the phone and called Sanders, as she was instructed to do in case there was an emergency with any of his guys. Sanders informed her when he first hired her that if things ever got out of hand in any manner that he was the first one to be called, and he would handle it, with no police or medical personnel involved.

"Hey, something's wrong with your guy here," she screamed.

"What's wrong?"

"I don't know. He's not looking good," she said, glancing over at him.

"I'll have someone there in ten minutes."

"Oh my God," she yelled as she watched him fall on his side.

"What now?"

"I think he just passed out."

Sanders hung up and had a doctor rush over to Cain's apartment. Heather ran over to Cain, who was now lying on his side on the couch. She lifted his eyelids open and checked his pulse. She really wasn't sure what she was doing, but it seemed like a good thing to do. She stood up and put her hands on her head, hastily trying to think of what else she could do. Two minutes later, Cain opened his eyes, not totally sure what was going on. He was breathing heavy and batting his eyelids, trying to get his wits about him.

"Are you OK?" Heather asked.

Cain slowly sat up and looked at her, unsure what had happened. Heather grabbed his arm to try to comfort him.

"Do you need anything?" Heather asked again.

A dazed and confused look appeared in Cain's eyes, still hazy from passing out. He had no idea who the beautiful woman sitting next to him was.

"Who are you?" he asked.

"You don't remember?"

"No," he replied with a shake of his head. "What happened?"

"I don't know. We were just talking and all of a sudden you just looked really bad and then slumped over."

"I passed out?"

"Yes."

"For how long?"

"Maybe two or three minutes. I called Sanders. He's sending a doctor here to check you out."

"Who's Sanders?"

"Umm... your boss," she responded, unsure of what else to say.

"Oh. Who are you again?"

"I'm Heather."

"Do I know you?"

"We just met earlier," she told him.

Cain leaned forward and attempted to get up but was met with resistance from Heather, who gently held him back.

"Just sit back until the doctor gets here," Heather said. "What do you need? I'll get it for you."

"I'm thirsty."

Heather grabbed the bottle of water from the coffee table and helped Cain take a sip of it. She laid him back down on the couch and kneeled down on the floor next to him, watching over him. A few minutes later they heard keys rattling in the door, a second later the door opening to reveal Sanders, Lawson, and the doctor. The trio rushed into the apartment and immediately checked on Cain's condition.

"I said give him a good time, Heather, I didn't say kill him," Sanders remarked.

Heather rolled her eyes, ignoring the comment, and watched as the doctor looked at Cain. Several minutes later the doctor got up and approached Heather, Sanders, and Lawson, who were standing in a circle.

"He had a seizure," the doctor noted as he turned to look at his patient.

"I thought the drugs were supposed to stop that," Sanders said.

"For most patients, the drugs will control them, but it doesn't mean he can't have additional seizures. The drugs also have side effects, including dizziness, nausea, vision problems, and memory issues."

"Is this gonna be a frequent problem?" Sanders asked.

"He might have a few a year or he might never have another one. No one can say with any amount of certainty. Everybody reacts differently."

"Just great. Every time this guy's out in the field we're gonna be wondering if he collapses and falls off a cliff somewhere."

"What do we do from here?" Lawson asked.

"Well, I'd give him a couple of days to rest and recover. No strenuous activity," the doctor replied. "After that he should be able to resume normal activities."

"What about his memory, doctor?" Heather asked.

"What about it?"

"Well, when he woke up, he didn't know who I was or recognize Mr. Sanders' name."

"Oh, well, that's quite normal. Often when someone has a seizure, their mind is still cloudy and can't recognize names or faces. It usually wears off within thirty minutes or an hour and he should be able to recognize anyone he knew before."

They talked amongst themselves for the next few minutes trying to decide how to proceed. They didn't feel comfortable leaving Cain by himself in case anything else happened.

"I guess I'll stay here with him," Lawson volunteered.

"No, you're too valuable to stay here. You've got work to do and ten other agents to take care of. I can't have you sitting here being a nursemaid," Sanders responded.

"Who do you have in mind then? Who else is aware of his problem and will be able to stay with him?"

Sanders walked over to the window, looked down at the traffic below, and thought about who he could get.

"I could stay with him," Heather blurted out.

Sanders raised his eyebrows, surprised at the stripper's suggestion. He turned around and locked eyes with Lawson, also shocked at Heather's offer. Heather knew that as soon as she said it they would look at her strangely and wonder why she was making the offer. She wasn't quite sure herself, except it just seemed like the right thing to do. Sanders could tell by Lawson's face that she was not in favor of it. He then walked over to Heather to discuss it further with her.

"Why would you wanna do that?" he asked.

"He seems like a nice guy."

"Strange coming from you."

"Sir, I really don't think this is a good idea," Lawson said.

"Why not? Someone's gotta look after him. Who else do you have in mind?"

"We can get someone at the office to swing by. One of the secretaries maybe."

"And who's gonna take their spot? There's a lot of important work to be done. I'm not sure that's the best and most productive use of time."

"What does she know about taking care of someone? Plus, we can't afford to have any information slip out by accident."

"What of your other job?" Sanders asked.

"I'll take a few days off," Heather replied.

"Everything here is top secret information, you understand that? Any slips about his condition to the wrong people could mean his death. Or yours. Nothing leaves this room."

"Who am I gonna tell?" Heather said, incredulous that he suspected her of revealing anything. "I don't even know anything other than you work for the government."

"I'm just making sure we understand each other."

"We do. Nobody will know of his condition."

"I can't reimburse you for your time, other than what you were already here for."

"I'm not asking for anything."

Sanders took a step back and paced back and forth for a few moments, deliberating and considering his options. It didn't take long for him to come to a conclusion.

"Well, I don't think we have very many alternatives to Ms. Lloyd's offer. I think we should be appreciative of her being a good Samaritan. So, considering that, I think it'd be in our best interest to accept her kind offer," Sanders said.

Lawson slightly opened her mouth, ready to continue fighting against the notion, but she thought better of it. She rarely went against Sanders' wishes, and when she did, it was something she really believed in fighting for. She wasn't sure this was a big enough deal to go against him. She sighed in disapproval, looking Heather up and down in her revealing outfit, but didn't fight the directive any further. Although she disagreed with his decision, she understood.

"Well, we have other matters to attend to, so we're gonna get going," Sanders said. "Anything happens, anything you need, you call me."

"I will," Heather said.

As the trio of officials got to the door, Sanders stopped and looked back at Heather.

"Remember what the doctor said, no strenuous activity," Sanders said sarcastically.

"I heard," she shot back.

5

Heather walked back over to the couch and placed her hand on Cain's forehead. She then helped him take another sip of water and sat on the sofa across from him. About a half hour later the fuzziness began wearing off and he finally recognized the woman in his apartment. He started to ask more questions but Heather wanted to make sure he just took it easy the rest of the night. Cain continued to lay there, lethargic for the next couple of hours, as the two of them watched TV. Heather watched him fall asleep as the midnight hour approached. She went into the bedroom, grabbed a blanket off the bed, and placed it over him. She fell asleep on the sofa a short time later.

Cain woke up the next morning much more alert, the cloudiness seemingly gone from his head. He actually felt pretty good as he lay there looking up at the ceiling, waiting for the sleepiness to wear off. Something smelled pretty good, encouraging him to finally get up. He walked over to the kitchen to find Heather making breakfast.

"You can cook too, huh?" Cain asked, smiling.

"I've been known to cook a few things," she said, smiling back. "It's only eggs and bacon. It's kinda hard to mess that up."

"I've known people who could mess up peanut butter and jelly."

Heather let out a good laugh, "I'm sure you have."

"Smells really good," Cain admitted.

"Sit down. It's almost ready."

Cain sat at the table and noticed that Heather seemed to be wearing a man's shirt. Most likely his. He couldn't complain too much since it did look pretty good on her. It only covered a third of her thigh, but he certainly had no qualms about looking at her nicely tanned legs.

"Nice shirt," he blurted out. "Something looks familiar about it."

"Oh. Yeah. Sorry about that." She sheepishly smiled. "I wasn't planning on being here more than a few hours last night so I had no other clothes. Hope you don't mind."

"No, I don't mind. Can't say it doesn't look good on you. Probably looks better on you than me," he teased.

A wide smile overtook her face as she was pleased to hear him say something that sounded like he was attracted to her. She finished making breakfast and brought their plates over to the table.

"How are you feeling?" Heather asked.

"Pretty good right now."

"You gave me a pretty good scare last night."

He laughed. "Probably gave myself a bigger one."

"Do you have many of them?"

"That was the first one. Hopefully, it's the last."

"Do you know why it happened?"

"I was shot in the head," Cain said bluntly.

"Oh my God."

"Yeah."

"What happened?" she asked, putting her hand on his arm.

"I can't really say. I don't remember anything about it. One day I just woke up in an army hospital with a bandage on my head and people telling me how lucky I was to survive."

"I can't even imagine what it was like. You seem like everything is fine."

"For the most part, it is. I feel healthy. My memory is gone though. I can't remember anything about my past. Names, faces, dates... it's all gone. I can't tell you anything about where I've been or what I've done before I woke up in that hospital," Cain explained, his eyes swelling up with tears. He wiped his eyes with the sleeve of his shirt to prevent him from crying.

"That's terrible. I feel so bad for you," Heather said, gushing. "Isn't there anything you can do to get your memory back?"

"Not that I know of. They say it might just come back one day out of the blue," he replied. "Or it might never come back again."

"Can't they bring in a family member or something? I've heard seeing a familiar face sometimes jogs people's memories."

"There isn't anybody."

"Nobody?"

"Well, I saw my file, and it seems I'm all there is. Parents were killed and I have no other family to speak of."

"I'm so sorry," Heather said, rubbing his arm.

He gave her a warm smile that seemed to thank her for the comforting wishes without him saying a word. They continued talking as they ate, Heather feeling more connected to the man sitting next to her with each sentence he spoke. Even though she proclaimed she liked what she did, and the money was too good to pass up, she really yearned for a serious relationship. It was something she figured she'd never find in her line of work, at least not one worth having. She'd had a few boyfriends, but she knew they were mostly interested in her for the sex, and they thought it was cool to have a stripper for a girlfriend. Hardly the type of guys you brought home to mother. She could tell Cain was a different type of guy. One with standards and morals. That was obvious since he didn't ravage her the night before.

"What do you do for Sanders?" she asked.

"I don't think I'm supposed to tell you."

"Oh yeah. I forgot. Are you gonna be in New York for a while?"

"I don't know. I can live anywhere I want but I don't know where else I would go."

Cain got up from the table and put the dishes in the sink once the pair finished eating.

"That was really good, thank you. I really appreciate it."

"You're welcome. It was nice," Heather replied. "I enjoyed cooking for someone else for a change. Gets a little boring when you're only cooking for one all the time."

"That's surprising."

"Why is that surprising?"

"I dunno. I figured a girl like you would have guys banging down your door or begging at your feet to be with you," Cain surmised.

"A girl like me. You mean a stripper?" she asked without a hint of anger.

"No. I meant a girl as pretty as you."

"Oh. Well, there are plenty of guys banging down my door every day. But it doesn't mean anything. They're only after one thing."

"Sounds like you're not as into your profession as you made it seem last night."

"Well, I don't just go around talking about my feelings with everybody."

"Why are you talking about it now?" he asked.

"I don't know. I guess you're pretty easy to talk to," Heather admitted. "You're not like most guys I run into."

"I'll take that as a compliment."

"I meant it as one."

"So how long are you planning on staying? I mean, when do you have to get back to work or whatever?"

"Well, I told Sanders I'd stay for a couple of days to make sure you were OK," she said. "But if you don't want me to then I completely understand. I can leave whenever you want."

"It's fine."

"I can leave now. I'll just get dressed," she said as she got up from the table.

"Heather..."

"I mean, I really don't wanna feel like I'm imposing."

"Heather..."

"So, I'll just get dressed and then I'll be out of your hair."

"Heather..."

"I'll just tell Sanders you seem perfectly fine," she said nervously, not hearing anything Cain was saying.

"Heather," Cain yelled, finally succeeding in getting heard.

"What?"

"You can stay."

"I can?" she asked, surprised.

"Well, you already told Sanders you'd stay a couple days so you might as well. Plus, I'd like you to stay."

"You would?"

"Yeah. I mean, I told you I have memory issues. I forget how to cook," he joked.

A little sense of relief came over Heather as she never felt so comfortable and at ease with a man as she did with Cain. She was glad he wanted her to stay for a couple of days. She sauntered over to the couch in the living room, hoping to get a few lusty glances from him as she walked. Cain stood by the kitchen counter watching her every move. He couldn't remember much, but he was certain he hadn't seen legs that looked that nice in a long time. He sure didn't see anything like that in the army. He didn't feel right about having sex with her the minute he saw her but he felt no shame in undressing her with his eyes.

"I think you have one problem," he said.

"What's that?" she asked anxiously.

"If you're gonna be here a couple days, then I think you need your own clothes to wear. I mean, my shirt looks good on you but I don't think you can walk around the whole day like that."

"Don't bet on it."

Heather went to the bedroom and got dressed into her clothes from the night before. She came out about ten minutes later and told Cain she was going to her apartment to pack a few things.

"Want me to come with you?" Cain asked.

"Come with me? Why?" Heather asked, surprised by his request.

"Uh... I dunno. I thought maybe you'd need help or something."

"Umm, I think I should be OK."

She was a little reluctant at having Cain see her apartment. For the first time since she started stripping she seemed a little embarrassed about it. The only guys who'd been inside her apartment were guys she dated or paid for the privilege. For a few brief moments when they were talking at the table she felt like she was someone else. Like they were normal people just having a conversation and she kind of liked it. She'd hate for him to see her apartment and have the reality of her profession smack him in the face and change his opinion of her. She walked toward the door and thought about what might happen if he had another seizure while she was gone. She'd only be gone an hour or two but what if he had one and she wasn't there to help? What would Sanders say?

"I guess under the circumstances it'd be better off if you came with me," she reluctantly agreed. "I mean, with your seizures and all, I probably shouldn't leave you alone."

"Oh, yeah, you're probably right."

They took the elevator to the ground floor and walked out of the building. Almost immediately a beautiful blonde woman walked past them. She was rather tall with long hair and a striking figure. She gave Cain a slight smile. He was mesmerized by her and watched her walk past him. Heather noticed Cain continuing to watch the woman as she kept walking.

"I wish I'd gotten that kind of response from you last night," she deadpanned.

She expected some type of reply but he kept silent.

"I wasn't really serious," she said. "Most men would be falling over themselves if she walked past. I couldn't blame you."

After a minute, she realized she was basically talking to herself because he seemed like he was in another world. His head was still turned in that woman's direction though she was fading from view and barely noticeable at that point. Heather put her hand on his arm and shook it a little to try to break him from his trance. She shook it gently without success before putting a little more weight into it. It worked as he finally turned his head back to her. Heather was a little alarmed by the blank look that overtook his face.

"Are you OK?" she asked.

"Yeah, I'm fine."

"What's the matter? Don't remember seeing a pretty woman before?" she kidded.

"No. I mean, I saw something."

"What do you mean?"

"It was an image," Cain said.

"An image of what?"

"A woman."

"Well, she just walked by you, it's understandable. Most men would probably have the same image in their head."

"No, it wasn't of her. It was somebody else."

"Who?"

"I don't know. I just saw her face. She had blonde hair, a little past her shoulders, and a pretty face."

"What was she doing?"

"Nothing. It was just her face. Everything else around her was just white space. Like a picture of a face on the pages of a book and that's all there is."

Heather could tell he seemed troubled by this vision. He seemed genuinely disturbed by it.

"I feel like I should know who it is. Like she's connected to me somehow," he said.

"Maybe it was a high school girlfriend or something. Maybe a friend that you knew from before."

"Maybe."

Heather made sure that Cain was all right before they started walking toward her apartment. They could've taken a cab, but they decided to walk the half hour to her place. It'd give them some time to talk along the way. With each step they took they seemed to grow a little closer to each other. In another time and place Heather thought about how things might be different. Maybe they'd be holding hands or exchanging playful glances with each other. But she knew that at this point in time there was no chance of anything ever developing further. After a half hour of walking, sidestepping bustling people who seemed to be charging at them, they arrived at a nice looking building that stretched up fifteen floors.

"I'm impressed," Cain said.

"I told you I was paid well."

They went inside and went up to her apartment on the eleventh floor. Heather put the key in and unlocked it, taking a deep breath before opening the door, hoping he wouldn't change his opinion of her after seeing it. There was nothing unordinary about the place, nothing that anyone would associate with her profession like poles attached to the ceiling, furry handcuffs on the couch or kinky fetishes. But to her, it was a stripper's place, and she attached a stigma to it even if no one else did.

"Well, here it is," she said, walking in.

"Very nice. I like it," Cain replied, looking around the living room. "Not quite what I expected."

"Which was?"

"Well, I, uh, I was kind of half expecting some unflattering things to be out and about."

"Most people do," she said dejectedly.

"Well, I'm gonna go pack a few things. Sit down and make yourself at home if you want. Kitchen's over there if you want a drink or anything."

Cain sat on the black leather couch, shifting around into different positions to get a feel for it. It was so comfortable that he didn't want to sit on it for too long or else he probably wouldn't want to get up. He walked into the kitchen and opened the refrigerator to see what was available. He poured a couple glasses of orange juice for the two of them. Just as he finished pouring there was a loud knock on the door.

"You want me to get that?" Cain asked.

"No, no," Heather huffed, scurrying into the room. "I'll get it."

She turned him around and told him to wait in the kitchen. The loud knocking continued.

"Come on, Heather, let's go," a deep voice yelled from the other side.

"Coming," she replied.

Heather opened the door to reveal a large, bald man with a Fu Manchu. She took a deep sigh, obviously displeased to see the heavyset man before her.

"Hi, Tommy," she said.

"So, what's this about you not working tonight?" he asked as he pushed past her.

"Sure, come on in," she said sarcastically.

"Why aren't you working? You don't look sick."

"I just feel like taking a couple of days off, OK?"

"Boss doesn't think that's a good idea."

"I don't really care what he thinks. I'm taking a few days," Heather insisted.

"Maybe you just need a little something to pick you up."

Tommy took some drugs out of his pocket and placed them down on the coffee table. Heather looked at him curiously before glancing down at the table.

"I don't know what you think you're doing but take that stuff and get out of here," she said.

"What, you don't have time for some old friends?" he asked cheerfully.

"Please, just leave."

Cain was still in the kitchen, listening to the entire conversation, and was beginning to worry about his new friend. She didn't sound particularly pleased to have him in her apartment and he didn't appear to be leaving anytime soon. He assumed she asked him to stay in the kitchen because she didn't want him to get involved in it. With each passing second of Tommy's bullying, Cain grew wearier of his presence. Another minute elapsed and Cain had heard all he could stomach. He couldn't stand bullies, especially when it was a woman involved. He emerged from the kitchen to the surprise of Tommy, who smiled as he looked over to Heather.

"Got a little something happenin' on the side, Heather?" he asked.

"Shut up," she replied.

"I believe the lady would like you to go," Cain said.

"She ain't no lady. Listen, buddy, just go back in the kitchen and mind your business," Tommy warned. "And maybe I won't bust you up some."

Cain didn't feel at all threatened by the burly man and continued to walk in his direction. Heather quickly looked at both of the men before her and tried to diffuse the situation before it got out of hand.

"Tommy, please just go," Heather said.

She put her hand on Tommy's arm to persuade him to leave but he shoved it aside. Cain kept walking closer to his adversary, who also wasn't about to back down. He looked like he was in good shape but Tommy had been pitted against plenty of guys who were in good shape but couldn't take the power of his punches.

"I really don't want to have an altercation with you," Cain told him. "But the lady asked you to go several times. I do believe it's best if you take her advice."

Tommy simply laughed at Cain's suggestion. He felt the implied threat Cain was giving him was just some tough guy bravado, and he didn't have the stones to back it up. Cain, on the other hand, was ready to toss the meathead out the door. He wasn't itching to fight, but could tell that the bald bruiser in front of him wouldn't have it any other way. Heather tried one more time to separate the pair, but it was falling on deaf ears.

"Matthew, please don't," she said.

"I'm not doing anything. If he leaves then there's no problem," Cain replied.

Heather looked up at him and sighed knowing there was nothing else she could do. She worried that one of them was going to get seriously hurt. She was fearful of Cain getting injured, and though she didn't personally care for Tommy, she didn't want Cain to get in any kind of trouble for anything he might do. Just as she turned around to face Tommy once more, he shoved her out of the way, pushing her into the wall. That gave Tommy the distraction he needed to catch Cain by surprise. He stunned Cain with a couple of big right hands, causing Cain to stumble backwards. After Cain regained his composure, he blocked a couple of Tommy's blows, countering with a few of his own. Cain quickly got the upper hand using a combination of strikes and kicks to get Tommy off balance. Cain unleashed some moves that he didn't even know he had in his arsenal. Now Tommy was the one trying to stave off his attacker, albeit unsuccessfully. Using a combination of punches, MMA holds, and kickboxing maneuvers, Cain had Tommy in a world of hurt. A few minutes of brutality elapsed with Cain showing no mercy on the thug lying before him. He bounced Tommy's head off the floor a few times with his punches.

Heather shook off the pain from hitting her head against the wall and watched as Cain continued his assault. Tommy was bleeding profusely from his nostrils, along with the bridge of it, which by now was broken. Blood was pouring out of cuts from above his right eye and both sides of his mouth. He coughed up a few teeth and was certain to lose consciousness any minute. Cain was showing no mercy and Heather was getting concerned about the carnage she was witnessing.

"Cain, stop!"

It was no use. She yelled a few more times for him to stop but he didn't hear a word of it. He was in such a zone that he had blocked everything out. There could've been trumpets playing behind him and he wouldn't have heard a single note. Heather worried that Cain was going to kill Tommy unless she stopped him. She was a little afraid of getting in the way and possibly catching some of Cain's wrath but felt she had no other choice. She raced in between the two men, catching hold of Cain's right arm in the process.

"Stop," she told him.

Cain immediately snapped out of whatever trance he was in, noticing the concerned look on her face. He released his curled up fist and dropped his arm, signaling the end of his confrontation. He slowly backed away, his face showing remorse for the amount of pain he just inflicted. He walked over to the window and reflected on what he'd just done. He was reminded of it by the blood stained on his knuckles. He was sure that Heather would think he was a monster now, and he wasn't sure if she'd be wrong. He realized he took it too far.

Heather had taken the next few minutes to get Tommy somewhat stable and help him back on his feet. She was sure he had some broken bones and probably a concussion. She wasn't really as concerned about his well-being since he was a major jerk, but didn't want anyone dying because of her. As soon as he was able to stand on his feet, she hurried him to the door to prevent any other problems. Not that Tommy was looking for anything since he now knew that his opponent could easily have killed him and was not close to being a match for him.

"You can consider yourself done," Tommy painfully whispered. "You'll never work again in this town as long as I can help it."

"Just go," Heather replied, shoving him out the door.

She knew he wasn't just giving an idle threat. He was connected to all the owners of the major clubs and would badmouth her to the point where she'd have to work in run down joints that hardly paid anything of substance. She closed the door behind him and sighed heavily as she wondered what she'd do now. Cain turned around to face her, somewhat shamefully, as he waited for her to snap at him. She looked at him a little differently now, seeing what was inside him, as opposed to just half an hour before that when it didn't seem like he was capable of such a vicious beating. Neither person said a word, both waiting for the other to start the conversation, as Heather slowly walked to the couch. She sat down, still not quite believing what she just witnessed. Cain could see the hesitation she now had with him and attempted to alleviate her fears.

"I, uh," he started. "I apologize."

Heather didn't respond. She wanted to, but just didn't know what to say. She leaned on her side, with her hand on her head, her arm being supported by the couch. She looked at him and could see how remorseful he was. He didn't look like a man who was proud of what he'd just done.

"If you're having second thoughts about anything, you don't have to worry," Cain said. "I'll let Sanders know I told you to stay away. He won't give you any problems."

"Sanders is the least of my problems now," she said with a laugh. "Tommy was right. He knows all the major players in this town. He'll make sure I don't work again. Looks like I'm unemployed now."

"I truly am sorry."

Cain was certain Heather didn't want to be near him anymore and started to make his way toward the door.

"Hey," Heather shouted.

"Yeah?" Cain replied, turning around.

"I really wasn't worried about him. I was worried about you."

"I wasn't in any danger."

"I know. That's what I was worried about. You made it look so easy."

Cain nodded and turned back around to head for the door. He put his hand on the knob before Heather stopped him again.

"Where are you going?" she asked.

"Back to my place."

"Aren't you forgetting something?"

"Like what?"

"Like me."

"You still..." Cain started to say.

"I'm not afraid of you," she responded, trying to calm his fears. "I know you were only trying to protect me. And I really am thankful and grateful for that."

Cain nodded in reply, not wanting to actually say words in response.

"The fact is that nobody's ever defended me like that before, or at all really," she stated. "It felt kind of good that you were there to protect me. I just got kind of scared at how far you were taking it."

"I guess once I got caught up in things..." Heather interrupted him before he could complete his thought.

"It's OK. You don't have to explain anything. Really, you don't."

"OK," he relented.

"I guess I saw what makes you so valuable to Sanders, huh?"

"I guess so."

"Where'd you learn all those moves?" she asked.

"To be honest, I have no idea. An hour ago I didn't even realize I could do some of those things."

"Well, just give me a few more minutes to pack and I'll be all ready," she said.

Heather went back into the bedroom to finish up as Cain sat down to wait for her. A few minutes later she emerged with a rolling suitcase and a duffel bag. As they left the apartment Heather wondered if she'd ever come back to it. She really didn't have many ties to it and intentionally kept the place devoid of too many personal items. They kept talking once they were in the cab as they drove back to Cain's apartment.

Heather sighed. "I hate all the traffic in this city."

"Isn't this normal?"

"Yeah, I suppose so. The Rangers play tonight so it's gonna be even worse since it's a playoff game."

"Oh."

"You like hockey?"

"Who? Me? I love hockey," Cain said. "That's a silly question. Why would you even ask that?"

"Have you even watched a game before?"

"Seriously? I feel a little insulted now," he joked. "Questioning my hockey knowledge."

"When was the last game you went to?" Heather insisted.

"Uh, well, you know, it's been a while."

"Who played?" she asked, smiling.

"It was, uh... the Rangers," he paused. "And the... Devils. The Devils, that's right."

"You have no idea, do you?"

"Well, you know... I have that whole memory thing going on right now."

They both looked at each other and burst out laughing.

"We should go to a game sometime," Heather said.

"Yeah. I'd like that."

Once they got back to Cain's apartment, Heather put some of her things away. Once she finished she went into the living room, sitting on a chair. Cain still felt bad about what transpired at her apartment and wondered what he could do to make it up to her.

"You know, I was thinking that maybe it's a good idea if you didn't go back to your apartment for a little while," Cain said.

"Why?"

"I dunno. Just in case your friends come back around for some reason. I'd feel better if you didn't go back."

"Where am I supposed to go?" she asked.

"Well, you could stay here for a few weeks."

"That's really nice of you... but I couldn't impose on you like that."

"You're not imposing. I'd like you to stay. Besides, it's kind of my fault about what happened. I wouldn't want to worry about you staying there by yourself."

"You'd worry about me?" Heather asked, a little amazed.

"Yeah. I would."

"Well, I guess I could stay a couple weeks. I mean, just until I get a new job and find a new place. Luckily I only have two months to go on the lease so I'm not losing out too much."

"So, if you can't keep, uh, doing what you're doing," Cain started, "then what're you gonna do? Move somewhere else?"

"I don't know. Maybe. Or maybe I'll actually try to find a real job. It's kinda scary not having a job."

"Well, like I said, you can stay here as long as it takes."

6

S anders was in a meeting with his five deputy directors going over new files and information on possible targets. Every week they went over pertinent information about new targets or anything that was learned about targets they were actively seeking. Each director had a touch screen computer embedded in the oval table at his location, to which the information could be transferred and seen by everybody via a screen on the wall. Each deputy director was in charge of a different region which included North and South America, Europe, Asia, and Africa. Tim Wells, Deputy Director of South America passed a file over to Sanders and began going over the information, using the computer at his location.

"Mario Contreras," Wells began, as Contreras' name and picture popped up on the screen. "He's a guy who first popped up on our radar several months ago."

Also appearing on the screen was his list of offenses, physical description, marks or scars, aliases, and photos.

"This outstanding citizen is a Honduran national who was one of three men involved in the kidnapping, rape, and murder of a six-year-old girl in New York seven years ago. He was 23 at the time. It was planned as a ransom that went bad. The other two men were captured, sentenced, and are currently serving time in federal prison. Contreras, however, managed to avoid capture and disappeared without a trace. It was assumed he went back to South America, probably back to Honduras, though there was never any evidence to suggest that was so. Until last week," Wells continued, waiting for the photos on the screen to load. "These pictures were taken of Contreras in Honduras in the city of San Pedro Sula."

"What's the FBI's take on it, Tim?" Sanders asked.

"He was on their top ten for two years but they have no leads on him and he's seemingly falling off their radar. They have other fish to fry."

"Makes him a good target for us," Sanders mused.

"I was thinking it might make a good first assignment for Cain," Wells stated.

Sanders stared at the screen, only taking his eyes off it to look at Wells momentarily, his fingers stroking his chin, deep in thought.

"I agree," Sanders finally said. "Hand the file over to Shelly and have her work out the details with Cain."

"Right."

"What else you got?"

Wells spent the next half hour going over various forms of information he'd received, not all of it deemed reliable or anything that could be acted upon soon. Anything that was agreed on to be relevant was saved for future use so they could acquire more information or scheduled to be handed out to a handler. Once the meeting ended, Wells went back to his office and emailed the entire contents of the Contreras file to Shelly Lawson. All handlers got automatic text messages when they received emails so any new information or cases were handled promptly.

Lawson was in a small coffee shop when she got the text alerting her to a new email. She was going over logistics of a mission of another agent when she logged onto her tablet to check the email's contents. As an agency, Contreras was usually not the kind of target that they went after. He was not a threat to the safety and security of the United States, which was their primary goal. But he was the perpetrator of a major crime that escaped punishment, which they sometimes decided worthy of pursuing if time allowed and it could be done quickly. They also usually picked these cases for new agents to get them acclimated to the agency and how things were done. Lawson began working immediately on the file and quickly engulfed herself on the contents. While working on it she decided to give Cain a heads up to let him know a mission was coming his way so he could start mentally preparing for it. She took her phone out of her purse and dialed his number.

"How you feeling?" Lawson asked.

"OK, I guess."

"Getting tired and bored of sitting there?"

"A little bit," he replied.

"Well, looks like that'll be ending soon."

"Why's that?"

"You're being given a mission."

"Where?"

"Honduras," she said.

"What's the target?"

"I'll go over everything with you tomorrow. Come into the Center at ten o'clock and I'll give you the details. I'm still working things out right now."

"I'll be there."

Cain walked into the Center at 9:55, greeting the reception- ist, before swiping his card to go through the door located in the back. He was greeted by Lawson.

"Anxious or excited?" she asked.

"Neither, really," Cain solemnly said.

They took the elevator up to the fourth floor to go to Lawson's office. Almost all offices in the building were surrounded by glass except for the director, deputy directors, and offices used for special purposes such as interviewing or interrogation. They sat down at her desk and she handed him copies of all the information she had about the case. Cain opened the folder and started reading the file.

"When do I leave?" Cain asked.

"Tomorrow. Your plane ticket's in there."

Cain looked in the back of the folder and took the ticket out, holding it up, looking at both sides of it. He looked somewhat confused.

"There's no return ticket?" he asked.

"It's up to you to purchase one to get back once the mission's been completed. We don't like to rush our agents into making decisions that aren't in their best interests just so they can catch a plane. Take your time to do it right and come back when you're done. You'll fly down to Miami from JFK here in New York and take a connecting flight to Honduras from there on American Airlines. Your flight from JFK is 2:00pm on Monday. Should take a little over six hours to get there. With the two- hour time difference you should be there around seven."

"What do you want me to do when I get him?"

"Eliminate him. He's not to be taken, captured, or transported. We only work one way."

"Dead," Cain said.

"Other agencies worry about capturing and all that stuff."

"Too much red tape?"

"Take him out and it's done. That simple."

"How will I know where to find Contreras?"

"You'll be flying into the Ramon Villeda Morales International Airport, which is about seven miles outside of San Pedro Sula. Once you arrive, you'll be greeted by a man named Javier Ruiz. He'll update you on the situation when you arrive."

"Why not just have this Ruiz take care of it then if he's already there?" Cain asked.

"Because he's not trained to eliminate targets. He lives and works there and feeds us information. We can't have locals doing the jobs themselves and risk compromising them," Lawson said.

"Is this Ruiz trustworthy?"

"Very. We've worked with him before. He's very reliable. There are absolutely no issues with that. Once you arrive, Ruiz will supply you with whatever weapons you need."

"I'm going unarmed?"

"While it is possible to get a gun through security, there's no need to take risks when you can be supplied with one as soon as you touch ground. But I do suggest obtaining a weapon be your first priority once you arrive."

"Why's that?"

"Because Honduras has the highest murder rate in the world and is one of the poorest countries in Latin America.

Crime is widespread and foreigners are deemed to be wealthy and frequently targeted. In the last 17 years there have been 113 U.S. citizens murdered there with only 29 resolved cases. There are roughly three murders in that city alone every day. Be aware of driving at night as carjacking is prevalent, as well as crimes of opportunity."

"Great. I'm excited already," Cain deadpanned.

"Contreras has been seen in the tourist city of San Pedro Sula which has seen armed robberies against cars traveling from the airport, most likely on tips received from someone working at the airport. Several citizens have been murdered shortly after arriving so it's quite possible you'll be targeted as soon as you arrive."

"And I'm not going armed?" Cain asked sarcastically.

"You'll be fine. Don't worry," Lawson replied.

"Oh, yeah, can't see any reason why I wouldn't be."

"Also, don't drink the water."

"And I thought that was just a bad punchline."

"They lack the substantial infrastructure to maintain water purity so only buy bottled water," she continued. "I also wouldn't eat any raw fish, fruit, or vegetables."

"Right."

"Hot foods, fresh bread, coffee, tea, beer, and dry food like crackers are usually fine to eat."

"Well, that's encouraging."

"Assuming you don't get them from street vendors," she said, smiling.

"Wow, this is a regular vacation destination."

"Remember, the sooner you get it done, the sooner you get home."

"These are the photos of Contreras that were taken of him

last week," Lawson said, putting them down on the desk. "And just in case you have second thoughts about killing him, this is the photo of the little girl he raped and killed."

Cain stared at Lawson for a few seconds before putting his eyes on the picture of the little girl. He picked the photo up, and focused on it, her image burned into his mind.

"It'll be done," Cain stated plainly.

After leaving the Center, Cain went back to his apartment. Heather was already in the kitchen preparing lunch for them.

"You know, I was thinking about getting tickets for the Rangers game on Tuesday. What do you think?" Heather asked.

"Umm... I'm gonna have to take a rain check on it," he regretfully replied. "I'm going out of town for a few days."

"Oh," she said, a hint of disappointment showing in her voice. "For your work?"

"Yeah."

"Where are you going?"

"I can't really say. It shouldn't take long though. I should be back in a couple days."

"OK. Well, I hope you have a good trip."

Cain sat down at the table as Heather continued making their lunch. She brought over a couple of turkey sandwiches, chips, and sodas for the both of them.

"So, when are you leaving?" Heather asked.

"Monday."

They ate in silence for a few minutes, neither able to figure out the right words to say. Cain could tell she seemed uneasy about something, though he wasn't sure what it was.

"Are you gonna be OK here by yourself for a few days?" Cain asked.

"Yeah, I'll be fine."

"Are you sure? Because I could try to get someone to come stay with you while I'm gone."

"Really? You're acting like I'm in witness protection or something. I've been living on my own for a few years now. I think I'll be fine a few days without you."

"Sorry. I guess I've got that whole protecting thing going on," he said.

"It's OK. It's cute. Besides, you leaving will help me out, anyway."

"How's that?"

"I won't have to look after you," she kidded. "I'll be able to spend a lot of time job hunting. I'll just check out Monster and some other job sites. Hopefully, I'll find a few things."

"I'm sure you will. At least you have a degree. That'll help."

"Yeah, but the gap on my resume won't help too much."

"What gap?" Cain asked.

"Well, I don't think that putting down stripping and other extracurricular activities on my resume will do much for my job chances."

"I see your point."

"I thought you might."

"Then don't put that down," Cain said.

"I have to put down something. If I don't, they're gonna ask what I've been doing the last few years."

"How about you just put down you had your own business?"

"My own business?" Heather asked.

"Well, it kinda is, isn't it?"

"And just what kind of business have I been running?"

He smiled. "Entertainment."

They spent a couple of days polishing up Heather's resume.

It'd been several years since she sent a resume out to anyone so she was grateful for his help. Cain enjoyed helping her even if he wasn't sure he was doing much good. He'd been in the army since graduating high school so he was fairly certain he'd never written one himself. The rest of the weekend they spent just trying to get to know each other. Cain was intrigued by the life of the beautiful woman he was now sharing an apartment with. Another place and time he might've made a move on her but he didn't think it was the appropriate time to do that. At least not until he was more certain of how his life as an agent would be. He knew there was going to be a good amount of travel involved and wasn't sure it'd be fair to make someone wait for him, not knowing when he'd be coming home.

Heather tried grilling Cain on his past to get a better idea of his life but he didn't divulge much. Not because he didn't want to but because he had no answers. He really didn't know what he liked or things he tried before. He tried to deflect most of her questions to avoid making it seem like he was trying to hide something from her.

The morning that Cain was supposed to leave on his trip he got up early, not able to sleep. He tossed and turned most of the night thinking about what it might be like. A lot of thoughts crossed his mind, knowing full well that it probably wouldn't be like anything he had envisioned. He tried to eat breakfast but only had a few bites as his stomach was too nervous to put any food into it. Cain was trying not to make too much noise so he wouldn't wake Heather, but she eventually walked out from the bedroom, anyway.

"I'm sorry," Cain said, noticing her standing in the door.

"For what?"

"Waking you up. I was trying to be quiet."

"No, it wasn't you. I just had to go to the bathroom and noticed that you were up," she said.

"Oh."

"I guess you're leaving soon?"

"Yeah, in a few minutes," Cain replied.

"I figured so. I'll make sure everything's good here."

"Oh, I know you will. I don't have any worries about it."

"Good," she said.

"Well, I should be going."

"You take care of yourself."

"I will."

Heather walked closer to him, trying to get a read on the situation. She really wanted to give him a hug but wasn't sure if he would push her away. She decided to go for it and awkwardly put her arms around him, barely touching each other. She wasn't sure what it was about Cain that made her so careful about both of their feelings as she'd never acted so gingerly around a man before. Maybe it was because of her past that she wanted to become a different person. Part of that transformation would include being more sensitive to her feelings. Heather assumed that when Cain looked at her, he still saw a stripper and she'd have to work at changing that perception. She knew that wouldn't happen overnight and that it'd take time. It would also take her being patient and not trying to force him into wanting her. She realized that if she tried to force herself onto him that it might make him think twice about her and back away. If she was ever able to get him to look past her background, it'd have to be a realization that came to him on his own.

7

Cain was walking through the Ramon Villeda Morales International Airport looking for the rendezvous point. He was instructed to meet his contact at a table in front of a Wendy's. Ruiz would be wearing a black New York Yankees baseball hat. It only took a few minutes before Cain located him. Ruiz was eating a Baconator as Cain approached. Cain sat across from him as Ruiz grabbed a napkin to get the grease off his hand, shaking Cain's as they introduced themselves.

"Ruiz?"

"Mr. Cain, pleasure to meet you," Ruiz replied.

"Your English is better than I anticipated."

"I speak it fluently. I owe it all to Rosetta Stone. Whoever made that program is a genius. I also speak French, Spanish, Russian, and German. Right now, I am studying Chinese."

"That's impressive. I still struggle with English," Cain joked.

"Can I get you something?"

"No. Thank you."

"Have you done this before?" Ruiz asked.

Cain stared at him momentarily, wondering if he should be truthful or lie about his experience. He didn't know the man sitting across from him, or know if his answer would make a difference in his help.

"This is my first assignment," Cain said.

Cain figured it was best to just be truthful. The agency trusted Ruiz, so he had no reason to doubt them. He looked around, surveying the airport, as Ruiz finished his dinner.

"You will do fine. I have good instincts for these things," Ruiz said.

"I believe you have some information for me," Cain said.

Ruiz nodded as he finished chewing. "I do. I have a rental car for you outside. I have the information you need in there."

"Good."

Cain followed Ruiz through the airport as they made their way to the car. Once inside Ruiz handed Cain a black duffel bag. Cain opened it, finding a file folder, as well as a sniper rifle and a Glock pistol. Cain began looking through the folder as Ruiz started driving.

"Where are we going first?" Cain asked.

"I'll take you to your hotel. You have a very nice room at the Hilton Princess. This way you can relax tonight after your journey plus map out your strategy."

"Very nice."

They'd been driving for about ten minutes on the highway when Ruiz spotted a white car following them.

"Get ready, my friend," Ruiz said.

"Why? What's going on?"

"I think we're about to have company."

The white car sped around them, then slowed down in front of them as a maroon-colored car took position behind them.

"We're being boxed in," Cain said.

"They most likely just want money."

The three cars slowly drifted to the side of the road, all of them eventually coming to a stop. Cain reached into the bag, slowly removing the Glock and putting it down by his side to conceal it. Cain's heart was racing as he waited for their visitors to make their move. He started sweating, anxious and nervous, hoping he'd make the right move. Two men got out of the car in front of them and started walking back to them. Cain noticed they both were carrying a gun in their hands. He checked the rearview mirror and saw two more getting out of the car behind them. They also had guns and started walking toward the rental. Cain put his finger on the trigger as he waited for the right moment. Two men stood near the bumper of their car as the other two stood by the driver and passenger side windows.

"Money," said the one by Ruiz.

Ruiz turned his head to look at Cain, not sure if he should comply with the demands or wait for Cain to make his move. Cain suddenly raised his pistol to the man by his window, blowing a hole through the man's chest. He then spun around and fired a shot past Ruiz, surprising their attacker before he could respond, fatally hitting him in the chest. Cain opened his door, jumping out onto the ground, firing a couple more shots. His target dropped to the ground, writhing in pain, the bullets lodging in his thigh and stomach. The other man ran back to the maroon car and sped off. Cain jumped up and steadied his aim as the man drove past. He was ready to fire but didn't have a clear shot and let him go. He walked closer to the wounded man on the ground to check on his status. He wasn't sure if the wounds were life threatening but Cain was beyond angry and the rush he felt overtook him. He aimed his gun at the man's chest and pulled the trigger, quickly ending the man's pain. Cain retreated back to the car, eager to move before police or witnesses showed up. As soon as he got in, Ruiz sped away.

"That was amazing," an overexcited Ruiz said. "Oh my goodness. Any doubts I had before are all gone now, my friend."

"Nice," Cain replied, putting the gun back in the bag. He sighed, amazed himself over what he'd just done.

They had a nice, quiet drive the rest of the way to the hotel. Ruiz grabbed Cain's luggage as Cain carried the duffel bag inside. He was led up to his executive room, Cain impressed at how lavish it looked. It was a very spacious room with a king-sized bed and marble bathroom. The men put Cain's bags down on the bed, Cain then checking out the view from the double wide windows.

"So, how'd you get involved in all this?" Cain asked.

"Me? It's a long story."

"I hope you get paid well."

"I do get paid well. But money is only secondary for me. It is not the reason I do this," Ruiz said.

"What is?"

Ruiz sat on the bed and took his hat off as he thought about the events that led him to this moment. He was a middle-aged man, probably in his late forties, who was bearing some emotional scars. The pain was evident on his face.

"It was about twelve years ago. One day I get a phone call from the police. They tell me my 16-year-old daughter had been raped and murdered. They had no suspects and no leads. The killers went free," Ruiz said.

"I'm sorry for your loss."

"I started trying to find out on my own but I got nowhere. No one would talk to me and everywhere I went the information got cold. Then one day I learned there were U.S. officials in the area on business. I went to them for help but they all refused. All except for one. He was a CIA officer and agreed to look into it. One week later he informed me he found my daughter's killer. It turned out to be a police official's son, and they were covering up the incident. He then contacted officials in our government and her killer was brought to justice. He was eventually executed for his crime. I owed this man for what he had done for me."

"I'm sure it wasn't easy for you and your wife," Cain said.

"I have no wife. We were eighteen when we had Maira. We were very young. She did not even want the baby once we found out. But, luckily, I convinced her that it was the right thing; even if she did not want the child that I would raise the baby on my own. She agreed. She stayed for a few months after Maira was born. One night while we slept she left, never to return."

"That's pretty tough."

"I shed no tears. She didn't want to be a mother, and it was best that she left before Maira grew up to see the person that she was."

"Well, sorry to hear it," Cain said, sympathizing. "Still, lucky for you that CIA officer showed up."

"Yes. You will enjoy working for him. He is a good man."

"I will? Who are you talking about?"

"Ed Sanders, of course," Ruiz said. "He is now your employer, is he not?"

"He is," Cain said.

"Several years later he contacted me once more asking to work with him again and he would pay me for my services. But payment is not what makes me do this. What makes me do this is justice. Bad men paying the price for their sins is what I do this for."

"I understand. Is this all that you do?"

"I have my own business. We export products such as coffee and cigars. I do not get wealthy off this but we make a profit. Along with what I get paid from your people, I do all right for myself."

Ruiz watched Cain as he continued looking out the window, trying to analyze him.

"You seem different than previous men I have worked with."

"How's that?" Cain asked.

"I am not sure yet. There is just something different with you."

"Well, when you figure it out, you let me know."

"I will do that," Ruiz said. "Now, let's get down to business."

Ruiz got the folder out of the duffel bag and took it over to the large desk against the wall. Cain walked over and sat down, examining the contents of the folder. There were pictures of Contreras in different spots around town over the previous two weeks along with information on where he'd been visiting.

"Who are some of these men he's been seen with?" Cain asked.

"I have not been able to capture the identities of these men. It is a mystery to this point."

Contreras had been photographed having discussions with

several different men. Ruiz thought these men looked like they were European. These were new pictures that Cain hadn't been shown before.

"What would he be doing meeting with Europeans?" Cain asked.

"That is the question," Ruiz said. "When will you go after him?"

"I'll start looking for him tomorrow."

"Then you will most likely find him."

"Why's that?"

"The last few weeks I have observed him eating lunch at Applebee's three days a week. Always arrives between twelve and one."

"Seriously? Applebee's?"

"What is wrong?"

"I just wouldn't picture a criminal from Honduras being addicted to an American restaurant chain."

"Yes, well, I suppose he enjoys the hamburgers, perhaps?"

"I guess so."

"He usually eats on the patio so that should give you a good visual on him."

They talked for the next hour about their target, discussing all the places Contreras had been. He was seen at Central Park, City Mall, The Francisco Saybe Theatre, The Old Train Station, and the San Pedro Sula Cathedral. All were within two miles of his hotel. They reviewed the dates and times, as well as who he met with, to see if there were any patterns. Almost all of the meetings he had occurred between twelve and four and none appeared to be with locals. Everyone Contreras met with was a foreigner. Cain and Ruiz finalized their plans before Ruiz left for the evening.

"Meet me for lunch at Applebee's tomorrow?" Cain asked.

"You think that's wise for us to be there with him?"

"Well, if he's by himself, it won't matter after a few minutes," Cain said. "And if he's with someone else, then I want to see who it is. Plus, we'll blend right in. I'll stand out more if I'm by myself. They don't know who we are, anyway."

A few minutes after Ruiz left the hotel, Cain called Lawson to update her on the developments.

"How's it going so far?" she asked.

"Fantastic. Killed three men so far."

"What?!"

"And the day's not even over yet."

"What happened?"

"They tried to hijack us on the way to the hotel."

"Are you in trouble?" she asked.

"No. No witnesses."

"Good. What else can I do for you?"

"I've got some pictures of Contreras meeting with a few people," Cain said.

"Send them over to me and I'll have them analyzed."

"Sending them now."

"I'll call you back in an hour or two."

Cain took photos of the pictures and uploaded them to his computer, then sent them to Lawson. He decided to lay down on the bed while he waited for a return call just to relax since he was still pretty jacked up from all the commotion in getting there. He closed his eyes and re-lived every second of the killings, from the moment he pulled the gun out of the duffel bag, waiting for his would-be victims. He surprised himself at how easily it came to him. There was no hesitation in his actions. He then imagined what it would be like killing Contreras. He envisioned Contreras sitting down to eat, Cain looking on from a distance in some window, then watching him drop to the ground after he pulled the trigger. Cain somehow stopped thinking of the gruesome images for a few minutes and dozed off. He was awakened two hours later by the ringer of his cell phone going off. It was Lawson.

"Hey," Cain answered.

"We've run some analysis on the three men in your photos."

"And?"

"We came up empty. We checked all our databases, ran them through our facial recognition software, and contacted a few people who might be in the know. Everything came back negative. Which means they're either insignificant players or they're low level guys, meeting with Contreras on someone else's behalf."

"So, do I still take him out?"

"Yes, but follow him for a couple of days. See if he meets with anyone else first. Him meeting with foreigners could indicate he's on the verge of something we aren't aware of and we'd like to know what that is if possible. Take pictures of anyone else he comes in contact with."

"OK. Will do."

Cain closed his eyes again, hoping to fall asleep quickly, knowing he could have an action-packed itinerary the following day. He turned his head from side to side as strange images started appearing. The blonde-haired woman from before popped up again. The first few images were like before, just her head floating around as if it were trapped in a television screen. Then her whole body appeared, wearing a red dress, walking down a busy street. She kept turning back as if she were looking for him. She then ducked into a store where he lost track of her. He opened his eyes, wiped the sweat off his forehead, and sat up in bed. He knew this woman must've been important to him at some point in his life. It couldn't have been just some random person he kept imagining. Cain took a few seconds to clear his head before lying back down. This time his mind was clear, and he fell asleep within a few minutes, no visions clouding his head.

8

Cain woke up early the next morning, around six o'clock, and immediately called for room service. He ate fairly quickly and decided to take a walk around, seeing some of the sights for himself. He grabbed the Glock pistol and tucked it in the back of his belt before leaving his room. He walked to each of the places Contreras had been seen to get an idea of his sight lines. At each location, he carefully looked around to see where he'd be able to set up shop as well as where he could position himself depending on where Contreras was. Cain spent the good part of the morning scouting out those locations, but he also walked around the area, just to see if there were any other spots he would be able to bury himself in. Once he saw it was eleven o'clock, he walked over to the Applebee's and waited for Ruiz to show up. He figured it was better to show up early in the event Contreras didn't stop by at his usual time. Cain grabbed one of the tables at the back of the patio, giving him a good observation point to see every other table out there. Ruiz came by five minutes to noon, still wearing his Yankees hat.

"You wear that everywhere you go?" Cain kidded.

"It's my good luck hat."

"I hope it is."

They sat and talked for a few minutes, waiting and hoping for Contreras to show his face. Cain was genuinely interested in the Honduran culture and what it was like to live there.

"This is a great place to be," Ruiz said. "Beautiful weather, good people, excellent food."

"Lots of murder."

"You are right, unfortunately, there is very high murder rate here. But is that so much unlike any of your American big cities like New York or Los Angeles? Crime is widespread in this world no matter the location. That is why we must not fail in our work here. To protect our children and make it safer for them."

"I suppose you're right."

Luckily for them their wait didn't last very long. Twenty minutes after twelve, Contreras walked into the restaurant, getting a table a couple rows in front of the American and his companion. With his sunglasses still on, Cain turned his head slightly to give the appearance he was looking elsewhere, but still kept his eyes glued to Contreras' table. Contreras appeared to be eating alone at first, as he ordered his food, but ten minutes later his company arrived. Two men sat at the table and also ordered food. They brought a briefcase and set it down in front of them. They took out some papers and handed them to Contreras who studied them carefully, occasionally stopping to take a drink. Cain could see Contreras' head nodding, without saying anything, appearing to like what he was reading.

Cain took out his cell phone and pretended to be texting, carefully positioning the phone to get a good picture of the three men seated in front of him. He was able to get a few pictures of the unknown individuals, a full face shot of the one, and a side shot of the other. Contreras had his back to the camera, but he was not important since he was already known. Cain sent the images to Shelly Lawson, letting her know the meeting was taking place right at that moment.

"Will analyze immediately," Lawson texted back. "Stay with them."

"Will do," Cain responded.

Cain and Ruiz kept talking as they ate their lunch, making it appear they were just regular people. Cain continued keeping an eye on the Contreras table in the process. Contreras was doing a lot of talking, and moving his hands around frequently, making it seem like he was incensed about something. Unfortunately, Cain wasn't good at lip reading, and couldn't even make a guess at what was being discussed. The other two men appeared to be staying calm, and not saying a whole lot, making it seem like maybe it was just something Contreras was passionate talking about. Cain did notice that the one man seemed to do most of the talking for the pair when they did speak, his partner mostly listening and looking around occasionally. As Cain studied the man, he came to the conclusion that he must've been a bodyguard. He figured someone in a higher authority would've had more to say. The fact he kept looking around made it seem like he was keeping an eye out for trouble. Both parties stayed at their tables until a little after one. Contreras concluded his meeting by shaking the hands of both his visitors, who left their briefcase behind as they walked away from the table.

"Should we follow them?" Ruiz asked.

"No. My target is Contreras," Cain replied. "Seems like something's going on, but we don't know who they are yet. Could be nobody."

"You are right, of course."

The briefcase changed Cain's plans slightly. Before, he was planning on killing Contreras with a sniper rifle. Now, he was thinking about what might be in that briefcase. If he took Contreras out up close, he could quickly snatch the briefcase. If he killed him from afar, he likely wouldn't have time to take it with onlookers and police converging on the dead body.

"Are you going to do it now?" Ruiz asked.

"Too many witnesses here."

About ten minutes later Contreras paid his bill and left the restaurant, briefcase in hand. Cain and Ruiz followed him out the door, watching him get into the back seat of a car, which then drove off.

"Damn," Cain said.

"What is wrong?"

"I walked here."

"We can take my car," Ruiz offered.

They raced over to his car and followed Contreras. It was a short chase as the Contreras car stopped a few minutes later in front of a cathedral. Contreras got out with his briefcase and walked inside. Ruiz parked his car in front as Cain debated going inside as well. He decided to wait until Contreras returned before either killing him or continuing following him. A half hour passed with no sign of Contreras, causing Cain to get a little worried that he knew he was being followed and ducked out somewhere. His driver was still parked in front, though, so Cain thought maybe Contreras was having another meeting inside with someone. It'd be a perfect place to have a meeting without having wandering eyes looking down at them. Patience wasn't Cain's strongest attribute, and he'd just about exhausted however much he had of it. He told Ruiz to wait for him to get back and exited the car.

Cain entered the cathedral and looked around, trying to spot Contreras. He started walking along the wall, spotting Contreras a few rows near the back, on the right-hand side near the end of a pew. He was sitting by himself, his head looking down, seeming to be in prayer. Cain quietly walked toward him, hoping he wouldn't notice him coming. He walked into the pew behind Contreras, sliding to the end, sitting directly behind him. Contreras, feeling the presence of someone behind him, slowly picked his head up.

"What can I do for you?" Contreras asked.

"There's not a thing you can do for me."

"Then why are you here? For the prayers?"

"I'm like a courier. Just here to deliver a message," Cain said.

"I'm listening."

"Where's the briefcase?" Cain asked, not seeing it next to Contreras.

"I don't see how that's of any importance to you."

"Who were you just meeting with?"

"Once again, I don't see how that is important to you."

"Well, in the grand scheme of things it really doesn't matter 'cause it's not gonna change your fate."

"Which is what?"

"You're dead."

"If you're planning to kill me, you could at least tell me why or who sent you," Contreras said, trying to buy time to think of a way out of his situation.

"There was a little girl in New York a few years ago that you sent to an early grave," Cain said.

"This is about that?" Contreras responded with a laugh. "Please, tell me how much they are paying you to do this and I'll double it for you to walk away. I'll put you on my payroll as we speak. I have big plans coming."

"No thanks."

Cain withdrew his gun from his belt, ready to put an end to Contreras' life. Just as he started to raise the pistol, Contreras slumped forward, part of his head exploding, pieces flying everywhere. Blood splattered onto Cain, who ducked for cover. Whoever killed him used a silencer since there was no sound from the shot being fired. Cain peeked over the pew, looking for the man who took out his target. He carefully raised his head above the pew, not wanting to expose himself too much in case the shooter intended to take him out as well. After being stationary for a minute, Cain assumed the shooter already left, and he raced toward the door. He wanted to quickly get out of there before police arrived.

As soon as Cain went through the door, he noticed a man getting out of the passenger side of Contreras' car. The man was holding a brown briefcase which looked like the same one Contreras had in his possession. He was a white man, about average height, short brown hair, and had a goatee. Once the man closed the car door, he looked around and noticed Cain standing at the cathedral's doors. The man smiled as Cain started running toward him. A car squealed its brakes as it rushed to the curb, the man getting in the back seat, rushing off before Cain got there. Cain slapped his leg in disgust, not believing what just happened. He walked over to Contreras' car and peered through the window. The driver was dead, as Cain assumed he would be, slumped to his side, his head resting against the window. He rushed over to Ruiz's car before anyone realized what happened and the pair drove away.

"What just happened?" Ruiz asked.

"I wish I knew."

"Is Contreras dead?"

"Yeah."

"The mission was successful then, no?"

"I'm not the one who killed him," Cain said, displeased.

"Oh. If you did not kill him, then who did?"

"That's the question."

"And why?"

Ruiz drove Cain back to the Hilton Princess so Cain could contact Lawson and figure out his next step. Cain thanked Ruiz for his help and told him he'd contact him if he needed anything else.

"Good luck, my friend, it's been a pleasure," Ruiz said.

"Same to you."

Cain went straight to his room and immediately called Lawson.

"Hey, we're still working on identifying the men in the photos," Lawson said.

"Contreras is dead."

"Oh. OK. A little faster than I anticipated, but that's OK."

"Except I didn't do it," Cain said.

"Then who did?"

"I don't know. I was about to and someone took a shot from behind me and blew his head off."

"Did you get a look at him?"

"Yeah, but he wasn't one of the guys from the pictures."

"Well, this is an interesting development, isn't it?" Lawson said.

"If you say so."

"We certainly didn't anticipate any complications on this mission."

"You're telling me."

"Well, sit tight until you hear back from me."

An hour went by without a word from Lawson. Cain took a shower then had food sent up to his room. As he sat down to eat, the phone in his room started ringing. A strange look came across him as he didn't know who'd be calling him there. He cautiously walked over to it, almost like he was afraid it might blow up, and after a few rings picked it up.

"Hello," Cain said.

"Mr. Mathews, we have an outside call for you, do you accept the call?" the front desk asked.

"Yeah."

"One moment."

"So, the room's registered to a Michael Mathews, is that your real name?" the mysterious man asked.

"Who's this?"

"Have you forgotten me so soon?"

"Who are you? You know my name, it's only fair that I know yours."

"Fair point. My name's George Wentworth. I'm sorry about interrupting your meeting at the church. It looked like it was about to end but I needed to be the one who finished it."

"Why was it so important that you needed to do it?"

"That's what I'm paid for," the man said.

"Who are you working for?"

"That's nothing for you to be concerned with."

"What was in the briefcase?"

"I don't know. I was just instructed to get it. What was inside was not my business."

"Are you with Specter?" Cain asked, not sure if he should've said the name, but he was curious if it was another test by Sanders.

"Specter? Ah, so you're a Project Specter agent," Wentworth said. "Now that makes it all the more interesting. That means Mathews probably isn't your real name."

"The same as Wentworth probably isn't yours. What do you know about Specter?"

"I was once in that boat, as you are now."

"You were an agent?"

"Yes. For several years. Now, I'm in business for myself. I freelance. Who is your handler?"

"Shelly Lawson."

"Shelly? She was my handler also. I loved Shelly. She was the only difficult part about leaving. If Shelly's your handler then you're in good hands. She'll take care of you."

"She seems like she knows her stuff," Cain said.

"Oh, she does. There's no one better. Just a word of advice from one agent to another; be careful."

"Of what?"

"Everything. Don't trust everything that's said or done," Wentworth added. "I don't know your particular situation but everything they tell you is not necessarily the truth or as it appears. They have their own agenda for things. They will play you for their own advantage. The same as if you're playing with fire... be cautious around it."

"Thanks for the tip. Maybe we'll run into each other again someday."

"If you're with Project Specter, it's more than likely."

"How'd you know where I was, anyway?" Cain asked.

"I followed you after the church. I wanted to see who the mysterious man was that I was competing with," Wentworth replied. "Some more advice for you, always make sure you're not being followed."

"I'll do that next time."

"You do that. Well, I have to go. Until next time."

Cain picked up his phone, ready to call Lawson, but put it back down. He figured she'd be calling him soon enough. He sat down to finish the rest of his dinner as he replayed the conversation with Wentworth in his mind. Just as Cain finished dinner his phone rang. It was Lawson.

"Looks like we got some hits on those pictures you took," Lawson said.

"What's the word?"

"The men Contreras was meeting with were definitely European, specifically Russian. The man he was talking to was Andrei Kurylenko. He is a burgeoning international arms dealer. He's been making contacts all over the world. He's someone we'll be having to contend with shortly. The other man with him was one of his top aides, Dmitri Butsayev."

"That seems like bad news."

"It is. If Contreras was meeting with Kurylenko that can only mean that Contreras was trying to acquire massive amounts of firearms."

"That doesn't seem like that was part of his repertoire," Cain said.

"Contreras dropped off the map after New York. He must've been trying to step up his notoriety."

"He did say he had big plans coming up."

"Kurylenko must've been what he had in mind," Lawson said.

"If Contreras was trying to get weapons then why would Kurylenko have him killed?"

"Maybe they disagreed on terms. Or maybe it wasn't Kurylenko."

"Who else would it be?" Cain asked.

"It's tough to say. We don't know exactly what else Contreras was into."

"So, what do you want me to do next?"

"Go home. Stay there for another day and relax. If you're able to pick up anything then all the better. If not, then come back on Thursday until we get another mission mapped out for you."

"OK," Cain replied, wondering if he should tell her about his conversation with Wentworth.

"Have anything else for me?" Lawson asked.

"Umm."

"What is it?" she asked.

"I dunno."

"C'mon, what is it? You can say anything to me. It's OK. If it's private, then I'll just keep it between us. You can trust me."

"Well, it's about the man who killed Contreras," Cain said.

"I've been checking on it. I've been checking into known violent people on our radar who arrived in Honduras the previous few days but so far, we've come up empty. Whoever it was must've slipped in quietly."

"I already know who it is."

"You do? How? That's good work by you but how did you find out already?"

"He called me."

"What do you mean he called you?"

"Apparently, he followed me to my hotel and called my room," Cain said.

"Well, that's highly unusual. What did he have to say?"

"He said he wanted to see who I was."

"And did you tell him?" Lawson asked.

"Just the cover name I was using."

"Good."

"I thought maybe he was from Specter, that it was another test for me."

"Absolutely not. I would know if it was."

"He said he was," he said.

"That's impossible. We have no other agents in that area. I would know if we did."

"He said he was a former agent who is now freelancing."

"I'm gonna have to check into it. As far as I know we have no former agents now freelancing," she said.

"He said his name was George Wentworth."

Lawson didn't reply, stunned by the name Cain just dropped on her.

"You there?" Cain asked.

"Yeah. Yeah, I'm here," Lawson stuttered, trying not to sound shocked.

"You seem surprised."

"George Wentworth is dead."

"Unless I was talking to a ghost, he seemed very much alive to me."

"George Wentworth was an alias for an agent named Eric Raines. He died six months ago in a warehouse explosion in Indonesia," she said.

"Can you send me a picture of him? I'll confirm whether that's the guy I saw or not."

"Uh, yeah, I'll send one over. I have pictures of all agents on my tablet. Just gimme a sec to pull it up."

Within a couple of minutes Lawson had pulled up a picture of Raines on her iPad. She looked at his face for a second, mixed emotions running through her. The thought of him being alive briefly made her excited for the possibility, cancelling the sadness she previously felt for his loss. She took a big sigh and e-mailed the picture over to Cain.

"OK. It's sent. Check your email," she said.

Cain grabbed his iPad and sat in a chair. He logged into his e-mail and downloaded the picture Lawson sent. With each percentage of the picture that showed on the screen, starting with the top of Raines' head, Cain could see the resemblance to the man he saw. Lawson eagerly awaited Cain's opinion, sighing and leaning on her desk, with her hand holding her head up.

"That's him," Cain said.

Lawson closed her eyes as soon as the words left Cain's lips. She couldn't believe the man they all thought was dead, that they mourned, was actually still alive.

"You're sure that's him?" Lawson asked.

"No doubt about it. That's the guy I saw. Exact same appearance except he's got a goatee now."

"I can't believe it."

"Well, better sink in soon. Because he's alive."

9

Cain's last day spent in Honduras turned up no new leads. He actually tried to soak up some of the country's culture and sampled some of their food, checking out some of their establishments. He contacted Ruiz to see if he could find out anything else on Contreras, like what he was trying to get into. Ruiz came up empty though. All leads died along with Contreras. After he was satisfied there was no further information to be had, Cain flew back to New York.

The entire plane ride home he thought about what Raines told him about not trusting what he was told. He thought about every detail that transpired from the moment he woke up in that army hospital bed until that very second on the plane. Cain closed his eyes as he relived everything. After a few minutes, he stopped thinking and just tried to relax. Relaxing didn't last long as more visions clogged his mind. He tilted his head as if he was trying to get a better view of what he was seeing. The woman who previously appeared was not there this time. On this occasion, it was a little boy. He must've been about four or five years old. He was smiling and laughing as he was playing on a swing set. The boy alternated between the swing and going down the sliding board. The captain's voice came over the intercom detailing the trip, breaking Cain's concentration on the boy. He opened his eyes, and the boy was gone. He closed his eyes again, but the vision was gone for good. He turned his head, looked out the window, and let his mind wander as they flew through the clouds.

A few hours later they landed at JFK airport in New York. Cain's plan was to grab his bag and then take a cab home. He strolled through the airport to the luggage area, where he spotted his bag. He grabbed it, then turned around and noticed Shelly Lawson standing about fifty feet away from him. Cain had told her what flight he was taking home so the agency would be aware of it though Lawson didn't tell him she'd be there waiting for him. He was a little surprised to see her there. He walked over to her, wondering what she wanted.

"Something wrong?" Cain asked.

"No, why?"

"I'm just surprised to see you. What are you doing here?"

"I just thought we should talk about some things," she said.

"Such as?"

"About what happened in Honduras."

"Already told you."

"I need more."

"Don't have anything else to tell you."

"Let's go to my place so we can talk," Lawson said.

Cain stopped walking, surprised at Lawson's request. A quizzical look overtook him, wondering what she was up to. Something didn't seem right. If she really wanted to talk about

Honduras, he was curious as to why they weren't going to the Center instead.

"What's this really all about?" Cain asked.

Lawson paused before answering. "I'll tell you when we get there."

"Is this an official request?"

"No. Just as a favor to me," she said.

Cain agreed to her request and continued walking with Lawson on the way to her car, still unsure what she wanted. There was something different about her, though he couldn't place exactly what it was. Maybe it was the determination exuding from her that indicated the seriousness of whatever matter she wanted to discuss.

They arrived at her house an hour after leaving the airport. She lived in a gated community, and judging by the looks of the houses, all the residents seemed to be doing well financially.

"Nice area," Cain said. "Anything up for sale? Maybe I'll move in."

"Not likely. There hasn't been a house for sale here since I moved in over two years ago and that was only because the previous owner passed away."

They went inside and she told Cain to have a seat on the couch while she went into the kitchen. She came back out a minute later, a bottle of soda and water in each hand. She offered Cain his pick of drinks. He grabbed the water, looking it over.

"It's not poisoned if that's what you're looking for," Lawson said, half kidding.

"Just checking," Cain smiled. "Wentworth... Raines, said to not trust anyone. I kinda believed him on it."

"What did he mean by that? Who was he talking about?"

"I don't know. He didn't elaborate."

"What else did he say?"

"Well, he did speak highly of you. He said how good you were and I was in good hands with you. He also said you were the most difficult part of leaving?"

Lawson's eyes started tearing up upon hearing how Raines spoke of her. She missed him since he'd been gone.

"He actually said he left?"

"That's what he said. Why all the questions about him?" Cain asked.

"Like I said, he was supposed to have died six months ago."

"It goes deeper than that, doesn't it?"

"In what way?" Lawson asked.

"Your eyes are tearing up, you seem emotionally involved, and we're here instead of at the Center. You had something personal with him, didn't you?"

Lawson choked back a few tears before answering. "Yes. We were lovers," she admitted. "Although we broke up about a week before he... a week before he died."

"I had a feeling."

"All this time I thought he was dead. I took a leave of absence for two months after his death because it hurt to go to the office knowing I would never see him again. And now he appears, seemingly alive, and if it weren't for you seeing him I still would think he's dead."

"I can see how that'd be upsetting," Cain said. "Seems pretty unusual. You break up, he dies a week later, six months later he shows up. Sounds like something he had planned in advance."

"But, but why? Why would he do that? What would he gain?" Lawson asked incredulously.

"I think it's pretty obvious. He wanted out. For some reason, he didn't think he could do that any other way. Which means he didn't trust that they'd let him out on his own. So, he cooked up a plan to make it happen."

"I just... I just don't know what to think. If he were alive, why wouldn't he contact me to let me know?"

Cain thought for a few moments, not sure if he should say what he was thinking. He finally relented. "Maybe your feelings for him were stronger than his feelings for you."

"I guess that's possible, isn't it?" she responded, hoping that wasn't the case.

"Or, maybe it's because of the trust thing he was talking about," Cain said. "Maybe something was going on when he died and he wanted to stay that way, not trusting anyone else to keep that secret. Or maybe he was afraid if he contacted you then he'd be found out or that he'd put you in danger. It's tough to know a man's reasons for something unless you're in his shoes."

"This is his file," Lawson said, bringing up his info on her iPad.

Cain carefully looked at each page on the screen. There was personal information, as well as documentation on every mission Raines had ever been on, who some of his known contacts were, as well as the case file on his final mission. Cain reread the information a few times to pick up anything he might've missed the first time around.

"Not a whole lot of information on the Indonesia mission," Cain said.

"That's 'cause we didn't know much about it. He contacted me a day before that and said he was meeting one of his contacts in a warehouse."

"And you don't know who that was?"

"He never said, and we never found out. There were two bodies found, badly burned, neither recognizable."

"How'd they identify him?"

"Dental records," Lawson replied.

"What does Sanders think?"

Lawson hesitated before answering, not really sure how to reply.

"You didn't tell him yet?" Cain inferred.

"Not exactly."

"Why not? What are you waiting for?"

"I don't know. I guess I'm waiting for the right time," she said.

"Don't you trust him?"

"Yeah, I guess," Lawson said. "I mean, I don't know. The whole organization is based on lies and secrecy, and lies based on lies, that it's tough to know what to believe sometimes."

"Wait," Cain said.

"What?" Lawson replied.

"He was in Indonesia before, about a year ago," he said, looking at his missions.

"Yes. He was following up on something about some arms dealer. Turned out to be nothing."

"Says he met with someone named Aditya Gutawa."

"We contacted him after Eric died to see if he knew anything about it. He said he didn't know and hadn't seen Eric since last year."

"And you believed him?"

"Why would he lie?"

"If Raines went to Gutawa and asked for his help, don't you think he'd help the man he worked with, developed a relationship with, help him disappear if that's what he wanted… or a government agency he probably doesn't care shit about."

"But we asked him—," Lawson started to say before being interrupted.

"But you're the government agency. He's not gonna tell you."

"You're right."

"You also need to accept another possibility," Cain said.

"Which is what?"

"That he's not the same man you once knew. The man you knew and loved, maybe he was a good man, maybe he had good intentions, I don't know. But you have to face that he might not be that man anymore. He dropped off the planet for a reason. And those reasons might not be all that pleasant once you find them."

"I know," she said solemnly, nodding.

Lawson leaned back on her sofa, letting Cain's words sink in. She knew he was right but didn't want to believe that Raines turned his back on her. Cain finished looking at Raines' file and turned off the computer, handing it back to Lawson.

"We need answers," Lawson said.

"We?"

"I mean the agency. We need to know what happened to him."

"You mean you need answers," Cain said.

"You're right. I do. But we also need to know if there's something bigger at work here. Not only that, but he knows everything we do. He knows how we think and act. If he has his own agenda now that doesn't mesh with ours, then he could put all our agents at risk. We need to find out what he's up to now."

"And how do you propose to do that?"

"How would you feel about going to Indonesia?" she asked.

Cain looked at her like she was crazy. He wasn't sure he bought what she was saying about the agency needing to find Raines as much as it was driving her insane that she didn't know what happened to him. Cain and Lawson talked for another hour about the situation and about how they'd present it to Sanders. Lawson offered to let Cain stay the night if he wanted, sleeping on the couch, but he wanted to get back to his place and relax. She drove him home, getting him to his apartment about seven o'clock. Lawson told Cain she'd let him know what Sanders said if she asked him about Indonesia.

He walked into his apartment, looking around for Heather, and shouting her name. He walked around from room to room, seeing how the place looked. The bed was made, and the rooms were clean, almost like she hadn't even been there. He walked over to the desk and noticed the PC was on. He awakened it from sleep mode and looked at the website that popped up. A couple tabs were on there, both job related sites. Cain then walked into the kitchen and noticed a couple plates in the sink. He looked in the refrigerator to see what there was to eat and pulled out some lunch meat, making himself a turkey sandwich. He sat down on the couch to eat and put the TV on, flipping channels until he came across a Yankees game. With almost every pitch thrown he wondered where Heather was. He assumed she would've been there when he got home. He hoped she didn't go back to her apartment or meet up with someone. An hour passed by when he heard some rattling just outside the door. It sounded like someone was fumbling with keys. Cain went to the kitchen drawer and opened it, putting his hand on the handle of his Glock, just in case it was an unwanted visitor. The door handle jiggled before opening, Heather walking in, a couple of bags in each hand. Cain took his hand off the gun and closed the drawer. She stopped and almost screamed when she saw Cain standing there, holding her hand over her heart and sighing like she almost had a heart attack.

"You almost scared me," she said.

"Almost?"

Heather continued walking into the living room, putting the bags down on the table.

"OK. Maybe a little bit. What are you doing here?"

"Umm, I'm pretty sure I live here," Cain said sarcastically.

"Obviously. I mean, I didn't expect you back so late at night."

"Well, I got back a few hours ago. I had to go over a few things first about Honduras."

"Oh. Was it a good trip?" Heather asked, not quite knowing how to ask about it.

"Had its good moments and bad."

"Oh. Anything you wanna talk about?"

"No," he responded, shaking his head. "Did you have fun while I was gone?"

"Oh yeah. Loads and loads."

"What'd you do?"

"Spent most of the time job hunting. When I got bored with that fun stuff, I did other exciting things, you know, like eating and sleeping."

"Sounds like a great time," Cain said.

"Oh. It was. It was."

"Whatcha got in those bags?"

"Oh, I went shopping," she said and smiled. "I've got two interviews tomorrow, so I wanted to get some new outfits for them."

"Good for you. What jobs are they?"

"One is for an entry level marketing position. And the other is for a payroll specialist at a payroll company."

"Nice. I hope you get one of them."

"Yeah, me too."

"I'm sure you'll do great."

"I don't know. I'm a little nervous."

"Just go in there prepared and show your stuff," he said.

"Well, I'm used to showing my stuff, but I'm not sure that's what they have in mind," she kidded.

Cain laughed, then reassured her that she'd be fine. Heather wanted to try the outfits on and asked him if he could tell her how she looked in them. In truth, she'd already tried them on in the store before she bought them and knew how they looked, but she wanted to get his opinion on them. Plus, she hoped it'd get Cain more interested in her. She went into the bedroom and changed into a blue skirt outfit that wasn't as revealing as most of the things in her wardrobe. After Cain gave her good reviews she then changed into a tighter fitting suit outfit, complete with black high heels. Cain looked her up and down, pleased with the view, and told her how good she looked.

"If you interview as good as you look, then you'll get the job hands-down," Cain said.

"Thanks," she replied, smiling ear to ear.

They talked a little more about the jobs, Cain helping her prepare for the interviews by asking her some questions. She knew the basics about each company and wrote down questions and some possible answers to them.

"Still nervous?" Cain asked.

"Yeah, but excited too. I feel like this is the beginning of a new chapter in my life. I feel good about moving on. But it's always scary when something new comes along."

"Yeah. You'll do great though," he said, putting his arm around her.

Heather hoped he'd take it further than that brief hug but was disappointed when he didn't make any other moves.

"Well, I guess I should get to bed. The first interview is at nine."

"When's the second one?" Cain asked.

"Noon."

"Maybe when you're done we could meet somewhere for lunch if you want?"

"Yeah, I'd like that."

They decided on a restaurant and agreed to meet at one, figuring Heather would be done with her interview. She then walked into the bedroom and brought out a pillow, placing it on the couch.

"What're you doing?" Cain asked.

"Going to bed."

"No, no, no. Get back in there," he said, pointing to the bedroom.

"What? I'm not sleeping in your bed."

At least not by herself, she thought. She wouldn't have minded sleeping in there with him, but she didn't want to take it on her own.

"Where'd you sleep while I was gone?"

"In your bed," she replied.

"Then there you go."

"But you're back now and I'm not gonna take your bed away from you."

"Heather, I was in the military, I'm used to not sleeping in beds. I could sleep in the bathtub if I had to."

Heather tried resisting one more time, but Cain wouldn't let her say no.

"Besides, you have a big day tomorrow, you need to get a good, comfortable sleep. You can't be scrunched up on the couch all night," he said. "Take the bed. Get a good night's sleep."

She finally relented, knowing she wasn't going to win the fight. She really wanted to give him a kiss and hug goodnight but wanted to give him space since he obviously was taking things slow.

In the middle of the night Cain started tossing and turning in his sleep while he was dreaming. He saw himself back in the army, in an old, abandoned building. It appeared that he was in some desolate town, very sunny with high winds, dust and dirt kicking up and swirling everywhere. He was in an upstairs window with a sniper rifle waiting for his victim to walk into his crosshairs. A man in a suit walked into his path but for some reason his face was blurry. He couldn't make out who the man was. The man stuck out, his suit seeming like odd attire for the kind of place they were in. Cain lined the man up for an easy shot, slowly pulling the trigger on his rifle. A shot rang out. The bullet moved at a snail's pace. Cain could see it traveling through the air, almost like a movie slowing the frame down. Once the bullet got close to its intended target it sped up like it was in fast forward, hitting the man square in the forehead, the bullet lodging in his head. The man instantly dropped to his knees before falling onto the ground, face down. Like he was transported, Cain was suddenly standing over the man's dead body. He knelt down to see who the man was and turned him over. It was him. He shot himself in the head. Cain suddenly woke up startled, screaming, almost jumping off the couch. He sat there, elbows on his knees, head down, sweat pouring off his body. Heather woke up once she heard Cain scream and stood in the doorway to the living room where she saw him sitting there. He was still sweating and heavily sighing. She ran to the couch and sat next to him, putting her arms around him, and then put his head on her shoulder as she stroked his head to relax him.

"It's OK," she whispered.

She was concerned because he was still breathing heavily and he was sweating like he just spent three hours at the gym. She thought of calling the doctor but decided to give him a few more minutes to calm down. He didn't seem like he was in pain, just startled.

"Are you OK?"

"Yeah," he replied.

"What happened?"

"I just had a dream."

"What was it about?" she asked, still clutching on to him.

"I was back in the military. A sniper," he told her, his breathing starting to slow. "And I shot someone in the head and killed him."

"It was just a dream."

"No. I went to check on him and when I turned him over and saw who it was... it was me. I killed myself."

"Shh. It's OK," she said.

Heather continued holding him until he stopped sweating, and his breathing returned to normal. About twenty minutes later Cain fell back asleep, in her arms, as she leaned back on the sofa. So much for getting a good night's sleep in bed, she thought to herself. She really didn't mind though as holding him was exactly what she was craving. If she lost an hour or so of sleep it wasn't a big deal. She'd rather have made sure he was OK first. She hoped he didn't have any more episodes for the night, not worrying about her sleep, but genuinely concerned for his well-being. She fell asleep a short time later, content to still be holding him.

Cain woke up a few hours later, free from any further dreams, and looked toward the light shining in through the window. He glanced at the clock which just turned seven. He picked his head up off Heather's shoulder and looked at her. She looked so peaceful lying there. She really was a beautiful woman, he thought. Cain was appreciative of her looking after him and taking care of him, especially after his latest episode. The alarm clock in the bedroom went off, Cain going in to stop it, then waking Heather up. She was one of those naturally beautiful women who looked great with no makeup or even with her hair messed up.

"Hey," she said. "How you feeling?"

"I'm OK."

"Good. You scared me a little last night."

"I scared myself," Cain said. "Thank you, though, for sitting with me and all. I appreciate it."

"You're welcome. That's what friends are for, right?"

"I heard the alarm go off, so I figured you wanted to get up now."

"Oh, yeah. Thanks. I have to shower. I probably look like crap," she said, running her hand through her hair.

"I don't think it's possible for you to look anything other than beautiful," he said.

A huge smile came over Heather's face, the compliment making her blush.

"Why are you blushing?" Cain asked.

"I dunno," she said, still smiling, looking away. "I'm used to fake compliments. You know, people who say something just because they think it'll get them somewhere."

"Maybe that's what I'm doing."

"No, it's not. I can tell. You say things because you mean them. It's genuine coming from you. That's a refreshing change."

Heather went in to take a shower, hoping someone would join her, though she knew it wouldn't happen. She was right, as Cain started making breakfast. He wanted to show her another sign of appreciation for what she'd done for him. It was nothing special, just pancakes, but he hoped she'd like it. He put the food on the table as she got out of the shower and changed. Once she came out, she saw breakfast waiting on the table for her.

"Aww. You're so sweet," she remarked, genuinely touched.

"Nothing fancy, but at least it's not burnt."

"No, it's great. Thank you," she said, kissing him on the cheek.

"Just my way of saying thank you for last night, and before," he said.

"Well, it's not necessary, but it's really nice of you."

They sat down and ate, talking some more about the interviews she was about to go on. Once they were done she finished getting ready and left by eight, wanting to get there in plenty of time. Cain passed the time by reading the news on the internet.

10

Specter Project Center—Ed Sanders was walking into his office when his secretary rushed in behind him before he even had a chance to sit down.

"Sir, there was someone looking at agents' files last night," his secretary said.

"Whose?"

"Eric Raines."

"Who was looking at it?"

"Shelly Lawson," she replied, looking at her paper, handing it to him.

Sanders sighed, disappointment covering his face, as he wondered what exactly she was looking for.

"Is Shelly in her office?" Sanders asked.

"I believe she is," his secretary said. "I'll double check for you, sir."

"Please do. If she is, will you please ask her to come in here?"

"I will."

"Thank you."

The secretary went to Lawson's office to find her. Lawson was just getting off the phone as her visitor walked in.

"Mr. Sanders would like to see you."

"OK. I'll be right there."

As Lawson walked to Sanders office, she wondered what he wanted to talk about. She thought about whether she should tell him about Cain finding Raines in Honduras, whether she should just keep it to herself for a while, or whether she should send Cain to Indonesia without telling Sanders. If she did and Sanders eventually found out she was withholding information from him, it could jeopardize her standing. She always tried to stay above board with everything.

Lawson walked into Sanders office, his eyes focused directly on her. She could tell he knew something. She could just see it in his face.

"Shelly, I was reading your report on Cain's adventure in Honduras," Sanders said.

"It's a little incomplete," she replied. "I have to revise some of it."

"Oh? I was under the impression this was all of it."

A slight hesitation engulfed her before she finally relented on telling her secret. She knew it was better to just come out with it like she was volunteering the information rather than have him dig for it, knowing it'd come out, anyway.

"I had to do some checking on something Cain told me," Lawson said.

"Which was?"

"Cain said the man who killed Contreras identified himself as George Wentworth."

"The alias of Eric Raines," Sanders said. "I noticed you looked into his file last night. You know those files aren't for general viewing."

"I pulled up his file and had Cain look at his picture to see if it was the same man he saw."

"And?" Sanders asked, seemingly convinced that it was a plausible explanation.

"It was," she said.

"And you believe it?"

"Cain said there's no doubt that's the man he saw in Honduras. Plus, he used one of his aliases so I tend to believe that he is in fact alive."

"Well, I don't even know what to say to that," Sanders puffed, stroking his chin in thought, trying to keep his composure.

"I believe we should send someone to Indonesia," Lawson said.

"You do realize we had confirmation of his death, do you not?"

"I do, sir."

"Then what makes you think by sending someone to Indonesia six months later, that we'll find out anything different?"

"I would like to send someone there to talk to one of his contacts he made over a year ago, a man named Aditya Gutawa."

"Did we not talk to him before?"

"Only briefly. There was no reason to question him further at the time. We thought Raines was dead," Lawson said. "Now that we know he's alive..."

"And you think Gutawa knows something?"

"I would like to find out."

"What are your reasons for this?" Sanders asked.

"To find out why he was presumed dead and six months later is found alive."

"Is that it? Or are your reasons more... personal?"

"I will admit I do have personal feelings," Lawson said. "But this goes beyond that. As much as I hate to admit it, we need to find out what happened and why. The fact that he shows up six months later in Honduras, and killing one of our targets, suggests he didn't just wanna drop off the map. He's still involved in some capacity and we need to find out where he stands in the game. If he's now playing on the other side, he could possibly compromise our entire operation."

"Who do you propose sending?"

"I'd like to send Cain," she said.

"Why him?"

"My other agents are deployed elsewhere, and I'd rather not pull them off. Plus, I believe Cain can get the information we need."

"You have a lot of faith in him."

"I do. He also is the reason we know Raines is alive."

"That's irrelevant," Sanders said.

"I know. I agree, but he's also a newer agent who has no opinion of him from before and has no ties to him which will not cloud his judgment on the situation."

"That I will agree with."

Lawson waited silently as Sanders sat there thinking about the best course of action. He agreed on what she was proposing.

"If you want Cain, you got him," he said. "When do you want to send him?"

"Within the next two or three days if possible."

"Get it done."

Lawson left the office to get to work on Cain's excursion. She needed to quickly get his flight together and the logistics of his stay. She also put out some feelers to people she knew to get the whereabouts on Gutawa. She didn't want to call Cain until she got more specifics on everything. Once noon came around, she started to get a better idea of what was happening. She was waiting for one more person to call her back on where Gutawa was.

Cain had just taken a seat at the restaurant he was meeting Heather at, waiting for her. The restaurant had outdoor seating, which considering the nice day that it was, Cain felt Heather would like. It was five minutes to one, so he was sure she would be there soon. He'd gotten a text from her fifteen minutes before that saying she was done with her interview and was on her way. He ordered drinks for the two of them while he waited. Just as he looked at the time on his phone again, it started ringing. Once he saw it was Lawson, he knew something was up.

"What's going on?" Cain asked.

"You're going to Indonesia," Lawson replied.

"When?"

"Tomorrow morning."

"Not much time to prepare."

"How much time do you need?" Lawson asked.

"None. It's good."

"Your flight leaves at 7:20am."

"Couldn't leave any earlier than that, huh?" Cain joked.

"It's a long flight."

"How long?"

"Better take some DVDs," she joked.

"Great."

"You'll fly to Heathrow Airport in Great Britain. From there you'll fly to Singapore and then to Jakarta, Indonesia, where you'll arrive at 6:05pm Saturday."

"Twenty-three hours?"

"That's the quickest they got."

"Fantastic."

"What are you doing right now?"

"About to have lunch," Cain said as he spotted Heather walking into the restaurant.

"Well, when you're done, come in. Sanders wants to have a word with you."

"I will do that."

Cain hung up just as Heather sat down. She looked like she was in a good mood, indicating the interviews went well.

"Who were you talking to?" she asked.

"Just business. How'd your interviews go?" he asked, brushing the question aside.

"I think they went really well. Preparing for them was the big thing."

"When are they gonna let you know?"

"Well, they both said they have other people to talk to, so it could be about a week or so."

"You'll get one of them."

"I hope so. Who'd you say you were talking to?" she asked again, knowing he tried to avoid telling her.

"Just someone from the office."

"You're just not gonna tell me anything, are you?"

Just as he was about to reply the waiter came over to take their order. They took turns ordering and Cain tried to switch the subject to something else, which Heather was not having any part of. It wasn't so much that she wanted to know the person who was calling more so than just wanting to be a bigger part of Cain's life and hoping that he'd eventually start confiding in her.

"Why won't you tell me anything?"

"Why do you wanna know?" Cain asked.

"I don't know, we're friends, and I'm living in your apartment right now. What you do kind of affects me."

"Listen, you know I can't tell you what I do."

"I didn't ask that. All I asked was who called. You can't tell me that?"

"It was Michelle," Cain finally said. "You remember her, right?"

"Oh yes. She doesn't like me too much. I guess I can't say I blame her."

"Maybe you two just got off on the wrong foot."

"I don't think there'll ever be a right foot with her. She called with good news I hope?"

"I have to go somewhere," Cain said.

"Where? Are you able to say?"

"Indonesia?"

"Indonesia? Where's that?" Heather asked.

"Southeast Asia."

"Oh. Important I guess?"

"I suppose so."

"When do you leave?"

"Tomorrow morning," Cain said.

"Oh," Heather said, dejected.

"What's wrong?"

"Well, you just got back from a trip. I just thought you'd be here for a while. Was looking forward to that hockey game," she said, trying to make it not sound like she was going to miss him.

"Yeah, well, I guess we'll have to try for a game once I get back. You'll look after the place while I'm gone?"

"Of course. How long will you be?"

"I don't know. Probably a few days."

Heather was so disappointed that Cain was leaving again, although she tried not to outwardly show it. She wanted to spend some time with him, whether it was going out somewhere, or just staying in the apartment, talking and hanging out. She was so upset about him leaving that she really didn't enjoy the idea of having lunch together. The fact Cain told her he was leaving the next morning made it more difficult for her to accept since he just got back. She knew it'd be tough for their relationship to grow to where she wanted it to go if he was always going away somewhere.

After having lunch, Heather went back to the apartment, while Cain went to the Center to talk to Sanders and get the rest of the mission from Lawson. He was directed to go to Sanders' office first. Sanders got off the phone a minute after Cain walked in.

"I'm gonna keep this brief," Sanders said. "First, good job in Honduras, good work."

"Thanks."

"I just wanna make sure we're clear about Indonesia. You're there to get information."

"Yeah."

"By any means necessary," he told him. "I don't care how you get the information we need. Just get it."

"I understand," Cain replied.

"Good. Do what you have to do. Shelly's waiting for you in her office."

Cain went straight to Lawson's office, who'd been waiting

for him. He sat down in the chair in front of her desk as she got out the paperwork.

"Here's your itinerary," she said.

"Such a long flight," Cain said.

"Well, that's why you're gonna have company."

"What?"

"You're getting a partner for this mission."

"Why? It's a pretty simple objective," he said.

"Well, just in case there are any unexpected surprises."

"Who is it?"

"They'll meet you at the airport."

Lawson talked about the culture of Indonesia, letting Cain know what to expect. The country consisted of over 17,000 islands and was the largest archipelago in the world. They also had the fourth largest population in the world, with over 85% of its inhabitants Muslim, also the largest in the world. They'd be flying into Jakarta, the capital and largest city. Robbery, theft, and pick-pocketing was common there, though most crime was non-violent and guns were rare. Indonesia was one of the most corrupt countries in the world as officials often asked for bribes to supplement their salaries. Though they had a corrupt legal system, they did deal with drug usage harshly. There's "Death To Drug Traffickers" signs at airports, and the death penalty was mandatory for those convicted of trafficking, manufacturing, importing, or exporting, and a person could be charged with such if drugs were found in their possession even if they weren't aware of it. Even though the penalties were harsh, drugs were common, especially cocaine, ecstasy, and crystal methamphetamine.

"So, where do I look for Gutawa?" Cain asked.

"Here," Lawson replied, handing him a paper with an address on it.

"What's this?"

"His address."

"You got his address?"

"Took some doing, and talking to a few people, but I tracked him down."

"Wow. You are good," Cain said, gushing.

"I know," she replied, and smiled.

Cain went back to his apartment to pack his bags once they finished going over their business in the office. Heather was on the computer looking up more jobs.

"Still going at it?" Cain asked.

"Well, just in case those other two don't pan out, I figured I should keep applying for other jobs."

"Good idea."

"How was your meeting?" she asked.

"Fine."

"When's your flight?"

"Early. I'll be gone by the time you wake up," he said.

"Oh. Don't know when you'll be back?"

"Shouldn't be long. Can't say exactly though. Takes a day just to fly there. So, it'll be two days just being in the air."

JFK airport—Cain was sitting in the terminal, waiting for his partner to arrive, though he didn't know how he'd know the guy since they didn't tell him who was going with him. About half an hour before they needed to board Cain looked around and noticed Lawson walking toward him. He noticed she was carrying a bag with her.

"Hey," she said.

"Hey. Going somewhere?"

"I did say someone was going with you."

"I assumed it was another agent," Cain said.

"I thought you might have a problem if I told you it was me."

"Does Sanders know about this?"

"I told him. He was fine with it."

"Why am I even going?" Cain asked.

"I'm an information girl. I know how to get it once I know what I'm looking for. I'm not trained in combat. In case something goes down, you're the muscle," she kidded.

"Reassuring."

11

Jakarta, Indonesia—Once Cain and Lawson touched down, they traveled using an AC minibus. It was night-time and was the most effective and easiest way of travel. Renting a car was dangerous in Indonesia, as they usually had very bad driving habits. They'd often drive on the shoulder of the road, making lane changes and passing other cars dangerously. They also often ignored traffic lights. Using the minibus was more expensive, but it was the safest way of driving. They immediately went to the address they had for Gutawa. He had a pretty nice looking two-story house that indicated he had some wealth. There was often a very stark contrast in Indonesia; you could see who was wealthy standing right next to those who were in extreme poverty. Lawson knocked on the door but there was no answer. There were no lights on so it appeared Gutawa was out.

"Come back later?" Lawson asked.

"You can. I ain't coming back later though," Cain said, as he picked the lock of the door.

"I'm not sure this is wise."

"Listen, I'd like to get out of this country as soon as possible. This isn't my idea of a vacation so the sooner we get this over with the better. Besides, how do you know when we come back he'll be here, anyway? We'll wait."

While they were waiting, they looked around for a computer. They weren't positive Gutawa had one, but they searched anyway. They looked through the living room and kitchen, before finally finding a laptop in a table drawer in his bedroom next to his bed. Lawson turned it on and searched through some files to see if there was anything of interest on there but she didn't notice anything important. She then installed tracking software on the machine that would pick up any e-mails that he received and immediately send a copy of them to her without being traced. Gutawa could find the bug they installed if he was looking for it, but it was likely he wouldn't discover it for quite some time. Their wait didn't last long, about an hour. Gutawa walked in the door and turned a light on, seeing Lawson sitting on his couch.

"What you doing here?" Gutawa asked. Most Indonesians spoke English capably.

"I want to talk to you. Come sit down," Lawson said.

"Get out of my house."

"I think you best sit down," Cain said from behind him.

Gutawa complied with their wishes, figuring they had other things on their minds if he did not.

"We're not here to hurt you," Lawson said. "We just want information."

"About what?"

"Eric Raines."

"What about him?"

"We know you were one of his contacts," she said.

"He died over six months ago."

"No, he did not."

Gutawa didn't reply to that, looking at both of his visitors, not seeming very surprised by the revelation.

"Judging by the look on your face, you already knew that," Cain said.

"I know nothing."

"Well, we think you do," Cain added, taking his Glock out of his belt, making sure Gutawa saw it.

"No. We don't need that," Lawson said. "Listen, we know he's alive. We've seen him. You don't have to hide it anymore."

"Why do you want to know where he is?"

"Because we need to know what he plans on doing. Whether he's in trouble and needs our help, or whether he's intending to do bad things. Either way, we need to find him."

Gutawa kept looking at Cain, who clenched the grip of his gun in front of his body. Gutawa seemed quite sure the man would use the gun on him if he chose not to give them the information they were seeking.

"What you want to know?" he asked.

"What happened to him?" Lawson asked.

"He came to me one year ago asking for my help. He said he was in trouble with some people and he needed to disappear."

"Trouble from whom?"

"He said the people he works for were getting close to him and were going to kill him soon."

"What? That's crazy," Lawson said. "Nothing like that was true."

"He come to me and asked if I could help him become a dead man. I say I cannot help in that matter but I know someone who can."

"Who'd you send him to?" Cain asked.

"His name is Guntur. You can find him at Ragunan Zoo. He works there sometimes."

Gutawa gave the pair Guntur's physical description so they could find him. The three of them continued talking about Raines, trying to get an idea of what he was working on.

"Have you heard from Raines in the last six months?" Cain asked.

"I have not," Gutawa answered.

"Do you know what his plans are?"

"No."

Lawson and Cain talked with Gutawa for another hour, trying to extract more information out of him, but they got to the point where he had nothing else to tell them. He seemed to be forthright with them and didn't appear to be holding anything back. He seemed rightfully afraid of the duo that broke into his house and knew they weren't playing games.

"Here's my info," Cain said, writing his number on a piece of paper, and handing it to Gutawa. "You hear from him, you call me."

"I will."

"If I find out he contacts you and you don't let me know, I'll come back and kill you," Cain said bluntly.

"I understand."

The pair left Gutawa's home and went back to their hotel for the night. They were pleased with what they got out of Gutawa. Not only did he divulge the name of the man who helped Raines, they were sure they'd wind up getting something useful from his computer.

"Do you think he'll contact Raines?" Lawson asked.

"I think it's likely he will at some point."

"Why?"

"If he feels loyal enough to him to help him disappear, then it's logical to assume he's likely to contact him at some point to tell him people know he's not dead and that they're looking for him," Cain replied.

"How long do you think it'll take?"

"Few days, maybe a week, maybe more. He'll probably wait until he's reasonably sure we've gone in a different direction."

The Ragunan Zoo didn't open until 8am the following morning so they had some time to wait. The zoo was a world class facility and housed over 500 species of plants and animals from around the world, including the Sumatran tiger and Komodo dragon. Once they got into their room, they discovered they had a bit of a situation.

"There's only one bed," Cain said.

"What?"

"You said it."

"That can't be. I booked..." Lawson started before realizing what happened.

"Yes?"

She grimaced. "When I made the reservations, it was just you going. Once I changed the plans, I forgot to change the hotel reservations."

"Fantastic," Cain added sarcastically.

"Wait, it's fine. I'll just call down to the desk and get another room."

Lawson called down to the desk and requested another

room. As she was speaking, her facial expressions indicated to Cain that she wasn't having much luck. She hung up the phone with an almost painful expression.

"Well? How'd that turn out?" Cain asked, already knowing the answer.

"Umm, not well. It seems they're all booked up for the night."

Cain sighed. "Well, I guess you take the bed and I'll take the floor."

"I'm really sorry."

"It's OK. I've been meaning to sleep on the floor lately. It's a good chance to get my back used to it again."

They both sat down and went on their computers for a little bit, Lawson to do some work on hers, Cain just surfing the internet. After an hour, Lawson put hers away and went to take a shower. After she finished, she came out in just a towel, barely covering her essentials. Cain tried not to pay attention but couldn't help but take a few glances in her direction as she sauntered across the room. She went to her bag on the bed and pulled out a brush, noticing that Cain was periodically glancing over at her. She hadn't been intimate with anyone since Raines broke up with her. It was nice to have someone still looking at her in a lusty manner. Cain, in an effort to get his mind off her, went in to take a shower as well. While he was showering Lawson had thoughts of surprising him in there, but she thought better of it, since it really wouldn't be professional or appropriate. She was attracted to him but she had second thoughts since she got burned the last time she had a relationship with one of her agents. She sat down on the bed and brushed her hair, getting thoughts of him out of her mind. He came out fifteen minutes later, just a towel covering his waist, and meandered over to the bed. His bag was next to Lawson's. She got up to give Cain some room, brushing up against him, accidentally knocking his towel off him. They looked at each other, both unsure that they should go any further.

"Oh, what the hell," Lawson said, leaning in to kiss him.

Cain returned her kiss and unwrapped Lawson from her towel. He picked her up and laid her on the bed. Though they both knew they shouldn't be doing it, neither was interested in stopping.

The following morning the two of them got dressed and headed to the zoo. Although neither was ashamed or embarrassed by what happened the night before, it was a bit uncomfortable between them.

"About last night," Lawson said. "It was great."

"But?"

"But we probably should leave it at that. It's not a good idea for either one of us to get involved."

"I agree," Cain said.

"Especially after what's happened with Raines, I just don't know if I can go through all that again."

"It's OK. Really. There's nothing wrong with leaving things as they are. We had a fun night. I'm OK with that."

"But it was great, wasn't it?" Lawson asked, smiling.

"Yeah."

They arrived at the zoo and went their separate ways, walking around trying to spot Guntur. If either of them spotted him they'd call the other to their location. They spent about five hours between walking and sitting, waiting to line Guntur up in their sights, before they finally got an eye on him. Cain was sitting by the Komodo dragon exhibit when he spotted him walking around, picking up litter, emptying trash cans. He called Lawson to let her know.

"I've got him," Cain said.

"Where?"

"Come to the Komodo dragon exhibit."

"On my way."

To prevent him from leaving the area before Lawson got there, Cain started to approach their target.

"Guntur," Cain said.

Guntur looked a little worried that the American knew his name. That could only mean bad news. He looked around like he was about to run.

"Let's sit down for a minute," Cain said, opening his jacket to show his gun.

Cain hoped that letting Guntur see his weapon would make him think twice about taking off.

"Now, about sitting down," Cain said once more.

Guntur nodded, agreeing to Cain's request. Cain grabbed hold of his arm to make sure he didn't take off on him. They sat down on the bench as they waited for Lawson to appear.

"First thing is I'm not gonna hurt you," Cain said. "All I want is information. You take off on me or feed me a bunch of crap and I'm gonna change my mind. Understood?"

"Yes."

Lawson quickly arrived, almost out of breath from scurrying over.

"How do you know me?" Guntur asked.

"Doesn't matter. We only want you to piece some things together for us," Cain said.

"What can I tell you?" Guntur asked the pair.

"Eric Raines, what happened to him?"

"He died six months ago."

"What'd I tell you?" Cain replied, shoving the gun in his side.

"What about him?" Guntur relented.

"We know you helped him fake his death," Lawson said. "How?"

Guntur seemed surprised his companions were asking about Raines, or even knew about him faking his death. Cain could see Guntur still had reservations about talking so he pushed the gun further into his side, causing the slightest bit of pain.

"I'm not telling you again," Cain said sternly.

"He was sent to me about faking his death."

"I already know that."

Guntur heavily sighed and resigned himself to telling the pair the information they were seeking. "We came up with blowing up a warehouse with him inside."

"How'd you get around verifying the body?" Lawson asked.

"You must understand, the Indonesian government is very corrupt. For a few extra dollars, you can find someone willing to switch records or create documents to say anything."

"What exactly did he need you for?"

"He came to me with what he wanted. I know the proper people who can make that happen. I am mostly a middle man."

"For a fee," Cain said.

"Of course."

"I'm assuming you get paid well for that sort of thing."

"Yes."

"Then what are you doing working here?" Cain asked.

"It's good cover. Plus, if I ever need to do business, I can blend in. Plenty of people walking around here. Easy to get lost in the crowd," Guntur explained.

"Did Raines tell you why he wanted to fake his death?" Lawson asked.

"No. Man who wants to do that has his own reasons. Not for me to know. Or to ask."

"Do you know where he was going after leaving here?" Lawson pressed.

"No."

"Is there anything else you can tell us about him? Anybody else he may have talked to while he was here?" Cain asked.

"No. As far as I know it was just me. I got the documents for him and off he went. What he did after me I couldn't say."

"OK." Cain sighed in frustration.

"Wait, one other thing," Guntur said. "When I let him know everything was taken care of he received a phone call in my presence."

"What'd he say?"

"I don't know. It was in a language I cannot understand."

"How long did it last?"

"Only few minutes. He kept saying nyet, nyet. He seemed a little angry after he was done though."

"Russian," Cain said to Lawson.

"Kurylenko," Lawson returned.

"They're working together."

Cain reached into his pocket and handed Guntur a 2,000 rupiah note. A big grin surfaced on Guntur's face, appreciative of the money. Cain also gave him his phone number, and received Guntur's as well, in case he ever had any information for him.

"You learn anything else, you call me," Cain said.

"You work for U.S. government?" Guntur asked.

"Maybe."

"I ever hear anything else about different things, maybe I call you about that too?"

"I don't wanna hear about old ladies getting hit in the street. But if it's big, you let me know," Cain said.

"And maybe I get more of these?" Guntur asked, holding the rupiah note up.

"Depends how good the information is."

He smiled. "Guntur only has good information."

"Well, you take care of yourself."

Cain and Lawson walked around the zoo for a little bit, looking at the animals, while also discussing Raines. They tried to figure out what his plans were or where he might be but didn't have much luck coming up with any answers. After the zoo, they went back to their hotel to continue brainstorming, Lawson trying to dig up anything she could on her computer. After still not coming up with anything, she called Sanders to let him know of their findings. Although finding out he was probably in league with Kurylenko was a good start, she wasn't prepared to hear the news that Sanders had for her.

"Well, we've just received some information here about Raines," Sanders said.

"Oh? What's that?" Lawson asked, surprised.

"We got word about eight or nine hours ago that one of our agents was killed in Mexico meeting with an informant."

"Oh my God. Who was it?" she asked, concerned.

"Danson. Both he and the informant were eliminated."

"Do we know who did it?"

"Not at first," Sanders said. "But we were able to get our hands on some surveillance footage of the building next to where they were located. Came in about two hours ago. It showed a man leaving that building minutes after the two of them were killed."

"Have we identified who the man is yet?"

"We have," Sanders replied. "It was Eric Raines."

Lawson was stunned to hear that Raines had killed one of their agents, someone who used to be on the same side as him. She didn't know what to say upon hearing the news.

"You there, Shelly?"

"Yes. I'm here. Are we positive it's him?" she asked, hoping it was a mistake.

"It is confirmed. The facial recognition software positively ID'd him. There's no doubt it's him."

"So, what's our next step?"

"His picture and file has been sent to every field agent, handler, executive, and support staff to get familiar with him. I've ordered a KOS on him. No questions asked," Sanders said.

"I see."

"I'm sorry, Shelly. I know it's difficult for you but we have no choice now that he's killed one of our agents. We now know which side he's on and it isn't ours."

"I know."

"Get back to New York as soon as you can."

"Our flight's leaving tomorrow," Lawson said.

As soon as Lawson got off the phone, Cain could see she was troubled by something. She was trying very hard not to break down and cry, though eventually a tear ran down her cheek. She quickly wiped it away, not wanting Cain to see it.

"What's wrong?" Cain asked.

"One of our agents was killed in Mexico."

"Who was it?"

"He said they have video of Raines leaving the building minutes after our agent was killed," she struggled to say.

"I'm sorry."

"Me too," Lawson said, managing to let a fake smile through.

"What's the next move?"

"We'll have to go back to New York and see. But in the meantime, Sanders has issued a KOS on Raines."

"KOS? What's that?" Cain asked.

"Kill on sight. It's very rare for that to be issued. It's only ordered for top priority cases where the other options are limited or exhausted. They don't like to issue it because it's dangerous for the field agents. If they run into a KOS target, then they're supposed to kill that target no matter where they are, whether it's in public or not. It could be in the middle of a crowded street. It exposes the agent as well as possibly compromising them along with the mission they were on. There's only been two other times the order's been issued since I've been working there."

"He's now a threat."

"You know, it was only a month or so ago where I stopped thinking about him every day and felt like I was actually starting to move on. And now this, just brings the hurt back even more," she said.

"It's gonna hurt again once someone finally kills him," Cain said. "And it will come to that."

"I know," she said sorrowfully.

"How did you break up?" Cain asked, trying to think of a way to tie everything together.

"Huh? Why does it matter?"

"Just curious."

"He broke up with me a week before he supposedly died. He said he felt like he had too much going on and just needed a break for a while."

Cain sat back in his chair, just thinking about Raines. He tried to put himself in Raines' shoes to get an idea of what he would do if he did the same thing. Cain shot a weird look over to Lawson that worried her.

"What?" she asked.

"Just thinking," he said, trying to think of the best way to phrase his thoughts.

"You got something?"

"I'm not sure."

"Well, just say it."

"He broke up with you a week before he died," Cain said.

"Yeah?"

"Well, we know he was planning this for at least six months to a year before that."

"What are you getting at?"

"That maybe he was using you to get information," Cain said.

"Information about what?"

"Where agents were located, types of missions being worked on, anything that might help him disappear."

"He never asked me about any other missions or files or anything."

"Maybe he didn't have to."

Lawson started looking all around the room trying to come to grips with everything. She so wanted Cain to be wrong but knew he probably wasn't. She had hoped that Raines' feelings for her were true but she was starting to realize that they most likely weren't.

"How often do you have your computer cleaned?" Cain asked.

"I don't know. I check it for viruses and bugs every week."

"No, I mean have the agency technician give it a complete check."

"Not in a while," Lawson replied.

"I think once we get back you should probably do that."

"You think he's got my computer hacked?" she asked, looking at her tablet.

"I think it's possible. If I was in his position, that's probably what I would do," he said.

"I would know if someone tampered with my computer."

"Would you?"

Lawson looked at him, knowing he was right again. She wouldn't have known, Raines would've been the last person she would've expected something like that from and likely would've overlooked any signs that her computer had been hacked.

"Love is blind," Cain said, trying to reassure her that it wasn't her fault.

12

On the flight back to New York, Lawson was in a very somber mood, unsettled that Raines may have been using her the entire time they were together. It was bad enough he broke up with her, then had to mourn his death, and then had to revisit everything upon learning he was actually alive. Now she was thinking that everything was a lie, and he had no feelings for her at all, which was the most upsetting, thinking she was just a pawn in whatever chess game Raines was playing.

While Lawson was having her own troubles, and not in a very talkative mood, Cain was trying to sleep on the long ride back to New York after having a brief layover in Great Britain. About an hour into the flight he had another vision. He'd seen a woman and a boy in his previous visions, in separate instances, but this one was different. In this one, the same woman and boy were together, playing together in a backyard. She was pushing him on the swing for a few moments, then waited for him to go down the slide. Just like the other visions he had, he couldn't hear any of their voices. He started moving his head around, hoping to get some clue as to who these people were. After a few minutes, Lawson could see Cain out of her peripheral vision having some type of problem. She assumed he was dreaming. She let him go for a few minutes until what appeared to be a painful expression came over his face. Lawson tapped on his shoulder to try to wake him to no avail. She then shook him more forcefully, finally able to awaken him from his sleep.

"Are you OK?" Lawson asked.

"Uh, yeah," Cain replied after taking a few seconds to get his wits about him.

"Having a bad dream?"

"No, not really."

"By the faces you were making it sure looked that way."

"No, I'm good."

Cain still seemed like he was out of it, his eyes a little glossy. Lawson kept a close eye on him for the next few minutes, unsure he was as fine as he claimed to be. He seemed like he was a little foggy to her. As the minutes went by Cain continued to shake the visions away, slowly feeling back to normal again. He looked at Lawson, wondering if he should tell her about the visions he was having. He thought if he told her then maybe she could help him in some way to figure out what was happening or who those people were. Cain knew he'd have to trust somebody eventually if he wanted help. With Lawson opening up to him about her troubles it seemed like she'd be a good candidate for him to open up to. Cain cleared his throat trying to think of a good way to talk about it.

"I, um, was wondering if I could talk to you about something," Cain said.

"Sure," Lawson replied, sensing something was bothering him.

"For the last week or so I've been having visions of people."

"What kind of visions? Of who?"

"I'm not sure. At first it was just of this woman, I don't know who she is. No voices. Just her face. Then a few days later she was walking somewhere. Then it was a boy playing on a swing. A few days after that both of them were together playing in a backyard."

"And you don't know who they are?"

"No."

"What do you think it means?" Lawson asked.

"I really don't know. Maybe I knew them before and I'm starting to remember, you know, get my memory back."

"Maybe so."

"I saw my file, but is it possible it wasn't complete?"

"In what way?"

"Maybe they're family, or friends," Cain said, hoping.

"I don't know. I saw the same file you did. All I know is that you weren't married."

"Maybe a sister."

"You're an only child," Lawson said.

Cain continued looking out the window, frustrated. Lawson could see the trying look on his face and felt bad for him. She wished she could do something for him but she didn't really know much more than what was in his file.

"Is there something that's been triggering these visions?" Lawson asked.

"No, I don't think so. Most of the time I was just sleeping."

"Maybe you should talk with a psychiatrist."

"I'm not doing that," Cain stated.

"No, listen, it might help you. Maybe he could get into your subconscious and figure things out," she said.

"I'll think about it."

"OK," Lawson said, knowing full well that he wouldn't.

"That's not all," Cain said.

"There's more?"

"I had a dream the other night that I was back in the army as a sniper."

"And?" she asked, knowing there was something he was troubled about.

"I shot someone in the head."

"Could've been something that happened while you were in the service."

"The person I shot was me."

Lawson didn't reply, not sure what to say to soothe his mind. She could see he was obviously upset by his dreams and visions but had no answers for him. She tried to calm him down.

"I know this isn't what you want to hear but it could be anything. You're trying to fit a five-letter crossword puzzle answer into a spot that's only got four spaces," Lawson said.

"What the hell is that supposed to mean?"

"That woman and boy could be anybody. Could've been an old girlfriend, a neighbor, just a friend, someone you saw on TV, maybe it's not even any of those things. Maybe it's just some woman you saw on the street and it stuck in your memory like you knew her."

Cain kept looking out the window, not wanting to hear what Lawson was telling him. She was right, but he desperately wanted it to mean something. Even if it was a little piece, at least it was a start. He stayed silent as Lawson continued talking.

"Right now, they're just visions of a woman. That's all they are. If you go around letting it eat at you like there's more to it, you're gonna drive yourself crazy. And everyone else around you."

"I don't have anyone else around me to drive crazy," Cain joked.

"OK, then me."

They dropped the subject momentarily as Lawson went back to work on her laptop. A few minutes later she still had more to say and turned it off, putting it away.

"Listen, I know you're frustrated, and I can understand. I know it's tough not knowing your past, and I can't say I know what it's like, but I am here for you. If you need help or just want to talk, don't hesitate to reach out to me."

"Thanks," Cain replied, giving her a smile.

"One more thing."

"Yes?"

"Is that woman still living in your apartment?" Lawson asked.

"You mean Heather?"

"Yeah, that's the one."

"Yeah, why?"

"It's not my business, but what is she still doing there?"

"It's not your business, but we have an arrangement," Cain said.

"She was only supposed to stay there a few days."

"So?"

"Are you two... involved?" she asked, trying to find the right words.

"She's a friend."

"People like that..." Lawson said, before being interrupted.

"She's actually a very nice person and very intelligent. You just have to get to know her. She actually has a degree you know."

"Really? That's surprising," Lawson said. "Are you hooking up?"

"That's not your concern."

"You are my concern. I'm your handler and it's my job to make sure your mind is in the right place," she said.

"Look, I kinda had an incident with the people she worked for," Cain said. "I didn't think it was wise for her to stay at her place so I told her to stay with me until she found a new apartment. They also kind of fired her so she's looking for a job."

"Like a real job?"

"Yes, a real job."

"You mean one that doesn't involve putting her ass in someone's face?" Lawson remarked.

"What is your problem with her?"

"I don't know. I know why Sanders uses her and I understand the reasoning behind it, I guess it just irks me for some reason."

"Why? Are you jealous?"

"What?!" Lawson said, her voice raising slightly. "No, I'm not jealous."

"Oh. I thought maybe you secretly wished you were in her shoes sometimes," Cain said, trying to egg her on.

"Yeah, right, don't be ridiculous."

"It just seemed like a little jealousy there."

"Listen, buster, I can get just as many men as she can if I wanted to," Lawson replied.

"Oh, I'm sure, I'm sure."

Once they arrived back at JFK airport, they grabbed their bags and started for their cars. Lawson invited Cain to her home for dinner and maybe a drink, but he thought it best to decline. He knew she was still in a highly emotional state and didn't want to complicate matters further. Besides that, he wasn't ready for any type of commitment with anyone and thought continuing any type of relationship that wasn't work related would lead in that direction. Before going home, Lawson went to the Center to drop off her computer to have it analyzed. The technician was still there as he often worked late nights and started working on it right away.

Cain walked through the door of his apartment to find it empty again. It seemed like every time he got back Heather wasn't there. He wondered where she was this time. Maybe she was out shopping again, he thought. He looked for something quick and easy to make himself for dinner and settled on macaroni and cheese. He sat down in the living room and turned on the Yankees game while he ate. As ten o'clock approached, Cain started to get concerned about Heather's whereabouts. He figured she would've been back by now. A few minutes after ten she came staggering through the door. Cain could tell right away that she was a little tipsy. He got up to make sure she didn't fall over and hurt herself. He put his arm around her shoulders and walked to the couch. By the smell of her breath she'd been drinking something fruity.

"Hey, you're back," she said.

"Yep."

"I, uh, I was gonna say something."

"You'll think of it later," Cain replied.

"You're such a cutie pie."

"Thanks."

Heather put her hand on his face and stroked his cheek. Cain sat her down on the couch and started to leave her when she grabbed his arm to sit him back down. She put her arms around his neck to move closer to him, hoping to get a kiss or two.

"You're pretty nice stuff," she said.

"You're pretty drunk," Cain responded, taking her arms off him.

"Why do you hate me?"

"I don't hate you."

"Then why won't you kiss me?" she asked, moving in on him again.

"Because I don't want to take advantage of you," he replied with a laugh.

"Please take advantage of me. I want you to take advantage of me."

"Not tonight. You need to sleep."

"What's a girl gotta do to get a kiss around here?" she stuttered.

"Be sober for one."

"And then you'll kiss me?" she asked hopefully.

"We'll see."

"Is that a promise?"

Cain laughed. "Just lay down."

"Not until you promise to kiss me."

"I promise."

"When?"

"We'll talk about it when you wake up."

"Sounds like a deal."

Cain finally eased her down on the couch, Heather falling

asleep within minutes. Cain went into the bedroom for a blanket and placed it over her. He stood over her for a few minutes, watching her to make sure she was OK.

"Seems like you started a little early," Cain said to himself, looking at his watch.

Cain was pretty tired and lay down on the sofa across from her. He figured he'd stay there instead of going to bed in case Heather needed anything during the night. It was a pretty quiet night though, as Heather slept straight through to the morning. She woke up holding her head and immediately went to the bathroom. Cain heard her getting up and got up himself to make sure she was all right. A few minutes later Heather emerged from the bathroom walking a little straighter though she was still rubbing her temples trying to make the pain go away. She noticed Cain standing by the sink in the kitchen.

"Hey," she said, forgetting she saw him the previous night.

"How are you doing?" Cain asked, smiling, somewhat amused with her condition.

"My head hurts."

"I can see that."

"When'd you get back?" she asked, putting her head down on the counter.

"Oh, I rolled in last night."

"Last night? Were you here already when I got in?"

Cain laughed. "Yeah."

"Oh. I'm so sorry."

"Don't be. Happens."

"I don't remember much. I really hope I didn't make a fool of myself," Heather said.

"You were fine."

"Wait, I think I remember a little bit," she said, straining to collect her thoughts. "Were we sitting on the couch or something?"

"Yeah."

"Did I try to, uh, throw myself onto you or something?"

"Well, it wasn't quite that bad," Cain said.

"Oh God. I'm so sorry. I feel so bad."

"Heather, it's fine. You didn't do anything wrong."

"I feel like such an idiot now," she explained.

"What were you celebrating? It's not New Year's."

"A girl I used to work with at the club is getting married. She wanted to go out for drinks with some of the girls to celebrate. I didn't have anything else to do."

"Oh. Sounds nice. Did you have a good time?" Cain asked.

"Apparently I had too good of a time."

Cain laughed as he started brewing some coffee for her. As they continued talking, Cain kept making a few jokes at Heather's expense. She could tell he was enjoying her agony and seemed to be having some fun with it.

"You're enjoying this, aren't you?" she asked.

"You know, maybe a little bit."

"Glad you're getting some laughs out of my pain."

"Hey, I'm sure you'd be doing the same to me," Cain said.

"Thanks for taking care of me though," Heather said, getting serious.

"I really didn't do much. Just put you on the couch and threw a blanket on you."

"Still. It's the thought that counts."

"Well, I recall you taking care of me the night before I left. I figured it was my turn to return the favor."

They just sat and talked in the living room for a few hours, trying to take it easy. Just after twelve Cain's phone started ringing. Heather walked over to the kitchen counter to get it and looked at the screen. She made a face when she saw who it was.

"Guess who?" she asked, handing it to him.

"Hey, what's up?" Cain asked his handler.

"Just got the findings back from the technician about my computer."

"And?"

"You were right. He's been looking at my emails, case files, missions, everything," Lawson said.

"Since when?"

"For about nine months."

"So, what now?"

"I don't know."

"Can you get the IP addresses from the computers he was using to hack it?" Cain asked.

"No. He's using a very sophisticated system that encodes his info. We can see what time and general location he looked at everything, down to the city, but that's about it. We might be able to nail it down further but it'd be kind of pointless by the time we find it. He's already long gone by that point."

"What's the last few things he's been looking at?"

"You," Lawson said.

"He knew you were in Honduras before you got there. He'd already accessed your file. He was waiting for you."

"I see."

"And he knows you and I were in Indonesia. He looked at our flight information a couple days ago. Hold on," she said, looking at her phone. "Sanders is calling. I'll call you back."

"You want some aspirin?" Cain asked his hungover companion.

"Yeah, I guess I'll take some more."

Cain went to the bathroom to get some Advil for her, bringing out a couple capsules along with a drink of water. As soon as he handed Heather the glass, his phone rang again.

"Hey," Cain said.

"We have something going on. Can you come here now?" Lawson asked.

"Uh, yeah, I'll be right there."

Whatever was going on sounded like it was important as Lawson seemed to be rushing her words. Cain quickly got his shoes on and grabbed his guns.

"What's going on?" Heather asked, concerned.

"Not sure. Have to go to the office."

"Be careful," she said, worried about the guns he was strapping on.

13

Cain rushed over to the Center, still unsure what was going on. Once he arrived he went to Lawson's office, who was waiting for him.

"C'mon, we're going to The Room," Lawson said.

"What's that?"

"It's kind of like an observation room. There's a bunch of analysts looking at information on their computers, and if there's an important mission going on, communicating with the agents in the field as things are happening."

"Oh," Cain replied as they swiftly walked.

"If we have video it's put up on the big screen for everyone to see. If there's a decision to be made then a higher up will make it... usually Sanders."

"So, what's going on now?"

"I'm still not sure myself," Lawson responded. "Sanders said he'd explain once we got there."

Five minutes later they entered The Room, Lawson swiping

her ID to gain entrance. Once inside, Cain looked around the room, impressed at the sophistication of the area. There were a bunch of mini workstations, all manned by analysts on headsets, with a bunch of small TVs all over the room, with a huge screen in the middle of the wall at the front. There were a couple of supervisors going from station to station to get the latest updates that the analysts had for them. Sanders' attention kept diverting between the TVs before he realized Cain and Lawson finally arrived.

"Glad you got here so quickly," Sanders said.

"What's going on?" Lawson asked.

"Well, considering both of you have gotten involved in this I figured you'd wanna be here to see its conclusion."

"Conclusion of what?"

"We've got Raines," Sanders said.

"Where?" Lawson asked.

"He's on a plane to San Francisco. He just left Mexico an hour ago and should arrive in about two hours."

"How do you know he's on it?" Cain asked.

"We got him on video from the Mexican airport boarding a plane. We then tracked the flight information. We're tracking the flight now so we'll know when it lands."

"What is he going to San Fran for?" Lawson asked.

"Just a layover," Sanders answered. "Going to San Francisco and then Hong Kong in lieu of his final destination... Indonesia."

"He's going back," Lawson said.

"Well, we're gonna make sure he's not."

"What's the plan?" Cain asked.

"We've got two agents en route to the San Francisco airport as we speak. They should arrive within a half hour."

"Are they capable of taking him out?" Cain asked.

"They both have considerable experience in the field. They're more than qualified," Sanders replied.

"Are they gonna kill him as soon as he steps off the plane?"

"No. As much as I'd like that it's too high profile. Our agents will be there waiting for him. They will take him into custody as soon as Raines steps off that plane."

"I thought custody wasn't sanctioned?"

"They will take him into custody and then they will immediately escort Raines into a bathroom. They will then proceed to lead him into a stall where they will promptly put two bullets in his head," Sanders explained.

"Oh."

"Then we will tamper with the surveillance footage in that time frame so there is no evidence that we were ever there."

"Sounds like it's all under control," Lawson added.

"This should be the end."

Lawson and Cain took a step back and just watched the proceedings as the time counted down. Lawson sat down in a chair and put her head down, mixed feelings running through her as she thought about what was about to happen. As much as she knew Raines deserved what he had coming to him, she still couldn't erase some of the feelings she had for him. Cain, on the other hand, was fascinated by The Room. He closely watched the analysts as they worked, magnetized by the complexity of their work. They all periodically looked up at the digital clock on the wall, anxiously waiting for that moment to arrive. As the time approached, just minutes from the expected deadly encounter, Lawson rocked on her chair, feeling like she was going to be sick.

"You all right?" Cain asked, noticing her discomfort.

"I'll be OK."

"Want some water?"

"No," she said.

Cain could see how anxious she was to the point it seemed like she might pass out. Her skin tone was getting lighter, her eyes seemed dilated, and she was heavily sweating. She was trying not to think about it but that was near impossible. Cain thought it might be best if she wasn't in the room as the incident went down to spare her feelings.

"It might be better if you weren't here," Cain said.

"I'm not leaving," Lawson replied.

"This isn't gonna do you any good."

"I wanna be here when it happens," she said, appreciative of his offer.

"Being here when it happens isn't gonna help," Cain insisted. "Your spirit isn't gonna feel lighter and angels aren't gonna come down and sing to you."

"Being in a different room not knowing what's going on isn't gonna help either. It's just something I'll have to deal with either way. I'd rather be here when it does."

Cain knew he wasn't going to win the fight, so he dropped it, hoping she knew what she was doing. Watching someone you once cared for die wasn't going to be an easy thing for her to swallow.

"All right. Here we go," Sanders said, looking at the time. The plane was due to land any minute.

They contacted their agents to check their status and were informed that they were already in the airport, heading to Terminal 1.

"This is Langston," the agent said through his earpiece a

few minutes later. "Rivers and I are in position to intercept the target."

"Good," Sanders replied. "Get it done."

The United Airlines plane finally touched down and passengers started exiting within a few minutes. The well-dressed agents stood there, waiting for Raines to show himself, prepared for a gun battle at any time if he saw fit to engage in such. Raines finally emerged, one of the last passengers to get off, and immediately noticed the two suits waiting there. He assumed they were there for him but he wasn't the sort of man who panicked at the first sign of trouble. He always calculated risks and determined when would be the right time to counteract any signs of trouble. He continued walking at a brisk pace, suitcase in hand, hoping to walk right past them. He wasn't past opening up on the two of them right there but usually was a little bit more cunning than that.

"You boys waiting for me?" Raines asked as the two men joined each of his sides, one of them grabbing his bag. They each grabbed hold of one of his arms to ensure he didn't rabbit on them. "Hope I didn't keep you waiting long," Raines joked.

"Let's go," Langston said.

"Where we going?"

"I have to go to the bathroom."

Raines knew exactly what that meant. Sanders and the rest of his crew were listening to every word on the speakers, somewhat surprised that Raines was cooperating so easily without a struggle.

"Something's wrong," Lawson blurted out, standing up.

"Everything's fine," Sanders replied, reassuring the group, though not so sure himself.

"He's going too easily. He knows there's a KOS order on him, he's seen it on my computer. He's up to something."

"Have your guard up in case he tries something," Sanders told the arresting agents.

"Roger," Langston replied.

"Maybe he just knows the game's up," Cain added.

"No," Lawson said. "That's not him. It's not in his makeup to just accept things as they are. He always has an idea to respond to a situation or an alternate way of doing things. That's just how he is. Just giving up and resigning himself to his predicament is something he's never done."

After a five-minute walk they found the bathroom. Static started blaring over the speakers in The Room.

"What's happening?" Sanders asked.

"We're losing the signal," an analyst replied.

"Why? Get it back up."

The agents and Raines walked into the bathroom and they all went to the sinks, the agents pretending to wash their hands as they waited for the bathroom to empty of witnesses. One man exited a stall, washed his hands and left, then another man finished at the urinal. As the final man left, Rivers went over to lock the door. As Rivers' back was turned to the pair, Raines produced a knife out of his sleeve, sticking it into the stomach of Langston. He grabbed Langston's gun out of his hand as Langston fell to one knee and fired two shots at Rivers as he turned around. The shots were muffled by the silencer on the gun so nobody would hear the shots and come running. Both bullets hit Rivers in his chest, instantly knocking him onto his back. Langston pulled the knife out of his stomach and got to his feet only for Raines to turn his attention to him. The first bullet entered Langston's body on the side of his head, blood splattering onto the sink and mirror. As Langston fell to the floor, Raines made sure the job was done and shot the fallen agent two more times in the chest. Langston was already dead by that point, the headshot terminating his life. Out of the corner of his eye Raines noticed the leg of Rivers moving slightly and he walked over to him. He stood over him, knowing he would perish shortly, but decided to end it quicker for him. He pointed the silencer at his head, putting one right in the center of the agent's forehead. There was no more life left within him and Raines quickly looked over his work. He grabbed the earpiece from Rivers' body and put it on. He washed the blood from his victims off his hands and quickly left the bathroom.

"Can we tap into the airport video?" Sanders asked.

"I'll get right on it," another analyst answered.

The silence was worrisome to the group, not knowing what was happening. Though they were confident of the plan succeeding, anytime something went awry that wasn't accounted for, it was a cause for concern. Lawson had sat back down with her hands together over her face, almost looking like she was praying. Cain periodically looked over to her to make sure she was OK and hadn't passed out or anything. They all anxiously waited to hear the words booming over the speakers again, hopefully that Raines had been eliminated

"Feed's up," an analyst noted as the video went up on the big screen. "That's the closest bathroom to the terminal. They gotta be in there."

Everyone intently stared at the screen as they waited for their agents to emerge. After a couple minutes of no activity they knew something was wrong.

"Something happened," Sanders said. "It doesn't take that long to put a bullet into somebody."

"Agent Langston, Agent Rivers, what is your status, over?" an analyst asked to no reply. He waited a few seconds before repeating the same question.

After a few more seconds of silence they finally heard a voice reply back.

"The target's been eliminated," the voice said.

"What took you so long?" Sanders asked, agitated.

"Just had to wait for people to clear out of the bathroom," Raines answered, hurrying out of the airport before they realized it was him.

"Where are you now? We've got video on the bathroom now."

"We already exited and are leaving the airport now."

"Well, good job," Sanders said. "We'll start erasing the evidence."

"It's been my pleasure."

Lawson suddenly stood up, alarmed at something she heard. Cain looked at her strangely, wondering if she was OK. He put his hand on her arm which she brushed off, indicating she was fine.

"It's him," she stated.

"What?" Sanders asked, turning around.

"Raines. He's alive. That's him you're talking to."

"How do you know that?"

"He said 'it's been my pleasure'."

"So?"

"Raines always said that. It was one of his quirky sayings that he liked to say," Lawson said.

"Are you positive?"

"That's him. Anytime someone said something to him that he felt like he should respond to he'd say 'my pleasure.' He's alive. Trust me."

Sanders turned back to the microphone on the desk and pushed the red button to talk.

"Raines," Sanders sternly said.

There was no reply as Sanders looked back at Lawson, who nodded that she was positive it was him. After a minute, Raines decided to respond.

"So, what tipped me off?" Raines asked.

"What happened to my men?" Sanders asked.

"I'm pretty sure you know the answer to that."

"I do."

"Shelly's there, isn't she? She has to be. She's the one who figured out it was me so quickly. Otherwise you wouldn't have known for a little while yet."

"She is," Sanders confirmed.

"May I talk to her?" Raines asked politely.

"Absolutely not."

"Tell her I'm sorry that it came to this."

"You're not one bit sorry."

"Well, that's for you to decipher. Tell her I did care for her."

"She can hear you."

"Well, it looks as though you've interrupted my plans. Now I'm gonna have to reach my destination in some other manner."

"We'll find you. Just like we did today," Sanders said.

"Even if you do, the results will play out just as they did today. You cannot out-think or outmaneuver me. I will always be one step ahead of you. So, beware of the obvious," Raines warned.

The connection cut out, ending the call, as a deafening

silence permeated through the room. A look of sadness and despair overtook the faces of everyone, angry and despondent over what just occurred.

"See if you can get video of the airport and parking lots to see if we can pick up where he's at," Sanders told an analyst.

"It's unlikely we'll find him. He's probably disguised himself or laying low for a while," Lawson said.

"I agree. But let's do our due diligence, anyway."

"Well, we know he was heading back to Indonesia," Lawson said.

"Yes, but I'd say it's a good bet he'll be changing his plans now that he knows we were on him," Sanders replied. "At the very least he'll be changing his method of getting there."

"Flying's the only way of getting there."

"He knows we'll be watching the flight lists. He'll come up with something."

A few people left the room though most of the analysts stayed to continue working. Sanders huffed and sighed as he exited the room. He stopped as he reached Cain and Lawson. Lawson seemed a little dazed, stunned that what she anticipated didn't come to fruition.

"I want you two to make finding him your top priority right now," Sanders told them before leaving. "You find him. I want him dead."

14

Lawson woke up a little after five in the morning after a pretty restless sleep, nightmares continuing to run through her mind throughout the night. She dreamt of various scenarios in which Raines was killed, sometimes by her shooting him, or by Cain finishing him off. She lay in bed for ten minutes, staring up at the ceiling, wondering where Raines was at that particular time. She looked over at Cain who was still sleeping, and smiled, pulling the sheets over his naked body. After Raines eluded their capture in San Francisco, Lawson and Cain went to her house to work. Cain mainly went to make sure Lawson was OK and didn't drink herself into a stupor. He somehow managed to let her get his guard down and started drinking along with her. After a couple hours of getting their mouths wet, they repeated the steps they took in that Indonesian hotel, and had a fun-filled night of passion. She got up and took a shower, then proceeded to go to her desk, working on her computer for a bit. She felt a little more clear-headed, the lustfulness of the evening taking some stress off her shoulders.

Cain started stirring once he heard her typing away on the keyboard. He sat on the edge of the bed, yawning, and holding his head.

"Hey, sleepyhead," Lawson greeted.

"Hey."

Cain got up and dressed, wondering to himself what he was doing. He didn't necessarily regret being there, but he wasn't sure it was the right thing they should be doing. He sat down next to Lawson at her desk, looking at what she was doing. They started talking but quickly stopped when a beeping sound started coming from her computer.

"What's that?" Cain asked.

"It's an alert from the tracking program I have on there. It picked up something," she replied, looking at the information that popped up.

By the look on Lawson's face, Cain could tell it was something big. Her mouth opened the way it does when someone gets a shock that they can't believe and her eyes stared at the screen, almost like she was afraid the information would go away if she blinked.

"It's from Gutawa's computer," she said, turning to him.

"And?"

"There's an email from Raines."

It read: *Will be in Indonesia Friday. I would like to meet with you if you're available.*

Cain looked at the screen as the two of them read the short e-mail together. There wasn't much to it or any complexities that they could see. They wondered if it was some sort of code but ultimately agreed that it wasn't. Lawson immediately called Sanders to let him know.

"Yes?" Sanders sleepily answered.

"Sorry to wake you, sir," Lawson said.

"That's all right. I was looking to get an early start this morning, anyway. I assume something's happened?"

"I just got a hit from the tracking software I put on Gutawa's computer in Indonesia," she said.

"Oh? Good news I hope?"

"I'm not sure yet. Raines just e-mailed him asking to meet with him. He said he'd be in Indonesia on Friday."

"Any reply back yet?"

"Not yet. We should look at the flight lists to see," Lawson started before Sanders interrupted her.

"There's no guarantee he's actually coming in on Friday. He might arrive Thursday. He also might not fly directly in. He could arrive via Singapore, or the Philippines, or even through Australia. Unless we have confirmed his path in, then the best course of action is to meet him there. Take Cain and go back. Get the earliest flight you can. When Gutawa meets Raines, so will you," Sanders said.

"I'll make the plans."

"Shelly."

"Yes?"

"I want you to be careful, understand?"

"I will."

"You are not an agent. I'm only telling you to go because you're directly acquainted with the way he thinks and you are probably the best person to track him. I do not want you getting engaged with him if something goes down. That's what Cain is for."

"I understand."

As soon as she got off the phone she started checking airline information and let Cain know they were flying back to Indonesia. Within a few minutes all the flight times were displayed, and she picked the one that'd get them there the fastest with the fewest layovers on the way. They wouldn't have much time to prepare as their flight would leave in six hours.

Cain immediately left to go back to his apartment. He walked in and saw Heather sleeping on the couch. A small amount of guilt slowly crept into his system for not coming home all night. He went into his bedroom and quickly packed some clothes, while also putting his guns into the secret compartment of his bag so that they'd go undetected through airport security. Heather woke up, the sounds of the drawers opening and closing waking her. She rushed into the bedroom, happy to see Cain, and hugged him. She thought she smelled a woman's perfume on him as he pulled away from her embrace.

"I was so worried," she said. "I sent you a bunch of texts but you never responded."

"Oh," Cain replied. He padded the pockets of his pants to feel where his phone was. He never even checked it once he got to Lawson's house, so he never got Heather's messages. "I, uh, forgot to check it."

"That's OK. I waited on the couch all night for you to get back. I must've fallen asleep while I was waiting."

The small amount of guilt Cain felt was growing by the moment. The fact that this woman was concerned about his whereabouts and well-being and he never bothered to even let her know where he was made him feel pretty crummy. He knew he wasn't obligated to tell her anything, but she was staying at his apartment and figured it was probably the proper thing to do.

"So, where were you?" Heather asked.

"Um, we had something important come up at the office. I just couldn't get away," he lied.

"All night? And you never checked your phone?" she asked, not quite believing his story.

"I just forgot."

A confused look came over Heather's face as she watched Cain finish packing. She wondered where he was going after rushing in from being gone all night.

"Are you going somewhere?" she asked.

He sighed. "I have to go back to Indonesia."

"Again?"

"Yeah. Looks like some unfinished business. Hopefully it won't take too long but I'm not sure."

"Oh. When's your flight?"

"A few hours," Cain answered.

"You were with someone, weren't you?" Heather finally asked, trying not to sound jealous.

"Uh," Cain mumbled, not sure what to say, and definitely not wanting to tell the truth.

"The perfume gives it away," she said.

"Oh."

"So, who's the lucky girl? Do I know her?"

Cain looked down at the floor, ashamed to look at Heather in her face. She could tell by his avoidance that it was some-body that she knew, which cut down the list of suspects dramatically. She thought for a second, then a look came over her face like she just solved a riddle. She remembered smelling that perfume before, not too long ago.

"It was Michelle, huh?" she asked.

Cain hesitated before answering, still not wanting to say. "Yeah."

"I remember that perfume. She was wearing it that night she came over here. The night we first met."

"Oh. Good memory."

"I usually don't forget things."

"I see that."

"So, are you two an item now?" she asked.

"No," Cain emphatically answered. "It just kind of happened. Nothing more than that."

They stood there in silence, both waiting for the other to continue, though neither one did. Heather knew she didn't have the right to be mad since they weren't a couple, but she couldn't help but be a little huffy. Lawson got what Heather wanted. Him. She couldn't figure out what Lawson had that she didn't. She figured she should stop peppering him with questions about it since they weren't together. He had the right to do what he wanted even though it made her heart ache. Cain could tell that Heather was a little annoyed, though he wasn't sure if it was more the fact he didn't come home or whether it was his little rendezvous with Lawson.

"Well, I should probably get going," Cain finally stated.

"OK."

"Um, I'll see you when I get back."

"Yeah," she replied, faking a smile.

"I'll let you know when I'm on my way."

Cain walked toward the door, turning around to see Heather once he reached it. He only saw her back as she was already walking into the bedroom. She had her head down and he could tell she was disappointed. Cain felt some remorse that he was the reason for her unhappiness and thought maybe he could make it up to her once he got back.

Once Cain arrived at the airport he met with Lawson, who was already waiting for him. She got there a half hour earlier and was on her computer working.

"Looks like we got some more news," Lawson said.

"About?"

"Gutawa replied to Raines' email," she said.

"What'd he say?"

"He agreed to meet with him. Ten o'clock at the Makam Perang Jakarta."

"Say that again?" Cain asked, not understanding what she just told him.

"The Jakarta War Cemetery."

"Convenient. He won't have to go far when we're done."

"I've downloaded a map of the cemetery so we can plan it out."

They looked over the plans during their long plane ride. The Jakarta War Cemetery contained the graves of almost 1,000 people, many of which died defending Java and Sumatra during the Japanese advance in 1942. Others died later in prisoner of war camps. The cemetery was in the suburb of Menteng Poeloe, almost seven miles from the center of the city. It was next to the Netherlands Field of Honour in South Jakarta. It was only open between the hours of eight and five, Monday through Friday, so Raines obviously picked the location for its seclusion. The entrance faced the cemetery where people from the local market often blocked the access, trying to sell their wares. The cemetery was entered from the north side by a short flight of steps which led into a memorial building. Two main grass areas went through the site, one which ran north and south, the other running east to west. The Cross of Sacrifice stood in the middle of where the grass areas met. In the southern part of the cemetery lay the graves from members of India's forces. A monument was set up in this part, with sculptured wreaths bearing the words "India" and "Pakistan" beneath them. The caretakers' quarters along with a garage were also in that part of the cemetery. All graves were marked by bronze plaques and concrete pedestals. There were many sub-tropical plants, trees, and shrubs that adorned the property.

"We're gonna be met by another agent once we get there," Lawson informed Cain.

"Why?"

"To have more parts of the cemetery covered. He was doing some work in Australia, so he was fairly close to bring over."

"What's the plan?" Cain asked. "Doesn't really seem like a lot of good places to take cover here."

"The meeting's scheduled to take place at the Cross of Sacrifice. Agent Stanton will be stationed by the garage where he can see the side entrance and the Indian Forces Monument if he should go that way."

"And us?"

"We're gonna have to be at the edge of the property. There are some shrubs at the back that we can take cover in," she explained.

"I'm not really liking this."

"Why?"

"Seems too exposed."

"It'll be fine."

"We'll see."

15

Jakarta, Indonesia—It was just about ten o'clock and everyone was in position. Stanton was by the garage guarding the side entrance. Lawson and Cain were taking cover behind some shrubs near the back of the cemetery. They were lying on their stomachs as the shrubs were small and they'd be exposed if they stood up. Cain had his sniper rifle out, targeting the area by the Cross of Sacrifice. A few minutes later they saw a figure emerge, walking in the main entrance through the memorial shelter. He reached the Cross of Sacrifice and sat there, waiting for his partner.

"It's Gutawa," Cain said, seeing him clearly through the scope of his rifle.

Gutawa looked very anxious and kept looking around as he waited for Raines to arrive. He got up a few times and walked around the monument, continuing to look for him. As the minutes ticked by, Gutawa seemed like he was contemplating leaving as he walked toward the entrance a few times before circling back to his location, looking at his watch. A half hour elapsed with no sign of Raines.

"Something must be wrong," Lawson whispered.

"Maybe."

"He should've been here by now."

"Maybe he's just being extra cautious," Cain replied.

"How long should we stay here if he doesn't show?"

"We'll stay here as long as Gutawa's here. As long as he's expecting him to show then we're not bailing either."

The time slowly ticked away, Lawson repeatedly looking at her watch, anxious for her former lover to arrive. It was just about eleven o'clock when Gutawa seemed to have had enough. He started walking toward the exit when Lawson stood up. Everyone seemed to believe that Raines was blowing the meeting off.

"What're you doing?" Cain asked, trying to grab her leg.

"Let's see if he knows more," she replied as she started walking.

"No," Cain said, flailing at her leg, just touching her heel.

Cain quickly regained his position, putting the entire area within the sights of his scope. He didn't think it was a good idea for Lawson to expose herself but there wasn't much else he could do. He figured they could've tailed Gutawa to see where he went after that. Gutawa could've led them to more information that would've led to Raines in some capacity. Lawson, though, figured Gutawa knew what the meeting was about and wanted to question him about it. Gutawa stopped as he noticed a dark figure moving closer to him. He closely watched the person moving in, eagerly waiting to see who it was. He squinted his eyes trying to make out who it was. His eyes opened wider, surprised to see Lawson emerge from the darkness.

"You look surprised," Lawson said. "Expecting someone else?"

"Why are you here?"

"Same reason you are."

Gutawa shrugged as if to say he didn't know why he was there.

"It's late, it's dark, and the cemetery closed over five hours ago. I know you're not here to just walk around," Lawson said.

"I have nothing to say to you."

"I know you were here to meet Raines."

"I still have nothing to say," Gutawa said.

"You don't have to say it. I already know," Lawson said. "Raines sent you an email asking you to meet him. You agreed and set up the time and place. So here we are."

Gutawa seemed stunned that she knew the exact details. "How do you know all that?"

"We have our ways. You're not leaving here until you tell us what we want to know," she said.

"I don't know what he wanted. He said he wanted to meet, so I agreed. The purpose of this meeting was unclear to me as well."

Just as Gutawa let the words out, a shot rifled through the crisp night air. He stumbled forward onto Lawson, who struggled to keep him upright, the pair eventually falling to the ground, Gutawa on top of her. Lawson pushed his lifeless body off her and looked down at her blood-soaked shirt. She then looked over at Gutawa, who wasn't moving and appeared to be dead. Cain frantically waved his gun around, desperately trying to find his target. He was unable to do so and turned his focus to Lawson. He looked at her through his scope and noticed she was moving.

"Just stay still," Cain said through his earpiece.

"I think Gutawa's dead," Lawson replied.

"Are you hit?"

"No, I don't think so."

"Just hold on until I get you. I don't know where the shooter is so I don't know if he's got sights on you or not."

Agent Stanton left his position and came rushing up the steps to get to Lawson. Once he got there, he bent down on one knee to check her condition. As he was doing so, another shot rang out, this one ripping through Stanton's chest. The force of the bullet knocked him back, killing him almost instantly. Cain noticed the flash of the man's rifle and saw it was coming from just beyond the fence. He took off running, hoping to catch the killer before he had a chance to escape. Once Lawson saw Cain running she quickly got up and ran after him. She wasn't going to let Cain get too far ahead of her. They heard the sound of a car door shutting, then squealing away, indicating Gutawa's killer had gotten away. Cain ran to their car, refusing to let their man get away. Lawson was right on his heels and got in the passenger side.

"What about Stanton?" Cain asked.

"I think he's dead."

Cain pushed the pedal to the floor to gain speed on the fleeing suspect. He could hear the squealing of the brakes so he could tell which direction the car was traveling. The two cars zoomed through the Jakarta streets in a short pursuit that felt like it lasted a while, but only took about five minutes. The car Cain and Lawson were following ended the chase prematurely as it reached a bridge that overlooked the Ciliwung River. The car just stopped and turned completely around to face the oncoming car. Cain stopped the car about forty feet in front of the other car as they waited for the occupant to make a move.

"What's he doing?" Lawson asked.

"I don't know. You stay down," Cain said as he pulled out his Glock.

The pair sat there staring at the other car, struggling to see who was inside. A few seconds later the other car door opened, though the occupant still sat in his seat. Cain opened his door also, mimicking the other driver.

"You have your gun on you?" Cain asked.

"Yeah."

"Get it out."

Lawson took out her gun, wondering what Cain had in mind. She usually carried a gun but seldom had any use for it. The only things she ever shot at were targets on the firing range.

"If something happens to me, do whatever it takes," Cain told her.

"What?" Lawson asked, surprised to hear him talking in that manner.

"I don't know what this guy's plans are, but if I don't make it, protect yourself."

Lawson checked her gun and got it ready, anxious and nervous about what was going to happen. Suddenly the other driver got out, revealing himself.

"Raines," Lawson exclaimed.

"Yep."

"You knew it all the time?"

"I assumed so. Who else would it be?"

"Why would he shoot his own contact? He helped him

disappear."

"Maybe because he found out that he talked to us. Besides, now that we know he's alive he's got no more use for Gutawa," Cain said.

"What's he doing?" Lawson asked.

Raines emerged from the car and just stood in front of it, gun in his hand, relaxed at his side. Cain and Lawson also got out, though Cain gave his partner a disapproving look, not wanting her to exit the vehicle. It was too late to argue as Cain wasn't about to take his eyes off of Raines and give him an advantage.

"It seemed as though I wasn't going to outrun you," Raines shouted. "So, stopping to face you seemed to be the proper course of action."

"You know this has to end," Cain replied.

"Does it? Why?"

"You just know it does."

"Yes, as Sanders has ordered," Raines said. "I've got no quarrel with you, Cain. We can both go our separate ways now."

"I can't do that."

"Why not? If I wanted you dead, I would've killed you in Honduras. And you know I could've. As for you, Shelly, I could've killed you in the cemetery just as easily as the others if I so desired. But my feelings for you wouldn't let me do that. I couldn't do that."

"Don't talk about your feelings for me," Lawson screamed. "You used me."

"I did. I apologize for that," Raines said. "But that doesn't mean my feelings for you weren't true because they were. Nothing I did or have done changes that."

"What is it you want?" Cain asked.

"For us to go our separate ways. You go back to New York and I'll once again disappear," Raines offered.

"Too much has happened for us to let that happen. You've killed some of our agents," Lawson said.

"Come on, Shelly, you're much brighter than that. To just accept what you've been told. Especially by those that perpetuate the lies. I killed those who attempted to kill me, in self-defense," Raines responded. "Tell me, Cain, have you yet figured out the lies that you've been told?"

"What lies?" Cain asked.

"To which there are too numerous to respond. In time, you will figure them out as I have. I assume that you will. The facts will at some point not come together the same as they used to. The memory will come back to you and reveal the things that you've lost. You will realize that things are not as they seem. That what you've been told is not necessarily true. One day something will just seem out of place and create a domino effect in which all the pieces fall down, revealing your true self. I hope you get to that place... as I have."

"What are you talking about?"

"I wish I could tell you. But I'm afraid our time here is up," Raines said, raising his arms in an attacking stance. "We've created quite a stir and the police will be here shortly."

Raines pointed his gun at the pair, which prompted Cain and Lawson to do the same. Raines slowly started moving away from his car and toward the edge of the bridge. Cain started circling around him as Lawson stayed in her position. Raines continued backpedaling until his back hit the bridge and he had nowhere else to go.

"Well, I guess I'll see you in our next life," Raines said.

Raines fired a couple rounds in Cain's direction before

quickly taking a shot at Lawson. All his shots missed as the bullets whizzed by Cain and the shot at Lawson grazed off the ground. Cain quickly regained his composure after dodging the bullets and fired at Raines. His shot hit his mark as Raines grimaced before the blow knocked him over the concrete railing. Cain and Lawson rushed over to the railing to see where Raines fell but couldn't see him in the water. Not only was it dark, but the Ciliwung River was a dirty, polluted river. Sometimes it was hard to see what was in it during the daytime. Cain put his hand on the railing as he kept looking and felt something. He pulled his hand up to see what it was and rubbed his fingers together before wiping the blood off on his pants.

"You think he's dead?" Lawson asked.

"I dunno but we gotta move," Cain replied, pushing her back to the car. "Stay here and we'll get some onlookers before you know it."

They drove back to the cemetery in the hopes of cleaning up the scene. In the event police were already there they'd keep on driving. Luckily, they had not yet arrived and Cain reached into the glove box for a spare gun.

"What are you doing?" Lawson asked.

"Fixing the mess."

Cain put the gun by Gutawa's hand and dragged Stanton's body a little to give the impression that they shot each other. He wanted to make it appear that there were no other people there and make it an open and shut case. He quickly finished his work and ran back to the car, driving back to the hotel with Lawson. Once inside their room Lawson called Sanders with an update.

"We cornered Raines on a bridge," Lawson said.

"And?"

"Cain shot him."

"Is he dead?" Sanders asked.

"I think so."

"You think?"

"The shot made him fall over the bridge and into the river," Lawson said.

"Did you see his body?"

"No. But there was blood all over the railing."

"Hmm. I'll put our sources to work to confirm it. If he's shot and bleeding he'll have to hit a doctor somewhere along the way if he's alive."

"You think he's alive?"

"Until his body is found we will go under the assumption that he is alive," Sanders said.

"Yes, sir."

"You two have done some good work on this. I want you to stay there for a few more days to see what you can find out. If his body is found it'll be all over the news."

Lawson told Cain about the instructions Sanders left for them. She could see something was wrong with him. He had this look on him that indicated something was troubling him.

"What is it?" she asked.

"It just doesn't seem right."

"What doesn't?"

"Raines is an expert shot. He fired three rounds and didn't hit either one of us," Cain said.

"Well, he was in a hurry."

"I don't think that was it."

"You think he missed on purpose?" Lawson asked incredulously.

"Maybe."

"Why would he do that?"

"You saw the result. He disappeared again," Cain said.

"You're assuming he's not dead. So, you think he staged that to disappear again?"

"Possibly. He realized he wasn't going to lose us so he set the stage at the bridge."

"That's quite a risk to take. If that's true then what would make him think you wouldn't kill him?"

"Maybe he thought it was a risk worth taking."

"No, I don't buy it. He's dead," Lawson said.

Cain continued to sit there silently, looking over to the wall. Lawson could tell something else was on his mind.

"What else?" she asked.

"I was just thinking about what else he was saying on the bridge. About all the lies."

"You don't seriously believe any of what he was saying, do you?"

"Why not?"

"He was just talking to divert our attention. Hoping to get the jump on us," Lawson said.

"I didn't get that impression."

"Trust me. I know him better than you."

"You didn't know him well enough to know he was playing you," Cain said, hoping not to offend her.

"You're right. But I do know him better than you."

"OK."

"Trust me. He knew this was the end and was just spewing crap out of his mouth trying to buy a few extra minutes to figure out his escape. We finally got him and put an end to it. This was the end," Lawson said.

"Could be. But, somehow, I doubt this is the end."

THE CAIN DECEPTION

16

I t'd been a year since the confrontation between Eric Raines and Matthew Cain on a Jakarta bridge in Indonesia. Cain and Shelly Lawson stayed for a week trying to get confirmation that Raines died that night. No body was ever pulled from the river and there were never any reports of an American man going to a hospital with a gunshot wound. The Project Specter agency went forward with the belief that Raines was still alive. Director Sanders would not allow the file to be closed on Raines until he showed up dead. Finding him again would prove to be problematic though. As he had done six months before, he effectively disappeared. There were no sightings, no chatter among informants, and no signs of where he went. He dropped off the grid.

Knowing that Raines was somehow involved with Andrei Kurylenko, the decision was made to put more pressure on Kurylenko and put him out of business. In doing that, if Raines was still involved with the Russian arms dealer, then he would eventually turn up along the way. In the year they followed Kurylenko there was never an indication that Raines was still in the picture. The agency got wind of a meeting taking place— courtesy of an informant—between Kurylenko and leaders of a Syrian rebel group near the Israeli border. He was trying to sell them several million dollars' worth of weapons. When the agency first heard of Kurylenko, he was a small player in the game. In the year since then he had increasingly upped his standing in the arms business. It was quite the rapid ascension for the Russian, who used a mix of intelligence, money, and violence to aid in his rise to the top.

It was decided that since there were still no leads on Raines, the time had come to eliminate Kurylenko. The assignment for killing him fell to Cain. His mission was to stake out the building that the meeting was going to take place in. If the shot was there, he was to take it. The caveat was that he was only to take the shot if he was sure he could escape. There were likely to be a lot of men on both sides. Kurylenko wasn't wanted badly enough to put an agent's life at risk if the odds weren't completely in his favor. His profile had been raised enough that they were sure they'd get eyes on him soon enough.

As the meeting drew closer, Cain took his position on the roof of a nearby building. There was a black tarp that he snuggled under, concealing his position. The meeting was happening in a building directly across from him. He waited for an hour before the two sides started to appear. First the Syrian rebels showed, the leaders going inside to wait as some of their men stood guard at the door. About five minutes later, a group that included Kurylenko appeared. He got out of a jeep and stood next to it as he talked to a few of his men. Cain surveyed the situation and knew he could take the Russian out fairly easily. He counted the rest of the men and didn't think he would have much of a problem. He figured he could take out between ten and fifteen men before they even realized where the shots were coming from. Cain looked through the scope on his rifle as he took aim. He suddenly pulled his head up and looked past the rifle, trying to look at the scene with his own eyes. He looked back through the scope and took his aim away from his target and located another man a few feet away from him. A weird feeling came over him, startled to see that Eric Raines was there. It was a complete shock to find him.

"Talk to us, Cain," Lawson said from her remote location in Israel. She was watching a satellite feed of the situation in her hotel room, along with Sanders who was watching and listening back in The Room in New York.

"I've got eyes on Kurylenko," Cain responded.

"Can you take him?"

"Yes."

"Take it when you're ready."

"There's a complication," Cain said.

"What's wrong?"

"Raines is here."

Sanders quickly interjected. "Are you sure that's him?" he asked.

"Positive. He hasn't changed a bit."

"Hold off on Kurylenko," Sanders said. "Wait for Raines. If you get a clear shot, you take it. If you get the opportunity to get Kurylenko after that then go ahead. If not, no big deal, we'll get him some other time. Raines is now your new target."

"Roger that."

Cain shifted positions and put his sights on Raines. He couldn't believe that he was actually there. Sweat started pouring off Cain's head, and he wiped it off with his sleeve. He put the scope on Raines who walked behind a few cars. Cain waited a few seconds to get a clear shot on him. Lawson started biting her nails as she waited for Cain's voice to tell them the mission was a success. Getting confirmation that Raines was still alive sent her for a jolt. Ever since that night on the bridge she clung to the belief that he was killed. She wasn't totally positive he was dead but wanted to believe it more than she actually knew it. She thought she had gotten all the emotions over him out of her system but they quickly flooded her system once more. She just wanted it to be over quickly.

Cain steadied himself as he peered through the scope. His eyes started feeling heavy though, like he was starting to fall asleep, and he began feeling sick. He tried to shake it off, continuing to look at his target. A vision appeared through the scope as he was about to fire. At the other end was a bunch of kids playing around in a backyard. It appeared to be a birthday party as they had party hats on and there was a cake on a picnic table. The same boy he saw before was blowing out the candles as he received a kiss on the cheek from the mysterious blonde. A few seconds later the vision was gone, and he tried to get himself right again. His eyes quickly closed, and he slumped forward, his rifle falling from the roof, causing slight panic from the group below.

"Cain, what's happening?" Sanders asked.

He waited a few seconds before he tried again.

"Cain, what's your status?" he asked.

"Cain, what's wrong?" Lawson said.

Through the satellite feed they could see the men on the ground start running for the building Cain was at. They could see Cain lying still and knew something had gone wrong.

Lawson started running her hand through her hair, concerned about Cain's condition.

"What just happened?" Sanders asked nobody in particular.

They could see men dragging a body away from the roof of the building. A few seconds later the satellite feed went down. Everyone in The Room hysterically worked to figure out what was going on.

"Shelly, find out what's going on," Sanders asked hurriedly.

"I'm on it," she frantically replied, shuffling papers around on her desk, grabbing her phone, and typing on her computer.

"Let me know if you get anything."

"Right."

She started finding all the contacts she knew of in the area that might be able to help figure out where Cain was being taken. She knew she had to work quickly or else they would most likely never see Cain again. Even if they didn't wind up killing him, Sanders would never authorize a rescue attempt. All agents and personnel knew that if they were ever captured they would be left behind, with no exceptions.

After a few minutes with no updates The Room got eerily silent, some people still looking at the blank TV, wishing what they just witnessed didn't really happen. Sanders tried to lift the mood to get them back into work mode.

"Everyone listen up," Sanders said. "We have an agent, Matthew Cain, down in the field. What his status is right now is uncertain. He's a very resourceful agent who's been in some tough spots before. Let's not assume the worst. His handler's on it and will do what it takes to get him out if possible."

"And if it's not possible?" an analyst asked.

"Let's pray it doesn't come down to that," he replied before leaving the room.

Lawson called every contact that knew and had those contacts get in touch with people they knew. She used any resource that she possibly could to get a lead on where Cain was. After two hours of calling or texting everyone in the area, or anyone who might know someone else in the area, she tossed her phone down on the desk in disgust. She was no closer to finding Cain than when she started. It seemed nobody knew where they might be taking Cain. Her surprise over the reappearance of Raines was now replaced by her concern over her agent. If there was any hope in reaching him they'd have to get a trace on him within a few hours while the trail was still hot. Once the days started going by they could go almost anywhere. Lawson tirelessly worked throughout the night, sleeping for only an hour or so, and barely eating. The rush of trying to find Cain kept her going. Sanders called her the next morning to get an update.

"What've you found out?" Sanders asked.

"I've got nothing," she replied, frustrated.

"No leads?"

"Nobody knows anything. It seems he's disappeared."

"Seems to be what Raines excels at."

"Either nobody truly knows or they're afraid of Raines or Kurylenko finding out they said something," Lawson said.

"Or they've been bought off."

"I'll keep working, but I don't know how much more I can do. I've basically run out of people to contact."

"Stay on it a few more days then head back to New York," Sanders said.

"Sir, if I get nothing else in the next few hours then I'd like to try and personally find him."

"How do you aim to do that?"

"I'd like to go into Syria myself."

"Absolutely out of the question."

"What other options are there?"

"We may have possibly lost one agent out there but I am not about to allow losing a handler on top of it. He's not the only agent you're in charge of. You have to think of your other agents and commit to them. I can get you another agent. I can't just instantly get another handler."

"Cain deserves whatever chance we can give him," she said.

"And he's getting that right now by what you're doing."

"I can't just give up on him."

"You're not. You've got three days to come up with something. If not, then you are to return to New York, do you understand?" Sanders said.

"Yes," she begrudgingly replied.

Lawson spent the next three days doing the exact same things she'd already done. She contacted the same people hoping someone would've heard something by then but it was no use. She'd gotten nowhere. Out of leads and time, she knew she had no choice but to return to New York. There was nothing else she could do. The entire plane ride home, obsessed over losing Cain. Only one other time had she lost an agent, other than Raines, but at least there was closure with that. The agent had died in a gun battle and there was a finality to it. With Cain, she didn't know if he was alive or dead or what was happening to him. She felt like she was giving up on him even though she knew there was nothing else she could do.

17

New York, one week later---Lawson was working in her office on missions for her other agents when her phone started ringing. She looked at the number but it was unfamiliar to her, and it wasn't in her list of contacts. She picked it up hoping that maybe it was a connection to Cain. It was, but not in the vain she was hoping.

"Hello?" Lawson said.

"Is this Michelle Lawson?" the woman asked.

"Yes. Who's this?"

"Um, I'm Heather Lloyd. I'm sure you remember me."

"Uh, yes, I do," Lawson replied, shocked to hear her voice.

"Yeah, I know I'm the last person you'd expect a call from, and I'm sorry to call you, but I really didn't know who else to turn to."

"It's OK. What can I do for you?"

"It's about Matt. I'm getting kind of worried about him," Heather said.

"Oh," Lawson replied, thinking of what she should tell her.

"He's been gone almost two weeks, and I thought he'd be home by now. I've been calling and texting his phone but he's not answering. Do you know where he's at?"

"Yeah, I do."

"Oh. Is he OK?" Heather asked.

"How'd you get my number?" Lawson asked. "Did Cain give it to you?"

"Oh, sorry. No, he would never do that. He never tells me anything about what he does. One time you called, and I grabbed his phone for him. Before I gave it to him I memorized your number in case I ever needed it for something," Heather said.

"I see."

"I'm sorry. I know I shouldn't have and I probably shouldn't have called you but I was just getting worried."

"No, it's OK," Lawson said.

"So, you said you know where he's at and he's OK?"

"Umm," Lawson stuttered, struggling between telling her the truth or covering it up and keeping her in the dark.

"Is something wrong?" Heather asked, starting to worry.

"Would you like to meet me somewhere?" Lawson said.

"Uh, why, what's wrong?"

"Let's just meet somewhere where we can talk. How about the Starbucks on 73rd?"

"Sure. That'll work."

"OK. Meet you there in half an hour?"

"Yeah, I'll be there," Heather replied.

Lawson immediately wrapped up what she was working on and left the building. She still wasn't sure what she was going to tell Heather, but she was leaning on telling her the truth. Or at least some version of it if not the exact truth. She could tell that Heather loved him. The pain in her voice over not knowing his whereabouts was quite obvious to her. Cain had always told her that Heather was just a friend but she could see that Heather did not share that notion. As soon as Heather put her phone down, she got a bad feeling about what was going to happen at this meeting. Usually people liked to meet in person instead of saying something over the phone when there was bad news. Like death. She feared that Lawson was going to tell her that Cain was dead or near dead. She left for their rendezvous with butterflies churning in her stomach. She got to the Starbucks a few minutes after Lawson did, who was already sitting at a table waiting for her.

"Hey," Heather nervously said, sitting down.

"Hey," Lawson replied, almost as nervous as her visitor.

"So, you wanted to talk about something?" Heather could barely get the words out, hoping not to hear what she feared.

"I did," Lawson replied.

Any doubt Lawson had about Heather's feelings for Cain were now erased. Her eyes were close to producing tears, she was fidgeting with her hands, and she could hardly sit still as she waited for the news about Cain. Those were the actions of someone who could barely function thinking about life without someone that they loved.

"Before I say anything I need to know a few things first," Lawson said.

"OK?"

"Are you two intimate?"

"What?" Heather asked, surprised at the question.

"I know it's a rather loaded question but I need to know before we go any further."

Heather looked down, then away, before answering. "No, we're not. We're just friends."

A half-smile came over Lawson's face. "That's surprising."

"Why is that surprising?"

"Because you love him. Don't you?" Lawson asked.

Heather didn't reply, unsure what this line of questioning was about. She didn't see what these questions had to do with anything.

"You're in love with him, aren't you?" Lawson repeated.

"Yes," she finally revealed.

"I thought so." Lawson smiled. "I could tell without you saying it. Does he know that?"

"No. At least I don't think he does. What does this have to do with anything?" Heather asked, clearly uncomfortable, starting to believe she was wasting her time. "I came here about Matt, not to have my feelings analyzed."

"It has everything to do with it. You know we work for a top-secret agency. Everything that I would tell you is highly classified. I couldn't discuss this with just a friend," Lawson said, trying to justify what she would say in her own mind, in case she ever needed to cover for herself. "But someone who's closer is a different story."

"Just tell me where he is," Heather pleaded. "Is he OK?"

"The truthful answer is I don't know."

"Oh my God," Heather said, putting her hands on her head, shaking. "You said you knew where he was."

"I know a general location. Exactly where I don't know."

"Where is he?"

"He was on a mission in Syria," Lawson said. "He was close to completing his assignment when something went wrong. We lost contact with him and haven't been able to pick up any leads on him yet."

"Syria? Aren't they having a lot of problems over there?"

"Yes. That's one of the reasons he was there."

"How long's he been missing?"

"Over a week."

"Oh my God," Heather said, starting to breathe heavily.

"Just relax," Lawson said, putting her hand on Heather's arm to calm her down. "We will find him."

"I'm gonna lose the only good thing that's in my life," Heather cried, tears rolling down her face. "Seems silly, huh? Shedding tears over someone you love who doesn't love you back? We've never even had a picture taken together. I can't help it though."

"What makes you think he doesn't love you?" Lawson asked, trying to console her.

"He's never said anything, or done anything. In the year we've known each other, he's never even tried to kiss me," she said, dabbing at her eyes. "Not like you two," she added.

"What?"

"I know you two have been intimate before. I've smelled your perfume on him."

Lawson was taken aback by her claims. She wasn't expecting to hear that, though she wasn't going to deny it either.

"Yes, we were. Not in a long time though," Lawson said.

"Do you love him?" Heather asked, not sure she wanted to hear the answer.

"No. I mean, I care about him a lot. But I don't love him the way you do. After the first couple times we were together, I thought maybe those feelings would turn into love."

"But they didn't?"

"No, they didn't. I always felt like he was resisting for some reason. Like maybe there was someone else he was yearning for," Lawson said.

"I was jealous of you for a long time."

"Why?"

"Because you had what I couldn't."

"But I've never had his heart. That belongs to someone else," she said, Heather looking surprised at what she was suggesting.

"I have to admit I was kinda surprised that you wanted to meet with me, knowing how you feel about me," Heather said.

"I know you think I hate you, but I don't. I never have. I maybe disagreed with some of your lifestyle choices, but that's about it."

"That's all in the past. I gave all that up when I met Matt. I have a real job now."

"I know."

"I guess I thought leaving all that behind would increase my chances with him," Heather added. "But it didn't."

Lawson's phone started going off. It was Sanders. He had some information on a different case she was working on for another agent. She told him she wasn't able to take the information at the moment and would come into The Center for it.

"Well, I need to get back to the office," Lawson said.

"Wait. What can I do?"

"For what?"

"If Matt's in trouble out there I need to help somehow. What can I do?" Heather asked.

"There's nothing you can do. Go home. If I hear anything I'll let you know," Lawson said.

"I have to do something."

"There is something."

"What?" Heather asked.

"Pray."

Syria---Cain blinked his eyes quickly, finally waking up, trying to get his wits together. He tried to move but his arms were restrained by the ropes that were wrapped around his wrists. His arms were spread out above his head as the ropes were nailed into the wall. He looked around the room but it was empty, with just one window. He sat on a dirt floor, wondering what was going on and where he was. The sun was shining brightly into the room. As he sat there reflecting on what would probably be his fate, he started having a vision. It was an older couple, probably in their fifties, setting up a Christmas tree. Though he couldn't hear, he could see they were smiling and laughing, having a great time putting up their decorations. Then the blonde-haired woman entered the room with that little boy that he always dreamed about. They started helping put ornaments on the tree. They had hats on with their names written in glitter across the white strip in front. Cain struggled to see their names, wishing they'd come closer to him so he could get a better look.

Noises from outside his door rattled Cain, breaking his concentration, making the visions slowly fade away. Though he could hear voices and people walking, nearly half an hour went by before he received any visitors. Two armed men walked in, followed by a man Cain was familiar with. The man sent the guards away so the two men could be alone.

"Mr. Cain, I've been waiting for you to come around," the man said.

"So, what do I owe the pleasure of your visit, Raines?"

"I just wanted to stop in and say thank you for helping me disappear in Indonesia."

"Why thank me? I didn't do anything for you. If I recall correctly, I shot you," Cain said. "We were hoping you were dead."

"Shoulder," Raines responded, patting his left shoulder. "Hurt like a bitch, too."

"Shame."

"Since that day, I told myself if I ever had the chance, that I would thank you properly."

"For?"

"You could've killed me but you didn't," Raines said.

"Missed my shot."

"Did you? Somehow, I doubt that. You seem to be an expert marksman. You can hit a man from a few hundred yards but miss from a few feet? Seems somewhat dubious to me."

"I was rushing."

"Or maybe it was because you know what I was saying was true, or at least got your curiosity aroused, thinking it might be true. You had doubts and deliberately missed your shot, didn't you?" Raines said. "You weren't sure I was the enemy, were you?"

"What about you?" Cain asked, ignoring his question.

"What about me?"

"I could say the same for you," Cain said. "You're just as deadly as I am, yet you fired two shots at me that weren't even close and a shot at Shelly that missed by just as much. How do you account for that?"

"That's a fair question. One in which I would answer that I was thrown off by the fact I had two targets to hit in a matter of seconds. I didn't exactly have time to aim properly."

"You know as well as I do you could've hit me, then easily shot Shelly. She's no match with a gun and she probably wouldn't have fired at you anyway with your history."

"Yes, well, hindsight is twenty-twenty as they say," Raines said.

"You deliberately missed your shot, didn't you? It was a big risk you took, letting yourself get shot in order to escape."

"One that apparently paid off, did it not?" Raines replied, acknowledging the truth.

"I suppose so. For a while anyway," Cain said. "What if I shot you in the chest?"

"Then I guess my plan would have failed, wouldn't it?"

"Why didn't you just try to kill us instead?"

"For a myriad of reasons. One is that although the belief is that I betrayed the agency, and perhaps I did, and in spite of my now mercenary status, is that I loved Shelly. Maybe I even still do. No matter her feelings for me now, I don't wish any harm to come to her and would never allow it to be at my hands."

"And me?"

"You remind me of someone," Raines said.

"Who's that?"

"Me."

"I don't see a connection," Cain said.

"Of course you don't. You haven't lived through it yet."

"You talk in a lot of riddles."

"I was once in the same position you're in. The young 'it' agent that the agency decides it can't do without. You get the top assignments, plenty of money, girls when you want. You go along with their game until you slowly discover that you are not the person you thought you were."

"How's that?" Cain asked. "How's that pertain to me?"

"That's only something you'll be able to answer. It's happened to us all. What that is for you specifically is only for you to say. In time, you'll discover the answers to questions you haven't even asked yet. Then one day it'll all fit together."

"Assuming I get out of here."

"You will."

"You seem pretty confident of my abilities," Cain said.

"Well, I am, but that has nothing to do with it in this situation. You will get out of here because I will help you," Raines said.

"Why would you do that?"

"Self-preservation, Mr. Cain."

"How do you figure?"

"I'm well aware there is a KOS order out on me. I will help you out of this predicament on the condition that you are to never execute that order should the chance arise," Raines said.

Cain looked at his opponent with a confused look on his face. He was sure there was some ulterior motive behind his statement. Raines could see the distrust in Cain's eyes and sought to reassure him.

"I assure you this is no trick," Raines said. "I'm offering you a deal."

"I'm still not sure what you gain from this."

"I'll put it in simpler terms. My only goal is survival. If I let them kill you now, the agency will simply send someone else in your place to terminate me when possible. If I come to terms with you, and they send you, I'm at a significant advantage. We both win. You get to leave here and go home to

Heather, and I get a reasonable assurance I won't be killed... at least by you."

"How do you know Heather?" Cain asked, concerned about her safety.

"Relax," Raines replied, trying to ease Cain's anxiety. "She's perfectly safe and will remain that way."

"Then how do you know her?"

"Well, she's sent you over fifty text messages and called you several times in the last week," Raines said, pulling out Cain's cell phone from his pocket. "She seems quite concerned about your safety."

"How do you know you can trust me? What makes you think if I line you up again I still won't pull the trigger?"

"You can pull the trigger, as long as you hit someone other than me. The man next to me, a goat, the wall, whatever you like. If I've misjudged you, then it's a gamble I will lose. But there's little risk for me. If it's not you pulling the trigger, it'll be someone else. At least with you, there's the chance you'll miss," Raines said.

"How will you explain my escaping to Kurylenko?" Cain asked.

"That's the least of my worries. Kurylenko trusts me implicitly. I could tell him a spaceship came down and beamed you aboard and he'd believe me."

"If I agree to your terms when would I leave?"

"I have a man stationed in back with a jeep ready to take you to Israel," Raines replied.

"And if I don't agree?"

"Then there's nothing else I can do for you. Kurylenko will torture you to extract any information he can and then he will kill you. It will be a long, painful process."

"Seems I don't have many options," Cain said.

"It would appear not."

"Then I guess I accept your terms."

"Excellent. Guards," Raines yelled.

The two armed guards came in as requested. Raines asked them to untie Cain. As soon as they did, Raines shot both of them, giving them two bullets each in the chest. Raines reached behind him and pulled out a gun from his belt, handing it to Cain.

"I believe this is yours," Raines said, handing Cain his Glock.

"Thanks," Cain said, accepting his gun, checking to see if there were bullets in it.

"It's loaded," Raines said with a smile.

"Just checking."

"My man will take you within a few miles of the Israeli border. After that you'll have to walk in," Raines added, handing Cain his phone. "The Israeli guards would most likely shoot him if he goes further."

"That's fine. I'll call Shelly to let her know I'm coming."

Raines led Cain out the back of the building where a jeep was waiting to take him away. A few seconds later the jeep sped off, Raines watching as it rode into the distance. Kurylenko and the rest of his men were away on business which made it the optimal time for him to get Cain out of there. Once Kurylenko returned, he'd just explain to him how a rescue mission must've been launched to help Cain escape. As Cain raced for the border, he called Lawson as they were en route.

Lawson was heavily involved in gathering information for an agent in Switzerland but dropped everything when she saw Cain's name pop up on her screen.

"Cain," Lawson said, hoping it was him.

"Hey."

"Thank God, are you OK?"

"Don't have time to talk. I was able to escape and I'm on my way to Israel. I should be there in a few hours."

"I'll contact the Israeli government and the American Embassy to let them know you're coming so there'll be no problems," she said. "Are you being chased?"

"No, I don't think they know I'm gone yet. I've got a good lead, I'll be OK."

"OK. Hurry up and get back."

Lawson immediately called Sanders to let him know about Cain's escape. She then contacted the appropriate government officials in Israel to let them know an American who worked for the U.S. government would be approaching their border. Cain reached Israel a few hours later and had no trouble entering the country since they were expecting his arrival. They got him a hotel room so he could relax for a few days before he flew back to New York. He sat down and looked through his phone, listening to his voicemails. There were fifteen on there from Heather, some just asking where he was and if he was OK, but each one increasing in the concern heard from her voice. He then scrolled through the text messages from her, also heavily laced with her worrying about his safety. He then lay on his bed, looking up at the ceiling, thinking about everything he'd been through. He thought about Raines, Heather, the visions he was having, and started lamenting that he couldn't remember things. He felt like these visions were trying to give him clues and he just couldn't understand what they were trying to tell him.

Lawson called him to see how he was doing and get a report

on what happened in Syria. He told her how he blacked out and woke up a week later.

"How were you able to escape?" she asked.

"Oh, I was able to bribe one of the guards," he lied.

"With what?"

"I told him I had some money. I was surprised how well it worked."

"Well, I'm glad you made it out. I spent a week looking for you but everywhere I turned I came up empty," Lawson said.

"It's OK. I know you did what you could. I didn't expect a rescue mission. I know the drill."

After he talked with Lawson, Cain wanted to call Heather before he went to sleep for the night. There was a seven-hour time difference between Israel and New York so he knew she'd probably be home. From her messages, he could tell she was almost sick with anxiety and worry. Heather was sitting on the sofa eating a sandwich when her phone started ringing. Every time her phone rang for the past couple of weeks she jumped at it, hoping it'd be Cain, telling her he was OK. This time was the same as the others. She eagerly lunged for the phone, sitting on the coffee table. Once she saw Cain's name, her eyes lit up, almost not believing it was actually him calling.

"Matt!" she shouted.

"Hey, you."

"Oh my God, I'm so glad to hear your voice," Heather said, wiping away some joyous tears.

"It's good to hear yours too," he replied, smiling at the happiness he could hear in her voice.

"Where were you?!"

"I can't really say."

"It doesn't matter. I'm just glad you're OK," she said. "You are OK, right?"

"Yeah, I'm fine. I'll be coming home in a few days."

"That's great. I'll be waiting for you."

"I got all your texts and messages so I just wanted to let you know I was OK so you'd stop worrying."

"I'm sorry. I probably shouldn't have sent you so many but I was just so worried. You said you'd be back in a few days and then it's a week later, then two weeks and I still hadn't heard from you," Heather said, trying to justify it to him.

"It's OK. I'm glad you missed me."

"Well, I did."

"Maybe you can make me some of your world-famous spaghetti when I get home. Haven't had much to eat lately," Cain said.

"One spaghetti dinner coming up."

"Thanks. Well, I'm gonna try to sleep. I'm really tired out from everything."

"OK. I lo..." Heather started to say before catching herself.

"What's that?" Cain asked, not sure what she was trying to say.

"Umm, I was just gonna say I'll be waiting for you."

"OK. I'll text you when I get up in the air."

18

Once Cain arrived back in New York he was met at the airport by both Sanders and Lawson, both eager to hear about what happened in Syria. Cain knew the debriefing would take a while and sent Heather a text, letting her know what was going on. He told her it was likely to take a while, and he'd probably be home really late and not to wait up for him. Even though they knew Cain would be tired, it was important for him to tell them his story while it was still fresh in his mind. They whisked him away back to The Center to talk to him. Cain was careful not to give too much information away and stuck to his story about bribing one of the guards to let him go. He wasn't sure about what was going on with the agency and Raines, but he made a deal and wasn't about to go back on it. Plus, he knew without Raines' help, it was unlikely he would've ever made it out of Syria alive. Cain knew he owed him his life and wasn't about to help Sanders end Raines'. Once Cain's supervisors were satisfied that he had nothing else to tell them they told him to go back home to get some rest. After his ordeal Cain was told he'd have the next week or two off to just relax.

It was about 2am when Cain finally got home. He quietly entered his apartment, slowly opening and closing the door so as to not wake Heather, assuming she was sleeping. Cain looked at the clock and then noticed Heather passed out on the couch. He smiled as he saw her phone on her chest, still in the clutches of her hand, knowing she was probably waiting for him. He walked over to her and slowly pried the phone out of her hand, careful not to wake her up. Cain placed the phone on the table and then picked her up, his bicep cradling her head, his right hand underneath her thigh. She was so tired that she didn't realize he had picked her up and was completely knocked out. Cain stared at her face, tempted by how close she was, and briefly thought about kissing her lips. It was the closest he'd ever been to doing so but thought there'd probably be a better, more appropriate time to do it. He'd always been attracted to her but always felt like he should wait to make a move on her, thinking there'd be a perfect moment, even though it never seemed to arrive. He took her into the bedroom and placed her on the bed, bringing the covers up to her chest. Cain then went out to the living room and crashed on the sofa, falling asleep within minutes.

Heather woke up around eight and once she got the sleep out of her eyes, rushed into the living room, hoping Cain would be there. Once she saw him sleeping on the couch, a huge smile erupted on her face. She was so happy to have him back that she couldn't contain the joy she felt. She quickly made herself a cup of coffee then sat down on the chair across from Cain and just watched him as he slept. As much as Heather hoped for him to wake up so she could talk to him, she was enjoying just watching him sleep. It was very calming for her, much different than the previous couple of weeks when she was in agony, terrified that she had lost him. She probably could've watched him all day and been content in doing so.

Cain didn't wake up until ten, immediately seeing Heather's smiling face staring at him. He smiled back at her as he sat up.

"Coffee?" Heather asked, holding her cup up.

"You know I never touch that stuff."

Cain got up to go to the kitchen, Heather following right behind him. He got a bottle of water from the fridge and took some sips from it as Heather did all she could to refrain from jumping all over him. She started moving her arms up as if she was about to hug him but awkwardly itched her face or her body, or pretended to fix her hair. She desperately wanted to kiss and hug him but couldn't bring herself to do it. He just didn't give off the vibe that he was into her like that. She would've been embarrassed if she tried to kiss him and he wasn't into reciprocating the pleasure. After a few minutes of small talk that she really didn't care about, she finally let loose with her feelings, not able to hold it in any longer.

"What is wrong with me?!" Heather cried.

"What do you mean? Nothing's wrong with you," Cain replied, confused.

"Then why won't you touch me?!"

Cain looked away momentarily, grimacing, not really wanting to get into the subject.

"See. You won't even look at me," Heather said. "Do you not think I'm pretty? Am I not caring enough? Don't like my cooking? What?"

"It's not what you think."

"How isn't it?"

"It just isn't," Cain said.

"For the past year I've been trying to do everything I can think of to make you want me. I don't know what else to do. If it's my past that's keeping you away then just say so. I can deal with it. If you just can't get over what I used to do, then I'll be disappointed, but at least I'll be able to move on eventually."

"It's not your past. That doesn't bother me. Well, I'm glad you're not doing it anymore, but what you did before you met me I can't control or let bother me."

"Then what is it? Are you just not attracted to me? I mean, if that's it, then just say you only look at me as a friend," Heather pleaded. "At least then I'll be able to move on."

"That's not it."

"God, you're so frustrating! You tell me nothing! I'm pouring my heart out and you say nothing! Every time I think maybe we're getting closer to starting something, you pull away. You say it's not what I used to do, it's not my looks, is it my personality? Am I not smart enough for you? Not enough fun? What?"

"It's complicated," Cain said.

"Please just tell me something! You're torturing me by letting me be so close to you without really being close. You seem like maybe you want to move closer but then take a step back. I can't keep pretending that all I want to be is friends. I have feelings for you and they're not subsiding, and they're not going away. So, if you have any type of feelings for me then please just let me know."

Cain stood there silently, staring at her, letting her words sink in. He already knew she had feelings for him, even a blind person could've seen it, and he knew it wasn't fair to her to keep leading her on. But there was something that just made him keep resisting, even if he didn't want to.

"I can't make you feel something for me that you don't," Heather added, her face wet with tears. "If this is all our relationship will ever be, then just say it so I can try to move on because I can't take being around you anymore and not touching you. You sit next to me and I want to hug you, you stand next to me and I want to hold your hand, I see your face enter a room and I want to kiss you. I can't take not acting on any of that anymore."

Cain continued with his silence, not knowing how to respond. He didn't want to hurt her but also wasn't sure moving into a romantic relationship was a good idea.

"Why won't you let me in? I want you to pull me close to you. I want to know what you think and feel but you won't let me. You push me away and make me feel like you're not interested in me at all," Heather said.

"Heather, it's just... there's just a lot I have to deal with."

"OK. Like what? What is it? Just tell me and explain it to me so I can understand. I want to understand what you're feeling."

Cain sighed, not wanting to reveal what he was thinking. Seeing the tears rolling down Heather's face was slowly breaking him down to the point he felt he should tell her his fears.

"What are you afraid of?" she asked.

"You," Cain finally relented. "I'm afraid of you."

"Me? How could you be afraid of me?"

"It's you... and me," he added, wiping some of her tears away.

"That makes absolutely no sense. Can you explain that a little?" Heather asked tersely, sitting down on the couch.

"What if we get involved and the person you go to bed with isn't the same person that wakes up?" he asked, sitting next to her.

"I don't understand," she replied, shaking her head.

"The reason I've never tried anything with you is because I don't trust myself. I don't really know who I am. Since I woke up in that hospital bed last year, I have no idea about my true self. Am I the person that I've always been? Am I someone different? What if the person you see now isn't the person I really am and not the person you fall in love with?"

"I'm willing to take that chance," she said.

"All I know is what I've been told. What if at some point I regain my memory and I'm a different person? What if I go back to who I used to be, and I was a jerk, or I'm just not a good guy?"

"You won't be."

"You don't know that," Cain reasoned. "I don't even know that."

"You're right. I don't know that. But I also know that you can't live your life worrying about what could be... and you miss out on something that could be better."

"For the last year I've been walking around with my head in the clouds. I walk around and it just feels like there's something missing. I see visions of people and I don't know who they are, yet it seems like they're close to me somehow. I have nightmares that won't go away. It just seems like everything is not what it should be. I feel like I'm close to discovering parts of my past but yet not close enough."

"That's not my fault."

"I know it's not," Cain said.

"Then let me in. Let me help you. I want to help you."

"I don't know, Heather."

"Let me help you figure out the missing pieces. We can do this together. You don't have to go it alone."

"You don't have to do that."

"I know I don't, but I want to. I want to help you if you'll let me," she said.

Cain sighed, feeling bad about all the pain he was causing Heather. It wasn't what he intended. He looked away, staring at the wall, wondering what else he could say to her. From Heather's standpoint, there was nothing more he could say, except for one thing. All she needed to hear was that he wanted their relationship to move to the next level. His continued silence felt like a knife penetrating her gut because she knew that meant that he wasn't ready. He wasn't ready for her. Instead of continuing their conversation, she got up to put her shoes on and walked to the door. She kept sniffling and wiping her eyes on the way. She knew the longer she stayed there, clinging to the hope that he'd come around to her way of thinking, that she was just continuing to torture herself and wouldn't be able to move on.

"Where are you going?" Cain asked.

"I don't know. Taking a walk, I guess."

Cain started to move his lips to say something, but didn't have any words. Nothing he'd say would have any impact, anyway. Cain watched as Heather walked out the door, staring at the door as it closed behind her. A piece of him wondered if he was going to see her again. He chalked it up to emotions since her things were there, so of course she'd be back. She probably just needed to clear her head, he thought. He knew she deserved better. Better than he could give her right now. He felt like the slimiest person in the world at that moment. Here was this beautiful, caring woman, who only wanted to love and help him in any way possible, and he seemed to be doing everything possible to push her away.

He waited about an hour for her to come back, hoping he could talk to her again. He wasn't sure what else he could say but maybe he could get her to understand the way he felt. The anxiousness proved to be too much for him and he felt he needed to get out some of his energy. He grabbed his guns and went down to The Center to get some shooting in at the firing range. Shooting usually seemed to calm him down. It was better than hurting his hand by punching walls, anyway. Hopefully she'd be back by the time he returned.

Cain spent the next hour firing round after round from his pistols, hitting his target almost every time, dead center. As he was finishing up, he heard the door opening behind him. He turned and saw Shelly standing there. He wondered what she wanted and why she was there but didn't acknowledge her with words. He figured she'd let him know soon enough. He turned his attention back to his guns and waited for her to speak.

"I heard there was an angry-looking guy that entered the building and was on his way to the shooting range," Lawson kidded. "So, I figured I'd stop by to see who it was. Kind of had a feeling it might be you."

"Looks like you were right," Cain said, not amused.

"What's going on?" Lawson asked, walking over to him.

"Don't wanna talk about it."

"OK," she replied, standing next to him, looking away. "How'd your shooting go?"

"Good."

"Maybe I can help."

"I don't need help shooting."

"I meant with what's bothering you."

"You can't," Cain stated.

"Is it personal or work related?" she asked.

"Doesn't matter."

"C'mon, let me help."

"Why does everyone keep asking to help me?" he said, perturbed. "I don't need anyone's help."

"By everyone, you mean who?" Lawson asked.

"Look, I know you mean well, but just drop it," Cain said, still tending to his guns.

"I could take a guess. Wanna hear it?"

"It's your dime."

"It's Heather, isn't it?"

The look Cain gave her was the only indication she needed to confirm her suspicion. It was the only time he looked at her to that point and the look he gave her wasn't a pleasant one, indicating Heather was who was on his mind.

"She's the only other person besides me that I could think of that'd say something to you about helping you in some way," Lawson added. "So, I figured it must've been her."

"Good guess."

"So, what's going on?"

"I don't wanna talk about it."

"Did you guys have a fight?"

His silence indicated she was right on the money again. He didn't like to admit when other people were right about him so he tended to be quiet when they were.

"She told you how she felt about you, huh?" Lawson guessed.

"You seem to know quite a bit about this for some reason," Cain said.

"It just stood to reason. Her and I had a talk about you," she said.

Cain was taken aback and finally stopped fiddling with his guns and turned to face his handler. "You and her talked? When?"

"When you went missing in Syria, she called me. She was concerned about you."

"How'd she get your number?" Cain asked.

"Apparently she memorized it one time when I called you."

"Yeah, well, she's pretty resourceful."

"She is. And she loves you. That much was clear."

Cain was starting to feel uncomfortable hearing about her feelings for him and started messing around with his guns again.

"You and I have a pretty good relationship but I don't really wanna talk about this with you," Cain said.

"Why does that bother you so much?" Lawson asked.

"It doesn't."

"Then maybe you should give things a chance."

"Why are you defending her? You don't even like her," Cain said.

"That's not true. I admit I didn't like her before, mostly because of what she did. But after talking to her, I could see how she felt about you. If only you could've seen how upset she was when she thought you might not be coming back."

Cain cleared his throat and looked at Lawson out of the corner of his eye, without turning his head, trying to fight a tear from showing. Hearing about her concern for him touched him, more than he wanted it to. He already knew from her texts and voicemails, but it somehow hit him differently hearing it from someone else. Doubt started creeping into his head, wondering if continuing to push Heather away was really the right move. Maybe he should let her in more, he thought. The more Lawson talked to him about Heather, the more confused he was getting. For the first time, he was letting his heart over-rule his head. For the last year he had convinced himself that shutting his heart off to the world was the best thing for him. Now, his heart was talking to him more than his brain.

"Why are you here?" Cain asked.

"Just here as a friend. Thought maybe you wanted to talk."

"So, what is it that you want me to do?"

"I don't want you to do anything. Just listen to your heart. I know for a long time you've acted very methodically, like you don't want your emotions to show or get the better of you."

"And?"

"And maybe that's what makes you such a good agent. But maybe letting your emotions show sometimes isn't such a bad idea."

"You think I should…" he started to say.

"It's not up to me to say you should do anything. All I'm saying is to look within yourself and really ask yourself what you want. Maybe she's not the person you need to help you heal. But if it's just that you're afraid to open up and be vulnerable, well, usually the biggest risks also have the biggest rewards."

Lawson didn't stick around any longer for Cain to reply. She left him with that thought, hoping it might help him somehow. She thought a girlfriend might've been good for him. She some-times worried that he was wound a little too tight, and he didn't get enough down time. She wasn't about to tell him what he should do but secretly hoped he gave Heather the chance that she wanted.

Cain looked over at the empty space where Lawson had just been standing, hearing her words again as if she was still standing there talking. He let those words penetrate through him as he tried to decipher what it was that he wanted. His stomach felt like it was in a thousand knots. He finally pushed his head to the side and started listening to what his heart had been telling him for a while. He kept thinking of Heather and the more he thought of her, the more he realized that he didn't want to be without her. He didn't have a lot going for him in his life, but he finally started to see that she was what he looked forward to. Coming home and seeing her face, talking to her, she was really what kept him going. All the times he was away on missions, it wasn't the apartment that he missed, or the things that entertained him between jobs, it was her. If she were no longer there, he'd have nothing to come home to. Just some empty walls, some furniture, and a TV. She was what kept him together. Cain knew what he needed to do and put his guns in his belt and raced out of The Center, hoping Heather would be at the apartment when he got there.

Cain rushed into the apartment, eager to see Heather. He quickly noticed a couple of bags packed, sitting on the coffee table. A few seconds later, Heather emerged from the bedroom, with a few of her clothes in hand. She looked at him briefly but wanted to make leaving as painless as possible, so she tried to avoid eye contact and walked over to her bags.

"Where are you going?" Cain asked, worried he blew it.

"I can't stay here anymore," she replied. "It's just too hard to keep staying here, living under the same roof. I'll stay at a hotel for a few days before I find my own place. I'll call you in a few days once I calm down."

"I don't want you to go. We can make this work."

"Please don't. Nothing's gonna change. Please don't make this harder for me than it already is."

Heather picked up her bags and started to walk past him, but he grabbed her bags and set them on the floor. She took a big sigh, wondering why Cain was punishing her by making it so hard for her to leave. She turned around, not really wanting to face him, looking at everything in the room other than him.

"Matt, I can't do this anymore," Heather said, starting to cry. "I just want to be happy and I can't really be that as long as we're living together but not really together."

"I want you to be happy too," he replied.

"It's torture living here with you, knowing you don't want the same things I do. I need more. And I know it's not gonna happen."

Cain grabbed her hands and pulled her closer to him, then wiped her face free of tears. He caressed her chin and gently lifted her head up, kissing her on the lips. Heather was so surprised that she almost thought she was daydreaming. She opened her eyes for a moment to make sure it was real. If it was some kind of dream, she sure hoped she never woke up from it. She wasn't sure what was happening, or what was causing him to act that way, but she wasn't about to object or do anything to make him stop. She put her arms around him, soaking up the moment. After a few minutes of passionate kissing, Cain started taking her clothes off, then picked her up and carried her into the bedroom, setting her on the bed. He made sure she realized what she meant to him.

They woke up a few hours later, Heather rolling over and placing a kiss on Cain's cheek. She looked at him and smiled, amazed at what just happened, still hoping that she wasn't dreaming it all. She rubbed his chest, waking him up, as she gazed into his eyes.

"That was amazing," Heather said.

"Yeah," he replied, kissing her.

"So, what brought all that on?"

"Complaining?"

"Not at all. This morning it just seemed like we were worlds apart. Then all of a sudden here we are," she said and smiled.

"I guess I just realized that I wanted you in my life and I couldn't stand the thought of you leaving. You're not still leaving, right?"

"Not if you don't want me to."

"I don't," he said.

"I do have a few questions for you though."

"Yeah?"

"About your work."

"I still can't tell you anything," Cain said.

"I know. I'm not asking for details. It's just the guns that somewhat bother me."

"Well, I can't do much about them. I need to have them."

"It's not that. I know you do some dangerous things. Just tell me that whatever it is that you do, you're doing it to bad guys?" she said.

"I promise I'm not doing anything to people that don't deserve it," Cain said, reassuring her.

They lay there for a little while, giving each other kisses, as Heather started dreaming about what might be. She knew she couldn't rush him into anything but she hoped that this meant their relationship had finally turned the corner. She'd been waiting for this day for over a year, and gave up that it'd actually happen several times, and now she found it hard to believe it finally came. They put their clothes back on and went into the living room to watch some TV. Heather grabbed ice cream from the freezer and sat down next to Cain on the couch with it. She took turns between feeding him and eating it herself. Though she dreamed of what it'd feel like to be intimate with Cain, it felt even better than she ever imagined it would.

"Wait, are you sure this isn't a one-time thing and you're gonna shove me out the door tomorrow?" she asked, her tone in the middle of joking and being serious.

He smiled. "I'm sure," he said, taking the spoon to feed her some ice cream.

"So, what changed your mind? I mean, besides my obvious good looks," she joked.

"I just finally realized that you were right. I know if I'm to overcome the things that are haunting me that I am gonna need help. I'll need some support to get me through it. And there's only one person who I can think of to help me do that," he told her, kissing her softly.

"I'm always here for you."

"I know that. Even if I didn't always see it."

"Wait, does this mean that we're a thing now?" Heather asked.

"A thing?"

"You know, a couple?"

"Umm, yeah, I guess so," Cain said, letting out a small laugh.

"All I ask is that you are honest with me. I know you're gonna have some bad days, and there are things that I don't and won't ever understand, but just let me know what you're thinking and feeling. Don't shut me out."

"I'll try."

"Good," she replied, kissing him.

"I guess since we're on this new honesty kick and opening up, I guess I should tell you that Matthew Cain isn't my real name," he said.

"What?" she asked, astonished. "What is it?"

"Thomas Nelson."

Heather was surprised and not sure how to respond. She didn't know which name to call him now.

"So," she started, "what am I supposed to call you now?"

"I'm Matthew Cain now. Thomas Nelson died fifteen months ago in Syria."

"Good. I like that name better anyway," she kidded.

Cain spent the next couple of hours telling her his story. She already knew bits and pieces but he figured he'd tell her the rest of it, the parts he'd been hiding from her. Although he wasn't sure before about telling her what he did, he figured it was time, especially if they were getting closer. He didn't want to be off somewhere in a foreign country and have her worrying, not knowing where he was or what he was doing. She at least deserved to know what was going on. Plus, he was growing tired of keeping secrets from her. Every time she asked where he was he'd avoid the subject and talk about something else. If their new relationship was going to survive, he knew he had to open up more and tell her everything.

The next morning, Cain woke up and looked to his right, expecting to see Heather's lovely face staring back at him. All he saw were a couple of deformed pillows. He got up to see where she was and was surprised to find her typing away on the computer already.

"Why are you on there so early?" Cain asked.

"Just checking something."

"What are you doing?" he asked, looking over her shoulder at the screen.

"This website has a list of soldiers killed in action in Afghanistan and Iraq. Has pictures and information on them. Just wanted to see if you were there," she replied.

"I'm not. I was in Syria, and I was part of Delta Force. The government doesn't publicly release the names of Delta Force soldiers."

"Oh. Why not?"

"Because they don't acknowledge their existence."

"Oh. I was hoping to see how cute you looked in your uniform," she joked.

"I looked horrible," he responded, smiling.

"No way. Well, I'm gonna keep looking on here, anyway. I'm determined to find you on here somewhere."

19

Cain knew something big was up. He had been summoned for a meeting with both Sanders and Lawson, which was highly unusual. Since Lawson was his handler and usually devised the mission's plans, he very rarely talked to Sanders about a mission unless there was a bigger reason for doing so. He entered the meeting room, where Sanders and Lawson were already seated, waiting for him to arrive. Cain took a seat across from Lawson as Sanders got up and walked around the table. Sanders had a clicker in his hand and started displaying information on the computer screen on the wall. The first picture was of Andrei Kurylenko, followed by a series of shots of a house.

"You're both aware of this man," Sanders said. "We received information about two weeks ago that this house was his place of residence. We've been trying to verify that since."

"Have we?" Lawson asked.

"We have. We have intel that he arrived late last night after his trip in Syria. Some of the information and pictures you're seeing is from what we found on previous real estate listings and some from men we put on the inside."

"Inside? We put people in there and didn't kill him?" Cain asked.

"They were not agents. They were there for information purposes. We didn't know who was there and couldn't take the necessary risks without verifying all the information. They entered the premises as pizza delivery men, TV repairmen, etc."

"So, what's the mission?" Cain asked.

"Now we know he's there, you're going to eliminate him."

"Doesn't seem like a great setup," Cain mused.

"We can't always hope for optimal conditions. There are anywhere from ten to fourteen men on the property at any given time. Two in the guardhouse, probably watching video surveillance, six to eight on the property grounds, and two to four inside the house with Kurylenko."

"That place looks huge."

"It's not tiny. Over 8,000 square feet, 5 bedrooms, 5 bathrooms, indoor swimming pool, private lake towards the back of the property, tennis court, and, of course, his own helipad. All at the not too shabby price tag of fifteen million dollars."

"How many men am I taking?" Cain asked.

"None. It's just you," Sanders calmly replied.

"You expect me to take out as many as fourteen men all by myself?" Cain asked incredulously.

"Yes, I do."

"Well, OK then."

"Sir, that seems like a really tall order for one man, no matter how good Cain is," Lawson said, speaking up.

"I'm only interested in one man. The rest are inconsequential," Sanders said.

"With all due respect, there's no way I can get to Kurylenko without taking out everybody, unless he's standing on a balcony or something," Cain said.

"Then take them out."

Cain sat there, taking turns between staring at the computer screen and Sanders, sure he'd lost his mind. He wasn't sure how Sanders expected him to take out so many men but he was beginning to think it was a suicide mission.

"There's more," Sanders said, throwing a tape recorder down on the table.

The three of them intently listened to the voices on the tape though Cain couldn't make out what was being said. The tape ended after two minutes. Cain and Lawson looked at each other with a confused look on their faces.

"I don't speak much Russian, what was all that about?" Lawson asked.

"That was Kurylenko speaking to a man named Valeri Medvedev," Sanders said. "It was recorded three days ago."

"Who's he?"

"He's a top enforcer for a Russian mafia group."

"Sounded like it was getting heated."

"It was. I had it translated, and Medvedev was basically threatening him. He said if he didn't get with the program he was going to come to his house and kill him and everyone who lived there."

"So, I take it that I'm to make it look like a Russian mafia killing?" Cain said.

"Yes. After you kill Kurylenko, you're going to drop this recording by his body."

"Getting easier by the minute."

"Listen, we can't send a team in there. First, that's not how we operate. Second, if things go bad and there's a firefight, who's going to explain why a group of Americans is in Moscow trying to kill one of its citizens," Sanders said. "All hell would break loose."

"But one man is expendable," Cain said.

"If it came to that."

Cain looked at Lawson, a befuddled look on his face, thinking the mission wasn't practical or realistic. Lawson also wasn't very keen on the details.

"As far as the specifics of the plan, as always, that's left up to you two to come up with something. Just make it good," Sanders said. "Any questions?"

"When do I leave?" Cain asked.

"Tomorrow. Any later than that and we risk Kurylenko leaving. Has to be done as soon as possible," Sanders said, giving Cain a pat on the shoulder as he walked past him. "Sorry about the rest of your leave. I know you've only been back three or four days, but it has to be done quickly."

"I understand. It's fine."

Sanders gave Lawson a folder that contained pictures of the house as well as a map of the property. He then left them to devise their plan and headed back to his office. He was only in there for a minute before his phone started buzzing.

"Yes?" Sanders said.

"Sir, we have a bit of a problem," a security agent said.

"What's that?"

"We've got some red alerts popping up in relation to one of the agents."

"Who's that?"

"Matthew Cain, aka Thomas Nelson, aka..."

"I'm aware of who we're talking about. What's the issue?" Sanders asked.

"Someone's looking up information about him. We've tracked it down to the location, and it's coming from Cain's apartment."

"Do you have times, dates, information they're looking at?"

"The last search was about half an hour ago," the agent said.

"Cain was here. That means it must be...," Sanders said, his voice trailing off.

"They're trying to get info on Delta Force and the time Cain was in Syria. It doesn't look like they've gotten anything substantial yet."

"OK. Keep an eye on it. Let me know if anything changes," Sanders said. "I'll start figuring out a plan."

"Yes, sir."

Lawson and Cain had gone to her office to figure out the details of the plan. They spent a few hours going over different scenarios and possible ways for him to enter and exit the property. They wished they had more time to prepare but more often than not they had to work on short notice and were used to it. After six hours of intensive discussions they finally agreed on a plan. Cain was to infiltrate Kurylenko's property via a river that ran behind it and kill the guards stationed on the outside before working his way into the house.

Once the plans were finalized, Cain left to go home. He was a little worried about telling Heather that he had to go on another mission so soon after getting home from a mission that went terribly wrong. He knew she'd be upset about it, especially since they just took their relationship to another level. But there wasn't much he could do about it and would just try to explain it to her the best he could and hoped she'd understand. Heather was waiting for Cain when he got back, hoping they could do something fun for the rest of the evening.

"Hey, sweetie," Heather said gleefully. "It sounds kind of funny saying that after all this time."

"I'm sure we could get used to it," he said, giving her a kiss.

"I can definitely get used to that."

"I bet."

"So, how'd your meeting go?" she wondered.

"Fine."

"Anything important?"

"Umm, you know, just the usual stuff."

"I was thinking maybe we could go out tonight, catch a movie, have dinner, make it a real date. What do you think?" she asked as she started wiping down the countertops.

Cain knew he'd have to tell her at some point that he was leaving and figured he might as well do it sooner and get it out of the way. He knew she was going to be crushed.

"Heather, I have to go," he said.

"You have to go? Right now? Where?"

"I've been selected for another mission," he said somberly.

"Again? You just got back," Heather replied, disappointed. "It hasn't even been a week. I thought you said they were giving you a couple weeks off?"

"That's what I thought too. But this is important."

"Why you? They have other agents. Why can't they send someone else?" she asked.

"Because it's my case."

"So where are you going?"

"Russia."

"Russia? They don't have anyone stationed there?"

"Heather, it's the guy I was after in Syria. It's my case. I have to go."

"Now I have to wonder if the same thing's gonna happen to you as in Syria?"

"It won't."

"How can you say that? You're after the same guy that just last week almost got you killed and almost gave me a heart attack wondering where you were," Heather said, getting hysterical.

"Just calm down."

"Don't tell me to calm down. You calm down."

"Umm, I am calm."

"So, I'm supposed to just sit here and wonder if you're ever coming back again?"

"You're getting emotional," Cain said.

Heather realized he was right, and that she was acting irrational. She felt like she was being foolish and tried to pull herself together.

"So, when do you leave?"

"Tomorrow," Cain said.

"How long will you be gone?"

"A few days."

"That seems to always be the standard answer," she said.

"That's 'cause it's always the plan."

Heather continued cleaning the kitchen, knowing nothing she could say was going to change the outcome. She knew he was going, and she needed to put on a better face and not pout about it.

Cain grabbed Heather's waist to turn her around so he could look in her eyes. "I promise I'll make it up to you."

"Yeah, until they tell you they're sending you somewhere else."

"Hey," he said, putting his arms around her, holding her close to his chest.

"I'm sorry," Heather replied, looking up at him.

She was enjoying the close affection from him though not under those circumstances.

"I know I'm acting foolish," Heather said. "I'm just gonna miss you."

"I'll miss you too."

"You will?"

"Of course. Every mission I've been on since I met you I've thought about you while I was gone."

"You have?"

"It's part of what made me realize I couldn't let you go. Every time I've been in some foreign country, in some broken down hole-in-the-wall, when it's cold, wet, hotter than hell, or wondering how I'll get out of a situation... you're what gets me through it," he said. "There's never been a time when I didn't think of you."

"Aww. You're so sweet," she replied, softly kissing his lips.

"You're the reason I always come back."

"Just make sure you do."

"Nothing could stop me from coming back to you," he said, kissing her.

20

Moscow, Russia-It'd been a long time since Cain had to swim. He needed to use his aquatic skills on a mission in South America a few months prior to this but it wasn't anywhere near as long a swim as this was. He was a little tired swimming from the other side of the lake but it was the best option to get on the property without being noticed. Once he got near the shore, he raised his head slightly out of the water so he could see, the water hovering above his lips. It was a pitch-black night; the moon tucked away, perfect for what he had planned. He had a bag full of weapons with him; the strap slung around his neck. Cloaked in black clothing to blend in with the night, he crawled onto land, surveying the situation. He heard some laughing coming from the side of the house. It wasn't especially loud, but the unison of several voices made it more noticeable. Still lying on the ground, he slowly opened his bag so as to not make a noise as it unzipped. He had two handguns which he put inside his belt and he quickly assembled a sniper rifle, complete with scope and night vision goggles. He probably could've swung around to the side of the house to take out the men there, but if he couldn't get them all before they returned fire, he'd have a tough time making it to the house. He needed to get to the men in the guardhouse first. Luckily there were some trees near the shoreline that he could use as cover as he made his way to the front of the property.

Cain slowly went from tree to tree to get around the side of the property, taking about five minutes, not wanting to make too many movements to get recognized. He saw several parked cars which he made his way to. He looked around for cameras and noticed one near the front gate, and a few fixed on different entrances of the house. He located the guardhouse and saw one of the men standing near the entrance smoking a cigarette. Cain quickly scanned the rest of the area to see if anyone else was near but didn't notice a soul in sight. He thought about quickly taking the one guard out but there was no guarantee whoever else was in the guardhouse would come out, compromising his position. He figured the best option he had would be to kill them from close range, taking them by surprise.

As soon as the guard put out his cigarette and turned his back to go inside, Cain quickly ran over to him. He got there in a few seconds and rushed through the open doorway. The two guards quickly jumped up from their seats, trying to grab their weapons off the table. Cain's presence was too much for them and he quickly gunned them down at the hands of his silencer. He shot each of them in the chest then gave them one more in the head to make sure they were dead. He looked at the cameras to see where the rest of the men were and noticed three on the side. He waited a few minutes to see if anymore appeared, but it seemed as though they were it. The rest must've been inside. It was past one in the morning so he assumed everyone else was sleeping. He shot the surveillance equipment, putting a bullet in each machine so he couldn't be later identified by the police when they investigated.

Cain left the guardhouse and knelt down in front of it so he could pick off the other men. He steadied his rifle and took aim at the men, who were loosely wearing their weapons. The scope of the rifle was aimed squarely at the forehead of the one man, Cain pulling the trigger, instantly dropping the unsuspecting victim. As soon as the bullet left the rifle, Cain took sights on the man next to him. The man watched his comrade drop in front of him and wasn't sure what was happening. A second later he joined his friend, the bullet penetrating his back and exiting through the left side of his chest near his heart. The third man was able to pull his weapon but not before Cain had fired his final shot, and though he missed what he was aiming for, still killed the man with a bullet through the neck. He shook his head, unhappy with his final shot, trying for a bullet through the man's head.

So far, everything was falling into place. Five of Kurylenko's men had been slain, with anywhere from seven to nine more inside. Cain quickly moved to the side of the house, pondering his next move. Going through the front door was risky, he felt, as there could've been someone stationed there on the inside. He walked down the length of the house and found an open window. He quietly pulled the large piece of glass open further so he could squeeze in and did so without banging into anything.

It was a bedroom, and Cain quickly noticed someone lying in the bed sleeping. He walked closer to the bed, ready to shoot the victim, but pulled back when he noticed it was just a boy. Probably no more than twelve or fourteen years old. He gently glided across the floor, hoping there were no creaks in it. He pulled the door open just enough to look down the hall. He started making his way down the hall, gun pointed directly in front of him, ready to take down anyone in his path.

He made his way to the living room, and upon clearing it, started toward the kitchen. Cain thought he heard a noise coming from it but wasn't positive. It was more like grumbling than voices. He peeked and saw four men passed out at the kitchen table. It was possible they were sleeping, but judging from the number of empty bottles on the table, countertop, and floor, they were most likely passed out drunk. Without hesitation, Cain entered the kitchen and promptly put a bullet in each man's back before returning to each one and firing one more round in the back of their heads. He exited the kitchen and started walking for the front door, clinging to the sides of the walls.

Once he got there, he peeked around the corner of the wall, and noticed two men sitting there in chairs, leaning back against the wall. Their eyes were closed and appeared to be sleeping. He moved in closer to finish them off but one of them jumped up and fired at Cain, barely missing him, the bullet flying past his head. Cain shot him in the face, instantly killing him, as the other man fell off his chair. He quickly grabbed his weapon, but it was too late, as Cain put two rounds into his chest. As the bullets entered the man's body, his gun accidentally discharged, a bullet firing into the floor. Eleven men were down and if there were any more, by now they knew he was there once they heard the shots fired.

Cain went back to the living room where he was met with a

bullet whizzing past his ear. He jumped behind a couch and returned fire in the direction the shot came from. He poked his head out from behind the sofa, just enough to get a look at the shooter. He patiently waited for the man to make his move. The other man didn't seem to be in much of a hurry either as the two of them tried to outlast the other. After a minute or two of waiting, the Russian grew tired of the inactivity and revealed his position as he tried to get a better angle of Cain. It was all Cain needed as he fired at him, piercing the man's shoulder, knocking him back a bit as he grimaced and grabbed his shoulder. Cain quickly seized the opportunity to finish him and ran over to him, shooting him point blank in the head.

As Cain stood over the fallen guard, a shot rang out, hitting Cain in the arm. He fell forward, rolling completely over, and firing a return shot in the process. He hit the man in the leg, completely shattering his shin, as he crumpled over in agony, holding his leg. Cain quickly jumped to his feet and walked over to his attacker and noticed it was Kurylenko.

"I knew we'd meet again someday," Kurylenko whispered, the pain almost unbearable. "I knew we would."

"Yep," Cain replied.

Cain didn't wish to continue the conversation any longer to prolong the inevitable and put two bullets into Kurylenko's head. Cain took out the tape recorder that contained Kurylenko's phone call with Medvedev and dropped it next to Kurylenko's hand. He assumed he was finished and relaxed for a moment only to hear one more shot, this one grazing his side. He stumbled but quickly turned around, ready to fire his weapon and kill whoever was before him, but hesitated once he saw who it was. It was the boy from the bedroom, holding a gun in front of him, aimed in Cain's direction, smoke rising from his pistol. Sweat was pouring off of Cain's body as he contemplated his next action, his gun pointed at the kid. Cain adjusted his grip on his gun, loosening his fingers before tightening them again. He knew he could easily kill the boy if he so desired but it wasn't what he wanted. He also wasn't sure what to do with him now. He wasn't about to shoot him down in cold blood, but didn't think he could just leave him there either.

"Who are you?" Cain asked without a reply. "What is your name?"

The boy still stood there, not answering his questions, with the gun still raised. Cain could see the kid was scared. The boy's hand started wavering, the gun moving side to side, as his nervousness increased. He was scared the hit man was about to kill him like he did the rest of the men.

Cain started asking the boy more questions, this time speaking in Russian. "What's your name? I will do you no harm. Just tell me your name. "

"Sergei Kurylenko," the frightened child replied.

"Is that your father?"

"Yes," he responded.

"Anybody else here?" Cain asked.

"No."

Cain put his hand out to the boy, palm exposed, and lowered his weapon, signaling to the boy he wasn't going to hurt him. He walked closer to him and gently eased the weapon out of the boy's hands. The younger Kurylenko didn't put up a struggle as the gun left his hands. He then rushed over to his dead father, sobbing hysterically, as he knelt down and held his father's head in his hands. Cain took his comm link out and called Lawson to see what to do with him.

"Is it done?" Lawson asked excitedly.

"Almost."

"What do you mean, almost? What's left? Is Kurylenko dead?"

"He is. There's a complication though," Cain said.

"What's that?"

"His son. He's about twelve or fourteen years old. I don't know what to do with him."

"Is he a problem?"

"Not at the moment," Cain said.

"Did he see anything?" Lawson asked.

Cain sighed. "Yes."

"That is a problem, isn't it?"

"That's why I called."

"Hold on, let me get Sanders on," Lawson said.

Cain exhaled and sat on the arm of the couch as he looked on at the boy sobbing over his dead father. It was the first time since Cain became an agent that he really felt guilty about a mission's outcome. Although he knew that there must've been some innocent people who were hurt over some of the people he killed in the past year, but he never saw their faces or heard their tears. This was different. He was looking in the eyes of a young boy, completely innocent of his father's ways, who had no idea what was going on. But Cain had just turned his world upside down. The boy went to bed feeling safe and woke up with his life now destroyed. Cain had a feeling that this would stay with him for a while. He wouldn't easily forget this. A minute later Sanders' voice boomed into his earpiece.

"Cain, you there?" Sanders asked.

"Go ahead."

"Shelly told me about your predicament. Unfortunately, there's no easy way around this."

"I figured as much," Cain replied.

"I was hoping the boy wouldn't be there when this happened but now we have to deal with it. Is he the last survivor?"

"Yes."

"I'm trying to beat around the bush here, son, but there's really no other way to say it," Sanders said.

"Which is what?" Cain asked, beginning to worry about what he was about to be told.

"You have to take the boy out."

"What?" Cain asked again, tapping his earpiece to make sure he heard correctly, though he knew he did.

"He has to be eliminated," Sanders repeated.

"No. I can't do that."

"I know it's a rough thing to hear, but it has to be done."

"There has to be another way," Cain said.

"There is no other way and we can't stand here arguing about it. You have to start moving before you get company."

"I can't do it."

"You can and you will," Sanders said, his voice rising.

"He doesn't deserve that just because of who his father is."

"It's because of who his father is that we can't leave him. His father has likely already started teaching him the ways of his business."

"You don't know that," Cain replied.

"I can almost guarantee that if you don't eliminate this boy that you will regret it in ten years when he starts seeking revenge on who did this to his father. And you'll be first on the chopping block," Sanders warned.

"You're assuming he's gonna turn out like his father."

"And you're assuming he won't. I think I'm more likely to be right on this than you."

Cain looked up at the ceiling briefly before he closed his eyes and took a deep breath. He looked at the younger Kurylenko and wondered what kind of a future he'd likely have. Seeing the death of his father was a traumatic experience and would probably haunt him forever. He was trying to accept Sanders' words as the truth but he just couldn't justify killing a child, no matter what kind of man he was likely to become. Even if Sanders was correct in his assumption, how could he live with killing a child? It was easy for Sanders to say since he wasn't the one who had to pull the trigger.

"Cain, you have to move," Sanders said.

Cain didn't reply and kept looking at the young boy, clutching his father's face in his hands. A sadness came over Cain as he looked away from the duo. He wondered how they could honestly expect him to shoot a child down in cold blood. He looked at the other body lying on the floor and thought about how much easier it was to kill when the other person had a gun in their hands.

"Shelly, talk to him," Sanders told his handler.

"Cain, are you there?" Lawson asked.

It took Cain a few seconds before responding, worrying his handler that they might've lost him. "I'm here."

"I know this isn't easy. I know it's not," she said, trying to appease him.

"Then don't ask me to do it."

"We all have to follow orders."

"We don't have to," Cain replied. "Not when it's something like this."

"I know what you're being asked to do is incomprehensible,

and if I were in your shoes, I don't know if I could do it either."

"Then we agree."

"You're only looking at this from one angle."

"Is there another one?" Cain asked.

"Yes. That boy can identify you. If you're identified as the killer then you will now become an international fugitive. Your picture will be everywhere and they will not rest until you're found. You will cause a stir in the international community, putting the U.S. government at risk and causing serious jeopardy to this agency."

"That's not my main concern."

"Well, it ought to be," Lawson reasoned.

"How can you ask me to do this?" Cain asked, struggling to accept his orders.

"Because there's no other way."

"What if I take him with me?"

"And do what with him?"

"That's not the business we're in, soldier," Sanders chimed in. "You do what you're told and get back here on the double, do you understand me?"

Cain's eyes danced around the room as the struggle he was dealing with was clearly evident on his face. His eyes stopped dancing around as they fixated on the gun he clutched in his hand, resting against his leg. He looked at the gun then looked over at the boy hugging his father.

"Get it done," Sanders yelled again. "That is a direct order."

"Please, Cain, just do what's asked," Lawson said, wincing as the words left her lips, not believing she was actually advocating for killing a child.

Lawson was now regretting getting Sanders involved. She called him hoping he'd have some ideas on how to proceed, not having any clue that his orders would be to kill the boy. She stayed silent for a minute as she waited on Cain to complete his mission. Cain started to think about just leaving and telling them he killed the boy, but he knew that wouldn't work. They'd find out in a matter of days that the boy was still alive, if it even took that long. He thought about maybe just going into hiding, as Raines had done, but he wasn't prepared to take that route. He wiped the sweat off his forehead as he started to come to grips with the inevitable. He knew the longer he waited the tougher it was going to be.

"Talk to me, Cain," Lawson said.

Cain ignored her and stood up from the arm of the couch, taking his earpiece out, letting it dangle across his shoulder. He squeezed the handle of his gun as he walked around the sofa, keeping his eyes on Kurylenko. He blinked rapidly several times as he wiped the sweat off his head again. His heartbeat was elevated, and he closed his eyes again, praying for forgiveness from whoever would eventually judge him from this life. Cain walked around the rest of the furniture so he could get behind the kid without him seeing what he was doing. He wanted to make sure it was over quickly so the boy couldn't see it coming.

Cain stood within a few inches from the boy and raised his gun to the back of his head, just barely missing touching his skull. Cain closed his eyes and pulled his finger back on the trigger. The shot rang out and he heard the body hit the floor. He licked his lips before opening his eyes as he tilted his head away from the scene, barely looking at the carnage that lay before him out of the corner of his eye. He backed away from the pair until he hit the wall, slowly dropping to the floor, letting his gun fall from his hand onto the floor. He raised his knees and set his elbows upon them, covering his eyes with his hands as he tried to come to grips with what he'd just done. He sat there motionless for a few minutes, not wanting to move. Lawson and Sanders both heard the shot and were trying to get Cain to respond. He heard their voices but had nothing to say to them. He wasn't sure how he could go on doing what he was doing and associate with them feeling the way he did. They kept on trying to get his attention which was starting to annoy him. He grabbed his com and put it back in his ear as he listened to their pleas.

"It's done," Cain bluntly told them, anger apparent in his voice.

"Good job, son," Sanders told him. "I know it wasn't easy."

"Yeah."

Lawson's heart sank, knowing how Cain must've been hurting. "Just get out of there. Get back as soon as you can, OK?" she said solemnly.

"OK."

He turned his com off, grabbed his gun, and stood up. He turned to leave when he suddenly stopped, hearing a creaking sound upstairs, startled at the thought of someone else being in the house. Cain stood there for a few moments, intently listening, hoping he didn't hear anything else. The thought of his work not yet being done for the night wasn't a pleasant one. He was emotionally drained. He didn't want any more trouble. All he wanted was to somehow be transported somewhere else. The creaking sound returned though, and this time it didn't stop, as it sounded like someone was walking across the floor over top of him. He thought of going up the steps to meet the person head on but it didn't seem like it would be necessary. Whoever it was, the sounds were getting louder, indicating the person was getting closer. There was a large bookcase against the wall that Cain rushed over to, taking cover next to it as he waited for the person to come down.

The bookcase covered Cain totally as he stood sideways, only the top of his head showing as he periodically peered out from it. The creaking stopped as it sounded like the person approached the top of the stairs. Cain was almost hoping it was an adult with a gun. Actually, hoping for someone who had a chance to kill him was a better thought than if it was another kid that he might have to eliminate. The thought of killing another child would probably be too much for him to bear. He heard a different sound, more of a thud, as the man's heavy steps took to heading down the stairs. Cain clenched the gun with the palm and fingers of his right hand, ready to pounce on the man once he was within his sights. The man stopped when he reached the halfway point of the stairs and called out to Cain. Cain was surprised to hear the stranger calling out to him.

"Cain," the stranger yelled. "I know you're down there. Don't shoot."

Cain looked bewildered as he tried to figure out who it was and why the man waited until now to show himself. He peeked out from the bookcase and saw the bottom of the man's legs, standing still in the middle of the stairs. Cain thought maybe it was some type of trap and looked around the room to see if anything was out of the ordinary. Nothing seemed different though.

"C'mon, Cain, we have an agreement not to harm each other," the man shouted. "I don't even have my gun out."

It took Cain a few minutes until he recognized the man's voice but the confused look on his face didn't disappear. He still wasn't sure what the man was doing there.

"I'm coming down," the man said.

Cain's eyes peeked around the edge of the bookcase as he watched Eric Raines reach the bottom of the steps. He waited until Raines got to the floor and saw that he had no gun in his possession that Cain could see until he showed himself. Cain emerged from behind the bookcase, his hand still clutching the gun.

"Ah, there you are," Raines said.

"What're you doing here?" Cain asked.

"Well, Andrei invited me to stay at his house for the week to talk about some business that he had lined up. It appears that it was an unwise decision."

"How'd you know it was me down here?"

"I heard your voice when you were talking about the kid," Raines said, looking down at Kurylenko.

"Is anyone else here?"

"No. The rest have been... neutralized, I should say," Raines said with a smile.

"Why'd you wait till now to show yourself?"

"Well, there was no point in doing so until now. Any sooner and I'd have risked ending up face down with splinters piercing through my lips."

Cain relaxed his arm and put his gun inside his belt, feeling relatively certain that Raines wasn't trying to play him.

"I must say that I'm impressed by your handy work," Raines said. "You do good work. Quick, efficient, and plenty of bodies."

"It doesn't seem to shake you up too much," Cain said.

"What's that?"

"Looks like you'll need a new employer."

"Oh. No need to worry about that. I've already got backup plans. You should know that about me by now. Always planning for the future. I've known Kurylenko was as good as dead for a year now. Ever since you showed up, I knew it was only a matter of time. I just had to make sure I didn't end up there with him."

"So, what now?" Cain asked.

"Now we go our separate ways. I'll drop out of sight for a little while and you keep on doing what you do."

Cain made a face that Raines could tell indicated he wasn't too keen on continuing with his profession.

"So, what's troubling you?" Raines asked.

"Nothing. I'm good," Cain replied.

"I don't believe that any more than you do."

Cain started to say something but stopped, not wanting to vent about his problems to Raines. Raines could tell what was bothering him though; he'd been there before, worrying about the same things.

"I can guess," Raines said. "You're starting to question your role and what it is that you do."

"Maybe."

"Maybe nothing… I've been there. I know what you're feeling and it isn't good. You get into this thing thinking that you're doing good work, protecting your country and all that, then one day it all goes out the window. Something happens, something goes wrong, something pulls at your conscience and all of a sudden your country isn't there for you."

Cain didn't reply and just sat on the edge of the couch, listening to what Raines had to say.

"I think once you get into this profession you know that eventually you're gonna be faced with a decision that you know you'll regret. We've all had them. I think all of us are tormented by 'that one'."

"The one what?" Cain asked.

"That one mission that keeps you up at night. The one decision that you made that you wish you could take back. The one victim that continually haunts you. That boy over there will be yours," Raines said.

"So, what's yours?"

"A woman. Four years ago. October 17th," Raines said, remembering every little detail. "Her only mistake was the man she married. She wasn't involved in his dealings, didn't know what he was planning, her only involvement was that she loved him for whatever reason. She was completely innocent."

"Why'd you do it?" Cain asked.

"She wasn't supposed to be there. Wrong place, wrong time," Raines said. "But it still needed to be done, I was told. Just like you were here tonight. So, I did it. And I immediately regretted it. I remember throwing up right after it and several times later. There were plenty of sleepless nights where I wondered what was wrong with me for killing an innocent person. There were also plenty of nights where I hoped, and wished, for someone to end the pain that I lived with."

"So, how'd you end up coping with it?" Cain asked.

"The pain stays with you for so long that it ingrains itself in you and becomes part of who you are. You never get over it and it never leaves you."

Cain put his head down trying to collect his thoughts, hoping Raines wasn't right that this would haunt him forever.

"Look at us," Raines said. "Look at the things they've made us do. And you... look at what they've turned you into."

Cain raised his head up and looked at Raines, knowing he was speaking the truth.

"Whatever kind of man you were before, whoever you were inside... you're not that anymore," Raines said.

"That's not true," Cain replied.

"Oh no? Look around," Raines gestured. "Look at the carnage that's been done here. Do you think the man you were before you got caught up in all this was the type of man who'd do this?"

"I don't know."

"Make no mistake, you are now a killer," Raines said, moving closer to Cain for emphasis. "Look at the man they've turned you into. You are now a killing machine. Just like they wanted."

Cain had no words to reply with. He looked up at Raines and worried that he might have been right. This wasn't the work of a normal person. Only a killing machine could do the things he was now capable of. His eyes started feeling heavy, tired from all of the night's festivities. All he wanted to do was just lay down and wake up somewhere else. Somewhere secluded where nobody knew him or what he'd done. If only it were that simple, he thought.

"Well, it's about time we started moving on, I suspect," Raines said. "Stay here any longer and we risk getting caught in a shootout with the police."

"I guess so."

"You take care of yourself," Raines said, extending his hand.

"You too," Cain replied, returning the handshake.

Raines smiled. "Always." Raines smiled.

Cain put his equipment back in his bag and the two of them left, Cain taking one more look at the guard station, making sure the video equipment was destroyed. He noticed Raines take off in an SUV, flying through the gates. He then went down to the river and slowly immersed himself into it, vanishing into the water.

21

The entire flight home all Cain could think about was pulling the trigger and killing Sergei Kurylenko. He kept thinking about what Sanders told him to try to justify it, but he couldn't make it seem right. There was no excuse in his mind for killing a child, no matter who it was. Raines was right. This was probably going to haunt him forever. He tried to sleep on the way but all he saw was the grisly images of the scene he left behind in Russia.

After Cain's flight landed back in New York, Heather was waiting for him at the terminal. As soon as she saw him she ran up to him and then hugged and kissed him. They held hands as they picked up his luggage and exited the airport. Cain wasn't usually the biggest talker to begin with but he was even more silent than usual. Heather sensed something was bothering him but didn't want to press him on it too much.

"Are you OK?" she asked as they started driving.

"Yeah. Why?"

"Just asking. You seem like something's wrong."

"I'm just tired. It was a long flight," Cain said. "I wasn't able to sleep."

"You should go straight to bed once we get home."

"Maybe I will."

The entire drive home, Cain just stared out the window, trying to forget the impossible. Heather turned the radio on, putting the volume low, hoping to relax him a little bit. They didn't talk the rest of the way as Cain focused on the scenery. His mind was so elsewhere that if Heather had said anything to him, he wouldn't have heard it anyway. Once they got back to the apartment Cain immediately went to the couch and plopped down.

"Can I get you anything?" Heather asked.

"No, I'm fine, thank you. I just wanna sit here for a few minutes."

"How was your trip?" she asked, reaching into the fridge for a bottle of water.

Cain didn't answer as he started spacing out, staring straight ahead, not really focusing on anything. Heather walked into the living room and noticed his lack of focus, waving her hand in front of his face.

"Matt," she said, without a reply. "Matt."

"Huh?" he asked, snapping out of it.

"Are you OK?"

"Yeah, why?"

"I asked you a question, and you didn't answer and you just seemed like you were somewhere else."

"Oh. I'm sorry. What was your question?"

"I asked how your trip was," Heather said.

"It was fine. Well, I think I'm gonna lay down for a bit," he said, not wanting to talk about it.

Cain went into the bedroom, closing the door halfway. Heather knew that something wasn't right, and it wasn't just his lack of sleep. There was something eating at him. Even when he wasn't in a talkative mood, he never seemed distant. She decided to let him have some space. Maybe when he woke up, he'd be a little more receptive to talking about whatever was bothering him. She just watched TV for a few hours until she started to feel tired. She turned the TV off about midnight and got ready for bed. She went into the bedroom and was surprised to see that Cain was awake. He was lying in the middle of the bed, staring up at the ceiling. Heather turned a light on and was concerned as his eyes looked a little bloodshot and he wasn't moving.

"Have you been awake all this time?" Heather asked.

She sat on the bed, trying to talk to him, but it was a one-way conversation. Cain wasn't hearing a word she was saying. The only thing he was seeing was the boy he had killed. All he heard were voices crying out to him for help. Heather gently grabbed his face to try to snap him out of whatever funk he was in. Her touch didn't seem to work, so she straddled him and looked directly in his eyes.

"Matthew!" she yelled.

Cain seemed startled, and he started squirming, his eyes blinking and shifting around. He sighed and licked his lips like he was dying of thirst. He took a gulp and wiped his eyes as they started to tear.

"What's wrong?" Heather asked with concern.

"Why are you on top of me?"

"Have you just been lying here for the last three hours?" she asked, moving to his side.

"Guess I was just thinking about things," Cain replied.

"Like what?"

"You don't wanna know."

"If I didn't wanna know I wouldn't have asked," she said.

"If I told you, it would change your opinion of me," he warned.

"Nothing could change my opinion of you."

"Don't be so sure."

"I thought you promised to be more honest with me and talk to me. We made a deal," she insisted.

"Please don't."

"You did something bad?" Heather asked.

Cain looked away, not wanting to tell her what happened. She reached over and gingerly turned his face to look at her again.

"It doesn't matter right now," she said. "Right now, you need to sleep. You're exhausted."

Heather took him in her arms hoping that would help him fall asleep. She caressed his hair as his head lay across her chest. Her arms and her touch was just what he needed to relax as Cain fell asleep in a matter of minutes, somehow blocking out the torturous memories he had trouble forgetting. Heather couldn't help but wonder what it was that seemed to be tormenting him. From how he was acting she knew it must've been awful. He seemed genuinely traumatized by whatever happened. She slowly drifted to sleep within the hour, still holding Cain tightly.

Around three in the morning Heather was awakened by the sounds of Cain screaming, still nestled in her arms.

"No. Don't do it!" Cain screamed. "Stop!"

"Matt!" Heather yelled as she put him on his back.

"I'm not a killing machine," he said calmly.

Heather looked worried, more about his condition than what he was saying, though his last line did concern her. He kept muttering things, most of which were only one or two words that didn't make much sense. She tried gently shaking him with no success before doing it with much more conviction, finally succeeding in waking him from his terrors. Cain snapped up, sitting up quickly as he wiped the sweat from his face. He looked over at Heather, who bore an obvious face of concern about him.

"What happened?" Cain asked.

"You were dreaming."

"Oh," he said, sighing.

Cain continued sitting there for a minute, in silence, trying to gain some clarity in his mind. His heart was racing, and he knew he must've said or did something to alarm Heather with the way she was looking at him.

"So, what'd I say?" Cain asked, turning his head without actually looking at her.

"Most of it was just talk, didn't make much sense."

"You said most. What was the rest?"

"You kept yelling no and stop. Then you said something about how you're not a killing machine," Heather said.

Cain looked frustrated, putting both of his hands on his head. He didn't even want to look at Heather, thinking she must've thought some awful things about him by now. He started to get out of bed but Heather grabbed his wrist, pulling him back down.

"Talk to me," Heather said softly.

Cain stared in her eyes and could see the care and concern that she had for him. He didn't try to pull away from her and figured he'd just lay it all out there for her and hopefully wouldn't make her back away from him.

"I... um," he muttered.

"Just take your time," Heather said, stroking his face. "I'm not going anywhere. I'm right here."

"I did something in Russia that I, uh," Cain said, moving his jaw around. "I did something that I don't know if I can forgive myself for."

"What was it?" she asked.

"I killed someone," he bluntly stated, avoiding the details.

"Without sounding too uncaring, I know you've killed people before. How was this different?"

"It was a child."

"Oh," Heather said, taking her hand off him.

Cain looked at her, ashamed, knowing that she likely would never look at him or feel the same way again.

"What happened?" she asked.

"My mission was to eliminate a man named Andrei Kurylenko. He was an international arms dealer. He was the man I was after in Syria when I was captured. My mission was to get into his house and kill him along with his men that were there and make it look like the mafia did it," Cain explained.

"And did you?"

"Yes. I killed him and his men. I killed Kurylenko. I killed his men. And I killed his son."

"Why?"

"I didn't know the boy would be there. I called and asked what to do with him and I was told that he needed to be eliminated too."

"How old was he?"

"Probably around twelve or so."

"Who told you to do it?" Heather asked.

"Sanders. He said the boy was a risk in identifying me and could cause an incident with the U.S. government if the truth was found out."

Heather struggled to find the right words to help him cope with what he'd done. She didn't condone the killing of a child but wanted to let him know she was still there for him. She knew he wouldn't have done it if he wasn't ordered to.

"I am a killing machine," Cain told her. "I killed thirteen men in a matter of minutes. It came so easily."

"Oh my God," Heather said, shocked at the sheer number of bodies he piled up. "That's uh, such a big number."

"I'm not normal. Normal people don't do these things."

"You're not a killing machine," she replied, trying to ease his fears.

"I am. Every mission I've ever been on, I've killed so easily, without hesitation. I don't even have to think about it. It just comes naturally. Like a machine."

"You're not," she said again, hugging and squeezing him tightly. "You were in the military. You were trained to do things like this. Of course it's gonna come more easily to you than it would someone like me."

"Maybe," Cain said, not wanting to admit anything else.

"You just need to rest for a little bit."

"How can you love someone like me? Someone who does the things that I do?" he asked.

"Because you're not a bad man. You said yourself that you only do the things you do to bad people," she rationalized.

"Except for now."

"You know, there are a lot of men who wouldn't have wanted to get involved with me, with my past. They would've run in the other direction. But you didn't. You saw something else in me and helped me see it too. You were there for me. So now it's my turn to be there for you."

"It's not even close to being the same thing," he said.

"Come here," she said, taking him in her arms again.

She wrapped her arms around him as they lay down. Neither one of them went back to sleep as they were both wide awake, but they lay there in silence, him thinking of what he'd done and her thinking of the pain he was going through. She couldn't imagine what it was like to have to do the things he did and didn't even dare to think she knew how he felt. Heather knew all she could do was to keep reassuring him that she was there for him and try to help him overcome his demons.

22

Heather was dead tired from the long night she shared with Cain and just felt like calling out of work but decided to be a trooper and drudge her way through it. She poured herself four cups of coffee to try to get herself ready for the day. Cain sat at the kitchen table as he watched Heather get ready.

"What are you gonna do today?" Heather asked, taking a sip of coffee.

"I'm not sure. Maybe I'll just lounge around or something."

"That sounds like a good idea."

Cain kept watching Heather as she frantically rushed around, complaining about how tired she felt, and how horrible she looked. He couldn't help but think of how beautiful she looked, her hair down to her shoulders, wearing a white blouse with a black skirt and matching heels. Even at her worst she looked like the sexiest woman alive to him. Heather noticed how his eyes were following her wherever she went. She stopped in the middle of the living room and looked at her outfit like something was wrong.

"Do I have something on me?" she asked.

"What?"

"You keep watching me like I have a stain on my top or something."

"Oh, no." Cain laughed. "I just like to look at you."

"Oh, I see. Enjoying the view?"

"Very much. You look beautiful," he gushed as he got up to move closer.

"You're a bad liar. I look ridiculously horrible of epic proportions. I've got bags under my eyes, my hair's a mess, and I just look hideous," she countered.

"You look unbelievably sexy," he said, kissing her on the cheek.

"You're gonna make me not want to go to work," she replied, passionately kissing him.

"That's the idea," Cain said, kissing her neck.

After a minute, Heather was able to regain her composure and gently pushed Cain away.

"You're really making it hard," she said.

Cain grinned. "I thought I was supposed to."

"I really don't want you to stop."

"Then I won't."

"As much as I'd love that, if you don't stop, I have a feeling I'll be a few hours late to work," Heather said.

"OK. You win."

She smiled. "Later. You know how to make me feel good though."

Cain finally was able to keep his hands off Heather, at least long enough to let her leave for work.

"You be good while I'm gone," she said.

Cain went on his laptop for a little while to pass the time while Heather was gone. He read mostly news and sports pages. He eventually noticed an ad that kept popping up occasionally for a trip to Hawaii. After seeing it a couple of times he clicked on it. As he continued looking at it, the thought of taking a trip became more appealing. He told Heather that he'd make it up to her before leaving for Russia and he thought a trip would be the perfect way to do it. Cain figured he'd earned a little vacation and would clear it with Lawson first and called her right away.

"Shelly, I need a favor," Cain said.

"What's up?"

"I wanna take a little trip."

"To where?" Lawson asked.

"Hawaii."

"What's there?"

"You know, sand, beach, water," Cain said.

"Is this business or are you asking for a vacation?"

"I think I need to blow off some steam for a while," he said.

"How much time do you want?"

"Maybe a week or two."

"I think it's a good idea."

"You do?"

"Definitely. You've earned it and you deserve it."

"Hmm."

"What?" Lawson asked.

"Well, I really didn't expect it to be that easy. I thought I might have to talk you into it."

"Nope. I support it totally. I do have a couple of questions though."

"Which are?"

"Are you going on this trip by yourself?"

"Why are you asking?"

"Well, I seem to remember some conversations I had with you about a certain woman and then you left for Russia. How'd that whole scenario play out?" Lawson asked.

"Umm. Fine."

"You didn't answer my question."

"I'll probably book it for two people," Cain replied.

"You aren't going with another man, are you?" Lawson kidded.

"Seriously?"

"So, you're going with a woman then?"

"Yes."

"Great. I'll start packing. When should I be ready by?" she joked.

"I actually had someone else in mind."

"Wow. I feel really let down now." She laughed. "So, you and Heather are a thing now, I'm guessing?"

"I guess you could say that," he answered.

"It is Heather!"

"Yeah."

"You're hard to get information out of sometimes," Lawson said.

"I know it."

"Well, I'm glad to hear it. I think it'll be good for you."

"The trip?" Cain asked.

"The trip... and her."

"Do I need to run it by Sanders?"

"No, I'll let him know. It'll be fine," Lawson said.

"I'll see you again in two weeks then?"

"Yeah. You guys have fun," she said. "Just don't bring her back pregnant or anything."

"Very funny."

Cain continued looking up information on Hawaii and was getting excited about going. He hoped Heather would be surprised and not opposed to going. He wondered if maybe it was too soon for them to plan a vacation together but it wasn't like they just met. He was about to book the reservations but then remembered Heather's work. She really enjoyed working at the marketing firm since she'd been hired, even though she was still in an entry level position. She was highly thought of and was a candidate to move up in the company at some point. Cain knew she wasn't going to be able to just go at a moment's notice so he thought about contacting her boss to make sure she could get away. He also thought he would wait in the lobby of Heather's building and surprise her when she got done since he'd never been there before. He printed out a picture of a beach in Maui to show her. This was the most excited he could ever remember being. He couldn't wait to meet Heather and show her what he was planning. Cain eagerly waited for the time to fly by, almost like a little schoolboy who was waiting for his father to come home from work with a toy. Cain was so into reading everything about Hawaii that he almost forgot to check the time at two o'clock. He wanted to make sure he had enough time to talk to Heather's boss before waiting in the lobby for her.

Cain got to the building located on 52nd Street, a tall building that was twenty floors high, and had several corporations running their businesses from it. The marketing firm was on the third floor. Cain went into the receptionist's office and asked to speak with Mr. Chaney, Heather's boss. The receptionist called Chaney, who told her he would be in shortly. Cain took a seat in the office as he patiently waited, watching a TV on the wall. It was a short wait as Chaney walked in within a few minutes. Chaney was an older man, probably in his late fifties, just a shade under six feet tall, with a full head of grey hair, and glasses. He was the kind of boss most employees enjoyed working for. He was a caring man who tried to look out for his people and help them when possible. He treated them fairly and expected their best effort while at work. As long as they gave that he was always there for them. Heather had always spoken highly of him to Cain so he hoped he'd be successful in securing her a week off.

"Mr. Cain, a pleasure to meet you finally," Chaney said, shaking his hand.

"You've heard of me?"

"Yes. Heather hasn't stopped talking about you in the last week."

"Oh. I'm sorry to hear that," Cain remarked.

"No, it's nothing bad. Quite honestly, it's nice to see her happy finally. Ever since she started working here, she seemed to be missing something. But now, for the last week, we can't seem to wipe the smile off her face. She's been walking around here beaming from ear to ear since she met you," Chaney told him as they walked into his office.

"Well, we were friends for a while. It took me some time to see what I was missing," Cain replied, sitting down.

"I'm glad you saw the light. She's a great girl. Wonderful personality. She's doing a great job here."

"I'm glad to hear that. That's kind of the reason I came."

"Oh? Anything wrong?" Chaney asked.

"Oh, no. It's just that I, uh, wanted to take her away somewhere on a vacation and I wanted to surprise her."

"Well, that sounds fantastic. Is there something you need from me?"

"I wanted to surprise her by going away in a couple days, but that'd mean taking her from work on short notice. She loves it here and I wouldn't want to do anything that'd get her fired or anything. So, I was just wondering if it was possible for you to give her some time off?" Cain asked.

"Well, that is a predicament. I did have some plans for her in the next week or so but I suppose it could wait until she got back. She hasn't taken any time off since she's been here so she's certainly deserving of it and she's due two weeks of vacation time. I've asked her several times about taking a vacation week but she's refused every time, always says she has no place to go," Chaney said. "If you want to take her away for a week, then you have my approval. It's about time someone got her away from here. I'm glad she's so dedicated but everyone needs to get away sometimes. Her job will still be here when she gets back."

"Thank you. I really appreciate it."

Cain left Chaney's office and proceeded down to the lobby, where he waited on a bench, constantly checking the time. Heather was done work at four and Cain just stared at the marble floors, watching people go by, as he waited for her to come down. It seemed like he sat there for an eternity but was only about an hour. Once he saw Heather walking in his direction he stood up to greet her. She saw him standing there and was surprised to see him. It was the first time he'd ever been there, so she thought something might be wrong.

"What are you doing here?" she asked, worried he was going to say something she didn't like.

"I just wanted to surprise you," Cain replied with a kiss.

"Nothing bad?" she asked, slightly turning her head, still looking worried.

"Nothing bad," he said, shaking his head.

"You're not breaking up with me?"

"Of course not."

"You're not going away somewhere?"

"No."

"Good. Sorry, I just had the feeling you were gonna tell me something disappointing," Heather said.

"Well, what I said isn't totally true."

"Which part?"

"About going away," he said.

"You have to leave?" she asked, disappointed.

"It's something I volunteered for."

"Why would you do that?"

Cain reached into his pocket and pulled out the brochures he printed on Hawaii. He handed them over to Heather, who reluctantly accepted, not sure she wanted to look at them. She unfolded them, and started to look them over, confused about what she was seeing.

"What's all this?" Heather asked.

"Just look at them."

"I don't understand," she said. "So, you're going off to Hawaii?"

"No," Cain responded. "We're going off to Hawaii."

"What?" she asked, still not convinced of what he was saying.

"If you recall, before I left for Moscow, I told you that I'd make it up to you. This is my way of making it up to you. I want you to go to Hawaii with me."

"Wow. I don't know what to say," she replied, astonished.

"Just say you'll go."

"When?"

"I thought maybe tomorrow."

"I'd love to..." she started.

"But?"

"But I don't think now's a good time."

"Why not?"

"It's very thoughtful, and you're so sweet," she said, kissing his cheek. "But it's such short notice. We have a lot of work going on right now. I really can't get away so soon."

"But you can. I already talked to your boss about it. He endorsed it," he explained.

"What? You talked to Mr. Chaney?"

From the sound of her voice, Cain thought she was angry that he talked to her boss and tried to explain his actions. "I'm sorry. I know I shouldn't have. I just wanted to surprise you and I wanted to make sure they were OK with taking you away. I didn't know of another way."

"No, it's OK," she said and smiled, her eyes getting teary. "It's incredibly sweet and thoughtful. Who knew under that rough exterior lay the heart of a sweet, romantic guy?"

"So, you'll go with me?" Cain asked.

"Of course," she replied, wiping her eyes, then kissing his lips. "How could I refuse an offer from an extremely good looking, hopelessly romantic man like yourself?"

"Hmm, not sure I like the sound of that," he kidded. "You might start expecting this kind of stuff all the time."

"I might at that," she replied, her tears still flowing.

"What's all those tears for?" he asked, wiping them away.

"I'm just really happy," she said, hugging him.

"Let's go home and finalize everything."

They left the building holding hands, excited about the trip they were about to share together. The entire way home they talked about things they could see and do. Once they got back to the apartment, they immediately went on the computer to book the plans.

"Wait, are you sure your work is just gonna let you go for a couple weeks?" Heather asked.

"Already cleared it. Relax," he replied with a kiss.

"There is one more small problem," she said.

"What's that?"

"I'm starting to get a little nervous."

"About what? I promise I'll take care of you."

"No, it's not you. I feel completely safe with you. That's not the problem."

"Then what is it?" Cain asked.

"I've never been on a plane before," she said.

"Don't worry. I'll be by your side the entire time. You know I fly all the time. It's completely safe."

"Right."

Cain talked to Heather about her fear of flying for a few minutes, seeming to relieve her fears, if only temporarily. She did feel a little better about it but she also knew she wasn't near a plane yet. She might think differently once it was time to board one. They booked their flight and hotel room, staying in Maui for seven days. That'd leave them a few days to relax once they got back before they returned to work.

They arrived at LaGuardia Airport the following morning for their 7:30am flight. As they waited, Heather and Cain sat next to each other, holding hands. Cain could tell she was

MIKE RYAN

getting more nervous as she started squeezing his hand tighter by the second.

"Trying to break my hand?" Cain chided.

"Huh?"

"My hand. It's starting to hurt," he playfully added.

"Oh," Heather replied, releasing his hand. "I'm sorry. Guess I'm nervous."

"Doesn't show."

Cain grabbed her hand again and smiled at her, rubbing her hand.

"Everything's gonna be fine," Cain told her.

Heather didn't respond, her nerves had gotten the best of her vocal chords, and she simply smiled back at him. She appreciated his calming influence and let him know that even if it didn't show, that he really did help put her mind at ease a little bit.

"I would not be able to do this without you," Heather said, taking big breaths.

"Once this is over you'll be able to do it again with no problem. The first time's always the worst."

The passengers started boarding the plane and Heather's anxiety was starting to get the best of her. She stopped, not sure if she could go any further, but Cain was able to coax her onto the plane after a minute.

"I can do this," Heather stated, pumping herself up.

They boarded the plane, Cain walking ahead of her, still holding her hand. "Want the window seat?"

"You've got to be joking," she replied.

Heather felt a little better once the plane got in the air, breathing somewhat easier. Cain helped her immensely by holding her hand or putting his arm around her the entire plane ride. They had one stop in Dallas before landing in Hawaii a few hours later. They had a jam-packed itinerary once they got settled at their hotel. They had activities lined up around the clock almost every day they were there. They planned a dolphin excursion, whale watching, helicopter tours, hiking, horseback riding, snorkeling, and surfing lessons, along with restaurants, shopping, and the beach. They decided to spend their final day just relaxing on the beach. They walked along the shoreline for a little while, holding hands and talking, just letting the water roll past their legs. The week they'd spent there felt like they were in heaven.

"You know, I almost don't feel like going back," Cain said.

"I know. This has been the most incredible week of my life," she said, kissing him. "This really does seem like paradise."

"Maybe one day when all this is over we can settle down in a place like this."

"That's a nice thought."

They walked for a few more minutes, Heather contemplating telling Cain exactly how she felt, though she was unsure how he'd take it. She definitely wasn't trying to rush into things but they'd known each other over a year and had been living together so it wasn't like a typical new relationship. After some thought she decided she'd just lay it all out there for him to interpret however he wanted without pressure from her.

"I have something I wanna tell you," Heather started.

"Well, that sounds ominous."

"I want you to just hear me out and let me finish. There's something I want to say and get off my chest and you don't have to respond. You don't have to say anything at all if you don't want to, OK?"

"Sure."

"You know this… us, is what I've wanted for a long time. I almost feel like pinching myself, like it's a dream, and if it is, one that I hopefully never wake up from. There's a million thoughts that are running through my head and it's hard to rationalize them all."

"Just say what's on your mind," Cain said.

"OK. I'm just gonna say it then," she said nervously. "You don't have to say anything back and I'm not expecting you or pressuring you to reply."

"Just say it, Heather." Cain laughed. "If you don't say it soon, you might bust."

"I love you," she blurted out. "There. I said it."

"Wow," Cain said.

"You don't have to say anything back. I just wanted to throw it out there so you know how I felt."

They stopped, turning to face each other. Cain was about to respond to her affection when a photographer suddenly approached them.

"Get together guys," he told them. "Smile."

"No, it's OK," Cain replied.

"Aww, c'mon," Heather objected. "We don't have any pictures together. We're here in Hawaii, let's get one."

"OK."

The photographer took a few pictures of them in a couple different poses. He gave them his card and told them he'd have them developed and ready to be picked up in a few hours. Cain and Heather stayed at the beach for another hour before going back to their hotel room. Heather was very excited to get the pictures of them. She'd been wishing for some photos of them together so she couldn't wait to get her hands on them. After getting something to eat, they went to the man's small photography store to pick up the pictures. Heather gave the photographer the ticket he gave them. The shop's walls were lined with pictures of people whose photos he'd taken over the years who never came back to claim them. He hung them up as examples of his work. As they waited, Cain went over to the wall and looked the pictures over. The photographer grabbed the pictures and handed them over to Heather. As the two of them looked them over, Heather started gushing over the pictures, though Cain didn't hear a word she was saying. As he looked over the photos on the wall, his eyes stopped once he saw a particular picture. He was mesmerized by it and couldn't take his eyes off it. The faces were familiar though he didn't know the names. They were the ones he'd had visions of. It was a picture of a blonde-haired woman hugging a little boy. Heather looked over at him and saw he was in a trance and called out to him. He didn't respond so Heather walked over to him, tapping him on the shoulder, startling him.

"What's the matter?" she asked.

"Umm, nothing," he said, not sure of what to say.

Heather looked up at the photos, wondering what had him so entranced. Cain looked at her and remembered his promise to be honest with her. He cleared his throat and looked back up at the picture.

"I know them," Cain whispered.

"Who?"

Cain reached up and grabbed the frame, taking the picture off the wall. "They're the ones I've told you about. The visions I've had."

"Are you sure?" Heather asked, incredulously.

"I'm positive. That's them."

Cain turned the picture over to see if there was anything

written on the back, a name or a date, but was disappointed to find nothing. He looked back to the photographer to see if he had any information about it.

"What can you tell me about this picture?" Cain asked.

"Not much," the photographer replied. "It was taken on the beach a few years ago. She never came in for it so I just put it on the wall."

"Do you know a name or anything?"

"No. Just like I did with you guys, I took their picture on the beach and developed it in case they came in for it. No names or dates or anything. If they don't come in, I just hang it on the wall sometimes."

"I see," Cain said, disappointed.

"What's so interesting about them?"

"I know them. Somehow. I just can't remember where."

"I know how frustrating that can be," the photographer acknowledged.

"How much for this one?" Cain asked.

"Twenty and it's yours."

Cain paid for the picture along with the ones that were taken of him and Heather. The excitement she had for the pictures she finally had of them was temporarily halted by jealousy of this woman in the photo. The woman in the photo was very pretty, and if it was a former girlfriend, maybe he'd go back to her once he found out who it was. As happy as she was that maybe Cain had found a link to his past, she worried that maybe it would be a link that would ultimately be their undoing. They went back to their hotel for the night, though they might as well have been in separate rooms. All Cain could think about was the photo, analyzing the faces, hoping something would eventually jog his memory. Heather spent most of the night in misery, watching Cain stare at the picture constantly. Even when they were talking, she knew that his mind was somewhere else. As the night wound down, Cain started to feel bad, knowing that he didn't make the night very enjoyable for Heather. It was their last night in Hawaii and Cain didn't make it a memorable one for her. As they got ready for bed, Cain snuck up behind Heather and wrapped his arms around her. She smiled and stroked his forearms, happy to be in his grasp.

"I'm sorry," he said.

"For what?"

"I know my mind's been elsewhere tonight."

"It's OK. I completely understand," Heather said.

"No. We've had a great time this week, and I made our last night here not very special for you."

"Listen, this whole week has been special. Nothing could change that," she said, trying to ease his mind.

"Thanks. That's what makes you special. You see the good in me no matter what."

"It's not hard to see."

"It's just that once I saw that picture I knew that I'm not crazy," Cain said. "At least not yet."

"That's comforting."

"It means that these people are connected to my past somehow. Now I feel like I've been here before. Maybe I subconsciously saw the ad for Hawaii and wanted to come here, because I was here before. Maybe everything is connected, these people in the picture, Hawaii, and maybe I knew that deep down."

"That's a lot of supposing," Heather added.

"Maybe you're right. But it's the only lead I have."

23

Cain and Heather had a relaxing night at home once they got back from Hawaii. They had a romantic dinner, Cain trying to put the picture aside and not think about it for the evening. He wasn't due to check back in at the agency for another couple of days but was thinking about seeing Lawson in the morning. Around midnight, Cain got out of bed, careful to not wake Heather up. He sent Lawson a text asking if she was still in New York. She replied almost instantly that she was. Cain asked if he could meet her at The Center around ten the next morning to which she agreed. As Cain read the message, he glanced over at Heather's naked body and smiled, the sheet barely covering her torso. He put the phone down and got back into bed, trying not to wake her. She felt the covers moving which woke her up as Cain slid under them.

"What's wrong?" Heather whispered, her eyes barely open.

"Nothing," he replied, kissing her cheek. "Go back to sleep."

"Then why were you on your phone?"

"You don't miss much, do you?" Cain asked, rubbing her back.

"I try not to."

"It was just a message from Lawson asking if I was back."

"Oh."

"I gotta go in for an hour or so tomorrow just to let them know I'm back."

"But you're still on vacation."

"I am. It'll only take an hour or so," he said, passionately kissing her lips, as they began their second round of the night.

The following morning, they got dressed and had breakfast, mostly still talking about their trip to Hawaii and how much fun they had.

"You know, as much as I like living here, I wouldn't have minded forgetting our way back," Heather said.

"I know."

"Everything was so perfect there."

"Well, I'll be back in a little bit. I'm just gonna go check in now," Cain said, buttoning his shirt.

"I'll miss you," Heather said.

"I'll only be gone an hour or two," he replied, chuckling.

"I'll still miss you."

"I'll be back before you know it," he said, giving her a hug and kiss.

She wrapped her arms around him, rubbing his back, before lowering her hands to his butt. She raised them slightly and sighed, feeling some type of paper tucked in the back of his pants. Though she didn't see it, she knew what it was and what he was doing.

"Thought we said no secrets," she said.

"We did."

"You don't have to hide the picture. I know what you're doing."

Cain sighed, before letting out a grin. "I'm sorry. I just didn't want to burden you with it."

"Listen, I know this is important to you. This might be a link to your missing memories. And if it's important to you, then it's important to me. You don't have to worry about what I might think. I'm with you all the way. I always will be."

"Have I told you recently how great you are?"

"Oh, stop."

"Really, you're the best," Cain said, holding her chin with his thumb and finger while kissing her.

Cain let out a sigh, and Heather knew something was wrong with him.

"What's the matter?" Heather asked.

"It's nothing."

"Matt," she said, giving him a look.

"It's just that sometimes I look at you and think about how much better you deserve than me," he said. "I don't know what the future holds for me but I wonder if it's fair for me to drag you along with me."

"All I want is you and I'm willing to go wherever you take me."

"I have so many flaws," Cain said softly.

"Everyone has flaws."

"Not like mine. I still think about that boy in Russia. That's never gonna leave me," he said, looking at the floor.

"We can get through everything, anything that comes up, we can get through it together." She reassured him with a kiss.

"The other day at the beach you told me something," Cain

said. "And you told me you didn't want to pressure me or anything."

"And I meant it. I won't ever pressure you."

"And I appreciate that. But now it's time for me to tell you something and you don't have to say anything back, it's just something I want to say."

"OK," Heather said, somewhat worried.

"I've been thinking for the last couple days about what you said. And the more I thought about it the more I realized that I feel it too. I love you. And no matter where this journey takes me to find the missing pieces of my life, that's not gonna change. Whoever this woman is, isn't gonna change my feelings for you. But I need to know where I've been, the people I've known, the places I've been. I need to connect the dots. But however those dots connect, the one person I know I can count on is you. That won't ever change."

Tears were streaming down Heather's face as Cain was talking. She couldn't believe he was actually saying the words, though she was ecstatic that he was.

"It took me a long time to realize what I wanted, what I needed, was standing in front of me all along. Now that we're together I'm not gonna lose the most important person, the only person that means anything to me. I want you to know that if I'm gonna do this, that I need you, and want you to be by my side."

Heather sniffled. "You never have to worry about me."

"And I do love you. You've been the only thing in my life for the last year that's been worthwhile. You're what keeps me going, what makes life worth living. I want you to know that."

"I do. And I love you too," she replied, kissing him.

Cain managed to pull himself away from his beautiful girlfriend so he could get down to The Center. He walked over to the door and turned around to look at Heather before he left.

"Tell Ms. Lawson I said hello," Heather said.

He smiled. "I will."

Once Cain arrived at the agency, he immediately went to Lawson's office, where she was sitting at her desk, sorting through some file folders. Lawson saw him enter and got up to greet him, giving him a big hug. He was a little uncomfortable with it at first, but knew it was a completely friendly greeting.

"You're looking a little tanned," Lawson said.

"A little bit."

"No baby pictures yet, right?" she joked.

"Not yet," Cain replied. "I do have a picture for you though."

"Oh. Is it safe for work? Some young strapping man who's barely covered."

"Umm... not quite."

"Well, let me see."

Lawson sat down at her desk again as Cain took the picture out of his pocket. He placed it on the desk for her to look at.

"Hmm. Not quite what I had in mind," she said, looking up at him, waiting a few seconds for him to explain what it was about. "So, what's this about?"

"I know them."

"OK. Who are they?"

"I don't know."

"Are you sure you weren't in the sun too long? Because that doesn't really make a whole lot of sense."

"These are the people in my visions," Cain said.

"Umm, wow."

"Yeah."

"I don't really know what to say to that."

Cain sat down across from Lawson as they began to discuss the picture.

"Are you sure it's them?" Lawson asked.

"Positive. It's them. It's not similar, or almost, or just about... that's them. Same hair, same eyes, same nose, chin, everything."

"So, I guess that means there's a few possibilities."

"A few?" Cain asked.

"Maybe you knew them before."

"I just get the feeling that me going to Hawaii wasn't an accident. Like it was already planted in my mind that I'd been there before and that's why I wanted to go back. Like I subconsciously knew everything was there and finding that picture wasn't just some fluke," Cain said.

"That's one possibility. There are others though."

"Like what?"

"Like maybe you were in Hawaii before and saw that picture while you were there. Maybe you never knew who they were, and they weren't part of your life. You stored the picture into your memory bank. Then you went back and saw the picture, remembered it, and now it's starting to come back to you, revealing itself in your visions like you knew them when in reality you didn't," she said.

"Why are you always such a downer?"

Lawson laughed. "I'm sorry. I'm just trying to be practical and realistic. Yes, it's possible you actually knew these people. But it's also possible you didn't. I'm just trying to be honest with you."

"I know."

"I don't want you to get your hopes up so much that you get let down."

"I have to go with the hunch that I know these people. At least until it's proven that I don't," Cain said.

"I can understand that."

"Can you help me?"

"You know I would if I could, but I don't know what I can do. All you have is a face. No name, date, nothing."

"What about facial recognition software? We can match it against every DMV in the country and try to get a hit on it."

"We can try it," Lawson said. "But this isn't the best picture to use for it."

"It's as clear as day."

"I know, but facial recognition software does have limitations. Full frontal shots are best as well as pictures with neutral expressions. Her head in this picture is slightly tilted and her smile's as wide as the Grand Canyon. We can try it; just don't get your hopes up, OK?"

"Understood," Cain replied.

They left Lawson's office, photo in hand, and went down to the desk of an analyst. Lawson asked if he could run the software check on the picture they had.

"It's gonna take some time," the analyst said.

"How much?" Cain asked.

"Am I checking against known criminals or everybody?"

"Everyone."

"I'll scan it into my system and start running the check on it now," he said. "Should have a match for you, or not, later tonight or sometime tomorrow."

"Wow. That's pretty quick. I was expecting next week or something," Cain said.

"Maybe in the old days of last year," the analyst said and laughed. "The software we run now can instantly scan thousands of pictures within a minute and automatically determine a possible match. We can access up to seventy million pictures within twenty-four hours depending on computer speed. Give or take a million."

"Call me when the scan's done," Lawson said.

"Will do," he replied, handing the picture back.

Cain and Lawson left to go back to her office to discuss the matter further when they ran into Sanders on the way.

"Mr. Cain, nice to see you back from your little vacation," Sanders said.

"Thank you."

"You look well rested. Ready for another mission soon enough, I take it?"

"I am."

"Glad to hear it. What do you have there?" Sanders asked, seeing the picture in Cain's hand.

"Just something I found in Hawaii," Cain said, handing him the picture.

"Pretty woman," Sanders said, looking troubled. "I was under the impression you went there with Heather."

"I did."

"So, who is this lovely young woman then?"

Cain hesitated before answering, not sure he wanted to tell him. "I'm not sure."

"You're carrying a picture of a woman you don't know? Come now, I'm sure there's more to this story."

Cain glanced at Lawson, wondering if he should tell him. She nodded back at him.

"For the past year I've had visions of people. People I couldn't identify. When we were in Hawaii, I saw this picture. These are the people in them. I was hoping to find out who they are to find a link to some of my missing memories," Cain said.

"I see. Have you had any luck with them?"

"Not yet. We're running it through facial recognition now."

"Well, hopefully we get a match on it," Sanders said. "However, if there is not, do you have contingencies?"

Cain sighed. "No."

"Then perhaps I could be of assistance. If you allow me to keep this picture for a few days, I can put the full power of this agency behind finding out who this woman and child are."

"You would do that?" Cain asked.

"Of course. You are one of the best agents we have. When we recruited you, I told you we could assist you in getting your memory back. I meant that. I meant every word," Sanders said. "If we can support you in that pursuit then I will use every power I possess in order to do so."

"I appreciate that."

"It's the least we can do."

Sanders went back to his office while Cain and Lawson went to hers. Once Sanders sat down at his desk, he immediately picked up the phone.

"Are you running the facial rec software for Michelle Lawson and Matthew Cain?" Sanders asked.

"Yes, sir, I am," the analyst said.

"I want to be advised of the results as soon as they come in."

"I will."

"You're not to call Lawson or Cain with the results. I will tell them."

"Understood."

Sanders hung up the phone and leaned back in his chair,

thinking of his next move. He stared at the photo on his desk and then picked up the phone again to make a call.

"This is Mr. Specter calling," Sanders said.

"One moment," the woman replied.

"You're a few days ahead of the usual schedule," the man said.

"We may have a situation."

"With what?"

"Matthew Cain."

"I assume this has to do with his Hawaii vacation?"

"Yes. He found a picture of..." Sanders started.

"You told me it was nothing to worry about."

"And I still believe that to this point. It'll be taken care of but I just wanted to keep you informed of the situation."

"How do you plan to take care of it?" the man asked.

"I have a couple ideas. I need to work out some of the details first before I put them into action. Once I flesh them out, I'll inform you of them," Sanders said.

"Do I need to remind you of the importance of this and what we're doing?"

"No, you do not."

"You better take care of this. Don't let it escalate," the man warned.

"I will have it contained within a couple of days."

"Good. But let me remind you that the organization is bigger than the individual pieces. If he becomes a problem, then you eliminate it before it becomes a major problem that we can't contain."

"I understand."

Sanders put the phone down and rubbed his forehead before resting his hand over his mouth, thinking about what needed to be done. He logged back onto his computer, adjusting details in some files. He stayed there working on the information for several hours, planning to stay in his office until the results of the facial scan came in. He didn't expect it to take much longer than that.

Cain didn't wait around very long and discussed a few things with Lawson before leaving to go home. He spent the rest of the night with Heather, the two of them trying to enjoy a romantic night together, having a candlelit dinner and a movie. Though he was eager to know the results, he tried not to appear too anxious, mostly for Heather's sake. They fell asleep on the couch together, Heather waking up around one. With her eyes barely open, she reached out for Cain, but she felt nothing but air. She sat up, wiped the sleepiness from her eyes, and scanned the room for him. The room was pitch black, and she didn't initially see him. She got up to search the apartment for him, starting with the bedroom. Even in the darkness she noticed a figure sitting in the corner of the room, not moving. Heather rushed over to him and knelt down in front of him. She put her hands on his knees and was startled to see a gun in his left hand, resting on his thigh.

"Matt, what's wrong?" she asked.

He continued staring ahead, not looking at her, her words bouncing off him. Cain seemed like his mind was in a different place, alarming Heather about his well-being. She tried for a few more minutes to snap him out of his funk though she was unsuccessful in doing so. She placed her hand on his, hoping to be able to slide the gun out of his fingers, but he tightened his grip upon feeling her touch.

"Matt, you're scaring me," she shouted, starting to cry. "Please."

Heather then reached up and touched his face, hoping her gentle touch would break his trance. She stroked his cheeks for a few minutes without having the desired effect. She put her head down and just started bawling uncontrollably. It was enough to get Cain to break his staring of the wall. He looked down at Heather sobbing and put his hand on top of her head. She managed to stop crying enough to look up at him and saw an incredible amount of sadness in his eyes. Cain released the grip on his Glock and let it fall off his leg. A slight smile crept over Heather's face, hoping that Cain's condition had changed for the better.

"Are you OK?" Heather asked.

"Fantastic."

"What are you doing?"

Cain wiped his eyes before tears could start forming. "I was just thinking about things."

"Like what?"

"Like the boy's life that I ended," Cain replied, shaking his head.

"I know it's hard, but you can't let it eat away at you."

"I don't know how I'm supposed to live the rest of my life without thinking about it constantly. I had a dream that instead of me shooting him, he shot me."

"It was just a dream," Heather said, caressing his face.

"I just can't stop thinking about what I did."

"What were you planning on doing with this?" Heather asked, picking up the handle of the gun with her thumb and index finger, almost afraid it'd go off.

"I don't know."

Heather walked over to the bureau with it and opened a

drawer, placing it inside. She closed the drawer and went back to Cain, grabbing his hands.

"Let's go to bed," she told him.

"I'm not sure if I can sleep."

"Just try. For me."

"OK."

Cain stood up and let Heather lead him to the bed. They lay down and Heather wrapped her arms around him, hoping she could get him to fall asleep. They faced each other and looked in each other's eyes for a while, without saying a word. She had the magic touch for him as he fell asleep half an hour later. Heather worried that he might have another incident before the night was over but luckily there was none as Cain slept straight through.

They woke up at eight o'clock to the sound of Cain's phone ringing. Thinking it might be news about the facial scan, he jumped out of bed and raced into the living room to grab his phone off the table. It was Sanders calling. He actually had gotten the results a little after midnight, but wanted to sleep on them, and decided to hold off on telling Cain until the morning.

"Yeah?" Cain answered.

"I got the results of the facial rec scan," Sanders said. "I thought it best you heard it from me."

"OK?"

"There was no match."

Cain sat down and closed his eyes, frustrated that there was no progress made. He put his hand over his head and let out a sigh.

"How is that possible?" Cain asked. "It was such a good picture."

"Well, it was a good picture. Too good as it turns out."

"How's that?"

"Well, her head was slightly turned to the side, and she had a big smile on her face. Those small movements distorted her facial features to the point that the scan didn't pick up the necessary points. Most people in their DMV shots are looking straight at the camera and don't show much emotion on their face. Apparently, it was just enough to throw the scan out of whack," Sanders said.

"I understand."

"I know it's a big blow for you but I don't want you to get too down about it. I'm still working on some other leads. I told you I'd help you out as much as I could and I still intend to do that."

"I appreciate it."

"I have some other news for you as well," Sanders said. "I've just had it verified within the last hour."

"What's that?"

"Well, I think it's best you come into the office to hear it."

"That doesn't sound good," Cain said. "What's it about?"

"It stems from your trip to Russia. There's been a few complications that've come up."

"What kind of complications? I made sure everything was buttoned up."

"There's a whole package I need to present to you. I'm gonna call Shelly in as well. You need to come in to get the full deal."

"When?"

"As soon as possible. Let's make it for ten."

24

Cain rushed down to The Center and quickly hurried into the meeting room, wondering what the big problem was. He got there ahead of schedule by about twenty minutes but Lawson was already waiting, fiddling around on her tablet. He sat down across from her and tried to get some details.

"Do you know what this is about?" Cain asked.

"I have no idea, do you?"

"No. All I know is it's about what happened in Russia."

"Russia? What about it? We wrapped that up," Lawson said.

"I know. I don't understand what could've come up," Cain said. "What'd Sanders say to you?"

"Nothing. He called me this morning and said he wanted to go over mission details."

"That's it?"

"Yeah. Did he tell you it was about Russia?" Lawson asked.

"Yes. He said there were some complications," Cain said.

"He didn't say that to me."

They kept talking, wondering what kind of problems could have possibly occurred. Sanders showed up about ten minutes later.

"Nice to see you both got here early," Sanders said.

"What's this about?" Lawson asked. "Cain said something about Russia."

"Yes," Sanders said, tossing some file folders down on the table.

"I took out everyone that was there," Cain said.

"I know you did," Sanders replied. "Unfortunately, someone found out about it."

"How?"

"We're not sure yet."

"So, what exactly is the issue?" Lawson asked.

Sanders stared at Cain for a moment before proceeding. "The issue is this man," Sanders said, putting a man's face on the big screen.

"Who's that?" Cain asked.

"His name is Dmitri Kurylenko."

"Kurylenko?"

"Yes. I know what you're thinking and you'd be correct. He is related to Andrei. He's his brother."

"That wasn't in his file," Cain said. "There was no mention of a brother."

"That's because we had no information on him. Technically, he's his half-brother," Sanders told the pair, handing them info sheets on him. "As you can see, he's a former member of the Russian Foreign Intelligence Service. He left the SVR about two years ago to go into business for himself."

"Which is what?" Cain asked.

"Apparently, he'll do whatever you have the money for," Sanders said. "Security, assassinations, guns, drugs, he's into pretty much everything."

"Why are we just getting this information now?" Lawson asked.

"He's been flying underneath the radar," Sanders replied. "I just got most of this information this past week and got official confirmation this morning, which is why I'm bringing it to you now."

"This is all very informative but I'm still not seeing the complication," Cain said.

"As I said, he's been flying underneath the radar. I imagine his background in intelligence has benefited him in laying low. Until now," Sanders said.

"How so?" Lawson asked.

"He's made it known to several sources, some of whom work for us, that he intends to find his brother's killer. And he says he will stop at nothing to find him."

Cain took his eyes off the screen and looked at the information on Kurylenko before glancing at Lawson. They couldn't believe the revelation.

"There's more," Sanders said. "In retaliation for the death of his nephew, Sergei, he has vowed to exact revenge on his death by killing the family of the man responsible."

"So, what are we going to do?" Lawson asked.

"We're going to find Dmitri and take him out before he has a chance to make good on his plans. These are photos of his latest work," Sanders said, tossing them on the table. "He believed they knew who his brother's killer was and tortured them."

Cain and Lawson studied the photos for several minutes.

They were of two men and a woman in various poses of pain and punishment. They were bound, bloodied, tortured, and eventually killed.

"How'd we get these?" Cain asked.

"They were taken from the crime scene a few days ago. It was actually a little bit more involved than that, but we'll just say we got them in an exchange of sorts," Sanders said.

"So, how do I find him?" Cain asked.

"We're in the process of verifying an address right now. While it is unlikely he still resides at that location, it is a starting point," Sanders said.

"When do I leave?"

"As soon as possible. Within twenty-four hours if practical. We need to find him. For all of our sakes."

"OK."

"Let me be clear. This cannot come back to us. Don't come back until you've found him or all possible leads are exhausted."

"Understood," Cain replied with a shake of his head.

"Any other questions?"

Cain sighed deeply as Sanders gathered up his folders and left the room.

"Well, that was a big kick in the chins," Lawson said.

"A kick somewhere. But it ain't the shins," Cain said.

"Go home and get ready. I'll get the flight arrangements and as soon as Sanders gets me the address I'll forward it to you."

Lawson pushed her chair out to get up but noticed Cain still seemed troubled by something. There was something on his mind that he wasn't saying.

"What is it?" Lawson asked. "You look like you're worried about something."

"I am."

"What?"

"If Kurylenko has vowed to kill the family of the man who did this..." Cain began.

"You don't have any family. What are you worried about?"

"Do girlfriends count?"

"I wouldn't worry too much about that," Lawson said. "We'll have tabs on him, we have a picture now, his info's on file, and if he shows up within our border, we'll know it."

"Yeah, I guess so."

"Concentrate on finding him first and the rest doesn't matter."

Lawson left, leaving Cain alone with his thoughts. He sat there thinking about how it could've come back to him and he was sure he made no mistakes. Then it dawned on him. There was one person who knew he was there... Raines. Cain thought of all the possible scenarios and though he didn't want to believe it at first, he had to admit the possibility that perhaps Raines decided to terminate their deal. Raines could've killed him in Syria if he had wanted to so it was a mystery as to why he'd try to take Cain out now, if in fact he was responsible for letting the information slip out to Kurylenko. But he also knew that Raines was a strange fellow who did things unconventionally. The moves he made couldn't always be understood at first glance. While Cain didn't want to jump to conclusions, and wasn't certain that Raines had betrayed him, he at least had to consider the possibility.

Cain went home to pack for his trip. Heather was cleaning the apartment when he got there. She could tell something was wrong by the expression on his face. He was trying so hard to put on a good show for her but she could tell he was faking it.

"What's wrong?" Heather asked, turning off the vacuum.

"Nothing," he replied, pretending to look for something in the drawers to avoid her questions.

"I know you better than that. What's wrong?" she insisted.

"I have to leave on an assignment."

"I can't say I'm not disappointed, but I knew it'd be coming soon after having some time off."

"Yeah."

"When are you leaving?"

"Waiting on flight information now. Probably within the next twelve hours I'd say," Cain replied.

"Oh. So soon. Where are you headed?"

"Umm, Russia."

"Again? Didn't you just come from there?" Heather asked.

"Yeah. Just cleaning up some loose ends."

"Be careful," she added, walking over to him for a kiss.

"Always am."

Cain was kind of surprised she was not upset about him leaving. He assumed that she was starting to come to grips with the fact he was going to have to go on these trips sometimes. The vacation probably helped to clear her mind also as their relationship grew. He thought of telling her about Kurylenko but decided she didn't need to know yet. If the threat proved to be credible and Kurylenko found out about them, then he'd discuss the situation with her. But he didn't believe her life was in danger yet. Besides, he intended to find Kurylenko before it reached that point, anyway. They spent the next few hours just hanging out together, avoiding any topics about his work or him leaving. Heather knew that complaining about it wouldn't change anything and would just put a strain on them so she was trying to be more supportive and accepting. They were sitting together watching a movie when Cain's phone rang. He saw it was Lawson and assumed the plans were finalized.

"What's the word?" Cain said.

"Hope you're already packed 'cause your plane leaves in three hours."

"I'll be ready."

"Good. You'll be flying into Pulkovo Airport in St. Petersburg," Lawson said. "I've also got you booked for a room at the Grand Hotel Emerald. Just a few minutes from the Moskovsky Train Station."

"Where am I going from there?"

"You're going to meet a contact in a café near the entrance of The Hermitage Museum."

"What for?" Cain asked.

"He's got information on Kurylenko. He was worried about his phones being tapped and was only willing to give the information in person."

"Who is he?"

"Not sure. He's one of Sanders contacts."

After getting the rest of his trip information Cain got ready in just a few minutes. This was one trip he was actually anxious about getting underway for. He was hoping for a smooth trip and wanted to take Kurylenko out of the picture quickly and not let it linger. He embraced Heather for a few minutes, kissed her, and told her he'd be back as soon as he could though he didn't know when.

"Be OK without me?" Cain asked.

"I'll just immerse myself in work," she replied. "Hopefully that'll help and you'll be back before I even realize you're gone."

25

St. Petersburg, Russia—Once Cain touched ground in St. Petersburg he immediately got in the taxi that was waiting for him. It was pre-booked to expedite time. The cab dropped him off at the famous Heritage Museum. The museum is St. Petersburg's major transaction, a palace sized museum that housed a collection of over three million pieces of art and artifacts. It was considered one of the world's greatest museums and was home to classic works by artists such as Rembrandt, Michelangelo, and Leonardo. Cain was told his contact would be wearing a white hat with the letters CKA on it with a star underneath it. The hat was in reference to the SKA, St. Petersburg's professional hockey team. He entered the café and scanned the crowd. Toward the back of the café to his left he noticed a man in a white hat with CKA on it sitting by himself reading a newspaper. Cain removed his cell phone and took some pictures of the surroundings, pretending to be sightseeing. He also grabbed a snapshot of his contact sitting at the table. Cain quickly moved to his location, maneuvering past a few couples getting up from their tables. He sat down as if he'd been directed to do so, blending into the environment.

"Anything interesting?" Cain asked, not knowing if the man spoke English.

The man broke his concentration from the paper and looked up at his newfound acquaintance sitting across from him. After studying Cain's face for a few moments, he focused his eyes back on the newspaper. Cain was slightly annoyed and looked at all the people around him as a calming mechanism to make sure he didn't lose his temper yet. After sitting there for another minute without a word from his contact, Cain was beginning to lose his patience. He'd had enough of the silence and decided to bring an end to it. He slammed his hand down over the paper, flattening it on the table.

"I didn't come here for the pleasure of your miserable company," Cain said angrily. "I don't know if you can understand me but I came here for one reason, Dmitri Kurylenko. I came here because I was told you had information for me. You will either share that information or I will make you regret ever laying eyes on me."

"I understand you very well," the man responded. "I just want to make sure you are the man I'm supposed to talk to."

"Who else would it be?"

"I need to be very careful. The man that sent you is?"

"Sanders."

"OK, then."

"And who are you?" Cain asked.

"It is not important. What is important is the information I have."

"Which is?"

The man looked around at the crowd while he simultaneously reached into his coat pocket to pull out a white piece of paper. He didn't look at it and placed it on the table, pushing it in front of Cain. Cain turned it over, revealing an address and some numbers written on it.

"What is this?" Cain asked.

"You wanted Dmitri Kurylenko," the man replied. "There he is."

"He resides at this address?"

"As of three days ago, yes."

"How far away is this?"

"From here a ten-minute walk or so," the man answered.

"Can you take me there?"

"Me? No. I'm afraid no."

"Why not? You were supposed to help and give information," Cain said.

"Information I have given you. A tour guide I am not."

Cain reached into his pocket and took out a handful of money, quickly placing it underneath the newspaper. The man reached under the paper, quickly sized up how much it was and grabbed it, putting it in his pocket.

"I will take you there," he told Cain.

"Let's go."

"First you must know this. I will take you to the building. Once we arrive I will go my separate way. You are on your own from there."

"OK."

"Second, Dmitri Kurylenko is a very dangerous man. You must tread carefully if you are to beat him."

"Treading carefully is not what I do," Cain said.

"That is up to you. I have done my duty and warned you. From there it is your call."

The pair got up to leave the café and started walking toward Kurylenko's apartment. Cain followed the man but kept looking around in case something wasn't right. Though he was hopeful, there was a part of him that had doubts about the information as it seemed too easy. He kept his eyes open in case it was a setup. The two didn't share another word as the Russian led Cain to his target. After ten minutes of walking, they arrived at Kurylenko's apartment. It was a large building with five floors and a brick exterior.

"This is where it ends for us," the man said.

"What about getting in?"

"The other numbers on that paper is the code to get in the building. As for getting into his place, I cannot help you."

"OK. Thanks," Cain said.

"Good luck."

The man turned and left, quickly walking away like he was afraid something bad was going to happen before he was able to leave. Cain watched him for a few minutes to make sure he really was leaving, not totally trusting him. Satisfied that the man had no interest in coming back, Cain entered the building and saw a silver metal box on the wall. He took out the paper with the code on it and punched the numbers in. The door buzzed, signaling that it was unlocked and Cain quickly opened it before it locked again. He went inside and walked down the hallway, passing the elevator until he got to the end, reaching the stairs. Cain disliked using elevators as he never knew if someone would be waiting for him when the doors opened. There was less of a surprise factor when using the stairs. He walked up the steps until he reached the fourth floor. He went to the end of the hall until he found door 42.

Cain slowly turned the handle of the door in case it was unlocked, trying not to alert anyone inside of his presence. Since it was locked he decided to just knock to see if someone was there. He waited for a few minutes but nobody answered. He looked around to make sure no one was coming and then jimmied the door open by picking the lock. He took his gun out in case someone was waiting inside to surprise him. The apartment was remarkably clean, almost like it wasn't even lived in. There was no excess junk anywhere to be seen in the living room. There were no paintings on the wall, books or magazines on the tables, or a single picture anywhere. The couches didn't even seem to have any creases on indents from people sitting in them. He moved on to the kitchen. He opened the refrigerator but there wasn't much in there. A container of milk along with some juice and fruit lined the bare shelves. He checked the freezer which had just as little inside it. The cabinets contained a loaf of bread and a few cups. Either Kurylenko barely lived here or he'd been clearing the place out and moved just prior to Cain's arrival. Cain went to the bedroom and discovered more of the same as the rest of the place. A bed that looked like it wasn't slept in much and no clutter on the floor.

He checked behind the door to see if anything was behind it. He noticed some pictures pinned to the door and closed it to get a better look at them. Once he saw them he took a step back as he frantically shifted his eyes toward them all. He gulped and stared at them, eyes widening by the second as he stared at them in horror. They were pictures of both him and Heather, about twenty in total. Some were of them individually and some were of them together. He could tell they were recent. In a few of them they were holding hands. A couple pictures were of Heather in the lobby at her work. Cain was horrified that Kurylenko had apparently been watching them without their knowledge. He took a few steps back and took a few photos of the collection adorning the wall. He removed the pins that stuck them to the door and stacked them in his hands, carefully going through them one by one. With each one he looked at his temperament turned from anger to concern and back to anger again. He wished Kurylenko was standing right in front of him at that very moment so he could strangle him. Well, he wouldn't have killed him by strangulation. He would've let him recover his breath just long enough to put a bullet between his eyes. There was nothing else that he wished for more than getting Kurylenko in his sights as soon as possible. He took the photos into the living room and continued looking at them as he paced about the room. Cain then thought about his contact and wondered if he knew what he was going to find. He scrolled through his cell phone numbers until he got to Shelly's.

"Hello," Lawson answered.

"Hey. I need you to do something for me."

"Sure."

"I'm sending you a photo. Need you to see if you can iden-tify him for me," Cain said.

"Send it over."

"OK," Cain said, attaching the picture into a message. "Sent."

"I'll see what I can do."

"Umm, one more thing. Try to keep this between us," Cain said.

"Why? What's up?" Lawson asked.

"I'm just not sure about some things. Something seems off."

"Did you meet your contact?"

"That's the picture I'm sending."

"What are you not telling me?" Lawson asked.

"He led me to Kurylenko's apartment."

"That's great. So, what's the problem?"

"Well, he took off before I went inside. Once I got into the apartment it looked pretty clean, almost like no one was living here," Cain explained.

"And?"

"And I found some pictures."

"What kind of pictures?"

"Pictures of me. And Heather. Some of us separately and some where we're together," he said.

"Oh my God."

"Yeah."

"You think your contact knew what you were gonna find?" Lawson asked.

"I'm not sure. Something doesn't feel right. And if he was sent by Sanders I'd rather keep it between you and me until we figure out what's going on."

"We have to tell him about the pictures."

"I don't know."

"If he's got pictures of you that means he already knows you did it. He's further along than we thought he was. So that means we're gonna need the full power of the agency to find his whereabouts."

"I guess you're right," Cain said.

"If he's got pictures of you guys that means he's been in New York in the past couple of weeks. That means we can try to get a trace on him and see where he's been."

"My contact said Kurylenko was here as recently as three days ago," Cain said.

"Well, come back home and we'll figure it out."

"What if he's still there?"

"In New York?" Lawson asked.

"Yeah," Cain said, thinking about Heather. "I gotta come back now and make sure Heather's all right."

"I'll make sure she's OK. I'll go over to your place myself and check on her," Lawson said.

"OK."

As they continued talking, Cain kept pacing around the room until he stopped by a table in front of a window. He put the photos down as he leaned over to continue looking at them. The window suddenly shattered, a bullet piercing through it, whizzing past Cain's head. The suddenness of the window bursting knocked Cain to the ground, his phone flying out of his hand. Lawson heard the glass breaking and kept calling for Cain though she got no response. Cain slowly got up amidst dozens of pieces of glass on the floor. He felt his forehead and winced, wiping his head and seeing blood on the tips of his fingers. He then touched his cheek and wiped more blood off his hand. A couple pieces of glass had sliced through his forehead just above his right eye and on his right cheekbone. They weren't deep cuts and were more of just an annoyance to him. He peeked above the bottom of the window to see where the shot came from. There was a building across the street that appeared to be some type of warehouse, though from the looks of its exterior, probably wasn't being used currently. Cain shook the cobwebs loose and looked for his phone and crawled over to it.

"You still there?" he asked, breathing heavily.

"Yeah. What happened? You OK?"

"Yeah, I'm fine. Someone took a shot at me through the window."

"Are you hurt?" Lawson asked.

"No, not really. Got cut a few places on my head from the glass shattering, but it's nothing too bad. Other than that, I'm OK," Cain said.

"Did you see who it was?"

"No. Must've come from the building across the street. I'm gonna go check it out."

"Be careful. Keep me updated."

"I will," Cain replied.

Cain quickly gathered up the pictures and put them in his pocket. He rushed out of the apartment and scurried down the steps. He exited the apartment building and ran across the street, clinging to the side of the brick warehouse. He pulled on a glass door but it was locked. He peeked in, careful to not expose too much of his head in case someone was waiting to blow it off. Cain pulled his gun out and looked around to see if anyone was nearby. He thought about blowing a hole through the glass but was concerned the gunshot would alarm anyone nearby and put him in a compromising situation. He looked toward the ground and found a loose brick on the side of the building. Cain wrestled it free from the others and in one motion threw it through the door, shattering the glass. He stepped through the door and combed his way through the warehouse, ready to take on anyone he came across. The building had two floors and as soon as Cain was satisfied the first floor was empty, he made his way up to the second floor. After a few more minutes of searching, he concluded that the shooter was no longer there. He likely knew he only had one shot and immediately split whether he hit Cain or not. Cain did fall to the floor so maybe the shooter thought he hit him. Cain sighed as he looked around the empty warehouse and then noticed an open window. He quickly walked over to it. It was on the side the shooter must've been on, facing the apartment window. Cain looked over the area to see if the shooter left anything behind. There was a shell casing on the ground that Cain picked up. He looked it over for a moment before putting it in his pocket. He called Lawson to let her know what he found. She instructed him that as long as he had no other leads to follow up on that he was to get back to New York as soon as possible. Cain went to his hotel while Lawson booked a flight for him. She wound up getting him a flight for later that night. Cain worried about Heather's well-being and called her as soon as he got back to the hotel.

"Hey honey," Heather exclaimed.

"Hey."

"How's your trip going?"

"Oh, it's going," he said.

"Well, I hope you'll be back soon. I miss you already."

"Good, 'cause I'm already on my way back."

"What? Already?"

"I'm leaving here tomorrow morning," Cain said.

"Oh, wow. I definitely wasn't expecting you to get back so soon but I love it."

"I mean, I guess I could stay here another week if you want."

"Don't you dare," she said.

Cain started thinking about Kurylenko and the pictures he had of them. Heather kept talking but stopped after a minute when she realized that Cain wasn't listening or responding.

"Matthew?" she asked.

"Hmm?"

"You're not listening to a word I just said."

"Oh. Sorry," Cain replied.

"It's OK. What are you thinking about?"

"Just some things."

"What kind of things?"

Cain sighed, not wanting to tell her the truth, but knowing he needed to. "Listen, I need to talk to you about something."

"Sounds serious," Heather said.

"It is. I want you to stay home from work until I get back."

"What?"

"Please just trust me," Cain said.

"Why? What's going on?"

"Do you trust me?"

"Of course I do. You know that," Heather said.

"Then just stay home and don't answer the door or pick up the phone for anybody other than me."

"Matt, you're starting to scare me."

"I'm sorry, but it needs to be done. You have to listen to me," he said.

"If you want me to do what you're asking, then you have to tell me what's going on."

He sighed. "OK. I'm in Russia trying to find the half-brother of the man I killed the last time I was here. Apparently, he threatened to get even with the person responsible by killing them and their family."

"Oh," she said, stunned.

"There's more. I found his apartment and inside were pictures of me. There were also pictures of you and of us together."

"Oh my God."

"That means he knows where we live. While I was in his apartment someone shot at me through a window," he said.

"Are you OK? Are you hurt?"

"I'm fine. Just a few cuts. I'm assuming it was him that shot at me, though, which means he's not there. But I don't want to take any chances."

"OK, um, I'll call my boss and tell him an emergency came up and I'll be gone for a couple of days," Heather said.

"Good. There's one more thing."

"What's that?"

"I have a gun in the kitchen drawer should something happen before I get there. Use it if you have to," Cain said.

"I don't know how to use that."

"It's easy. Just pull the trigger."

"OK."

"Heather?"

"Yeah?"

"I work alone," he said. "The only other person that may stop by is Shelly. If she does, that's fine. Other than that, don't let anyone in. If anyone else stops by and tells you I sent them, then you give them two in the chest and one in the head."

"I'm getting scared," she said.

"Try to stay calm. I will protect you at all costs."

"I know. It's just a little scary."

"I know it is. But I won't let anything happen to you. I promise."

26

New York—Cain and Heather continually texted each other on his way back. She let him know she was doing OK and to ease his concerns. Lawson had stopped by their apartment to stay with Heather and keep her company for a few hours until Cain returned. Nothing happened that was out of the usual but it was better that they played it safe. Cain called them when he reached their building. He just wanted them to know it was him coming so they wouldn't get a little haphazard with their trigger fingers thinking it was someone else. Once he entered the apartment, Heather rushed over and gave him a big hug.

"I'm so glad you're here," she whispered.

"Me too," Cain replied, giving her a passionate kiss.

Cain looked over at Lawson who was sitting on a chair watching TV. "Thanks for being here."

"Don't mention it," she said.

"Here's the casing."

Cain handed her the shell casing he found from the warehouse so she could take it in to The Center and have it analyzed.

"And the pictures?" Lawson asked, holding her hand out.

"What about them?" Cain said.

"I'll take them in too."

Cain hesitated for a few seconds, not sure if he wanted to turn them over or if he wanted to just hang on to them. He looked at Heather, not wanting her to see them.

"It's possible we can get some prints off them," Lawson said.

"I think we already know who it is," Cain replied.

"What if we find prints of someone else? Maybe an accomplice or a girlfriend or something. Maybe someone we can find easily who can take us to Kurylenko."

"You're right," Cain said, handing her the photos so Heather couldn't see them.

"Sanders might want to see you."

"I'm not leaving here," Cain said, looking at Heather.

"I'll let him know," Lawson said, putting her jacket on. "I'll let you know if we come up with anything."

"Oh, did you get anything from the picture I sent you?" Cain asked.

"Not yet. I'm still working on it though."

Cain saw Lawson to the door and thanked her again for sitting with Heather. He then went back to join Heather on the couch. Once he sat down, she gently touched his face where the cuts were, causing him to grimace slightly.

"Does it hurt much?" she asked.

"Nah. It's not too bad. I guess I'll have to put my modeling career on hold now," Cain joked.

Heather tenderly kissed his cheek and forehead. She

worked her way down to his lips and then his neck before Cain pulled away.

"I'm sorry I got you into this," he said.

"It's not your fault."

"Yes, it is. I'm not sure this is gonna work."

"What?" Heather asked, hoping he wasn't saying what it sounded like.

"I can't do this to you."

"You're not doing anything to me."

"By being with me, by being part of my life, I'm putting yours in danger," Cain said. "I should've realized that before. Maybe I did. Maybe that's why I kept you at bay for so long."

"It's not just your choice you know. I have a say in it too."

"I'm in this life because I chose to be. You didn't. You're locked in a room right now because of me."

"And there's nowhere else I'd rather be right now than here with you," she said.

"You deserve better."

"All I want is you. My life before I met you really wasn't worth living. I pretended to be happy, but I wasn't. Now I have a reason to get up every morning. As long as I have you I know we can get through anything."

Cain smiled at her and began stroking Heather's hair. He couldn't remember being with any other women but he was sure it would've been tough to find one as devoted as her. He couldn't imagine someone else being so attached to him even in the face of danger. They began kissing, slowly at first before getting more passionate. They quickly ripped each other's clothes off as they lay down on the couch. They enjoyed the closeness of their bodies for the next hour before they drifted off to sleep. They were awakened by Cain's phone going off a couple hours later. He stood up to answer it as Heather rubbed her hand over his naked butt.

"I want you to come down to go over some options with you," Sanders said.

"Can't do that."

"Why not?"

"I have Heather here. I'm not leaving her alone," Cain said.

"Well, we still need to talk."

"Fine. I'll bring her with me."

"I'm afraid that's out of the question. It's completely against the rules and regulations of this office. Non-personnel are not permitted to be here. It's not possible."

"Then I can't come in," Cain said.

Sanders realized he was fighting a losing battle and knew Cain wasn't going to go anywhere without Heather so he attempted a compromise.

"I'll station a couple guards outside your building and one inside the lobby to make sure she's safe while you're gone," Sanders offered.

"OK. Once they're here I'll come in."

"I'll send them now. I'll expect you within the hour."

Cain got dressed immediately as Heather got up, wondering what was wrong.

"Where are you going?" she asked.

"Just going down to the office. They wanna talk about some things."

"Can I come?"

"I'm afraid not. They won't let you," Cain said.

He could see a little bit of fear creeping into Heather's eyes as she wondered what she was going to do without him.

"Don't worry. There's gonna be a team here before I leave to make sure no one gets in this building. There'll be two guys outside and one in the lobby so you don't have to worry," Cain said.

"I probably still will, anyway."

Half an hour later the agents assigned to guard Cain's apartment building arrived and called to let him know they were there. He kissed Heather on his way out the door and met with each agent to shake their hands and get an initial impression of them. Once satisfied that they'd do an adequate job of protecting Heather, he left to meet Sanders.

Sanders was in his office waiting for Cain and had summoned Lawson to meet them as well. Sanders had been increasingly relying on Lawson when it came to Cain. He could tell that she was able to get through to him when others had a harder time. He could tell that Cain trusted Lawson more than anyone, which was how it was supposed to be between an agent and handler, and wanted Lawson there to reinforce anything he told Cain. Once Cain arrived, he took a seat next to Lawson in front of Sanders' desk.

"So, what's up?" Cain asked.

"We've identified some fingerprints off the pictures you found in Russia," Sanders said.

"Kurylenko?"

"Not quite. The only fingerprints that could be identified belong to a man named Darren Ackers."

"Who the hell is that?"

"Small-time crook who lives here in New York," Sanders said.

"Am I the only one who doesn't get this?" Cain asked.

"What's that?"

"A small-time crook, who's American, is mixed up with a Russian and has fingerprints on photos that I found in Russia?"

"There's one possibility," Sanders said. "It's possible that Kurylenko, knowing his movements here would be tracked, hired someone to take the pictures. He somehow got connected to Ackers who did the work for him, took the pictures, then sent them to Kurylenko in Russia."

"How would he get matched up with Ackers?"

"That's unclear right now."

"You're quiet," Cain said, looking at Lawson. "What do you think?"

"Well, we have no hits on Kurylenko either entering or leaving this country in the past two months. Your contact in Russia said he was there as recently as this past week. It would seem to lend credence to him hiring someone to get him what he was after without risking showing himself," she said.

"But how would that happen?" Cain asked again.

"I'm not sure that's really the question we need to find the answer to," Sanders said. "How he got into contact with him is irrelevant at this point. The real question is finding Ackers in hopes he can still contact Kurylenko."

"Have any leads on him?" Lawson asked.

"We are running a few things down now. If we get confirmation on anything I'll let the both of you know," Sanders said.

"So that's it?" Cain asked.

"What else would you like?"

"Our only lead on finding Kurylenko is some small-time hood?"

"Most times you catch the big fish by dangling the little ones," Sanders responded. "Find the little fish and start piecing together some of the puzzle."

Cain sighed, thinking there must've been something else they could've been doing, something more.

"There is one other thing I can think of," Sanders said.

"What?" Cain asked.

"You'll probably meet what I'm about to say with some resistance but hear me out first."

"OK?"

"There is one surefire way I can think of to get Kurylenko out into the open."

"How's that?"

"Give him something he wants," Sanders replied.

"Which is what?"

"Bait."

"What kind of bait?"

"It seems that in retaliation for his brother and nephew's deaths, he's after two people. One of which is you. The other is your girlfriend. I'm suggesting you give him what he wants. Make it easy for him."

"You're saying I make myself a target for him?" Cain said.

"Not quite."

"Then what are you saying?"

"I'm saying you give your girlfriend up in order to take him out," Sanders said.

"You're asking me to sacrifice her?"

Sanders threw his hands up. "It's a small price to pay, isn't it?"

"No, it's not," Cain said.

"Trading the life of a stripper for a chance to take out someone as dangerous as Kurylenko? Seems worth it to me."

"Well, it doesn't to me," Cain replied angrily. "First, she isn't a stripper anymore. Second, her life is in my hands and it isn't negotiable."

"Cain, I know you care for this girl," Sanders said. "But she's not the only one in the world capable of taking your pants off, if you know what I mean. There are other women out there."

"It's not an option."

"Talk to him, Shelly."

Cain looked at her and raised an eyebrow, looking irritated, not believing that Lawson would actually try to talk him into giving Heather up. Lawson was not in favor of the Director's plan and tried to downplay the situation and relieve the tension by trying the original plan first.

"Instead of doing something so dramatic that could cause friction amongst everyone, let's just try to find this Ackers first," she said.

"Tell me, Cain, how are you going to protect this girl when you're out there on a mission or trying to find Kurylenko? Or you're tracking down some lead?" Sanders asked.

"That's my problem. I'll take care of it."

"I hope you're right. Because I can't spare men every day to be her personal bodyguards."

"I don't need help in protecting her," Cain said.

"I hope so. For your sake."

Cain angrily stormed out of the office and started walking down the hall when Lawson caught up to him. She grabbed his arm and pulled him into her office.

"I can't believe he actually just suggested what I heard him say," Cain said.

"I know," Lawson replied, trying to calm him down. "Just forget about it and let's concentrate on finding Ackers and

Kurylenko and getting this thing over with so you and Heather can move on."

"I still don't get the connection between the two," Cain said in angst. "I mean, how would they get together? Kurylenko didn't just grab a copy of the phone book, close his eyes, and pick out a name."

"There is one other thing," Lawson said.

"What?"

"Just before we went in there I got a hit back about your contact in Russia."

"Who is he?" Cain asked.

"His name is Alexander Yushkevitch. He does have an arrest record. Beyond that, his association with Kurylenko is unclear. Perhaps he was a former associate of his. There's not much more information about him."

"I know how we can find out," Cain said.

"How?"

"By asking."

"Huh?" Lawson muttered, not making sense of his comment. "Ask who?"

"Someone who worked for Andrei Kurylenko," he said, purposefully being vague.

"Who would that be?"

Cain raised his eyebrows and tilted his head, hoping Lawson would get the hint without him having to say the name.

"Please tell me you're not suggesting what I think you are," Lawson said.

"I'm not suggesting anything."

"I think I know what you're hinting at," she said, raising her voice in anger. "Do you really think it's a good idea to go looking for him in order to get information? First, he's got a KOS order on him which means, technically, you're supposed to kill him the minute you lay eyes on him. Secondly, do you really think he would help you in any way figure this thing out? Thirdly, what makes you think you can even find him to begin with? And fourth, you must be crazy if you're gonna try to meet him without the agency finding out about it."

"Do you have another option?" Cain asked.

"Yes. We do what we said we would and find Ackers and go from there."

"That's not good enough."

"Why isn't it?"

"Because our boss just suggested to me that I intentionally trade in the life of my girlfriend," Cain said, getting heated. "How can I just sit back and wait for everyone else to track down leads and hope they find something? Leads that I'm not even sure are worthwhile to begin with."

Lawson sighed and sat in her chair. She rubbed her face in her hands in frustration, trying to think of what to do next.

"And if you find Raines, then what?" Lawson asked. "What makes you think he'll talk to you and not kill you himself?"

"It's a chance I'm willing to take."

"How do you plan on even finding him?"

"I know someone who might know his whereabouts," Cain said.

"Who?"

"I'll worry about that. The less you know the better. If Sanders finds out what I'm doing, you won't have to cover for me."

"I don't like this. If you don't tell me anything how will I know if you get into any sort of trouble?" Lawson asked.

"Easy. If I don't come back within a week, I'm probably dead."

Cain left Lawson's office and started walking down the hall. He took out his cell phone and scrolled for Guntur's number. He figured Guntur might still know where Raines was or how to get in touch with him. He helped Raines disappear once before, Cain thought it likely they still had connections. Cain dialed his number as he left the building, dodging oncoming walkers as the phone rang.

"Hello?" Guntur answered.

"Remember me?" Cain asked.

"Of course I do, Mr. Cain. Pleasure to speak with you again."

"I'm sure."

"What can I do for you?"

"Eric Raines," Cain said.

"What about him?"

"I need to find him."

"Why come to me?" Guntur asked.

"Because I think you know where he is. Or at least know how to get in touch with him."

"I'm afraid I can't help you with that request, Mr. Cain."

"Guntur, don't make me fly halfway around the world just to beat you to a bloody pulp. I'm not asking you to set him up for me or anything. I just want to meet with him. You get in touch with him and let him decide. I need some information that only he can provide. I'll meet with him on his terms, whenever and wherever he'd like. You relay that information to him and I'll make sure you're taken care of."

"Of course, Mr. Cain. Why didn't you say so before?"

Cain rolled his eyes. He knew Guntur was a master bullshitter who could talk out of both sides of his mouth, depending on who was the recipient. But Guntur obviously knew how to play the game which was why he was so good at what he did.

"So, you do know how to contact him," Cain said.

"You did say there would be something in it for me? How much you say?"

"You just get him. You do that and you won't regret it."

"Excellent, Mr. Cain. I will call you when I hear something."

"I'll be waiting for you," Cain said.

Cain walked the rest of the way home, hopeful that Guntur would have some positive news for him within the next couple of hours. Once he got back to his apartment, the team of guards dispersed when they saw him. They were directed to only be there while Cain was gone. Heather greeted him with a kiss as he came in.

"Anything good?" she asked

"Huh?"

"At the office. Good news?"

"Oh. Umm, I'm not sure yet. There's a couple of leads they're working on but I have something of my own I'm waiting on," Cain replied.

"When will this be over?"

"Soon I hope," he said, taking her in his arms. "I'm sorry again."

"I swear if you apologize to me one more time..."

Cain let out a slight smile, amazed at how perfect she was. He was equally amazed at how fast Guntur got back to him. He didn't expect a return call for at least a few hours but he called back about forty-five minutes later.

"Hope you have good news for me, Guntur," Cain said.

"Indeed, I do, Mr. Cain. I have word from Mr. Raines that he is willing to meet with you."

"Where and when?"

"You are to take a flight tomorrow morning to Heathrow Airport in London," Guntur told him.

"Where do I go after that?"

"From there you will be contacted on a direction. Mr. Raines has arranged the details. Even I do not know more than that. Do you agree to these terms?"

"I do," Cain said.

"Very well. I will inform Mr. Raines of your acceptance. He looks forward to your discussion."

"As do I."

Cain put his phone down after he hung up and sighed. It wasn't out of frustration though, more of feeling like he was actually getting somewhere. He hoped Raines would be able to help. He turned and looked at Heather, who was reading a magazine, and wondered what he was going to do with her while he was in London. Leaving her at home could be dangerous and he didn't trust tasking Sanders with her protection. Taking her with him could be as equally dangerous, though if she was with him he could at least keep an eye on her. After thinking about it for a few moments he thought there was only one way to go.

"Pack your bags," Cain said.

"Huh?"

"We're going to London."

"What? Why?" Heather asked.

"We're going to meet someone."

"Do you know this person?"

"I've met him a few times. He might have the information that I need," Cain said.

"Why not just call him and ask?"

"Doesn't quite work that way. First, he's actually on the agency's most wanted list, and I'm supposed to kill him on sight."

"Oh, wow. But you're not?"

"No. So I can't risk the agency finding out, never know if they have phones tapped or monitored."

"Oh."

"So why are you supposed to kill him?" Heather asked.

"It's a long story."

"Why are you taking me with you?"

"I can't leave you here if I'm there. The best way I can protect you is if you're always with me. I don't think I'd be able to stand being on a different continent knowing you were in danger. I'd worry too much."

"Guess I'm growing on you, huh?" she said with a smile.

"Guess so," Cain replied, returning the smile.

Heather initially felt a little nervous about going on a trip with Cain. She loved going away with him but this was business, not a romantic getaway like Hawaii. After a few minutes, she felt a little better about it, not quite as anxious, knowing that she was better off being by his side. Being by herself while he was in a different country might have been a little hard for her to take, especially under the current circumstances.

London---Cain and Heather flew into London where they were met by one of Raines' associates. They were directed to a train station where they boarded the train on their way to Liverpool. From there a car was waiting for them and drove them to a popular restaurant. Cain and Heather were led to a door in the rear of the restaurant. They entered the private room and saw Raines sitting at the rounded table. He had food already prepared for all of them as he waited for their arrival. The men who brought Cain and Heather to the room left once their visitors were inside and closed the door behind them. They sat at the table, eager to hear what Raines had to say.

"Nice place," Cain said.

"Yes, it is. Good food and the service is outstanding. I didn't anticipate you bringing a friend but there is more than enough for everybody."

Cain and Heather hesitated as they weren't really up for eating. They were more interested in what came out of Raines' mouth, not what he put into it. Raines could see they had reservations and tried to make them more at ease.

"Please now, you must have something," Raines told them. "After I went through all this trouble to welcome you, you have to sample the fine cuisine."

Cain and Heather relented and put some food on their plates and started eating, hoping their eagerness to please him would result in some information to their liking.

"I must say I was intrigued when I heard you wanted to have a meeting," Raines began. "I was caught a little off guard. I had thought our business was finished."

"So did I. But I didn't know who else to turn to. I figured you were the best option I had," Cain said.

"Had I known you were bringing a lady with you I would've tried to make your journey a little easier," Raines said, looking at Heather. "And you are?"

"Heather," she said.

"Ahh, yes, I remember the name. The woman so concerned about your well-being when you were in Syria. Am I to assume you two are a couple?"

"That's not why we're here," Cain said. "Our relationship is irrelevant."

"Maybe so. I just like to be well informed. The implication is clear anyway, whether you confirm it or not. Unless she is an agent, which seems unlikely, she wouldn't be here otherwise. Which also begs the question of why you've brought your girl-friend with you? Seems highly peculiar."

"OK. Can we get down to business?" Cain asked.

"Absolutely. What can I help you with?"

"A problem's come up relating to my work in Russia," Cain said.

"Yes, several groups of rebels and militia are now scram-bling to find a new supplier," Raines joked.

"That's not the problem I'm referring to."

"So, what is this problem you speak of?"

"It seems as though someone, somehow, found out about my work there."

"And you thought maybe I had something to do with it," Raines concluded.

"It crossed my mind."

"I hope you immediately crossed it off your mind."

"Well, you are the only person who personally witnessed what happened," Cain said.

"I sincerely hope you are not considering me as a suspect. I assure you that if I wanted any harm to come to you, I would've killed you myself on at least four different occasions. In Russia,

Syria, that bridge in Indonesia, and Honduras. So, you see, if I wanted you dead, you would be."

"And I understand that. Which is why I didn't put much stock into you being the one," Cain said, tossing the Kurylenko file on the table.

"What is this?"

"The man who supposedly is after me... Dmitri Kurylenko."

"Kurylenko?"

"Andrei's brother," Cain said.

Raines looked at the file and picture of Kurylenko then quizzically looked back up at Cain. It wasn't making sense to him either.

"I worked for Andrei Kurylenko off and on for over two years. I never heard him say anything about a brother," Raines said.

"There was no mention in any of his files either."

"Very strange."

"I met a contact in Russia, a man named Alexander Yushkevitch, who led me to an apartment that was rented by Dmitri. I went inside and after a few minutes a sniper tried to eliminate me through a window."

"How unfortunate."

"Do you know Yushkevitch? Maybe he worked for Andrei at some point?" Cain asked.

"I can't say I'm familiar with the name. If he did work for Andrei, then I am unaware of it."

"Well, before the business at the window happened, I found these," Cain said, putting a couple pictures near Raines.

Cain had given most of the pictures he found over to Lawson but he'd kept a couple for himself in case he needed them for anything.

"So, you think Kurylenko took these?" Raines asked.

"Apparently they had fingerprints on them that were traced to a small-time hood named Darrin Ackers. It's believed that Kurylenko hired this Ackers fellow to take the pictures and send them back to him."

"But you're not so sure?"

"It doesn't make sense. Kurylenko hires someone like Ackers? Dmitri apparently used to work for the SVR, I'm sure he's got better contacts to use than this guy."

"It does seem like shoddy work. Unless he assumes this man will be found rather quickly and doesn't want to burn one of his normal contacts on such a low-level assignment."

"I guess that's possible," Cain said.

"Interesting predicament you've gotten yourself into."

"I need to find Dmitri soon and put an end to this now. If he wants a piece of me that's fine, but I can't risk Heather's life any more than I already have."

"I understand your concern. Would you mind if I kept these for a bit?" Raines asked of the pictures.

"Sure."

"I would like to run them by a few people I know. Perhaps I can shed some light on your situation for you."

"I would appreciate it."

"Well, I need to go," Raines said, putting the pictures in an envelope. "You two stay and enjoy the rest of your meal. Don't worry about the bill, it's already paid for. I have a driver waiting outside for you when you're finished. He'll take you wherever you want to go."

"How will I get in touch with you, or you me, if you find anything out?" Cain asked.

.   .   .

Raines reached into his pocket and pulled out a cell phone, sliding it across the table. Cain picked it up and wondered what it was for.

"What's this?" Cain asked.

"My number is pre-listed in there under Wentworth. If you ever need to contact me for anything you may do so through that. Or if I need to contact you, I will call you on that phone. Don't worry, it's completely untraceable and could never come back to me. I prefer you use that than to use your phone and call my contacts. Just in case the agency traces your phone calls," Raines said. "I don't want them to get burned or have it get back to me."

"Understood," Cain replied. "I really appreciate you checking into this. Thanks. I'll owe you one."

"No need to thank me. That's what friends are for."

Raines stood up and nodded at his guests before he left. Cain and Heather looked at each other once he left the room.

"OK, I just have to say that that guy borders on the edge between creepy professor and psycho dangerous," Heather said.

Cain just nodded in agreement, raising his eyebrows, agreeing with the assessment.

"So, what do we do now?" Heather asked.

"I guess go back home. Nothing really else to do here," Cain replied.

27

New York—Cain and Heather had just gotten back from their trip to London when Cain's phone started going off.

"Yeah, Shelly?" Cain answered.

"Where are you?"

"Just got home an hour ago."

"Good."

"Why? What's up?"

"We found Ackers," she said.

"Where?"

"Through an informant. We've set up a trade. We're supposed to meet him in a warehouse to complete a drug transaction. He's bringing a large supply of drugs and we're supposed to bring a very large supply of money."

"I'm going."

"I knew you'd want in. That's why I called. Each side can bring one backup person," Lawson said.

"What time?"

"I'll come pick you up now."

"I'll be ready."

Cain told Heather they found Ackers and that he was going to leave for a while. While she was initially scared about being left alone, he assured her that he'd be back within a couple of hours. He went to the kitchen drawer and took out one of his guns, placing it on the counter.

"Don't answer the door for anyone," Cain said. "Not for anyone."

"I won't."

"Remember, I work alone. If someone comes through that door you put two in their chest and one in their head."

"I'll try."

"It'll be fine," Cain said, kissing her forehead. "Just don't shoot yourself in the foot."

"That's comforting."

"I'm sorry," he said, kissing her again.

"I'll be OK. Just hurry back."

Lawson drove over to pick Cain up and rushed to the meeting place with Ackers. They were about twenty minutes early and waited outside the building. It was a small warehouse that hadn't been used in several years. It'd previously been used for a small factory until a fire destroyed most of the building. The company then decided to move to a new location, leaving the partially torn building behind.

"So, how'd you find him?" Cain asked.

"We put the word out to some of our low-level informants, showed his picture around, and eventually someone recognized him."

"And?"

"One of the informants said he occasionally dabbled in drug sales so we contacted him to set something up," Lawson replied.

"What are we buying?"

"Heroin."

After waiting for ten minutes the two of them got out of the car and went inside to pass the rest of the time. Cain grabbed a briefcase from the backseat that contained the money they were supposed to be trading with. The roof wasn't totally intact and some of the windows were missing or broken, causing all of nature's elements to create a very displeasing odor inside. It smelled like a mixture of rain, sewage, and animal waste. There were small pockets of puddles throughout the warehouse. The broken windows allowed beams of light to shine in.

"This has gotta be one of the more unpleasant smells I've ever come across," Cain said.

"I would say so."

A few minutes later they noticed a Grand Marquis pull up in front of the building. Two men got out, one of them carrying a duffel bag. They entered the warehouse and removed their sunglasses. The man in front was Ackers. The picture they had of him was dead on. There was no mistaking him.

"Do you have the merchandise?" Lawson asked, not wanting to waste time.

"Of course," Ackers replied, pointing to the duffel bag.

"Let's see it."

Ackers nodded to his associate, who put the bag on the ground and unzipped it. Lawson walked over to it and kneeled down, putting her hand inside to look it over.

"It's good," she said.

"And now I believe you have something for me?" Ackers asked.

"Oh, we do," Lawson replied, standing up and motioning for Cain.

Cain walked forward and set the briefcase down, allowing Lawson to open it for them. Their eyes widened and could hardly contain the smiles on their faces, excited to be receiving all that money.

"Shame you're not going to collect any of it," Lawson told them.

"What?" Ackers asked, not sure what she meant.

"I mean this transaction's over."

Cain quickly drew his gun and fired, hitting Ackers' associate in the chest three times, killing him instantly. Ackers drew a gun from the back of his pants but was too slow for the lightning fast Cain. Cain shot Ackers in the shin, dropping the criminal to the ground, screaming in agony. Lawson and Cain walked over to him as he lay there, writhing in pain. Cain stood over him and pointed the gun at his head, making Ackers think his life was about to come to an end.

"It doesn't have to end the way you think it's about to," Cain said.

"What do you mean?"

"Give us the right information and we'll call you an ambulance and get you fixed up in no time."

"What kind of information?" Ackers asked, barely able to get the words out.

"You don't remember me?" Cain asked.

Ackers squinted his eyes to make him out better but was unable to remember him. "No. Am I supposed to?"

Cain took out a picture and held it up for Ackers to see.

"Remember now?"

"Yeah."

"Thought you might," Cain said.

"I thought you looked familiar. Just couldn't place you."

"Where's Kurylenko?"

"Who?"

"Dmitri Kurylenko. The man that hired you," Cain shouted.

"Never heard of him."

Cain kicked Ackers in the shin, causing him to yell out in excruciating pain.

"I can put you through a whole lot more," Cain said.

"I don't know him."

"Who hired you?"

"I don't know his name. He just told me he wanted some pictures taken. I took them and gave it to him and he gave me the money," Ackers said.

"You gave it to him? In person?"

"Yeah."

"That means he was here," Cain said to Lawson.

"There's still no record or proof of it," she replied.

"What'd he look like?" Cain asked.

"Black hair, brown eyes, no facial hair, tough looking."

"Fits Kurylenko's description."

"If the guy you're looking for is Russian, it wasn't him. This guy was American. No accent," Ackers said.

"Is this him?" Cain asked, holding a picture of Kurylenko up.

"Yeah. That's him. That's the guy."

"What name did he give you?"

"Stevens, I think," Ackers said.

"Where'd you deliver the photos?" Cain asked.

"Was told to put them in a drop box and an envelope with money would be waiting for me."

"What else?"

"That's it. I don't know anything else."

"How'd he pick you for the job?"

"Don't know. Never said. Just said someone recommended me for it," Ackers replied.

"Know where we can find this guy or how to contact him?"

"No idea. He contacted me. Don't have a name, address, or nothing."

Cain looked at Lawson and put his hands up, exasperated, thinking they weren't going to get any more information that was useful out of Ackers. He seemed like a perfect patsy. Someone who'd do anything for money and didn't ask too many questions and wasn't wise enough to cover his own tracks. He was too dumb to be in charge of anything or have much knowledge of it.

"I think that's about all we're gonna get from him," Lawson said.

"Probably."

"Hey, wait, you guys gonna call an ambulance?" Ackers asked, worried he'd get left behind.

"How about a hearse?" Cain asked, raising his gun at Ackers' head.

"Cain! He's not who we're after," Lawson yelled, hoping to get Cain to stand down.

Cain looked at her and nodded, dropping his gun. "I know."

Cain then suddenly brought the gun back up and fired, hitting Ackers in the thigh on his other leg. Lawson jumped, shocked that Cain actually fired, though somewhat relieved that he didn't kill the man.

"Now it seems you're shot in both legs. Looks like you ain't going anywhere for awhile," Cain said.

"You gotta call an ambulance," Ackers shouted painfully.

"Well, here's the deal," Cain started. "There's a dead man there who's been shot. You can't move because you've been shot. Looks like you two turned on each other."

"You're crazy!"

"Could be. I'm gonna take that bag of heroin. Except for one pack. I'm gonna leave that here between the two of you. Between the drugs, the guns, and the dead body, I wouldn't put too much stock in your future."

"You can't get away with that."

"If you mention a word about us being here, I will find the hospital they take you to and I'll put a bullet in your head," Cain warned. "And since I'm calling the ambulance, I'll know where that is."

"My legs feel like they're on fire!" Ackers yelled.

"Good. Well, you take care."

Cain and Lawson gathered up the bag of drugs and the money and left the warehouse, Ackers still rolling around in agony. As they drove away, Cain called 911 and let them know there was a big drug deal going down at the warehouse.

"So, what do we have now?" Lawson asked.

"A whole lot of nothing."

"Well, we now know Kurylenko was the man who hired him. He identified his picture."

"But we're not any closer to finding him than we were before. Not one bit closer," Cain said. "He could be anywhere."

"That reminds me, how was your trip?"

"It was OK."

"Productive?" Lawson asked.

"We'll find out."

Lawson dropped Cain off at his apartment and went back to the office. Cain went up to his apartment, concern hitting his face as he got to the door. There was a white envelope taped to it with Cain's name written on it. He ripped it off the door and hurried inside, worried that something happened to Heather. He barged in and didn't see her anywhere. The hairs on the back of his neck were standing at attention.

"Heather!" he yelled out.

Cain rushed into the bedroom, half expecting to see her lifeless body draped over the bed. To his relief, his fears were unfounded. He double checked the closets and under the bed but there was still no sign of her. Partly easing his fears was that there were no signs of a struggle and no blood either. He thought maybe she'd taken a shower, but he didn't hear the water running. He went into the bathroom and stumbled back against the wall, seeing Heather's body in the bathtub.

"Heather!" he shouted.

Heather opened her eyes and jumped, startled by Cain's shouting.

"You're OK?" Cain asked, kneeling down beside her.

"Yeah. Why wouldn't I be? I figured since you were gone I'd take a bath. I guess I fell asleep," she casually replied.

Cain looked up at the ceiling and sighed, thankful that she was OK.

"What's the matter with you? Why do you seem so jumpy?" Heather asked.

"Well, I saw this envelope taped to the door, then I come in and couldn't find you anywhere and you didn't respond to me calling you, then I guess I just feared the worst."

"Aww, I'm sorry, baby," she said, kissing his lips to make him feel better.

Cain helped Heather get out of the tub as she put a towel on. They kissed a little longer, helping Cain to calm down as his heart was still racing.

"So, what's in the envelope?" Heather asked out of curiosity.

"I don't know. I didn't look inside yet."

"I guess I'll get dressed," she whispered. "Unless you have some other plans?"

"Maybe later," Cain said and smiled.

Cain went into the living room to check the contents of the envelope as Heather got dressed in the bedroom. He opened it and took out a piece of paper. It was typewritten with just a single sentence on it.

"I know who the girl in the picture is," Cain read aloud.

Cain turned the paper over to make sure nothing was written on the back side and double checked the envelope in case something else was in there but he came up empty. Just that single sentence was all there was. Heather came out a minute later brushing her hair dressed in shorts and a tank top.

"Anything good?" she asked.

"You mean besides you?"

"In the envelope, silly."

"How am I supposed to concentrate when you come out looking like that?" Cain asked.

"Like what?"

"Sexy and beautiful."

"Oh stop," Heather said. "I'm just wearing shorts and a tank top."

"That's what I mean. Something so simple and you still look like a runway model."

"Well, I don't really agree with you but I'm not gonna stop you from saying it," she said. "So, what was in the envelope?"

Cain handed her the letter so she could see it for herself. She read it and also looked on the back to see if something else was written.

"Is this it?" she asked.

"Seems like it."

"That's weird."

"Did someone knock on the door?" Cain asked.

"No. I didn't hear anything."

"A noise or anything?"

"No. Nothing. Who do you think it came from?"

"I don't know."

"Well, how many people know about that picture?" Heather asked.

"It's a small list. Us, the guy that took it, Lawson, Sanders, and the analyst that cross checked it," Cain replied.

"Could there be more?"

"I don't know. Sanders kept it and said he was gonna keep checking on it. Maybe he showed it around and somebody knows something."

"Maybe you should tell him about this. He might know who it was," Heather said.

Cain listened to Heather's advice and grabbed his phone. He called Sanders to ask him about the photo.

"Yes, Mr. Cain?" Sanders said when he answered.

"I was just out chasing down a lead," Cain started before being interrupted.

"Yes. I know all about what happened with Ackers. Shelly turned a report in already."

"Well, when I got back I found an envelope attached to my door."

"What was in it?"

"It just said they knew who the girl in the picture was," Cain said. "Only a small group of people know about that picture. I thought maybe you had showed it around and someone recognized it or something."

"Hmm. Well, I guess that's possible."

"You don't know who it might've been?" Cain asked.

"Not off-hand I don't. I'll keep checking on it for you though," Sanders replied.

Cain hung up and put the phone down then faced Heather.

"You know, every time I talk to him I feel like he's giving me the runaround. Like he's just saying stuff to appease me," Cain said.

28

It'd been a few days since Cain interrogated Ackers. Since then no new leads had developed. It was a frustrating couple of days for Cain, waiting around for something to happen. He couldn't stand just waiting for Lawson or Sanders to call with a lead. He was getting tired of being cooped up in his apartment, knowing there was a target on their backs. Cain and Heather had just finished eating lunch when he heard a phone going off. It wasn't either of theirs though. Cain remembered the phone Raines gave him and rushed into the bedroom where he had it sitting on the bureau. He eagerly answered it, hoping Raines had something good to tell him.

"Nice to talk to you again," Raines greeted.

"Since you're calling, I assume you got something for me."

"Well, it is something. Exactly what, I cannot say for sure. It appears that you have a phantom targeting you."

"What do you mean by that?" Cain asked.

"Because as far as I can tell, Dmitri Kurylenko does not exist," Raines said.

"He doesn't? You can't find anything on him?"

"I cannot. As a matter of fact, I cannot find a trace of evidence of him ever being in existence."

"Don't you find that a little strange?" Cain asked.

"Absolutely. So, I took it one step further."

"How's that?"

"I have a contact that works for Russian Intelligence," Raines said.

"That must come in handy."

"It does. I asked him to check their records to see if Dmitri ever worked for them."

"And?"

"As far as he can tell there has never been a Dmitri Kurylenko that has ever worked for the SVR or any branch of Russian Intelligence," Raines said.

"How can that be if we have a file on him? Is it possible they're covering the information up and are trying to hide his existence?"

"With Russian Intelligence that is always a possibility. However, in this instance, my contact strongly denies that it's being done in this case."

"Maybe he's not really a brother. Cousin or something like that," Cain reasoned.

"I asked him to check everything they have on Andrei, and they've been tracking him for a long time, and they have no record of a brother. They claim Andrei was an only child, which coincides with my knowledge of him. Their unofficial stance is that Dmitri Kurylenko is a fictional character and does not exist. He's a ghost."

"Well, then who the hell is after me?"

"That is a very good question. One that I cannot answer at the moment."

"We found the guy who took the pictures, and he said the guy who hired him was an American. He said the man spoke with no accent and he identified the picture we had of Kurylenko as the guy who hired him," Cain said.

"That is interesting. I do have another suggestion."

"I'm open to anything."

"This man we know as Dmitri has been in America but has not shown up on your radar."

"Correct."

"He talks with no accent that we know of."

"Yeah."

"That would seem to suggest to me that you're looking for the wrong thing."

"What should we be looking for?" Cain asked.

"Instead of a Russian who has somehow eluded your sensors, perhaps you should be looking for an American who's posing as a Russian."

"What about the apartment in Russia with the pictures?"

"You said yourself it looked like it'd hardly been lived in. We both know it's easy enough to set up a dummy apartment. You could hire anyone to plop down a payment and throw up some pictures."

"If that was the case, then it would mean they expected me to find it at some point," Cain reasoned.

"Yes, it would."

"But why?"

"That is the million-dollar question," Raines said.

"What about this Yushkevitch character that I met with? Find anything on him?"

"I did."

"Well, at least we didn't come up totally empty," Cain said.

"I'll preface it by saying there's not much to tell about him. As far as working for Andrei, there are no records of that, and no reason to believe that is the case. As far as anything else, he's a low-level criminal who's spent time in a psychiatric unit. It's highly unlikely he's aware of anything going on."

"Does it seem possible he's the one who took a shot at me?"

"Tough to say. Considering that they missed, I'd say it's a good bet they didn't use a professional. Since he was in the area, it's conceivable that they might've paid him to try his hand at you, though I can't say with conviction in either scenario."

"OK. Well, I'll run Kurylenko's face through our facial rec scan and see if we can pull something up," Cain said.

"I would say that's a good idea," Raines agreed. "I would also be careful if I were you."

"In what way?"

"If it is true that Dmitri Kurylenko does not exist, which appears to be a strong possibility, then somebody's trying very hard to deceive you. I would trust no one with what you're about to do. Not Sanders, not Shelly, maybe not even your girl-friend. You cannot afford to take chances with their loyalties. I would say that someone close to you is not who they appear to be. You must be discreet."

"You might be right."

"Whatever you decide to do please let me know of your findings. I'm curious," Raines said.

"I will."

"Of course, for my part, I will continue to sniff around to see if I can come up with something. If I do, I will be sure to let you know."

"I appreciate it."

Cain went back into the living room and sat next to Heather on the sofa as she was reading the newspaper.

"Who was that?" Heather asked.

"Oh, just a contact."

"Anything that'll help?"

"Maybe. Too soon to say," Cain replied. "Listen, I'm gonna have to go to the office for a little bit. Do you mind staying here by yourself for an hour or so?"

"Course not. I'll be fine. Just like usual."

"I'll be back before you know it," he said, giving her a goodbye kiss.

Cain left for The Center and once he entered the building immediately headed for the analysts' room. He spotted the same guy that ran the picture for him before and figured he'd ask him to run the picture he had on Kurylenko since they were already familiar with each other.

"Excuse me? Do you have a few minutes?" Cain asked politely.

"Sure," the analyst replied.

"I don't think I ever caught your name before."

"Oh, it's Bill. Bill Heyward," he replied, shaking Cain's hand.

"I have another favor to ask of you."

"Name it."

"I have a picture here of a man I'd like you to run," Cain said, handing him the photo.

"OK, no problem. It'll probably take about the same time as before."

"Just one other thing. Don't tell anyone else about this. If you get any info on him call me directly."

"This is highly unusual. Most requests come from handlers or the directors and they usually always need to be informed of any results we get," Heyward said.

"I'm gonna tell you the truth. I received a file of this man who is supposed to be in Russian Intelligence. I have a contact who says he never heard of him. He doesn't exist. So, if we find a match in the U.S. database that means someone's lying. Someone in this agency. We can't afford to tell the wrong person about this. Once I get the information, I'll decide how to proceed and who we can trust," Cain said. "You with me?"

"Wow. That's heavy stuff. You really think someone in this agency is covering stuff up?"

"I'm not sure. If there's no match then maybe not. But if there is... then we got a problem. Either someone is giving this agency bad information on purpose or someone in this agency is intentionally giving out bad info. Either way, we need to find out."

"All right. I'm in," Heyward said. "I'll let you know if anything comes up."

"Thank you."

Cain slipped out of the room quickly before anyone caught him there and wondered what was up. It seemed like a quiet day there as it didn't seem as busy as usual. It appeared that most of the directors and handlers were out of the office which made it easier for him to go unnoticed. He was back home within the hour, surprising Heather at how quickly he made it back.

"That really was fast," she said.

"I just couldn't stand being away from you."

346

"Sweet talker."

Cain and Heather spent the next few hours passing the time. They watched TV, played some card games, and just talked. They were starting to get ready for dinner when Cain's phone rang. It was Heyward. He just started running the scan about six hours ago. If he was calling so soon that must've meant that he got a hit already. Cain excitedly answered his phone.

"Hey, what'd you find?" Cain asked.

"Some pretty interesting stuff. I mean this is just crazy."

"Did you get a match?"

"We did."

"Who is it?"

"Comes up as a man named Brian Chapman. Ring a bell?" Heyward asked.

"No. Does he have a sheet? Any Russian aliases?"

"No aliases. But it seems this guy has been arrested and jailed more times than you can shake a stick at."

"For what?"

"Robbery, assault, murder, rape, extortion, burglary, intent to sell, and drug trafficking," Heyward said.

"Wow."

"Yeah. This guy's a bad dude all the way around."

"Send me his info," Cain said.

"Sending it to your phone now."

"How'd you find him? DMV?"

"No. I had a feeling he wouldn't pop up so easily through there so I did a backdoor check and got a hit from an NYPD arrest photo," Heyward said. "I was able to piece everything together from there."

Cain's phone beeped indicating he had a new message. He briefly looked at it to make sure it came through.

"OK. Got it."

"So, what are you gonna do now?" Heyward asked.

"I'm gonna go pay Mr. Chapman a visit. Then I'm gonna find out who hired him," Cain said.

"Be careful."

"I will. Thanks for the help."

"Don't mention it," Heyward said. "Oh, by the way, don't hang up."

"Yeah?"

"Did you find that girl yet?"

"No, not yet," Cain said.

"Well, I'm hoping I have it narrowed down for you in the next few days," Heyward said.

"What?"

"The first scan came back negative, but I put it through again, and I ran it through some filters and came up with a list of possibilities. Before I was just checking for the woman but this time I put the boy's picture through a scan as well. Still a good bit of work to be done though."

"I wasn't told anything about this."

"Oh. Really? I'm sure I told Director Sanders about it. Unless I forgot. But I'm almost positive I mentioned it to him and he said he would let you know," Heyward said.

"He didn't mention it."

"Oh. I'm sure he probably just forgot or something. He's got so much information passing through his desk every day it probably just slipped his mind."

"Yeah. Probably," Cain said.

"Anyway, I'll keep working on it. Still can't promise anything or make any guarantees."

"I understand. Just let me know."

Once they hung up, Cain let the phone slip down by his side as he stared straight ahead, not focusing on anything. He had serious doubts about whether Sanders simply forgot to tell him about the picture. Sanders always had a reason for doing, or not doing, anything. He didn't just forget. Cain went back into the living room to get ready and let Heather know he was leaving soon.

"I'm afraid I'm gonna have to skip dinner," Cain said.

"Oh no. Where are you going?"

"New Jersey. It could be the break we've been waiting for."

"How long will you be gone?" Heather asked.

"Probably a few hours at least. Take the same precautions as usual."

"I will," she replied, giving him a kiss.

Chapman's address was just over the state line into Jersey and would probably take Cain an hour to get there. But there was no telling whether Chapman was still there or even lived there at all. Cain left around six, in a hopeful mood that everything was coming to a conclusion soon. If Chapman was there, then he could end the entire matter in as soon as an hour or two. He hoped so, if only for Heather, so she could get back to a normal life and not be cooped up inside all the time with a bodyguard.

The address Cain was given was a two-story house located in a residential neighborhood. Most of the houses looked pretty similar. Once he located the house, he parked his car on the next street over and cut through the yard in the back. He swiftly moved through the yard, the darkness cloaking his movements.

He reached the back door of the house and located the security system, quickly rendering it useless. He was inside within a minute, almost instantly picking the lock. He was amazed that someone of his ilk wouldn't have a better security system but he probably felt most people wouldn't be trying to mess with him too much. Whatever the case, Cain used it to his advantage as he started poking around inside. Once he established that Chapman wasn't there, he began going through every room, trying to find any information he could that could shed some light on what was happening. He went through every file cabinet, closet, and table drawer he came across until he finally found something interesting. Cain sat down at the desk in the living room and started ransacking the drawers, pulling out everything he saw. He pulled out an unmarked file folder and opened it, revealing pictures of both Cain and Heather. They were copies of the pictures he found inside Kurylenko's apartment in Russia. That seemed to make it a slam dunk that Chapman and Kurylenko were the same person. He couldn't come to any other conclusion as to why he'd have the same pictures. There was no other explanation. As far as any other information that was useful, there was none. Just the pictures, which really didn't help him any. He'd already suspected Chapman was the guy he was looking for but what he didn't know was who else was involved. Cain had doubts that Chapman was the leader in this little game and figured somebody was above him calling the shots. He put the pictures back in the folder and closed it, leaving it on the desk as he swiveled around in the chair, facing the door. He pulled his gun out and let it rest on his leg as he waited for Chapman to return. Cain took turns between staring at the door, waiting for the knob to start turning, and looking at the window, waiting for the headlights of his car to shine through. After a couple hours of waiting, he sent Heather a text, wanting to make sure she was OK, and just asked how she was.

"I'm good. Miss you," she wrote back. "Wish you were home."

"I will be soon hopefully," he replied.

"Love you."

"Love you too," Cain messaged.

After putting the phone down, Heather started cleaning the kitchen to pass the time. She was really hoping that Cain would be back soon. Though she could take care of herself, she did feel better, and safer, when he was around. After cleaning for a few minutes there was a knock on the door. Startled, Heather jumped and knocked a glass off the counter, shattering it once it hit the floor. Her heart started racing, wondering who was there. She remembered what Cain had told her and raced to the drawer that had the gun in it. She picked it up, her shattered nerves making it shake in her hand. She tried to be still for a minute, careful as to not make a sound, hoping that whoever was there would go away. It didn't help though, as her heart started pounding even more when the knocking resumed a few seconds later.

"Pizza delivery," a man shouted from beyond the door.

Heather scrunched her face, confused, since she knew she didn't order anything. She tip-toed her way over to the door, still trying to not make a sound. Her mind raced with different thoughts of what she'd do if the man was dangerous and broke in. Would she be able to do what Cain instructed her to? Would she actually be able to pull the trigger and shoot someone?

She wasn't sure if she could actually squeeze the trigger and do what was necessary.

"Pizza," the man shouted again, knocking.

Heather stood to the side of the door wondering what she should do. She could feel the sweat pouring off her body. The person didn't seem to be going away. Though if it was someone dangerous, she assumed they'd be trying to force their way in by now. Maybe it was just an honest mistake, she thought. Maybe they were delivering to the wrong address. After knocking again, Heather figured she'd just tell them it was the wrong address.

"Pizza delivery," the man yelled again, knocking even stronger.

"I think you've got the wrong apartment," Heather yelled back. "I didn't order any pizza."

The man replied with her address and apartment number, saying that's who the order was for.

"But I didn't order it," Heather restated.

"Maybe someone else ordered it for you," the man replied. "It's already paid for, ma'am. I'll hold it up to the peephole so you can take a look at it."

"OK."

She looked through the peephole and saw the man, who didn't look dangerous, holding a pizza box. He held it up and opened it so she could see it was a pizza.

"Can you see it?" the man asked.

"Yes."

As soon as the words left her mouth, the man withdrew a gun from his jacket and fired three shots through the door. He knew she was standing in the middle of the door, looking through the hole, so he was sure he'd hit her. He heard something that sounded like her body dropping to the floor. He dropped the pizza box and kicked the door open, only opening part way, as Heather's leg blocked it from opening entirely. The man squeezed his way inside and looked at her. Such a shame for a woman as beautiful as that to come to such an end, he thought. Blood was pouring out of her stomach as the life began draining out of her. She hardly moved an inch.

"Sorry, lady," the man said softly. "It's just business."

He took one last look at her as she gasped for breath. Satisfied that his work was done, he left, closing the door behind him as if nothing happened. Heather lay motionless on the floor, blood staining the floor underneath her, two bullets lodged inside her. She wanted to crawl along the floor to get to her phone to call for help but had no energy left within her. Her eyes slowly flickered until she could no longer keep them open.

29

Although Cain had gotten tired of waiting after sitting there for four hours, he was determined to wait it out a little while longer. It didn't look like Chapman was clearing out his house and the refrigerator was packed so Cain figured he wasn't leaving anytime soon. He assumed Chapman was out on some kind of business. Cain's wait finally came to a close during the sixth hour as he finally saw the headlights flashing through the window. He had to control his emotions, though, as his first instinct was to rip a few bullets into Chapman's body as soon as it emerged through the doorway. Cain needed answers first. Answers that he hoped Chapman could provide. Cain took cover in the corner of the room, tucked in between a couch and a sofa. There was no lamp in the vicinity which made it pretty dark, perfect for Cain to wait until he was ready to pounce.

Chapman walked through the door and locked it, including

the deadbolt, then proceeded to go into the kitchen. Cain could hear him getting something to drink from the sound of the pop from the beer can. He peered around the edge of the couch and saw Chapman walking into the living room from the kitchen. Chapman grabbed the remote from the coffee table and turned on the TV. His back was to Cain which provided Cain the opportunity he was looking for. He sprung up from between the furniture and rushed at Chapman's back, getting him in a stranglehold. Chapman immediately dropped his beer as he tried to get his attacker off him. Chapman managed to elbow Cain in his gut, causing Cain to loosen his grip. Chapman wriggled his way free from Cain's grasp and punched him in the jaw, making Cain stumble backwards. Chapman saw the opportunity to end the struggle quickly and reached for a gun he had stashed by the TV stand. Cain noticed the gun before Chapman grabbed it and quickly withdrew his gun. It wasn't quite how he envisioned it going down, but Cain had no other choice but to fire, striking Chapman in the shoulder. It temporarily stunned Chapman, knocking him to his knees. It didn't deter him though, quickly getting back to his feet, as he made a move for the gun again. Cain fired once more, this time hitting Chapman in the leg as he stumbled to the ground, grabbing his thigh.

"Bitch," Chapman moaned.

"Don't make me kill you," Cain said.

"Go to hell."

Chapman once again made it back to his feet. Cain knew he wasn't going to stop reaching for the gun. Cain quickly cut him back down, firing one more time, hitting Chapman in the stomach. Chapman dropped to the ground, clutching his stomach as he fell to his knees. Chapman's hands were drenched with the blood coming out of him as he looked up at Cain. Cain turned on a light so Chapman could get a better look at him.

"It's you," Chapman whispered.

"Sure is. Why'd you come after me?"

"It was never about you," Chapman said.

"What?" Cain asked, astonished.

"Not you. It wasn't you," Chapman said, falling on his side.

Cain knelt down beside him and put his hand on Chapman's arm.

"You weren't the target," Chapman said. "You can't protect her anymore."

"What's that mean?" Cain asked, agitated.

"You'll find out," Chapman replied, struggling to get the words out.

"Who hired you?" Cain asked angrily, pulling on the dying man's shirt collar.

It was too late to get an answer out of him. Chapman's eyes closed, and he stopped breathing, Cain letting him roll face forward on the ground. Cain immediately thought about Heather and knew she was in more danger than he had realized. He pulled out his phone and dialed her number, his fingers not quite going as fast as his mind was racing.

"Please pick up," he said to himself.

With each passing ring that she didn't answer, he increasingly grew worried. Maybe she just fell asleep, he hoped. Or maybe she went to the bathroom. He came up with half a dozen reasons why she wasn't answering her phone. Each time it went to voicemail he just hung up and immediately dialed again. Five separate times he rang her phone. Each time was more frustrating than the previous try. He tried not to let the negative thoughts overtake his mind but he couldn't shake the feeling that something was seriously wrong. Cain took one last look at Chapman and sighed. He was an hour away and if something had happened, he was worried he couldn't get there in time. He then called the only other person he trusted.

"Shelly," Cain said.

"Hey."

"Listen, I think something's wrong."

"What's the matter?" Lawson asked.

"I've been following up on something and I can't get a hold of Heather. I'm worried something's happened."

"Calm down, I'm sure she's fine. Probably sleeping."

"I'm about an hour away, do you think you could stop at the apartment and check on her?" he asked.

"You realize it's after midnight, right? If I go knocking on her door, I might scare her half to death."

"But what if she's in trouble? Please?"

"All right," Lawson said. "I'm only doing this for you though. I'll grab one of the security guys and go check on her. I should be there in about fifteen minutes."

"I appreciate it."

Cain hung up and raced out the back door, jumping over a couple fences to get to his car. He sped off, hoping he could shave off a few minutes of driving time.

Lawson called one of the security agents and had him meet her at Cain's apartment. Lawson walked up the steps to Cain's floor, not really expecting any issues. She was actually kind of nervous about being there so late and maybe startling Heather. They walked down the hall and Lawson instantly noticed a pizza box lying by the door. They both withdrew their guns as they slowly walked toward the door. Once Lawson saw the holes in it, she knew Cain was right to be worried. She hoped that whatever happened here that Heather somehow managed to get away. The security agent held Lawson back so he could get ahead of her. He turned the handle of the door and slowly opened it, though Heather's fallen body prevented it from opening fully. The agent went in and immediately noticed Heather and motioned for Lawson to come in and check on her while he cleared the rest of the apartment. Lawson knelt down beside her and checked for a pulse, which was faint, but at least she still had one. She pulled out her phone and called for an ambulance.

"We're getting help, just hang in there," Lawson said.

"Everything's clear," the agent informed her.

"Get Sanders on the phone and tell him what happened."

"Right."

Lawson dreaded telling Cain about her condition. She wasn't sure how she could tell him. She was undecided whether she should've called him right then and told him what was going on or if she should wait until he got there. She worried about his state of mind driving if she called him immediately. After a few minutes of debating with herself, she just figured she'd wait a little before she called him. At least until the ambulance got there and she could update Heather's condition. Luckily, the paramedics arrived within five minutes. They put her on a stretcher and wheeled her down to the ambulance, hoping to stabilize her. Lawson was by her side the entire way until they put her in the truck. She wiped her eyes as they closed the doors. Her vitals were not looking good, and they raced to the hospital.

Cain called her once he was about twenty minutes away, wondering what was going on.

"Hey, did you get there? Is she OK?" Cain asked.

"How far away are you?" Lawson asked.

"About twenty minutes."

"We'll talk when you get here."

Cain's heart almost dropped out of his chest. He knew that response meant it was bad. "What are you trying to tell me? Is she OK?"

"I'd rather just talk to you when you get here," Lawson insisted.

Cain immediately hung up, angrily tossing his phone on the floor of the passenger side of the car. He wished Lawson would've just told him something about her condition. Was she alive? Was she dead? Hurt? His mind wandered in a million different directions, wondering how Heather was. He wiped a few tears from his eyes, assuming the worst had happened and that they'd tell him when he arrived that she was gone. It seemed like he got there in a matter of minutes because he couldn't even remember driving in the time it took him, his thoughts only concerned with Heather's well-being.

Cain rushed up the steps in his apartment building, getting there faster than if he had used the elevator. Seeing men standing in the hallway that looked like they worked for the government didn't help to put his mind at ease. He saw the bullet holes in the door and ran into his apartment. He saw blood on the floor and looked around, seeing Lawson and Sanders talking in the kitchen. They halted their conversation once they saw Cain enter the room. Cain walked up to them and looked at Lawson, his sorrowful facial expression obviously expecting the worst of news.

"What happened? Where is she?" Cain asked.

"We're still trying to piece everything together but it looks like someone posing as a pizza delivery man lured her to the door. Once they knew she was there, they fired a few times through the door," Lawson said.

"Where is she?" he asked somberly.

"She's been taken to the hospital. She's alive but in critical condition. She was unconscious."

"Any leads on who did this?"

"We're gathering up leads now," Sanders said. "We also have a few cameras in the area that we are analyzing now. I would think we should be able to have some concrete answers within a few hours."

"Good. I wanna see her."

"I figured you would," Lawson said. "I'll drive you there."

Cain wasn't much for prayer, but pray was all he did on the drive to the hospital. He didn't utter a single word to Lawson. Instead, he stared out the window and thought of what he could've done differently. All he could think about was how stupid he'd been for leaving her alone. He was beating himself up over how she paid the price for his lack of awareness. For all he knew they could've been waiting outside his apartment, just waiting for the chance that he'd leave and they could get her alone. Lawson fought to hold back tears as she was driving. She didn't figure her crying would help matters any. It wasn't a long drive to the hospital but for Cain it seemed like an eternity. Each red light seemed to take forever to change to green. Twenty minutes later they arrived at the hospital, Cain rushing in. A few minutes in the waiting room didn't help his mind from wandering. After pacing around the room for five minutes a doctor came in to update him.

"Are you the victim's boyfriend?" the doctor asked.

"Yes. How is she?"

"Well, I'm not gonna sugarcoat things for you or give you false hope. She's got some major abdominal trauma going on."

"Will she make it?" Cain asked.

"I'm afraid that's a question I can't answer right now. In abdominal trauma cases eighty percent of deaths occur with twenty-four hours of admission and sixty-six percent die during the initial operation. So, she doesn't have that going for her."

"Where did the bullet hit?"

"It penetrated her stomach and hit portions of her liver and intestine. Luckily it didn't go through the center of either organ but it still did some pretty extensive damage. She suffered a rather large amount of blood loss and was going into shock when she was brought in. Another issue is the possibility of infection," the doctor said.

"How likely is that?"

"I would say it's probably more likely than not at this point."

"What are her odds?"

The doctor made an agonizing face, the kind that Cain recognized as a face of someone who didn't want to be the bearer of bad news.

"Truthfully," Cain said.

"It's difficult to say. I don't do percentages as a rule as there are so many variables that come into play, but if you want my honest opinion, I would say she's gonna have a tough go of it."

"Less than fifty percent?"

"I would say that's probably accurate. But that doesn't mean it can't happen and she can't overcome it. As I said, the next twenty-four hours are the most critical. If she can hang on that long, her odds will keep increasing past that point."

"I understand," Cain said.

"So, we're preparing her for surgery now. Between the

surgery and post-op, it'll most likely be a few hours before we update her condition again."

"Thank you, doctor."

"Sure. I'll keep you updated and let you know if anything changes."

Cain wiped his eyes and finally sat down next to Lawson, feeling pretty helpless. He wished he could do something but knew there was nothing he could do except wait. And hope. And pray. Lawson put her hand on Cain's knee to let him know she was there for him.

Sanders stopped by for a visit an hour later to see how everything was going. He tried calling their phones first, but neither answered and he assumed they either didn't have their phone on them or weren't getting good reception. Cain was a little surprised to see him walking through the doors. He knew Sanders didn't really care about Heather and had no feeling on whether she lived or died.

"How's she doing?" Sanders asked.

"No change yet," Cain said.

"I tried calling first, so I just decided to come down to let you know what was going on. We've got some footage from a building only a couple doors down from yours."

"And?"

"It's a clear shot of Kurylenko. He was wearing some type of hat and was holding a pizza box. I don't think there's any question who the shooter is," Sanders said.

Cain wrestled with whether he should tell him that Kurylenko was dead. That he shot and killed him earlier that night. But something was nagging at him, something that was telling him not to say anything. He wasn't sure who was behind the Kurylenko deception but until he knew who it was, he thought it was best not to say anything about it.

"I have a few analysts trying to pin down his location now so we can get rid of this son of a bitch," Sanders said. He broke from his thought pattern as his phone started ringing.

"Yeah?" Sanders said.

Cain watched him intently as Sanders seemed to answer everything in short sentences without revealing much. Sanders smiled once he hung up and put the phone away.

"Looks like good news," Sanders said.

"What's happening?" Lawson asked.

"Looks like we've got him cornered."

"Really?" Cain asked.

"Some abandoned warehouse a little east of here. I'm gonna head down there and take charge of the situation," Sanders said. "Wanna come?"

"No. I'm sure you guys will take care of it. I think I'd be better off staying here in case anything changes," Cain replied.

"Understandable. I'll let you know what happens."

"Thanks."

"Well, at least there's some good news," Lawson said.

"I guess so."

"Hopefully it'll be over soon."

"I doubt it."

"Why? You don't think they'll get him?"

"No."

"Why not?" Lawson asked.

"Because I don't think they have him cornered like they think they do," Cain said.

He contemplated telling Lawson what happened but quickly

reconsidered. It wasn't that he didn't trust her but didn't want to put her in a position to have to lie or cover things up for him. So, it was easier to just keep her out of the loop for the time being. The pair continued waiting, waiting for word from either a doctor or Sanders to let them know what was going on. Though Cain's mind was predominantly focused on Heather, he did wonder how they had a man cornered that he had already killed. Either Sanders was deliberately lying to him or Sanders himself was being duped. Either way, he was interested in what the final result would be.

Two hours went by and Lawson was starting to get a little antsy about Kurylenko, waiting there for information. Cain, though, knowing Kurylenko was already dead, was calm and nonchalant about hearing from Sanders. Lawson couldn't believe how calm Cain was being about Kurylenko. She figured he'd be angry about what happened and either try to kill him himself or be waiting on the edge of his seat until he found out what happened to Kurylenko. A few minutes later, Lawson's phone started ringing. It was Sanders.

"Did you get him?" Lawson asked.

"Afraid not. We thought we had him but he somehow managed to escape," Sanders said.

"That's too bad."

"We'll get him. We'll keep our eyes and ears open and get a fix on him soon enough. He's not going to be able to evade us for too long."

"Well, let's hope you're right."

"Any change there?" Sanders asked.

"No. Still the same."

"Well, I'm going to go home for the night. If anything changes you know where to reach me."

"I will," Lawson replied.

Lawson hung up and looked over at Cain, who already knew what she was going to say.

"Didn't get him, huh?" Cain asked.

"No. How did you know that was gonna happen?"

"Just a hunch."

"Some hunch."

The doctor then entered the room and walked over to Cain, sitting down next to him. The somber look on his face told Cain not to expect good news. The anxiety was almost too much for him as he waited for the doctor to tell him about her condition. As many times as Cain had come close to death and stared it in the face, nothing was as bad as this. The feeling he had now was a hundred times worse than if he'd been in the situation himself.

"So, we were able to get the bullet out," the doctor began. "Unfortunately, the damage we found inside her was a little worse than what we originally expected."

"Which means what?" Cain asked wearily.

"Her condition is deteriorating. I'm sorry, but there is no easy way to say this."

"Say what?"

"At the rate she's going now, we don't expect her to last much longer than another hour or two," the doctor said.

Cain opened his mouth to respond but couldn't formulate the words in his mind. He looked away, first at the wall and then the floor. He forcefully closed his eyes and sighed, tears starting to flow. Lawson came over to him and put her arm around him. Cain was able to compose himself after a minute.

"Can I see her?" Cain asked.

"Of course. Just give us a minute and I'll have someone come out to bring you in."

"Thank you."

"I'm sorry, Matt," Lawson said. "I wish there was more we could do. I wish I had gotten there sooner."

"You did everything you could. If you didn't get there when you did she probably would've already been gone by the time I got there."

"I just wish there's something else that could be done."

"There is," Cain said.

"What?"

"We can find the person who's responsible for this."

"We're looking. We'll find him," Lawson said.

"No. I'm not talking about Kurylenko," Cain said.

"What are you talking about?"

"This goes beyond Kurylenko. He's just a pawn in this. Someone set this up and got him to do the dirty work and I'm gonna find out who."

"How do you know there's someone else?" Lawson asked.

"I can't tell you yet."

"You have information that you're not sharing?"

"It's something I have to keep to myself for a while. I'll let you know when it's time," Cain said.

"Well, what can you tell me?" Lawson asked.

"Just that there's someone above Kurylenko. I don't have proof of anything yet. But when I get it... that person's as good as dead."

"Matt, you need to let me help you. Don't shut me out."

"I'll let you know when I put two bullets in his head. I'm not gonna concentrate on that until this is over."

A nurse came over and led Cain into Heather's room. He was visibly shaken upon seeing her lying there, unconscious, hooked up to various machines. He slowly walked over to her and kissed her on the forehead. Cain sat next to her and held her hand as he softly talked to her.

"I'm sorry for everything. This is all my fault. If we meet up again in another life, I hope you'll be able to forgive me," he said. "Until then, I will find out who's responsible for this and I will even the score. Your death will not go unpunished. I promise you that."

THE CAIN DIRECTIVE

30

Cain was sitting at the kitchen table having a bowl of cereal when he went into a zone. He started reliving some of his most painful memories. Any noise in the apartment was blocked out as he was completely immersed in his past, staring straight ahead. An emotionless expression was trapped on his face as he once again was in that Russian house where he terminated the life of Andrei Kurylenko and his young son. For a while he was able to somehow keep that regretful night out of his mind, but lately it had returned, and more often than before. It seemed he had dreams about it at least once a week.

Once Cain pulled the trigger on the younger Kurylenko, the memory slowly faded into white space and a new memory began. He imagined Dmitri Kurylenko firing those shots that penetrated the door and lodged into Heather's midsection. The vision was just as vivid as if he was there himself when it happened. He was suddenly in the hospital, watching as they put Heather in a body bag, zipping it over her head. Cain pulled out a gun and began firing, shooting the hospital attendants, yelling about not taking Heather away from him.

He felt a hand wrap around his wrist, trying to break him from his trance. The touch on his skin snapped him out of it as he grabbed their wrist. Cain looked up, a little dazed and confused, taking a few seconds to recognize who it was standing next to him.

"Are you OK?"

"Yeah," Cain answered, not sure whether he actually was or not.

"The visions again?"

Cain sighed. "Yeah."

She reached down and hugged him, holding him tight.

"I wish there was something I could do to help you get rid of them," she told him.

"I don't think there's anything you can do. I don't think there's anything anyone can do. They're just part of me now. I have to live with it."

"But you shouldn't have to."

"I'll gladly deal with it every day for the rest of my life as long as I still have you in it," Cain said.

Heather smiled. Even after surviving a near death experience, she never wavered in her love for Cain. An hour away from death, once Cain entered the room and sat next to her, holding her hand, her vitals improved. He stayed by her side, day and night, for four months until she was well enough to leave the hospital. He didn't go on any missions, and basically refused to do anything at all, until she was out of danger. Though Heather never blamed him for anything, Cain always felt he was responsible. If she wasn't with him, then she never would've been put in that situation, he thought. They figured that was partly why he kept having his nightmares, because he felt everything that happened was his fault.

"When are you gonna stop blaming yourself?" Heather asked.

"I don't know. I don't know if I ever will."

"Matt, not one time have I ever questioned us or you. Not once. My life before you was nothing. You know that. I've never blamed you for what happened and I never will. It's been a year since it happened. So why do you keep beating yourself up over it?"

"Because I can't get over that I almost lost you. You're the only person that's meant anything to me and I just can't accept that you were almost killed because of me. You lost nine months of your life because of me. Four months in a hospital bed and five more of rehab and recovery. I just can't pretend that it didn't happen," Cain replied.

Heather sighed and looked down, upset in knowing that she was unlikely to change his outlook no matter how hard she tried. Things weren't quite the same between them since she got out of the hospital. Though they still loved each other and hardly argued, Cain brooded more. Heather was still pretty much the same person she was before, always trying to see the positive and staying upbeat, but Cain's darker side had emerged a little more. He never unleashed it in her direction but she sometimes found him just sitting in a corner staring into space, waking up in a bad mood for no reason, punching holes in the wall, or walking around like he was about to knock the head off of the next person he saw. She worried about him getting worse.

Heather looked at her phone and started moving.

"Oops. I didn't realize what time it was," she said, putting her phone in the back pocket of her jeans. "I gotta get going."

"Where are you going?"

"I told you this morning. Were you not listening?" Heather asked playfully.

"Umm. I uh... no, I guess not."

"I told you I'm going to the park to meet a friend."

"Oh. What are you gonna do?" Cain asked.

"I dunno. Just walk around and talk about girl stuff, I guess."

"Who are you meeting?"

"Just a friend. Don't be so nosey," she said, kissing his cheek.

"OK. Well, have fun."

"I don't wanna see any holes in these walls when I get back, understand?"

"Yes, Mom," he kidded.

Heather left to go to the park to meet her friend. She sat on a bench and looked at the time. It was 11:35. She wondered where her friend was as she was usually on time. Just as she contemplated whether to call her she looked up and saw her walking toward her.

"Hey Shelly," Heather said, smiling.

"What's up, girl?" Lawson returned, hugging each other.

"Thanks for meeting me."

"No problem. It's been a while. You look great."

"I feel good," Heather said and beamed.

"I can't believe it's been three months since I saw you last. That's the tough part about this job, so much going on that you sometimes can't get away from it."

"Yeah, I know. I completely understand."

"So, what's up? When you called I detected something other than just wanting to meet and catch up," Lawson said.

"Yeah," Heather said, looking at her and offering a frustrating type of smile.

"I'm all ears."

"It's Matt."

"Had a feeling it would be."

"I don't know what it is. Well, maybe I do. I'm just so worried about him. He's not the same man he was before," she said.

"In what way?" Lawson asked.

"Last week I got home from grocery shopping to find three holes in our living room wall that he punched out. Some days he wakes up like he's already mad at the world. This morning I found him sitting at the kitchen table staring at the wall, thinking about all the things that led up to what happened."

"He's dealing with a lot."

"He blames himself for what happened to me. No matter how hard I try to convince him that it's not his fault, it doesn't seem to do any good. It's like it goes in one ear and out the other. I could never blame him for anything. He saved my life when he met me," Heather said. "Any bad that comes up is just something we have to deal with and I completely accept as something I choose in order to be with him."

"I wish I had some answers for you. But I don't. Matt is always going to have to deal with things that you and I won't. Just from the beginning, being shot in the head and his memory, then everything else, he's got to figure out how to deal with things that you and I will never have to," Lawson said. "No matter how much you and I sometimes want to just shake him and get out those negative connections he has... we just can't."

"I know," Heather said dejectedly.

"I don't know there's much more you can do other than what you're doing. Just love him for who he is and keep being there for him. Hopefully, one day he'll be able to put all the demons behind him."

"I guess you're right. I'm sorry for being such a worrywart."

"It's OK. Sometimes it helps to just talk about things and vent."

"Thanks for being a good friend," Heather said.

"No problem. It's nice to talk about normal things instead of the usual government stuff I do all the time," Lawson replied, stopping as she thought of something. "Hey, what about moving?"

"Moving? To where?"

"I don't know. Anywhere."

"What for?"

"Maybe that would help. Something new, something different, something else to get his mind off things. New environment, new location, I dunno, just something different."

"Hmm. It's an idea. Maybe I'll kick it around with Matt a little bit."

The two of them continued walking around the park, talking about Cain mostly, but also other things, such as Lawson's love life.

"So, where's your Mr. Right at?" Heather joked.

"I think he drowned," Lawson replied.

"Oh, c'mon, there must be someone that you're interested in."

"No, not really. This job doesn't really lend itself to much matchmaking."

"Aww, I'm sorry."

"Hey, it's OK. I'm not sad or anything. I don't need someone in my life right now. If it happens, great, but if not, that's OK too. I'm OK with being on my own right now,'"she told her.

"You know, work keeps me pretty busy most of the time ,anyway."

The two had started becoming friendlier even before Heather's hospital stay, but while she was in there, Lawson visited her frequently. At first, Lawson figured she owed it to Cain to visit and show her support, but after a while she was visiting more because of the friendship that she and Heather were developing. It was quite a transformation from their initial encounters when they couldn't stand each other. While Lawson wasn't there at the hospital as much as Cain was, she visited as often as she could, usually four or five days a week, unless she was away on business.

They talked for about an hour before they had to go their separate ways. They gave each other a hug and promised to see each other again soon. Heather went back to the apartment, happy to find nothing destroyed, and Cain watching TV. She looked at him then turned her head to a kitchen drawer. She walked over to it and stood in front of it, contemplating whether she wanted to take the envelope out.

"You know, I was thinking about going back to work next week," she blurted out.

Cain immediately got off the couch and walked to the kitchen. "You think that's a good idea?"

"Matt, it's been a year."

"I know. I just want to make sure that you're ready and all."

"I've been ready for two months," she said.

"As long as it's what you want."

"It is."

Cain turned to leave before he looked back as Heather started to speak.

"There's something else that I want."

"What's that?" Cain asked.

Heather opened the drawer and pulled out a white envelope and placed it on the counter between them.

"What're you doing?" Cain asked.

"When are you gonna get back to this?" Heather asked of the note proclaiming to know the woman in Cain's picture from Hawaii.

"Heather."

"What? You need to do this. For yourself."

"Stop."

"What? You don't wanna know anymore?"

Cain looked away, not really wanting to get into it. "When everything happened with you last year, I told myself that nothing was more important than getting you back. I said I'd put everything else aside to be there for you and support you. I didn't want any distractions or anything getting in the way of you getting healthy again. That was my number one goal."

"And that's great, and I appreciate everything you've done, and every second you've been there for me. But I haven't had therapy in two months," Heather said. "Matt, I'm back. I'm fine. You need to do this for you. And for me. Because nothing would make me happier than for you to find out who this person is and what she meant to you. To start connecting the pieces of your life."

"I'm fine," Cain said, trying to reassure her.

"No, you're not. You've been slowly torturing yourself for a long time. About the choices you've made and the things you've done. You can't go back in time and change them."

"Wouldn't that be nice?"

"Yeah, but you can't. You have to learn to live with what's happened. You have to accept it."

"Easier to say than to do," Cain said.

"I know it is," Heather replied. "I just want you to be happy. And I know you're not."

"I'm happy as long as I have you."

"I wish that was enough."

"You're not leaving me, are you?" Cain asked with worry in his voice.

Heather laughed. "If a bullet couldn't get rid of me, then nothing will."

She leaned over the counter and kissed Cain, holding his face in both of her hands.

"Will you please get back to this?" Heather asked, looking deep in his eyes, holding up the envelope. "For me?"

"OK."

Heather smiled and gave him another deep, passionate kiss. She thought about bringing up the topic of moving but then thought better of it. She figured one breakthrough was enough for the day. They sat around talking for the next few hours before Cain figured it was time to get out of the apartment. As he was going out the door, he got a call from Lawson about a mission they might have for him. She said it was urgent, so he got down to The Center right away. Cain went to her office, where she was sitting at her desk, working on her computer.

"So, what's this big mission all about?" Cain asked.

"It's Kurylenko," Lawson said. "After all this time, he's finally popped back up on our radar."

"Oh?"

"Two days ago, we got a hit that he's back in Moscow."

"That's impossible. What kind of evidence is there?" Cain asked.

"We have photographs of him," Lawson said, pulling the photos out of a folder and putting them on her desk.

Cain picked them up and carefully studied the three pictures. "This isn't him," he calmly stated.

"How can you say that? It is him."

"The pictures are grainy. It could be anybody."

"It's him. Our analysts have gone over it and have confirmed it's him," Lawson replied, steadfast in her assertion.

"Did you talk to the analysts?" Cain asked.

"No."

"Then how do you know?"

"Sanders sent me all the information."

"Shelly, this isn't him," Cain said, pushing the pictures away.

"I called you because I figured you'd be happy we finally found him. That maybe this would help bring some closure for you and all you can say is that it isn't him?" Lawson said, getting annoyed. "You're not even willing to consider the possibility that this is him."

"Because I know it isn't him," Cain said, raising his voice.

"And how do you know that when everyone else says it is?"

"Because I killed him!" Cain said with a sigh.

"What?" Lawson asked, not believing what she just heard.

"I killed him," Cain repeated softly.

"How? When?" she asked, shaking her head in disbelief.

"Last year, the night Heather got shot, that's where I was when I asked you to check on her. I got one of the analysts to run another scan of Kurylenko and they matched it up to a prison photo of a man named Brian Chapman. He was a big-time thug. So, I went to his house and waited for him. I guess while I was waiting there he was already at the apartment and shot Heather. Once he got back, I didn't have a chance to question him, he immediately went for his gun and I shot him three times, I think."

"Are you positive you killed him? Any chance he could have survived?" Lawson asked.

"No," Cain answered with a shake of his head. "I watched him die in front of me. His last words were something about how it wasn't about me."

"Why didn't you say anything before now?"

"I don't know," Cain said, throwing his hands up in the air. "I wasn't sure about this whole Kurylenko thing and when I found out his name was actually Chapman, I wasn't sure what to think."

"Or who to believe," Lawson said.

"That too."

"Although I would've thought you would've built up a little trust in me by now."

"Shelly," Cain replied, throwing his hands up again, not sure what else to say.

"It's OK. I guess I don't really blame you." Lawson paused for a few moments before speaking again. "So, what do you think he meant when he said it wasn't about you?"

"The only thing I can figure is that I wasn't the target. He was after Heather all along."

"But what sense would that make? She's not a threat to anybody."

"I don't know. I've tried to wrap my head around it but I can't figure it out. Somebody fabricated Kurylenko's existence and tried to kill my girlfriend. The meaning behind it is just something I don't know. As for the person who set this up, I can only assume it is someone within this agency," Cain said.

"But who? Why would someone want to do all that?"

"I guess I pissed someone off."

"So that's how you knew Sanders wasn't gonna catch him that night?"

"Yeah."

"Which brings up the latest question," Lawson said.

"How do they have information on the whereabouts of a man I killed a year ago?"

"Right."

The two of them brainstormed for a little while and threw out some ideas at each other to try to figure everything out.

"What's the one constant in all of this?" Cain asked.

"I'm not sure."

"Who's the one person who knows me, Heather, where I live, both Kurylenko's, the missions, everything?"

Lawson thought for a second before a surprised look came over her face. "You're not suggesting what I think you are?"

"Why not?"

"Director Sanders?"

"The only person other than him who knows everything and would have the means to do something like this... is you."

"Well, I hope you've put that thought out of your head," Lawson said.

"I have."

"Well, that's a relief."

"So, we're back to the same person as before."

"I don't know, Matt."

"Who else would it be? Who else knew about Andrei? Who else could've created a fictional brother weeks later that nobody had ever heard of? Who else knew where I lived so they could take pictures of us?"

"OK, even if I agree with all of that, and it does make sense, why would he go through all of that? You're one of our best agents. Why would he want to do this to you?" Lawson asked.

"I don't know, Shelly. I just don't know. Maybe I've become a liability somehow. Did something I wasn't supposed to. That's all I can come up with."

"Well, that's all certainly plausible."

"I feel a but coming on," Cain added.

"But how are you going to prove this? I mean, this is a very delicate situation that needs some stroking. You need concrete evidence."

Cain scratched his face as he thought for a minute. "Russia," he blurted out.

"What about it?" Lawson asked.

"I need to go back. I'll take this mission and see what I can dig up."

"If this is all true, then it's quite possible, even likely, that it's a setup."

"I know. I'm counting on it. I can try to use it as a springboard toward getting some answers."

"Well, you know you can count on me for anything."

"I know. While I'm there, I can see if I can track down Yushkevitch. If he's Sanders' contact, it's possible he knows something about what's going on."

"I'll ask Sanders if he could arrange a meet with you."

"Good. If this guy knows anything, I'll get it out of him. One way or another."

31

Moscow, Russia--Cain had just stepped off the plane when his phone went off. It was Lawson. She told him she'd call him as soon as she got confirmation about a time to meet Yushkevitch.

"What do you have, Shelly?"

"Yushkevitch will meet with you in one hour on a bench inside the Moscow Metro," she told him.

"Doesn't give me much time."

"I know. Hey," she added.

"Yeah?"

"Be careful."

"I will. You're not gonna get rid of me this easy," Cain said.

"Just be sure you come home."

"I promise."

The Moscow Metro was the second most heavily traveled subway system in the world. It opened in 1935 under the leadership of Joseph Stalin and his Communist Party. The system was actually mostly built by British engineers, who were later charged with espionage because they had learned so much about the city's layout while working on the project. It opened with thirteen stations and a six-mile line and had since grown to 190 stations and a 197-mile line. It was known for being one of the most beautiful subway systems in the world with marble walls, high ceilings, mosaics, stained glass, and chandeliers. It was almost like walking through a museum.

Cain spotted Yushkevitch sitting on a bench, wearing a hat, reading a newspaper. He quickly walked over to him and sat down next to him.

"Nice to see you again," Cain mused.

"Mr. Cain," Yushkevitch replied, still reading the paper, holding it in front of his face.

"So, I hear you have information on Kurylenko's whereabouts?"

"Of course."

"Where can I find him this time?" Cain asked.

"I must say you're a persistent man. Most people would not be so interested in finding a man so dangerous as him."

"I guess I just love the danger."

"Indeed. You Americans are always such thrill seekers," Yushkevitch said.

"His location?"

"An apartment a few minutes from here."

"So how do you know he's there?" Cain asked.

"I have my ways of finding things."

"I'm sure. Are you sure he's still there?"

"Positive."

"When did you see him last?"

"He was there as of last night," Yushkevitch said, handing him a piece of paper with the address on it.

"Interesting," Cain replied, thinking about telling him he knew the truth.

"What is so interesting?"

"How do you know Sanders?"

"We have mutual contacts."

"I see."

"Something bothering you?" Yushkevitch asked.

"Actually, there is."

"What is it?"

"Well, I'm just wondering how it's possible that you saw a fictional character?" Cain asked, figuring it was time to try to get the truth out of him.

"What do you mean?" he asked, looking at Cain concerned.

"You and I both know Andrei didn't have a brother. Dmitri Kurylenko doesn't exist and never has. So, I find it puzzling that you say you saw a man as recently as last night who doesn't exist."

Yushkevitch laughed. "I don't know where you get your information, but he does exist."

"Oh, he existed in the form of Brian Chapman, the American whose face was used to perpetuate this lie."

"Well, maybe you should talk to this Chapman fellow you speak of."

"I did. I already killed him last year," Cain said. "So again, tell me how you saw, and how I'm supposed to meet, someone I killed over a year ago?"

Yushkevitch was deeply concerned at how Cain seemed to

be piecing everything together. He simply looked at him, not wanting to reveal any more information. He got up to leave but Cain grabbed his arm to prevent him from standing up. Cain pulled out his gun and jammed it into Yushkevitch's side, grabbing his paper to cover the gun.

"And considering there's no record on you, why don't you start by telling me who you really are?"

"I really don't think you're going to pull the trigger, Mr. Cain," Yushkevitch said. "Right here in a public place would not be the best of options for you."

"I got nothing to lose. If you feel like tempting fate, then you go right ahead and test me," Cain warned. "Once again, your real name?"

Yushkevitch sighed, knowing he didn't seem to have many options other than telling Cain what he wanted to know. He could tell Cain meant business and every word that came out of his mouth. Cain pushed the gun into his side a little more to spur him on.

"Mikhael Fedorov."

"Why are you using an alias?" Cain asked.

"Standard procedure."

"Standard procedure for who?"

"For who I work for."

"Who is?"

"You really expect me to tell you that?"

"Whose idea was it to come up with Dmitri Kurylenko?" Cain asked.

"I do not know," Fedorov replied, Cain shoving the gun deeper to show his displeasure with the answer.

"Gotta do better than that."

"I do not know. I just do as I have been instructed. The reasoning behind this maze was not made clear to me."

"Who do you report to?"

Fedorov sighed again.

"I swear if I have to repeat myself again you're gonna find yourself eating two pounds of lead," Cain said angrily. "I'll leave your body in a pool of blood right here in this station. So, who do you report to?"

"Sanders."

"How did you meet up with him?"

"I work for him," Fedorov said defiantly.

Cain wasn't expecting that answer as the shock on his face showed. "You're a Project Specter agent?"

"No. I'm a freelancer. He hires me when he needs something."

"Why would he do that?"

Fedorov shrugged. "Something you need to ask him. Those are reasons I do not know."

Fedorov suddenly jerked his head up and looked past Cain as if he spotted someone noteworthy. Cain turned his head to look back which gave Fedorov the opportunity he needed to get away. He knocked the gun out of Cain's hand and sprung off the bench as he ran towards the train. Cain quickly reached down for his gun before racing after Fedorov. Fedorov stood in the doorway as the open door closed just before Cain arrived. The two men stood there staring at each other through the glass, each having a stoic expression on their face. A few seconds later the train started moving and Fedorov was gone. Though he lost Fedorov, Cain was not unhappy with the developments. He at least felt like he was starting to get some answers. Though he only had Fedorov's word, for whatever that was worth, he now knew that Project Specter, or at least Director Sanders, was behind the whole ordeal. He took out the paper Fedorov handed to him and looked at the address. Maybe there were some more answers there. He equally knew it could've been some kind of trap but it was worth the risk. Cain promised Lawson that he'd keep her updated every step of the way so he gave her a call to let her know what was happening.

"Did Yushkevitch tell you anything?" Lawson asked.

"Quite a bit, actually. His real name is Mikhael Fedorov, and he's a freelance agent."

"What?"

"He told me he reports directly to Sanders. Have you ever heard of that name before?"

"No. But handlers don't usually know the agents outside of their own. He just volunteered this information to you?" Lawson asked, sounding unconvinced.

"Well, there might've been some persuasion with a gun," Cain replied.

"Are you sure he was being truthful?"

"People have a tendency to tell you the truth when you threaten to kill them."

"Wow. I don't even know what to say to that."

"Before all that went down, he gave me an address that he said Kurylenko was at as recently as last night," Cain said.

"Did you go there?"

"Not yet. I'm on my way now."

"Maybe you should back off. This doesn't sound right. If everything he said was true, then this could be a trap," Lawson said with worry.

"I know it. I have to go though. I have to see what's there."

"I know."

Cain left the subway and started walking to the apartment. It was about twenty minutes away on foot. On his way there he tried to think of the possible scenarios he might be walking into. He also realized that it was possible that Fedorov might've alerted whoever was there that he was on his way, making it an even riskier event. Once he got there, he wished he were James Bond with an arsenal of hidden, powerful weapons that he could use to his heart's content. But as it was, he had his gun and his fists. That would have to be enough. Cain waited outside the building for half an hour, hoping to see some type of movement to give him an indication of what was in store for him, but there was nothing. Finally, his impatience got the better of him and he figured it was time to make a move. He went up to the sixth floor and walked to the apartment door. He listened at the door for a few moments as he gripped his gun. He took a big sigh before taking a step back and then kicked the door open. Ready to fire, Cain was surprised to find himself alone, no guns looking back at him or staring him in the face. He walked through each room to make sure there was no one hiding or waiting for an opportunistic moment. He looked for any papers scattered around, or pictures hanging, anything that would give an indication that the place was actually being used. But there were no signs that anyone had lived there at any point in time. Dejected for the moment, he was startled when he suddenly heard a phone ringing. He looked over to the desk along the wall and walked over to it. After the fifth ring, he answered it.

"Mr. Cain, I'm sorry to disappoint you if you expected a little something more for your troubles," the voice said.

"Who is this?" Cain asked, not recognizing the voice.

"That, I can say, is of no importance. What is important is that I can be of assistance to you."

"In what way?"

"If you go into the bedroom and look under the bed, you'll see a box. The combination is 221. Open the box and you'll be blown away by what's inside," the man said, laughing hysterically as he hung up.

Cain put the phone down and walked into the bedroom, looking under the bed. He saw a small grey box and pulled it from under the bed. He looked at it intently, wondering what could be inside. He knew it could've been a trap but the curiosity of possibly finding some answers was greater than the fear of the alternative. Cain closed his eyes for a moment and then reopened them. He punched in the code and slowly opened the lid. The soft beeping upon opening told him all he needed to know without actually seeing it.

He raced out of the room and through the apartment, rushing down the hallway and running down the stairs. He wasn't sure how much time he had but he assumed it was only a few seconds before the building was leveled. It seemed like an eternity, but he made it to the ground floor and sprinted out the door. As soon as the door closed behind him he heard a blast coming from the apartment, flames shooting out the windows as they shattered. The building started crumbling within seconds as Cain was catapulted across the hood of a nearby parked car, landing on the pavement on the other side of it. He lay there motionless for a minute as he tried to shake the cobwebs loose. He slowly blinked his eyes and turned his head side to side as he licked his lips, not sure where he was for a second. After a few more seconds he began to get the feelings back in his limbs. A nearby onlooker rushed over to him to make sure he was OK and helped him to his feet. Cain assured the concerned citizen that he was fine and brushed himself off, thanking the man for his assistance. Parts of the building were still standing but the side of the apartment the bomb was in was torn apart. Cain wondered how many people inside and had lost their lives as a result.

32

New York---Cain had just stepped off the flight and was getting his bag when his text message ringer started going off. He assumed it was Lawson, wanting him to check in, or even Heather. He was surprised to see it was a number that he wasn't familiar with. He was almost floored when he read the message.

It read: "I know everything. Your real name, the girl and kid in the photo, Kurylenko, why your girlfriend was shot, and the person behind it all. I'll be in touch shortly."

Cain stopped walking and sat on a bench to try to comprehend everything. He tried to send a return message, but it came back as blocked. He called Lawson to see if she could run a trace on the number.

"Hey, can you run taps on this number?" Cain asked, giving it to her.

"Sure, what's up?"

"I just got a text message from that number saying they knew everything that was going on."

"Really? What else did they say?" Lawson asked.

"That was basically it. They said they'd be in touch shortly. Might help if we can figure out who it is ahead of time to see if they really know or if it's just someone blowing smoke up my ass."

"I'll get right on it."

"Thanks."

Lawson got right to work on tracking down the phone number. She used every means the agency had at their disposal to find who it belonged to but it was a worthless effort. Whoever it was had used extreme caution and knew exactly how to remain untraceable. By the time Cain got home she called him with the regrettable news. He'd just barely gotten himself settled, not home for more than five minutes, when he eagerly took her call.

"So, it looks like whoever it was is pretty sophisticated," Lawson said.

"How so?" Cain asked.

"Well, it's a prepaid number that I tracked to a New York location. The message was sent from a shopping mall, not much chance of finding him."

"How about surveillance from the mall?"

"We can tap into the surveillance feed and feed it through the facial scan but that won't tell us much. Even if we get some hits, it doesn't mean they sent the message," she explained.

"Figures. What about a trace on other calls or anything?"

"No, it's no good. It was bought two days ago at a Staples store, paid in cash, and there's no video in that store. There's no history of any other calls or messages that we can tell. Looks like it was purchased just for you."

"Well, at least we know it's someone local," Cain said.

"True, but we don't have anything else to go on. We'll have to wait until he makes his next move."

It didn't take long for that next move to come to fruition. The next day, as Cain and Heather were eating lunch, his phone rang. He was somewhat shocked that he was hearing back from the person so soon and that he was actually calling and not just giving him a message.

"Hello," Cain answered, hope evident in his voice.

"Mr. Cain, are you somewhere where you can talk right now?" the digitally altered voice asked.

"Yes. I'm at home," he replied, looking at Heather, who was intently watching him as he conversed.

"Good."

"How do I know I can trust you? I mean, deception seems to be a fact of life for me these days. How do I know you're any different?"

"You don't. And you shouldn't. At least not right now. I wouldn't trust anyone right now either if I were you."

"You said you had all the answers that I'm looking for."

"I do. Not now though."

"Why not?" Cain asked.

"I'm trying to stay off the phone as much as possible. The longer we talk the more they'll be able to trace me through you."

"Who are you?"

"We don't need to go into that. Let's just say I'm on your side," he told him.

"If you really do know everything, why are you doing this?"

"Because I don't like what's been done to you. You deserve to know the truth. You've been deceived from the moment you had your surgery in that army hospital."

"So, who's behind it?" Cain asked.

"You already have your suspicions. In a few more days you'll have your answers and the proof."

"When can you tell me everything?"

"In two or three days. First, I'm working on a backup plan to ensure my survival if this gets found out. I've contacted a reporter with the *New York Times* and am meeting with him tomorrow to go over all of my findings. Not just of you, but the entire Specter Project. If something happens to me, I will instruct him to contact you so you can pick up where I left off. His name is Roger Falk."

"I can help you now."

"No, they might be watching your place. That's all I can say for the moment. I have to go before they get a beat on me. I'll be in touch," the man told Cain.

Cain stood there for a few moments, his phone still pressed to his ear as he struggled to comprehend everything he was just told. Heather was still watching his every move and could tell he just received some major news.

"So, what's going on?" Heather asked.

"He said I'd know everything in two or three days. That'd he'd have proof of everything."

"That's great. Finally, a break."

"He said he was contacting a reporter in case anything happened to him," Cain added.

Waiting for a few days was going to be excruciating for Cain, knowing that all the answers he'd been looking for could be laid out in front of him. Heather did what she could to keep his mind from locking in to that and tried to keep him relaxed, no matter how difficult it was. Cain avoided all contact with anyone other than Heather because he didn't want to get distracted from the meeting and possibly get caught up in something else. He simply told Lawson he was going to be unavailable for a couple of days so he and Heather could relax and get some rest. Whatever he did worked as the time seemed to fly by. Three days went by and he woke up that morning hoping he'd hear from the mystery man. Cain had just finished taking a shower and was drying off when he heard his phone ringing. He bolted into the bedroom, not even bothering to put clothes on, to answer the call.

"It looks like today's the day," the man told Cain. "Are you able to meet?"

"Just name a time and place and I'll be there."

"Train station at twelve. Get on the train that's headed for Baltimore. I'll be in the third car wearing a white Mets hat, blue David Wright jersey, and a copy of yesterday's *New York Times*."

"I'll be there."

"I'll give you three minutes. If you're not there three minutes after twelve then I'll assume there were complications and I'll be gone," he warned.

"Don't worry, I'll be there," Cain said.

Cain finished getting dressed and told Heather what was going down. They spent the next hour going over plans to make sure Cain got there in time. He was starting to feel paranoid that maybe the apartment was being watched. They'd have to come up with a diversion to make sure that when he left, he wouldn't be followed. They anxiously stared at the clock, seemingly watching every minute tick away. Once eleven o'clock came around, they started getting ready. They left the building with the assumption that Cain would be followed. Cain noticed a car across the street with two men sitting inside.

"All right, let's stick to the plan," Cain told Heather.

"OK."

"Sure you're up for this?"

Heather answered him with a kiss. "Be careful."

"Always."

The two of them got in their SUV and drove off.

"They're on the move," one of the men radioed in.

"Stay with them," a man replied.

They continued following the pair through several streets, side streets, and detours. Cain could see the car tailing them the entire way. He toyed with them for about ten minutes before he decided they weren't going to lose them this way. He stuck to the plan and drove to a nearby cab company. They parked and went into the office.

"My name's Cain. I called earlier," he told the person at the desk.

"We've been waiting for you. We have five cabs ready to go," the person replied.

"Fantastic. Thank you," Cain said, handing over a credit card. "I really appreciate it."

"Thank you, sir. It's not every day we get to charge a thousand dollars."

"It's worth it for what I need. Two hundred per driver for a ten-minute drive."

"Come with me and I'll introduce you to your driver," he told Cain.

He led Cain to the garage, where all five cabs were waiting for the go ahead. All the drivers were standing against the driver side door of their cabs, ready for their instructions.

"I know you've all been informed of what's happening but I just want to reinforce how critical it is that you all head away from the train station. If you're stopped or pulled over, you don't know me, never met me, and have no idea what they're talking about. Don't worry, you're in no danger. Any questions?" Cain asked.

The drivers all got into their cabs, ready to execute their missions. They were all pretty excited about it; it was something more interesting than their usual mundane routines of picking up fares and dropping them off.

"This is Mike Patel."

"Glad to know you," Cain said, shaking his hand.

"Mike knows the best ways to the train station. Short cuts, alternate routes, he's the best man to get you there quickly."

"Excellent."

"Ready to go?" Patel asked.

"Let's get it done," Cain replied.

He turned to Heather and gave her a kiss.

"I wish I was going with you," she said.

"I'll call you when I'm done. You'll be OK?"

"Don't worry."

Cain got into the back seat of the cab and lay down on the floor.

"If you see a black Cadillac following us, let me know," Cain said.

"Don't worry. This isn't my first rodeo trying to lose someone," Patel responded. "We'll give them the slip."

The two men in the car were still waiting outside the cab company. They called in to let Sanders know what was happening.

"They're still inside," one of them said.

"Give it a few more minutes, then go in and check," Sanders replied. "He's up to something."

They never got the chance to check as a few minutes later all the cars came zooming into the street. One by one they raced off. Heather was in the lead in the SUV, followed by the five cabs, with Cain in the second one.

"Oh, shit," the man bellowed.

"What's happening?" Sanders asked.

"The SUV and five cabs just came roaring out. Who do we follow?"

"Who's in the SUV?"

"Looked like just the girl."

"Forget her. He's in one of the cabs."

"Which one do we pick?"

"Just pick one and hope you're right," Sanders told them.

"Pick that one," the man told the driver, pointing to the fourth one. He figured Cain wouldn't be in the last one as it'd be the easiest to follow. The plan worked to perfection as there were too many cars moving in different directions for their followers to keep up with them. Patel got Cain to the train station in about twenty minutes, plenty of time for Cain's meeting. Cain got out of the cab and thanked Patel for his service.

"My pleasure," Patel said, writing his number down on a piece of paper. He handed it to Cain.

"What's this?"

"If you ever need me again, this is where you'll find me."

"Thanks again," Cain replied, putting Patel's number in his pocket. "I'm sure you'll hear from me at some point in the future."

Cain went to the ticket booth and bought a pass to board the train. He looked at the time and he still had ten minutes to wait. He kept looking around, almost waiting for someone to jump out at him. He stayed alert until the time hit noon. They called for the final boarding on the train to Baltimore and Cain got on. He boarded the second car and instantly looked for his contact. His gun was stuffed inside his belt and he kept one hand on the handle just in case he would need to use it in a hurry. He walked the length of the car until he spotted a man wearing the Mets hat and jersey. He was seated at the end with his arms folded and head down as if he were sleeping. Cain sat down next to him and started talking as he looked at the rest of the passengers.

"You have something for me?" Cain asked.

Cain waited a minute for him to respond but got no answer. He looked over to him, wondering why he was staying silent. He put his hand on the man's forearm and instantly felt some type of liquid on his fingers. Cain pulled his hand off the man's arm and rubbed his fingers together. The blood dripped down off his fingers and Cain took a closer look at the man. He unfolded the man's arms which were becoming redder by the second. The man's arms flopped down to his sides and Cain noticed two bullet holes in his chest. Cain took the sunglasses off the man's face, flipped his hat off, and tilted his head back to see his identity. He was taken aback when he saw Bill Heyward, the analyst he'd worked with several times. Cain went through Heyward's pockets and looked around him to see if he had any documents with him. He came up empty. If he had anything with him, whoever killed him took them. Cain was so intent on trying to find something that he didn't notice the onlooking crowd. He was finally alerted when he heard a nearby woman scream in horror at the scene in front of her. Cain saw several people staring at him and heard a couple people calling 911 on their phones. He knew the police would be there any minute. He knew he couldn't stay. He was going to become the prime suspect, and he'd have a hard time talking his way out of it. With Heyward's death, he knew that the agency wanted him gone. If he stayed, he knew that they'd see to it that he hung for this. The only thing he could do was flee.

33

Cain spent the hour after Heyward's death wandering around the streets, trying to stay low. He knew his picture would be up everywhere as a person of interest since there were cameras at the station. He wasn't sure where he could go to lie low but knew he couldn't go home. He walked to a nearby clothing store to buy a baseball hat, sunglasses, and a new shirt, hoping that would help to disguise him, at least for a little while. It was only temporary until he could figure things out more clearly. He figured he should call Heather to let her know what was going on.

"Hey sweety, how'd it go?" she asked.

"It didn't."

"What? He didn't show?"

"It turned out to be Heyward. He was dead when I got there," Cain said.

"Oh my God."

"I can only assume the agency knows what was going on and killed him before he had a chance to tell me anything."

"So, what are you gonna do?"

"If they knew what Heyward was gonna tell me I have to assume they're coming after me next. They'll pin his murder on me since I was there at the station," he said.

"This can't be happening," Heather cried.

"I can't go back home. I'm gonna have to figure something out. I'm gonna need to get a new phone too or else they'll track me down through this," Cain said.

"So, when am I gonna see you?"

"I don't know. I don't know how I'll get in touch with you but I will soon. Just wait for me, OK?"

"What if they come after me?" Heather asked, worried.

"Go to your sister's."

"I haven't seen or talked to her in over five years."

"Just explain to her what's going on and see if you can stay there for a while," Cain said. "Leave as soon as you can."

"OK. I love you."

"Love you too. I'll find a way. I promise."

Cain walked to the park and sat on a bench to contemplate his next course of action. He kept his head down just in case there was a roving patrol that came by. He wondered how it could've come to this so fast. Just a short time before he was hopeful of getting all the answers he needed to figure out his past and who was after him. Now, all that seemed to be gone. Now there were even more questions. He was a little startled when his phone started ringing. He hesitated to look at it, not sure he wanted to see who it was. He figured it wasn't Heather since they'd just spoken, but checked anyway, just in case it was her. It was Lawson. He wondered if she was in on everything.

Cain thought about not answering and letting it go to voicemail but picked up at the last minute, curious of what she knew.

"Hey," Cain answered.

"What the hell is going on?!" she asked.

"Don't you know?"

"I just got a call from Sanders saying you just went rogue. That you killed one of our analysts inside a train and now you're on the run," she hurriedly said.

"The mysterious text I got was from Heyward. He instructed me to meet him at the train station where he'd give me all the information about what was going on. I went there to meet him and he was dead when I got there," Cain told her.

Silence swept over both ends of the phone as Cain wasn't sure what else to tell her and Lawson wasn't sure what else she could do to help.

"Were you in on this, Shelly?" Cain asked bluntly.

"What?"

"I need to know."

"How could you even ask that?!" she asked defiantly.

"I don't know who I can trust now."

"When you went missing in Syria, I was the one who kept looking for you when nobody else did. I was the one who kept on tracking down leads for you on Kurylenko. I was the one who went to check on Heather when you weren't there. I have always been the one constant who's always tried to help you. How could you even think that I've turned my back on you and had a hand in setting you up or framing you?"

"I'm sorry. I just don't know what to think now."

"It's OK. We can talk about that later. Let's just use our heads and think."

"Wait a minute," Cain said.

"What? You got something?"

"Heyward said he was contacting a reporter in case he was killed. I need to find him."

"You better do it quickly. If they know who he contacted, and if they don't, they will soon enough, they'll kill him next," Lawson warned.

"Do me a favor?"

"Sure."

"I sent Heather to her sister's. Can you just keep an eye on her and make sure nothing happens?"

"Of course. Don't worry about her. If I hear something, I'll move her."

"Thanks."

"What are you gonna do?" she asked.

"Find this reporter. I'm gonna have to ditch this phone. I'll contact you later when I have some answers."

Cain figured his only other option at that point was to find the reporter and see if Heyward had already given him the documents he had. He knew he had to do it quickly because Sanders would have the reporter killed as soon as he learned of his involvement. Because he knew he probably didn't have a lot of time at his disposal, he figured the surest way to keep Sanders away from the reporter was to create a diversion. Give him something else he wanted more. That would be him. He took out his phone once more and scrolled down to Sanders' name. He sighed before his thumb hit the call button. It only rang two times before Sanders picked up.

"I must admit I'm a little surprised at this phone call," Sanders began, motioning to an analyst to start tracing it.

"Not as surprised as I am."

"Are you looking to turn yourself in?"

"So, why'd you do it?" Cain asked.

"Do what?"

"Set me up."

"I don't know what you're talking about," Sanders replied.

"Oh, yes, you do. You've been behind everything, haven't you? The entire time."

"I think all the excitement has gone to your head and giving you delusional thoughts."

"I don't think so. When you suggested having Heather killed, that was a warning to me, wasn't it? Eliminate her or eliminate the both of us," Cain stated.

"Couldn't be further from the truth."

"Gonna lie to the bitter end, huh?"

"Why don't you come in and we'll talk about it?" Sanders asked.

"If I come in, I'll never see the light of day again."

"You know if you stay out there that this can only end one way," Sanders warned.

"You created Dmitri Kurylenko to make it seem like it wasn't you. You tried to kill Heather for some reason and then you killed Heyward because he knew the truth," Cain said.

"Even if that were all true it doesn't matter now. You know you're not going to be able to escape."

"Who said I was looking to escape?" Cain said, putting his phone down on the bench without hanging up.

Cain knew they were tracing the call and figured he'd make it easier for them. He had to lose the phone anyway, so by leaving it, they'd track it to the park and give him the time he needed to get to the reporter.

Sanders dispatched a security team to the park's location. He knew Cain wasn't likely to reveal his position like that unless he had something up his sleeve so he told the team to use caution. While waiting for them to report back when they'd arrived at the park, Sanders had Cain's information pulled up.

"Get into the system and freeze his bank account," Sanders told an analyst.

"Pulling it up now," the analyst replied, looking at the information. "Uh, there's a small problem."

"What problem?"

"There's no point in freezing his account."

"Why not?" Sanders asked.

"There's no money in it," the analyst explained. "Well, fifty dollars, but I assume you don't care about that?"

"Fifty dollars?! How can that be? Pull it up again."

"It's still the same."

"He's made a couple million over the last couple years. How can he only have fifty dollars? What's he been spending it on?"

"Doesn't look like anything."

"Say again?"

"Going over his records it looks like he's been withdrawing fifty thousand every two weeks for the last two years."

"Great." Sanders sighed, knowing that would make tracking him harder. "That means he's got enough cash to hold out for years."

"I would say he most likely opened a different account that was untraceable," the analyst offered.

"Any way to figure out where that account might be?" Sanders asked, hoping for a positive response.

"Unless he opened it in his name, or one of his aliases, it's gonna be really tough. Probably impossible."

"Any other way?"

"Banks have security cameras that we can try to pull footage from. That's gonna take a lot of time to go through every bank in the city's camera system though. And the odds of finding him are not strong. If he was smart enough to be doing this, I would bet he used some type of disguise to hide his face so as not to be recognized by anything."

"It's all we got right now. Do it."

"You got it."

"Keep me updated," Sanders said.

It took the security team about twenty minutes to reach the park. They tracked the location of the phone and took the necessary safety steps to ensure they weren't being ambushed. After they secured the area and were sure that Cain was no longer there they informed Sanders of their findings. He wasn't surprised that Cain was gone but wasn't sure what else he had in mind. Sanders wasn't sure if Cain was just toying with them by leaving the phone and irritating them by coming after it, or if it was just part of a larger scheme he had. Sanders continued going over information in The Room with the analysts when Lawson burst in, looking for a confrontation.

"Can I talk to you for a minute, sir?" she sternly asked.

Sanders hesitated, slightly surprised at her presence. "We do have a lot going on here."

"It'll only take a few minutes."

"Certainly," Sanders said after taking a few seconds to think it over. He directed everyone to keep going with what they were doing while he was gone.

Sanders led Lawson into his office. He sat down at his desk and waited for Lawson to get out what was on her mind.

"I talked to Cain a little while ago," Lawson told him.

"And?"

"He proclaims his innocence. He said Heyward was dead when he got there.'"

"And you believe him?" Sanders asked.

"I have to. He's never lied to me before."

"Well, this is also a unique situation that hasn't occurred before."

"I don't believe he did this."

"There is footage of him at the station," Sanders stated.

"I'd like to see it," Lawson said, not believing the implications.

"It's still being analyzed right now."

"Still being analyzed? It's either him or it isn't."

"There are some other things we're looking at," Sanders replied.

"Such as?"

"Such as things I'm not at liberty to discuss. It's above your level right now."

"Above my level? I am Matthew Cain's handler. I should be included in every detail that involves him," she said, her voice rising.

"I'm beginning to wonder if your loyalty to your agent is a bit blinded," Sanders said. "Your first loyalty should be to this agency, not an individual."

"I would like access to all of his files," Lawson stated.

"Absolutely not."

"Maybe I can use it to our advantage."

"I fail to see how it'd be of any use to you," Sanders said.

"I want to be in on finding him."

"I'm not sure that'd be a good idea. You have other agents to take care of. You have to accept that one of them has gone rogue. It's happened before. You deal with it and move on."

"I'm not sure I can do that," Lawson replied.

"You better learn to do that. Matthew Cain has a KOS order on him now and there's nothing you can do about it."

"Don't do that," she pleaded.

"Shelly, he killed a government agent. You know as well as I do that when that happens a KOS order is automatic. It can't be changed," Sanders said.

"You're in charge. You can change anything if you wanted to."

"But I don't want to," Sanders told her. "Listen, I can tell it's tough for you to wrap your head around this. It's happened so suddenly. I know you've been through some tough times with him, we all have, but you have to accept reality. If you want to take a few days to get your head right, you're more than welcome to."

Lawson knew her pleas were falling on deaf ears and angrily stormed out of the office. She wasn't surprised that Sanders shot down her offers for help. If he really was the one behind everything he wasn't about to let anyone help Cain in his quest for the truth. But she did hope that Sanders would agree to her request out of courtesy, even if he didn't expect her to do much. She paced up and down the hallway until she saw Sanders leave his office and go back into the analyst's room. As soon as he was out of sight, Lawson approached his secretary with a bold idea.

"Hi, Mary," Lawson said in a very friendly manner.

"Hi, Shelly. What can I do for you?"

"Umm, I'm gonna ask you for a favor that's completely against protocol and you'll probably say no."

"Try it on me."

"I need to get into Sanders' safe," Lawson said.

"What? I can't do that."

"You know the code, don't you?"

"That's irrelevant. He would kill me if I did that without his knowledge and approval," Mary said.

"That's why he won't find out."

"I'm sorry, Shelly. I can't do that."

"How much do you know about what's going on right now with Matthew Cain?" Lawson asked.

"I know what I've been told."

"That's just it. I don't think what you've been told is the truth. I know him. I know he didn't do what they're accusing him of."

"There's a camera in there, you know," Mary stated.

"I actually did not know that. Can you disable it?"

"Well, yes, I can, but that's not the point."

"You're right, it's not the point. The point is that I think he's being set up by this agency. I think Heyward found out something and was gonna give it to Cain and when they found out about it, Sanders had him killed and framed Cain," Lawson said.

"And you think what's in that safe will prove it?"

"I don't know for sure. But it's a start."

Mary continued sitting at her desk in silence, unsure about letting Lawson in. She needed more convincing for her to aid in helping someone break into her boss' safe.

"If we do nothing and they kill him, and it later comes out that he actually was innocent, how would you feel knowing you had a chance to clear an innocent man and didn't?" Lawson said, appealing to her.

Mary sighed. Lawson finally pushed her over the edge. "You sure know how to hit a girl beneath the belt."

"So, you'll help?" Lawson asked, hoping.

"I can disable the camera for two minutes. Anything longer than that and security will get suspicious."

"Be in and out before you know it."

"The code is 2212," Mary told her, disabling the camera through her computer. "You've got two minutes."

Lawson hurried into the office and immediately went to the safe, putting the code in and unlocking it. She quickly took out all the files and put them on the desk to rifle through. The files were in reverse alphabetical order. She saw Raines' name on one of them. She stopped for a second, curious as to what it contained, but quickly moved on. As curious as she was, Raines would have to wait. Lawson knew she didn't have enough time to go through every folder that piqued her interest. She only had time for Cain's. She finally found his and opened it, laying it on the desk. She took pictures of every piece of paper with her phone. She didn't read any of the information yet. At that time she was only concerned with getting a picture of everything for her to look over later. Lawson finished a minute later and put everything back in the safe and locked it up. She rushed out of the room and nodded at Mary as she walked down the hall, just a few seconds before the two-minute mark. Mary immediately turned the camera on again and went back to work as if nothing happened.

Lawson went into her office and locked the door. She sat down, plugged a USB cord into her phone and transferred the pictures to her computer. She eagerly read each document, most of which contained the information on Cain's transformation from Thomas Nelson to Matthew Cain. Just when she started thinking that there was nothing to be gained from his file, she froze, stunned by what she'd just read. She stopped and read the passage again from the beginning. She stopped and reread the page five more times, almost like she expected the words to change and say something else the next time she read it. She couldn't believe what was appearing on the screen in front of her.

"Oh my God," she said.

34

Cain stopped in front of the *Times* building and looked up at it, amazed at the sheer size of the skyscraper. It was a 52-story building that housed the *Times*, real estate companies, and some law firms. There was also an auditorium and banquet hall on the first floor. He walked into the building and asked the receptionist where he could find Roger Falk. She directed him to the fourteenth floor. He bypassed the elevator as usual and used the stairs. Once Cain reached the fourteenth floor, he looked around for Falk's desk. Since he didn't know Falk by sight, he was at a little bit of a disadvantage. After a few minutes of unsuccessfully searching, he asked the closest person near him.

"Excuse me?" he asked someone searching through a file cabinet.

"Yes?"

"Could you tell me where I can find Roger Falk?"

"Depends who's looking for him."

"Oh, my name's Bill. I was supposed to meet with him on a story but I've never met him before so I don't know what he looks like," Cain said.

"Oh, OK. Well," the man replied, looking around. "Looks like he's about to get into the elevator over there."

Cain hurried over to the elevator, hoping to get to Falk before he reached it. The elevator doors slid open and Falk stood to the side so a few people could get off. Cain snuck up behind Falk and locked arms with him, spinning him around and walking toward the stairs.

"Excuse me, who are you and what are you doing?" Falk asked, agitated.

"My name's Matthew Cain and we have to go."

"Go? Go where? Do I know you?"

"I believe you have something that interests me," Cain said.

"I'm not going anywhere with you," Falk said, stopping and breaking Cain's grasp of his arm.

"I know you met with Bill Heyward," Cain revealed.

"Cain. You're the agent he was telling me about. He, uh, didn't tell me your name. But he said if something happened to him that you'd be making an appearance. Is he um..."

"Dead? Yeah."

Falk sighed. "Oh, man."

"So, we have to go now before they realize that he met with you."

"I'm not going into hiding," Falk objected.

"Just for a couple of days until we figure things out."

"I can publish what I have now. They can't touch me."

"Listen, they will kill you once they know who they're dealing with," Cain bluntly said.

"So, what do we do then?" Falk asked.

"Right now, we need to find a place to lay low for a day or two so we can figure out our next move without panicking or rushing into something."

"OK."

Cain led Falk to the stairwell, and the pair started walking down the stairs. Falk adjusted his backpack, which was slung over his right shoulder. He used the backpack to carry most of the stories and ideas that he was working on.

"Umm, can you tell me why we're going down the stairs when we could just take the elevator?" Falk asked.

"I hate elevators."

"Any particular reason why?"

"Sure is."

"Mind telling me what it is?"

"Never know who or what's gonna be waiting beyond those doors when they open," Cain told him.

"How do I know you're not the one who killed Heyward?"

"Because I say I didn't."

"Not to be difficult, but how do I know I can trust you?" Falk asked.

"Because if I wanted to kill you you'd be dead already."

"So, do you have any idea where we're going?"

"Let me use your phone," Cain said.

Falk handed him his cell phone and Cain dialed a number as they kept walking.

"Can you meet us at the corner of 43rd?" Cain asked. After getting a positive reply, he hung up and gave the phone back to Falk.

"Who are we meeting?" Falk asked.

"A contact of mine. We can't just walk around the streets. They'd eventually spot us."

After a few minutes of briskly going down the flight of steps, they finally reached the ground floor. Falk was a little out of breath, not used to the physical activity. He was a slender man, in his mid-forties, with black hair and greying temples. He couldn't wait to get to work on this story since he thought it could've been his big break. Falk wasn't usually assigned to the big stories and usually wound up working on the background stuff. If he could break a major story like this about a secret government agency, it could catapult him into a lead story writer. Once the two of them hit the lobby, Cain went first to make sure everything was clear. If not, at least he was armed well enough to put up a fight. With no obstructions in sight, the two of them left the building and walked toward their destination.

"Keep your head down," Cain told him. "Tougher to get a look at your face."

"Do you think they're here?"

"They will be soon enough. And trust me, you don't wanna meet them."

Once they reached 43rd street, they waited inside a small bookstore until Cain's contact arrived. Cain stood near the front window so he could see the street and pretended to look through a book. After fifteen minutes flew by Cain started to get a little anxious. His contact said he'd be there in ten minutes. Cain wondered what was holding him up. He was about to call him again when Cain saw him pull up to the curb.

"Let's go," Cain told Falk.

"That's what we're waiting for? A taxi?"

The pair got in the back seat, Cain giving the driver a tap on the shoulder as a greeting and in appreciation.

"Nice to see you again," the driver said. "I didn't think it'd be so soon though."

"I didn't either, Mike."

"What happened? It's all over the news about a man getting shot at the train station," Patel said.

"He was dead when I got there. They're trying to make it look like I did it," Cain explained.

"Wait a minute. I heard about the train station murder. That was you they were talking about?" Falk asked.

"Yeah. I went there to meet Heyward to get the documents he had. He was dead already, and the documents were gone."

"That's a shame. He seemed like a decent guy when I met with him."

"Did he give you the documents?" Cain asked.

"He gave me something sealed in an envelope," Falk said.

"Did you open it?"

"No. He said don't open it until I heard from him again or if something happens."

"Do you have it?"

"It's in my backpack," Falk said.

"As soon as we stop somewhere, we'll take a look at it," Cain responded.

"Where to, my friend?" Patel asked.

"I'm not sure. We have to hold up somewhere for a day or two. They're gonna hit surveillance cameras at buses, trains, planes, and be on the lookout for hotels probably too."

"I think I know of a spot," Patel said.

"Go ahead," Cain replied.

"It's a small motel on the other side of the border, in Jersey. It's a little shady, a lot of people use it for drug transactions and prostitutes and things like that, but I don't think it's a spot they'd look for you."

"Sounds good. Seems perfect. Can you take us there?" Cain asked.

"Of course. It will take us about an hour to get there," Patel told them.

"So, what are we gonna do?" Falk turned to ask Cain. "We can't stay at some cheap hotel forever."

"We'll open up the envelope and see what kind of information Heyward had. Then we'll go from there."

Cain kept looking out the window, his eyes focused on the road for any sign of problems. Every now and then his mind wandered to thoughts of Heather. He hoped she was making out OK. He figured she was safe, for a little while at least. Cain assumed they'd leave her be for the time being, that he was their main priority. But it occurred to him that if they were unsuccessful in finding him after a few days or a week, that they may turn their attention towards her. If she was staying with her sister, it wouldn't be a hard thing for Sanders to trace. They could either try to use her as bait to lure him out into the open, or extract any information from her that they could. Or they could just eliminate her. In any scenario that played through Cain's head, he knew he was going to have to get her relatively soon. She wasn't going to be able to fend off the agency alone or stay ahead of them without help.

After an hour of straight driving, they finally reached their destination. The motel looked pretty much like Patel had described it. There was some graffiti on a wall, a broken bench in front, and a sign that was partially off and hanging down. It did look a little better in the daytime though. It was a small motel that housed sixteen rooms. Cain and Falk bid their friendly taxi driver goodbye as they went to the office to rent a room. Cain checked in under an alias and used the name Jerry Anderson.

"Couldn't have used something original like Smith or Jones?" Falk teased.

"I strive to be different," Cain replied.

The pair went to their room and Cain immediately locked the door and closed the windows and curtains. Falk put his backpack on a small round table near the wall and pulled out the envelope he got from Heyward. Falk opened it and split the papers in half for each of them to read. They each eagerly read the documents, fascinated by the information contained in it.

"Wow. This is really good stuff," Falk stated after five minutes of reading.

Cain could tell Falk read something that either bothered him or was really interesting as he kept shifting positions. Falk was making faces and squirming in his seat, leading Cain to believe he found something disturbing. Falk looked up at Cain briefly before going back to reading, but it was tough for him to keep concentrating without telling Cain what it was. He wasn't sure the best way to tell Cain about it so he just decided to let him read it for himself.

"You might want to take a look at this," Falk said, handing the papers to Cain.

Cain hesitated before taking them. He looked at the papers and then Falk. "What's in it?" Cain asked.

"It's probably better if you read it for yourself."

Cain took his advice and started reading, though he wasn't looking forward to whatever it was Falk was referring to. He assumed it was something bad that he'd probably wished he hadn't read. He finished reading the first page without anything jumping out at him and then turned it over to move on to the next page. There it was. The entire history that the agency had on him. He read it quickly, wanting to see everything at a moment's notice while still trying to slow down and decipher what it was saying. Cain felt a mix of happiness, sadness, anger, and rage all at the same time. While it felt good to finally know the truth about his past, he was beyond enraged at the fact the agency had been deceiving him the entire time he'd been with them. Instead of helping him with his memory loss and remembering his past, they contributed in trying to destroy it. With each line read, his eyes widened, his fists clenched, and his jaw tightened. Falk watched as Cain read the information about himself and saw the anger boiling over. While he assumed Cain was a good man, since he was helping him, he felt sorry for what the Specter Project had done to him. Falk could see that he was a man who you got out of the way from when he was angry. Cain reread the pages on himself a few times, letting it sink in, getting angrier each time he read it. He focused in on one part:

Name: Matthew Cain

Also known as: Thomas Nelson

Real name: Justin Clifford

Family: Wife, Deanna; Son, Justin Jr.

He could hardly believe what he was reading. All along he'd been told he had no family. Nobody at home to help him overcome his memory loss when he was shot in the head. It was the only reason he agreed to join the agency to begin with. He had no other options. Now he knew it was all a lie. Not everything, as they were truthful about his parents being killed when he graduated high school, leading him to join the military. He had no brothers or sisters as he'd been told. But it was right there in black and white.

He was married with a son. And Nelson wasn't even his real name either. Sanders even fabricated that. Cain knew he probably never would've been able to uncover all of this on his own. He thought of Heyward's demise and felt a sense of sorrow for him, while still being thankful and appreciative of what he'd done for him.

"I'm, uh, sorry for what you've been through," Falk said.

"Thanks. We don't have time for that though," Cain responded, trying not to seem depressed over it. "Now we need to figure out how to bring them down while staying alive."

"Well, with all of this I can write a story and submit it. Might take a few days."

"We don't have that kind of time. We need to fax this to members of the media, Congress, the Senate, that will ensure our survival."

"But that would kill my story. This is my chance to make a name for myself," Falk objected.

"You won't have a story if you're dead," Cain told him.

"Give me two days. Just two days."

Though it was against his better judgment, Cain agreed to give Falk two days even though it might mean their lives. Cain pulled out the phone Raines had given him and wondered how untraceable it really was. He was about to find out.

"Who are you calling?" Falk asked, seeing Cain dial a number.

"Ed Sanders."

"What? Umm, is that the same Ed Sanders that I'm reading about in here?" Falk nervously asked.

"I don't know any others."

"Are you crazy?" Falk asked, getting a cold stare from Cain in response. "Well, what I mean is, won't he trace the call? I mean,

I'm obviously not as up to date on all this spy stuff as you, but it seems like that would be common practice."

"The phone's not traceable," Cain told him.

"Oh."

"Satisfied?" Cain asked sarcastically.

"If you had that phone the whole time, how come you had to use mine to call the cab?"

"Forgot about it," Cain replied with a shrug.

"I think it's still risky."

"Riskier than giving you two days?"

"Point taken," Falk replied, going back to the documents. "Don't mind me; I'll just keep going over this stuff. Just pretend I'm not here."

"Already have."

Calling Sanders again probably wasn't the smartest thing to do, even if the phone wasn't traceable. Though he wasn't totally positive it couldn't be traced, he only had Raines' word for it, he was prepared for the consequences if it wasn't. Cain was still seething about what Sanders had done to him, and took away from him, and he wanted him to know he now knew the truth. He hesitated before pushing the call button, making sure it was really what he wanted to do. He only paused for a couple seconds before finally pushing the button. He anxiously waited for Sanders to pick up as it rang for the third time. Cain wasn't sure what he was going to say but figured his anger would take over.

"Hello?" Sanders answered, wary of who was on the other end of the line. It came up as a private number, which always made him uneasy when he didn't know who it was.

"Justin Clifford," Cain calmly stated.

"I see you've been busy," Sanders replied, snapping his fingers at an analyst to get the call traced.

"My real name is Justin Clifford. I had a wife and a son, you son of a bitch," Cain said angrily.

"Let's not get irrational. Why don't you come in and we can talk about it nice and calm?"

"I had a family, and you took that away from me!"

"To them you were already dead. What kind of life would you have had with a family you couldn't remember?"

"They could've helped me remember! Why me? Why choose me?"

"Because you were a perfect candidate. You had a significant injury, you couldn't remember a thing, and were unlikely to ever remember. You still wouldn't know, and never would, if not for whatever Heyward gave you," Sanders said. "I needed agents. You were an elite trained soldier who didn't remember his past. I couldn't have asked for a better or more ideal situation. You still remembered your skills which meant training time was very little."

"If I could reach through this phone right now, I would strangle the life right out of you," Cain seethed.

"I know you would. It's the little details that make you who you are. One of the things I love about you is that you don't make idle threats."

"If it's the last thing I do, I'm gonna make you pay for what you've done to me."

"You may think I took your life away, but that's not true. I gave you a life," Sanders explained. "I gave you a job. I gave you money. I gave you an apartment. You wound up with a girlfriend. What do you think you would've had if you just went back home?"

"A family who loved me," Cain replied.

"You would've had nothing. No money, no job, and a family who would've been frustrated that you couldn't even recognize them which would've eventually led to a divorce. It seems to me like I saved you a lot of heartache."

"You've got a lot of gall."

"I didn't get to my position by being soft. I make hard decisions that can impact a lot of lives. I do what's best for this agency and this country. That's the only thing that matters," Sanders said. "If some people get hurt along the way, well, that's just the way it goes."

"How many other people have you done this to?" Cain asked.

"That's irrelevant. You were a special case."

Sanders looked over to the analyst and threw his arms up, wondering how they were making out with the trace. The analyst replied with a shake of his head and a painful-looking expression, letting Sanders know they were having a hard time.

"So, how are we going to solve this little problem we have here?" Sanders asked.

"How about you stand in the middle of Times Square and I'll blow your head off? I think that'd solve everything."

"Well, outside of that there are some things that may sway your opinion."

"Nothing could change my opinion," Cain said.

"I wouldn't be so sure of that. I know you've got some files you shouldn't have and I know you've got a reporter with you."

"I don't see the problem."

"The problem is that I'm sure you're probably planning on doing something stupid with that information and reporter. I'm sure you're equally aware that I'm not gonna let that happen."

"That's your problem," Cain said.

"No, it's yours. But just to show you there's no hard feelings between us, I'm gonna give you an out."

"You're gonna give me an out?"

"If you go down the road you're on, I can promise you that you and everyone with you is as good as dead. You, the reporter, Heather, and anyone else you may come into contact with."

"And the alternative?" Cain asked.

"You kill the reporter for us and come in and we'll forget about this matter," Sanders said. "You and I can sit down like men and talk about this and decide where to go from here. If you want to be mad at me or angry with what I've done, that's fine. Whether you want to continue with us, try to go back to your family, I'll support you and help you in whatever decision you come to."

"So, I just kill him and everything's good?"

"You know it's the only way. I will not allow anyone to bring this agency down," Sanders said. "No matter what the cost."

Cain looked over at Falk and hesitated before answering.

"C'mon, Cain, it's your only option," Sanders said.

"Not my only option."

"What else can you do?"

"I can't do that. I won't sacrifice the life of someone else just to save my own," Cain told him.

"Cain, think about what you're saying."

"I have. The only way you're getting to him is if you go through me first."

"If that's the way you want it."

"And you can tell them to stop tracing the call, it won't work," Cain said before hanging up.

"Anything?" Sanders asked his team.

"It's a very sophisticated blocking system he was using," an analyst replied.

"So, you've got nothing?"

"He could be in any of fifty different places."

"In New York?"

"In the entire country."

"Damn."

Cain put his phone down and sat on the edge of the bed and started thinking. Falk could tell Cain had a lot weighing on him.

"Didn't sound like a very pleasant conversation," Falk said.

"Never had one with him that was."

"So, did he say anything that might help in some way?"

"He told me I could have an out if I wanted it," Cain said.

"Really? Really? Well, what would you have to do for that?"

"Just kill you."

"Oh. You're, um, you're not gonna do that right?" Falk asked.

Cain just rolled his eyes. "Just hurry up and finish your story."

35

Heather was nervous. It'd been several years since she'd seen or talked to her sister. They stayed in touch by sending each other birthday and Christmas cards, but that was the extent of their dealings with each other. Cassie didn't approve of the choices Heather made involving her work, and most of the people she associated with. At the same time, Heather wasn't thrilled with Cassie's choice of men, or that she stayed pretty close to their father. Heather took a cab to Cassie's place, a small ranch house located in Rochester. She got out of the cab, a backpack slung over her shoulder, and stood across the street. Her feet felt like they were glued to the concrete sidewalk as she stared at her sister's house. She was nervous and anxious at what Cassie would say or do once she saw her. It had been a long time. Maybe too much time had passed for them to overcome the differences they had. Heather mostly just hoped that her sister wouldn't close the door in her face and would give her a few minutes of her time.

After a few moments, Heather finally was able to move her legs. She walked across the street and up the driveway. She took a deep sigh before she knocked on the door. It was a half-hearted knock, without a lot of force behind it. It was almost like she didn't want Cassie to hear it and answer. Heather looked around nervously as she heard someone coming to the door. The door swung open, Cassie standing there with her jaw dropped, surprised at her sister's appearance.

"Hey," Heather sheepishly said.

"Hey. What are you doing here?"

"Umm, can't a girl just drop in on her sister to say hi?"

"Uh, yeah, sure. Do you wanna come in?" Cassie asked.

"Sure."

A baby started crying in the background, and Cassie quickly rushed into the kitchen. Heather was taken a little off guard. She followed her sister into the kitchen and saw a baby sitting there in a high chair. Cassie had never mentioned anything about a baby in any of her cards. Not that they really divulged much about their lives to each other, but that seemed important enough to at least mention.

"Is she yours?" Heather asked.

"Yeah," Cassie replied, picking her daughter up. "This is Emma. She's eight months old."

"Oh, my God. She's beautiful. How come you never mentioned her before?"

"I don't know. Just didn't seem like something you just reveal in a greeting card."

"So, where's David?" Heather asked of Cassie's boyfriend.

"He's not here."

"Is he at work?"

"I don't know. He left me two months ago," Cassie said.

"Oh, I'm so sorry."

"Yeah. Me too. Being a father didn't seem to fit his plans, so he ran off with some Hooters waitress."

"How could anyone not wanna be around something so precious as this?" Heather asked, stroking Emma's blonde hair.

"He sent me money last week so I guess that's about as good as I can expect from him."

"Well, if you ever need help with her, babysitting or whatever, maybe I could if you ever need it," Heather offered shyly, unsure of how it'd be received.

"Aren't you busy with your job and all? That used to keep you pretty busy."

"I don't do that anymore," Heather responded, her eyes tearing up.

"Oh?"

"Yeah," she replied, dabbing at her eyes to dry them. "I met this great guy, and I got a different job working at a marketing and advertising company."

"Really?" Cassie asked, surprised.

"Yeah. Decided to finally put my degree to use."

"That's great. Really great. I'm happy for you."

"Thanks. Yeah, so I've been doing that for a couple years now. Well, not this past year."

"Why not? What happened?" Cassie asked.

"Oh. I was in the hospital for like eight months."

"Oh, wow. Are you OK?"

"Yeah. I was shot and in a coma and unconscious for a while. Almost died, but, you know, no big deal," she said with a laugh, trying not to make a big deal of it. "I'm still here."

"You were in the hospital for eight months and nobody told me?"

"Once I woke up Matt asked if I wanted him to bring you down but I figured you were busy and had other things to do."

"I would drop everything to make sure you were OK. So, who's this boyfriend of yours?"

"His name's Matt. He's a really great guy," Heather told her, smiling. "I couldn't live without him."

"I can tell you have something special. You smile when you talk about him."

"Yeah. He's made my life so much better. He's made it worth living."

"So, why are you here? Are you in some kind of trouble?" Cassie asked.

"I could really use a place to stay for a day or two if you have the room," Heather said nervously.

"Uh, yeah, I have an extra room you can have."

"I promise I'll be gone in a couple days."

"You sound scared. What's going on?"

"The less you know the better off you probably are," Heather told her.

"Well, if you're gonna stay here, then I think I deserve to know what's going on," Cassie said. "It's been a long time since we've talked like this. Let's start back up on the right foot."

Heather sighed and sat down at the kitchen table. "It's a long story."

She told Cassie to sit down as she explained. Heather started by going back to the first day she met Cain. She remembered every little detail and didn't leave anything out. Every incident they encountered, every mission she knew he'd been on, their entire relationship, and every bump in the road. She remembered it all and explained it in great detail. By the time Heather was done, Cassie felt like she was there with them the entire time.

"So, your boyfriend is some secret government agent hit man?" Cassie asked.

"I wouldn't put it quite that way, but I guess you could say that."

"Leave it to you. This would only happen to you."

"What do you mean?"

"Only you would finally get your life turned around by falling in love with a man who kills people for a living."

"Hey, he only does that to bad people," Heather said, objecting. "It's not like he has fun doing it and knocks off everyone he sees. It's to protect our country."

"I guess so," Cassie replied. "Well, the bedroom's down the hall to the left. You can stay as long as you like."

"Thanks. I really owe you."

"You don't owe me anything. That's what family is supposed to be for, right? It'd be nice just to get my sister back," Cassie told her, wiping her eyes.

"It would," Heather said, reaching over to hug her sister. "It's been too long."

Heather grabbed her backpack and walked down the hall to the bedroom. She felt much better now that she and Cassie had talked. She felt like they could actually have a relationship again. Though she was happy about how things went with her sister, she was worried about Cain. She wished she was still with him. If he was caught, or worse, how would she know? It would just be covered up, and she'd never know what was going on with him. All she wanted to do at that moment was to call him on the phone and talk to him to make sure he was OK.

Heather sat on the edge of the bed and put her head in her hands and started to cry. The severity of everything was beginning to overwhelm her. Cassie walked in to see if Heather needed anything else and felt bad that her sister was crying. She took a seat next to Heather and put her arm around her to comfort her.

"I'm sure he's fine," Cassie said to reassure her.

"I just feel lost without him right now." Heather sniffled. "I don't know what to do."

"We'll figure it out," Cassie responded, putting Heather's head on her shoulder.

New Jersey---Cain was contemplating their next move as he let Falk try to make sense of the information for his story. Cain took a shower and had just come out when he saw Falk fiddling with his phone, putting it down as soon as Cain appeared.

"What were you just doing?" Cain asked.

"What? Nothing."

"I just saw you using your phone."

"Oh, that? I was just sending my boss a message," Falk replied. "He was wondering where I was so I told him I was working on an explosive story."

"How many messages?" Cain asked, looking deeply concerned.

"I don't know. He sent two, and I sent two."

Cain started moving quickly to gather his things, causing Falk to wonder what was wrong.

"What are you doing?" Falk asked.

"We gotta go."

"What? Why?"

"They'll get a beat on your phone and track down what cell towers your messages came from. That'll eventually lead them here," Cain said.

"Oh my God, I had no idea."

"I told you to stay off the phone."

"I thought you just meant phone calls. I didn't know they could trace texts!"

"Get your stuff together."

"Are you gonna call Mike again?" Falk asked.

"No. We only used him twice so if they find him he's probably safe if he sticks to the story. If we use him any more than that, then they'll probably assume he's thrown in with us which'll put him in danger."

"So, what're we gonna do?"

"Stay here. I'll be back in a few minutes."

"Where are you going?"

"Gonna steal a car," Cain replied.

Cain returned ten minutes later with a two-year-old silver Honda Civic.

"Couldn't have found something sportier, like a Porsche or Camaro or something?" Falk joked.

"The goal is to blend in. Not stick out."

"So where are we gonna go?"

Cain took a minute to think before answering. "Rochester."

"What's there?" Falk asked.

"Someone I need to help."

"There's more people out there?"

Cain couldn't help but think that Heather was in an increasing amount of danger. He thought she'd have some time before they turned their attention toward her but what if he was wrong? If they went after her right away he wouldn't be able to live with himself. She shouldn't have been out there left to fend for herself, anyway. He got her into it and he'd get her out. Thoughts of his wife and son crept into his mind as he wondered about them. He had ideas about going to see them but quickly realized this probably wasn't the best time to be doing that. The last thing he wanted to do was put more people in danger. It was a six-hour drive from New Jersey to Rochester. Cain hoped he wouldn't be too late. He got out his phone to make sure she was at her sister's and to let her know he was coming so she'd expect him.

Heather was helping Cassie clean the house. She figured it would help pass the time, plus she felt like she should help do something since her sister was letting her stay there. Heather was in the kitchen cleaning dishes when she heard her phone ring. She rushed out to the living room, drying her hands on her shirt on the way. She was so focused on the phone, which lay on an end table, she almost tripped on a couple boxes and some baby toys that were on the floor. She saw it was a number not in her phonebook and knew, or hoped, that it was Cain.

"Hello," she answered eagerly.

"Hey. It's me," Cain replied.

"Thank God. I've been so worried about you."

"No need to worry about me. I'll be fine."

"So, what's going on?" Heather asked.

"Are you at your sister's?"

"Yeah."

"OK. Stay there. I'm on my way."

"When will you get here?" she asked.

"I'm about six hours away."

"Six hours? Where are you?"

"New Jersey."

"What are you doing there?"

"I've got the reporter Heyward was working with. Was gonna stay low for a bit but it didn't work out."

"Well, I'm glad you're coming. I miss you," Heather told him.

"Don't answer the door for anyone until I get there."

"I won't. Won't even get close. I'm not gonna make that mistake again."

"If anyone does come and they get in, you know what to do," Cain said.

"Two in the chest and one in the head."

"You got it."

As soon as Heather put the phone down, she went back into the kitchen to finish the dishes and talk to Cassie.

"Matt's on his way," Heather said.

"Well, that's good."

"Yeah, he'll be here in about six hours he said."

The two continued cleaning for a while, trying to get the house in order. Once Cassie got Emma to lay down for her nap, the two sisters sat down to watch a movie.

"Remember when we used to sit in your room and watch movies together?" Cassie asked.

"Yeah. I miss those days."

"I guess high school couldn't last forever."

"I guess not."

"When Matt gets here what are you guys gonna do?" Cassie asked.

"I don't know. Whatever he thinks is best, I suppose."

"Well, if you leave right away when he comes, or..." she said, stumbling over the right words. "What I'm trying to say is if you do leave, I don't want another five years to go by without seeing or talking to you."

"It won't. I promise," Heather replied with a smile. "Whatever our differences were before were silly and stupid and shouldn't have driven us away like it did. That's not gonna happen again. I wanna be a part of your life. And Emma... I wanna be part of hers. I want to be the best aunt ever."

"You'll be great. She's gonna love you."

36

New York---Ed Sanders had stepped out of The Room for a few minutes to get a cup of coffee and clear his head. Whenever he felt the tension of his job was getting the better of him he'd go sit down with a cup of coffee and try to find a peaceful setting to relax. It worked as well as it usually did, and once he began to feel better, he went back to The Room to get a beat on Cain. As soon as he walked in, an analyst informed him of the breaking developments.

"Sir, we got a hit on the reporter's phone. He sent and received some messages to his editor at the paper."

"Were you able to trace it to his location?" Sanders asked.

"It comes back to a tower in New Jersey."

"Most likely is a decoy. Cain's too smart to get tripped up by something like that."

"Unless he didn't know Falk used the phone."

"Get some people out there just in case but he's probably

gone by now," Sanders said dejectedly. "Did you try that number Cain used before to see if he used it any other times?"

"We did. It's no use though. It's the weirdest thing I've ever seen," the analyst said. "One minute it traces to Los Angeles, the next Miami, the next Chicago, the next Beirut, then Paris, it just goes around in circles with fifty different locations. I've never seen anything like it."

"We're going to have to change tactics," Sanders stated.

"How so?"

"Cain's too smart and too good. He's using an untraceable phone number, he's withdrawn everything from his bank account so he's got unlimited resources, and he knows how we operate. He could stay a step ahead of us for a long time."

"What else could we do?"

"Go after the only thing that matters to him," Sanders replied, staring at a monitor.

"Which is what?"

"His girlfriend. He won't sacrifice her. He's proved it and told me that himself. We get her. And we get him."

"Any ideas on where to start?"

"The first place you usually start. Family."

They ran the background check on Heather and within five minutes found the only family she had, her sister.

"Cassidy Fleming. Married for three years, one daughter, lives in Rochester," an analyst said.

"What's the husband do?" Sanders asked.

"David Fleming... works in construction. Nothing to worry about."

"Good. Who do we have that's near there?"

"Closest agents we have are about an hour away," the analyst replied, checking the computer.

"Send them over and check the place out."

"And if they find her?"

"Heather Lloyd is to be brought in alive. We need her to set the trap for Cain," Sanders said.

"And her sister?"

"If Heather's there, we don't need any witnesses. Eliminate the rest of them."

"And the child?"

"Same policy as always. Nobody is left behind who could cause a problem in ten or twenty years," Sanders coldly explained.

Sanders then left the room and went to his office to do some paperwork while he waited for word from the agents dispatched. Once an hour went by and the agents arrived at Cassie's house, Sanders went back to The Room to oversee everything. They finally got word from the agents sent to New Jersey, who finally were able to track Cain and Falk to the motel they were in.

"They're five or six hours ahead of us," Sanders said with a shake of his head.

"Agent James and McNabb are in position," an analyst said.

"Tell them to move in when they're ready."

Rochester---Cassie had just put the outside light on when she caught a glimpse of something across the street. The lights of a car driving by revealed two men sitting in a dark car across from the house. Frightened, she retreated into the living room where Heather was reading a magazine.

"I think someone's here," Cassie said quickly.

"What?"

"Someone's sitting in a car across the street."

"Are you sure?"

"Positive."

Heather looked at the time. Nine o'clock. She didn't expect Cain for probably another hour. One thing was for sure, nobody would have a reason for being there at that time of night unless they had bad intentions. She got up to look for herself, peering through the curtains. She did see a car sitting across the street, but wasn't ready to jump to the conclusion that they were there for them.

"Maybe it's someone that lives across the street waiting to go in or something. Maybe had a date or something," Heather said calmly.

"The only person that lives over there is a seventy-four-year-old woman. I don't think she's done any dating recently," Cassie dryly joked.

They kept watching out the window for a few more minutes until their worst fears were realized. They saw two men get out of the car and start walking toward the house. They paired off as one approached the front door while the other appeared to be going around the back.

"Oh my God, what are we gonna do?!" Cassie yelled, freaking out.

"Calm down!" Heather replied, grabbing her sister's arms. "Go to Emma's room and lock the door. Get your phone and call 911."

"What are you gonna do?"

"Hold them off until the police come."

"You can't do that."

"Just go! Emma's the first priority. Keep her safe," Heather told her.

Heather ran to her room and went into her backpack and pulled out her gun. She ran back to the living room, breathing heavily, hoping Cassie called the police. She had no delusions about being better than a couple of professional agents; she just hoped to be able to hold them off long enough for help to arrive. There was a knock on the door as Heather stood beside it. She learned her lesson from the last time she stood in front of a door. She wasn't gonna make that mistake again. The man knocked on the door again.

"Hello?" the man said.

"What do you want?" Heather replied.

"I'm looking for David Fleming."

"What do you want him for?"

"I'm a friend of his. I really need to talk to him."

"He's sleeping right now."

"I really need to talk to him. I just had a fight with my wife and she left me and I don't know what else to do. I could really use someone to talk to," the man said.

"Leave your number and I'll have him call you when he wakes up."

"Is he here? I don't see his car in the driveway."

"It's in the shop."

"Are you Cassidy?"

"Yeah. Why?"

"He talks about you all the time about how much he loves you," the man said.

"OK, I think it's time for you to go."

"I can't."

"If you don't go now I'm gonna call 911."

"Go ahead."

"I'm calling," Heather said.

"I think their system's down tonight," he said with a laugh.

Heather pulled out her phone and looked at it but it wasn't getting a signal. They must've somehow jammed the phone lines.

"So, who else is in there?" the man asked.

"Nobody."

"Open the door so I can take a look."

An idea came to Heather about doing what had been done to her. She took a deep breath and went to the door and looked out the peephole. She pointed her gun at the middle of the door and fired a couple shots through it. The shots must've hit their mark as the man screamed then dropped to a knee. Unfortunately, the man got back to his feet and angrily started beating on the door. Heather turned around as she heard the back door being kicked in. She ran into the hallway, hoping to get a shot at him before he got in. The door was already open when she got there and as she turned around she got slapped in the face with an open hand. It knocked her against the wall and she dropped her gun. Heather reached down for it but was met with a closed fist which knocked her to the floor. They were joined a minute later by the man from the front, who finally got in.

"Looks like we found our target," one of the men said.

They were startled when they heard a noise coming from the bedroom. They kicked the door in and saw Cassie crunched down in the corner holding her daughter. One of the men pulled them out and led them into the living room. The other pulled Heather in by the arm, dragging her along the floor as she was still dazed from the punch. They dropped

Heather in front of the couch as they shoved Cassie onto the couch.

"You wanna do it or should I?" one of them asked.

"You can do it. I don't wanna shoot a kid."

"Please, no!" Cassie yelled. "Not my baby!"

Just as the one agent was about to pull the trigger they heard a noise coming from the back door.

"What was that?"

"Nothing. Don't worry about it."

They turned their attention back to Cassie to get the deed over with. Cain rushed in through the front door, firing his gun. He immediately dropped the agent holding the gun on Cassie then quickly fired at the other. The agent was able to get a shot off at Cain though it missed, the bullet lodging in the wall. Cain did not, however, and fired several shots that ended the man's life. The other agent was still on the ground, breathing heavily, until Cain put an end to that. He stood over him and shot him in the forehead as if it was no big deal. Falk peeked in through the front door, amazed and somewhat impressed at what he'd just witnessed from the lead character in his story. Cain walked around the couch to check on Cassie and the baby.

"Are you all right?" Cain asked.

"Yeah. I'm fine," Cassie said, holding her head. "Just a little shaken."

"The baby OK?"

"Yeah. She's fine," she said after checking her.

"Good."

Cain then turned his attention to Heather as she had just sat up, leaning against the end of the couch to steady herself. She raised her knees and rested her elbows on them as she put both hands on her head. Cain knelt down beside her to check her over.

"Looks like you got the worse end of things," Cain said.

"Not as worse as it could've been."

Cain started to get up to find an ice pack but saw Cassie had beaten him to it and was coming over with one. She handed it to Heather who put it across the side of her face that felt the wrath of the punch. Cain moved her jaw up and down to make sure it wasn't broken. She was lucky that her biggest issue was the big red welt on the side of her face. Her cheek was a little puffy but the swelling would go down in an hour or two with the ice.

"We need to go," Heather blurted out, sounding concerned.

"What? Why?" Cain asked.

"I told Cassie to call 911 before this started. The police will be here any second."

Cassie shook her head. "I never got to call them. It wouldn't go through."

"My cell had no signal too," Heather replied.

"They probably jammed your signals before they got here. They figured you'd try something like that. It's pretty standard procedure," Cain told them.

"Thank God you're here," Heather said, putting her arms around him.

Cain gently rubbed her back as they hugged. His thoughts turned to his wife and son and almost felt guilty about hugging Heather. Cain wasn't sure how he was going to tell her about it. There probably would never be a right time for it. As much as he thought he loved her, how could he continue on with the relationship when he had a family waiting for him at home?

"As soon as you feel well enough to move, we're gonna need to get going," Cain said.

"But if the police aren't coming, what's the rush?" Heather asked.

"Because once these two don't report back they'll know something happened. They'll probably assume I'm here and try to close in on us. They'll create a radius search and start closing off escape routes. We need to move as soon as possible to stay ahead of them."

"I'm good. Let's go now," Heather replied, standing on her feet.

"Are you sure you're OK? We can wait a few minutes."

She smiled. "No, let's just go now. I'm fine."

"Grab your stuff."

"What about them?" Heather asked, nodding at her sister. "We can't leave them here. They might come after them again."

Cain looked at Cassie and Emma and sighed, knowing he had a big problem. It was hard enough being on the run by himself, but now he had a reporter to look after. Plus, trying to take care of Heather and now he had another woman and a baby. It was getting harder by the minute. Cain knew he was going to have to think of something. There were too many people now to stay low. He'd have to find a spot quickly, and he was running out of ideas. He wasn't sure he could keep them all safe if they stayed with him. In the meantime, he didn't want to just leave a couple of dead bodies in Cassie's house to implicate her in anything.

"Go get their car and back it into the driveway," Cain told Falk.

Falk dug for the keys in one of the agents' pockets and did as he was instructed and brought the car over. Cain had Falk open up the trunk, and he brought the dead men out, one at a time, slung over his shoulder to place them inside. Cain put them in then went back inside to talk to Cassie.

"Well, it's up to you what you wanna do," Cain said to Cassie. "If you stay here, I can't guarantee that they won't show up here again. If they do, I can't protect you. If you come with us, there's a good chance you'll see more of what went down here tonight at some point."

Cassie looked at Heather before looking back at Emma, tears starting to flow. Heather felt horrible knowing that she placed her sister and niece in jeopardy and now they were forced to make a life altering decision.

"Can you give me a couple minutes so I can pack a bag of her things?" Cassie asked about Emma.

Cain nodded, sympathetic of her decision.

"I'll help you," Heather told her.

"On the way here I saw a Target. Do you remember it?" Cain asked Falk.

"Yeah, why?"

"Take that car and park it there. As soon as they're ready, we'll come over and get you. Stay low, don't get out, and don't park near anybody," Cain said. "We'll be along in a few minutes."

Falk left, taking the car full of dead bodies with him. Heather and Cassie were quickly packing Emma's things, knowing they didn't have much time. Heather packed a bag of her clothes while Cassie went to the kitchen to pack some of her baby food and bottles. Heather joined her sister in the kitchen once she got Emma's clothes together.

"I'm so sorry for dragging you into this," Heather said sorrowfully. "I never thought it'd end up like this."

"It's not your fault."

"I'll never forgive myself for this."

"Hey, I don't blame you. I'm not mad at you or anything. I'm just worried," Cassie said, putting her hand on Heather's shoulder. "Everything just happened so fast. I just can't believe all this is happening."

"Matt will do everything he can to protect you guys. And so will I."

"I know."

While the women were in the kitchen, Cain thought of the only person who could help them that might be able to conceal their whereabouts. Eric Raines was the only person he could turn to. Cain wasn't sure he could totally trust Lawson anymore, and even if she was on his side, it was likely they'd have her staked out too. Nobody else would be as equipped to help them as much as Raines. It was ironic that the only person that he could turn to was the man he was supposed to kill. He dialed Raines' number, unsure what he could do, but hopeful he had an idea.

"What can I do for you, my friend?" Raines answered.

"I can use your help," Cain said.

"What do you need?"

"I'm not sure."

"You sound flustered. What is going on?"

Cain sighed. "I've got a host of problems right now."

"Tell me what's going on," Raines said.

"You want the short or long version?"

"Preferably the short version without leaving anything out."

"I tried to meet my contact who was already dead. They're framing me for it. He gave everything he had to a reporter who I've got with me now before they had a chance to kill him. I sent

Heather to her sister's while I was with the reporter and they tried to kill them. Luckily, I got here in time. That leads me to right now."

"Sounds like you have a rather sticky situation on your hands."

"So, I'm on the run, have a reporter, Heather, her sister, and a baby in tow."

"You couldn't have found a dog on the way?" Raines joked.

"I figure that's next."

"How can I help?"

"I can't keep them all with me. There's no way I can move fast enough with them all," Cain stated.

"Figure on dropping two or three of them off on the road-side and let them take their chances?" Raines asked sarcastically.

"Obviously I can't just leave them. They won't make it on their own."

"Which is where I come in."

"You're the only person I know who I can trust right now," Cain said.

"What did you have in mind?"

"I know it's a lot to ask but would you be able to hide them out if I sent them your way?"

"You want to put them on a plane and have me take care of them?"

"Like I said, I know it's a lot to ask, but you're the only person I know who they don't have tabs on. They don't know where you're at," Cain said.

"They will once they find out what plane they're on."

"I'm out of options. Sanders screwed me, Eric. I'm actually married with a son. I need to repay him for that," Cain said.

Raines felt badly for him and offered another solution. "You realize that if you put these people on a plane overseas that there's a very real possibility, I'd even say more likely than not, that there will be agents waiting for them when they arrive."

"Yeah."

"So how about if you send them to France? I can meet them there and get them into England."

"What's the difference?" Cain asked.

"Once I get them, they'll have no idea which way I'm going. If they think I've settled in France, then let them look. If you send them to England and Sanders thinks I'm stationed there, then things can get rather hot very quickly," Raines told him.

"I'll owe you one."

"Kill Sanders and I'll consider the debt repaid."

37

Once Heather and Cassie were ready they all got in the stolen car to go meet Falk. Heather wondered about the information that the reporter had and quizzed Cain about it.

"Does Falk have everything Heyward had?" she asked.

"Yeah," Cain answered.

"So, what was it?"

"Just stuff about the agency."

"There had to be stuff about you in there, right? I mean, he contacted you about it," Heather said, pressing him.

"We can talk about it later," Cain replied, knowing her heart would be broken when he revealed the facts about his past. "First, let's just get out of here."

"Where are we going?"

"The airport," Cain said.

"The airport?" Heather asked, confused. "Why?"

"It's hard enough to do this on my own. With all of you it's almost impossible. I need to send you all somewhere where I know you're safe and they can't find you," Cain explained.

"You're sending us away?" Heather asked with disappointment.

"It's the only way I can think of."

"So what airport are you taking us to?"

"Syracuse. It's about two hours away."

"Is that the closest?" she asked.

"No, the closest is about four miles from here, but that's where they'd look first."

"I don't wanna leave you again," Heather said.

"It'll only be for a little bit."

"Why can't I just stay with you?"

Cain didn't answer her, and she knew that it was useless arguing. She knew he wasn't going to change his mind no matter how much she objected to it. Heather looked out her window, silently steaming about being sent away. She felt she could help him and that he needed at least one person that he could depend on. Cassie stayed silent in the back seat, mostly just tending to her daughter, but still listening to the conversation up front. She was scared not knowing what was happening, but her main priority was protecting Emma. If this was the best way to do that, then she was fine with it. She saw how skilled Cain was and had to put her trust in him.

"Where are we being sent?" Heather asked, breaking the silence.

"Paris and then you'll make your way into England."

"Are we just supposed to know where to go when we get there?"

"Eric Raines will meet you," Cain replied.

"Raines? That's reassuring," she said, not thrilled.

"Hey, he's the only person we can trust right now."

"When's the flight?"

"Tomorrow morning at 5:45. That's the soonest," Cain told her.

"I can't believe you're getting rid of us," she objected.

"It's not about getting rid of you. It's about protecting you."

"I can take care of myself."

"You think so?"

"Yeah, I do."

"Not against these people you can't," Cain said. "If I hadn't gotten there when I did you would all be dead."

"That's why we should stay with you."

"No, that's exactly why you can't, because I can't always be there to protect everybody. If you stay here, you're gonna have to see me do things that... things you shouldn't have to see. You'll have to see me kill."

"I've seen that already."

"Not in the way I'm gonna have to. What you saw earlier was killing in self-defense, to protect those I care about. To get out of this I'm gonna have to kill unprovoked, violently, and without a second thought. I don't think you're ready to see me like that. It will change how you look at me."

"Nothing could change how I look and feel about you."

"I wouldn't be so sure of that," Cain said.

"What's that supposed to mean?"

Cain sighed and waited to answer. He waited long enough that they pulled into the Target parking lot to find Falk so that he was able to avoid the question.

"There he is," Heather said and pointed.

Falk immediately got in the car, and they quickly drove out of the lot. It was a long, quiet car ride. It'd been a long day for everyone and their energy levels from the rush and all the excitement had finally started to dwindle. For Heather, though, it was something more. Maybe it was just the stress from the situation, but she got the feeling something else was going on. Though he wasn't talking, Cain seemed different. Maybe that was what was bothering her. He wasn't talking. She just assumed that a man who was sending his girlfriend away for an indefinite period of time would have more to say to her. She knew Cain wasn't the type of guy who usually spilled his emotions out onto his sleeve but this was an extraordinary circumstance. For all she knew, these would be the last few hours she'd ever spend with him. The least she thought he could do was talk to her about what was in his head.

"Everyone should probably get some rest while you can," Cain told the group.

"I'm fine," Heather said sternly.

Falk and Cassie both agreed, though, and figured a few hours of sleep would do them good. After a few minutes, Cain looked at the backseat passengers and noticed that they'd fallen asleep. He then looked over at Heather who was still very alert, staring out her window. He could tell that she was still steaming. He debated whether he should tell her about what he found out in the files but it just seemed like it wasn't the right time. Cain also wondered if he should just not tell her at all. If things went bad and he wasn't able to survive this mess, maybe it'd be better for her to not know his past, and just remember what they shared together.

"I'm sorry," Cain blurted out.

"For?"

"I know you're pissed about leaving."

"It just seems like there should be another way," Heather

said. "I can understand Cassie and the baby, and even the reporter, but I can help you."

"Heather, you've been through so much already. Helping me has almost got you killed twice already. I'm not gonna take a chance on a third time."

"You never did say what was in the files you got from Heyward."

"Just stuff about the agency," Cain quickly replied.

"And the stuff about you?"

"I don't think right now is the best time to talk about it."

"You're sending me away and I might never see you again. When exactly will it be the right time to talk about it?" Heather asked, slightly agitated.

Heather could sense there was something Cain didn't want to say. It wasn't just about the right time to talk. She knew it must've been something bad. Maybe he had a criminal record in his past. It seemed like a thousand things flashed through her mind of what might've been keeping him from opening up to her. One thing she knew, she wasn't going to keep pestering him about it. Whenever people kept bothering Cain about stuff he truly didn't want to talk about, he clammed up even further. Heather wasn't going to do that to him, mostly because she knew it wouldn't do any good. But it also made for an uncomfortable car ride the rest of the way to the airport. Cain felt badly about what he was putting Heather through, but honestly thought it was for the best that she didn't know just yet.

Cain got to the airport a few minutes under four hours. He pulled into one of the lots and waited a few minutes before waking up the others. They got out of the car to stretch their legs and grab their bags.

"How are we gonna make it through security?" Heather asked. "They're looking for us."

"They're really only looking for me. And they're looking for Matthew Cain, not Thomas Nelson," Cain replied, taking out a different ID.

With his hat on, and wearing a pair of glasses, he didn't think there was much of a chance of him being spotted. They went into the airport and through the security checkpoints without incident. They took a few seats as they waited for the plane to board. Cain got up to move around, not liking sitting in one spot for too long. As he walked around, he pulled out his phone to make a call. While he was talking, Heather figured it might be her only chance to know what was in those files. She turned to the reporter for answers.

"We've never really been properly introduced," Heather started. "I'm Heather."

"You can call me Falk," the reporter replied, shaking her hand.

"Did you get a chance to study what was in those files from Heyward?"

"Oh yeah. Some really good stuff in there."

"Is it enough to bring the agency down?" Heather asked.

"To its knees. It'll crumble once some of the things in there get released."

"Great. What about Cain? Did he get the answers he was looking for about his past?"

"Yeah. Poor guy. I feel sorry for him," Falk said.

"Why?"

"Well, I'm not sure I should say. I don't think he'd want me to talk about it."

"Oh. It's OK. You can tell me. I've been there with him since the beginning. We actually lived together. Kind of roommates, I guess," she said.

"Oh. You're not dating or anything are you? Because that'd be kind of weird and uncomfortable with... well, you're not together, right?"

"Oh. No. Of course not," she stumbled. "No, we're just friends. Nope. Never dated."

"OK. I'll tell you then. Just promise you won't tell him I told you."

"Yeah. Sure. I promise."

"Well, it looks like he was actually married and had a son," Falk said.

Heather was stunned and not sure how to reply. "You mean he got divorced before he enlisted in the military?"

"No. He was still married when Project Specter recruited him. They faked his death and made his wife a widow and his son fatherless. They used his injury to get him to join. Then they gave him more drugs to compound his memory issues to make sure he'd never remember them."

"Oh my God," Heather whispered, looking at Cain.

"Yeah. I can't even imagine what the guy is going through. They even lied to him about his real name."

"It's Thomas Nelson, isn't it?"

"No. His real name is Justin Clifford. They told him it was Thomas Nelson, but that was a lie too."

Heather looked down at the floor and stared at the tiles. All she wanted to do at that point was cry. She couldn't believe what she'd just heard. Cain had a wife and son. She imagined that would mean that their relationship would be over. She couldn't blame him if he really did have a wife and son. But it sure did feel like someone just drove a knife through her heart.

That must've been why he seemed a little bit colder and more distant than usual, she thought. Her eyes started to tear up, but she quickly got her emotions under control and tried to put on a brave face. She didn't want Cain to know that she knew. Cain started walking back toward the group and she wiped her eyes to make sure there were no tears on her face. Cain was about to say something but stopped when he noticed Heather's face. It appeared her eyes were a little red which made him think she was beginning to cry.

"You OK?" Cain asked.

"Yeah, why?"

"It looks like something's wrong."

"I'm fine. Just worried about everything. Guess it all just hit me at once," Heather said.

Cain nodded. "OK."

"So, who were you talking to?" Falk asked.

"Eric Raines. Just wanted to let him know where we were and everything was still good."

"I'm not going," Falk told him.

"What?" Cain said, giving him his icy stare.

"I look at it like this. The person they want most after you is me. Maybe they even want me more right now with my paper contacts. So, if I go with the ladies that makes them a target," Falk said. "I don't want that on my head. If I stay with you, then maybe they won't even bother with them and stay on us."

Cain looked at the women and Emma for a few moments, thinking about Falk's thoughts. He couldn't believe it but Falk's words actually made sense to him. He agreed that maybe it was for the best if Falk stayed with him.

"Raines knows you are coming," Cain told the women. "He'll be there waiting for you at the airport and will keep you safe."

Cain was still somewhat expecting an argument from Heather and was a little surprised when there was none. It wasn't like her to just give up on something she wanted. Cain stood there, not moving, almost waiting for her to come up with some other plan. He knew something was wrong with her when she just sat there staring ahead, not even looking at him. He wrote down Raines' number and handed it to Heather in case she needed to call him once they landed if something wasn't quite right.

"What's wrong?" he asked.

"Nothing."

"It's not like you to be silent like this."

"I guess I know when I'm beat," she said.

Cain looked at Cassie, wondering if something was said while he was talking on the phone. He let it go, figuring if it was really important she would say something to him. They waited ten more minutes before they announced the plane was boarding. Cain walked the sisters toward the entrance.

"See ya, little one," Cain told Emma, touching her nose

"Well, thank you for saving us," Cassie said. "I never did thank you properly for what you did back at the house."

"Thanks aren't necessary. Hopefully, I'll see you all soon."

"Yeah. Well, thanks again," Cassie said, kissing him on the cheek. "Be careful."

"I will," Cain replied before turning his attention to Heather.

"So how long are we staying with Raines?"

"Till it's safe for you to come back."

"Well, I guess just let me know how you're doing from time to time if you can," Heather said, her voice starting to crack.

"I will," Cain replied, not sure what else to tell her.

"You take care of yourself," she told him, tears starting to flow.

"I'll try to end this as soon as possible."

"I know."

Heather gave him a final hug. She turned around and joined her sister as they walked toward the tunnel. Cain waited for her to turn around and give him one more look, or a final wave, but she never did. He thought it was weird that she seemed a little cold as it wasn't in her nature to act that way. He couldn't afford to think too much more about it, though, and turned around. He grabbed Falk, and they began walking through the airport. They only walked a few minutes before Falk's phone began ringing. Falk took it out of his pocket and looked at it, unsure if he should answer the private number calling. He looked at Cain who nodded to answer.

"Hello," Falk said.

"Put Cain on the phone."

"It's for you," Falk said, handing Cain the phone.

"Who is this?" Cain asked.

"Did you really think you could get away from us?" Sanders asked.

"It crossed my mind," Cain replied, recognizing the voice instantly.

"I just want you to know that it's all on your head."

"What's that?"

"Well, let's start with a certain cab driver that we both know of," Sanders said. "Oh, what's his name? Patel, is it?"

"Never heard of him," Cain replied.

Sanders laughed. "You're gonna pull that one, are you? We know he helped you. As a matter of fact, he's about to meet one of our finest interrogation officers. Care to stop by and watch?"

A lump went down Cain's throat knowing that Patel was in the clutches of Sanders and his men. He knew that meant Patel would never see the light of day again.

"So, let's talk exchanges," Sanders said.

"Unless you're talking the stock exchange, you're wasting your time."

"Such a sense of humor," Sanders responded, laughing. "No, I'm talking an exchange for Patel. Give me something I want and I'll let him go."

"We both know that if you truly have Patel that you'll never let him go no matter what. You can't afford to let him walk out of that building. He means nothing to me, anyway. He's just a cab driver. So why don't you just skip the nonsense and get on with it," Cain said.

"Fine. If that's the way you want it."

"It makes no difference to me," Cain responded. Outwardly, he was saying all the right things and what he thought Sanders needed to hear. Inside, though, he was beside himself that another person was losing their life because of him.

"So, did you kiss her goodbye?" Sanders asked.

"What?"

"Heather. Did you give her a final goodbye before sending her away?"

"I don't know what you're talking about," Cain replied, a little worried about his reference.

"You think we don't know where you are right now?"

"Just where would that be?" Cain asked, grabbing Falk's arm as they both stopped. Cain did a three sixty as he looked for any signs of Sanders' men. He didn't notice anything, which probably alarmed him more than if he did.

"What do you think the chances are that you're gonna walk out of that airport?"

"I dunno. What do you think the chances are that I'm gonna rip your throat out?"

"I would say they're not real good. You're never getting out of there alive. Your reporter friend is gonna go down with you, and your girlfriend and her sister will never reach their destination," Sanders said.

Cain had enough of Sanders' innuendo about their demise and hung up.

"Do they really have Patel?" Falk asked.

"Yeah."

"Are we gonna get him?"

"No. Can't," Cain replied. "If they have him, he's as good as dead. There's nothing we can do for him."

"He seemed like such a good guy." Falk sighed.

"Yeah. We got other things to worry about now."

"Like what?"

"Like they know we're here," Cain said.

"What? How?"

"Don't know. We gotta get out of here though."

They began walking quickly until Cain suddenly stopped and turned around, thinking of what Sanders told him. He looked in the direction they just came from, worried about Heather's safety. His head was telling him to just keep going, to make sure Falk made it out OK, but his heart was still thinking of Heather.

"We have to go back," Cain said.

"What? Why?"

"They're in danger."

"OK. How about you go back and I'll go wait in the coffee shop up there," Falk said.

"I can't leave you alone. It's not safe."

"Well, hate to break it to you, but being around you isn't exactly safe either," Falk joked, smiling. "Plus, they're looking for us to be together. Might be wiser to split up for a few minutes."

"Point taken," Cain replied. "Fine. I'll be back in five minutes. You see anything that looks like trouble you call me and I'll be right over."

"No problem. Good luck," Falk said, tapping Cain's shoulder.

Cain wanted to run but knew that was probably a bad idea since that would bring attention to himself. He briskly walked, pulling his hat down just above his eyes to further conceal his face. He got to the terminal, but it was already closed. The plane had just started making its way down the runway. Cain went to the window and watched as the plane took off, the wheels lifting off the ground. He envisioned when this moment happened that some weight would be lifted off his shoulders, that he would feel some relief. But he actually felt just the opposite. Sadness overwhelmed him and he couldn't help but feel that maybe he'd seen Heather for the last time. He thought he was a step ahead of Sanders but he apparently knew they were there. Splitting up now almost seemed like he was sending Heather and her sister to their doom. If he'd only known Sanders already had a beat on them, he wouldn't have sent them away. It was too late now to keep dwelling on it. He had to turn his attention back to Falk and focus on getting the two of them out of there. He walked past the flight board and saw her plane information and put his hand on it.

Cain got back to the coffee shop Falk was supposed to be at within a few minutes but was rattled when he saw a bunch of empty seats. Falk wasn't there. He cursed himself for being so stupid and leaving him alone when he knew Sanders' men were out there. Cain turned around and tried to look through the crowd to see if he could spot Falk walking. It was too tough a task though with the crowd. Who would've thought it would be so busy at six in the morning, Cain thought to himself? He was only gone for five minutes but Falk could've been anywhere by now. It wouldn't take long for them to be completely out of sight and stuffing him in a trunk somewhere at this point. Just as Cain was beginning to lose hope and think it was a lost cause, he felt a tap on the back of his shoulder. He spun around and threw a punch to which his intended target quickly ducked the blow.

"Hey there, tiger. Ease up," Falk said. "That was mildly uncomfortable."

"Yeah, well, you were almost comfortably dead."

"Sorry about that."

"Why'd you sneak off?" Cain asked.

"Went over to the newspaper stand," Falk replied, holding up a paper.

"That was kinda stupid."

"Figured I'd check out the news."

"Do something like that again and I'll kill you myself," Cain said plainly.

"Umm... understood."

"C'mon, let's go," Cain said, pulling Falk's arm.

"Did you get to the girls?"

"Plane already took off."

Cain and Falk continued walking the concourse in the

hopes of getting out of there quickly and without incident. They reached the escalator to go down to the first floor. Before getting on, Cain stopped and took another look around to see if someone was watching. He couldn't shake the feeling that someone had tabs on them. Unable to see anything suspicious, he nodded to Falk to get on. Just as Falk got on, he stumbled against the railing, a trickle of blood starting to show on his shirt. Falk briefly looked at his protector and wondered if this was the end for him. Cain looked on helplessly as another bullet ripped through Falk's body, causing him to fall on the steps and violently roll down the escalator out of control. Cain immediately dropped to one knee and removed his gun, pointing it in different directions to try to distinguish his target. With no subject in sight he quickly ran down the escalator before the bullets came in his direction. At the bottom of the escalator he briefly checked on Falk's lifeless body. Falk's shirt was covered in blood and there was no trace of life left. He was gone. Cain quickly rooted through his bag and took out the folder he was carrying with the files.

Cain flew down the concourse until he got to the doors and noticed a couple of rough-looking fellows approaching. There was no stopping him though; he was going through whoever was in his path. Cain bolted out the door, surprising the three suits coming toward him. The men quickly realized who was coming at them and removed their weapons. Cain already had them beat, though, and fired his gun before they even had a chance to respond. He fired one round at the chest of the first two agents who were walking side by side and then two more rounds at the agent walking behind them. Cain didn't bother to check on their condition and kept running to his car. He reached the car without a problem and sped off. As he peeled out of the parking lot, the windshield shattered, a bullet ripping through it as Cain moved his head. The bullet made its way through the headrest before stopping in the cushion of the back seat. Cain wasn't fazed and kept driving, another bullet going through the trunk. A few minutes later he made it out of the airport and was flying down the hallway. He couldn't tell if anyone was following him but he wasn't taking chances by slowing down.

Sanders was in The Room watching everything unfold. He watched as the events in the airport went down via the airport cameras. They were able to tap into the parking lot feeds but couldn't see every inch of the lot. Sanders anxiously waited for word from his agents, hopeful that they'd inform him of Cain's demise. After a few minutes of silence, he got tired of waiting.

"Somebody talk to me about what's happening," Sanders said.

"We have three agents down."

"I'm not concerned with that. What about Cain?"

"It looks like he's escaped, sir."

An obviously angry Sanders took a step back and looked up at the ceiling as he sighed.

"Can someone please explain to me how we managed to bungle this?" Sanders calmly asked, controlling his anger.

"He's a world class agent, sir."

"Don't give me that! We knew where he was, we knew where he was going, we had men in place to take him out, tell me how we didn't get the job done. I don't want excuses."

"We have no explanation, sir."

"And can someone please tell me why the first shot was to kill the reporter? Why was Cain not the first target? I can kill a reporter any day of the week. You might only get one chance to take out Matthew Cain."

"It was just a poor decision, sir."

"Well, all isn't lost. We have a couple hours until the plane is over the Atlantic," Sanders grimly stated. "Get everything cleaned up there and try to find him."

A frustrated Sanders quickly left the room, irritated by the turn of events. He went back to his office to try to form a new plan. Cain, meanwhile, was still flying down the highway trying to figure out where to go. He wasn't sure what to do now. He figured the only person who might be able to help him now was Lawson. He told her he'd check in with her anyway, so he was about due. He dialed her number, hoping she was available.

"Hello," Lawson answered, picking up on the first ring.

"I need help."

"What's going on?"

"What happened to keeping an eye on Heather for me?" Cain asked, referring to the incident at Cassie's house.

"I don't know what you're talking about. Did something happen to Heather? After we talked last, I went to Sanders and tried to get some information but he shot me down completely. He told me to take a few days off so I'm completely out of the loop."

"Oh."

"Did something happen to Heather? Is she OK?" Lawson asked, worried.

"She's fine. They tried to take them all out but luckily I got there in time."

"Thank goodness. Where are you now?"

"Driving down the highway."

"Who's with you?"

"Nobody. I just came from the airport. I sent Heather and her sister to Europe. Raines will hide them and keep them safe for now."

"Are you sure about him?" Lawson asked.

"About as sure as I am about anybody."

"Did you ever find that reporter?"

"He's dead."

"Oh."

"He was at the airport with me. Somehow Sanders found out our location, and a sniper got him," Cain said.

"Oh no. Did he have the information you were looking for?"

"Yeah, I have it."

"Well, that's good at least. Where are you heading now?"

"I don't know. I'm just driving," Cain replied.

"Just lay low for a few days. Take whatever documents you have and fax them to every government official and newspaper office there is."

Cain thought about the documents and suddenly realized where it was he needed to go. Virginia. His last known address, according to the records. Where his wife and son still lived.

"I figured it out. I know where I'm going," Cain said.

"Please don't tell me you're going to the office."

"No. Somewhere much more important."

"Which is where?" Lawson asked.

"I'll call you later, Shelly."

"Matthew," Lawson said, before hearing the silence of the phone. She thought about where he might be headed and had an idea where it was.

It was about an eight-hour drive from New York to Virginia, giving Cain plenty of time to think about what he was going to do once he got there. It was a quiet ride for Cain, not a government man in sight. Once he finally crossed over the Virginia border, his first order of business was to find a hotel. He was pretty tired and just wanted to rest for a couple of hours since he seemed to be out of immediate danger. He found a Sheraton and checked in under an alias. Once inside the room Cain placed his bag on the floor and put his phone on the table. He then plopped down on the bed and lay on his back, staring up at the ceiling. As soon as he closed his eyes, his phone rang. He sighed and took a few seconds to get up, wondering what the issue was this time. It was a private number, which whittled down the prospective callers.

"Yeah?" Cain answered, thinking it might be Sanders.

"It's Raines."

"Oh, hey. Are you at the airport?"

"Have you heard the news?" Raines asked.

"What news?"

"There's been some complications."

"What complications? What are you talking about?" Cain asked, getting worried.

"The plane you put Heather and her sister on never arrived."

"Why not? Where's it at?"

"I guess I'm stalling and trying not to say the inevitable," Raines said sorrowfully.

"Please just say it," Cain stated, getting a hint of his news.

"The plane Heather and her sister were on blew up over the Atlantic two hours ago," Raines said, barely able to keep his composure. "Reports are saying everyone on board has been killed. No survivors."

Cain's eyes immediately filled up with tears and he had no words to reply back with. He simply let the phone drop to the ground as he fell onto the bed. He couldn't stop the tears from falling and he didn't even care to try. Everyone close to him was being eliminated and there was nothing he could do to prevent it no matter how hard he tried. The stress was overwhelming, and he fell asleep crying within a few minutes.

New York--- Sanders was sitting in his office watching TV, switching between channels to see what they were saying about the plane incident. His aides were bringing in reports every few minutes as they gathered more intelligence on it.

"So, what's the verdict?" Sanders asked.

"All 230 people were killed."

"And the cause?"

"It'll go down as engine failure," his aide replied.

"Excellent. Let's see what kind of response we get out of Cain once he hears about this."

38

C ain did a search on the internet and wrote down the address and phone number of every public and private school within the area that Justin could've possibly gone to. His plan was to call every one until he found out which school he attended. He picked up the phone and put his plan in motion. Cain called thirteen schools, each of whom told him they had no student by that name. The fourteenth school on his list was a Catholic school about three miles from the Baldwin home.

"Hi, I was wondering if there's a student named Justin Clifford enrolled there?" Cain asked.

"I'm sorry, sir, we don't give out student information to strangers," the secretary replied.

"Oh, I'm sorry, I'm not a stranger. Let me explain my predicament. My name is Matthew Clifford, I'm his uncle."

"Hold on a second, let me get the principal for you."

The sound of the secretary's voice gave Cain some hope. It

sounded unlike any of the other calls he'd made, like someone who knew the answer but just wasn't allowed to say. It was only a minute before he found out.

"Hello, Mr. Clifford?" a woman asked.

"Yes."

"Hi, I'm Mrs. Sadowski. I'm the principal here. I understand you're inquiring about one of our students?"

"Yes, Justin Clifford. I'm his uncle," Cain told her.

"Can I ask why you're inquiring?"

"Well, I know you typically don't give out student information and I totally understand that. It's just that I'm his uncle and I'm in the military and I've been gone for two years so I was hoping to surprise him by picking him up from school."

"You've not talked to his parents?"

"I'll be honest, I was in a Special Forces unit in deep cover and I wasn't allowed contact with anyone. I just got home on leave, arrived last night, and I wanted to surprise everyone, letting them know I was back. Justin's almost like my own kid, we're best buddies. I figured he'd be super stoked once he saw me," Cain said, hoping his lie worked.

"I see. That's a really sweet idea but I'm afraid it's not possible."

"Why not?"

"I don't think I can really say. I think it's best if you talk to Justin's parents," she replied.

"I don't understand. What's the problem?"

"I just don't think it's appropriate for me to say."

"Please, just tell me. I really would appreciate you being honest with me," Cain said.

"I'm afraid Justin is no longer with us."

"He's not there anymore? He got transferred to another school or something?"

"Well, not quite," Sadowski stumbled. "Justin passed away about eight months ago."

"Excuse me?" Cain asked, sure he misunderstood what she said.

"I'm sorry to be the one to tell you. Justin died."

Cain's mouth fell open, unable to formulate words for a response.

"He had a rare form of cancer. It took him quickly."

"I'm uh... well, thank you for telling me."

"I'm sorry for your loss."

Cain hung up and sat back in his chair, stunned and at a loss for words. His eyes immediately started tearing up as he thought about the son he couldn't remember. He wiped his eyes, trying to control himself, but was unable to stop the flow of tears. He folded his arms and put his head down on the desk as he bawled his eyes out. For the next half hour Cain sobbed uncontrollably. He couldn't believe his son was gone before he even got a chance to know him. Once the sadness began wearing off, anger started to set in. He grabbed a few things off the desk and threw them across the room. Cain then went over to pick them up and looked at the wall for a moment before proceeding to put three holes in it with his fist. He walked around the room for a few minutes to compose himself, the anger slowly leaving his body. Then Cain figured it was time to see some of the things he'd been missing and left the hotel.

Once Cain pulled onto Deanna's street, a little nervousness started setting in. It was a feeling he couldn't remember having before. He drove down the street, still unsure what exactly he was gonna do. He pulled alongside the curb on the other side of the street and stopped a few houses away. He was still able to get a good look at Deanna's house without being seen. He just sat there as he contemplated his next move.

Cain kept his eyes focused on Deanna's house, periodically looking around and checking the mirrors for signs of visitors. He looked in the rearview mirror and noticed a figure moving closer to him. He grabbed his gun, anticipating he would have to use it. The person in the mirror was trying to stick to the houses for cover, though not doing a very good job at it. He continued watching the person for a few minutes as they tried to sneak up on him. The person was wearing a hat and sunglasses, but there was something familiar about them. The way the person walked and moved, Cain knew who it was without having to see their entire face. He tucked his gun away as he waited for them to show their face. About five minutes later the person made their move toward his car, sprinting from behind one of the houses towards the passenger side door. They quickly opened the door and jumped in, a gun in hand, pointed at Cain. Cain slowly and calmly looked over, not phased in the least by the sight of the gun, and smiled at his visitor.

"What took you so long?" Cain asked.

"Huh?"

"You're a lousy spy, Shelly. I first saw you ten minutes ago."

"Oh. Well, sneaking up on people was never really my thing," Lawson explained.

"Is that really necessary?" Cain asked, nodding at the gun.

"I just wanted to make sure I didn't get shot before I got a chance to talk to you."

"And you thought that would make a difference?" Cain asked.

"Like I said, this has never really been my thing."

"It shows."

Lawson put her gun on the dashboard before taking off her hat and sunglasses.

"So, what do you think you're doing?" she asked.

"Just sitting here."

"Are you kidding? You better give me a better answer than that."

"What else do you want?" Cain asked.

"I want the truth."

"How'd you know I was here?"

"I've actually been here since yesterday. I kind of assumed you'd be here eventually," Lawson said.

"You knew? All this time, you knew?"

"No. I didn't find out till Heyward was killed. After I talked to you I went into Sanders' office and broke into his safe and looked at your file. Everything was there."

"You broke into his office? Not a wise career move."

"I'm not worried about that."

"You never kept anything from me, did you?" Cain asked.

"No. No. Of course not. When you were first recruited, Sanders told me how there were things in your past you were better off not remembering," she remembered. "I assumed it was related to your parents' death or something else. I never dreamed or imagined that he was driving you away from your wife and son. Please believe me."

"You've never been a good liar," Cain replied, believing her story.

"So, what exactly do you plan on doing here?"

"I haven't really figured it out yet."

"Well, if you plan on sitting here for a few minutes to think

475

about things, fine, have at it, but if you plan on actually going over there and knocking on the door, then I'd strongly advise against it," Lawson pleaded.

"Don't you think I deserve to know my wife? Don't you think she deserves to know that I'm still alive and didn't die?"

"Yes. Of course. But what you both deserve and what can actually happen here are two completely different things and you need to realize that."

Cain kept staring out the windshield, not looking at Lawson at all, thinking about her words.

"If she sees you, you will destroy her life all over again," Lawson said. "Losing you destroyed her life once. But she's picked up the pieces. She's found love again. She's gotten remarried. She's moved on. What do you think you're gonna do to her if she sees you again? What do you think you'll do to her life? You'll throw it upside down again."

"Point taken." Cain sighed in frustration.

"And what about Heather?"

"What about her?"

"You've created a new life with her. She deserves to have you back," she said.

"She deserved a lot more than me."

"What do you mean deserved?"

"You didn't hear the news?" Cain asked.

"Hear about what?"

"The plane I put her on went down over the Atlantic a couple hours ago."

"Oh God no," Lawson said, anguished. "Are you sure?"

"Yeah."

"I can't believe it," she said, distraught.

"Just follows the pattern."

"What pattern?"

"One by one they all wind up dead. Everyone close to me. If I were you I'd take off now and leave me behind. You're all that's left."

"Why are you so hard on yourself?"

"Because everything that's happened is my fault," Cain said.

"What? That's crazy. How could you blame any part of this on yourself?"

"Because everyone that's gotten close to me has gotten hurt. Anyone who's tried to help me has lived to regret it. Heather almost got killed once because of me. Because of this. Now it's happened for real. Heyward lost his life trying to help me. Patel's dead because he helped me."

"Who's Patel?" Lawson asked.

"Cab driver who made the mistake of helping me lose some of Sanders' men."

"Oh. Matt, nobody could blame you for feeling frustrated or upset about everything. But what's happened to you isn't your fault."

"I wish I could feel that way."

"You are such a stubborn, stubborn man. Over the last couple years, I've watched you beat yourself up over every mission, every kill, what happened to Heather, that boy in Russia..."

"You know you shouldn't be here," Cain told her. "If they find out you're here, they're gonna assume you're trying to help me."

"I'm not worried about that."

"I am. You need to go before they come."

"We can go together. Right now. I can help you," Lawson said.

477

"No. I can't let you. If they find out you're with me or helping me you're as good as dead. I can't let that happen."

"OK. I'll go. But you need to go too."

"I'll stick around a little while," Cain said.

"What? Why? Why would you stay here if you know they're coming?"

Cain didn't respond and simply looked at her. The cold, icy stare he gave her indicated he had something else in mind. Lawson knew what he was planning.

"You're not planning on walking out of here are you?" Lawson asked.

Cain smiled at her. "You should go."

"Think about this for a second."

"I have thought about it," Cain replied.

"There's another way. It doesn't have to end like this."

"Shelly, I'm tired of everyone close to me getting hurt and I don't want it to happen anymore. This whole thing has to end. The longer it goes on the more people will get hurt. I can't let it continue."

"You're talking crazy."

"I'm talking sense," Cain said. "I can't get my wife and son back. I can't have Heather. People are dead because of me. The missions, the kills, I don't wanna live with it anymore. There's really no reason for me to keep on with this."

"Except that you're a fighter. And if I know you, the reason you'll keep on is so they won't do this to someone else. Do you want someone else to feel what you're feeling?"

"Why should I care?"

"I know you're hurting and I know you want the pain to stop. But there's another way. We'll find it," Lawson said.

"The best thing you can do for me is to go back to New York and tell Sanders you found me here and turn me in."

"What?!"

"You're my handler; he's already having doubts about you. If you tell him you found me and tried to get me to come in and tell him where I'm at then you'll probably be safe. If I make it through this, I can use your help from the inside."

"I'm not turning you in and telling him where you are."

"Please, just do it."

Cain reached into the back seat and grabbed his duffel bag. He pulled out the files from Heyward and handed them to Lawson.

"What's this?" she asked.

"I think you know what it is."

"Why are you giving it to me?"

"You'll probably know what to do with it better than I will," Cain said.

"OK," Lawson replied. "When you're done here, you call me."

"Sure."

Lawson reached into her pocket and pulled out a piece of paper and handed it to Cain. He looked at it, unsure what it was.

"What's this?" Cain asked.

"Address to the cemetery where Justin's buried. Thought you might want to visit," she said. "It's in the northwest corner of the cemetery. I put some purple and yellow flowers, with one red rose, on his grave this morning so you'd know which one it was. You know, in case you wanted to visit."

Lawson took the folders and got out of the car. She had a nasty feeling that it'd be the last time she ever saw him. Cain continued sitting, and waiting, and watched as Lawson drove past him out of sight. Half an hour later Cain sat up at attention as a car pulled past him and into Deanna's driveway. He watched eagerly as a blonde-haired woman got out of the car. It was Deanna. She was even more beautiful than in Cain's visions or in the picture he had. He felt his heart skip a beat as he watched her reach into her car and pull out a few bags of groceries. Cain kept watching her until she brought all the bags inside the house. He was a little sad once she was done and disappeared from his sight.

After some angst and soul searching, Lawson wrestled with Cain's wishes about telling Sanders where he was. As much as it sounded like Cain was giving up and wanted to end everything, she thought maybe he actually had a plan, and he needed her to get it activated. As much as she hated doing it, she picked up her phone to call Sanders. She prayed that Cain had something else in mind.

"Shelly, what can I do for you?" Sanders said happily.

"Umm, I just wanted to talk to you about Cain."

"We've been over this already. I can't change what's been done."

"I know," she said. "I just wanted to tell you that I know where he is."

"What?"

"I was just with him an hour ago."

"Oh?"

"I thought I could get him to come in before he got hurt," Lawson told him, hating herself for what she was doing.

"And?"

"He won't."

"I'm not surprised. Well, I respect your feelings for him,

Shelly, I really do, but by calling me you're showing your loyalty to this agency. And I appreciate that."

"It's my job, sir," she said, barely able to get the words out.

"So, where is he?"

"Sitting outside his wife's house in Virginia."

"Glad to hear you say that."

"Why's that?" Lawson asked.

"Because we already knew that and have a team moving in his direction as we speak."

"What?"

"We actually got surveillance of him at a gas station just inside the border," Sanders said. "But I really do appreciate you calling and telling me. Just reaffirms my trust and belief in you."

"Well, thank you."

"I'll admit after our last conversation I wasn't sure which way you were going. But calling in with his location means that you put our organization first and foremost above any personal feelings you may have and that's an important characteristic."

"Thank you. One other thing," she said. "Was that plane crash in the Atlantic our doing?"

"Unfortunately, the cost of doing business."

"All those innocent people."

"Sometimes collateral damage is unavoidable. Besides, one of the first things you learn in this business, to make things more digestible, is that there are no innocent people. They all have skeletons."

"Understood."

"So, when are you coming back to New York?" Sanders asked.

"I'm on my way back now."

"Excellent. I'll see you when you get here."

Once Lawson hung up, she closed her eyes and shook her head, hoping the violent and painful visions she was imagining with Cain wouldn't come to fruition. A few minutes later her phone started blowing up with texts from different office personnel as well as field agents. Something big was going on. She couldn't believe what was happening. Then she started making calls to confirm what she was being told.

Sanders was still in his office when he got the word. His secretary brought him the memo. He uncomfortably shifted in his seat as he read it. He then crumpled it up and threw it on the floor.

"Why is it so hard to kill one woman?!" Sanders shouted.

He dialed the number of one of his top aides, John Parry, to get the lowdown. Parry had just finished up at the airport and was leaving the premises. He was the first to figure out that Heather was still alive.

"John, what the hell is going on down there?"

"Looks like her and her sister got off the plane two minutes after they originally boarded," Parry explained. "They weren't on the plane that took off and blew up."

"How many times do we have to try to kill one woman?"

"I don't know, sir."

"Well, I'll tell you how many. Two times too many. It shouldn't take three tries to kill one female civilian. It's unacceptable. We're looking like a third-rate organization here," Sanders said.

"I understand your concern."

"So where is Ms. Lloyd off to now?"

"Same as before. She took the next flight to Paris an hour later," Parry informed him.

"Wonder what the point of that was?"

"Don't know, sir."

"Well, we can't blow up two planes in one day and get away with it. One looks like an accident. Two looks intentional. What's its status?" Sanders asked.

"Should touch down in about an hour."

"You're positive she's on this plane?"

"Absolutely. I watched the airport footage of her getting off the first plane. Then they got off like they were looking for someone. They waited a few minutes in a coffee shop and then got tickets for the next plane. I watched them board, and they never got off."

"Good. We'll be waiting for them."

Sanders immediately got on the phone to a couple agents they had stationed in France. He directed them to meet Heather and her sister when they stepped off the plane. His instructions were to take them away from the airport to a secure and remote location to promptly put a bullet through each of their heads.

Heather and Cassie were discussing their situation aboard their flight. Cassie urged Heather to call their contact.

"Shouldn't you call this Raines guy to let him know we're coming on a different flight?" Cassie asked.

"Yeah. I guess I should."

"What's wrong with you? Ever since we left something's been bothering you."

"I guess I wasn't ready and prepared to hear stuff," Heather said.

"Like what?"

"The reporter told me what was in Matt's files."

"Oh. Was it that bad?" she asked.

"He's married," Heather said, her eyes tearing up. "And he has a son."

483

"Oh no," Cassie replied, putting her arm around her sister. "I'm so sorry."

"Things will never be the same."

"Give him time to sort things out."

"How could he choose me over a wife and son that were taken away from him?" Heather asked.

"Give him a chance."

Heather shook her head. "I know him. He couldn't live with himself if he chose to be with someone else after knowing he had a family."

Heather wiped her tears away and made the call to Raines. As much as she was upset about losing Cain, she knew she had to look after Cassie and Emma. At the very least, she had them to look forward to.

"Hi. Is this Eric Raines?" Heather asked.

"Yes, it is."

"This is Heather, Matt's girl... well, he told you we were coming."

"Uh... yes, he did," Raines replied, stunned. "Forgive me for, well, I'm a little bit at a loss for words."

"You knew we were coming, right?" Heather asked, concerned he wasn't going to meet them.

"I did. I'm just somewhat surprised and confused."

"About what?"

"You were supposed to be on an earlier flight. That plane blew up and crashed a couple hours ago over the ocean. So, you see, I was operating under the assumption that you were no longer among us," Raines said.

"What? I got off the plane and took the next flight."

"How fortunate for you."

"I think we should be there in about an hour. What should we do?"

"Exactly as we planned. We must assume that they know you're on that plane. If they blew up one, then it's a fair bet that they will try to eliminate you again. Let's go under the assumption that they will be waiting for you once you arrive."

"So, what do we do?" Heather asked.

"Nothing. I'll take care of everything. If they'll be there to meet you, so will I. I gave Cain my word I would take care of you and I will. You can count on me," Raines said.

"I'm scared."

"Fear is what keeps people going. I'd be more worried about you if you weren't. Try not to think about it."

"That's a little easier said than done."

"I know."

After Heather hung up, Cassie could see that she looked a little rattled.

"What is it?" Cassie asked.

"Umm," Heather stammered, unsure of whether to tell her sister the truth. "It looks like the original plane we were supposed to be on blew up."

"What?!" she replied, raising her eyebrows.

"Yeah," Heather affirmed, faking a smile like she wasn't concerned.

Before their plane touched down, Cassie had a few things on her mind she wanted to discuss. They'd always avoided talking about their father since their relationship started going downhill. Cassie figured it was time to change that. Being thousands of feet in the air, there was nowhere for either of them to go.

"So, when are we going to get rid of the elephant in the room," Cassie said.

"Huh?"

"Until we talk about Dad, there's always gonna be something unsettled between us. We've been apart for too long and we need to put this behind us once and for all."

"What is it that you want to know exactly?" Heather asked.

"Why did you leave so suddenly? What exactly was your problem with Dad?"

Heather sighed, still not really wanting to talk about it, but knew Cassie wasn't going to let up on the subject. Plus, she figured Cassie deserved to finally know the truth about everything. She'd been shielding it from her for too long.

"Because you two always got along so, well, and I didn't want to ruin your opinion of him. With Mom gone, I wound up taking on more responsibility. Part of that was making sure you were safe," Heather said.

"I'm not sure I understand."

"Dad drank a lot. Didn't help his temper much either," Heather said, her voice quivering. "So, a lot of times when I'd get home from work he would take that anger out on me."

"What?"

"He would threaten to do the same to you but I always egged him on enough where he was satisfied just doing it to me."

"Why would you never say anything?" Cassie asked, horrified.

"All the makeup and staying out late wasn't because I was partying like you thought. It was to hide the bruises," Heather explained.

"I can't believe it. I always thought you abandoned us."

"Ever since Mom died, you looked up to him so much, I

couldn't stand to tear him down for you. I didn't want you to lose both parents."

"You should've confided in me. I would've stuck with you," Cassie said. "I can't believe it. Why were you never around while I was going through college? I really could've used your help."

"I was too busy helping to put you through it."

"What do you mean?"

"I wasn't dancing and stripping because I enjoyed it. You always thought it was Dad who put you through college but it wasn't. Everything I made went toward your tuition," Heather said. "Dad never told me that."

"I know. I told him not to."

"Why would you do that?" Cassie asked.

"Because I knew you wouldn't approve."

"You're right. I wouldn't."

"I know. I figured if you knew where the money was coming from you wouldn't accept it. And I was determined to get you through college. Dad couldn't help and financial aid wouldn't have been enough," Heather explained.

"Dad had money saved up in investment accounts for us for school though."

"No," Heather replied, shaking her head. "Anything he had saved up he gambled away. His weekly casino trips cost him thousands. Including our school savings."

"I feel like such a fool for some of the things I said and thought about you. I always thought he paid for it through his savings account."

"I just figured it'd be better if you didn't know the truth about everything."

"I'm so sorry for ever doubting your feelings and intentions," Cassie said, giving her sister a hug.

"Well, my intentions have put you in a lot of danger right now. I wouldn't be too thankful for that."

"This has brought us closer than ever and I feel like I finally understand you again. And that's wonderful. I don't care how much danger we're in. Getting my sister back is bigger than anything."

Heather gave her a sheepish smile. Though she was grateful that they seemed to be on the same page again, she thought of the danger that was probably waiting for them at the airport terminal. She wasn't as worried for herself as she was for Cassie and Emma. As the plane came in for a landing, Heather looked over to Cassie to make sure she was ready.

"I'm not sure what's gonna be waiting for us," Heather said. "Hopefully it's Raines. If it's not, though, be ready to move, and move fast."

"I will."

39

Passengers started getting off the plane and Heather and her family were right in the middle of the bunch. As soon as they stepped through the gates Heather looked around for Raines. At least she had the advantage of meeting him before so she knew what he looked like. It would've been even more troubling if she had no idea who she was searching for. They stood there looking around for a minute, Heather's worries increasing every minute without Raines' presence. She was counting on him being there. Without him, she wasn't sure what they should do next. Heather wasn't sure exactly where they could go but she was fairly certain that they couldn't just sit there. Eventually, she knew Sanders and his men would arrive. Heather and Cassie agreed to wait five more minutes. If there was no sign of Raines, then they'd leave and take a cab to a local hotel to figure out their next move. As people moved around them, Heather started to worry that something happened to Raines. With the five-minute mark approaching, Cassie held Emma tighter, as her and Heather prepared to move on their own. Just as they were about to start walking, Heather spotted a few men in suits that had earpieces. They were the type of men who looked like the ones who tried to kill them before. The three men began walking toward them. Heather tensed up and thought about running, but knew they wouldn't get far. Cassie couldn't run quickly with Emma and Heather wasn't about to leave them behind. They would just have to take their chances and hope that Raines sent them.

"Heather?" one of the men asked.

"Yes."

"Hi. Cain sent us to meet you and take you to a secure location so you'd be safe."

"Oh? He didn't say anything to me about that before we left," Heather said.

"Change of plans. He called us while you were in mid-air," the man said.

"Oh. So where are we going?"

"One of our safe houses."

"So, did Matt call you from his cell phone?" she asked.

"Uh, yeah."

"Oh. His cell wasn't working before."

"He fixed it."

The men led Heather and Cassie away, pretending to be protecting them. Heather knew they were lying as Cain would never send anyone to meet them. Plus, she knew that Cain didn't have his cell phone anymore, so it was an easy trap. They were Sanders' men. She knew what was in store for her but could only hope that they'd let her sister and the baby go. She'd plead for their lives if she had to. She didn't have to think about it for long though. As they were leaving the airport and walking in the parking lot, Heather's eyes raised when she saw a familiar face coming closer to them.

"There's been a change of plans," the man told the agents.

"What change? Who are you?"

"My name's Wentworth. Sanders sent me to make sure these women were not eliminated."

"Why did he send you? Why didn't he just contact us directly?" the agent asked.

"Looks like they've got Cain pinned down in a warehouse right now. He's a little busy with that. If they can't smoke him out, he wants to use this pair as leverage and try to use them as bargaining chips. Their life for his."

"He thinks Cain will go for that?"

"He's sure of it," Raines replied, smirking. "Should we put them in your car?"

"Yeah. It's over here."

Raines gave Heather a wink and started walking to the side of them. Heather nudged her sister in the arm and gave her a look to let her know something was about to happen. Cassie understood the message. As they walked to the car, Raines gradually walked slower to let the group get completely in front of him. Once they got to the car, one of the men started to climb in before Raines grabbed his arm to stop him.

"Hey. Where are your manners? Ladies first," Raines told him.

The man shrugged and rolled his eyes but complied with the request. He opened the back door and let the two sisters get in. Once they were both sitting in the car, Raines had the opportunity he was seeking. He didn't want to get into a gunfight with the women possibly getting in the middle of it and taking a stray bullet. Getting them into the car by them-selves at least afforded them some protection.

"Well, I guess this is where we'll part company," Raines said.

"What? What're you talking about?"

"I'm switching teams."

Raines reached into his coat and pulled out a gun and commenced firing. Before any of the Specter agents knew what was happening, they were lying on the ground, blood pouring out of their bodies. Raines acted with such surprise and quickness that none of the other agents were even able to grab their guns. One bullet to each of them put them down. As they were lying there, just to make sure they were dead, Raines unloaded another round into each of their lifeless bodies. He then opened the car door and ushered the woman out.

"We haven't much time," Raines told them. "Once these men don't report they'll assume something happened and put the word out."

"Thanks. You're a little late though," Heather replied.

"Once I got here, I noticed these jokers roaming through the airport. I didn't want to engage in a shootout in there so I had to wait to get them into a better position."

"Well, thank you."

"Not necessary."

"Hmm. That's what Matt would say," Heather said. "Is Matt really pinned down right now?"

"No. I just told them what I thought would get the job done," Raines replied.

Raines' car wasn't parked too far away, and they rushed over to it, reaching it in a matter of minutes. He put them in the back seat and told them to get down to avoid being seen as he drove away. Once they were on the road for a few minutes Raines told them it was safe to sit up again.

"That was more excitement than I'd care to have again," Cassie said.

"Hopefully it will be the last you'll have of it," Raines replied.

"Can I ask you something?" Heather asked.

"If I say no will you ask it anyway?"

"Probably."

"In that case, go ahead," Raines said.

"Why are you doing this?"

"Cain asked me to."

"Yeah, I know that. But why are you really doing it? You don't owe him. Or us. What's it matter to you what happens to us?" Heather asked.

"It's complicated."

"I've got time."

"There are many factors involved."

"You're a wanted man. Aren't you taking a bigger risk of them finding you?"

"I take a risk every day I get out of bed."

"You're evading the question."

"One of my best qualities," Raines said.

"So, you're not gonna answer?"

"I don't know how much Cain has told you about this line of work, but things are hardly ever as clear cut as they appear. In fact, I'd say things are almost always not what they seem to be."

"So, how's that apply to you?" Heather wondered. "Are you not who you appear to be?"

"There are many facets to my involvement in this. Most of which I am not at liberty to go into with you," Raines answered.

"Is it about getting revenge on Sanders' men?"

"Only one small factor in the equation."

New York---Sanders was talking to one of his men on the phone when his secretary rushed into his office, putting a note on his desk for him. Sanders read it as he was listening to the agent talk.

"Hold on a minute. I just got handed something," Sanders interrupted. "I'll call you back."

Sanders immediately dialed the number of Pierre Proulx, the European Director, to get the full story.

"Pierre, what's this crap that I've just been handed. Please tell me it's not accurate," Sanders said.

"If you're referring to this mess in the airport here, I'm afraid it's very accurate," Proulx said.

"You're telling me that three of our agents have been killed by Cain's girlfriend?"

"You obviously have not gotten the whole story yet. Our agents were killed, but not by her."

"Who did it then?"

"Eric Raines," Proulx said.

Sanders didn't immediately respond, stunned by Proulx's answer. "You're totally certain that it was Eric Raines?"

"We got a facial rec on a parking lot security cam. There's no doubt it's him."

"And what happened to Lloyd and her sister?"

"I'm afraid it gets even murkier. From the video feed, it looks as though Raines talks to the agents and somehow gains their trust and starts walking with them. The women get put in the car and Raines killed all three of them," Proulx said.

"And what did he do with the women?"

"He took them to his car and drove off."

Sanders sighed in frustration and rubbed his forehead. "How is Raines involved in all this now?"

"I'm not sure we're gonna get an answer to that anytime soon."

"We need to get Raines and those women," Sanders said.

"Ed, we've been after Raines for several years now. We're no closer to finding him now than we've ever been. He's probably on his third car by now."

"Well, we need to step up our efforts. The fate of this agency could be in the balance here. I feel like things are starting to fall apart. We need those women. Especially Lloyd."

"I'll put every resource I have into it."

"OK. Let me know what you come up with."

Sanders was now more concerned than ever. Two of the most lethal agents he'd ever had were both on the run and eluding them. It seemed to him that the two of them had somehow aligned their efforts. It seemed obvious that Cain had enlisted Raines' help and had sent the women over to him. Things appeared to be spiraling out of control. He could only hope the agents dispatched to Cain's wife's house would finish him off. Sanders then left his office to go to The Room, wondering about the status of the agents near Cain.

"What's the ETA of the men near our boy?" Sanders asked.

"About two minutes."

Sanders let out a sigh. "Let's get this done finally."

Before going back to the office, Lawson stopped at a Staples store to use the fax machine. She knew she couldn't fax what Cain had given her in her office in case she was being monitored. She looked up the numbers of a couple senators and congressmen and faxed everything she had to them. She also sent a copy to the *New York Times*. After she was through, she headed to the office. Once she got in, there seemed to be a lot of commotion, people hustling through the halls as if something was happening.

"What's going on?" Lawson asked someone.

"Looks like they're moving in on Cain."

"Oh," she replied, hustling into The Room.

"Shelly, just in time," Sanders said, noticing her walk in.

"I hear we've almost got him?" she nervously asked.

"Almost."

Cain was still sitting in his car when he noticed a black Ford pulling onto the street behind him. He knew what was about to happen. As soon as it got behind his bumper, Cain sped off, leading them on a high-speed chase. He thought about engaging them right there but didn't want to endanger his wife in any way or have her see gunfire erupt in front of her house. He zoomed down the next street, his attackers closely following. Cain spun his car and did a three sixty, speeding past them. He raced out of the section and onto the highway. He reached over a hundred miles per hour with the agents still in pursuit. After ten minutes on the interstate, Cain took an exit and led his pursuers to a more remote location. Wheels screeching, he turned a corner into an abandoned set of warehouse buildings. He led them around a couple of buildings and once Cain got a little separation, he went down an alley between two of them. He waited a few seconds and as soon as the Ford entered his crosshairs, Cain put his foot on the gas. His wheels spun, smoke rising from them, and he sped into the black car. The front of Cain's car smashed directly into the driver's side door, spinning it out of control, airbags deploying. Cain quickly got out of the car to check on the condition of the agents. They were both knocked unconscious by the impact. Cain thought about just leaving, but knew he'd have to deal with them again at some point if he left them breathing. He raised his gun up, pointing it at the agents through the shattered window, and hesitated about pulling the trigger. Though he wanted to just walk away without killing two men who weren't even conscious, he knew there was a very good chance he'd have to do it again soon anyway once they got back on his trail. Regretfully, he pointed the gun at each agent and shot them three times, leaving no doubt about their demise. Cain turned to leave when he heard voices emanating from the car. He reached into the car and checked the driver and took out his earpiece. He placed it in his own ear and went back to his car.

"Six-two-seven, what's your status?"

"His status is dead," Cain broke in.

Lawson closed her eyes and breathed a sigh of relief upon hearing Cain's voice. Sanders slapped his leg and looked up at the ceiling, frustration once again setting in.

"Nice to hear your voice again, Cain," Sanders said.

"Save the crap. When are you gonna stop sending other people to do your dirty work?"

"As soon as you're dead."

"Sorry to keep disappointing you," Cain responded.

"Well, you know what they say... tomorrow's another day," Sanders joked.

"And you only have so many left."

Sanders immediately discontinued communications and angrily stormed out of the room. Cain drove off to the cemetery where Justin was buried, about ten minutes away. It was a large cemetery with a green metal fence that surrounded it.

Cain walked around some of the graves, glancing at them on his way to the back. After walking for a few minutes, he looked up and noticed the purple and blue flowers with the red rose nestled between them on a grave off in the distance. He cleared his throat and continued walking in the direction of the flowered grave. Just as Cain reached the grave, the skies grew darker and a light rain started coming down. Cain looked up momentarily before looking back down at his son. He licked his lips, unsure what he should do or say. He knelt down on one knee and fiddled with the flowers. He cleared his throat again.

"I, uh, I'm not quite sure what to say here so bear with me a few minutes," he started, his eyes beginning to tear up. He coughed as he tried to collect his thoughts. "I wish I had something eloquent to say, some poetry to recite, or some beautiful words to relay, but I don't. All I can tell you is... that I'm sorry," Cain said, tears rolling down his cheeks. "People keep telling me that none of this is my fault, but I can't help but feel that it is. I guess that even if I were around that none of this would be any different, but at least you would have died having your father around. If you're looking down, you probably already know everything that's happened with me, but I wish I could remember something about you. Your first words, your first steps, maybe when you first started crawling, or maybe even playing catch in the backyard. But I can't remember any of it. They took my life away from me and...," Cain stopped, not sure what else he was trying to say. The skies opened up a little more, and the rain started coming down a little heavier. "Is that my cue to leave? Trying to get rid of me already?" He laughed. "Well, due to my current situation I probably shouldn't stay in one spot for too long anyway. I'm not sure when I'll be able to make it back, or if I ever will, but if not... I just want you to know I love you."

Cain stood up and looked at the grave, letting the raindrops bounce off him, and watched as the flowers began getting soaked. He wiped his eyes and glanced up and noticed a flash over by a clump of trees. It looked like the type of flash that happened when something reflected off the scope of a sniper rifle. If Cain was being lined up, he sure didn't have much cover, and it was a long way to get back to the car. He hoped he was wrong, and a sniper wasn't waiting for him, but he couldn't take the chance of just standing there doing nothing. He pulled his gun out from the belt of his pants as he said his final goodbye to his son.

"If this is it, I might be seeing you sooner than I figured. If not, I'll talk to you soon."

Cain then took off and started running toward the front gate, passing some small headstones. He ran about thirty yards when the sound of a rifle being fired sounded. Cain almost instantly felt a shooting pain and fell to the ground. He lay there motionless, blood coming out of his left shoulder. He figured he'd lay there a little while, knowing the sniper would most likely leave rather quickly. The sniper would figure he was dead and take off, or if he thought he was still alive, would have to come closer to check. Cain lay face down, still clutching his gun in his hand, tucked underneath his stomach. Now all he had to do was wait.

The Room was abuzz with excitement when the agent called in to let them know he'd shot Cain. Sanders was quickly summoned from his office to survey the situation.

"Who do we have there?" Sanders asked.

"Agent Hester," an analyst replied. "While the other agents

went to Cain's wife's house, Hester staked out the cemetery where his son was buried."

"Excellent."

"He called in and said he'd just shot him."

"Hester, what's the situation down there, soldier?" Sanders asked.

"I was waiting by the cemetery and Cain showed up. He must've spotted me because he made a run for it. I shot him and he went down."

"What's his status?"

"He's still lying there," Hester replied.

"Where'd you hit him?"

"Not sure. Thought I nailed him square."

"Can you take another shot?" Sanders asked.

"Don't think so. Not from this angle and where he's lying. He's between a couple graves. The only thing I can do from here is shoot his feet."

"Well, we need to know for sure. You need to go check on him."

"Roger that."

Cain lay still for half an hour to make sure he was in the clear. With his shoulder needing attention, he knew he couldn't stay there too much longer. Luckily, his attacker was moving in and he didn't have much longer to wait. Hester had made his way to the front of the cemetery and was about to enter through the arch-shaped gate. He was taking his time and making sure he didn't rush and make a mistake. A mistake that might get him killed. By this time, he switched his weapon from the rifle to a handgun and was inching closer to Cain's body. As Hester moved in, he kept looking around to make sure no one else was there. He still saw no signs of life in Cain's body, causing him to relax a little.

"Cain," Hester yelled. "Doesn't look like he's alive," he replied back to Sanders.

"Don't take any chances. Put two more bullets in his back to make sure."

"Roger that."

Upon hearing Hester's voice, Cain could tell exactly where he was standing and that he'd relaxed a little by talking to Sanders. He wasn't entirely focused on him at that point. Cain rolled over as quick as lightning and fired a couple bullets that found their way into Hester's midsection. Hester dropped to his knees as he looked at Cain, shocked that he got the jump on him and made such a careless mistake. Hester raised his gun slightly but dropped it a second later as Cain put one more round into his chest. Hester fell onto his back and Cain got to his feet and checked on the man. He took the transmitter out of his ear and put it in his own. He waited a few seconds until someone spoke.

"I heard gunfire, Hester, is it done?" Sanders asked.

"Looks like you lost one more agent," Cain replied. "You failed again."

"This isn't over. I'm gonna keep coming and coming and coming. I don't care how many agents it takes, but your days are numbered. I guarantee you that. There's nowhere you can run, hide, or take cover."

"Heartwarming."

"And if I don't get you first, maybe I can get Raines. You know, since he seems to be hiding your girlfriend and her sister right now."

"You haven't been able to locate him in several years. I doubt you're gonna be able to do it now."

"I guess we'll see," Sanders said.

"We're done here," Cain said, tossing the earpiece on the ground and crushing it with his foot.

Cain held his shoulder and began running out of the cemetery when he stopped near the front gate. His mouth felt really dry, and he licked his lips. He felt a shortness of breath and grabbed one of the iron bars on the gate to keep his balance. He squinted his eyes as he had trouble focusing on anything and his vision was slightly blurry. Cain knew what was happening and knew he couldn't just stay there. He gathered up enough energy to stumble forward until he reached his car. His head was pounding and felt like it was about to explode. He wasn't sure how much time he had left but didn't want to pass out there. He got in the car and fumbled with the keys, finally able to start it after a few seconds. It was no use though. His breathing became very heavy, and he closed his eyes. He turned the car off knowing he couldn't drive anywhere without crashing into a tree somewhere. A second late he slumped over, his head resting on the passenger seat.

40

Cain woke up, still lying in the front seat of his car. After staying in that position for a few minutes, he finally was able to sit up. His head felt a little foggy, and he was breathing hard. It was dark out. He turned his car on and looked at the time. It was after ten. He wasn't sure exactly where he was, so he got out of his car and just looked at his surroundings. Cain saw the cemetery sign and thought for a few seconds to remember what he was doing there. After a minute, it came back to him. He remembered everything that happened. A pain came out of his shoulder causing him to wince and look down at it as he dabbed the wound with his hand. He'd forgotten he was shot until the pain reminded him. He looked at his phone and saw several missed calls from Raines. He thought about calling him back but figured he'd do it later. With Heather gone he didn't think he had much to discuss with him. Cain knew he needed medical treatment soon, though, and got in his car and started driving until he came across the first hospital he saw. Once he found one he went in and immediately got his shoulder looked at.

"You know, I have to report this," the doctor told him as he was getting the bullet out.

"Yeah."

"Wanna tell me what happened?"

"I was walking downtown and saw a couple guys trying to rape some woman. So, I tried to help and one of them pulled a gun and shot me."

"Wow. Good thing you came along," the doctor replied, not sure he bought the story.

"Yeah."

After the doctor finished, he instructed Cain to stay there for a little bit. Cain knew he couldn't risk staying in one spot for too long, especially once the authorities came after the doctor told them a gunshot victim was there. Cain stood up from the bed and stretched his shoulder. Another doctor came in to check on him, causing Cain to be a little suspicious.

"So, am I good to go, doc?" Cain asked.

"Sure am. I just have one more needle to give you to help with the pain," he replied, holding a needle in his hand.

"Should I sit down?"

"If you'd like."

Cain sat down and reached his right arm behind his back where his gun was tucked in his belt and gripped the handle. The doctor moved the needle closer to Cain's shoulder when Cain suddenly knocked it away, the needle flying across the room. Cain withdrew his weapon from his belt and pointed it at the doctor's chest as he stood up. The doctor backed away with Cain following until he backed himself into the corner.

"Who you working for?" Cain asked, the doctor's fate depending on his answer.

"What's it matter? If you're gonna shoot me, then just do it."

"Because I haven't decided yet if I'm gonna pull the trigger. So, I'll ask you again, who are you working for?"

The doctor huffed as he decided whether to answer. "I work for Sanders."

"You're part of The Specter Project?"

"Surprised?"

"No," Cain said as he pulled the trigger, firing three rounds into the doctor's chest as he watched him slump to the ground. "Not at all."

Cain then left, quickly walking down the hallway, taking care not to run to avoid drawing attention to himself. He couldn't be sure if anyone else was waiting but assumed he would've run into them by now if they were. Once he got out of the hospital, he ran to his car and sped off. As he raced down the highway, he realized that they seemed to be on to him no matter where he turned. His wife's house, the cemetery, the hospital, Specter seemed to know where Cain was going before he did. He slowed down and pulled out his phone and called Lawson.

"Shelly, where are you?" Cain asked.

"I'm at home. Why? Where are you?"

Cain sighed. "I can't seem to shake them. I just had a run-in with an agent at the hospital."

"Hospital? What were you doing there?" she asked.

"Shot in the shoulder. It's fine though. No big deal."

"So, what's your next move?"

"I'm not sure. Did you fax those documents?" he asked.

"Yeah."

"Hopefully that does something. Soon."

"Matt, depending on how far up this goes, they could take this operation down tomorrow or it could take months. If they do anything at all. We can't count on help coming from that," Lawson said.

"I know. I'm just not sure where to go next."

"Just lay low for a little bit. You don't have to engage every agent you come across or seek them out. Just wait and see what happens."

"Hiding out isn't exactly my strength."

"I know. But you can't take down this entire agency by yourself. You can't."

"What other options do I have?"

"Wait and see if anything happens with the documents. Lay low for a few weeks. Find a spot they can't find you and just sit tight," Lawson told him.

"Easier said than done."

"I know," she said, trying to think of something to make him think her way was right.

"Maybe I should just walk into Sanders' office and go down in a blaze of glory," he said.

"No. No. Don't do that," Lawson said, suddenly thinking of what might work. "Heather's alive!"

"What?"

"She's not dead. She got off the plane before it took off and grabbed the next flight. Raines has her and her sister right now. They're safe."

"Are you sure?" Cain asked.

"Of course I'm sure. Sanders is having a fit about why they can't seem to kill her."

"That must've been what Raines was calling me for. I'm sure it's killing Sanders that he can't take out one woman."

"His face gets so red when he's told she's escaped whatever plan he's put in place." Lawson laughed. "It's so funny. He looks like he's about to burst."

"You really think laying low for a few days is the ticket?"

"Yes, I do. All I know is that if you keep looking for trouble, then you will find it. And eventually, that trouble will be more than you can handle. You don't need to take down everyone in one day."

"OK. I'm gonna find a spot to settle down. I'm not sure where but I'll find something. I'll talk to you later."

Cain kept driving, not sure where he was traveling to, but knew that he just needed to be invisible for at least a few days. He drove for hours, careful to avoid anywhere he might be spotted by a camera that could be picked up by Sanders. Once he got to Maryland, he settled on a small hotel just on the edge of the Baltimore line. He figured if he could stay there for a few days, hopefully something would break for him while he was there.

Three days went by without any more incidents. Cain effectively hid without being tracked by Sanders and didn't try to engage any of his men. On Sanders end, they had no leads on where Cain or Raines went. They both seemed to just drop off the grid at the same time. Sanders was beginning to think that this was the beginning of the end. Two former agents that they just couldn't find or kill. It just seemed that the wheels were beginning to come off and things were unraveling.

Sanders was sitting in his office reviewing some files when he noticed a commotion on one of the security monitors in the lobby. His security team seemed to be detaining a large group of men until what appeared to be the leader of the group started getting animated with them and showed them some papers. Sanders couldn't quite tell what it was, but he had a pretty good guess. He noticed a few guns in the crowd and detected a shiny badge on one of them to indicate they were some sort of government personnel. A few minutes later his security team let the group pass. The group quickly moved through the building. Sanders logged onto his computer and sent a mass email to his deputy directors informing them of the situation. He then started deleting the information on his computer. A few minutes later he heard loud voices emanating from just outside his office. His secretary was unsuccessful in trying to prevent a man from barging into his office. Sanders leaned back in his chair as he waited for the man to come in. A younger man emerged, probably in his early thirties, opening the door.

"Director Sanders?" he asked forcefully.

"And who might you be?"

"I'm Special Agent Whitfield."

"By what right do you have barging into my facility like this?" Sanders asked angrily.

"Sorry to inform you that you are being placed under arrest."

"By whose authority? I only answer to one man," he said.

"By order of the President," Whitfield replied, putting the order on the desk. "Did you really think you could just blow up a plane with innocent civilians, Americans, and get away with it? That's not to mention the money laundering, gun trafficking, and other things you've been dabbling in."

Sanders gently picked up the papers and carefully read the contents. After he was done he nonchalantly put them back on the desk.

"So, the plane was what did me in?" Sanders asked.

"They've been keeping an eye on you for a while. Once we received proof of some of the things you were doing, things were set into motion. The plane was the final straw. They couldn't wait any longer to bring you in. Any man in control of a government facility who's willing to blow up a plane with civilians on it is a man they felt was losing his grip."

"These charges won't stick," Sanders noted, still feeling confident.

"Doesn't matter. I'm placing you under arrest and I'm afraid you're gonna have to come with me," Whitfield replied.

"This is my building," Sanders puffed. "You think you can just waltz in here and place me under arrest and get away with it?"

"Don't make this difficult on yourself. It'll be easier for you if you come peacefully."

"You mean easier for you," Sanders said, standing up. "Not one of these charges will stick."

"It's not up to me."

"I assume you have a car waiting to take me away?"

"Yep."

"Mind if I call my wife first just to let her know what's happening?" Sanders asked, starting to smoke a cigar.

"They'll be time for that later. First, we need to get out of this building," Whitfield told him.

"We have the first three floors secured," a voice called out over Whitfield's radio.

"I'm coming down with Sanders in a minute," he replied.

Sanders put the palm of his right hand on the edge of the desk as he puffed on his cigar, the index finger going underneath the desk and hitting a button.

"I guess I'm ready," Sanders stated.

Whitfield led Sanders out of his office as they walked down the hall to the elevator. People were looking on, wondering what was going on. For someone being arrested, Sanders looked extremely calm. Whitfield thought it was somewhat strange how carefree he was being but figured Sanders didn't really have much choice in the matter. They stepped on the elevator and Whitfield hit the parking garage button.

"You really think it's gonna be this easy?" Sanders asked, blowing smoke from his cigar into the air.

"What do you mean?"

"You really think you can just come in here and do this? This is my building. These are my people."

"We've got them taken care of," Whitfield responded.

"Oh, do you?" Sanders shrugged, amused. "I think you have no idea what you've gotten yourself into."

Whitfield was starting to become concerned that maybe Sanders had something up his sleeve. He pulled out his gun as the elevator stopped. The doors swung open and Whitfield was pleasantly surprised that there was nobody there waiting for him. He took Sanders' arm, and they stepped out of the elevator. They walked over to the black car with the tinted windows that Whitfield had waiting for them. He opened the door and put Sanders inside before getting in next to him. Whitfield was immediately horrified when he saw three of his men sitting there dead, bleeding out due to gunshot wounds. He quickly got out and pulled Sanders with him. As soon as he closed the door he turned around to find five guns pointed at him. Sanders took the gun off the young agent.

"As I said, this is my building. These are my people," Sanders said with a smirk. "Did you really believe I didn't have a contingency plan for the day this happened? I'm always two steps ahead."

"You're making a big mistake," Whitfield responded.

"I don't think so. I knew this day would eventually come. I used this agency for everything I could. Now it's time for me to disappear."

Sanders then took Whitfield's arm and led him back over to the elevator.

"You're gonna make the call saying you've got me and are on your way back," Sanders said.

"I'm not doing that."

"You will or you're dead," Sanders threatened. "Make the call and I'll put you back on that elevator unharmed."

Whitfield sighed, knowing he had no choice but to comply with Sanders' wishes. He got on the radio and told everyone that he had Sanders in the car and they were on their way. Sanders smiled and pushed the up button on the elevator.

"See, I'm not unreasonable," Sanders said, putting the agent in the elevator. "Unfortunately for you though... I am untrustworthy."

Sanders raised the gun he took from Whitfield and shot the agent with his own gun. He fired three rounds, all three hitting Whitfield in the chest. The force of the bullets knocked him back as he fell to the ground, blood smearing against the wall. Whitfield was dead as the bullets lodged inside his chest, the first one going through his heart. Sanders' security team whisked him away to his car and zipped out of the garage before anyone knew what had happened.

"Is my jet ready?" Sanders asked.

"Yes, sir."

"Excellent."

"What about Cain and Raines?" the agent asked.

"They're not our problem anymore. Let them deal with them. Our only focus is disappearing."

Lawson was in her office, sitting at her desk, talking with one of the agents in charge of the raid. They were having a very cordial conversation and Lawson was being extremely helpful and forthright. The subject turned to Sanders, Lawson very interested in what they were doing with him.

"So, Sanders is in custody?" Lawson asked.

"Yes. He's already on his way to detention," Agent Powell replied.

"How many men did it take?"

"Just one."

"One? Are you sure?" Lawson asked, surprised.

"Yeah, why?"

"Was there a struggle?"

"No. He went without a fight," Powell responded. "Why do you sound surprised?"

"Because I've spent the last eight years working for that man, going over reports with him, going over missions, everything you can think of. He's always aware of what's going on, always has a backup plan. The fact that he let himself be arrested without a struggle concerns me. Something's not right."

"Well, we didn't give him a chance. He never saw us coming."

"Sanders always knows what's coming," Lawson said. "Call your man."

"What?"

"Call whoever's with him and make sure everything's alright."

Powell was unconvinced that there was a problem but reluctantly called for Whitfield on the radio. After unsuccessfully trying to reach him for several minutes, Powell started to get concerned and come around to Lawson's way of thinking.

"Seems you've got a problem," Lawson told him.

"Come with me," Powell said, rushing out of the office.

Lawson quickly followed him as the two of them scurried down the hallway to the elevator. Powell pushed the button, and they waited for the doors to open. A few seconds later the doors opened, and the two took a step to enter before they were stopped in their tracks at the sight of Whitfield's dead body still lying there.

"Umm, is that the guy you were talking about?" Lawson sarcastically asked.

"Yeah."

"Looks like you've got a problem."

"Damn."

Powell immediately pulled out his phone and called his superiors to let them know what was going on and inform them of Sanders' escape. With Sanders gone, Lawson's thoughts then turned to Cain.

"What will happen with Matthew Cain? Do you know what's going on with him?"

"I believe right now he's a fugitive, is he not?"

"He's innocent. They set him up."

"That's not my call."

"Well, whose call is it?"

"Director Roberts," Powell informed her. Jim Roberts was the CIA Director. "He's personally reviewing all cases and records involving Project Specter."

"How long will that take?" Lawson asked.

"Probably months."

"That's not acceptable. His case needs to move to the top of the pile."

"How do you know there aren't others like him? Why should he get top priority?" Powell asked.

"Because I'm not familiar with anyone else. I am with him. I also know that he's a very dangerous man and if the CIA looks for him and treats him as a criminal, dead bodies will begin to pile up," Lawson said.

"If he's really innocent then I'm sympathetic to your case. All I can do is put you in touch with Director Roberts' secretary so you can make your plea personally."

"I would appreciate that."

Powell gave her the CIA Director's office number. Lawson walked back to her office and dialed the number. She paced back and forth in her office as she waited for someone to pick up. After a few rings, the secretary answered.

"Hi. My name's Michelle Lawson. I'm with Project Specter, which the CIA apparently just shut down. I need to talk to Director Roberts immediately. I'm sorry, I know I'm talking fast here and probably not making sense, and the Director probably doesn't even know who I am, but I really just need to talk to him. It's extremely important."

"Director Roberts is very aware of who you are and Project Specter," the secretary responded.

"Oh. Really? Is there a way I can talk to him for a few minutes? I know he's extremely busy, but it's about an agent named Matthew Cain. Ed Sanders set him up and now he's a fugitive but he's really completely innocent and I'm just afraid something will happen to him before Director Roberts gets to review his case. I'm sorry, I'm Cain's handler and I'm just very worried for his safety."

"I completely understand your concern for your agent's well-being. Director Roberts has been reviewing Project Specter records exclusively for the last week, eighteen hours a day."

"So, can I talk to him? Please?"

"It usually requires more effort than simply calling me for an appointment. Especially for someone who's not in a high government position."

"I know. If I could just have five minutes of his time. That's all I ask," Lawson pleaded.

The secretary stayed silent for a few seconds. "Hold on a minute."

She was only on hold for a couple of minutes but it seemed like an eternity. Lawson kept pacing, nervously waiting for an answer to her request. She sat down for a second but got back up once she heard the secretary's voice return.

"Director Roberts will see you at nine o'clock tomorrow morning in his office here in Washington. Can you make it?"

"I will definitely be there. Thank you so, so much. I really appreciate it," Lawson replied.

"Good luck in pleading your case."

"Thank you again."

Lawson immediately went to her computer and made the travel arrangements to go to Washington. She'd get there later that night and stay in a hotel so she'd make the meeting in plenty of time. The CIA was now fully in control of the Project Specter building and began clearing employees so they could leave or hold them for further questioning. Lawson was cleared rather quickly. As soon as she left, she went home to pack for her trip. She then went to the train station and headed down to Washington.

The next morning, Lawson was sitting in the waiting room in Director Roberts' office, fidgeting with her fingers as she anxiously waited for her name to be called. She looked at the clock on the wall. Five minutes to nine. She prepared a little speech to make but just hoped she wouldn't forget it once they started talking. She looked at her notes for a few minutes until she heard her name called. She got up and sighed, then headed into Roberts' office where she was directed to take a seat. Roberts was looking at some files on his desk and writing on a pad of paper. He stopped what he was doing as soon as Lawson sat down.

"So, Ms. Lawson, what brings you here?" Roberts asked.

"First of all, Director Roberts, thank you for agreeing to meet with me on such short notice. I know you're extremely busy. I'm here to talk about one of my agents, Matthew Cain. Where to begin? Well..." Lawson started, before Roberts put up his hand to stop her from continuing.

"No need to proceed, Ms. Lawson. I'm familiar with the case of Matthew Cain. I've already read his file."

"Then you know he's completely innocent and has been framed by Sanders."

"What is it that you'd like me to do?" Roberts asked.

"Remove the KOS order out on him and clear him of all charges."

"To be honest, I'm not sure it's in our best interests to do that."

"What? Why not?"

"We've already discussed Cain's case internally and there are those who question his status."

"His status? What does that mean?"

"He could be viewed as a liability," Roberts said.

"A liability? That's crazy, uh, sir," Lawson replied, raising her voice. "Matthew Cain is one of the best agents we've ever had. How could he ever be viewed as a liability?"

"He has memory issues and seizures. There are some that would consider this a severe liability. He was on a mission in Syria and had a seizure that could've gotten him killed or tortured into divulging secrets."

"But he escaped and has helped this country immensely with the things he's done."

"He only escaped because of Eric Raines."

"What?"

"Raines freed Cain and helped his escape," Roberts told her.

"Why would he do that?" Lawson asked, astonished.

"Because Eric Raines works for us."

Lawson sat back and raised her eyebrows, blindsided by Roberts' revelation. "Eric Raines works for you?"

"I'm sorry you had to find out this way. I know it must be a shock considering your history with him. Yes, Eric Raines works for us. He's been on a deep cover mission for the last several years. We recruited him to work for us and helped him fake his death in order to infiltrate some targets we'd been trying to destroy."

Lawson sat there with her mouth open, stunned. She wasn't sure what to say.

"It's a lot to take in right now, I know. Especially with your history with him."

"Uh, yeah, yeah it is," Lawson said before she got back on topic. "Besides that, back to the point of why I'm here, Matthew Cain is an excellent agent, and it's to this country's benefit that he is cleared of these charges against him and reinstated."

"And of his issues?" Roberts asked.

"Those issues were in part helped by bad medication that Sanders gave him. They wanted him to have these problems and helped foster them for their benefit. If we save him, we can help alleviate those issues by giving him proper medication and eliminate the risks involved."

"What if it's too late? What if he can't be saved?"

"He can be. It's not too late," she begged.

Roberts rubbed his chin and thought about the options he was facing.

"You feel strongly that Cain's issues can be corrected and that he can still be an asset and a strong agent?" Roberts asked.

"Yes, sir, I do."

"I do as well. I believe it's at least worth the risks. I told you that there were some who thought he may be a liability. However, I am not one of those people. I was glad you called and asked for this meeting. As much as I can study a file, it's not the same as talking to someone such as yourself, who has intimate knowledge of him and his abilities."

"So, you'll lift the charges?" Lawson asked with hope.

"Consider them dropped."

"Wow. That's great. Thank you so much."

"Bringing him in might be a bit of a challenge but I'm sure we'll manage," Roberts said.

"Well, I can just call him and tell him."

"In his state, he'll think it's some type of setup."

"Yeah, you're right. I just wish I knew where he was," she replied.

"Oh, we know where he is. He's in a small hotel in downtown Baltimore. I have agents just waiting for my orders. The trick is to get to him without getting any of my men killed in the process."

"How about if we tranq him? Get him in the open and shoot him with some darts and then bring him in?"

Roberts nodded in approval. He got on the phone and told the agent in charge of the plan to bring Cain in.

"Roger that, sir. We'll move in shortly," the agent replied.

"Keep me informed," Roberts said.

Cain had been resting but suddenly sat up in bed, then looked out the window. He had a feeling something wasn't right. Nothing definite. Just a feeling. When your life revolved around a gun and danger on every corner, you learned to trust your instincts, regardless if there were any facts to support it. He looked out the window for several minutes, hoping to see movement to support his paranoia. He did not though. Everything seemed clear. He went back to the bed, but before he got to sit down, he was startled when the window shattered. Tear gas was shot in through the window, the smoke starting to fill the room. Cain went to the window but still had a hard time seeing anybody. The smoke was getting into his mouth and eyes, making him cough. He opened the door and stood to the side of it. The car was about thirty yards away. It'd be tough to get there, but he figured it was probably the only chance he had. He took a big sigh and took off, running. Cain got about ten yards when he felt a tingling in his shoulder, followed by what felt like sharp needles being stuck in his back. He stopped in his tracks and looked back and saw the dart sticking out of the back of his shoulder. He assumed the other two in his back were the same. He looked up at his attackers but still couldn't see where the shots were coming from. His eyes were growing heavy, but he started walking toward the car. He was stopped by a dart to the front of his shoulder. He looked at it and put his hand on it to pull it out when he was shot again in the top of his back between his shoulder blades. The gun fell out of Cain's hand as everything started spinning. He was starting to lose consciousness. He finally saw a few men in black SWAT outfits moving towards him and a few seconds later Cain dropped to the ground. The men put cuffs on him and tied him to a stretcher as they loaded him in a black van.

"Director Roberts?" one of them called.

"Yes?" Roberts answered.

"We have him. Cain's in custody."

"Any casualties?"

"No. Went without a hitch. We're loading him in the van now and will begin the transport."

"Great work."

Roberts hung up and smiled at Lawson. "They have him."

"Is he hurt?" Lawson asked eagerly.

"No. They're bringing him in now."

"What are you gonna do with him?"

"He'll be taken back to New York to the Specter building. Agent Conlin will be taking charge of the facility and will talk to Cain upon his awakening."

"Conlin? What's his story? Cain doesn't take to new people all that well. He has trust issues."

"As well he should. I have no worries though. Agent Conlin is a very highly thought of agent. He's young, but is intelligent, has experience, and trusts his people. You'll like him. Everyone who remains there will need a new voice, a different voice, one that can be trusted. He's that guy," Roberts told her. "I fully expect he will be embraced."

"I will trust your judgment."

41

Cain was brought back to New York and put in a detention cell on the twelfth floor. He stayed there for a few hours until he woke up. It took him a little longer than most to wake up since they used so many darts on him. Typically, only one or two were needed to get the job done, but they used six on Cain. Six hours after being brought back, Cain woke up. He sat up in the bed and looked at the bright white walls. It was an entirely white room. White walls, a white bed, and a white door. That was it. There was a window, tinted, unable to see through it, which Cain assumed was for observation purposes. Cain sat there and wondered how it could've ended like this. He envisioned the end coming in a flurry of bullets, him getting killed in a huge gun battle in which he took at least ten men down with him. Instead, he wound up locked in a white room for crazy people with who knows what about to happen. Agent Conlin, now appointed Director, had been alerted to Cain's condition and came down to watch Cain through the glass for a few minutes. After five minutes, Conlin decided to go in and talk to him since Cain seemed calm and not violent as some prisoners would be. Cain stood up as the door opened, wondering who he was going to see. He backed up a couple steps like he was getting ready to fight. Conlin stepped in the room with a couple of metal folding chairs and a couple of armed guards behind him.

"You men won't be needed. You can wait outside," Conlin told them. He then set the chairs up in the middle of the room. "Join me?" he asked Cain.

Cain was a little unsure what was going on. It seemed strange that some guy would come into his cell with no guards and want to sit down with him.

"Please," Conlin said, offering Cain a seat. "I understand your hesitation, but I assure you all I want to do is talk."

"Who are you?" Cain asked, moving closer to the chair.

"Greg Conlin. I'm the new director of this facility," Conlin stated, holding his hand out to shake.

"Just what facility are we in?"

"The Specter building," Conlin said, sitting down.

"What? Where's Sanders?"

"Gone. That ship has sailed."

"You expect me to believe that?" Cain asked in disbelief, also taking a chair.

"I know it's not easy to accept, but it's true. He's been relieved of his duties and is currently a fugitive of justice."

"Him and this agency have been hunting me down as little as three days ago and you think I'm gonna buy that?"

"Well, here's how it shook down. The CIA had been keeping an eye on him for some time, gathering evidence against him for several transgressions. Apparently, the plane he blew up looking for your girlfriend was the final straw. They decided he could no longer remain in power, capable of killing innocent civilians and planned to bring charges against him with the evidence they had. Some of which was contained in the documents you had a hand in faxing over, I suspect," Conlin explained.

"So, you're telling me he's on the run?"

"Him and his deputy directors. We invaded the building and thought we had him but he managed to escape. Cunning man, apparently."

"Seems to have happened rather suddenly."

"These types of things usually do go down rather quickly, without warning."

"So, if this is true then what am I doing here?" Cain asked.

"We needed a way to bring you in safely without you killing anybody, or yourself for that matter."

"What are you gonna do with me?"

"Well, that in large part depends on you," Conlin responded.

"In what way?"

"As I said, I'm taking over this building. This will still be a black ops facility but with additional oversight. Before, Sanders only reported to the President and Vice President. This was initially something they created off the grid. It is now being listed under the direction of the CIA under Director Roberts. There will still be limited knowledge of this building but I need good agents and men I can trust. If the aura of internal shadiness, for lack of a better word, continues, then they will shut this operation down. You can help keep it going and successful."

"How?"

"All charges against you have been dropped. I'd like you to come back and work for us. For me."

"How do I know I can believe all this?" Cain asked. "How do I know I'm not being baited to step outside and be shot or something?"

"How would you like me to prove it to you?"

"I don't know."

"I have a way," Conlin said, getting up and going to the window, motioning to someone on the other side. "I believe I have someone you can trust."

The door opened, and Shelly Lawson walked in. She immediately went over to Cain and gave him a hug.

"Not professional, I know, but I'm just glad you're OK," she said.

"You see, if you decide to stay, Shelly will still be your handler," Conlin said.

Cain looked at Lawson. "Is all this true?"

"Yes. Every word. Remember when I told you faxing those documents could take days or months? Well, it took days. Sanders is legitimately on the run. He's gone," she told him.

"I need some time," Cain said.

"Of course. I don't blame you," Conlin replied. "You've earned it and deserve it. Take a few days or a few weeks. However long you need. You should know that Ms. Lawson really pleaded your case. She even went to Washington to speak to Director Roberts personally on your behalf."

"I guess I owe you one."

She laughed. "You owe me more than one."

Cain smiled.

"What about Heather?" Cain asked Lawson.

"She's on her way back. She should be arriving sometime today. She knows everything."

"What?"

"I talked to her yesterday to inform her of everything. She already knows about your wife and son."

"How'd you find her? Raines was hiding them."

"Director Roberts informed me that Eric Raines has been working undercover for the CIA for the past several years," Lawson said.

"Really?"

"Yeah. Apparently, his death was the beginning of his cover."

"Have you talked to him?" Cain asked.

"No. I'm not sure what I'd even say at this point."

"Well, I guess I'll leave you two to discuss things further," Conlin told them. "Matt, you're free to leave, walk around the facility, whatever you'd like. I do hope you decide to rejoin us and I'll be waiting for your decision when you decide to make it."

"Thank you," Cain said, shaking Conlin's hand.

Lawson and Cain walked out of the room and down the hallway as they meandered down the corridor to talk about their futures.

"So, what now?" Lawson asked.

"I don't know."

"There's a position for you here if you want it. They want you in."

"I know. I need some time to think. To get away for a little while and just take it easy for a bit," Cain said.

"They're willing to wait for you."

"There's some other things I have to take care of first."

"Heather?" she asked.

"Yeah."

"What're you gonna do?"

"I have to let her go," Cain replied.

"Why? You've always been happiest when you're with her. You love her."

"I do love her. That's why I have to let her go."

"Is that some kind of reverse logic?"

"Since she's been with me she's never been in more danger. She's been shot, put in a coma, almost blown up, her sister and baby almost killed, God knows what else," Cain said.

"But Sanders is gone now. She'll be safe," Lawson said, trying to reason.

"He's not gone. He's still out there. As long as he's out there I'll always be a target. That means she will be too. I can't risk it anymore. I won't. I won't put her life in danger anymore. Everyone associated with me has been killed at some point. I care too much about her to let it happen to her. As long as I do this, there'll always be a Sanders in some form."

"Sounds like your mind is pretty well made up."

"It is. Nothing you can say will change it. I'm doing it for her."

"I hope you're doing the right thing."

"She'll get over me. She'll move on and find someone better. Maybe another marketing guy or an accountant or banker or something. Someone who can give her everything she deserves," Cain said.

"I always thought that was you."

"Everything but keeping her safe. I obviously can't do that."

"You're not thinking of giving it a shot with Deanna, are you?" Lawson asked.

"No. You were right about her. I can't go back. If she remarried, it means she's happy, and she's moved on. Me coming back into the picture can only mess things up for her. Besides, I'm not the same man she knew. I don't remember anything about us and our time together. I don't know how to be the man she knew or the husband she married. I'm dead to her and that's the way it should stay."

"I agree. So, how are you gonna tell Heather?" Lawson asked.

"I don't know. I guess I'll just tell her it isn't working."

"Oh."

Their conversation was interrupted by the ringing of Cain's cell phone. It was Heather. Lawson handed him his phone back and walked away so they could talk in private.

"Hey," Cain answered.

"Hey. How are you?"

"Good. Tired. This has all been pretty exhausting."

"I know. Our plane landed a little while ago and I'm taking Cassie back to her house. I'll be there in a few minutes. The agent's said it's safe for her to go back. After I drop her off, I'm gonna head back to the apartment."

"OK. I guess I'll meet you there," Cain said.

"OK. I suppose we have some things to talk about," Heather said.

"Yeah. I guess we do."

"I'll see you there then," she said, a hint of sadness in her voice.

"Yep."

Cain hung up and leaned his back against the wall. He looked up at the ceiling and sighed. He knew what needed to be done. He felt it was the right thing to do. The best thing for Heather was to be with someone else. But it wasn't a conversation he was looking forward to. It would have been easier if Cain didn't love and care for her as much as he did. After standing against the wall for a few minutes thinking about what he was going to say to her, Cain left to go back to the apartment.

Heather dropped her sister off at her house and Cassie could tell her mind was on Cain. Heather hardly said anything the entire drive.

"Do you wanna come in for a few minutes?" Cassie asked.

"No. Not right now. I just need to talk to Matt first."

"I know. What do you think you guys will do?"

"Well, he's married. So, unless he gets a divorce, I think that's kind of an issue," Heather replied, her voice cracking.

"Maybe he won't go back to her," Cassie said.

"I tried thinking about what I would do if I were in that situation," Heather said, her vision getting blurry from her eyes tearing up.

Cassie hugged her. She felt bad about what her sister was going through. "I'm here for you if you need me. You know that, right?"

"I know." Heather smiled. "I might need a place to stay later."

"You can always come here. Emma would love having you here. So would I. Kind of make up for lost time," Cassie said.

"Thanks. I should go."

Heather left, dabbing at her eyes on the way back to the car. She needed to stop crying. She didn't want Cain to see her like that. She wanted to seem strong, even if she wasn't. She had a little bit of a drive to dry her eyes, get rid of the redness around them, and compose herself. She tried thinking of what she was going to say when she saw Cain but her mind had too much going on and really couldn't focus. Though she wasn't in a hurry to hear what she thought was going to happen, she drove quickly to get there. She'd rather just get it over with than agonizing over it and delaying it.

Once Heather got there, she slowly walked up to the apartment, her stomach feeling like it was in knots. She felt a little queasy, like she might throw up all over the steps. She finally made it to the door and fumbled with the keys, her nerves getting the better of her. Heather was able to steady her hand and opened the door. She walked in and saw Cain sitting on the edge of the couch, his legs bouncing up and down like he was nervous or anxious. She walked over to him and sat down next to him.

"No new holes or anything?" she joked.

Cain smiled. "No."

The chemistry that they usually shared wasn't there. It was almost like they were meeting each other for the first time. There was an uncomfortable silence as neither was quite sure what to say or where to begin. Finally, Cain figured he should be the one to start the conversation.

"You know how much I care about you right?" Cain asked.

"Yeah," she replied, knowing the bomb was about to come.

"All of this... what I do, who I am... the danger I'm constantly in, I'm not sure is conducive to a relationship."

"Just stop. You don't have to lie to me to protect my feelings," Heather told him, trying not to cry.

"I don't?"

"No. I know, um, with your wife and all... that maybe you want to see what you had with her and I get that. I really do. I get it. You were married, and they took it away from you and as much as it hurts me to see you walk away, I completely understand that you want to get back the life you had. If it were me I'd probably feel the same way."

"Umm, yeah," Cain stammered, following her lead. "I just

feel like maybe I can reconnect some of the missing dots and piece some things together."

"And I don't blame you for it," she said, sniffling. "Let's not make this a long goodbye though, huh? It's painful enough as it is."

"Sure. Whatever you want."

"I'm gonna go now. I'll come back in a few days for my things if that's OK?"

"Yeah, that's fine."

"Are you moving anytime soon or anything?" Heather asked.

"No, I don't think so. Your stuff will be here whenever you want it. I can help you if you want," Cain offered.

"Thanks, but it'd probably be better if you weren't here."

"Whatever's best for you. Just let me know."

"OK, well, I'm gonna go."

"Do you have somewhere to stay?" Cain asked, not wanting to throw her out on the street.

"Cassie said I can stay with her. It'll be good for us to help reconnect with each other."

"That'd be great for you two. You can get to know Emma better too."

"Yeah. So, I'll be fine," she replied, standing up.

Cain also stood up as Heather told him goodbye. She gave him an innocent, friendly, final hug and turned to leave. Cain knew the best thing in his life was walking out the door, but in his heart, he knew it was for the best, no matter how much it hurt the both of them. As Heather got to the door and opened it, she turned around one final time and gave Cain a smile. Cain forced a return smile as she closed the door behind her. He closed his eyes and clenched his fists, gritting his teeth as a single tear rolled down his cheek. Heather walked down the hall and simply stopped once she got to the stairwell. She put her back against the wall and slid down to the floor, crying uncontrollably. She tried to make it the easiest she could for the both of them by not prolonging their separating but it still hurt.

Cain walked into the kitchen for a bottle of water. He started feeling a little lightheaded. He thought maybe it was just the stress of the situation taking its toll on him. He walked back into the living room as dizziness started settling in. The room was spinning, and he knew what was about to happen. His eyelids started drooping down and his eyes felt heavy. His grip on the bottle loosened, and it fell to the floor. Cain tried to take a step but couldn't even accomplish that as he fell over, hitting his head hard on the floor.

After a few minutes of crying, Heather composed herself and stood up. She looked back toward the apartment door and started walking back to it. She thought maybe she should at least take a few clothes with her. She got to the door and closed her hand to make a fist, holding it up near her head ready to knock. Before her fist hit the door she suddenly stopped, wondering if it was the right thing to do. Heather put her ear up to the door, trying to hear what Cain was doing. A few seconds of silence convinced her to just wait to come back. Seeing him again would just make it tougher for her. She backed away from the door and quickly walked down the stairs, exiting the building. Before getting in her car she took one last look up at the apartment window. She sort of hoped Cain would be watching at the window so she could give him a final wave or something, but it was probably just as well that he wasn't. Without any last-minute detail to deter her, Heather got in her car and drove off to her sister's.

42

Lawson had just gotten off the phone with one of her agents when Conlin walked in. She'd been trying to contact Cain for the last several hours just to make sure he was OK. She figured it was a lot for him to take in, breaking up with Heather, the news about Sanders, being cleared of the trumped-up charges against him, and she just wanted to be there for him if he needed it.

"Have you gotten hold of him yet?" Conlin asked.

"I've texted him three times and called him twice. Still no answer."

"Is that normal?"

"No. He usually always responds to his messages fairly quickly," Lawson replied.

"You think something might be wrong?"

"I don't know. He just broke up with his girlfriend. Maybe he just wanted some alone time for a little bit."

"How about you go over to his place just to make sure? If he needs some time that's fine. I just want to make sure though," Conlin said.

"Right on it," Lawson responded, getting out of her chair immediately.

Lawson headed over to Cain's apartment. She didn't let on to Conlin, but she was pretty worried about Cain. It was after ten at night and he almost always responded to her messages. She couldn't think of a time he didn't answer within a few hours. She knew breaking up with Heather was tearing him up so she wasn't sure what state of mind she'd find him in. Once she got there, she saw his car was still there. She went up to his apartment and knocked on the door. Several minutes elapsed without a response from him. It was always possible he walked somewhere, but she had a feeling he was in there. She called his cell phone again and listened at the door. She could hear his phone ringing. He was in there. Lawson kept knocking on the door with no answer. What was more alarming was that she didn't even hear any movement. Luckily, she had a key for his apartment. Sanders gave her one when Cain first joined just in case there were ever any problems. Lawson didn't want to use it but now was the time it seemed to come in handy. She hurriedly opened the door and once inside instantly saw Cain's lifeless body lying in the middle of the floor. She rushed over to him to check his condition. Since the agency's previous doctor was now in confinement due to his relationship with Sanders, and his questionable practices, Lawson called Conlin to tell him about Cain. Conlin had a doctor rush over to Cain. Just as the doctor got there Cain started coming around. He sat up, though he had a dazed look and glassy eyes. The doctor did what he could from there but was concerned about his blood pressure and heart rate.

"I understand this has happened to him quite frequently?" the doctor asked Lawson.

"Yeah. He was intentionally given bad medication to fight it initially which made his symptoms worse," she replied.

"And it's happening more?"

"He told me he's been having them a lot lately. In the beginning, it was sporadic, one or two a month. He said in the past couple weeks he's been having them almost daily."

"That's very concerning," he said, scratching his cheek. "He needs to just rest for tonight. But I'd like for him to come down tomorrow for some testing."

"I'll stay here tonight and make sure he's OK and I'll bring him down tomorrow."

"That's fine. Let's make it for nine o'clock."

"We'll be there," she told him.

Lawson and the doctor helped move Cain to the couch where he lay there for a little while until he fell asleep. Lawson stayed there with him, sleeping on the chair across from him, in case he needed anything. It was a quiet night, however, and Cain woke up at seven the following morning without a lot of recollection of what happened. He had a splitting headache but otherwise felt pretty good. His stirring woke Lawson up.

"So, what are you doing here?" Cain asked.

"It's nice to see you too," she replied, stretching. "Have you ever tried sleeping in that chair? Not very comfortable."

"Well, good morning, Shelly. How was your night? Sleep well? No? OK. So, what are you doing here?" he sarcastically asked.

"You had another seizure. I tried contacting you all day. When you didn't respond, I came over and found you on the floor."

"Oh."

"So, we have a meeting with the doctor at nine," Lawson informed him.

"We who?"

"We. You and me."

"I'm not going to a doctor," Cain said.

"Oh, yes, you are."

"Oh, no, I'm not."

"Matt, they're getting worse. You need help."

"Just let it be."

"Will you please just go for my sake? Just see what he says. I'm not asking you to do anything other than that. Just see what he says."

"Fine, but I won't make any promises other than showing up," he said.

They arrived at the Specter Project's medical facility on the 9th floor, which was higher tech than most hospitals, where Dr. Ellison was waiting for them. He led them into his office where he described in detail what he wanted to do.

"First off, I know what was done previously to you by other doctors," Ellison began. "I'm well aware you probably have trust issues."

Cain nodded in acknowledgment.

"So, I want to get out of the way that I'm a doctor first. My patient's health and well-being come before any government work and involvement. I will not allow agents to be cleared for duty unless I'm fully convinced of their well-being and will not be pressured into doing so under any circumstances. That's my diatribe."

"So, what is it you wanted to see me about?" Cain asked.

"After my basic findings last night, and with Ms. Lawson

telling me your seizures are happening almost daily, I think it's time to do further testing to determine how we can treat the problem better."

"What did you have in mind?"

"Well, there are several procedures designed to first measure where exactly in the brain the seizures are originating from. It's quite intensive. In no particular order there's a PET scan, subdural and depth electrodes, amobarbital, several EEG recordings, neuropsychological tests, sphenoidal electrodes, and an MRI."

"Sounds like a lot."

"It is."

"Why can't we just try other medication for it?" Cain asked.

"Because I believe that you're too far gone for medication to be helpful at this point. I've dealt with seizures before and in my experience, I believe surgery will be your best option. But testing will show our options."

"I'm still not sure why we can't just try other medication first for a few months."

"I'm going to be blunt and tell you what I'm thinking. The amount of seizures you're having is increasing and the length of time you're having them is also increasing. My worry is that if we just try medication, and it doesn't work, that at some point you're going to have a seizure that you just won't wake up from," Ellison said.

"You think the seizures may be killing him?" Lawson interrupted.

"I think it's very possible. Further testing will show. I'm not suggesting we take any action right now other than doing the tests to see exactly what we're dealing with. If we find nothing major, then perhaps medication is the right way to go. If we find something concerning, perhaps surgery will be the best option."

"You seem like you have your mind made up about what you'll find," Cain said.

"I have my suspicions which are based on the fact that your seizures are lasting hours at a time and in rapid succession. That's not normal. For most people, they don't typically last that long," the doctor explained. "That makes me believe we have another issue at stake."

"When do you want to do these tests?" Cain asked.

"As soon as you would like. We can start right now if you're ready."

"How long will the tests take?" Lawson asked.

"Depending on breaks... probably well into the night."

"I don't need breaks. Let's get it done," Cain said.

Ellison took Cain into a room for him to get undressed so they could start the testing process. The doctor then told Lawson to go home or to the office and that he'd call her when they were done. It was a long day for Cain that ended roughly fifteen hours later. Lawson waited around the office doing work until he was finished so she could drive him home. Cain didn't want to talk much about the testing other than to say the results should come back in another week or so.

"Do you want me to stay the night?" Lawson asked as she stopped in front of his apartment.

"Nah. I'll be fine," Cain said.

"OK. I'll see you tomorrow?"

"Probably."

They gave each other a quick hug and Cain went up to his apartment. He turned the lights on and looked around the apartment. He couldn't help but think it felt a little weird without Heather there. It just seemed so cold and lifeless without her presence. Cain went to the kitchen and grabbed a bottle of water. He sat down at the table and started to drink it. He sighed deeply and closed his eyes tight. He felt another one coming on. He put the bottle on the table and braced for it. He started to feel light-headed and dizzy. A minute later he passed out, slumping off the chair onto the floor. Cain didn't wake up for another nine hours, with nobody knowing of his condition. Lawson had called him the next morning to see if he needed anything but Cain told her he was fine. He didn't mention the seizure he had. He didn't see the point in worrying her further. Until Cain got the test results back, he figured he'd just stay in his apartment. He worried about going out and having a seizure in public. Not that he was ashamed or anything, he just didn't want anyone going into a panic over him if he did have one.

In the week that followed, Cain had three more seizures. Each lasted at least eight hours. He knew that wasn't good. Lawson stopped by a couple of times to keep him company and bring him some food if he needed it. She came over the day his results came in, mostly she just wanted to give him some support if he needed it. Though he was typically a very stoic person, even she was surprised at how calm he seemed to be handling everything.

"I guess today's the big day, huh?" Lawson asked.

"Guess so."

"I can't believe how nonchalant you've been about this all week. I'd be a nervous wreck."

"The worst part of anything is not knowing. I already am prepared. Makes it easier that way," Cain explained.

"You're expecting the worst, aren't you?"

Cain stood silent for a few moments, not sure about

whether to tell her about the additional seizures. "I wouldn't be surprised at the worst-case scenario. And neither should you."

"But why? Why would you think that?"

He sighed. "I've had three more seizures this week."

"What?! And you didn't tell me until now?"

"I didn't want to worry you."

"Well, that's kind of a big deal, don't you think?" Lawson asked.

Cain put his hands up, not having an explanation.

"Have you talked to Heather about any of this?" Lawson asked.

"There's nothing to talk about."

"You know she still loves you."

"That's the problem. She thinks I'm going back to my wife. She needs to distance herself away from me. This wouldn't help that," Cain replied.

The pair spent the next couple of hours quietly passing the time away, watching TV and reading as they waited for the doctor's phone call. It came about two o'clock. Cain put the call on speaker so Lawson could hear too. The tone of Ellison's voice was a good indication of the conversation that was to follow.

"So, what's the verdict?" Cain somberly asked.

"It's not good, I'm afraid."

"Didn't think it would be."

"The tests have proven, rather conclusively, that you have pressure building up in one spot in the brain which is causing the seizures. The good news is that we've pinpointed the issue and we know the exact cause of it. The bad news is that the only real way to stop it from causing additional seizures is surgery."

"Which entails what?"

"Removing that part of the brain that's causing the block-age," Ellison told him.

"How tough a surgery is it?" Cain asked.

"Well, any time you have brain surgery I wouldn't say it's a walk in the park, but I don't foresee any problems. It's a surgery I've done before without complications."

Cain looked at Lawson to gauge her reaction to the news. She had a worried look on her face but nodded at Cain to go through with the surgery.

"I have a date that's opened up if you want me to pencil you in. Three days from now," Ellison said.

"I think I'd rather skip the surgery for now," Cain said. Lawson's eyes ballooned, not believing what just came out of his mouth. "I'd prefer trying different medication."

"I can tell you with a hundred percent certainty that medication, in any form or variety, is not going to solve your problem. Surgery is the only option to fix this."

"OK. Let me think about it."

"Absolutely. Take some time to mull it over. Brain surgery is not something to be done whimsically. Give me a call in a couple of days and we'll set something up."

"OK. Sounds good. Thank you, doctor," Cain said.

As soon as Cain hung up his eyes met Lawson's. He knew she disapproved without even looking at her.

"What are you doing?" Lawson asked, perturbed.

Cain looked down at the ground. He didn't have an answer for her. He just shrugged.

"Do you not understand that surgery is the only option?" Lawson repeated.

"So I heard."

"Then I don't understand what you're doing. Medication isn't going to help."

"I know," Cain replied.

Lawson looked him up and down, a disgusted look on her face, before she took a step back. Then it dawned on her what he was doing.

"You're giving up," she whispered. "You're just going to do nothing."

"Sometimes you have to know when to give in."

"What? Since when has that ever been your attitude? You're a fighter. You always have been. Now's not the time to change," Lawson shouted.

"Sometimes you have to be realistic and face facts."

"What's this really about?"

"I don't know what you're talking about," Cain replied.

"Is this about Heather?" she asked.

"No. Why would it be about Heather?"

"Well, let me ask you a question then."

"OK."

"Would you be doing this if Heather was here right now?"

"That's not the point," Cain said.

"It's exactly the point. Why won't you give yourself a chance?"

"I've had my chances."

"All this time you've been fighting to remember your past, fighting for other people, fighting for yourself, fighting for survival... and now, after all this time, you're just gonna give up?"

"Maybe this has never really been about me. Maybe it was just about stopping a man from doing to others what had been done to me."

They continued arguing about his lack of will to keep fighting. Lawson was increasingly getting angry with each passing second. After a few more minutes she realized that she wasn't going to change his mind and thought maybe it'd be best if they separated and continued the conversation later. Neither was giving any ground, and they were getting nowhere except annoyed with each other. She angrily stormed out of the apartment, slamming the door behind her, as Cain watched her leave. He did feel bad that he was upsetting her so much as he could tell she cared about him, but he did feel it was the best course of action.

Lawson kept trying to get a hold of Cain for the next few days to continue their conversation, but Cain wasn't answering his phone. With no success from Lawson, Conlin decided to finally interject. After a meeting with Lawson where she explained everything, Conlin gave Cain a call. Upon seeing Conlin's name appear on his screen, Cain wasn't sure whether he should answer or not. To his credit, the few times Cain had talked to Conlin he seemed like an up-and-up guy. Maybe he owed him one last conversation to explain himself. Cain decided to answer.

"Cain, nice to get a hold of you," Conlin said. "Shelly's been telling me she's had a heck of a time getting through."

"Yeah. Tell her I'm sorry about that. Everything's already been said though. No need to keep going over it."

"Maybe you could explain it to me then. I'm not sure why you don't want back in. What else do you plan on doing?"

"I've got a lot of money saved up. I don't need to do anything," Cain replied.

"So, you're just gonna stay cooped up in your apartment and be a vegetable?"

"Honestly, I don't know what I'm gonna do. But I know I don't wanna keep living the life that I am. That I have been."

"Things can be different now. I promise you that," Conlin said.

"Listen, you seem like a decent guy who's got good intentions, and I don't wanna seem ungrateful for the time and effort you're putting in to me, but I think you should put it elsewhere."

"My job is to get the very best men and women that I can find to help this agency. You're one of those people."

"Maybe I used to be. I'm not sure about that anymore."

"I know a lot has happened, you've had a lot to process, and it's happened pretty quickly. Don't make any rash or hasty decisions. Take some time," Conlin said.

"I don't need any time," Cain responded. "I'm done. I'm walking away forever."

THE CAIN REDEMPTION

43

It'd been three months since Matthew Cain gave Director Conlin his final answer on rejoining the Specter outfit. He'd spent that time doing what he envisioned he would. Absolutely nothing. Though he was still having seizures regularly, they were a little more sporadic. Instead of almost daily seizures they'd whittled down to two or three a week. He put his personal appearance on the back burner as well. He grew his hair long with a matching beard that indicated he hadn't shaved in a long time. Probably in three months. If he got any mail, he usually threw it out without even looking at it and he rarely even glanced at his phone. Sometimes if he heard it ringing, he just socked it away in a drawer to forget about it. His apartment was a mess, clothes all over the place, dirty dishes everywhere; cleanliness wasn't something he was overly concerned with anymore. Cain only ventured out once or twice a week, and that usually was to get food or buy some groceries. He really didn't care about his former life anymore. As far as he was concerned, he was done. But his former life wasn't quite done with him.

Director Conlin had called an emergency meeting that required the presence of his high-level assistants as well as several handlers, including Michelle Lawson. The meeting consisted of about fifteen people. The purpose was to discuss Ed Sanders and his former cohorts that used to run The Specter Project. They had gotten close to finding them at various points but every time ran into a dead end. Someone would just narrowly escape or throw them off their trail at what seemed like the last minute before they closed in. Everyone was seated, waiting for Conlin to appear, wondering what the gist of the meeting was about. It was rare for all of them to be in the same room at one time. Conlin came in a few minutes later, file folders in hand, and walked around the oval table to his spot.

"Thank you all for coming on such short notice. I don't want to keep you too long from your duties so this won't be a long meeting," Conlin began. "The purpose of our meeting here today is to discuss these men," he continued, the pictures of Sanders and his henchmen being shown on the board.

"We're doing the best we can to find them," a handler stated.

"I know you are. But with all due respect to your efforts, it's not good enough," Conlin calmly replied. "These just came in this morning," he said, showing the pictures of three dead bodies to the group.

"Who are they?" Lawson asked.

"They are the bodies of agents who worked for us. Until now, we haven't gotten that close to them. Not really. This shows how close we are. Unfortunately, it's still not good enough. Three agents, all killed sometime yesterday. One in Italy, one in

France, and one in Russia. We believe the perpetrators to be Booth in Italy, Proulx in France, and Collins in Russia."

"What about Sanders?"

"We have no idea where he is. But we all know he's still pulling the strings on these men."

"So, what's the plan now?"

"That's what we're here to discuss. We lost three men yesterday. I'm not about to lose any more. I believe we've been going about this the wrong way. We've been sending men all over the place following whatever leads we've had, none of which have really panned out."

"How else would we go about it?" Lawson asked.

"Systematically concentrate on one target at a time. Once we find one, we'll find the others."

"You're saying to go up the food chain. Get the lower level guys first which will lead us up the food chain."

"Exactly. It's unlikely we'll find Sanders until we find the rest. It's proving to be too difficult to get a handle on his location. Let's start with the lower tier guys. Once we find Booth, he'll lead us to Proulx, who'll lead us to Collins, who'll then lead us to Sanders. We have to start small and work our way up. Trying to get the top dogs first hasn't yielded results yet. We have to try something different," Conlin told the group.

"So, who do we target first?"

"Booth. We know he's in Italy. I want this to be everyone's top priority in this office. Track down every lead, every contact you have, even the most remote possibility. This agency will always have something hanging over its head until these men are eliminated. I want this to be the beginning of the end."

Conlin spent the next forty-five minutes presenting some of the leads they had for the group to brainstorm. It also gave them a starting point to focus their efforts on. There was still something else on his mind, though, that he wanted to discuss in private with Lawson. After the meeting adjourned, he asked Lawson to stick around a few extra minutes. The room cleared out until it was just the two of them.

"I want your honest opinion," Conlin started. "Do you think this'll work?"

"I do. With the right men tracking them down," Lawson replied. "To be honest, even the best plan can only get us so far if it isn't executed properly."

"What are you saying exactly?"

"Even if we know exactly where each of these men are, we can't send just anybody to capture or kill them. With these men, nothing will be as it seems. If we find them too easily, it's because they want to be found. Once we get a lead on them, we have to send the very best we have."

"I agree. Which brings me to what I wanted to talk to you about," Conlin said.

"OK?" Lawson responded, having a good idea where he was going.

"We need Cain back. He's the most dangerous agent we have. Nobody is better qualified than him to do this. Nobody would have a bigger stake in this than him."

"Or he's too personally involved to think clearly and wouldn't be his normal self."

"I guess that's always a risk when a mission becomes personal. But I think he's too good to let that get in the way of doing his job."

"Even if that's true, there's still the problem of getting him to come back," Lawson said.

"You still keep in contact with him?" Conlin asked.

"I've tried," she told him, throwing her hands up. "I call him once a week but he never answers or returns my call. I send him a few texts too with no response. I've even gone to his apartment a few times, but he doesn't answer the door. There's no way to get to him."

"Well, he has to go out at some point, right?"

"Well... yeah."

"Put someone on his apartment twenty-four hours a day. The moment Cain leaves I want us to be notified."

"I will."

"One more thing... what about his ex-girlfriend?"

"Heather? What about her?"

"Does he still talk to her?" Conlin asked.

"No. I talk to her once or twice a week. They haven't communicated since they broke up."

"Maybe it's time we changed that."

"Why?"

"He's obviously not the same without her in his life. For whatever reason, that was his choice. If she walks back into his life, maybe he walks back into ours," he reasoned.

"You want us to play matchmaker?"

He smiled. "In a word... yes."

"I didn't think the United States government cared about their employee's love life," Lawson joked.

"If that's what it takes to get him back, we do. He needs to have meaning in his life. Right now, he has none. She can bring that. Is she still single?"

"Yes. She is."

"You think she still loves him?" he asked.

"She does."

"Good. Make it happen."

"I'll see what I can do."

"One more thing, Shelly."

"Yes?".

"Eric Raines is wrapping up his mission within the next week or so."

"OK?"

"That means he'll be coming back here and working out of this office again."

"I'm not getting your meaning," Lawson said.

"I know you two have a history. I trust that won't be a problem?"

"I don't see how it would be unless... are you assigning me to be his handler again?"

"Any reason why I shouldn't?" Conlin asked.

"I'm sure there are other handlers equally as capable of having him," Lawson objected.

"I'm sure there are. But is there another handler who knows him better than you do? You know his strengths and weaknesses, and what he's capable of better than anyone. Isn't that true?"

"Yeah. I guess it is," she agreed reluctantly.

"So, you can make it work?"

"I have a feeling no matter what I say you're going to assign him to me anyway."

"That's pretty accurate." He smiled. "I just figured I'd give you the courtesy of letting you know beforehand so you could prepare for it."

"Thank you," she replied, faking a smile. "I'll be as professional as I can be."

"I know you will."

Lawson got an agent to stake out Cain's apartment to see if

he went anywhere. The agent stayed on Cain for two weeks. Cain went grocery shopping on Mondays, Wednesday he went to the corner restaurant for breakfast, and Fridays he went to dinner at the same restaurant. He followed the same pattern each week. The following Wednesday, Lawson waited for Cain outside the restaurant so they could finally talk. She got there about five minutes before he usually arrived. Right on cue, Cain showed up a few minutes later and was taken to his usual table towards the rear. As he was looking at the menu, Lawson made her move. Cain had the menu in front of his face and never noticed his old handler walking toward him.

"Hello, Matt," Lawson said as she sat at his table.

Cain lowered the menu slightly, just enough for his eyes to peer over it to see his acquaintance.

"You know, if you wanna hide from people and not be found, you shouldn't be predictable and go to the same places every week," Lawson said.

"So, you've been following me."

"Not me. But we've had someone keeping an eye on you."

"What are you doing here?" Cain asked.

"Well, since you haven't returned any of my calls or texts in the last three months, I figured it was time for us to chat."

"I think everything was said the last time we talked. Nothing has changed."

"Well, I wouldn't say that. You've uh, changed a little," she said, noting his appearance.

"You haven't. Still look as pretty as ever."

"Flattery will get you nowhere with me. You know that."

"Just checking," Cain said, still looking at the menu. "For the record, I'd recommend the French toast. It's ridiculously good."

The waitress came by and took their order, Lawson taking Cain's suggestion. Once she left, Lawson got down to business.

"Can we talk about what you don't want to talk about?" she asked.

"Seems like you've already started. Anyway, I don't suppose it'd do any good if I said no."

"It wouldn't."

"So, what is it now?" Cain asked.

"We need you."

"I'll give you the same answer I did before. Not interested."

"Does this interest you?" Lawson asked, tossing pictures of the dead agents in front of him.

"What are these?"

"Dead Specter agents. They were killed by Sanders and his cronies."

"I'm sorry to hear that," Cain said sorrowfully.

"Yeah, and they'll probably be a few more in the coming weeks and months unless you come back and help us."

"Don't put this on me."

"I didn't mean it like that. I'm sorry. But we need you."

"You have other agents who are capable."

"Not as dangerous as you," Lawson replied.

"Shelly, I respect and love you, you know that."

"I feel a but coming on."

"But with my condition you can't expect me to be able to do the things I used to do," Cain said.

"I don't. That's why you'd have to get it fixed first."

"That's not gonna happen."

Lawson could tell that the conversation was going nowhere again. But it was basically what she expected out of him. She didn't think she'd just roll back into his life after a couple months and get him to change his mind.

"I'm meeting Heather tomorrow for lunch," she blurted out.

"Oh? How's she doing?"

"As well as can be expected, I guess. Still dealing with a broken heart."

"She'll be better off in the long run for it," Cain said.

"So you say."

A few seconds later Lawson faked a surprise look, spotting Heather walking towards their table.

"Oh my gosh, look who it is," Lawson said.

"Who?" Cain asked, turning to look.

"Gee, I hope I didn't get my days and times mixed up. I could've sworn I said tomorrow. Hmm."

"I bet." Cain sighed, looking down at the ground away from the table, hoping not to be recognized. "Wow. This doesn't feel the least bit orchestrated."

"Hey, Shelly," Heather said, not initially recognizing the shaggy-haired man with the long beard across from Lawson. She stood next to Cain without really looking at him.

"Aren't you two gonna say anything to each other?" Lawson asked.

Heather looked confused as she was sure she didn't know who the man was, at least not from the back. She looked down and was shocked at the face looking back at her, wearing a grin.

"Hey," Cain said.

"Oh my God, Matt?" Heather asked, astonished at his appearance. "What happened to you? Have you been on a secret mission or something?"

"Uh, something like that."

"Wow. I didn't even recognize you."

"Yeah, that was kind of the idea."

"So... how are you?" Heather asked uncomfortably.

"Great... and you?"

"Very well, thank you."

"You look good," Cain told her.

"Thanks. Should we make this another time, Shelly? I don't want to interrupt you two talking business," Heather asked.

"No, sit down," Lawson said.

"Yeah, it's OK. I was just about to leave anyway," Cain said.

"You were?" Lawson asked.

"Yeah. I have some business to attend to. Remember?" Cain replied, raising his eyebrows, hoping Lawson would play along.

"Oh. Sure."

"It was nice to see you again," he told Heather as he stood up.

She smiled. "Yeah, you too."

"I'll talk to you later," Cain told Lawson as he turned to walk away.

"Yes, you will," she said, smiling back.

Heather sat down, taking Cain's seat as she put her purse on the ground next to the chair.

"Well, that was certainly unexpected," Heather noted.

"I know. I got here a few minutes early and saw him sitting here."

"He doesn't look well. Hope that wife of his is taking good care of him."

"Yeah, well, that's one of the things I wanted to talk to you about today."

"What?"

"I didn't ask you here just to have breakfast and catch up. Most of it is about him," Lawson said.

"Shelly, if he's having problems at home or whatever, I really don't think I should be getting involved. And I don't want to," Heather said.

"He doesn't have any problems at home."

"Then what's the problem?"

"The problem is that he doesn't still have you in his life and it's killing him," Lawson said.

"I don't understand," Heather said, shaking her head. "That doesn't really make any sense. Why would I be a problem for him?"

"Because he still loves you."

"Please, Shelly, I assure you that he doesn't. He made his decision a long time ago, and I respected and understood the choice he made. I don't fault or blame him for it."

"There's so much that you think you know that you don't know," Lawson said.

"You know, I really don't have time for this," Heather said, standing up and pushing her chair out, ready to leave.

"He's dying, Heather."

Heather's jaw dropped, and she froze, struggling to consume the information. She slowly sat back down, staring at Lawson, waiting for her to say more.

"What did you say?" Heather asked, hoping she heard incorrectly.

"Matt's seizures have gotten worse."

"How bad?"

"They've gone from one every couple of months to four or five a week," Lawson said. "And some of them are lasting eight to ten hours at a time. And that's just what I know. He hasn't even talked to me in weeks so who knows how much worse they've gotten."

"Oh my God. So, what's being done?"

"Right now, nothing."

"What? Why not?"

"It's complicated," Lawson said.

"So, what can I do?" Heather sighed, obviously still in love with Cain, though she didn't really want to get involved since he was with someone else.

"He needs surgery to remove a blockage inside his brain. If he doesn't get it, the doctors think he'll eventually just have a seizure that he won't wake up from."

"And he's fighting having the surgery?"

"Yes."

"Why?"

"Because he feels he has nothing else to live for," Lawson said.

"He's got a new life now with his wife again. I don't understand why he'd feel that way."

"First, you need to know the truth about everything. Matt won't like me for telling you this, but I think you need to know."

Heather's eyes were focused directly on her friend and didn't notice a single other person in the restaurant at that moment.

"Matt never went back to his wife," Lawson said.

"What?" Heather asked, raising her eyebrows in disbelief.

"It's what he let you believe because it was easier that way."

"Easier in what way?"

"Easier for you to distance yourself from him."

"Why would he do that?" Heather asked.

"Well, I can't say I know all the reasons, but I do know maybe the most important one."

"Which is?"

"He believes that everyone close to him or helps him is eventually hurt or killed. And he mostly blames himself for that."

"I never have."

"I know. He knew he could never go back to his wife and spin her world upside down again. But he didn't want to put you in danger anymore either. If you were with him you'd never be truly safe. He believed that by sending you away he was protecting you, saving you."

"I can't believe this," Heather said.

"Truth is, he hasn't worked a day for us since the two of you split up. He only leaves his apartment a couple hours a day, three days a week. He's letting himself go."

Lawson could see that Heather was having a hard time processing everything she was throwing at her. It was a lot to take in so suddenly.

"Are you OK?" Lawson asked.

"Uh, no, no I'm not OK."

"Do you still love him?"

Heather closed her eyes as they started to tear up. "Of course I still love him. I've never stopped loving him."

"Then you'll help me get through to him?"

"I don't know what I can do. Yes, I still love him, but I can't make him listen to me or want to be with me."

"Yes, you can. Be passionate. Say what you're thinking. Say what you're feeling. Say what's in your heart. Don't hold anything back. I can arrange for you two to bump into each other. If you truly love him, you'll find a way."

Heather sighed and looked down at the table.

"You're not seeing anyone else right now, are you?" Lawson asked.

"No. Of course not."

"So, you'll do it?"

"Of course I'll do it. I'm just not sure he'll listen," Heather replied.

"He'll listen." Lawson nodded, grabbing her friend's hand. "He'll listen. We've gotta have faith."

They talked for a few more minutes and then ate breakfast, continuing to discuss Cain and his condition. After their discussion, Lawson felt much better about Cain's future. She thought they actually had a chance to finally get through to him with Heather in the loop. As soon as they finished breakfast, Lawson called Conlin to keep him updated.

"So, how'd it go?" Conlin asked.

"It went well. She wants to help."

"Fantastic. What's your next step?"

"They're going to accidentally bump into each other the next time he steps out of his apartment," she explained.

"Sounds like you have things under control."

"Let's hope so. Getting Heather in was the easy part. Convincing him, well, that's the part that'll be hard."

Though Lawson knew she'd have Heather's help in trying to convince Cain to get the surgery, she still wanted her to talk to the doctor first. That way she knew exactly what was involved without hearing second hand information. Plus, the more information she had to work with the better her chances would be at getting through to Cain. Lawson arranged a meeting with Dr. Ellison at a nearby outdoor restaurant near The Center. The doctor was already sitting and waiting as the two women sat down across from him.

"Thank you for meeting us," Lawson said.

"No problem. What can I do for you?"

"Well, this is Heather, Matthew Cain's uh... better half," Lawson stumbled, getting a look from Heather.

"Nice to meet you," Ellison said, getting a smile in return.

"The reason for the meeting was so we could discuss Cain's health," Lawson said.

"You know I can't discuss a patient's health with anyone else."

"Doctor, the only one... the only one who can help convince Cain to get this surgery is Heather. He won't listen to anyone else. Not you, not me, not anyone. If your top priority is really saving him, then the only way to do that is to get her help. And she needs to know what we're dealing with. I know you have your ethics, which is really encouraging considering most in our line of work do not, but please just put them to the side this one time," she pleaded.

Ellison sighed as he digested her words and looked over at Heather, who had a hopeful, but worried look on her face.

"OK. You win," he said, putting his hands up in the air. "How much do you know?"

"Just that his seizures are worsening and that he could eventually die from them," Heather replied.

"First, there are several things to consider. He's having prolonged seizures, which is very disconcerting. A seizure should last no more than a minute or two. His are lasting for hours. About 50,000 people die of prolonged seizures every year. A good majority of them occurring within thirty days of their prolonged seizure."

"So, we probably don't have much time," Heather said bleakly.

"He needs to get into that operating room as soon as he agrees to the operation."

"What exactly would be done?"

"I'll try to say as much of this in plain English and not doctor speak. What we'd do is remove the brain tissue that contains the seizure focus without damaging the other areas of the brain."

"How complicated of a surgery is it?" she asked.

"Well, I would never say any surgery involving the brain is easy. But it's a surgery I've done before, and done successfully."

"What's the recovery process like?"

"Usually two to four days in the hospital. After that, he should be able to resume his normal activities in six to eight weeks. Though after meeting him, and with what I've heard of him, I'm sure it would be the lesser of that."

"And that's it?"

"Well, he'll need to continue taking anti-seizure medication for another two years or so, which can be reduced as his condition stabilizes. The surgery is successful in eliminating seizures in close to ninety percent of the patients," Ellison said.

"Well, that's very encouraging."

"With all that being said there are some risks and complications involved."

"Which are?" Heather asked.

"The complications can be numbness, nausea, headaches, feeling tired, depressed… though they generally go away after a while. The risks… the surgery doesn't work… infection, bleeding, pain, changes to his personality."

"How likely is any of that?"

"It is likely he will have some of the complications. That's perfectly normal. The risks are small, but they are there. Though in his condition as it is now, the risks are much greater if he does not have the surgery," Ellison said.

44

A s soon as Lawson and Heather were done with Dr. Ellison, they continued talking about Cain as they walked along the sidewalk.

"I figure we'll wait a few more days and I'll arrange for you to bump into him. We've had him under surveillance for a while now so we know his every move," Lawson said.

"We don't have a few more days to wait. You heard the doctor. What if he has a seizure tomorrow that doesn't go away?"

"What do you suggest?"

"I'll just go to his apartment now and talk to him," Heather said.

"No. We can't just go barging over there. You know how stubborn he is. If we just go over there now and start blasting away at him, we'll lose him. You know he'll withdraw."

"No, he won't. Not with me."

"What makes you so sure?" Lawson asked.

"Just trust me. I'll go over there by myself and talk to him."

"I don't know. I think we need to be more calculated than that."

"Shelly, trust me. I know him. Let me go over there and talk to him. He won't ignore me. He'll talk. He'll let me in," Heather said.

Lawson stopped and sighed as she pondered the best solution.

"We don't have a lot of time," Heather told her. "He will talk to me. I'll get him to listen."

Lawson nodded in agreement. She wasn't sure it was the best course of action but she reluctantly agreed, anyway. "Just let me know what he says if you do talk to him."

"I will," Heather replied as she headed for Cain's apartment.

Heather wasn't exactly sure what she was going to say to convince Cain that surgery was the best option. She figured she'd just say whatever was in her heart. She hoped he still had enough feelings for her that he'd listen. Once she finally got to his apartment, the nerves started shuffling around in her stomach. She walked up the stairs, hoping to burn off the extra excitement she was feeling. As Heather reached Cain's door, she put her hand up to knock but suddenly stopped before hitting the door. She took a few more seconds to collect her thoughts. She took a gulp and sighed before finally knocking three times. She didn't hear any movement inside the apartment. Lawson assured her that Cain was in there. Heather knocked three more times, a little harder than the first time. She thought she heard someone moving this time.

Cain had quickly gotten a gun out of a drawer and quietly moved toward the door. He stood to the side of it as he readied himself for a battle.

"Matt, it's me," Heather yelled.

Cain raised his eyebrows, surprised that Heather was there. Without standing in the middle of the door, he looked through the peephole and saw that she was alone. He cleared his throat as he wondered what to do.

"Matt, I know you're in there. Please let me in," Heather yelled again.

Cain sighed and put the gun inside the belt of the back of his pants. He wasn't sure talking to her was the best idea. But seeing her there brought back some pleasant memories and actually made him feel good for a bit. After a few seconds, he closed his eyes and unlocked the door. He opened his eyes as he pulled the door open. Cain gulped as he stared at Heather, still looking as beautiful as always.

"Hi," she said, smiling.

"Hey."

"Mind if I come in?" Heather asked hopefully.

"Uh, yeah, sure."

"Thanks."

Heather looked around and was a little surprised at how messy the place was. There were clothes on the floor; the kitchen table was a mess, dishes piled up in the sink, magazines and newspapers on the furniture. It looked like the place hadn't been cleaned in months. But after seeing how Cain had let himself go, she figured that was probably a pretty good assessment.

"I'd ask you to sit down but..." Cain said, looking around at the mess. "I've been on missions left and right and haven't really had a chance to clean lately."

"It's OK. I really didn't come to critique your cleaning skills."

"Why are you here?"

"I just wanted a chance to talk about some things," she said.

"Like?"

"Like us. Matt, I know about everything. You don't have to lie to me anymore."

Cain's mouth fell open a little bit, stunned. "What do you mean, everything?"

"Shelly told me that you never went back to your wife, and that you haven't been on a mission since we broke up, and about your seizures."

"Shelly talks too much. I'm surprised she sent you over to do her dirty work. I thought she was above that."

"She cares about you. And you're lucky that she does."

Cain went over to a chair and moved some newspapers off of it and tossed them on the coffee table.

"So, what exactly do you want?" Cain asked.

Heather rushed over to him and knelt down on her knees in front of him, grabbing his hands. She figured this was the moment to hold nothing back, no long drawn out conversations, just passionately express what was on her mind.

"I want answers from you. I want the truth," she said, wiping her eyes. "I want you to tell me exactly what's going on and not lie. All these months I've felt one thing and then one day I'm told something else and it wasn't even from you. I think I deserve to know the truth. I think I deserve that much."

Cain wiped his eyes as well. He was never comfortable being around her when she was upset. It always made him vulnerable. He licked his lips, knowing that she was right and deserved to know the truth.

"You're right. Shelly was right. I never went back to my wife," he told her.

"Why not?" she asked, tears now freely flowing.

"Because with my son dead I didn't think she needed me back in her life. She remarried and moved on. Me coming back into it would probably only make things worse. Besides, I've no memory of her or us. What kind of life would we have had?"

"So why move on from me?"

"Because I thought it was better for you to be as far away from me as possible. You've almost been killed multiple times because of me. I can't keep putting you in more danger. I can't," Cain said sorrowfully.

"Don't you think that should've been my call?"

"You wouldn't have left."

"Of course I wouldn't. I loved you," she replied, still sobbing.

"Plus, with you knowing about my past, I thought maybe it'd make you uncomfortable if we stayed together."

"Why would you think that?"

"Because I wouldn't want you to think that even though we were together I was wishing to be back there or have my old life back. I didn't think it'd be fair to you," Cain said.

"Would you please stop making decisions for me and let me decide what I'll think and feel? Let me decide what's best for me."

Cain stopped looking into her now red eyes and looked toward the floor, unable to continue watching her cry. Heather wasn't gonna let him off the hook though. She gently grabbed his chin and pushed his head up to look at her as she dabbed her eyes.

"Why are you living like this? Why are you not working? Why are you not getting the surgery?"

Cain cleared his throat as he thought of what to tell her. "Because working no longer had any meaning for me. I was only working to find out what happened to me. Once I found out, I lost any edge that I had."

"And the surgery?" Heather asked.

"I just didn't feel there was a need to keep on going," he softly said.

"That's not like you," she said, shaking her head. "You've always been a fighter. You've never been one to just give up."

"Everyone has their limits."

"Can you please get the surgery?"

"Heather…"

"Please? If you won't do it for yourself will you do it for me?" she asked.

"I've already made my decision."

"Matt, please, don't do this. How many times do I have to lose you until you realize how much you mean to me?"

"Please don't try to guilt me into this," Cain said.

"I'm not trying to guilt you into anything. I want you to do this for yourself. And for me."

"Heather, I really don't wanna talk about this right now."

"Well, we need to talk about this right now. This is your life. And I'm not just gonna let you throw it away. Let me tell you something… I have been miserable without you. Miserable. I pretend that I'm fine and I'm moving on, but I'm not. I accepted the fact that you went back to your wife because it was what you really wanted and I was OK with it. But now that I know the truth I feel a little hurt, a little angry, and confused as to why you won't accept my help."

"I never meant to hurt you."

"Then don't. I have a question for you and I need to hear the answer. Truthfully. No lies. No deception. Just the truth."

"OK?" Cain said, unsure what she was getting at.

"Do you still love me?"

Cain sighed and gulped, knowing he couldn't lie to her anymore. "Yes."

Heather smiled, though she could barely see with all the tears coming from her eyes. "Because I still love you. I always have and I always will. And that's never gonna change, whether you want it to or not. If you do truly love me, then you'll stop doing this to yourself. You'll let me back into your life and start living again."

"Heather..."

"I'm not accepting excuses," she interrupted. "If something happens to you because you chose to do nothing, I would be devastated. Seeing you again and being this close to you again... I can't just put my feelings aside without fighting for us. I want you and need you in my life. I don't want to keep on living without you. I would hope you feel the same about me."

As much as Cain thought about continuing to push her away, she had quickly broken him down. Now that she was here in front of him, it reminded him of everything they had together. He realized that he missed her terribly. Heather caressed both sides of his face and gently kissed his lips.

"We probably shouldn't do this," Cain reluctantly told her.

"Probably not," she responded with another kiss.

"I don't ever want to put you in danger again."

"Then don't ever leave me."

She kissed him a few more times, Cain not resisting at all. She'd broken down his defenses. They kept passionately kissing a few more minutes until Heather took Cain's shirt off. She then moved to undoing his pants.

"Do you want me to stop?" she whispered.

"No," he replied.

Cain began undressing Heather as well, taking off her top and bra. Once they got each other completely undressed, Cain scooped her up in his arms and carried her into the bedroom.

"Don't worry. It's much neater in here. Haven't gotten around to messing up the bed yet," he told her.

"I guess we'll have to fix that, won't we?"

Heather woke up a few hours later, a smile permanently attached to her face, and rolled over to look at the clock. She turned back over to look at Cain. She gently stroked his body with her fingers, alternating between his face and his chest. She then leaned over and kissed him, waking him up.

"It's almost five," she told him.

"So?"

"Can't lay in bed all day."

"Why not?" Cain asked.

"This wasn't just a one-night thing, was it?" Heather asked.

"Huh?"

"I wanna be with you. For good. No more games and nonsense. I don't care about any risks, or anything that's happened before. All I know is that when I'm with you, I'm happy. And when I'm not with you, I'm not happy. Judging from the way you and your apartment look, I hope you feel the same."

Cain responded by kissing Heather on the lips several times.

"Does this mean yes?" she whispered.

"This is what you really want?"

"You're what I want. Before I met you, I was nothing. The happiest I've ever been was when I was with you. And I want it back. Didn't you miss me?"

"Of course I did. Every second of every day," Cain replied.

"But as much pain as it caused me to not have you in my life, I thought it was the best thing for you."

"I love you," she said. "So, can we start again?"

"You're positive this is what you want?"

"I think you just like hearing me say how much I want you," she kidded.

"Maybe."

"So, you still haven't said yes yet. What else do I have to do to convince you that we belong together?"

"Just one more thing," Cain said.

"Anything."

"Just kiss me."

That was the easiest request that Heather had ever heard. They passionately kissed for several more minutes before they decided they needed to get going. Heather wanted to tell him to get the surgery set up as soon as possible.

"So, you are gonna get the surgery, right?" Heather asked.

"Yes. If it's what you really want."

"I do. I'll be with you every step of the way."

"I know."

"One more thing..."

"Yes?" Cain asked, wondering what else she had in mind.

"This," she said, running her hands through his longer hair and bushy beard. "This has gotta go."

"Right away."

"And one more thing," Heather added.

"You have another request? What else is there?"

"You ever try to get rid of me again and I will hurt you," she said with a laugh.

He smiled. "I think that might be the scariest threat I've ever gotten."

45

Lawson was trying to be patient, keeping her phone near her, waiting for Heather to tell her how it went. It'd been six hours since Heather left her to go to Cain's apartment. She hoped it was going well, but the waiting was excruciating. She was trying to do some work when Conlin popped into her office.

"Anything yet?" Conlin asked, hopeful.

"No. Unfortunately not."

"OK. That's a good sign. Means she hasn't been flat out rejected yet. Unless she's been too busy crying her eyes out. Just to keep you in the loop, your newest agent will be here tomorrow to meet with you."

"Newest agent?"

"Raines. He'll be here tomorrow. I want you to go over things with him."

"What things?" Lawson asked.

"I want him as lead agent on tracking down the Specter remnants," he said.

"I thought we were waiting on Cain."

"Can't wait forever. Besides, even if we get him back, he'll need surgery first. That'll put him out of action for a couple months. We can't wait that long. Raines is our best bet in the meantime. You need to bring him up to speed. Any problems?"

"Uh, no. No problems." she sighed.

"Good."

Lawson stared at Conlin as he walked out of her office. She continued staring at the wall, wondering what she was going to say to Raines when she met him again. There was so much that she was thinking that she couldn't process it all. Her concentration was broken a few seconds later by the ringing of her phone. She jumped at it when she saw Heather's name on the screen.

"Hey, everything OK? What happened? Where've you been? I thought you would've called by now," Lawson said, grilling Heather..

"Relax. Everything's fine."

"Did you talk to him?"

"Yep. Told you he'd let me in," Heather boasted.

"You've been talking all this time? Wow. You're good."

"Well, I wouldn't say it was all talk," she teased.

Lawson's eyes widened, surprised by the insinuation. "You guys didn't..."

"We did," Heather said with a smile..

"Oh my God. So... so... so...," Lawson stuttered, trying to collect her thoughts.

"I'll put Matt on the phone so he can tell you."

"That was a dirty trick sending her over here," Cain told Lawson.

"Desperate times call for desperate measures, pal. Besides, all's fair in love and war, right?" Lawson said.

"I suppose so."

"So, does this mean you're back?"

Cain took a few seconds before answering. "I guess I'm in."

"Yes!" Lawson shouted, smiling ear to ear. She was trying not to get too emotional and shout into the phone.

"When can we do the surgery?"

"Doctor said tomorrow morning if that's convenient for you."

"Good a time as any, I suppose."

"OK. I'll call the doctor to let him know and I'll get back to you with the time."

"Sounds good."

"I'm glad to have you back, Matt. And I don't just mean as an agent," Lawson said.

Cain smiled, realizing how good a friend she was. "Thanks. I appreciate all you've ever done for me. I may not have ever said this or let you know... but you mean a lot to me. You've always been there."

"Don't go getting mushy on me. I'll talk to you later."

Lawson immediately called Conlin to let him know of Cain's decision. After she was done telling him the good news, she stepped out of the office to get some coffee. While she was pouring a cup, she heard a few voices discussing Raines. A buzz was permeating throughout the office once word leaked that Eric Raines was scheduled to return in the morning. It'd been the dominating water cooler talk for the entire week since the rumors started flying that he was returning soon. Now that the day was confirmed, everyone wanted to be around when he finally showed up. When he worked there previously, he'd been widely recognized by most as one of the best agents in the company. But for the previous couple of years he'd been one of the agency's top targets. A man Director Sanders wanted so badly, but always seemed to be a step behind him. Lawson stood there for a few minutes listening to the talk about Raines but finally had enough and went back to her office and closed the door. She really wasn't ready to see him again. She went through it in her mind over and over again. What she'd say, what she'd do when she saw him again. But now that it was almost a reality, she didn't know what she'd say. Since they'd be working together again, she would have to be somewhat professional and probably couldn't say everything she wanted to. She knew she wasn't going to get any work done if she just spent the rest of the night remembering their past. She turned back to some mission prep work, hoping that would get her mind off him. Even though what she was working on was for him, he wasn't the focus of her work. She just hoped she'd be able to keep herself together once she started talking to him again. Lawson worked deep into the night and actually wound up sleeping in her office, her couch coming in handy as it sometimes did.

The following morning, Cain and Heather headed over for the hospital wing of The Center. The entire 3rd floor of the building was a dedicated hospital floor. It had its own private elevator that didn't stop anywhere other than the parking garage. Because of its black ops status, friends and family members weren't allowed to see any other part of the building, but could still see their loved one with the private access. Once they arrived they were immediately sent to a separate room where Cain got undressed. Heather was able to wait with him until they came to take him for surgery.

"Are you nervous?" Heather asked.

"No. Not really," Cain calmly replied.

"OK, well, I am."

Cain smiled and gave her a kiss to relax. "It'll be fine."

"How can you be so calm?"

"I dunno. What good would worrying do?"

"You're sure this is what you wanna do, right?" she asked.

"Yeah. Why? Do you not want me to get it done anymore?"

"Of course I do. This is the only way you'll get better. I just wanna make sure that it's what you really want and that you're not just doing it for me or for us, that you're doing it for you too."

"I've never done anything I didn't really wanna do. I don't succumb to peer pressure. You should know that by now."

"True. You are the most stubborn person I've ever met," she kidded.

"Hey, insulting me before a major operation? Not cool."

Heather smiled. "You know I'm joking," she said, kissing him.

"I know."

Lawson exited her office and was on her way down to see Cain before he went under the knife when she saw Raines get out of the elevator. She stopped dead in her tracks, unable to move as she watched him walk. They locked eyes before Lawson broke contact, going back to her office. She knew she'd have to talk to him but she didn't want it to be in such a public setting. She'd be more comfortable in the confines of her office. A few seconds later, Raines knocked on the open door.

"Can I come in?" he asked.

"It's open," she replied, shuffling some papers around on her desk.

Lawson started typing on her computer, trying not to look at him. He still looked as good to her as he did the last day she saw him. Her heart felt like it was doing back flips and it scared her a little as she was determined not to be nice to him.

"You still look as good as ever," Raines said, trying to thaw the air.

"I don't wanna hear how good I look, OK?"

"I guess I owe you an explanation about…"

Lawson was starting to get pissed and wasn't about to let him explain anything before she told him how she was feeling. "About what? The fact I thought you were dead? Or was it that I was seriously depressed for months? Or maybe it was the one day finding out that you were suddenly alive. Maybe for the deception?"

"Deception is a major component of what we do. Of what I do," Raines said.

"But not from me!"

"What was I supposed to do, Shelly? I was ushered into a secret meeting with CIA Director Roberts where he informed me they wanted me to go undercover. Cut off all ties with everyone I knew."

"You could've trusted me."

"I did trust you."

"Funny way of showing it."

"If I had told you what I was doing and you let it slip to the wrong person, or your computer was hacked into by Sanders, then my cover was blown and my safety put in jeopardy," he explained. "Nothing I did was because it was what I wanted. I never wanted to be away from you."

"You think you can just walk in here after all these years and talk to me like this never happened? That I'm just gonna say, 'OK, Eric, no problem. All's forgiven?' No, that's not gonna happen. I don't forgive you for what you put me through."

"I don't blame you for feeling the way you do."

"Well, that's nice of you," she said sarcastically.

"I just hope one day we'll be able to get back to…"

"No, just stop right there. You and I will never get back to where we once were. Not ever. You had your shot, and you blew it. The only reason we're having this conversation right now is because I was given no choice. Director Collins wants me as your handler and I wasn't given an option. So, I don't wanna hear about old times or anything. I don't want to hear from you under any circumstances unless it's work related. And if you ever call me out in the field… your fingers better be on fire when you're dialing."

"Understood," he said dejectedly.

"We have a mission to go over but first I have to go down to the hospital wing. Cain's getting surgery soon and I want to see him first."

"I'll go with you," he said, getting an icy stare in return. "He's my friend too."

Lawson didn't reply and stormed out of the office, Raines following her. The eyes of anyone in the office who happened to be there, eagerly watched their cold exchange as they walked through. They got on the elevator and went down to the third floor without saying another word to each other.

"Wait here," Lawson said to Raines, directing him to stay outside Cain's room while she went inside.

Raines sighed, but did as she wished. Lawson went inside and gave both Heather and Cain a hug.

"So, how are you feeling?" Lawson asked.

"Fine. But I haven't been knifed yet either," Cain replied.

"Good point. Can I get you anything?"

"No. I'm good."

"Heather? Anything?"

"No thanks, Shelly."

"Eric Raines is outside. He wanted to see you before the surgery," Lawson said.

"Oh? I didn't know you two were..."

"We're not. Anything. Actually, he's lucky I didn't rip his testicles out the moment I laid eyes on him."

"Wow," Heather said, raising her eyebrows.

"Did you two talk?" Cain asked.

"I did most of the talking," Lawson said.

"So, you pretty much just bitched him out," Cain assumed.

"Yes."

"Shelly."

"I don't wanna hear it. Especially from someone who was a hermit and ignored me for months. I needed to get it out of my system. I've been carrying around all this emotional baggage for the last three years," Lawson said.

"I know."

"OK. Well, if you don't need anything, I'm gonna head back upstairs and do some work. I just wanted to make sure you were OK."

"You just wanted to make sure I actually showed up," Cain quipped.

"That too," Lawson said and smiled. "Let me know as soon as he's out," she told Heather.

"I will," Heather said.

"OK. Love you both," Lawson told the pair as she left the room.

Lawson passed Raines in the hallway without saying a word. He then went into Cain's room.

"Hey, buddy," Raines said with a handshake. "You look... good."

Cain laughed. "Liar. So I see your chat with Shelly went well."

"Uh, yeah."

"Could it have gone worse?"

"I guess it could've. She could've stabbed me, shot me, chopped my fingers off, and then blew off my legs," Raines joked.

"Well, there's something to look forward to," Heather added.

"I'm actually kind of surprised I made it down here in one piece. I guess I had it coming."

"She just needs to be mad for a little while. She'll come around eventually," Cain said.

"I don't know about that. I don't blame her. That's why I didn't really argue. I betrayed her trust. In this business, we trust very few people, if any. When that happens it's very difficult to get back."

"I can try talking to her if you want," Heather offered.

"I appreciate that but I think she just needs to sort it out for herself for a while. I'm not looking to get back to where we were right away and jump into her bed. Right now, I'd just like for us to be civil towards each other."

"Time heals all wounds so they say," Heather said.

"So it does. Just look at you two," Raines said. "You two are back together again I take it?"

"Yeah. I was pretty foolish trying to push her away from me all those times," Cain said.

"We all have our weak moments I suppose, don't we?"

"So, they got you on anything yet?"

"I'm going after what's left of the Specter group that's on the run."

"Thought that's what they were bringing me back for," Cain said.

"Well, I guess I'm on point until you return. Who knows, maybe I'll eliminate them all by the time you get back," Raines said.

"Don't get greedy. Save Sanders for me," Cain said with a smile.

As soon as the words left his mouth, Heather looked at him concerned, worried that revenge on Sanders would consume him.

"Be careful, Eric," Heather told him.

"Yes, ma'am," he said and nodded. "I'm afraid I won't be here by the time you get back from surgery so I just wanted to wish you good luck with your recovery."

"You're leaving already?" Cain asked.

"My plane leaves in a few hours. Just take your time with getting healthy. Don't rush. I'll take care of things," Raines said.

"Trying to hog all the fun for yourself, huh?"

"Make sure he doesn't go too fast," Raines said to Heather.

"You really think I'll be able to stop him?"

"Probably not. I would be just as anxious if it were reversed."

"I'm more worried about you being out there without me backing you up than me coming back too quickly," Cain said.

As soon as he was done visiting with Cain, Raines headed

back up to Lawson's office, where he found her hard at work. She had numerous folders set out on her desk, shuffling papers back and forth between them. Raines knocked before entering. Lawson looked up briefly before going back to her work. Raines sat down and waited for her to finish. After a few minutes of being ignored, he finally spoke up.

"I know this is difficult for you, but the sooner you go over the mission with me, the sooner I'll be out of your hair," Raines told her.

"Fine. Your first target is Frederick Booth. We last had him pegged in Italy."

"Is he still there?"

"We're not certain but we think so. We have a contact there named Enrico Vasari. He's a tour bus operator. He gave good intel to our previous agent in the area who was able to corner Booth somewhere in Florence. We lost contact with him and then we received word our agent was dead."

"How long ago was this?" Raines asked.

"A few days ago."

"And no word he's been on the move?"

"We've got no hits on any of his passports or aliases and no chatter about him moving anywhere. That's why we believe he's still there," Lawson explained, handing him a file.

"Any idea if he's with anyone?"

"We just don't know. He could be by himself. Or he could have an army with him."

"When do I leave?" Raines asked.

"Your plane leaves in three hours."

"Good thing I didn't unpack yet."

Raines took another minute to look over the information he had in case he had any more questions. Once he was satisfied with everything he got up to leave, Lawson stopped him once he reached the door.

"Eric," she said.

"Yes?"

"Be careful."

Raines smiled and nodded. He grabbed his bag and immediately went to the airport. He hadn't even checked into his hotel room yet, so leaving so quickly was not an issue for him. It was something he'd gotten used to.

46

Cain woke up from the surgery, his eyelids fluttering quickly as he tried to get his bearings. He felt someone holding his hand and slightly turned his head to the left, seeing that pretty face of Heather's looking at him. He smiled at her.

"You're as beautiful as an angel. If I didn't know better, I think I might've died and went to heaven," Cain joked.

Heather smiled, somewhat relieved that he still had his sense of humor. "How do you feel?"

"Feels like someone hit me with a hammer."

"I'll get the doctor and let them know you're awake."

Heather returned a minute later with Dr. Ellison, who was happy to see his patient coming to.

"Mr. Cain. Glad to see you've rejoined us. How are you feeling?"

"I don't know. It hurts. A lot. But I feel different," Cain said.

"How so?"

"I'm not sure," he said, struggling to find the right description. "Lighter almost."

Ellison smiled. "That's a good sign. The pressure's gone so you should feel some relief."

"Can I get out of here now?"

"Wow, that was earlier than even I had predicted." He laughed. "No, you'll have to stay a few more days. It won't be long."

After Cain and Ellison were done talking, Heather called Lawson to let her know that he made it through the surgery. There were still a few tests that had to be done, but she was very upbeat about his condition.

Florence, Italy---Raines had been in Italy before, though only briefly, but he'd never been to Florence. It was a city rich in history. It was the most populous city in the region of Tuscany, and along with being the capital, over a million people resided in the area. It was also considered the birthplace of the Renaissance. Currently, tourism was the chief economic industry of the city. The city was famous for its buildings, architecture, and art. It housed numerous museums, churches, art galleries, and religious buildings.

Raines flew into Florence using the Pisa International Airport. Eager to get to work, he skipped checking in to his hotel and went straight to find Vasari. He went to the location Vasari was supposed to be working and waited for him to appear. After waiting an hour, he saw a man getting into a bus. Raines took a picture out of his pocket to compare and confirmed that it was Vasari.

Vasari was busy looking at some papers and never noticed Raines coming toward him. Raines walked in front of the bus and quickly went in, closing the door behind him as he took a seat behind the driver. Vasari was startled as he could tell the stranger wasn't some tourist or someone who was lost.

"Can I help you?" Vasari nervously asked.

"You can. I need whatever info you have on Frederick Booth," Raines said.

"Who are you?"

"My name's not important. You gave this information to someone recently. Unfortunately, this man has turned up dead. I've been sent to rectify that mistake."

"You're the U.S. agent?"

"Yes."

"I have not heard about his whereabouts in the last several days. Before that he was living in a church a few minutes from here," Vasari told him.

"A church?"

"Yes. I am not sure of the connection myself, but he was there."

"Not alone, I'm sure. Who's he have with him?"

"At least two that I know of. Possibly more but I cannot say with much certainty."

"Thanks," Raines said, putting some money in the man's shirt pocket.

"Be careful. As I told the previous agent, the church is protecting him. You must proceed with caution."

"Where's this church at?"

"If you go to the next street, go eight blocks down, turn right, three more blocks, turn left, it will be on the right. Saint Martin's."

Raines nodded in acknowledgment and tapped Vasari on the shoulder as he exited the bus. Raines started walking toward the church Booth was staying at and began formulating a plan along the way. He figured he could barge in and force the situation or he could just sit back and survey it for a while. If he barged in, there was no way of knowing if Booth was still there, or how many men he had with him. If he waited and staked it out, he could wait there for days without seeing anything, which would seriously delay him if Booth had already moved on. As he got closer, he made the decision to wait. He wasn't usually the kind of agent who kicked ass first and took names later. Raines always wanted as much information as possible before making a move of any kind. That's how he'd survived as long as he had. He got within a block of the church and walked around the perimeter, surveying potential spots he could watch from without being seen. There were several big problems though. The church was so massive that no matter what side he was on he couldn't see the other sides. He could possibly see the front and side, but the other side and back weren't visible from any location. Raines' other problem was that there were so many tourists going in and out that it would be tough to pinpoint Booth. Now he could see why the last agent got killed. There was no other way but to go in there. He'd have to be smart about it. He went back to his hotel and started to formulate a plan. He contacted Lawson to give her an update on what was happening. They did some brainstorming to come up with something that wouldn't get Raines killed.

"So, have you come up with anything yet?" Lawson asked.

"Yeah. I walk in the front door and ask where Booth is."

"I mean something that won't get you killed."

"You're concerned for my safety and well-being? I'm touched," Raines said.

"Don't be too touched. I'm more concerned about Booth killing another agent and escaping without us knowing where he's going."

"Oh."

"Let me see where the next available agents are and I can see if I can swing them your way."

"Do you really think there's time for that?" Raines asked.

"You can't go in there alone. It's too risky. You need backup."

"We don't have time to wait a day or two for other agents to arrive. Booth could be gone by then if he isn't already."

"And if we lose you because you're being impatient then we'll lose him anyway," Lawson argued.

"I have an idea that I think might work."

The following morning Raines left the hotel and went back to St. Martin's. He had what he thought was a pretty good plan. At least he hoped it was. He figured it was either so brilliant that he could have Booth in custody before the day was over, or it was so stupid he'd probably be killed in a matter of minutes. Raines thought it was a chance worth taking though. He stood outside the church's walls and simply looked at the massive structure, wondering how it could be harboring a wanted fugitive. After pondering it for a few seconds he went inside. He found someone who worked there and asked to see the priest who was in charge. He was told that Father Marino was the person he was seeking, but he was currently engaged in other business. Raines showed a badge and said he was in law enforcement and had important business to discuss. He asked if he could wait and was led to Marino's office. Raines walked around the office, looking at everything that was visible to see if there were any clues for the taking. He came up empty. He waited for about ten minutes before Marino was able to meet with him. Upon meeting, they shook hands and sat down at a desk across from each other.

"I understand you're from the law enforcement community?" Marino asked.

"I am," Raines replied. "I'm not supposed to say from where but I'm sure you can make a pretty accurate guess."

"So, what can I do for you?"

"I tend to be blunt and honest and get straight to the point so I won't beat around the bush or play some type of game to get the information I want."

"OK?"

"Frederick Booth. We know he's here and we know you're shielding him. We haven't figured out why yet but that really isn't my concern," Raines said.

"I can assure you that I haven't the faintest idea of what you're talking about."

"Father, I'm not really in the mood to engage in a debate about it. There's been one agent of ours killed here already."

"I am sorry for that."

"I'm not here for you or your apologies," Raines said. "Your reasons for helping him are yours and not my concern. My only concern is apprehending him as quickly as possible. He's a dangerous man and a wanted fugitive who needs to be brought to justice."

"Justice? What justice? Yours?" Marino asked. "There is only one that is supposed to give justice."

"Well, until that day arrives, I guess I'll just have to do my part."

"And if he were here as you suggest, the reasons for

shielding him as you put it, may not appear to be what they seem."

"Things usually aren't."

"I would say there are many reasons for doing the things that we do. They may not always make sense to those who aren't privy to all the information."

Raines stood up and put a piece of paper down on the desk for the priest.

"What is this?" Marino asked, reading the address that was written on it.

"I'm staying at the Waldorf Astoria. Room 913. I'll be there until tonight."

"And why would I have any use for this?"

"Because I expect that you'll contemplate our conversation and at some point, you'll do the right thing and give me the information I'm looking for," Raines said before walking to the door.

"What makes you think I will? Or that I wouldn't just give this to this Booth person that you're seeking?"

"Trust, Father. Trust."

Raines left the office and walked straight out of the church. Everything went exactly as he thought it would. Marino's defiant stance proved to Raines that Booth was there somewhere. It was such a big place, though, that finding him there would be near impossible. He'd have to get Booth to come to him. He was counting on Marino giving Booth his address and him paying Raines a visit. He figured Booth would have to try to take him out since Raines knew where he was. The only thing he didn't know, and it could've been a big problem, was how many men Booth had with him. But there was no way of telling until it was time to battle. And Raines was as ready as he ever was for that.

Once Raines got back to the hotel, he got an idea on how to even the odds a little if Booth brought more men with him. He immediately sought out an employee at the main desk.

"Will you be working all night?" Raines asked.

"I'm here until ten, sir," the employee replied.

"Here's my problem... I have a very dangerous job and I think at some point today I may be receiving a visit from some very unsavory characters. If you see a group of rough-looking men come in and head straight for the elevator for the ninth floor, I'd appreciate an immediate phone call," Raines said. He reached into his pocket and took out a hundred-dollar bill, offering it to the employee.

The man took it and nodded. "It'd be my pleasure, sir."

Raines smiled. "Do a good job and there'll be another one of those before your night's over."

"How will I know when I see them?"

"Trust me. You'll know."

Raines went up to his room and got himself ready for some visitors. He had three guns with him that he put silencers on. One for each hand plus a backup that he put in the back of his pants. Now all he had to do was wait. While he waited, he called Lawson to let her know how it was going. If Booth really was in hiding at the church, Raines was sure he'd get paid a visit relatively quickly. Booth couldn't afford not to. A few more hours went by without a peep. Raines looked at the time hitting four o'clock just as the phone rang. He quickly answered.

"Four men just got into the elevator for the ninth floor," the desk person told him.

"Thank you."

"Wait... there's a fifth guy waiting down here in the lobby."

"Thanks again."

Raines went over to the sliding door that led to the balcony and opened it slightly. He then went into the bathroom and turned the shower on. Then he proceeded into the bedroom and turned the TV on, making sure it was loud. He put a couple pillows in the middle of the bed and pulled the covers over them. Raines was doing anything he could think of to give himself an advantage. Even if it gave him an extra second, any pause that the intruders made, it could be the difference that he needed to survive. He closed the bathroom and bedroom door before sliding under the bed. A few minutes went by. Raines went through the probable chain of events in his mind. He pictured how he'd kill each man, going from room to room. It helped to relax him so he didn't overthink things. His concentration was interrupted a minute later as he thought he heard the front door open. He patiently waited for someone to come through the bedroom door.

The floor creaked slightly as the men tried to quietly walk through the room. Quickly surveying their surroundings, the leader of the group motioned for one man to check the kitchen, and the other two to check the bedroom and bathroom. He was heading for the open door on the balcony. The intruders stopped at each of their respective doors, listening for any kind of sound that would indicate Raines was on the other side of it. The man at the bedroom door went first, quickly rushing in and waving his gun around in a circle. The man at the bathroom door watched his partner go into the bedroom and assumed Raines wasn't there since there were no shots fired. He heard the water running in the bathroom and slowly opened the door. The man in the bedroom saw the lump on the bed and focused his gun on it. He gradually pulled the covers off, revealing the stacked pillows. Feeling at ease, he put his gun in his holster. Raines turned to his side and put his gun within an inch of the man's leg and pulled the trigger. The man instantly fell to the ground, holding his shin in agony as pieces of the bone flew off. As soon as he hit the ground, Raines put two more bullets in his chest. It happened so fast the man didn't even have time to scream.

Raines rolled out from under the bed and scurried to the door. He had a clear line of sight to the bathroom as it was right across from the bedroom. The man had just checked the shower and let the curtain fall back into its position. Raines held his weapon out in front of him and aimed at the man's chest. As soon as the guy turned around Raines fired a shot, hitting him in the chest. He fell back into the tub as the water dribbled over his lifeless body.

"You alright in there?" a voice shouted from the main room.

"In the bathroom," Raines replied, putting his hand over his mouth to disguise his voice, hoping he sounded like one of them.

Raines waited to the side of the bedroom opening. As soon as he saw the outline of a man rounding the corner he fired two rounds into the man's back. He let out a grunt just before he passed away, hitting the ground face first. The last surviving member of the group heard the commotion and came rushing over just as Raines peeked his head out the door. The two men exchanged fire, neither one hitting their intended target. A piece of wood splintering off the door frame hit Raines in the side of the forehead but he brushed it off. He entered the hallway towards the main room, ready to fire again.

"You've got nowhere to go," Raines yelled.

"You don't either," the man shouted back.

"Perhaps. But there's no way you can get to the door without running past me. And there's no other way out of this room."

"I could say the same for you."

"Let's make a deal then."

"I'm listening."

"Instead of either of us taking the chance of getting killed, let's agree to call it a stalemate and we'll both go our separate ways," Raines offered.

"If I leave this room without you dead, I might as well be dead myself."

"I'm only after Booth. If I get him you're in the clear. I'm not after you. Don't even know who you are."

"You'd let me walk?" the man asked.

"All I want is Booth."

"How do I know I can trust you?"

Raines thought for a few seconds to determine how to handle the situation. "Tell you what. Let's both slide our guns out at the same time. Sound good?"

"I guess so."

"On three. One... two... three," Raines said, sliding his gun into the open spot of the floor. The gun of the other man slid at the same time, hitting his as they spun around.

"Now, let's both come out with our hands up to show there's no funny business," Raines said.

Raines raised his hands and walked to the end of the hallway and peeked around the corner. He saw the other man walking closer, his hands in the air as well. They both lowered their arms as they only stood a few feet from each other.

"So, we just both go our separate ways now?" the man asked.

"Unless you'd like to change the terms of our agreement."

"As a matter of fact, I would. You should always carry a backup weapon," he said, reaching for a gun tucked inside his jacket.

Raines quickly removed his gun from the back of his pants and shot the man three times in the chest. He wasn't even able to remove his own gun from his jacket before he hit the ground and died. Raines walked over to him and stood over his body.

"I agree," he stated, reloading his gun.

Raines reached down into the man's pockets to see if he was carrying anything of value with him that would help get Booth. He noticed his phone and pulled it out. Raines scrolled through his list of contacts and saw a listing for Booth. He tried to think of a way to draw him up to the room.

"It's done. Raines is dead," he texted. "There's another guy here. His ID says his name is Cain. He's hurt but still breathing. What do we do with him?"

He figured that by including Cain's name he raised the stakes a little bit. He didn't think Booth would be able to resist coming up knowing Matthew Cain was there and in their custody. A few seconds later the room phone started ringing. Raines went over to the table and answered it.

"Hey. Just wanted to let you know the other guy down here's on his way up," the desk employee said.

"You just earned yourself a raise," Raines replied.

Raines wanted to make sure he'd get the jump on Booth, not quite sure he'd just walk into the room. Raines left his room and went down the hall to stand next to the elevator. He'd surprise Booth as he walked off. A minute later he heard the sound of the elevator stopping. He turned his back, put his head down and pretended to start walking away. A few people stepped off the elevator first before Booth. Once he did, he did a quick look around then turned left to head to Raines' room. Raines propped his head back up and turned around once he heard the elevator doors closing. He saw where Booth was and quickly walked toward him, making sure he was quiet enough to surprise him. Just as Booth got to the door, he turned around, only to get the butt end of a gun hitting him in the face. His back hit the wall as he stumbled. Once he regained his footing, he clearly saw Raines standing in front of him, a gun staring him right in the face.

"Should've known," Booth said. "Stupid mistake on my part, coming up here."

"Yes, it was. But then again, desperate people who are on the run sometimes do stupid things, don't they? Drop your gun on the ground."

Booth did as he was instructed and reached for his gun. He gently removed it and tossed it on the floor. Raines motioned with his gun for Booth to go inside the room. Raines reached down to pick up Booth's gun as he followed him inside. Booth immediately saw the first man lying on the ground, then turned his head and saw another lying in the hallway.

"Looks like you didn't send enough," Raines told him.

"Harder to find good help now than it used to be."

"Sit," Raines said, pointing to a chair.

Booth complied and sat down, fairly certain in knowing what his fate would be.

"So, what now?" Booth asked.

"This is the part where you talk and give me the information I want."

Booth just laughed. "We both know you're gonna kill me, regardless. So why do you think I'm gonna tell you anything?"

"Don't they say something about dying with a clear conscience or something like that?"

"Yeah. Something like that."

"Do you want a drink before you start?"

"There's nothing you can do or say that'll get me to say anything. I know you're gonna kill me so just get it over with."

Raines didn't say anything. He moved closer to his adversary and simply shot him in the left kneecap. Booth grabbed his knee, screaming in pain.

"Now, I can do this all day, putting you in just enough pain and agony as to keep you alive for days in a severe amount of pain. Or, I can end it quickly so you won't have to go through all that," Raines said.

"Go to hell."

Raines fired his gun again, this time hitting Booth in his right shoulder.

"Now, I have enough bullets to shoot you another sixteen or seventeen times if you prefer. I can drag this out for days until you're in so much pain that you eventually succumb to it. Or you can just tell me what I want to know," Raines said. "You already know how this ends. So why not save yourself the pain? You can't save it for another chance somewhere down the line."

Booth sighed. "All right."

"Where are the others?"

"Proulx' in France."

"We already know that."

"He's living with his girlfriend. Near Paris. Not sure the exact address."

"How do I find him?"

"Find her. She'll lead you to him," he said.

"What does she do?"

"Some kind of artist. Photography, I think."

"Have a name?" Raines asked.

"Maxime something. Never did get her last name."

"Does she know he's on the run?"

"Yes."

"What about the others?"

"Collins is in Germany," Booth answered.

"Where?"

"Don't know. Last I heard was he was trying to start up his own operation there."

"What kind of operation?"

"The usual stuff. You know, drugs, money laundering, guns."

"Anything else?"

"That's all I got."

"What about Sanders?" Raines asked.

"No idea. Haven't talked to him in months."

"You don't have any idea where he might be?"

"Could be anywhere," Booth replied.

"Would the others know where he's at?"

"Collins might. He was like his right-hand man. If he was still talking to anyone, it'd probably be him."

"That it?" Raines asked.

"Told you all I know."

"I'll give you the courtesy of choosing where you want the fatal blow to be. Head, chest, back?"

"Just make it quick."

"Want to see it coming?"

Booth just shook his head. Raines walked around behind him to give him the fatal shot.

"I'll count to five if you want to say any prayers," Raines

said.

"Thanks."

"One... two...," Raines said, pulling the trigger early and firing into the back of his skull. The blast knocked Booth out of the chair and onto the floor, blood and brain matter flying everywhere.

Raines didn't see the need to prolong Booth's suffering any longer than it needed to be. He thought it'd be better for him to get it over with quicker. He stepped over Booth's body and grabbed his bag, putting two of his guns in it. He took one last look at the carnage he'd left before walking out the door. Once Raines got down to the main floor, he saw the employee who'd helped him. He walked over to him and handed him six one hundred-dollar bills.

"Appreciate the help," Raines told him. "I wouldn't let anyone go in that room until tomorrow."

"Are you checking out, Mr. Ferguson?"

"I am. My business here is finished."

47

Lawson tried calling Raines again. Still no answer. It was the fifth time in the last thirty minutes that she tried to reach him. Seven texts also went unanswered. She tried using the computer to get a fix on his location using the GPS coordinates but that also turned up nothing. She ran her hand over her face in frustration as she feverishly worked to find him. A tear started forming in the corner of her eye but she quickly wiped it away, determined to not get emotional. She called a few contacts she had in France but nobody had any information for her.

It'd been over a week since Raines flew out of Italy after killing Booth. He touched down in France a day later and immediately started looking for Proulx via his girlfriend Maxime. He expected to be able to find her without much of a problem but it proved to be more difficult than he thought. Either Maxime wasn't her real name or she wasn't a photographer because he wasn't able to find one that matched her description. After five days of searching, Raines finally thought he'd found someone who could lead him to either Maxime or Proulx. He'd told Lawson that he was meeting with a contact and would follow up with her after he was finished. That was over nine hours ago. Lawson knew his lack of communication was for only one reason. He ran into trouble. Hopefully, it wasn't the deadly kind.

After Lawson exhausted every option that she had at her disposal, she finally called Conlin to fill him in. Conlin dropped what he was doing and came into The Center. He met Lawson in her office.

"How long's it been?" the Director asked.

"Over nine hours."

"Nine hours? Jesus. Why the hell did you wait so long to tell me?"

"I was using all my resources to find him first," Lawson said.

"You should've let me know two hours after he didn't check in. Then I could've directed all resources on this immediately," he told her, fuming.

"I bungled it," she admitted.

"This has never happened before with you. Why now? Is it the personal thing you had with him?" Conlin asked.

"No. I don't know why it took so long. I guess I was giving him the benefit of the doubt and was just trying to find him on my own."

Conlin paced around the room as he thought of their next move. Lawson stood there at her desk like a kid in school, waiting to be reprimanded by their teacher. She knew she blew it and wouldn't have been surprised if she was sent home and taken off the assignment.

"All right, let's get everyone in The Room and start working on finding him. Right now, everyone's top priority is finding Eric Raines," Conlin said.

"Right away."

Lawson rounded up all the analysts who were there and coordinated their efforts into finding Raines. They spent the next several hours retracing his steps and looking into the information that he had previously relayed to try to locate him. They'd gotten no closer to finding him than Lawson had. Everyone in the room was getting frustrated by their lack of progress.

"What now?" Lawson asked.

Conlin put his hand over his mouth and blew into it as he tried to formulate a plan. "We need to send someone in."

"Who? The last time we sent agents into these places three of them ended up dead."

"I know," Conlin replied. "We need an edge."

"What kind of an edge?"

"We need Cain," the Director plainly stated.

"We don't have anyone else like Cain," she rebutted.

"I don't mean someone like him. I mean... him."

"Sir, with all due respect, you can't ask Cain to go back out in the field already. He won't survive," Lawson said, animated.

"He'll survive. Because he has the will to do so."

"The doctor said he'll need at least six weeks of recovery. He's only through week one," she said, continuing her argument.

"Well then, I guess we'll just present our case and see which side of the coin he falls on."

"And if he feels he's not ready?"

"Then I guess we'll have to send someone else," Conlin said.

"But I don't think it'll come to that. Tomorrow morning, go to his apartment and see what his willingness is."

The following morning, Lawson begrudgingly went to Cain's apartment. It was a visit she didn't want to make. A question that she didn't want to ask. She could always say that she asked and he said no, but she knew somehow the truth would come out and put her in a bigger jam than she was already in. She almost hoped that when she knocked on the door nobody would answer. Not that it would change anything, it'd just delay the inevitable. Heather quickly answered the door. She gave Lawson a hug as soon as she saw her. Lawson faked a smile to try to hide the way she was really feeling, though she wasn't very good at it. Heather picked up on it right away.

"What's wrong?" Heather asked.

"I, uh, just need to talk to Matt for a minute," she replied.

"He's over on the couch," Heather said and pointed.

"Listening to doctor orders?"

"Yeah, right. You know him as well as I do."

Cain was lying on the couch watching TV. He saw Lawson come in and was glad to see her. He watched her come closer and could tell she looked troubled by something. He slightly propped himself up so he wasn't flat on his back.

"You look like someone who's bringing bad news," Cain said.

"That obvious, huh?"

"Yeah. Pretty much."

"How are you feeling?" Lawson asked.

"Pretty good actually. I get tired easily. But I know that'll get better in time. My head feels good though. Clearer, if that makes any sense."

"No other symptoms or anything?"

"Not really. Just tired. Feels like I sleep sixteen hours a day. Why?"

"Just wanted to make sure you're OK."

"I'm doing good. Now are you gonna tell me why you're here?" Cain asked.

"Can't I just stop in to say hi and see how you are?"

"Could've just picked up the phone to do that. I imagine there's something that you didn't want to say over the phone."

"I hate how you know me," Lawson said.

"It's a gift," he joked.

Heather sat in a chair close to them, listening to their conversation, not liking where the talk was going. It felt to her like someone was about to drop the other shoe. Like a bombshell announcement was about to go off. She feared what was about to come out of Lawson's mouth.

"First off, I want you to understand, both of you, that me coming here to talk about what I'm about to talk about was not my choice," Lawson said.

"OK?" Heather replied.

"I'm doing what I was ordered to do."

"Shelly, stop running in circles and just say what you need to say," Cain calmly told her. "We're all friends. Nobody's gonna bite your head off."

"Well, nobody's heard what I'm about to say yet," she said, continuing to dodge.

"Shelly...."

"OK. OK," she said, pausing for another minute. "Eric's missing."

"What?" Heather asked.

"What do you mean he's missing?" Cain asked.

"He hasn't checked in in almost twenty-four hours," she said.

"Where is he?"

"France. He found Booth in Italy. Before he died, he told Eric that Proulx was with a girlfriend named Maxime. She's supposed to be a photographer there but we haven't been able to locate her."

"Can you pinpoint his last location?"

"No. He said he had a meeting with a contact. He didn't say where though. We haven't heard from him since."

"So where do I come in?" Cain asked.

"They want to send someone in to find him."

"They can't just send in anyone. Has to be someone highly skilled, knows the people, can get things done quickly. Someone with experience," Cain said, knowing full well he was hinting at himself.

"Yeah."

Heather looked at the two of them for a few seconds before finally picking up on what they were referring to.

"Please tell me you're not suggesting that Matt go in there?" Heather said.

"I'm not suggesting anything. The Director would like you to be the one to go in there," Lawson said.

"Absolutely not! That's ridiculous," Heather replied. "He just had brain surgery. He's only been out of the hospital over a week."

"I know. I'm not pressuring you, Matt. I told him this was out of the question. I didn't even wanna come here and talk to you about it."

"I know," Cain said.

"Please tell me you're not considering this," Heather said to him.

"Heather, if Eric's in trouble then he needs my help."

"Matt, I understand the relationship you two have, but you're not in any condition to travel yet."

"He saved my life. More than once. Yours too."

"I'm not saying he deserves to be left there. Obviously someone needs to go find him. But why does it have to be you?"

"Because I'm the most qualified."

"I can't believe we're even having this conversation," Heather said, rubbing her forehead. "Are you even able to fly yet? What about the air pressure? Couldn't your head explode or something?"

"My head's not gonna explode. Doctor said give it two weeks before I can fly. We'll just have to bump that up a few days."

"Seriously?"

"Worst that could happen would be blood clots," Cain said.

"Oh, well, that's just fantastic."

"What do you want me to do? Just sit around here and do nothing while Eric's out there in trouble?"

"Are there no healthy agents available? I just don't understand why you're the only one who can go."

"Because he's the best," Lawson said.

Cain stood up, slightly dizzy, but quickly regained his balance. He started walking around the room, trying to shake the listless feeling he had by just lying around for days. Heather's leg began shaking, moving it up and down. It was a trait she had when she was annoyed but didn't feel like talking yet. She watched his every move as he walked.

"Your mind's already made up, isn't it?" Heather asked.

"You've already decided that you're going. Not even gonna talk about it or anything, are you?"

"Nothing to talk about," Cain replied. "A friend's in trouble. He needs me. That's all there is."

"Just like that? No care or concern for your own well-being?"

"Just like that."

"You still don't care about what happens to you, do you?"

"Heather, right now, this isn't about me. It's about saving someone who we all care about," he told her. "If I didn't, I wouldn't have gotten the surgery to begin with."

Heather nodded, knowing she wasn't going to talk him out of going. The best she could do was try to help him to ensure he'd get home safely.

"Fine. I'll go with you then," she said.

"What? Absolutely not," Cain replied.

"Matt, I may not be able to stop you from leaving, but you won't be able to stop me from going with you. You leave me here and I'll be on the next flight out after you."

"What do you think?" Cain asked Lawson. "Your personal opinion. Not your professional one."

Lawson contemplated a few seconds, trying to sort out her thoughts. "I agree with Heather. I think she's right. I don't know if Eric's gone or not but I don't want to lose both of you."

Cain stopped roaming around the apartment and settled back down on the couch, sitting and listening intently to his handler's thoughts.

"So, what would you have me do?" Cain asked.

"I know you're your own man and you're gonna do what you want. But she's right. If you're gonna do this, then I think we should take precautions to make sure you're as least vulnerable as possible," Lawson said.

"Which means?"

"Someone should go with you. If you have some type of complication? What if you're there and you pass out and nobody's there to help you? We have to think about these things."

Cain sighed. He knew she was right. Needing help wasn't something that he usually sought. Asking for help was something even more unnatural.

"So, who do you suggest I pair up with?" Cain asked. "It can't be you," he said, nodding to Heather. "I love you and I couldn't do my job properly, I couldn't do what needs to be done, if I'm there worrying about you and trying to keep you safe."

Lawson looked at Heather, knowing there was only one solution. "I'll go," Lawson said. "Nobody else would know you like I do, what you need, what you've been through. It wouldn't be my first time out in the field."

"I can't believe this is happening," Heather said, a few tears starting to run down her cheeks.

She wiped them off her face as Cain looked over at her. He got up and came over to her, squeezing next to her on the chair as he put his arm around her shoulders.

"I'll be OK," he told her, their heads touching.

Heather nodded, not able to formulate any words. She wasn't sure she believed he would be. She knew it was time to stop fighting and arguing; it wasn't doing any good. Cain was going to do what he wanted, and she just had to hope and pray that it would work out for the best. She didn't like long arguments or anything that would dampen his mood before leaving on a mission. Heather always feared that if he left after a fight with her it'd weigh on his mind and possibly interfere with his mission and prevent him from coming home.

"So, when do we leave?" Cain asked.

"I guess as soon as you're ready," Lawson answered.

"Might as well make it as soon as possible. The longer we wait the more trouble Eric's likely to be in."

"I'll uh... I'll make the necessary arrangements."

Lawson took out her phone and called Director Conlin to let him know Cain was on board and that she would be accompanying him. Conlin had already anticipated Cain's answer and had a private jet on standby. It'd be ready as soon as they got there. She walked over to Heather and put her hand on her shoulder.

"I'm sorry," Lawson said.

Heather put her hand on top of Lawson's, nodded, and smiled. "It's OK. Just bring him back home to me."

"They've got a private jet. It's ready when you are," she told Cain.

"I guess give me a few minutes to put some things together," Cain replied.

"They've already put some gear and weapons on the plane."

Heather stood up to put on a brave face and was greeted with a hug from Lawson.

"Be careful," Heather told her.

"I will. You need anything?"

"Only thing I need is him coming back in one piece."

"He'll be back. I promise," Lawson said.

"Make sure you do the same."

Lawson moved over to the door as she waited for Cain to emerge from the bedroom. He came out a minute later with only a backpack as was his custom. He preferred traveling light just in case he ever had to move in a hurry. Or if he had to leave anything behind there was nothing of value that he'd regret losing. Cain took Heather's hand, and they walked together to the door before he leaned in and kissed her.

"You'll be OK?" Cain asked.

"I will be. Just make sure that's not the last one of those I ever get."

"Not a chance. Nothing will stop me from coming back to you. I... we... haven't come all this way to let something stand in our way now. I will be back."

Heather smiled and kissed him one more time. There was sheer determination in the tone of his voice that at least provided a little bit of comfort to her, even though she knew it wouldn't necessarily come down to just that.

48

Cain and Lawson arrived at the airport and immediately boarded the twenty-three-foot-long private jet. The jet was big enough to transport thirteen people, though the main advantage for its size was that it could get to France without stopping to refuel. The jet would save them several hours, all of which would be critical in finding Raines, as they could get to France in just over seven hours. The jet started up the engine, ready to take off. Lawson looked at Cain to make sure he was all right. She gave him some pills to help prevent any complications from the flight and the air pressure.

"Nervous?" Lawson asked.

"Not about the flight," he replied.

"What about then?"

"Heather."

"What about her?"

"Just hope she'll be OK while I'm gone and not stress out too much."

"She'll be fine. She's strong. She'll get through it."

"Yeah."

"Anything else? Not worried about the flight at all?" she asked.

"Nah. You should know by now that I don't worry about myself all that often. I'm more worried about Eric."

"Think he's still alive?" Lawson asked, the concern evident in her voice.

"Well, the fact that he hasn't turned up yet would suggest two things."

"Which are?"

"He's either being held for some reason, and probably tortured, or he's at the bottom of a river somewhere," Cain said.

"No room for a third option in there?"

"Not likely. In any case, the first possibility doesn't worry me as much; he can handle that. It's the other option that concerns me."

Lawson looked over at Cain every so often just to make sure he wasn't having any problems. She was probably more nervous about it than he was. He pretty much just rolled with whatever situation happened in front of him. They were about two hours into their flight and everything seemed to be going pretty smoothly. Lawson was working on her laptop when she looked over at Cain, who was rubbing his eyes. Cain leaned back in his seat and looked up at the ceiling of the jet. He started breathing a little more heavily and his eyes opened wider like he was having trouble seeing. Lawson rushed over to him and grabbed his hand.

"What's the matter? What's happening?" Lawson frantically asked.

Cain moved his mouth like he wanted to speak but started blowing air through his mouth to help breathe a little better. Lawson quickly left to grab her phone so she could call the doctor and came back over to him. Cain, though still having quite a bit of difficulty, managed to say a few words.

"Everything's spinning," he blurted out, still breathing heavily. He was also sweating profusely. He unbuckled his seat belt and stood up, though his balance wasn't very good.

"What are you doing?"

Cain took a deep breath and gulped as he struggled to balance himself. He wiped the sweat from his forehead and turned around. He quickly stumbled to the back of the jet where the bathroom was located. Just as Lawson got through to the doctor, she could hear Cain throwing up in the toilet. She kept talking to the doctor as she waited for Cain to reemerge from the bathroom, keeping her eyes glued in that direction. After waiting a couple minutes for Cain to return, she didn't hear any noises coming from the back of the jet. She started walking back there to make sure he was OK. As she got there Cain walked through the doorway, looking much better, though he was still sweating a lot. He wasn't having any balance issues and seemed to be breathing normal. He saw Lawson on the phone and motioned to her to put it away; he was OK and didn't need any help. He walked past her and wiped the moisture off his forehead as he returned to his seat like nothing happened. Lawson informed the doctor of his status and told him she'd call him later if anything changed. She also returned to her seat and looked over at her friend, analyzing his every move.

Cain felt her eyes watching him and turned his head toward her. "I'm fine."

"Had me worried for a minute," Lawson said.

"Nothing to worry about. Easy as pie, right? Nothing to it."

"I'll never get how you can be so calm about everything."

"Practice."

Lawson went back to her work on the computer but kept shifting her eyes over to Cain every few minutes as she worried that his symptoms might return. Cain on the other hand seemed as calm as ever. Didn't worry him in the slightest that he might have another complication. Didn't worry about the last one either. He took turns between staring out the window and staring at the wall in front of him.

"Thinking?" Lawson asked.

"No."

"Most people would listen to music or watch a movie or something to calm themselves down."

"I'm not most people," Cain replied.

"Boy, do I know that."

"I'm already calm."

"Then what are you doing?" she asked.

"Visualizing."

"Visualizing what?"

"Situations."

"Like what?"

"Situations we might find ourselves in. Things or people we might face. If I visualize dangerous situations that we might be placed in, I visualize in my mind what I would do. Then if those things actually happen, I already feel like I've been through it before. Helps to minimize any hesitation I might have if I've already been through it in my mind and gone through the possible scenarios," Cain explained. "Helps to not panic."

"I can't imagine you panicking over anything."

"Not in a fearful way. Panicking over finding a solution."

"How many times have you visualized things that actually took place?"

"More times than you'd think."

Another two hours in the air went by without a hiccup. Lawson's work was interrupted by a phone call that she received from Director Conlin.

"How's everything going?" Conlin asked.

"Fine."

"Got a call from the doctor saying there were some issues."

"Minor stuff. Nothing to be concerned about," Lawson replied.

"Good. We've just gotten word from an informant who says he knows what happened to Raines and that he's willing to meet with someone to relay that information... for a price, of course."

"A reliable source?"

"That we cannot say with much certainty. It's a little iffy at this point. But it's a lead we can't turn down."

"I agree."

"So, he'll be awaiting a female agent to meet him. I only told him one agent would be meeting him just in case things aren't what they seem. I want Cain in a sniper position in case things go sour. That way this guy doesn't suspect we have an extra man there," Conlin said.

"What's his name?"

"Joseph Cardullo. Not much on him. Small-time operator.

Be careful with him. If he's got something useful, then agree to transfer funds however he agrees."

"And if he's playing us?" Lawson asked.

"Then have Cain take him out. We don't have time for games with these people."

"What's the address?"

"I'll email it to you with the file on this guy."

As soon as Lawson's call ended she informed Cain of the latest developments. The email came in a minute later. She downloaded Cardullo's file and studied his picture and criminal accomplishments. She took the computer and sat next to Cain so he could look at the information with her. As Cain read the man's file, he knew it was likely he'd have to use his gun. Cardullo had a violent past. Cain felt it was unlikely he was someone who was interested in sharing information.

"It's most likely a trap," Cain said.

"Why do you think so?"

"Robbery, murder, attempted murder, guns, drugs... hardly seems the informant type. Wouldn't you agree?"

Lawson sighed. "I guess so. Unless he knows how valuable this is and just wants the money."

"How would he know how valuable it is unless he's connected to it somehow?"

"Well, aren't you a Debbie Downer," Lawson said.

"I didn't say he couldn't be useful in some way. I'm just doubting he's going to tell us anything of substance. Unless it comes from beating it out of him."

"Looks like the meeting's at a clothing warehouse."

"What is it with bad guys and warehouses? Can't they ever find someplace else for these meetings?" Cain joked.

Three more uneventful hours until they got to France.

Cain's mind took him to that warehouse where he envisioned twenty different scenarios of how the events would unfold. Over ninety percent of them ended with him putting a bullet in the target. As they circled over the airport and started their approach toward the runway, Cain wanted to make sure Lawson's mind was right.

"You all right with this?" Cain asked.

"Yeah. Why wouldn't I be?"

"Meeting with an unsavory character isn't your usual cup of tea."

"This isn't my first time in the field, Matt. You should know that," she responded.

"I know. But the reason for that is circling that brain of yours, I think."

"What's that mean?"

"We're here because of Eric. You have a very personal connection. It's not like we're here for some agent you don't know," Cain said.

"I'm here to do my job. Nothing else."

"And if this guy tells you that Eric's dead?"

The question brought back a deadly stare from Lawson. Cain raised his eyebrows in an I told you so manner in response.

"My point exactly," he told her.

"What point is that?"

"Eric may be dead. He may be alive. We don't know. But when we're in that warehouse you need to be focused on the man in front of you and not worrying about Eric. Make sure you're focusing."

"I will."

"I don't want to lose both of you."

"Aww... you care about me," Lawson teased.

"Oh stop. You already know I do. Can I ask another question?"

"I suppose so."

"Do you still love him?"

Lawson paused before answering. "I really don't know. Why?"

"Just wondering."

"Why? What are you, some love expert now?"

"I dunno... maybe. Thought maybe I could give you a few tips and pointers. Maybe a little bit of advice," Cain teased.

"From you?"

"Yeah. You know, since my love life has gone so well I thought I could impart my wisdom upon you a little."

The two of them shared a laugh as the jet touched down on the runway. As soon as they exited the plane, there was a car waiting for them. Cain sent Heather a text message to let her know he got to France safely. He didn't think there was a need to worry her about the hiccup he had since it didn't turn out to be anything serious. As long as he was there in one piece that was all she really needed to know since he didn't want to worry her any more than she already was. As they drove to the rendezvous location, Cain checked his weapons to make sure they were working properly.

"We have about an hour," Lawson said.

"How long will it take for us to get there?"

"I think about half an hour."

"Should be enough time for me to find a good spot," Cain said.

"If things start going bad, do you want me to give you some type of signal?"

"No need. If things start to go bad... I'll know."

"Just the same, how about if I run my left forearm over my forehead?" she asked.

"If it makes you feel better."

They made better time than they thought they would, arriving at the warehouse in only twenty minutes. Just before they got there, they pulled over to let Cain out. He put his guns in a duffel bag and walked to the warehouse on foot just in case Cardullo, or if he had any men with him already waiting at the spot, wouldn't spot Cain and give away the element of surprise that they were counting on. Cain would find another way into the warehouse and set up shop wherever he felt appropriate and would be able to cover as much as he could. After Cain exited the car, Lawson continued on to the warehouse, sitting in front of the building for a few minutes. She waited about ten minutes, looking for any sign of activity inside. She started walking towards the door when she heard it unlock and slightly open. She stopped as she waited to see an outline of someone standing there. She felt a sigh of relief when she saw half of Cain's face emerging from the shadows.

"C'mon," Cain told her. "Place is clean. Nobody else is here yet."

Lawson quickly ducked inside, closing the door behind her.

"How'd you get in?" she asked.

"Window. As you can see, there's a second floor," Cain said, pointing to it. "I'll be right up there. Gives me a pretty good vantage point of the middle of the floor and the door."

"What if he brings friends?"

"I'll worry about them. If shooting starts you just take cover behind some of those boxes over there."

It appeared to be some kind of clothing warehouse. Not a

huge place but it had two floors. The second floor had no offices or rooms. It was mostly just a narrow walkway that had boxes lined up around it. The first floor had the offices around the sides but the main floor had clothes on racks and boxes that were ready to be shipped out. There were a few pallets that were highly stacked and some boxes were just piled up in different sections on the floor, waiting for their invoices to be ready.

Cain noticed that Lawson kept turning her head around. He wasn't sure what she was looking at but also noticed she was fidgeting with her hands a lot. Then she started rubbing her arms up and down as if she were cold.

"Nervous?" Cain asked.

"Uh, no."

"Look nervous."

"I'm not," she told him.

"Seem nervous."

"Well, I'm not."

"OK," Cain said. "But you're acting nervous."

"OK. Fine. I'm nervous."

"Relax. Nothing to be nervous about."

Lawson rolled her eyes. "Easy for you to say."

"You got me here with you. What could go wrong?" Cain asked.

"You really want me to answer that question?"

Cain grinned then left her alone as he made his way back up to the second floor. He settled on a spot off to the side and piled up a few boxes next to each other to try to conceal his gun. He left a slight opening that he could fit his rifle through. He hoped they stayed in the same area otherwise the boxes would restrict his movement and he'd have to relocate. He looked through the scope of his rifle and simulated how far he could move it within the confines of the boxes. He lay on the floor to see if it was a better look but the metal railing blocked his rifle. He would've had to prop it up over the railing and he thought it could possibly give away his position. He decided just to kneel on his right knee as they felt the most comfortable.

Twenty-five minutes elapsed until Lawson saw the head-lights of a car pull up before turning off. She looked at the time and if it was Cardullo, he was fifteen minutes early. Maybe he had ideas of doing to them what they already had set up, she thought. It didn't take long for her visitors to introduce them-selves as they immediately went to the warehouse. She saw the handle of the door jiggle and then the clanging sound of the keys as the door unlocked. Four men walked in. Lawson recog-nized one of them as Cardullo from the photo that was sent to her. He was rougher looking than the picture had indicated as he had a newfound scar just under his left eye. Made him look a little tougher.

"I see you have your own key to the place," Lawson said.

"I know the owners." Cardullo smiled, looking his counter-part over. "How did you get in?"

"Girl can't tell her secrets, can she?"

"You're early."

"So are you."

"I always like to be punctual when meeting with a lady friend."

"So thoughtful," Lawson said as she looked at his friends. "I didn't realize you were bringing company. I thought this was going to be a one-on-one meeting."

"Don't worry about them. They're like my bodyguards. They follow me everywhere."

"Bodyguards, huh? Are you so hated that you need them?"

"Dangerous line of work that we're in."

Lawson faked a smile as she noticed the guns Cardullo's men were carrying with them.

"Did you bring anyone with you?" Cardullo asked as he looked around.

"Do you see anyone?"

"So, what's your name?"

"Bond."

Cardullo laughed at her sense of humor. "Funny. I like that. What do you say you and me have a few private moments in one of those offices over there?"

"What do you say we get on with what we're here for and get down to business?"

"I'd love to get down into your business."

"You don't have anything for me, do you?" Lawson asked.

"Now just hold on there, sweetie. I didn't say that. Calm down. Just trying to have a little fun first."

"Information first. Fun later."

"All right. I can dig it," Cardullo said, nodding to his men to spread out and check the area.

Lawson noticed they were moving. "Where are they going?"

"Not that I don't trust you, but I just wanna make sure that we're by ourselves here."

Lawson wiped her forehead with her left forearm, hoping that Cain would see the signal. Unfortunately for her, Cardullo noticed the signal too. He quickly lunged at her, taking her by surprise as he took hold of her, putting his arm around her neck as he stood behind her.

"What was that?" Cardullo asked. "Some kind of signal to somebody?"

"Just hot in here," Lawson replied, trying to pull his arm off of her to no avail.

"Crap," Cain whispered as he saw what was going down.

Cain set the rifle on the floor as he removed a handgun from his pants, readying himself for a visitor. He stayed low to keep himself covered from view on the first floor. He heard the sound of footsteps walking up the metal stairs. Cain put both hands on his gun as he took aim at the top of the steps, waiting for the outline of whoever was coming. As soon as the man stepped into his crosshairs, Cain fired his gun. Three booming shots rang out in quick succession, all landing in the chest and midsection of the oncoming man. He fell backwards and landed a couple of steps down from the top one. Everyone on the main floor flinched when they heard the shots.

"You do have someone here!" Cardullo angrily yelled.

"You thought I'd be dumb enough to trust you?" Lawson replied.

"I don't care what Proulx said, I'm killing you as soon as we take care of your friend up there."

"Where is he?"

"Shut up!"

Cain quickly went back to his rifle to see if he could line up a shot of Cardullo to free Lawson from his grasp. As soon as he looked through the scope, his vision started getting blurry. He closed his eyes for a moment and shook his head to try to shake it loose. He looked back through the scope and the image of Cardullo and Lawson became doubled. He sighed in anger and wiped his eyes, hoping his problems wouldn't cost Lawson her life. As he was wiping his eyes, he heard someone running toward him. One of Cardullo's men had snuck up the other side of the steps. As soon as Cain opened his eyes more fully he saw a blur of a fist raining down on his head. The blow knocked Cain completely over. The man pulled out his gun to shoot Cain as he lay there. Out of instinct, Cain rolled over as much as he could, though between the boxes and the wall he was only able to roll halfway. The bullet went into the floor as Cain kicked out the legs of the man standing over top of him. Both men stood up and exchanged punches. Both men were now visible to Cardullo.

While he was still holding Lawson with his left arm, Cardullo steadied his right hand as he took aim at Cain. He fired a round that went through one of the boxes near Cain. He fired another bullet that whizzed past Cain's head, lodging into the wall. Cain continued struggling with the other man for another minute as they continued exchanging face and body shots. If Cain were perfectly healthy, the man probably wouldn't have lasted more than a few seconds as Cain was a much better fighter. But in his confused state, Cain would've had problems with just about anybody. The punches hitting his head felt like cinder blocks smashing against his temple. After a few more minutes of struggling, Cain was finally able to get the upper hand on his opponent. Cain staggered him, knocking the man to his knees after kicking him in the stomach. Cain maneuvered himself behind him and grabbed him by the collar of his shirt. Cain spun around and tossed the man over the railing. It wasn't a huge drop, only about twenty feet or so, but the man landed on the back of his neck, breaking it and dying instantly. Cardullo fired another shot at Cain that once again missed as Cain took cover behind some boxes. Cardullo backed up with Lawson as he waited for his other guy to get Cain lined up. Cain knew there was still one more guy out there but he had no idea where he was.

Cain crawled over to his rifle and tried one more time to get a look at Cardullo. He felt his head to see if he was bleeding anywhere and where his stitches were to see if any had come out. Luckily and miraculously they were still in place. His vision was still a little blurry, and he was hesitant about taking a shot just in case he hit Lawson by mistake. He squinted his eyes, trying to concentrate and force himself into seeing normally. After a few more seconds his vision returned. Most of Cardullo's body was blocked by Lawson as he was using most of her for cover. His right shoulder was exposed and part of his head. Cain knew a better shot might not materialize and figured he had to work with what was presented to him. He steadied himself and pulled the trigger. A second later Cardullo screamed in pain as his right shoulder felt like it was almost torn from his body. Cardullo was knocked back slightly from the impact of the blast and he loosened his grip on Lawson's neck. It was just enough for Lawson to get away as she headed for the boxes Cain told her to go to. As Cardullo was holding his shoulder and trying to right himself, the lack of a human shield was perfect for Cain to finish off his target. Cardullo started to move for some cover but was stopped in his path by a bullet that entered into the middle of his chest. He dropped to his knees, the life slowly draining out of his body. Cain hurried up his demise by firing one more round into his chest, only a centimeter away from the other opening. The second shot knocked Cardullo flat onto his back for his final resting spot.

Cain, careful as to not expose his head too much for fear of getting it shot off his shoulders, looked through the scope of his rifle to spot the location of the last man. After coming up empty, he lowered the rifle to his side and peered over the side of the railing. He saw no movements, and he didn't hear any sounds.

He didn't want to call out to Lawson and expose her position to the guy in case he didn't know where she was. Cain knew he couldn't stay in his position and wait the guy out. If he were by himself, he might've been able to. But with Lawson there he didn't think he had the luxury. As long as Lawson and the other guy were on the first floor, there was a danger that he'd find her before Cain found him. He took the strap of the rifle and put it over his shoulder, letting the rifle fall to his back. He took out his handgun and started moving down the steps. Cain noticed when the men came in that none of them had rifles so at least he knew he wasn't going to get picked off on the way down. Cain made sure he didn't make a peep as he made his way down the steps.

Once he got to the main floor, he squatted to make himself as little a target as possible as he looked around for a spot. He looked to his left and saw the faintest trace of Lawson's hair sticking out from the corner of the boxes that he told her to hide behind. He thought about crawling over there but it was too much of an open space to be sure he'd get there in one piece. Cain quickly stood up and sprinted over to the boxes, diving over them and twisting his body to make sure his shoulder and back absorbed the blow of the concrete floor. Lawson was startled by the sight of someone diving over her and had her gun ready to fire but she recognized Cain immediately and lowered her weapon.

"Hey," Cain said as he got up and scooted over to her.

"You all right?"

"Yeah. I'm good. You?"

"I'm fine."

"Any idea where the other guy is?" he asked, still a little out of breath.

"I don't know."

"Well, we're gonna have to draw him out somehow," Cain said, his breathing returning to normal.

"How about a diversion?" Lawson asked. "I can maybe run for the door or something and try to draw his fire. Then you can see where he's at and take him out."

"No way. I'm not putting you at risk."

"Well, we can't stay here all night."

"I know," Cain said as he considered the options.

"You all right? Your head looks a little bruised," Lawson said, noticing a few welts on him.

"I'm fine."

Cain peeked around the side and over the top of the boxes to try to find the last guy but couldn't pick him up at all.

"He didn't slip out the door or something when the other stuff was going on did he?" Cain asked.

"Not unless there's a side door or something. Nobody went out this way."

"There's not."

"What do you wanna do?" she asked.

As soon as she asked the question the other man rose from his position and sprinted for the door. He was firing his gun as he was running to try to give himself some cover. He figured if they were too busy ducking they wouldn't be able to return fire, giving him just enough time to reach the door and get outside. Cain pushed Lawson to the ground as he dove to his right, giving himself a line of sight to the door. As soon as he saw the man's outline enter his sight, Cain furiously pulled the trigger of his gun, unloading six shots in rapid succession. Four of the bullets found their target as the man fell short just inches from the door. Two shots hit him in the chest, one in the stomach, and one in the leg. The shots took him off his feet as he fell, settling against the base of the door. Cain got up and went over to Lawson to help her to her feet. He then checked on each of the victims to make sure they were all dead. Lawson scurried over to Cardullo and started searching through his pockets.

"What are you doing?" Cain asked.

"Looking for anything significant," she answered, pulling out a few pieces of paper. "He mentioned Proulx' name, so he has to work for him."

As Cain watched her, he got a chill and started shaking. His eyes started getting glossy, and the dizziness returned.

"Hope you're finding something good," Cain said just before he passed out and dropped to the floor.

49

Lawson had just walked into the room as Cain was finishing putting his shirt on. They sat down next to each other as they waited for the doctor to come in and explain the results of the MRI and CT scan that he just had. They didn't have to wait long as the doctor came in within five minutes, holding his results.

"I'm Doctor Joyce," he said.

"You're American?" Cain asked.

"Yes." He smiled. "Americans do live and work in France, you know."

Cain let out a laugh and shook his head. "Sorry. Didn't mean any offense to that. Silly question."

Joyce waved his hand at him as he took a seat. "Ahh. No apologies necessary. I'd probably wonder the same thing if I were you. Anyway, I have your results. Your girlfriend told me you recently had brain surgery, correct?"

Cain slowly turned his head in Lawson's direction, who shot a smile back as she tried to maintain their covers.

"Yes. Yes, I did," Cain told the doctor.

"She said you got your current injuries trying to prevent her from getting robbed by three men. Very noble of you with your condition."

"I'm still a little hazy on that part. I don't really remember much of that... at all," he said as he looked at Lawson again.

"Well, it's to be expected."

"So, I'm good? No problems?"

"Well, I didn't say that," Joyce replied. "The results of your tests indicate that you have a very small blood clot in your head."

"Oh no," Lawson said.

"Do I need surgery again?" Cain asked.

Joyce put his hands out to each of them to prevent them from getting too worked up. "Let's just calm down. It's a very small blood clot. At this time I don't believe surgery will be necessary."

"How do I get rid of it?"

"Well, before we get to that let me explain the different ways to go about getting rid of a blood clot because they're treated differently depending on the size and location of the clot and the patient's health. I'll try to give the least amount of doctor speak as possible for you."

"I'd appreciate that."

"There are anticoagulants, which is medicine that helps prevent blood clots from forming. There is thrombolytics, which is medicine that dissolves the clot. There is also a procedure in which we could surgically insert a catheter and direct it to the clot where it would deliver clot dissolving medication. Then there is just surgery itself to remove it."

"And where do you stand?" Cain asked.

"Typically, surgery to remove it, or inserting a catheter, are more for clots that are considered life threatening and need to be aggressively treated," the doctor said.

"Mine isn't?"

"No. Yours is pretty small. I think treating it with medication should do the trick."

Cain nodded in approval. "I'm on board for that."

"You must exhibit extreme care for the next several weeks as far as taking care of your head. I know in this instance it perhaps was unavoidable, but if you sustain more serious blows. It could become a much more serious situation."

"I'll do the best I can."

"Let me get the medication sorted out for you and I'll be back in a few minutes."

"No problem. I'll just sit here with my girlfriend till you get back," he said sarcastically, looking at Lawson.

"Well, I had to come up with some kind of story," she told him. "I couldn't exactly just say you're a secret agent who got into a shootout with some bad guys in a warehouse, could I?"

"I suppose not. What exactly happened anyway?"

"You don't remember anything?" Lawson asked.

"Umm... I remember standing there watching you and that's about it."

"Well, you dropped to the floor. I dragged you out of the warehouse and got you into the car and took you to the nearest hospital I found."

"I guess I should say thanks for taking care of me again," Cain said.

"You can take me out to dinner when we get back to the States for repayment," she kidded.

They waited another ten minutes for Dr. Joyce to return with the medication he was prescribing for Cain. While they were waiting, Lawson got a call from Director Conlin about the information she had gotten from Cardullo before Cain passed out. While she was tending to Cain, Conlin had other analysts run down the information she'd given them. Once Dr. Joyce came back, Lawson exited the room to continue her conversation and get the rundown from Conlin. Cain remained seated as the doctor began speaking to him.

"I would say that when you get back to the States, get your head checked again just to make sure the clot hasn't gotten bigger," Dr. Joyce told him.

"I will. Could it be gone by then?"

"Sure. No way to say for sure, but it's possible."

The doctor gave Cain his prescription for some pills and as soon as he left Lawson came back into the room.

"What was all that?" Cain asked.

"Conlin. I had them checking on some things while we were here."

"Like what?"

"Cardullo had a key for the warehouse. He also mentioned Proulx by name. There has to be a connection there. Turns out the warehouse is owned by a subsidiary of a subsidiary of a subsidiary and so on and so on which finally links to a Global Industries," Lawson explained.

"Which means what exactly?"

"Now we find a link between Global Industries and Proulx."

"You know, I was thinking, Proulx probably isn't in one specific spot," Cain said.

"Why do you say that?"

"Seems like a safe bet. Can't get a fixed location on his girl-friend. Raines couldn't seem to find either of them. They must be moving around a lot."

"I don't know. That seems pretty risky don't you think? Moving around a lot in a country like this. Seems like some-one's bound to spot you at some point."

"You'd have to have a very secure travel system in place."

"You mean like maybe he's living on a bus?" Lawson asked.

"Yeah. Something like that. Bus, train, something where he's somewhat sheltered and doesn't have to be seen in public much."

"I'll get them looking into it."

As Lawson called Director Conlin to get them checking on any links to a bus or train, Lawson and Cain left the hospital. Once they got in the car, Lawson turned to Cain for direction.

"So, where to now?" she asked.

"Let's see what we can dig up on Global Industries," Cain replied. He then put his hand on Lawson's arm to stop her from starting the car. "Wait, you didn't tell Heather I was here, did you?"

"Of course not. Why?"

"Just checking. I don't want to worry her unnecessarily."

"You don't think she needs or has a right to know?"

"I'll tell her when we get back," he said.

"Why not now?"

"Because I'm sure she's already a nervous wreck. Telling her I passed out, was just in a hospital, and have a clot in my head, without me being there in person is probably not the wisest move."

"Yeah. You're probably right."

"I'll tell her when we get back. That way I'll be there and she can see everything turned out fine. Telling her now will just make her worry."

"As if she isn't already."

"Well... worry more."

Lawson started the car, and they drove to a hotel, checking into a room. They got their computer equipment started and immediately went to work on finding out anything they could on Global Industries. Director Conlin had his analysts checking the dozen subsidiaries while Lawson and Cain checked Global. They sat next to each other at a desk, each working on separate laptops. Lawson was able to hack into records and financial information for Global Industries as the two tried to find the smallest detail they could turn into a lead.

"What was that girlfriend's name again?" Cain asked.

"Maxime. Why? You got something?"

"I'm not sure," he replied, typing away on the keyboard.

Cain continued plugging away at the keyboard for another minute before he stopped, something gaining his attention.

"Hey. Look at this," Cain said. He pointed to the entry that was intriguing. "Last year Global hired someone named Maxime Bisset."

"Hmm. Doesn't say what for."

"Doesn't list an address either."

"That's gotta be her though," Lawson said.

"It'd make sense. Either that's how they met or he's using the company to give his girlfriend work."

"Let me see what I can find on her. You keep digging on Global," Lawson said.

After a few more minutes, Lawson was able to find a web

page that had Bisset's information on it such as an email and the type of work she did.

"I guess I could email and see if she responds," Lawson said, hoping that would work.

"Wait, look at the date on the bottom. What's it say?"

"Two years ago."

"That's what I figured. Hasn't been updated in two years. If she's with Proulx, no way he's letting her advertise her trade. The email will probably bounce back to you," Cain said.

"Well, let me try anyway. It's worth a shot in the dark, I guess."

Lawson typed a short email to Bisset explaining that she was interested in hiring her for some work that she was doing. She hit the send button on the message and a few seconds later got a return message saying the email was undeliverable due to a wrong email address. Lawson sighed, thinking they hit a dead end with her.

"Thought we might've had something," she lamented.

"Still might. Have examples of her photographs on there?"

"Yeah. Mostly nature type pictures. Landscapes and such."

"If there's one thing I know about photographers, it's that they rarely just stop. They love what they do and they love taking pictures. Even if she's not doing it professionally anymore, she's most likely still taking pictures."

"And given the types of pictures she seems to like to take, where could she still do that?"

"Let's see if we can tie her into any bus or train passes or tickets," Cain said. "You take buses and I'll take trains."

They each looked up every bus and train that operated in France. It took them over an hour as they tried to track down any tickets sold to Bisset, but each of them came up empty in their searches.

"Well, that was a no-go. How about we just try Global now? Maybe it's company linked," Lawson said.

"OK. I got trains again."

It didn't take quite as long this time since they both already had their respective databases pulled up and they already knew what they were looking for. After half an hour, Cain's face lit up like a small child who just received a new bike for Christmas. He stopped typing and lowered his hands to his lap as he just looked at the information on the screen. Lawson was still typing but noticed that Cain had stopped and looked at him, wondering what he was looking at. By his face she could tell that he had something.

"What is it?" she asked.

"Six train tickets sold to Global Industries three months ago," Cain answered.

"What names are listed?"

"Just lists one name. Probably a guy in the company who bought them and distributed them to Proulx."

"So, it'd be Proulx, Bisset, and four more?" Lawson asked.

"If I had to guess I'd say it was four bodyguards."

"What train?"

"Railway France. Looks like the train goes through several countries," Cain said, bringing up information on the train on the computer.

"How can they just keep someone stashed there for months?"

"Probably have their own car. Kinda like how companies pay for office space. They're paying for train space."

"That'd make sense with Bisset and her photography. What

photographer wouldn't love snapping pictures of the country-side on a cross-country trip of Europe? How are we gonna get aboard?"

"Well, it's not gonna run forever. It's gotta stop sometime."

"I know but don't you think they'll be on the lookout? I mean, I'm pretty sure Proulx knows your face."

"Maybe."

"Plus, I'm sure they know what happened to Cardullo by now. They must know we're closing in. They might not even be on the train anymore."

"They're on the train."

"What if they're connected to the ticket database somehow and can screen everyone who comes on?" Lawson asked.

"I really wouldn't be surprised if that was pretty accurate. I'm sure they do somehow."

"So, how are we getting on?"

"It'd have to be by surprise," Cain said.

"Well, how's that gonna work? Only way you're getting on a train by surprise is if you drop in out of the sky," she said with a laugh.

Cain looked at her with a grin on his face and simply nodded like he agreed with what she was saying. Lawson scrunched her face together trying to understand what his head shake meant.

"Wait a minute. Tell me you're not actually implying that you can just fall out of the sky onto a moving train."

"Well, you just said it yourself," Cain said. "The only way we're getting on a train by surprise is if we fall from the sky."

"I was obviously joking."

"It makes sense though."

Lawson put her hands on each side of her head as she tried

to comprehend what he was saying. "Matt, I don't know if you're aware of this, but this isn't the movies. You're not Tom Cruise, this isn't *Mission Impossible*, jumping onto a moving train isn't what I'd call a sound strategy."

"It'll work though," he calmly replied.

"Oh my God. I need a drink. Something heavy."

"Relax."

"Relax? You're seriously telling me to relax? You're telling me we should jump onto a moving train. Matt, I haven't jumped onto a moving anything since I was ten years old. And that was a skateboard that was moving two miles an hour. I fell off and cut my elbow. Ever since then I swore I'd never jump onto anything that's moving ever again. Maybe I'd try a skateboard again but not something traveling over two hundred times faster than that was. Maybe jumping onto a train is your idea of a good time but it's certainly not mine," Lawson sputtered.

"Shelly, calm down. I'm not asking you to jump on the train. I'll do it."

"How can you be so calm about it like falling off doesn't even enter your mind?"

"Because it doesn't," Cain responded.

"Are we sure you're human and not a robot or something?"

"Well, I can't guarantee that," he kidded.

"You're unbelievable. I am not gonna be the one to tell Heather that you died because you did something horrifically stupid like trying to jump onto a moving train and oops... he missed."

"Shelly, get a hold of yourself. Look," Cain said, pointing to the screen.

"What's that?"

"That's the Rhine Bridge at Kehl. It connects France and

Germany. The train will be re-entering France using that bridge tomorrow morning."

"And?"

"There's steel beams over top of it. I can sit on top of it and drop down when the train comes through."

"Oh. Well, as long as it's easy," she replied with an eye roll.

"The speed limit on the bridge for trains coming through is a hundred miles an hour. It'll probably be even a little less than that."

"And if you miss?"

"If I miss, which I won't, it's a thirty or forty foot drop into the water. I can withstand that easily. People have been known to withstand drops into water up to a hundred feet," he said, trying to lessen her worries.

"And what if you hit one of those steel beams on the way down?"

"Uhh..."

"Exactly."

Cain continued researching both the train and the bridge. Lawson, though, couldn't stop thinking about what could go wrong.

"And what if you are able to jump onto the train? What if you jump on the train and hit your head and knock yourself out? Or you cause that clot to burst or cause massive bleeding or something. You're as good as dead if that happens," she warned.

"Well, I wasn't planning on jumping head first."

"I have to run this by Conlin."

"You can run it by whoever you want, but it's not gonna change what I have to do."

Lawson immediately called Conlin and informed him of

what they found with Global Industries, Bisset, and the train tickets bought by Global. Conlin had no reservations and agreed with Cain that it was the best way to catch them by surprise. He fully supported whatever action Cain recommended. Cain was his best agent. If he thought it was the best course of action, Conlin was not going to stand in his way. Lawson briefly fought it, throwing out a few arguments against it, but knew she didn't stand a chance of changing anybody's mind. She knew Conlin would side with Cain's viewpoint but just wanted it on record that she opposed it and it helped her to vent while arguing against it. As soon as she hung up, Cain had another plan for her to consider.

"What about if we do it like the old west?"

"What?" a bewildered Lawson asked.

"You know. I could ride alongside the train on horseback and leap from the horse onto the train," he said sarcastically.

"Don't mock me."

"I mean, I could always hold up the train while I'm on it. Rob everyone of their valuables. Maybe after that we could find a stagecoach and steal some mailbags or cattle ranch payrolls."

"Are you through yet?" Lawson asked, not amused at his sense of humor.

"Uh... yeah, I think so."

"Why can't we just board the train like normal people again?"

"Because you said they were probably monitoring who comes on the train," Cain answered.

"What do I know?"

"And you were right. They know we're closing in and they probably have people monitoring who boards. So, we have to find another way on."

"I really hate this job sometimes."

Cain started making plans to attempt his train jumping, though he didn't get much assistance from Lawson. She was still trying to think of some alternate scenarios that would be a little safer and still be effective.

"Are you gonna help with this?" Cain asked.

"I'm thinking."

"Is that gonna take all night?"

"I've got it," she said enthusiastically.

"What?"

"What if we were able to make the train stop, and we swooped in from a helicopter?"

"And you don't think they'll notice a helicopter landing next to it?"

"Well, don't you think the engineer is going to notice a guy standing on top of a beam as he goes through it?"

"I'm not really concerned about the engineer," Cain said. "Won't have time to stop by that time. And I wouldn't be standing. I was planning on lying down."

"Whatever. Well, if the train stopped while on the bridge, we could get the helicopter to drop you onto it from just a few feet."

"As soon as they see that helicopter come close they'll know I'm coming," Cain warned. "And how are you gonna get the train to stop?"

"I don't know. Put a car on the tracks or something."

"And what if the train doesn't see it and crashes into it? A lot of innocent people could get hurt or killed."

Lawson sighed, knowing her pleas were falling on deaf ears. "I could call it in that there's something on the tracks."

"Then who knows where they'll stop."

"How are you going to get in? A lot of trains don't have windows that open, you know," Lawson noted.

Cain looked up pictures of the train that Proulx was on. Getting in would seem to be problematic until he noticed that the last car of the train had a ladder to the roof of the train. He pointed it out to Lawson who just rolled her eyes.

"Seems like you've got an answer for everything," Lawson said.

"No, I don't. Just seems that way," Cain said, turning to her and smiling.

"So, what comes next?"

"Time to hop a train."

50

Conlin had arranged for the use of a personal helicopter, flown by a pilot that had been used by them before in a few situations. The pilot wasn't the law-abiding type but was an excellent flyer and could be counted on to keep his mouth shut. For an extremely high price, of course. Specter was willing to pay him good sums of money for one or two jobs a month. All he had to do was fly the chopper and be quiet. And with the money they were paying him, it was good enough for him. Lawson was in the passenger seat in the helicopter as Cain was in the back getting ready.

"Tell me again why you feel the need to have these death wishes?" Lawson asked. "Why couldn't you just climb up?"

"One, I've never climbed a steel bridge before," Cain replied.

"Is there another reason?"

"Yeah. I left all my bridge climbing equipment at home," he sarcastically added.

"Funny."

"Seriously. We don't just carry bridge climbing equipment in our duffel bags, you know. Can't really pick that stuff up in a moment's notice."

"But we can find a chopper and a pilot on a moment's notice," she stated, looking at the pilot. "Where'd they find you, anyway?"

"Doesn't really matter, does it?" the pilot asked. "Long as I can fly this thing."

"You got a name?"

"Not really important, is it?"

"Wow. You can tell this guy's worked for us before," Lawson noted.

The pilot chuckled as they were approaching the bridge. He quickly looked back at Cain as they got closer.

"If you get on the landing skids, I'll get you right next to that sucker," the pilot told him.

"Get on the what?" Cain responded.

"The things under the chopper that you stand on."

"Oh. Right."

"I can hover right next to that thing. It'll be just like rolling out of bed."

"I can't look," Lawson chimed in.

Cain carefully maneuvered his way onto the landing skids so he had both feet firmly planted onto them.

"You got your earpiece in, right?" Lawson asked.

Cain felt his ear to make sure it was in securely. "It's in."

"I'll see you down the line I guess."

"You know it," Cain said, taking off his chopper headset.

The pilot looked back at Cain and gave him a thumbs up as he hovered the chopper's landing skids right against the steel bridge. He got the chopper so close to the bridge they were almost touching each other. Cain stepped off the skids and onto a steel beam, quickly maintaining control of his balance. He lay flat on the beam and untangled the rope that he had across his midsection and wrapped it around the beam to connect himself to it. He figured an extra security step to ensure he didn't fall off was warranted. Once Lawson and the pilot saw he had secured himself to the beam, they slowly pulled away.

"Remember, the train should be by in about an hour. Don't let a strong wind gust knock you off or something," Lawson told him.

"Thought that was what the rope was for?" Cain replied.

"I can see why they chose you for this," Lawson told the pilot.

"You should see me on the tough assignments," he said with a laugh.

The helicopter flew further up the line to make sure the train was still running on time. They flew off in the distance so they could keep it in sight without getting so close that anybody on the train would think they were stalking it. They followed along with it for about half an hour.

"There she is," the pilot said. "Right on schedule."

"Train's not gonna get away from us, is it?" Lawson asked.

"Not a chance, sister. Average speed for this chopper is about 145. I can push it even further if need be. Don't worry about it though. We'll be fine."

"Matt. Train should be there in a few minutes," Lawson told him.

"No worries," Cain responded.

"Maybe for you."

As the train approached the bridge, it slowed its speed to about seventy-five miles per hour. Cain was still lying flat on the beam and could tell the train had decreased its speed.

"He should be able to make that at that speed," the pilot noted.

It was a twelve-car train. Just before the train hit the bridge, Cain removed a knife from his pocket and cut the rope binding him to the beam. He quickly put it back in his pocket so there was no chance of cutting himself as he jumped and landed. As soon as the first car hit the bridge, he got to his knees, steadying himself on the beam with his hands. When the middle of the train passed beneath him he jumped onto it, his feet touching the top of the train first, but the force of the jump and the speed of the train caused him to lose balance, knocking him to his hands and knees.

"There you go," the helicopter pilot said. "He made it."

Lawson breathed a sigh of relief knowing that part of the assignment was over. Saying it was the hardest part wouldn't have been quite right as he still had four bodyguards, a girl-friend, and Proulx to take care of.

Cain was able to balance his weight and got to his feet, standing right in the middle of the train. He started walking towards the back when he noticed a pair of hands on the ladder on the last car.

The helicopter pilot peeled the chopper back to let the train get ahead of it and noticed the man coming.

"Matt. You're about to have company," Lawson said.

"How many?" Cain asked.

"Just one."

Just as the words left Lawson's lips, the man's head poked up from behind the cover of the train. Cain kept walking in his direction, getting one car closer to him. As the other man got on top of the train, he stood on the last car and removed a gun from his jacket. He pointed it at Cain and fired a shot. Cain ducked as the man fired though it would've missed him, anyway. Cain planted himself face first on the train and removed his gun. The man started making his way toward Cain. Cain put the gun in front of him and steadied it with both of his hands on the weapon. He fired a round that missed. He tried to steady the gun a little more to improve his aim. His next shot also missed the target. The man kept walking toward him and was only three cars away by that point. Cain closed his left eye as he concentrated on hitting the mark. As soon as the man stepped onto the next car Cain fired his gun. This time the bullet hit its intended target, ripping through the man's left leg and into his shin. The bullet went through his leg, shattering bones with pieces of flesh and blood flying off his body. As the man lay there in excruciating pain and holding his leg, he became an even better target to hit since he wasn't moving as much. Cain fired another round, hitting him in the left shoulder. The man screamed in anguish as he relinquished the gun from his hand, sending it flying into the wind and off the train. Cain regained his feet and hopped the next couple of cars until he reached the injured man. He was still breathing though he was in an incredible amount of pain. Cain put his hand on the man's back to check on him. The man hit Cain in the leg with his right hand though it didn't do much damage.

"Ever wonder what it was like to be Superman?" Cain angrily told him.

Cain punched him in the face, temporarily stunning the

man, before he got down to his knees. He put both his hands on the man's arm. He was about to push him off the train but was concerned that if someone saw him fall off the train that the train would be stopped. The easiest and probably best thing for Cain to do would be to just kill him there and leave him lying there until they got to the end of the line. Cain stood over the fallen man and removed the knife from his pocket again. The man saw what Cain was doing and yelled and pleaded for him not to do it, though he wasn't in much of a position to defend himself.

"No! Please!" the man screamed.

His pleas fell on deaf ears as Cain calmly drove the knife into the man's chest. The man picked his head up briefly before the life was quickly taken out of him. His arms fell limp as he perished from the blow. Cain removed the knife from the man's chest and wiped the blood off on the sleeve of the man's arm. He shook his head, not really pleased that he had to take the man's life. He knew it was necessary and had to be done but he didn't take any pleasure from it. He continued walking along the roof of the train until he reached the last car.

"I can see why they picked him. Your man's good," the pilot said as they watched the events unfold.

"No, he's not," Lawson responded. "He's the best."

Cain climbed down the ladder, not sure who or what he'd run into. He was ready for anything though. He entered the train but was slightly surprised that no one was there to greet him.

"How's it going down there?" Lawson asked.

"OK so far," Cain answered.

Cain started walking through the train but was quickly

halted as he peeked into the next car in front of him and saw two beefy looking men guarding a door. There was no doubt about who they were or what they were doing. He put a sound suppression device on his gun assuming he would have to use it.

"Found Proulx' room," Cain said. "Two guys standing outside his door."

"What's your plan?" Lawson asked.

"I don't know. What makes you think I got a plan? I'm open to suggestions."

"Can't you just shoot them from where you are?"

"Soon as they hit the ground whoever's inside knows I'm here. I figure my best chance is to surprise all of them at the same time."

"Why don't you walk up to them casually and ask them for a light or a cigarette?" the pilot chimed in.

"Might work," Cain replied.

"Do you even know how to walk up to someone casually?" Lawson remarked. "Have you ever done that before?"

"Not my usual style or preferred choice, is it?"

Cain intently watched for a few more minutes to get a better read on the situation. He finally noticed the door open, and a woman walked out. It looked like Bisset though her hair was a little longer than the pictures they'd seen of her. Cain thought he might be able to use her to get inside. He wasn't sure how he was going to accomplish it though. He'd still have to go past the guards somehow. He was beginning to think he'd just have to take his chances and go right up to them. Hopefully, they wouldn't shoot first and ask questions later. A few minutes went by until Bisset returned. It looked like she brought back a couple bottles of alcohol. Cain noticed that the guards seemed to be a little restless, kind of bouncing back and forth in their stances. The one guard tapped the other one on the arm and said something, motioning with his thumb like he was going to leave. A second later the one guard left and Cain knew he had to seize the moment. There was no telling how long the guard would be gone, maybe only seconds.

Cain tucked his gun into the back of his pants and started walking towards the remaining guard. Cain walked slowly and put his head down and his arms by his side, not wanting to give off an aggressive posture. As soon as the guard saw him, he tried to wave him on.

"Keep walking, buddy. Can't be back here," the guard told him.

Cain lifted his head up and pretended he didn't hear the guy. "Oh. What's that you said?" he asked.

"C'mon, can't be back here," the guard repeated, grabbing Cain's arm and pushing him forward.

Cain stopped and turned back toward the guard. "Oh... um... you got a light or a cigarette or something?"

"Nah, man. Don't smoke. Beat it."

"Oh. OK. Sorry to bother you," Cain said as he kept walking closer.

Cain wriggled his nose like he was about to sneeze. He went through all the gyrations of a huge sneeze coming on. He put his head down and his arm out as if he was about to hold on to the guard for assistance in keeping his balance. Just as he was about to let a fake sneeze out, he reached his right hand behind him and removed his gun and bumped up against the guard, pressing his gun against the man's midsection and firing into his stomach three times. The guard never even saw it coming and was caught by complete surprise as he slid down to the ground, dying in an upright position. Cain snapped his head to his left as he heard a noise that sounded like it was close. The other guard had returned with a stool for each of them to sit on. He was holding a stool in each hand as he saw his partner sitting there on the ground, blood pouring out of his shirt. He looked at Cain and dropped the stools to draw his gun but it was no use. Cain already had his weapon out and fired two more times, hitting the guard in the chest and killing him before the stools had even hit the ground. The guard didn't even have time to remove his gun from the holster.

Cain wasn't sure how much commotion was being made, or how much they heard, or if they assumed what might be going on outside the door. He knew he had to work quickly and not give them any more time to be ready for him if they already were. He quickly reloaded his gun and took a step back. He then launched his leg up and gave a good healthy kick against the door, busting it wide open. As soon as he stood in the doorway he ducked, just as a shot came whizzing past his head, splintering the door. Cain quickly found what he hoped was the last guard and fired two shots, both entering the front of the man's head. The first shot went through his forehead and burst out the back of his head, the second shot completely shattering and dismantling his nose, lodging somewhere in the middle of his skull.

Bisset was nearby and rushed over to Cain and tried to attack him with a knife that he easily knocked away. Cain saw Proulx rush over to a desk drawer that he could only assume had a gun tucked in it. Cain put his arm around Bisset and held her in front of him, using her as cover. He wasn't sure how much resistance she'd provide but it was better than nothing. Proulx pulled out a gun and pointed it at Cain, who had effectively shielded himself with Bisset's body. Only the corner of his head and right eye was visible. Cain assumed, and hoped, that Proulx wasn't a good enough shot to make it count. Cain wasn't even sure he'd be able to make the shot if he were in the other position.

"How'd you get on board?" Proulx asked. "I was expecting someone at some point. We had all the entrances watched."

"Oh, I just hopped on," Cain remarked.

"I had a feeling you were gonna show up soon. How's your memory these days?"

"Never better."

"I don't suppose there's a way we can work this out?"

"Nope."

"Not even if I told you where the others were?"

"We already know Collins is in Germany," Cain said.

"What about Sanders?"

"We'll find him."

"I can tell you where both of them are precisely. You could have them both captured in less than half an hour," Proulx said.

"And what would you want for your good deed?"

"My freedom. Tell them you killed me and I'll disappear from public forever."

"What makes you think I would do that?"

"I don't know. I guess I'm hoping the others are more important than me. Sanders is the one who put everything together."

"I don't need you for that," Cain said. "I'll find them on my own."

"I guess it was foolish of me to think you could be persuaded," Proulx said, suddenly firing his gun.

Proulx wasn't even trying to hit Cain. He was aiming directly at Bisset. He was hoping that the bullets would travel through her and hit Cain too or that she'd just drop out of the way and give him a clear line of sight. The bullet hit Bisset in her side. She suddenly bent over and Cain lost his grip on her as she dropped to the floor in pain. As soon as she fell from his arms, Cain returned fire, the first shot missing Proulx. Cain quickly fired again before Proulx had a chance to and hit him in the shoulder causing Proulx' gun to fly out of his hand. Cain quickly looked down at Bisset and saw her eyes were still open and she was moving a little. He turned his attention back to Proulx and walked over to him.

"Where's Raines?" Cain asked his injured counterpart.

"Dead."

"Where's his body?"

"I dunno. In a river. In a ditch. Burning along the side of a road for all I know," Proulx said.

Two shots suddenly rang out from behind Cain as he jumped and turned around. Bisset was sitting against the wall and breathing heavily as smoke rose in the air from the gun she just fired. Cain noticed the gun was pointing at Proulx and he turned his head to look at him. Proulx was now dead, thanks to two fresh bullet holes that appeared in his chest. Bisset began crying and looked at Cain, slowly raising the gun in his direction. Cain knew he could kill her if he wanted to before she ever got a shot off.

"Put the gun down," Cain calmly told her.

Bisset shook her head. "No. You'll kill me if I do that. I don't wanna die."

"If I wanted to kill you you'd be dead already."

"I can't believe that bastard shot me," she said, still holding her side. "I thought he really cared about me."

"Not likely. He was just using you for his own personal gain. You're gonna need to get that looked at," Cain said, looking and nodding at her wound.

"How do I know you won't kill me?"

"Because I didn't come here for you."

"What about the rest of them?" she asked, nodding at the others.

"I came here for one man. He was my target," he replied. "The others were a necessity based on the situation. And they would've killed me first. Besides, how could I kill someone who takes as good pictures as you do?"

"You know about me? What I do?"

"Yes," Cain said, moving closer to her. "Just give me the gun and I can help you."

Bisset, though still holding the gun in front of her, had lowered it slightly so it wasn't pointed directly at Cain's chest. He knew she had no intention of pulling the trigger and knelt down beside her, gently taking the gun out of her hand. He tossed it across the room and moved her hand from her side so he could take a look at her wound.

"Doesn't look too bad," he told her.

"Easy for you to say."

Cain smiled. "Take it from me. I've been shot in the head before. This is nothing."

"Really? I guess I'm pretty weak then because it feels like I'm dying."

"You'll be fine. Doesn't look life threatening."

"He's not dead you know," Bisset said.

Cain turned and looked at Proulx, though he wasn't who

she was referring to. "Not him. Your friend. The one you were asking about."

"Eric Raines? He's still alive? You're sure?"

"Yes. They're holding him at some house or apartment I think. I'm not sure where."

"How do you know?" Cain asked.

"Proulx called them earlier today to check on them. I can't believe I let him use me," she lamented.

"You wouldn't be the first girl to get fooled by a smooth talker."

"I'm gonna get blamed for all this, aren't I?" she said, looking around at the carnage. "It's always the one who's left that gets blamed for everything."

"I doubt anyone would believe you could do all this," Cain told her. "Just tell them what happened and you'll be fine."

"Tell them the truth?"

"Yes. A long-haired man with a beard, who's in his late forties, broke in and started blasting away. You heard someone mention the name of Stern," Cain said and smiled.

"The truth, huh?"

"Yeah. That is the truth, isn't it?"

"Yeah. I suppose it is."

"I'll keep an eye on you the next few days to make sure you're OK."

"You would do that for me?" Bisset asked, surprised that he'd take an interest in her.

"Yeah. I've got to make sure you tell the truth, don't I?"

Bisset smiled and tried to laugh but coughed instead.

"So, what would you do if I didn't tell the truth?" she asked.

"Why would you wanna tell a lie?"

"Just curious."

"Someone like me would be sent to pay you a visit," Cain said.

"I thought so. Don't worry. I'll tell the truth."

"I know you will... and I never worry."

Cain tore a piece of fabric off of one of the dead men's shirts and placed it on Bisset's wound. He found a tape dispenser on the desk and tore off a piece to keep it secure on the wound. Once he did that, he went back to Proulx' lifeless body and went through his pockets until he found his phone. Cain slipped it into one of his own pockets and went back to Bisset.

"I'm gonna have to go now," Cain said.

Bisset nodded and smiled at him. "Thank you."

"No thanks necessary. I'll see you around."

"Will you?"

"Never know."

Cain exited the cabin and quickly ran to the next car.

"Shelly! Need to get out of here fast," Cain yelled.

Lawson looked at the pilot to make sure he heard Cain's plea. He needed no spurring on and brought the chopper down in an instant.

"Comin' in hot," the pilot told everyone. "Drop the ladder down," he said to Lawson.

Cain hastily made his way through the train car until he reached the back. He rushed up the ladder and kneeled on top of the train until the chopper got close enough. He slowly stood up as he gained his balance. The pilot hovered the helicopter over top of the train as the ladder got into the position Cain needed. Cain grasped one of the rungs and jumped on it as the pilot veered off.

"You all right?" Lawson asked.

"Yep," Cain replied.

"Proulx dead?"

"Yep. I didn't kill him though."

"What? What happened?"

"I'll explain everything when we land."

"Everyone else taken care of?"

"All dead except one," Cain answered.

"Who's left?"

"Bisset."

"Why didn't you take care of her?"

"Wasn't necessary."

"What if she puts the finger on you?"

"She won't."

"Hope you know what you're doing," Lawson said.

"She'll be fine. She's the one who actually killed him."

"Oh. Guess that relationship went down in flames."

"Just keep tabs on her to see what happens to her," Cain said.

"Will do."

Cain turned his head to look back at the train, still perched on the ladder as they flew further away. After a few minutes of being in the air, Cain climbed the ladder and got in the helicopter, taking a seat in back.

"You get anything about Eric?" Lawson asked.

"Yeah. He's alive."

"What? Are you sure?"

"Well, no, I'm not sure. That's what Bisset told me, so I'm kind of taking her word for it."

"Think she was telling you the truth?"

"Yeah. I do," Cain answered. "She didn't have to tell me anything so I don't think she was leading me on. Plus, she was shot and pissed off at Proulx so I'm pretty sure she was being truthful."

"Shot? She gonna make it?" Lawson asked.

"Yeah. Nothing too serious. Day or two in the hospital and she should be as good as new."

Cain took the phone out of his pocket and nudged Lawson in the shoulder with it.

"What's this?" she turned around and asked.

"Proulx' phone. Bisset said he called whoever was holding Raines earlier today," Cain explained. "If we can trace all the calls, maybe we can figure out where he's being held."

"I'll start working on it as soon as we land."

They eventually landed on an airfield near the city of Reims. As the chopper was powering off, Cain and Lawson started unbuckling themselves.

"You're lucky my French is so good," the pilot said.

"Why's that?" Lawson asked.

"Pilots who don't speak French... man, that can be lethal," he replied. "A lot of these places don't speak a good second language."

"Good to know."

The three of them got out of the helicopter and started going their separate ways. Cain and Lawson stopped and turned around to look at the pilot walking away.

"Hey!" Lawson shouted. "Thanks for the ride."

"Anytime."

"Maybe we'll bump into you again someday."

"I could dig that." He smiled. "I'll fly with you two anytime. By the way, my name's Chris."

"Chris what?"

"Just Chris."

"If we could ever use you again, how would we find you?"

"Just look me up. I'm in the book," Chris replied. He then turned away to continue walking.

Cain and Lawson looked at each other. "What book? There's a book?" Lawson asked. "How come no one ever told me there's a book? Don't you think that's something I should know?"

"Yeah. It's probably big and black too," Cain sarcastically said. "Let's go."

51

With the help of the analysts back in New York, Lawson was able to trace the call Proulx made the previous day to an abandoned building just outside the city of Nancy. The building was a few minutes outside of town. It was close enough to the city in case they needed anything but in a remote enough area to provide enough privacy that nobody would notice a hostage being there. Cain and Lawson had driven to the area, parking on the edge of the city before walking the rest of the way. Cain had stolen the car during the night to avoid having to use a rental. In situations where they knew something bad was going to happen, such as a shooting, or any type of violence where the police were likely to come in afterwards, they tried to avoid using anything that would leave a trail leading to them. Even if they used false names and identifications, there was still a chance of an investigation leading toward them, even the slightest chance. But with the stolen car that they'd only need for a few hours, there was a high probability it'd never get linked to them. There were a few other buildings of various sizes surrounding the one Cain and Lawson were interested in, giving them enough cover to move without the fear of being spotted.

"What time you got?" Cain asked.

Lawson looked at her watch. "Ten."

"You're sure he'll be here?"

"Talked to him an hour ago. Said he'd touch down ten minutes after," Lawson said.

"You're sure we can trust him to be on time? I mean, we've only flown with him one time."

"I guess we'll find out, huh?"

"That's not very reassuring."

"Only answer I got for you. He said he'd be here."

"If we go in there guns blazing and come back out and he's not here, we could be in a world of trouble," Cain said.

"I know. He'll be here."

Lawson had contacted Director Conlin with their plan of attack and wanted to use Chris again as their method of escape. They figured if they had to leave in a hurry, it was their best chance of success with not knowing how many men they were going up against. Before proceeding, Cain turned to Lawson to go over the final plan.

"We all leave together," he said. "Or none of us do."

Lawson nodded. "Agreed."

"You stay behind me until we find Eric. Then you get him and I'll provide cover for you."

"Got it," she replied, looking at her watch again. "Two minutes after. We need to get moving."

"Roger that."

Cain checked the suppression device on his gun to make sure it was on tight and made his way to the empty-looking building with Lawson right on his tail. They clung to the outer wall of the building and followed it around to the back. Cain peeked around the corner and saw a man standing there reading a newspaper. He had a gun in a shoulder holster. Cain sprung around the corner and fired two times, hitting the man point blank, killing him before he knew Cain was even there. Cain quickly moved to the brown wooden door that was slightly ajar and peered inside. He could make out a few voices in the background though he couldn't quite hear what they were saying. He motioned to Lawson that he was going in and to stay on top of him. They were moving down a very narrow hallway that had a door on both sides of them plus one straight ahead. Cain motioned they were going left first. Cain turned the handle and pushed the door open, ready to come up firing, Lawson scurrying to his left to make sure she was out of the frame of the doorway. Cain had told her to avoid having her back to an open door in case anyone came up behind them so she wouldn't get shot in the back. He quickly scanned the room, but it was empty. They went to the door across from them. Cain slowly pushed it open, revealing two men playing cards on an old looking wood table that had a few holes in it. As soon as the men saw the intruders, they immediately rose up from the table but were instantly met with a couple of bullets from Cain's gun. He fired one shot at each of them initially to put them down. Cain checked on the status of both men. One was dead, but the other was still moving. Cain put the gun to the man's head and pulled the trigger. They couldn't afford to have any survivors.

Cain and Lawson walked out of the room and towards the last remaining door. Cain took a heavy sigh and looked at his partner. They both knew that it was likely that they were about to encounter a lot more resistance. Cain opened the door a sliver so he could see what they were about to run into. A voice grew louder, and it was apparent that someone was about to come their way. Cain and Lawson took a step back as the door swung open all the way. Surprised to find intruders, the man reached for his gun but was quickly gunned down by Cain. He fell completely inside the hallway allowing for Cain to close the door again.

"That's four so far," Lawson whispered. "How many do you think are here?"

Cain shrugged and opened his hand to reveal all five fingers. He closed his hand and put all five fingers up again. Lawson wasn't sure if that meant he figured ten total or ten more. Either way, it seemed a rather daunting task. Cain opened the door and rushed through it and turned to his left as it opened up into the kitchen. Three men were sitting there eating sandwiches. Cain scurried into the room firing his gun, hitting one man in the back, one in the side, and the other dead in the chest. The two men that were hit in the back and the chest immediately died. The one hit in the side fell to the floor but was still breathing. Cain told Lawson to watch the door to make sure they didn't get a surprise guest. Cain knelt down beside the fallen man to try to get a few answers.

"Listen, from the amount of blood you've lost, it looks like you'll live," Cain said. "As long as you tell me what I need to know, you'll stay that way. If you don't give me the answers I'm looking for, then I'll end your miserable existence right here, got it?"

The man nodded. "Yeah," he answered.

"How many men were stationed here including you?"

"Twelve."

"Five left. Where's Raines being held?"

"Basement."

"Where's that?"

"Over there," the man answered, nodding to a door off the kitchen.

"Anybody down there guarding him?" Cain asked.

"No."

"You sure?"

"Yes."

"I find anybody down there when I come back up I'm gonna shoot you on the way out," he threatened.

"No guards. That's what we were here for."

"Can he walk?"

"Yes."

"I assume he's tied up?"

"Handcuffed. Keys are on the hook by the door."

"That the only door in or out?" Cain asked.

"Yes."

Cain got up and went to the door and grabbed the keys that were hanging there. He went over to Lawson and handed them to her.

"You go get him and I'll stay here in case we have any company," Cain said. "If we both go down there and the rest of his friends stop by and realize we're down there then we're all dead."

"What if there's someone else there?" Lawson asked.

"Well, if you scream, then I'll know someone's there and I'll come running."

"You might hear a gunshot first."

Just as Lawson opened the basement door and started going

down the steps, Cain heard the sound of a helicopter coming closer. Lawson flipped on the light switch and raced down the steps. As soon as she got to the bottom, she immediately saw Raines sitting in the middle of the room. She glanced around the room just to make sure there was no one else there. There was a hood over Raines' face and his arms were cuffed behind his back to the chair. She removed the hood, startling him as he struggled with the light. His face had a few bruises on it along with a few cuts and some dried blood on his cheek.

"C'mon. Matt and I are here to get you out," Lawson said as she uncuffed him.

"Shelly?" he asked, looking behind him. "What are you doing here?"

"Saving you. What do you think?"

"I had everything under control. I was just about to get out."

Lawson laughed. "Yeah. I can see that."

"I was just breaking their defenses down."

"Come on. We have to hurry. Can you stand and walk?"

"Yeah," Raines replied, standing up and walking, though a little slowly.

Lawson put his arm around her neck and hers around his waist to help him move a little faster as they walked back up the steps. Cain had made his way towards the kitchen door, opening it to make sure that nobody entered the hallway they came in at. He'd have hated to have one of them get picked off in an area that they thought they'd already cleared. It took a minute for Lawson and Raines to emerge from the basement. Once Cain saw them, he rushed over to help Lawson.

"Give me a gun and I can help cover us," Raines said.

"You can barely walk," Cain replied. "You worry about getting out of here. I'll worry about covering us."

The three of them exited the kitchen and proceeded toward the hallway door. They were met halfway there by another of Raines' captors. Cain quickly released his grasp of Raines and shot the man two times. The man died without getting a shot off but screamed in the process.

"There goes the neighborhood," Cain said. "Get him out! Move!"

Lawson and Raines kept moving toward the door, Cain moving in unison with them but staying in front of them to prevent them from getting hit. Cain heard the sounds of men running in their direction.

"Company's coming," he said.

Lawson and Raines reached the door and were able to get into the hallway as Cain knelt down near it. The rest of the men had gotten there and Cain was now in a hail of gunfire, successfully holding the men off. He knew he had to wait it out another couple of minutes to give Raines and Lawson enough time to get to the chopper. Lawson and Raines finally made it out of the hallway and through the back door. Chris had the helicopter sitting there waiting for them. He got out and helped Lawson with Raines as the two of them put him in the back of the chopper.

"Matt, where you at?" Lawson asked.

"Busy," he replied, still engaged in a barrage of bullets.

"We just got in the chopper. Hurry up. Need me to come back?"

"No. Stay there. I'm coming."

Cain knew he had to make a move. He dove through the open door and quickly sprung to his feet. He closed the door and ran to the back door. Just as he got there he heard the other door open. Cain turned around and fired, hitting the first man that came through. Cain ran out and raced toward the helicopter. Lawson was tending to Raines in the back. Just as Cain was about to jump in, a man emerged from the back door, ready to fire upon him. Chris had his eyes glued to the door and reached under his seat, removing a gun. He fired a few times; the bullets whizzing past Cain. One of the bullets hit the man in the leg, temporarily stunning him, giving Chris enough time to get the helicopter in the air. A few bullets glanced off the chopper as Chris took it higher.

"Much obliged," Cain told the pilot. "Didn't know you carried a gun."

"Helps to carry in case of emergencies," Chris replied with a smile. "Never know when you might need one."

"I can see that."

"Man, you guys sure know how to operate."

"We do?"

"Yeah. I hate simple pick up and drop off stuff. No excitement. But you guys... you guys know how to throw a party. I love it."

"We certainly do."

"How's everyone doing? Anyone hit? Any problems?" Chris asked.

"No. We're all good," Lawson replied. "Thanks for the assist."

"Oh, no problem. Like I said, you guys are my kind of people. How'd you guys find me again so soon?"

"Like you said, you're in the book," she told him.

Chris started laughing, amused by her humor. On their way to the rundown airfield that Chris was flying to, Lawson tended to Raines. He was taken care of pretty well while he was being held other than the cuts and bruises on his face. His eyes were adjusting back to the light, and he felt some strength returning to his legs. Chris had some water that he passed back to him so he could get some fluids into his system. It didn't look like he'd need any further medical attention.

"What were they keeping you for?" Lawson asked.

"I think they were hoping more would come looking for me and they could take them as well," Raines said.

"Well, that was a lousy plan."

"Only because it was you two who came after me."

"Well, you saved my life a couple of times already. I guess I owed you some," Cain said. "I think I might still owe you one or two more."

"I'll consider us as even."

It took another hour before the helicopter touched down in the closed off, rundown airfield that Chris kept the chopper in. Cain, Raines, and Lawson got out as Chris was still in the helicopter, powering it down.

"Hey. Here you go," Chris said, handing a business card to both Cain and Lawson.

"What's this?" Cain asked.

"Contact info."

"Thought we already had it."

"No. Right now you just have a way to get in touch with me via a third party," he explained. "That right there is my personal, private number. You guys ever need me, you let me know."

"How far do you travel?" Lawson asked.

"As long as I can get there in the air I'll get there."

"Good to know. Thanks. Appreciate it," Cain told him.

"Good luck to you both."

The Specter crew checked into a hotel so they could get

some food into Raines as well as figure out a plan moving forward. They knew Collins was supposed to be in Germany but didn't yet have a lead on him.

"Anything on Proulx' phone? Like a call to Germany maybe?" Cain asked hopefully though he knew it was doubtful.

"No," Lawson responded. "Nothing but local calls and texts. It's possible he had no idea where Collins is. They might not have communicated with each other at all."

"Yeah. It's possible." Cain sighed. "I just wanna get this over with."

"I know. You know these things take time."

"It's also possible that once word of the deaths of Proulx and Booth leak out that an associate may decide to up the process for a financial gain," Raines interjected.

"That's true too. Maybe one of Collins men will figure it's better to turn traitor in exchange for a payoff than wind up dead with him," Lawson said.

"But we can't count on it," Cain reminded them.

Lawson went back to her computer and started digging for information. She also checked on Bisset to make sure she was complying with what Cain had told her. Lawson had a contact in the Judicial Police who she had asked for a copy of the report that Bisset made. Cain noticed some pictures of the cabin on the train on her computer and took a closer look.

"What are you doing?" Cain asked.

"Oh, this is the official police report from the train incident," she explained.

"What train incident?" Raines asked.

"We'll tell you about it later," Lawson said.

"How'd you get this?" Cain asked.

"I have a contact in the DCPJ. Told him we were interested

in the events though we weren't involved. Guess I'll owe him a favor later."

"What'd Bisset say? They suspect her of anything?" Cain wanted to know.

"No. Looks like she told police a long-haired, bearded man in his mid-forties broke in asking about money that was owed to him. When Proulx declined knowing anything, this strange guy who only spoke French started shooting."

The littlest of smiles crept over Cain's face as he read along with Lawson.

"Guess you were right about her," Lawson said.

"She's probably still in the hospital," Cain stated.

"Yeah."

"Can you find her?"

"What? Why?"

"I'd like to pay her a visit," he said.

"Any particular reason for that or anything?" Lawson asked, confused.

"She knew Proulx had taken Eric. She knew he placed a phone call that day. Maybe she knows other things."

"Like whether he knows anyone in Germany?" Raines asked.

Cain nodded. "Yeah."

"All right. Give me a few minutes to track her down."

While Lawson tried to find the hospital that Bisset had been transported to, Cain and Raines talked about the mission.

"Want me to go with you?" Raines asked.

"Nah. You stay here, rest up. I should be fine. Not expecting any gunplay or anything."

"You never know."

"It'll be OK. You just get your strength up," Cain told him. "How'd you ever get captured, anyway?"

"Got a call from an informant that he knew a guy who was willing to meet with me. He supposedly knew where Proulx was. Met with him in the back of some restaurant. Within a minute of meeting him I got jumped from behind and they must've injected me with something to knock me out because I don't remember much after that. I woke up in that place you found me."

Lawson interrupted their conversation a few seconds later. She'd found the hospital Bisset was staying and wrote it down on a piece of paper, handing it to Cain.

"I'll be back in a little bit," Cain told them. Once he reached the door, he looked back at the pair. "Maybe you should use the time that I'm gone to get reacquainted."

Cain drove to the hospital, which was over an hour away, hoping Bisset would have something for him. Even if it was something that she thought was insignificant, it could turn into the lead that they needed. When Cain got to hospital he went into the flower shop that was located on the ground floor and picked out some flowers. He didn't know much about flowers but figured the brightest would work the best. He asked at the desk if Bisset had any other visitors and was told that she hadn't. He wanted to make sure they were alone and would've waited if others were there.

Bisset smiled as soon as Cain entered her room. Her face lit up at the sight of a visitor. Cain was the first one she'd received.

"Are those for me?" she asked.

"They are," Cain replied, handing them to her.

"Thank you."

"Figured they'd brighten up the room a little bit," he said, finding a chair at the end of the bed.

"I guess you're here to see what I told the police," Bisset said.

"No. I already know what you told them."

"You do?"

"Yeah. I read the report."

"How'd you do that?"

"I have my ways," he told her.

"I'm sure you do."

"So, how you feeling?"

"Not bad. They said I should be able to go home tomorrow."

"That's good. Where you gonna go?"

She laughed. "I don't know. As you can see, I'm not that popular."

"No friends or family?" Cain asked.

"A few friends but nobody I'm that close with. It's been over a year since I talked to my parents or sister."

"Might be a good time to reconnect."

"Yeah, maybe. I don't suppose you could use a thirty-five-year-old, plain looking photographer in your life, could you?"

Cain smiled. "I have someone waiting for me at home."

"Of course you do. I kind of figured you might. Is she pretty?"

"Yeah. She is."

"She's a lucky girl," Bisset said.

"Not as lucky as I am. She's the reason I breathe."

"Sounds like a special girl. I'm jealous."

"She is."

"Hey, maybe if you ever get married and need a photographer, I could do your photos."

"Not a bad idea. Maybe I'll take you up on that," Cain said.

"Where do you live? Or can't you tell me that? Is that top secret?"

"New York."

"I've always wanted to go to New York. Is it just like everyone says it is?"

"I guess so," he said unenthusiastically.

"I'm sorry. I know you didn't come here to listen to me babble on about anything and everything. Just been kind of lonely in here."

"It's all right."

"So, what brings you here? I'm sure you didn't come just to bring me flowers and tell me to reconnect with my parents."

"I was hoping you might be able to help me."

"I doubt there's anything I can help you with," she said.

"You never know," Cain said. "I'm looking for someone."

"I kind of figured you were. And you think I can somehow help you with that?"

"Maybe. Maybe you overheard something somewhere along the way or saw something that'll come back to you."

"I don't think so."

"Something that seemed out of place. A conversation you heard where the words didn't make much sense," Cain said. "A piece of paper that had something written you didn't understand. We could be talking months."

Bisset put her head down to think, replaying events in her mind to try to come up with something. After a few minutes, she shook her head. She couldn't think of anything. Nothing that seemed out of the ordinary. Cain continued pressing her for a few minutes, though not hard, just trying subtle techniques to get her to remember something. A few more minutes of racking her brain produced nothing of note. She was about to give up with the exercise when she suddenly remembered something. It was a conversation she'd overhead, and it was only the tail end of it, but she replayed it for Cain.

"I don't really remember too much of what he said except for one part," Bisset said.

"What part was that?"

Bisset closed her eyes tightly as she tried to remember. "It was... blah blah blah... blah blah blah... you should be happy with Thor."

"Thor?" Cain asked.

"Yeah."

"You should be happy with Thor?"

Bisset nodded. "Yeah. That's what he said."

"Hmm."

"Think it could be important? Maybe what you're looking for?"

"I don't know. Maybe."

"What do you think it could be?" she asked.

"Well, I doubt he was going to the movies. I'll have to do some checking on that."

"I guess you're going to be leaving soon?"

Cain nodded. "I have to get back to work. I just wanted to see how you were doing."

"Well. Thanks for coming. Means a lot," she said and smiled.

Cain got up and walked over to the bed and touched her hand. "You take care of yourself."

"I don't suppose I'll ever see you again."

"Not likely."

"Hey, if you ever want those wedding pictures."

"I'll look you up."

52

Cain went back to the hotel and as soon as he walked inside the room wondered where everyone was. He expected them to be busy at work but their computers were at the desk, turned on. He didn't get a text or call saying they were going anywhere. He heard a noise coming from the bathroom and a giggle that sounded like Lawson's voice. She then emerged from the bathroom in only her bra and underwear, and holding a towel to dry out her wet hair.

"Matt," she said, startled. "I didn't know you were back."

"Obviously."

Raines came out a few seconds later with only shorts on, just as wet as Lawson was. He looked happy and was about to say something to Lawson when he noticed Cain standing there.

"Oh. Hey, buddy. How long have you been here?"

"Not long," Cain answered. "Luckily for you."

"We didn't think you were coming back so soon," Lawson said.

"Yeah, I came back a little too soon, apparently."

"It's not what you think."

"Oh no?"

"No," Lawson stumbled. "I, uh, had something in my hair and I couldn't get it out so I had to wash it. Eric was just helping me."

"And you both decided to take your clothes off for it?"

"Well, we didn't want to get them... wet," she replied, knowing just how ridiculous she sounded.

"Well, I was hoping you guys would be productive while I was gone. I just didn't realize... how... productive... you'd be," Cain kidded.

Raines took a big sigh trying to think of something but quickly closed his mouth when he realized he had nothing and would only sound more foolish than they looked.

"So, how'd things go with Bisset?" Lawson asked, trying to change the subject.

Cain smiled. "Productive. Though I'm not quite sure as productive as here."

Lawson looked at Raines. "Uh... why don't we get our clothes on and we can get back to business."

"Good idea," Raines replied.

They went back into the bathroom and put their clothes back on. Cain looked at them as they walked away and smiled, laughing to himself. Though he was kidding them, he was happy that they had seemed to get themselves back to a good place with each other, even if it was only for a few moments. He hopped on a computer and started searching Google. Lawson and Raines reappeared after a few minutes and joined him at the computer.

"Nice to see you guys again," Cain teased. "Though not as much of you."

"Sooo, what are you looking for?" Lawson asked.

"Bisset mentioned that she overhead Proulx on the phone once, though she didn't know who he was talking to."

"What'd he say?"

"Something about you'll be happy with Thor."

"Thor?"

"Yeah."

"What's that mean?" Lawson wondered aloud.

"Well, I'm pretty sure he wasn't calling for The Avengers," Cain remarked sarcastically. "Though they definitely could be of assistance right about now."

He turned back to his search on the computer. He had typed in Thor just to see what popped up. The first two pages had nothing but references to the superhero. The third page had some other interesting possibilities though. There was a manufacturer and distributor of biocides and chemicals, a manufacturer of recreational vehicles, and some kind of computer toolkit command. Cain's eyes immediately went to the RVs.

"This is interesting," he said.

"What?"

"Thor Industries. The world's largest manufacturer of recreational vehicles," Cain said, reading off their website.

"You think he's living in an RV?" Lawson asked.

"I don't know. Maybe. I mean, it would make sense, wouldn't it? They're not hiding in normal places. Proulx was on a train, Booth was in a church, why couldn't he be on an RV? Makes him mobile, hard to spot, never stays in the same spot, seems like a pretty good cover to me," Cain reasoned.

Cain continued pouring over their website, looking at all the vehicles they sold. Most didn't seem like they'd be a fit for Collins. At least not until he saw the motor homes.

"I can't see him hooking up a trailer or hitching something on to the back of a truck," Cain said.

"Doesn't really seem like his style, does it?" Raines confirmed.

"But a Thor Motor Coach?" Cain asked, clicking on some of the images and floor plans. "Yeah, I could see him in one of these."

"Those have got to be three or four hundred thousand dollars," Raines said.

"How about if we dig on Thor motor home sales to anybody in Germany, or even the surrounding countries if he decided to get cute?"

"I'm on it," Lawson replied.

"That can't be that big of a list," Raines noted.

"Motorized RV sales from their last quarter was over 250 million," Lawson informed him.

"OK. So maybe it'll take a little longer than I thought."

It actually turned out to not be as long a list as they thought it might be. Cain also turned up a few interesting things that would help in their search.

"Looks like you can't register a vehicle in Germany unless you're a resident and have a bank account," Cain said. "Without registration, it can't be insured or taxed, so it wouldn't be legal to drive."

"OK. Here's a list of German names registered as buying a Thor RV," Lawson said.

Lawson wrote down a list of names on pieces of paper and handed a few of each to Cain and Raines. All three of them started doing background checks on all the names to see if they were legit or possibly aliases. If there were no aliases, then they'd have to check to see if any of them had a possible connection to Collins. After a couple hours of actively searching, none of the names appeared to be aliases. They started checking the other names to find a connection. Lawson appeared to have found one.

"Wait, I think I got something," she told them.

"What do you have?" Cain asked.

"Markos Hochberg. Bought a five hundred thousand-dollar Thor Challenger Class A motor home, approximately two weeks after Collins went missing."

"That must be it," Raines said. "For five hundred thousand he must've ordered it custom made."

"Or just had some modifications done to his specs. Maybe an intricate alarm system or bulletproof glass or something," Cain added.

"Paid with a certified check. Let me check his background info," Lawson said. "Last known occupation was a security guard."

"He ain't buying a Thor on that salary," Cain said.

"Collins must've hired him as some muscle and had Hochberg put everything in his name," Raines said.

"That should make it pretty easy to find," Lawson noted. "You're not going to be able to park something that big just anywhere. You're going to have to use a campsite."

"That should narrow it down pretty quick. Find the Thor. Find the campsite. Find Hochberg or any combination of the three. Then they'll all lead us to Collins," Cain said.

Lawson was the best out of the three at running down that type of information and took the lead. If she needed anything, she'd direct the other two to get it for her. It took her about an hour but she finally got the break she thought she needed.

"Got him," she said excitedly.

"Collins?" Cain asked.

"No. Hochberg. But it's basically the same thing, isn't it?"

"Well... hopefully."

"I tried to track him through the check they gave for the RV. But they tried to cover their tracks because that account closed right after the sale," Lawson explained.

"Probably knew we'd find them someday."

"Most likely. Anyway, I was basically just trying to get a beat on Hochberg. I got a hit from the registration number and traced it back to a house. Then I used that address and was able to use it to find a bank account number, which I then was able to link to a bank card."

"I'm presuming you're going a step further with this," Raines said.

"And that bank card was used at a grocery store about two hours ago."

"Which tells us what?"

"Nothing in itself," Lawson told him. "But when you combine it with the fact it was also used at a gas station a half hour after that... gives us a good indication of where he's going."

"What campsites would be in his line of travel?" Cain asked.

Lawson turned around and hit a few more buttons on the keyboard of her laptop before spinning back around with a smile on her face, knowing she seemed to have all the answers.

"Camping Park Bielefeld," she said.

"How far is that from here?" Cain asked.

"By car... about five hours. Plane... nine hours... with two stops."

"What about train?"

"A little over three hours. And that's from Paris to Cologne, which after the travel to and from the train stations, will probably be close to five hours, anyway."

"Might as well take the car ride."

"It's cool. We can bond," she said.

"I think you two already did that," Cain replied.

"Ha ha."

They wasted no time starting on their journey. Cain and Raines packed up all their stuff while Lawson called in to Specter to inform them of their findings. Analysts back at Specter would continue to monitor Hochberg while the agents were driving. If his information popped up anywhere else besides Bielefeld, the agents could alter their direction of travel without delaying them. While they drove, they tried to formulate a plan of attack.

"It's possible he could see us coming if we go right up to the RV," Cain said.

"Other people might spot us too," Lawson added.

"Have to do it from a distance," Raines said from the back seat.

"What if the windows are tinted and we can't see inside?" Cain asked.

"That does pose a challenge."

"What if we break in overnight while he's sleeping?" Lawson suggested.

"How do you know when he sleeps?" Cain asked her. "Plus, it's an RV, very compact. He's gotta hear us. It's not like a house where you can break in at the far end where nobody is."

"Hochberg," Raines said.

"What about him?" Cain asked.

"We use him to get Collins. He can set him up for us."

"Why would he do that?" Lawson asked.

"Money of course. And our promise that he won't die or go to prison."

"Might work," Cain said. "We'll have to get him alone first."

They continued finalizing their plan, believing that it would work and they could turn Hochberg against his employer. They arrived at the campsite a little close to nine o'clock. If they'd had all the information they needed, the time would've worked out perfectly. They decided that the kill would be better to do at night when there was less activity. But first they had to find the Thor that Collins was in, plus determine if anyone else was in there with him, and figure out if Hochberg could be of any use to them. The three of them walked around the park to find the RV they were looking for. Most of the bigger ones were parked near each other and it didn't take nearly as long as they assumed it would. Once they found the one that looked like Collins', Lawson walked closer to it as Cain and Raines stayed behind in the distance. Lawson put a hat on to disguise her appearance a little. Though Collins was familiar with each of them, they thought that he'd be less likely to notice Lawson. They didn't think Cain or Raines would have a chance of getting close to the RV without Collins spotting them, figuring he'd recognize them no matter if they were disguised or not. Lawson went around the back of the motor home and verified the tag number as the one they were looking for. She didn't linger and chance being spotted herself and immediately went back to her partners as they huddled amongst each other.

"That's it," she told them.

"Well, I can see a light on," Cain noted.

"Damn tinted windows," Raines said.

"What if we wait until he steps outside? Get him on the way out," Lawson said.

"What makes you think he'll step outside?" Cain asked.

"Well, he has to sometime. Doesn't he?"

"He has someone get groceries for him. There's a bathroom and shower in there. All the comforts of home. Somehow I don't think he has to ever step foot outside if he doesn't want to."

"And we can't rush in there," Raines said. "He might blow us up as we get in the door."

"And who knows if he's even got some type of booby trap. Unauthorized access to the door and it blows up or something," Cain replied, getting a look from Lawson. "Can't count it out. He's got the money, and had the time to rig something like that up."

"He's right," Raines confirmed. "Can't take the chance of rushing in there. It's a cinch he's taken some kind of precaution."

"So, what do we do then?" Lawson asked.

"Stick to our original plan," Cain answered. "Wait for Hochberg. He'll tell us what we can do."

Raines nodded in agreement.

"Who knows how long that'll be?" Lawson sighed.

"Patience," Cain said. "He's in our sights. Everything's going our way. No need to rush and make a mistake."

"Wait," Raines said, putting his hand up. "Looks like the door's opening."

The door to the RV opened and Hochberg came walking out.

"Ask and you shall receive," Raines said.

"Maybe I should try that more often," Lawson said.

Hochberg walked around the Challenger and toward the woods.

"Where's he going?" Lawson asked.

"Looks like he's taking a walk," Cain answered.

"This is our chance," Raines told them.

"You guys go for him," Lawson said. "I'll keep eyes on Collins."

Cain and Raines agreed and started walking in Hochberg's direction. They were careful to not get too close to either Hochberg or the RV. They didn't want to get into contact with Hochberg until he reached the woods, assuming that's where he was going. If he stopped short of that they'd figure it out. He kept on walking until he reached the woods as he puffed on a cigarette. Cain and Raines continued following him and also looked around to make sure nobody else was within distance of them. They started walking a little faster as Hochberg walked past the first couple of trees. Cain and Raines rushed over to him as he disappeared from the view of the campground. Hochberg heard noises like someone was close to him but he wasn't fast enough to turn around in time. They both took a healthy swing at the back of Hochberg's head, who didn't see them coming. Hochberg fell face first onto the ground. Cain pulled him over.

"Hey. What's the idea?" Hochberg asked, looking up at his attackers and holding the back of his head.

"We just wanted to get your attention," Cain said.

"You've got it," Hochberg replied, still rolling on the ground.

"I see you speak English."

"Maybe."

Cain and Raines looked at each other and laughed.

"I don't have much money if that's what you're after," Hochberg said.

"We know," Raines replied.

"What is it then?"

"We'd like you to work for us," Cain said.

"I already have a job."

"With that job, you're gonna be unemployed soon," Cain quipped.

"I don't understand."

"You're employed as a bodyguard slash assistant for a man named Collins, correct?"

Hochberg didn't reply and just looked, somewhat fearfully, of the two men standing over him.

"What do you want?" Hochberg asked.

"You have two choices and you've got less than five minutes to pick the one you want," Cain explained. "You're gonna help us get Collins. Or you're gonna be buried with him."

"Which would you prefer?" Raines asked.

"Neither," Hochberg answered.

"Not one of the options," Cain said. "Listen. We're not here for you. We don't care what you've done or what you're doing. Right now, you're just a guy who's working for a living. I can understand that. But you're working for a man who's living on borrowed time."

"So, if you help us, you'll get paid for your troubles, and you get to walk away," Raines chimed in. "If you don't, then you'll get the same treatment as your boss."

"How do I know I can trust you?"

"Because if we were lying you'd be dead already," Cain told him. "We're here for one man. We'd rather not add to the body count though we can if that's the only choice we have."

"You said I get paid. How much?" Hochberg asked.

Cain and Raines looked at each other again, realizing that their tactic was working. He wouldn't be asking about money if he wasn't interested.

"I believe the going rate is two hundred thousand dollars," Cain said.

"For what? I have to kill him?" Hochberg asked.

"No. We'll do that."

"Then what you need me for?"

"We need you to set him up for us. Windows are tinted. Can't see in. We assume he's not coming out anytime soon. And rushing in and possibly taking a bullet isn't real high on our list either. We also want to keep it as low profile as possible. A sniper shot is preferable."

"So, what do you want me to do?"

"We were hoping you could tell us," Raines said.

Still lying on the ground, Hochberg's eyes looked to different places on the ground, trying to think of a way.

"I know a way," Hochberg said.

"We're listening," Cain responded.

"He has breakfast every morning at five. Sits at the table and eats pancakes, eggs, whatever. It's right in front of the window. I can have it opened for you."

"Sounds good."

"When will I get my money?"

"At four o'clock call your bank. Money should be in by then."

"How do I know you won't kill me after you kill him and take the money back?" Hochberg asked.

"First, stay out of the line of fire. Second, it's not my money, so I don't really care to get it back or care who has it. Lastly, I guess you'll just have to trust us."

"You need my bank info?"

"We have it. Just as a reminder, you tip him off we're here or warn him in any way, you'll wind up just as dead as he is."

"Don't worry. Your money is better than his," Hochberg stated.

"Five o'clock, window open?" Cain asked as a reminder.

Hochberg nodded to confirm. He started to get up but was interrupted when Cain and Raines grabbed him, stopping him in his tracks.

"One more thing," Cain said.

"What?"

"We'll have to confirm his death afterward."

"Which means what?" Hochberg asked.

"Immediately after the shot, two people will enter the RV and check to make sure he's dead."

"I could just tell you."

Cain smiled. "Yeah. Don't quite trust you either."

"They won't be there to kill me?"

Cain shook his head. "No. They'll be there to check his body. They will also check any papers he might have and go through the trailer for any other evidence."

"What kind of evidence?"

"We're also looking for another man. Collins might know where he is or have had some type of correspondence with him."

"What's this man's name?" Hochberg asked.

"Ed Sanders."

Hochberg shook his head and scowled. "I don't know the name. He's never mentioned him."

"It's not surprising. But he may have something written down that may lead us to this man. They'll check everything out and when they're done, they'll leave... with you alive. So, don't get antsy."

Hochberg nodded. "OK."

"Just as a warning, if anything happens to my associates when they enter that trailer, you won't make it out alive to spend that money. Understand?"

"I understand. I will hold up my end of the deal."

Cain and Raines then turned around and walked out of the woods. Hochberg finally got up after the pair disappeared from his line of sight. They rejoined Lawson near the bushes that faced Collins RV.

"How'd it go?" Lawson asked.

"As good as could be expected," Cain said.

"Is he playing ball?"

"He's not only playing, he's the starting pitcher."

"What's the deal?"

"Wire two hundred thousand to his bank account at four o'clock," Cain told her.

"What then?"

"Once he verifies it's there, he'll open a window that Collins always sits in front of to eat breakfast. At five o'clock Collins will sit down and I'll take the shot."

"OK. I'll call back to Specter and let them know what's going on and to do the transfer," she responded.

As Lawson called Specter, Cain and Raines continued talking about how they'd take Collins out. They agreed that Cain would be the one to pull the trigger. Though Raines was quite good, Cain was the better shot.

"What about afterwards?" Raines asked.

"I'm thinking you and Shelly go in and see if you can dig anything up."

"What about you?"

"I'll stay in position just in case Hochberg decides to go in business for himself," Cain said.

"OK."

"I don't think it's wise if all three of us go in there just in case something happens we don't foresee."

"I agree."

"I can cover you guys while you're in there. It'll still be dark out so there shouldn't be too many people up and about but you still probably won't have too much time," Cain said.

"Shouldn't take too long. Everything's pretty compact in there. It'll almost be like searching a small office."

"Just remember to grab his laptop or phone in there if he has one and you can find it. We can go through it later."

"Right."

Cain volunteered to stay and watch the trailer through the night so Raines and Lawson could get a couple hours of sleep. They both went to the car and nodded off for a few hours, Lawson lying down across the back seat, Raines leaning the seat back in the passenger side. Cain kept his eyes glued to the RV just in case Collins stepped outside for a breath of the night air. If he did, Cain would have to think about whether it made sense to shoot him ahead of schedule. It'd depend on if anyone else was around. As the night progressed, it was a decision that Cain would never have to make. It was a quiet night. There really wasn't much activity anywhere in the campground. Cain saw a person walking around every now and then but nothing that caused him much concern.

Raines and Lawson set the alarms on their phone for three.

They got up and Raines got some duffel bags out of the trunk of the car. They walked over to Cain's position and Raines handed him his bag. They each looked at their watches to make sure they had the time synched.

"What you got?" Cain asked.

"Three twenty-eight," Raines replied.

"Check."

"Half hour."

"You guys as nervous as I am?" Lawson asked.

"No," Cain and Raines replied in unison.

"How can you be so calm like this?"

"Easy," Cain answered.

"Where's your shot?" Raines asked.

"I figure right over there is best," Cain said, pointing to some bushes near the woods. "Good cover. Good line of sight."

"Right."

They looked at their watches once four o'clock rolled around. They continued watching intently, waiting for a sign that everything was in place, waiting for that window to open. They waited another half hour. Then they got what they'd been waiting so patiently for. A light turned on and the window on the RV slid open.

"There we go," Cain said.

"Looks like we're in business," Raines replied.

"I'm gonna go set up," Cain said, putting a communicator in his ear.

Cain grabbed his bag and calmly walked over to his position, looking around to see if anyone was nearby, careful as to not rush and draw any attention to himself if anyone was out walking. He put the bag down in the bush and kneeled down as he opened the bag, putting the pieces of the rifle together. He pointed the gun at the trailer and looked through the scope of the rifle as he prepared for the shot he was about to make. It was actually one of the easier shots he ever had. It wasn't a long distance, his target wouldn't be moving, and there were no obstacles in his way. For the next half hour, as he usually did, Cain visualized taking the shot and hitting the target over and over again. He was snapped out of it when he heard Raines' voice talking in his ear.

"Ten minutes to go," Raines said. "How are you making out?"

"Ready to go," Cain answered.

"Should be any minute now. Take the first shot you have."

"Roger that."

Cain immersed himself in the bushes, concealing himself and the rifle amongst the foliage. He peered through the scope of the rifle, ready to pull the trigger as soon as Collins' head appeared.

"Five minutes," Raines said.

"What happens if he's not on time for once?" Lawson asked.

"Then we'll wait," Cain replied.

"What if he changes his routine today for some reason?"

"Then we'll wait."

"I see movement," Raines noted.

It was 4:58. Cain noticed a body walking through the trailer. It looked like Collins. He probably could've taken the shot and hit him but he waited for the easier shot and an unmoving target once he sat down. Hochberg emerged into view, putting a couple plates of food down on the table before moving away. A minute later, Collins sat down, preparing to eat as he put down a magazine next to the food. Cain had a clear shot of the back of Collins' head.

"Get ready," Cain told everyone.

"Ready when you are," Raines replied.

Cain looked through the scope one final time. He had the back center of Collins' head lined up. He gently pulled the trigger. Cain continued looking through the scope as he saw pieces of Collins' head fly off and his body slumping forward, his head smacking the table as its final resting spot.

"Target down," Cain calmly stated. "Move in. Still covering."

"On our way," Raines replied.

Cain watched Raines and Lawson move toward the RV while he scanned the perimeter to make sure nobody would interfere with their plans. Everything was going perfectly. Cain moved his sights back to the trailer to make sure Hochberg didn't try to alter the deal somehow. Raines was the first to the trailer and knocked on the door with the back of his hand three times to let Hochberg know they were there. He turned the handle of the door and it opened. Raines removed his gun and led the way inside. He went in slowly just to make sure Hochberg wasn't greeting them with a surprise of his own. As Raines got to the driver seat, he noticed Hochberg standing toward the back of the RV. Both of his hands were in plain sight and he made no sudden movements. Raines walked over to the table that Collins was resting on and checked his pulse. He slightly pulled his head up off the table so he could see his face.

"It is Collins," Raines stated. "He's DOA."

"Roger that," Cain replied.

"Check your account?" Raines asked Hochberg.

Hochberg nodded. "Money is there."

"Good."

"Mind if I go now?"

"Just wait outside. Don't go anywhere until we come out," he told him. "Remember, there's still a gun on you if you try to alert anyone."

"No need to worry about me."

"Hochberg's coming out and waiting so he's not in the way," Raines told Cain.

"Roger that. I see him," Cain said as Hochberg came into view.

Hochberg stopped once he stepped out of the RV and just leaned against the trailer as he waited for the others. Lawson put a black bag on the table to put inside anything they thought might be of some use to them. They wouldn't have time to check everything right then and there so if something looked interesting, they could check it later. Lawson went over to a desk and looked at a few papers. Nothing looked important, but she took them anyway. Raines found a laptop near the couch and put it in the bag. They quickly went through the entire RV, looking in every open spot imaginable. They'd found a few things that may have given them something but nothing jumped out at them. They made sure everything was put back the way they found it and exited the RV, taking their gloves off as soon as they stepped outside.

"We good?" Hochberg asked.

Raines nodded to confirm. "We're good. I'd get away as far as possible if I were you."

"I'm already gone."

"Pleasure to do business with you."

Hochberg started walking away towards another car in the parking lot as Raines and Lawson rejoined Cain near the bush. Cain disassembled his rifle and put it back in his bag as the three of them quickly walked back to their car. Raines took the driver seat as Cain lay down in the back seat to catch some sleep. He wouldn't be able to get too much since they decided to drive to the Netherlands, but it'd suffice for the time being. Once they got into a hotel there, he'd be able to get some more rest. They could reach the Netherlands in just about two hours, which they figured was plenty of time to get out of the country. The usual method of operation when killing someone was to leave a country as quickly as possible before the body was found. Once the body was found and a manhunt started it was more difficult to leave. Once they got out of Germany, they'd check into a hotel and start going over the stuff they grabbed out of the RV.

53

Raines and Lawson had started pouring over the information they gathered from Collins as Cain got some much-needed sleep. Lawson called Conlin to let him know that they could check another name off the hit list. Raines began going over the documents they'd taken while Lawson went through the laptop. Cain slept for about six hours and by the time he woke up and saw his associates working, he could tell it wasn't going well.

"You guys look frustrated," Cain said as he walked out of the bedroom, noticing a few heavy sighs from the both of them.

"I guess you could say that," Lawson responded, sitting back in her chair. "I've looked at this computer for over five hours and I've gotten nowhere. There is absolutely nothing in this thing that's going to get us any closer to Sanders. I don't see a link anywhere."

"Eric?"

"Not going much better with me," Raines replied. "I've

694

looked over most of these papers two or three times, none of them really do us any good. Most of them are from when he was involved with Specter. Some are financial papers and look like a few bank accounts he's got scattered around a few different places. I can't find Sanders' name mentioned in any of them though."

"So, we basically got a whole lot of nothing," Cain said.

"That's pretty much it in a nutshell."

"Why don't you try going over some of this stuff and see if you can come up with anything," Lawson mentioned. "Maybe you can find something we overlooked."

"I doubt that'll do any good. You're much better with computers than I am. I doubt I can find something you didn't."

"Still, doesn't hurt to have an extra pair of eyes to double check."

"OK," Cain said. "I guess I'll take a crack at it."

Cain did his best to come up with something that the others couldn't, looking at both the computer and the documents, but ultimately, he came up empty just as the others did. They spent the better part of the day re-checking all the information they had in front of them but it didn't do them any good. Without any credible leads to follow up on, Conlin directed them to come back to New York the following day. Conlin sent a private jet to the Netherlands to fly them back home.

"Getting another private jet?" Cain asked. "We must've done a good job or something."

"Well, he's still a little concerned about the air pressure and your head. Don't want it exploding or anything," Lawson joked.

"Ha ha."

"He just wants to make sure you're in a controllable situation while flying. Harder to do that in a commercial plane."

"I just flew several times in a helicopter and nobody said a word."

Lawson shrugged, not having a good response. They boarded the jet the following morning and had a nice, dull, uneventful ride back to New York arriving in the afternoon. A car was waiting for them to take them back to The Center once they got off the jet. The laptop and documents they'd taken were handed over to other analysts as they took a crack at trying to uncover a lead they could work with. Cain texted Heather that he was back but had to take care of a few things before coming home. Lawson went into a debriefing meeting while Cain and Raines both went to the hospital wing. They wanted to make sure Raines had no lingering effects from being taken prisoner and Cain had to get his head scanned once more to make sure the clot hadn't gotten any bigger. He still hadn't told Heather about it and wasn't sure he was going to. Raines got cleared pretty quickly and was given a clean bill of health. Cain's results came back and his clot was still there but it had decreased slightly in size. Doctors were not worried about it, and with medication, thought that it'd wind up going away on its own within a month or two. He spent almost two hours in the hospital and after getting released, checked in with Lawson to see if he was needed for anything. Lawson told him he had the rest of the day off and to go spend time with his girlfriend and come back the next day.

Heather had a nice dinner ready for Cain by the time he got back home. She had a sexy dress on and was waiting to smother him with kisses. Once Cain walked through the door, not only did he smell something good in the kitchen, he immediately noticed candles lit on the table and the lights were not as bright.

"What's all this?" Cain asked with a smile.

"Oh, just a little something special for the man in my life," Heather replied, rushing over to hug and kiss him.

"Did something exciting happen that we're celebrating?"

"Why yes, there is. My super handsome boyfriend just came back after a little trip and I'm just really happy and excited that he's back so I decided to do a little something special for him."

"Wow. He's an extremely lucky guy."

"He certainly is," she said, kissing him.

"You look ridiculously beautiful," he told her, looking her up and down.

"Aww. I thought you'd never notice."

"I hope you haven't been looking like that while I was gone. Driving all the other men in this city crazy," Cain said, kissing her.

"Well, you know, just a couple," she teased.

"Not that I'd blame them for looking."

"No, actually I've made sure I was looking so ugly and frumpy, and wearing like oversized pajamas every day, that way I could transform into a beautiful-looking princess just for you when you got back," she said, with some passionate kissing.

"Well, whatever you're doing is working."

"Should I go back to ugly and frumpy?"

"Absolutely not."

"As much as I'd like to stay in your arms all night, I gotta get dinner out of the oven," Heather said, slipping out of his arms and going into the kitchen.

"Do you want me to do anything or get anything?" Cain asked.

"No, no, no. I've got everything," she happily said, bringing their plates of food in. "Sit down."

Cain sat down as Heather rushed back into the kitchen to bring out their drinks. She brought them in and put them on the table and then sat across from her boyfriend. Cain stared at her for a minute, unable to take his eyes off the glowing beauty that was in front of him.

"What?" Heather asked, noticing his stare.

"I'm just... you just mesmerize me."

A huge smile overtook Heather's face. She just wanted to wow him when he got back and show him how much she loved him. It seemed like her plan was working.

"You look so happy," Cain noted.

"I am happy. You're here."

"You're so beautiful. I'm so lucky to have you. I don't know what I'd do without you. Well, I guess we both know what I'd do. We kind of went down that road once already, didn't we?"

"Well, we'll never have to find out for sure or do that ever again, will we?"

Cain thought about telling her about the clot in his head but decided against it. At least for a couple of hours. She'd obviously spent a lot of time trying to make a special night for them with dinner and getting dressed up for him. He didn't want to ruin it by making her worry about him. Especially since he thought it was a minor thing. They both avoided talking about his work throughout the entire dinner. He was never real anxious to talk about it; he knew the questions were going to come at some point. Though Heather wanted to know how things went for him while he was away, she didn't want it to be the main focus between them. He was home and fine and that was the main thing for her. She didn't want to seem like she was constantly nagging on him or think she was worrying too much. Once they finished dinner, they cleaned up the table and put the dishes in the sink.

"Hey," Cain said, grabbing Heather around her waist. "Did you really think I was gonna be able to go through the whole night without touching you like this with how good you look?"

"Well, I was hoping not," she said, putting her arms around his neck.

"You know, I feel underdressed with you looking like that."

"A few more minutes of this and you're really gonna feel underdressed," she teased.

"So, I should keep this up?" he asked, kissing her some more.

"Oh, yes," she whispered. "You know the best part of dressing up and feeling sexy is when your boyfriend takes it off you."

Cain picked Heather up, his arms wrapped around her waist, her legs wrapping around his back, as he carried her into the bedroom. He laid her down on the bed as they continued making love and they began taking each other's clothes off. After a few hours of lovemaking, they got dressed and went into the living room, cuddling on the couch as they watched TV. As he held her in his arms, Cain thought about finally telling her about the clot in his head. As much as he didn't feel it was a big deal, he could've just not said anything realizing that it was probably going away, and she'd never know anything about it. But he didn't want to keep secrets from her, no matter how big or small, or how trivial it may have seemed. He thought she had a right to know if their relationship was going to work.

"I'm a little surprised you didn't ask anything about my trip," Cain started off.

"It's not really that important. You're home, everything's fine, that's what's really important."

"Yeah."

"Nothing happened, right?"

Cain didn't answer right away, trying to think of the right way to tell her. The fact he didn't talk immediately, Heather automatically thought something was wrong. She broke from his grasp, sitting up to talk to him.

"Nothing happened, right?" she asked again.

"Umm... well..."

"Oh my God. What happened?"

"Well, on the plane ride I got a little dizzy and threw up," Cain revealed to her.

"You were OK though?"

"Yeah. Just the altitude I guess."

"OK. Is that it?"

"Umm..."

"What else?"

"Well, uh, I got into a little trouble and got hit in the head a few times and passed out."

"Oh my God!" she exclaimed, putting her hands over her mouth.

"I was taken to a hospital and checked out."

"And nothing was wrong?" Heather asked, sensing there was more to it.

"They discovered I had a small blood clot in my head."

Heather's mouth fell open and Cain could already tell there were a thousand bad thoughts going through her mind. He gently took her hands to try to calm her.

"You need to relax. Everything's fine," he said calmly. "I had another scan when I got back earlier today. The clot is already smaller and they believe it's going to go away on its own."

"You're sure?"

"Well, all I can do is go on what they tell me. The doctor in France and the doctor here both said the same thing. It's relatively small, and with medicine, it should disappear on its own."

Heather sighed. "Why do you make me worry so much about you?"

Cain smiled at her. "I'm just that kind of guy I guess."

Cain pulled her closer to him and passionately kissed her.

"It's nothing to worry about. I just figured I should tell you because I thought you'd have a right to know. Not because there's something to worry about."

"Well, I'm glad you did," she told him.

"You're sure? You're not gonna worry more?"

"I'm always gonna worry about you. That's not gonna change. But it's not just because of your head and what you've been through with that. It's also because of what you do and I worry about you not coming home. And it's partly because I'm a girl and that's what girlfriends who are in love do... we worry about those we care about."

"You know I'd be lost without you?"

"I know." Heather smiled before giving him a kiss.

"I was thinking... maybe we should get a dog."

"A dog? Why?"

"Why not? You like dogs, right?"

"Of course I do. Just wondering why you think we should get one now."

"Well... I think it'd be fun to have one. And I think it'd be good for you," Cain said.

"Good for me? How?"

"Well, when I'm gone, you'd still have some company. I mean, he's not gonna talk back to you or anything, but he'd help keep you busy."

"And help not to worry about you so much?" Heather asked.

Cain shrugged. "Just an idea."

"You know I've always wanted one."

"Maybe we should look at some breeds and see which one we'd like."

Heather raised an eyebrow and smiled. She seemed happy and pleased with the idea. "Yeah. Yeah, I think that might be a good idea."

The following morning, Cain made breakfast for his lovely girlfriend, having it ready by the time she woke up.

"What's this?" Heather happily asked.

"Just figured I'd make breakfast for you. Return the favor since you made dinner."

"Well, aren't you sweet? Very thoughtful. Better not let this get out. People might think you're a bit of a pushover," she teased.

Cain laughed. "Yeah. They might take advantage of my sensitive nature. It's nothing extravagant. Only pancakes."

"It's not what it is, it's the thought that counts," she said, giving him a quick kiss. "And I love you for it."

Cain cleared his throat before saying what he knew she wouldn't want to hear. "I'm gonna have to go into work for a little bit."

"What?" Heather asked, clearly disappointed, and not even trying to hide it. "I thought maybe we'd be able to spend the whole day together."

"I don't think I'll be gone that long. Shelly wants me to

come down and brainstorm a little bit. We still have one more person to find."

"OK." She sighed. "I'll just wait here for you like the patient, loving, understanding, girlfriend that I am," she playfully replied.

Cain laughed and leaned over to kiss her. "And I love you for that."

"Maybe I'll do some research on different dog breeds while you're gone."

"That's a good idea."

"Maybe by the time you get back I'll have it narrowed down for you," she said.

"Why don't you get a list of your top five and we'll go from there?"

"I can do that."

Cain then left and went down to The Center where he was called in for a brief meeting with Lawson, Raines, and Director Conlin. They each took a seat in the meeting room as Conlin began the session.

"I wanted to have this meeting with you guys because you're the point people for this. You guys are responsible for Booth, Proulx, and Collins. It wouldn't have happened without you. You're to be congratulated for your speed and quality of your work. It's unprecedented how well you've completed your missions. You deserve more accolades than I'm capable of throwing out at you right now," Conlin told them.

"Thank you, sir," Lawson replied.

Cain and Raines just nodded in acknowledgment.

"But that being said, it's still not over. We have one man left," Conlin continued.

"What's the status of the stuff we brought back?" Lawson asked. "Has it been analyzed?"

"I've had ten analysts going over it all with a fine-tooth comb since you got back. They worked all through the night. They came up with nothing," he revealed. "Not a single piece of evidence in any of the documents or his laptop that connects him to Sanders in any way. Doesn't even look like they've communicated since they hit the road. At least, not in a way that we can understand."

"So, what now?" Lawson asked.

"I want you three to figure out where Sanders is. I don't care what it takes, but he is not getting away and vanishing into thin air. He used this office for his own personal gain. That's not acceptable and we're not going to let him get away with it."

"Without a lead, how are we supposed to figure out where he is?"

"That's what you guys get the big money for," Conlin said bluntly. "Find him. Today. Any questions?" he asked, looking around the room.

Lawson and Raines shook their head while Cain just kept staring at the table.

"Keep me updated," Conlin told them as he exited the room.

"I guess we need to find him soon, huh?" Cain cracked.

"Talk about the impossible task," Lawson responded. "Let's head back to my office and come up with something."

The three of them went back to Lawson's office as they started to brainstorm and throw some ideas out at each other.

"I have a feeling this is going to be a long day," Raines said.

"Even longer night probably," Cain replied.

Several hours of bantering back and forth produced no

results. They tried going on the computer to track Sanders down, but that too was done to no avail. Lawson went and grabbed some sandwiches for them as they worked through lunch. Having full stomachs didn't help much as they ran out of ideas. They had no idea where Sanders was and didn't know how they could find him. It seemed as if he'd successfully disappeared. There wasn't a trace of him anywhere. Conlin eventually called to get a status update.

"So where do we stand?" the Director asked.

"Well, uh, you know, we're still working on it," Lawson stumbled.

"So, in other words you've got nothing so far."

"Well, uh, so far we don't have much. But we're still digging and we'll crack something sooner or later."

"I'd prefer sooner."

"Yeah... well... um... we'll um...we'll keep going."

"Don't stop til you get something."

"We will do that. Yes. We certainly will."

Lawson hung up the phone and threw her head in her hand as she leaned on the desk.

"Seems like that went well," Cain joked.

"Yeah. About as well as a.... I don't know what," Lawson replied. "But it wasn't good!"

"So I gathered."

They continued for several more hours, feeling like they were beating their heads against the wall, while still coming up with nothing. They worked right through dinner without getting anything, eager to find something, anything.

"This can't be it," Lawson stated. "There has to be something else. Something that we're missing."

"We've been over the same information a dozen times. Two

dozen times. It is what it is. We're at a dead end. Our contacts have no more information for us and the leads have dried up. Sanders is a ghost at this point," Raines said.

"He's out there somewhere. Where is he?"

Cain just sat there, listening to the others speak, his eyes bouncing between the wall and the desk as he soaked in their words.

"You're being awfully quiet, Matt," Lawson said.

"Thinking..."

"Anything you care to share?" Raines asked.

"Wherever he is, it has to be somewhere where he feels safe. Somewhere you've been before...," Cain said, his voice trailing off.

"What? Think you have something?" Lawson asked.

"Somewhere you feel safe. Somewhere you've been before. To completely drop off the grid, as you know," Cain said, gesturing to Raines. "You need to have the support of people around you. People you know, people you trust, people you think would never betray you. You can't do that in a place you've never been before. Too many unknowns and variables you can't control. If you're already familiar with the places and people, you can control it."

"So where does that leave us?" Lawson asked.

"We would need to dig up his past before he became the director of Specter," Raines added. "Find out where he's been, who he knows."

"We might not have to," Cain said, his face lighting up the way a person's does when they find out a secret nobody else knows.

"Why are you looking like that?" Lawson asked.

"I think I might know where he's at."

"Well, clue the rest of us in."

"Honduras," Cain revealed.

"Honduras?" Raines asked. "Why would he be there?"

"Ruiz."

"What?" Lawson said. "You need to be a little more specific."

"My first mission was in Honduras. That's where we first met, remember?" Cain asked Raines.

"I remember."

"My first contact there was a man named Ruiz. I still have his contact info."

"How does this relate to Sanders?" Raines asked.

"Ruiz told me that's where he first met Sanders. In Honduras, before Sanders joined Specter. Ruiz told me Sanders was responsible for getting his daughter's killer when the local police failed. Ruiz thought Sanders was a good man. Spoke very highly of him. He always felt indebted to him after that," Cain explained.

"And who better to ask for help in hiding than a man who will always be thankful of what you did for him," Raines said.

"And a man you know will never betray you. Not after what you did for him. Not after getting your daughter's killer. If the man who got justice for my daughter's killer came knocking on my door and needing help... I'd help him. No matter what."

"So, it looks like we're going to Honduras," Raines said.

"Back to where it all started," Cain replied, cracking his knuckles.

"So, should you contact Ruiz and see what he'll tell us?" Lawson asked.

"No. The minute I say anything to him about Sanders, he's gone," Cain said. "He'll just assume I'm on to him and he's out of the country and we've lost our best shot of getting him."

"We need to just show up at his doorstep and confront him," Raines said. "He'll tell us what he knows."

"It's gotta be it," Cain said.

"I'll call Conlin and tell him what we got," Lawson told them.

Conlin had already left for the day but Lawson reached him at home. They kicked back-and-forth Cain's idea that Sanders was in Honduras. Conlin needed a little more convincing.

"What do you think?" Lawson asked.

"I think it makes some sense but I can't send agents down there on a whim."

"But it's all we got right now."

"I understand that. Before I authorize people going down there I'd like to try to get some kind of evidence that he's there."

"I don't know if we can get it."

"How about if we go on the assumption that he is in fact there. I'll call the assistant director and have him get everyone there working on seeing if they can get something on Sanders entering Honduras. I mean, he would have had to enter there by either boat or plane. Let's see if we can get something there," Conlin said.

"I think it's likely he would've disguised himself somehow and used false papers."

"No question. You guys go home and get some rest. We'll turn it over to the analysts overnight to see what they can turn up. When you guys come back in the morning we'll see where we stand."

"And if they get nothing?" she asked.

"Then we'll decide at that point. Let's give the analysts a chance to work their magic first though, OK?"

"OK. Will do."

"Good job. Get some rest."

· "Thank you."

"Well?" Cain asked as soon as she hung up the phone.

"He wants to get the analysts involved to see if they can dig him out entering Honduras at some point. He wants to try to get some type of evidence before blindly sending people down there," she said.

"They won't find anything."

"Maybe."

"You think he's hidden this long by being sloppy? He's not gonna make a mistake like that. They're not gonna find him," Cain insisted.

"Maybe not but they're gonna try. Our work for tonight is done. He wants us to go home and get some rest then come back in the morning and see where we stand."

"I'll tell you where we'll stand... same place we are right now."

54

Heather had just gotten off the computer a few minutes before Cain got home. She was sitting on the couch with a notebook, writing things down. As soon as she saw him come through the door, she rushed over to him to hug and kiss him.

"So, what've you been doing?" Cain asked, noticing the notebook in her hand.

"I've been looking up dogs and stuff all day long," she excitedly answered. "I can't wait to get one."

"OK. I think I might have created a monster. What'd you write down?"

"My list. And some notes on each breed that I think are important."

"You really are excited."

"I am. Don't you want me to be? I mean, it was your idea," she said.

"No. I'm glad that you are. What'd you come up with?"

Heather led him over to the sofa and sat down next to him as she opened the notebook and looked inside.

"So, my top five breeds are a yellow Labrador Retriever, Golden Retriever, Boxer, German Shepherd, and a Rottweiler," Heather said.

Cain scrunched his eyebrows together as he thought about her list. "Seems like they're all bigger type dogs."

"Yeah. I don't want a small dog. Not that I have anything against smaller dogs. I just think a bigger dog would be more fun."

"Why a yellow Lab? Why not black or brown?" Cain asked.

"I dunno. Just like yellow better."

Cain simply nodded.

"Do you have thoughts on it?" Heather asked.

"Not particularly. Let me see what you've got written down," he told her, grabbing the notebook from her.

"So, what do you think?" she asked after a few minutes of him looking at her notes.

"Uh... I'm thinking one of the retrievers or the Boxer."

"I'm thinking the same thing. I think the yellow Lab is my first choice. They're great family dogs. Especially if we ever have kids or anything," she said, peeking up at him to gauge his reaction, realizing what she just said.

"Uh, yeah, yeah," he stammered, unsure of how to reply.

"What do you think?"

"The Lab is fine with me."

"I meant the kids part," she asked, hoping she wasn't coming on too strong.

"I don't know. I haven't really given it much thought."

"I don't mean right now or even in the next year or two. But, you know, maybe in a few years or something."

711

"I don't know. Maybe. Honestly haven't thought about it at all. I guess if you haven't tired of me in a few years, we can talk about it."

"That would never happen," she replied, giving him a kiss. "So, when can we get the dog?"

"Whenever you want."

"How about tomorrow?"

"Uh... I have to go back to work tomorrow."

Heather sighed. "Of course you do."

"We may have finally found something about where Sanders might be," Cain said to try to alleviate her frustration.

"Really?"

"I came up with something and they're checking on it overnight."

"Well, that's good... I guess."

"You guess?"

"Well, I guess that means you'll be leaving again soon if you did find him," Heather replied.

Cain simply nodded. "As soon as this is all over I'll ask for a month or two off so we can just spend time together. Us and the new puppy."

"Puppy? You want a puppy instead of an adult dog?"

"Yeah, why not? Let's get a puppy and see how much of the place he tears up. It'll be fun having to replace our shoes every week and stuff," Cain said with a laugh.

"Oh... should we get one or two?"

"Let's just start with one for now and see how that goes."

They spent most of the rest of the night talking about their impending arrival of a puppy. They wrote down in Heather's notebook all the supplies they'd need, looked up different types of food, and finally, where to get the dog. They decided on getting a puppy from a breeder as they knew a lot of pet store dogs came from puppy mills, which they would not support.

Heather was on the computer the following morning, still looking up different dog breeders. She was compiling a list of ones to contact. Cain walked up behind her and kissed her on the neck as he looked at the screen.

"Find anything interesting?" he asked.

"A few."

"Good. I'll be back later."

"OK. I'll miss you," she said, returning his kiss.

Cain and Raines arrived at the building at the same time and went up together. Once they checked in they walked to Lawson's office. She was on the phone but hung up shortly after they got there.

"What's the word?" Cain asked.

"I'm not sure myself yet," Lawson responded. "I just got here about ten minutes ago and had a couple other issues to deal with. I was told Conlin was going to call me in about five minutes for something. I'd imagine it has something to do with the Sanders info."

"Let's pray for a positive result," Raines said.

Conlin called two minutes early and asked for the trio to come down to the meeting room as they had things to discuss. They promptly went down there where they were greeted by Conlin and another man who were both already seated.

"Come in," Conlin told them. "Sit down. This is Martin, one of our expert analysts and one of his specialties is facial recognition."

"Facial recognition?" Lawson repeated. "Did we get a hit on something?"

"Well, we're not sure. We've got no paper trail that suggests

Sanders is there. Nothing turned up. We've checked all video surveillance that we could find over the last few months and ran it against the facial rec software. We got no hits."

"I didn't think you would," Cain interjected.

Conlin put his hand out to let him finish his thought. "In saying that, we did get a list of partial matches. Martin has been combing through that list. I'll turn it over to him."

"OK. We had a list of twenty-three possibles, all of which were under a thirty percent match. I've looked at every one and tried to reconstruct the features the best I could and I've got one I think stands out from the rest," Martin told them as he looked at his computer. "I'll bring it up on the big screen now. As you can see, we only have the side profile of him. That makes it more difficult."

"You think that's him?" Lawson asked, observing a man in a hat, sunglasses, and a beard.

"Well, here's what I was able to do. Using pictures we had of him, I manipulated the software and took off all that other stuff, and came up with this," Martin said, putting the manipulated photo on the screen next to the real one.

Silence filled the room for a few seconds as they all intently studied the photos. Martin magnified the photos so they got a real up-close shot. Cain stared at each photo, glancing back and forth between the two. It was him. He knew it.

"That's him," Cain stated.

"I will say that it's a pretty close match," Conlin admitted. "But it's only thirty percent."

"Thirty percent, a hundred percent, or no percent, that's him."

"Possibly. I do agree that it's the best lead we have right now."

"Are we gonna act on it?" Lawson asked.

"We will," Conlin answered. "We have to. We can't afford to reject anything at this point. Cain and Raines will go down to Honduras and check it out."

"What about me? I wanna go," Lawson said.

"You're not a field agent, Shelly. You've performed capably when it was necessary for you to go out and when it was required. But two agents on this assignment I believe is enough. Especially when it's these two. You'll coordinate from here."

Lawson nodded. She was a little disappointed but completely understood the decision.

"When do we leave?" Raines asked.

"Plane leaves in three hours," Conlin replied, sliding an envelope with the tickets in it across the table.

"Commercial?"

"Yes. If Sanders is there, we don't know if he has any contacts working for him at the airport. It's possible he'd be alerted if a private aircraft landed as a precaution. I think it'll be wiser to go in as regular passengers and try to blend in with the crowd to avoid detection."

"Agreed."

"Any questions?" Conlin said.

"Any special instructions if we find him?" Raines asked.

"No. Same as anything else. Do what you think is necessary," Conlin told him, though making it obvious what he wished the end result to be. "If there are no other questions, get yourselves ready. Keep me updated," he said, looking at Lawson.

"Will do," she responded.

Everyone left the room to go back to their respective offices.

Once they got back to Lawson's office, she gave them a few final words before they left for their assignment.

"You better get ready," she told them.

"I'm already packed," Raines replied. "I'm always ready."

"I guess I need to go home and let Heather know," Cain said. "I'll meet you at the airport."

"I'll get all the information you'll need and give it to Eric for you guys to look at on the way down," Lawson said.

As soon as Cain got home, Heather could tell by the look on his face that he had something to tell her. He had that apprehensive look that he sometimes got when he was unsure how to tell her something.

"So, what is it?" Heather asked.

"What's what?"

"What you need to tell me. I can tell by now when there's something on your mind. You get a certain look on your face."

"I'll have to work on that," Cain said.

"Don't you dare. Then I'll have to figure out a new face all over again."

"We do believe we found Sanders in Honduras."

"So that means you're leaving," she figured.

"I'm afraid so."

"How long?"

"Plane leaves in a couple hours. So, I probably need to get there soon."

Heather faked a smile, not sure what else to say. She was trying very hard not to sound disappointed or frustrated. Cain went to the bedroom and packed a suitcase. He usually packed light, and it only took him about fifteen minutes to be ready.

"I probably should go," Cain told her. "There's some information I should look over before I get there."

"Anyone else going with you or are you going by yourself?"

"Eric's going."

"Good."

Cain grabbed his bag and walked it over to the door, setting it on the floor. He turned around to look at Heather, who was watching him, a nervous smile settling on her face.

"Please be careful," she said.

"Aren't I always?"

"I guess."

"What's wrong? You seem like something's bothering you. You've never looked so nervous before when I went on a mission," Cain said.

"A piece of me is always nervous. I just don't always show it."

"I'll be fine."

"I hope so."

"Relax. You should feel better now. You shouldn't have to worry about me having a seizure out there and something bad happening as a result of it."

"I know. It's just... this mission's different from the rest," Heather said.

"How?"

"The other missions were just jobs you were assigned. This one's personal. You're hunting the man responsible for your condition, for everything that you've gone through," she explained.

"I'll be careful."

"Just don't let your feelings cloud your judgment. Come back to me in one piece and the same man that you are now."

"Why wouldn't I be the same person?" Cain asked.

"I just know that sometimes people do things that change

them. Things that they can never erase from their memory. You already have a few of those. You don't need any more."

"OK."

"Don't kill him if you don't have to."

"I'll do what's necessary," he replied. "Nothing more and nothing less."

Cain leaned in and passionately kissed her before ending their embrace with a hug. As Heather watched him leave the apartment and walk down the hallway, she worried that it'd be the last time she saw him. She knew that Sanders was craftier than the others that Cain went after. Though she knew how good he was, she always worried about his safety, and she worried that he'd let revenge get in the way of good judgment.

Cain met up with Raines at the airport as they waited for their flight to be ready. It was about a six-hour flight to Tegucigalpa with a fifty-minute stop in Miami.

"Why are we flying into Tegucigalpa instead of San Pedro Sula?" Cain asked.

"Not as busy an airport I guess," Raines answered.

"I thought that's what they wanted? To blend in."

Raines shrugged. "Don't know."

"Where's Ruiz' house?"

"Looks like it's in La Ceiba."

"La Ceiba? That's all the way on the coast," Cain said, frustrated. "That's a lot closer to San Pedro Sula than where we're going."

"Maybe they thought Sanders would be watching there more closely."

"What's the report on Ruiz?"

"House built last year, so he just moved in. Gated community, mountain view, ocean waterfront, large lot," Raines replied. "Think Sanders is there with him?"

"I don't know. I kind of doubt it. I mean, Sanders isn't really the kind of guy who would be hiding in someone's basement, you know what I mean?"

"Yeah."

"I think it's more likely he used Ruiz for help in getting him situated and he's probably living in a beach house somewhere. What's the distance to La Ceiba from the airport?" Cain asked.

Raines plugged the information in to his computer. "Between five and six hours by car."

Cain groaned. "Fantastic."

"Should we get a rental when we get there or use a taxi?"

"Let's get a rental. That way we don't have to worry about getting a taxi every time we have to go somewhere. Plus, some of those cab drivers are shadier than the people we go after."

"True."

After an hour of waiting, they were finally able to board the plane. They had plenty of time to talk, about both the mission and life in general.

"So, how is Heather with everything?" Raines asked. "Frustrated with you already being away so much after the surgery?"

"Yeah. How'd you know?"

"Just stands to reason. She's a good woman. Sticking with you the way she has."

"Better than I deserve, probably."

"Any woman who has the misfortune of loving men like us will always be getting the worse end of it. Because of what we do and who we are."

"Shouldn't have to be that way."

"But it is. And it most likely always will be."

"As soon as this is over I'm taking time off and taking her somewhere," Cain said.

Raines laughed. "That's the way to keep a woman happy."

"She deserves more than I can ever give her."

"As they all do."

Raines continued talking for a few minutes but noticed that Cain wasn't responding. He looked over at his partner, who seemed to be in another world. Cain was deep in thought and could hear Raines' voice but couldn't really hear anything he was saying. Raines shook Cain on the shoulder to break his trance.

"Deep thinking?" Raines asked.

"What?"

"Your mind is somewhere else. Anything important?"

"Yeah, maybe," Cain replied.

"What's the matter?"

"Ruiz just bought a beach house in a gated community within the last year, right?"

"Yes."

"Is it possible that Sanders fronted him the money and also bought a house for himself?" Cain asked. "Especially a place with a view. A mountain or a beach or something. I can't see Sanders living in a dump of a place."

"Interesting theory. Plausible I guess."

"I'll text Shelly and see what she can dig up."

Cain texted Lawson, asking her to research home sales within the last year, specifically checking on sales closer to La Ceiba, or homes that had sold with a mountain or beach front view. Lawson texted back a few seconds later that she would look into it.

Five hours later they landed in Honduras at the Toncontin

International Airport in Tegucigalpa. They both had a sigh of relief as they touched down since the airport was considered one of the most dangerous in the world. It was considered very difficult to navigate, though more so in inclement weather. Luckily, they were able to fly in perfect weather. They donned baseball caps and sunglasses to maneuver through the airport without being spotted in case Sanders had eyes watching. They constantly glanced around and surveyed their surroundings without giving the impression that they were looking for something. They rented a car and started driving for La Ceiba with Raines behind the wheel.

La Ceiba was a port city on the northern coast. It had a population of over two hundred thousand and was the fourth largest city in Honduras. It was surrounded by jungles, mountains, rivers, and beaches. It was a very popular vacation spot.

Once they got closer to La Ceiba, Cain received a text from Lawson. There'd been homes sold in the area but she couldn't find any evidence to suggest Sanders was one of those purchasers. Cain wasn't quite satisfied with the response and called her.

"Shelly, you gotta dig deeper," Cain said. "There's something there. I can feel it."

"Matt, Ruiz bought his home with a mortgage and is making payments. It wasn't a cash sale to suggest he was fronted the money, and he didn't buy anything else to suggest one house was for Sanders."

"Check his bank account. Where'd the money come from? Check the names of whoever bought houses and see if one is an alias. The answer's in there, Shelly."

Lawson sighed, though she knew he was probably right and she could've dug deeper. "I'll do what I can."

"I take it she didn't find anything?" Raines asked.

"Not yet. He's here somewhere. Just have to find the link."

They arrived an hour later in La Ceiba and drove near the gated community that Ruiz's house was located in. They got out of the car and surveyed the situation.

"If people only realized that they're not as safe as they think they are in these things," Raines offered.

"I guess it's more a state of mind than anything."

"Well, let's find a spot."

The duo went around to the side of the community and found a portion of the wall that they were easily able to scale and go over. The night would be able to conceal their movements and within ten minutes they were at Ruiz's house. Cain took the front of the house while Raines went around to the back. They looked at the perimeter of the house to make sure there wasn't another type of alarm system but there was none. The lights were off as they started to make their entry. Cain was able to get in through the front door relatively easily while Raines came in through the back door. They slithered through the house undetected, checking each room as they passed through it. They came across a closed door that they figured to be the bedroom. Cain gently turned the handle to avoid making any noises as he slowly opened the door just a crack. He looked in the room and noticed a man lying on the bed with his back to them. He nodded to Raines to follow him in. Cain walked around the bed to face the man as Raines stayed in back of him. Cain looked at the man and confirmed it was Ruiz, nodding to Raines that they had their target. Cain shook his shoulder slightly to wake him up. As soon as Ruiz's eyes opened a little, he jumped up in bed when he recognized Cain. Ruiz looked in back of him and saw the other agent standing there and began to worry what they might do.

"Matthew Cain. It's good to see you again, my friend."

"Good to see you. Been a long time," Cain said.

"Much too long. What brings you down here?"

"We're looking for someone and we think you can help us with that. But you probably already knew that, didn't you?"

"I'm afraid I don't know what you are talking about," Ruiz said.

Cain looked down at the floor and sighed, a frustrated look covering his face. "I was hoping you wouldn't take that approach. I don't want to beat it out of you or force you in any way, but the man behind you, he doesn't have the personal history with you that I do. He probably wouldn't feel as badly as I would."

Ruiz slightly turned his head, seeing Raines out of the corner of his eye. "I know why you are here," he regretfully admitted. "But I will not ever turn on him. You know what he did for me."

"I know. But I also know, and maybe you don't, that he's done a lot of things that he needs to pay for."

"That is not my concern."

"But it is mine. And one way or another we will find him and he will pay. You can make it easier for all of us if you help us."

"I will not. Torture me if you must. Beat me up if you will. But I will not turn on my friend."

"I admire your loyalty even if I don't agree with it," Cain said, thinking of another way to get the information they wanted. "Did he buy you this house?"

"Why do you ask?"

"Just curious."

"Yes. He did."

Cain nodded to Raines to call Lawson with the information that they now knew for a fact that Sanders had given Ruiz the money for the house. Hopefully, they'd be able to trace a bank account. Though Cain knew that most people would talk if they were beaten or tortured, especially if they weren't trained to withstand such things, it was a path he really didn't want to go down. Ruiz helped him during his first mission and Cain didn't forget that. Though Raines could take over and Cain could technically wipe his hands of the matter, he still wanted to try other ways first. They tried for another two hours to pry some useful information out of Ruiz but he stayed firm in his stance of not giving them anything. Though Raines understood Cain's approach he was starting to lose his patience for the process.

"I think it's time to try something else," Raines told his partner.

"Not yet."

"He's not giving us anything doing it this way. It's time to try it my way."

Cain put his head down and looked at Ruiz. "If you don't give me something, I can't stop what is about to happen," he warned. "We're not going away until you give us something."

"And it better be factual or else I won't be so kind hearted anymore," Raines said.

Ruiz knew he had to start talking or else they wouldn't leave. "He bought a house near Santa Cruz."

"That's on the other side of the country. Why would he do that?" Cain asked.

"I do not know. He did not make me privy to such decisions," Ruiz answered.

"You're lying," Raines said. "We all know he's not there. Do you really think we're just going to take your word and leave here, leaving you to contact him that we're on our way, giving him enough time to escape?"

"I know my fate, regardless."

"No, you don't," Cain told him. "All we want is Sanders. We understand why you've helped him. But nobody can hide forever. If it's not me that gets him, they'll send someone else who won't understand your situation like I do. I can't guarantee what would happen after that."

"You'll let me go if I help you?" Ruiz asked.

"You have my word," Cain replied.

"He was here. He left two months ago because he thought you were getting close to him."

"Where'd he go?"

"El Salvador."

Raines didn't believe a word he said and had now lost whatever patience he had left. He walked around the bed and looked Ruiz in the face. Without saying a word, Raines delivered an uppercut that landed flush on Ruiz's jaw, knocking him over across the bed and down to the floor. Ruiz quickly got his wits about him and scurried to a box underneath the bed and opened it, pulling out a gun. He stood up to fire but Raines was one step ahead of him. Once he saw Ruiz reach underneath the bed, Raines assumed it was a gun and already removed his. As soon as he saw Ruiz with the weapon in his hand, he quickly fired, hitting Ruiz in the right shoulder. Ruiz dropped back down to the floor in agony as he clutched his shoulder. Cain watched the sequence of events unfold and was disappointed that it had to come to that. He wished Ruiz would've just told them what they needed and be done with it. Just as Cain was about to walk over to Ruiz, his phone started ringing. It was Lawson.

"I think I got him," Lawson exclaimed, not giving Cain a chance to say hello.

"Sanders?"

"Yeah. I was able to track the bank account number that was used as a down payment on the house Ruiz bought. It's not his bank account."

"Whose is it then?" Cain asked.

"Belongs to a man named Ramos. I can't find any info about this guy so it must be a cover."

"Could be."

"Anyway, a house was bought twenty minutes away from where you are, a down payment made through the same exact bank account," Lawson said.

"What's the address?"

"I'll send it to your phone."

"OK."

"How are you making out there?" she asked.

"Just about finished."

"He tell you anything?"

"Not really," Cain replied, hanging up.

He walked over to where Ruiz was and knelt down beside him, checking out his wounded shoulder. A few seconds later the text came through with the address they thought Sanders was at.

"Looks like you'll be alright," Cain told him. "It'll just hurt for a while."

"Did you find him?"

Cain nodded. "Does a man named Ramos ring a bell?"

726

Ruiz smirked, and though he didn't confirm or deny the name, his face conveyed the message that it was true.

"You never heard it from me," Ruiz said, somehow managing a smile.

"I know."

"It was important to me. I knew this day would come. And I knew it'd be you. But after all he's done for me, I couldn't be the one to give him up."

"I know. If you were to get this visit, were you supposed to contact him in some way to warn him?" Cain asked.

Ruiz nodded. "Just supposed to call him."

"Where's your phone?"

"On the table by the bed."

"We're gonna have to take it with us."

"I understand."

"I'll get it back to you somehow," Cain said.

"Don't worry about it. I'll get another."

"Can I trust you to not try and contact him after we leave?"

Ruiz nodded again. "Only other phone I have is the landline in the kitchen."

"You'll have to get it fixed."

"I understand. It was good to see you again, my friend."

"You take care of yourself."

Cain propped him up against the bed before they left. On the way out, Raines cut the cord to the phone in the kitchen as a precaution. Their mission was just about over. They could feel it coming to a close.

55

"You ready for this?" Raines asked.

"Let's just hope he's still there and doesn't know we're coming," Cain replied.

They'd just arrived at the outskirts of the property they believed Sanders to be living at. It was a two-story white beach house. A light was still on. They approached as they usually did. Cain in the front, Raines in the back. The front door was on the upper level, steps leading up to the deck. With his gun gripped steady in his hand, he slowly walked up the steps, almost expecting something to jump out at him. Once he reached the front door he jiggled the handle, surprised that it wasn't locked. He slowly pushed the door open, ready to start dodging bullets. The room was dark as Cain kept walking through, trying to stay close to anything he could use for cover if the need arose. Once he cleared the room, he went into the hallway, instantly noticing a light on in a room at the end of it. Cain walked past a couple of closed doors, making his way toward the room with the light. The door was slightly open but Cain couldn't make anything out as he looked through the crack. The only thing he noticed were some books on the wall. He assumed it was a study room or a library. He pushed the door open a little further only to see Sanders sitting directly in front of him in a chair, locking eyes with him. Cain quickly pulled his gun up, ready to exchange fire. To his surprise, though, he wasn't dodging any bullets. Sanders sat there calmly as if he hadn't a care in the world. Cain thought it was odd behavior for a man on the run. He thought maybe he was being set up and Sanders had a trick up his sleeve. The men remained in their respective positions for a minute, neither saying a word to the other. Cain knew he had Raines coming any minute, so he wasn't going to rush into anything.

"Matt, you in there?" Raines asked from the hallway.

"Yeah," Cain replied.

Raines walked in and also quickly brought his gun up as he saw the image of Sanders sitting before them.

"You get the other rooms in the hallway?" Cain asked.

"Yeah. Everything's clear."

"What tricks do you have up your sleeve?" Cain asked the man sitting in front of them.

"I have no tricks," Sanders answered. "I'm fully prepared for whatever punishment you're prepared to dish out."

"Seems strange coming from someone like you."

"Why? I've known this day would come for a long time," a seemingly defeated Sanders said. "The only question was when and who."

"Well, now you know."

"I always assumed it'd be you."

Raines looked behind him, not quite sure he believed there

wasn't another shoe to drop. "Excuse me for being skeptical, but do you expect us to believe you were just waiting here for us?"

"I was alerted to your presence about two hours ago. I knew there was insufficient time for me to escape. With you two, I knew you'd track me down in a matter of days, if not hours. Why delay the inevitable?"

"Why didn't you come up shooting?"

"Because you're both better shots than I am. I would stand no chance in a gunfight with you two, we all know that," Sanders responded.

"I'm a little surprised at your defeatist attitude," Cain said.

"It's not a defeatist attitude. It's a realistic one. And as I said, why delay the inevitable? Now, if I had known in advance you were coming, that'd be one thing. I'd have had some time to plan my escape. But with only a two-hour lead, with you two on my tail, we both know how far I'd get."

Sanders got up from his chair and started walking around the room, Cain and Raines somewhat expecting him to try something.

"If I may ask one thing, what led you here? How'd you find me?" Sanders asked.

"I remembered something Ruiz told me on my first mission," Cain replied.

"Which was?"

"He told me what you did for him in regards to his daughter. I figured the one man you knew you could trust who would never betray you... was him."

Sanders smiled. "I wasn't aware he told you that story. If I had, it may have changed my itinerary slightly. Have you been to see him?"

"Yes."

"Is he still alive?"

"Yes."

"Good. He's a good man."

"Still wouldn't give you up. All the way to the end," Cain said.

"I don't suppose you would be willing to walk away and forget you found me?" Sanders asked.

"You gotta be joking."

"I mean, after all I've done for you?"

"All you've done for me? You took away everything I had," Cain said angrily. "I had a wife and a son."

"Still carrying around that narrow-minded and false sense of being wronged attitude of yours, huh?"

"Only with you."

"You never did completely understand my plans for you."

"Your plans? Destroying my life was your plan?"

"I gave you a life!" Sanders yelled. "Look at you now. You've got a girlfriend. You've got a career. You've got a life. All that is because of me! Because of what I gave you!"

"You gave me nothing."

"So you'd like to think. You brood about your memory... your memory wasn't coming back. Bits and pieces, sure, but your life was already over by that point. You could've spent years in some hospital, toiling away, being visited by a wife and son that you had no memory of. I gave you a purpose to keep on living!"

Cain aimed his gun at Sanders' head, ready to pull the trigger and end his miserable existence. His thoughts suddenly turned to Heather, telling him not to kill him if it wasn't necessary.

"You know I'm right, don't you?" Sanders asked, still pacing around the room. "You'd like nothing more than to pull the trigger and kill me, but deep down inside, you know what I'm saying is true."

Raines looked at his partner and could tell he was having some conflict about what to do. He'd never seen Cain so conflicted before. All Cain could see was Heather's disapproving face if he pulled the trigger. Cain took his finger off the trigger and pulled the gun down to his side.

"Maybe you're right. Maybe you did give me a life. Maybe I should be more appreciative of what I have instead of what I lost," Cain stated.

Sanders nodded, sensing that his speech was working on his former agent.

"But in spite of that, you have crimes that you've committed that you need to be punished for."

"Oh, come on," Sanders objected. "We all know that's a bunch of crap. We're all intelligent men here. We can work something out."

"Maybe. But in spite of all that, all that you've given me, a life, a career, a girlfriend... you didn't give it to him," Cain said, pointing to his partner.

Sanders looked at Raines, worried about what Cain was inferring. As soon as the final words left his mouth, Cain turned around and walked out of the room. A smile formed on Raines' face as he finally saw the look of fear on Sanders' face that he was hoping to see. Cain kept walking down the hallway, not stopping until he reached the front door. He heard two shots ring out. He started to turn around to look back but thought better of it. He exited the house and went back to the car to wait for Raines. While he was waiting, he let Lawson know it was done.

"It's over," Cain texted.

"YES," she replied.

"We'll be back tomorrow," he told her.

Raines came back to the car a couple minutes later. Cain let him know that he told Lawson that Sanders was dead.

"What took you so long?" Cain asked.

"Just tying up loose ends," Raines replied with a smile.

A few seconds later Cain noticed some flames shooting out of the windows of the Sanders house.

"Sorry I left it on you," Cain said.

"Nothing to apologize for."

"Don't know why I let him get to me."

"Probably because there was a semblance of truth to what he was saying," Raines told him.

"Yeah. At least it's done."

"Yes. Though I was surprised he didn't try some shenanigans."

"I guess it's like he said. Why delay the inevitable?"

"Indeed."

Since it was the middle of the night, they found a hotel to get a few hours of sleep before heading back to New York. They took the first flight they could out of San Pedro Sula and got back to New York around 3 in the afternoon. Lawson greeted them at the airport when they got in and had a car waiting to take them back to The Center. As soon as they arrived, they could tell there was a more upbeat feeling in the building, like a world of pressure had been lifted off the shoulders of everyone. Several people shook their hands as they walked by. They walked into Lawson's office and almost immediately, Director Conlin followed them in.

"Job well done," Conlin told them, shaking each of their hands.

"Thank you," Raines replied.

"Just got the report in from down there. Whose idea for the fire?"

"That was mine," Raines answered.

"How come? Not gonna hide the fact there's a dead body with a bullet hole in his head."

"Just for kicks."

"Who got him?" Conlin asked.

"Eric did," Cain said without hesitation.

"I'm sure you would've liked to have been the one."

"Just happened that way. As long as it got done, that's the only thing that really matters."

"You're right about that. Good job team," Conlin said as he walked out the door. A second later, he popped his head back in. "By the way...vacations all around," he said with a smile.

Lawson clapped her hands excitedly and put her arms in the air. "Yes!"

"Lawson and Raines... you each got two weeks. Cain... take a couple months. Just make sure you're completely healthy when you come back."

"I will."

"Just make sure you come back," Conlin joked. "I don't wanna have to send someone after you again."

"Don't have to worry," Cain replied.

As soon as Conlin disappeared for good, Cain looked relieved. He knew Heather would be ecstatic about going away for a while. He'd offer her the option to go anywhere she wanted.

"So, will you two be taking separate vacations?" Cain jokingly asked.

Lawson smiled and then walked over to Raines, kissing his lips firmly. "Does that answer your question?"

"She can't resist my charm," Raines joked.

"Who can?" Cain replied.

They all had a laugh before Cain left the office, Lawson and Raines soon following. Cain went back to the apartment, eager to tell Heather the good news. As soon as he walked in she rushed over to him, giving him a big hug and kiss.

"I'm so glad you're home," she told him.

"Me too."

"So, what happened?" Heather asked, eager to know the details.

"We found him," Cain said, reluctant to provide specifics.

"And?"

"And he's dead."

Heather's face had no expression as she thought about the events. "Did you do it?"

"No," Cain said after a slight hesitation.

"You didn't?"

"No. Eric got him."

"Are you OK with that?"

Cain nodded. "Yeah. Yeah, I am."

"Good." She smiled, taking a few steps back. "I have a surprise for you."

"Wait," Cain said, taking her by the hand. "I have a surprise for you first."

"OK?" Heather asked, not knowing what it could be.

"I've been given a vacation."

Heather smiled and hugged him. "That's great. How long?"

"I don't know. Director said a couple months. He said not to come back till I'm fully healthy."

"That's fantastic."

"Yeah. So, wherever you wanna go. Hawaii, Mexico, Florida, California, Bahamas... it's up to you."

"Not Hawaii," she remembered from before.

"Oh. Yeah. Hawaii's out."

She gave him another hug. "That's so exciting. But I can't go."

"What?" Cain asked, confused. "Why can't you?"

"I mean we can't."

"Why not?"

"Because of the baby."

"Uh... what?"

"Well, I call him a baby," she said, going to the bedroom.

Heather opened the bedroom door, letting loose a little yellow Labrador Retriever puppy. The puppy sprinted for Cain, jumping up at the bottom of his legs. Cain looked down at the puppy then back at Heather.

"Surprise!" she yelled.

Cain reached down and picked the puppy up. As soon as his face was within range, the puppy unleashed a barrage of wet kisses for its new owner. Cain smiled as he cradled the dog in his arms. "So, you see, we really can't go anywhere right now," Heather said.

"I thought you would've liked going somewhere."

"I would have. But this'll be fun too. Just us three hanging out at home together for a couple of months. Are you mad?"

"Of course not."

"So, you don't mind just staying here?"

"No," Cain answered, seemingly enjoying the sloppy kisses he was receiving from the energetic puppy.

"I was thinking... what do you think of the name Champ?"

Cain thought about it for a minute before nodding. "I like it."

Heather rushed over to him and kissed him, then gave Champ a kiss on the bridge of its nose. "Our own little family."

Cain thought about what Sanders had told him about giving him a life. Everything he had now was because of what happened to him before. He looked at Champ then looked at Heather and kissed her. He stared at Heather's face for a minute as she smooched the dog. Though he always appreciated her, and loved her, he always felt there was something hanging over him that brought him down. As he looked at Heather, he thought of how much he loved her and how much she stood behind him. That empty feeling that hung over him was gone. He had his life back. And he couldn't have been happier.

AUTHOR NOTES

First, I'd like to thank everyone who has read and enjoyed the series. I really do appreciate your support. I thought it'd be fun to address some questions I've received in regards to the books, so I've answered a few down below.

As far as the ending itself, I had this idea early on about someone other than Cain being the one to kill Sanders, because it was always just assumed that Cain would be the one to do it and I thought it'd be neat to change that around. Then I thought it'd be a really cool scene to have Cain and Raines in the same room with Sanders, then Cain just walks out as Raines kills him. And for anybody wondering if maybe Sanders was just wounded and got out when the fire started... he's dead. Dead. Dead. Now let's get on to the questions I've gotten.

These are some actual questions I've received and are reprinted with permission from those who asked them.

Q: Did everything happen in the books the way you imagined it or did things change during the course of writing?

A: Things definitely changed from my initial outline of the series. As a matter of fact, there was initially only going to be three books. Conspiracy, Deception, then Redemption. But as I worked on the first two, I just thought I had too much material for three and I didn't want to cram in stuff that I didn't think belonged in those books.

Q: Which was the most difficult book for you to write and why?

A: I would say either Directive or Redemption was the most difficult. I feel like Conspiracy almost wrote itself. I mean, everything just flowed in the story. I really had no difficulties with anything. Deception was pretty similar. Directive had an issue or two that I had problems with, but nothing too bad. I guess I just talked myself into saying Redemption was the hardest to write. I had to rewrite it, and I wasn't sure which direction to go a couple of times, so I guess I just made the case for Redemption.

Q: How did the characters change, if at all, and which ones, from the way you originally dreamed them up?

A: Well, Cain was always supposed to be the way he was. Sanders was always set up to be the bad guy. I would say the only characters that really differed from the way I drew it up was Heather Lloyd and Eric Raines. Neither was supposed to be the major supporting characters they wound up being. Heather was actually what I call a throw-away character. She was only supposed to be in the one scene where Cain goes to his apartment and the stripper's there. It was meant to show that Cain was a different kind of guy. You know, here's a beautiful stripper taking her clothes off in front of him, but he's not really interested. It wasn't the kind of guy he was and it wasn't what drove him. But the more I wrote that scene and they started having dialogue, it just seemed that there was a chemistry between the two of them that I couldn't ignore. Then Heather went and volunteered to stay with him after a seizure, and I just couldn't get rid of her after that! Raines was meant to be just in Conspiracy as a minor character but he kind of just stuck around and I really liked the character and what he brought to the books that he wound up being more important than I thought he would be.

Q: I was wondering how you view the relationship between Cain and Heather because I think she's his rock and I'm not too happy about them splitting up at the end of Directive. Hopefully it's just a bump in the road and they'll have a happy ending in Redemption.

A: You should love Redemption by this point! But I really do agree with your point. Without her, without her love, I really think Redemption would have a different ending. If they had never met, if she wasn't in his life, I think the events he's gone through would've taken such a toll that he would not have recovered. And even with her, at the beginning of Redemption, he'd sent her away so she could find someone else and live a happy life without him. He was planning on dying. He'd given up. It was really because of her that he kept on living and fighting.

Q: I really love the series! I read your blog and subscribe to your newsletter but I've never heard you discussing whether there are more books in the series planned? Is this it or are you planning on doing more?

A: As of right now, I have no plans for more books in this series. I have no thoughts, no ideas, nothing written down on paper about anything else. If that ever changes, I do have an idea for an opening scene from a 5th book, but that's just in my head, something I've thought about, but nothing written. That being said, if I get deluged with emails from thousands of people asking for more books in the series, then I'll give the fans what they want. But even if that were to ever happen there's a few other things I'm working on before that. I have several other projects in the works: a new series called The Lazarus Series, which will again involve a secret CIA black ops group. Task Force 88 will be a military sci-fi series. Within the next year I'll also finish the last book in the CIA Ghost series called Ghost Fall. There's also a couple individual titles I have some thoughts on.

Q: I saw you said that you wrote The Cain Redemption a while ago but didn't like it and then rewrote it. What happened and why didn't you like it?

A: Well, I didn't rewrite the whole thing, just part of it. Everything was the same in both up until Cain gets the surgery. In the first draft, Cain was sidelined for about six weeks. That meant other people had to step up and do the things that Cain was meant to do. In doing that, that took Cain out of the book essentially for most of it. He wouldn't have come back until going after Sanders. After reading it, I thought the book became less about Cain, and I didn't think that was the right direction to go. I mean, he's the series. Everything's about him and what happened to him. I thought taking him out of a big chunk of the book was a disservice to readers and followers of the series. I think most people are reading for him. So I rewrote it that he only missed a week and was basically only out of the book for a chapter while Raines went to Italy.

Q: All the major characters basically made it through the

book (Cain, Heather, Lawson, Raines), did you ever consider killing any of them off?

A: Loaded question there! Actually, the only one of that bunch I never considered killing off was Lawson. The others I always had a few questions about. I'll take them one at a time. With Raines, I almost killed him off in Conspiracy. Then I wanted to include him in Deception. I almost killed him in Deception, but wanted to bring him back for Directive. I had no plans of killing him in the last two books, as he was vital to the cause. Heather almost got killed, and I did have some serious thoughts about her not making it through those gunshot wounds she received. It would've drove Cain to an ever darker place than he was. As I said earlier though, I don't think Cain could make it through the series without her support, so I just couldn't do it. As for Cain, I had a few thoughts about him going out in a blaze of glory, but it was just a fleeting thought. I didn't really think too hard about it. In the end, I wanted to leave things on a good note. This will go for most of my books in that I really want to end on a positive. Now if it makes sense for the main character to go, then I would, but only if it was really necessary. Now, if I had decided to kill Heather a book or two before, then I think it would've made a lot of sense for Cain to die at the end of Redemption, because he would've felt he had nothing to come back to. Once his mission was over, that would've been it for him.

ABOUT THE AUTHOR

Mike Ryan is a USA Today Bestselling Author. He lives in Pennsylvania with his wife, and four children. He's the author of the bestselling Silencer Series, as well as many others. Visit his website at www.mikeryanbooks.com to find out more about his books, and sign up for his newsletter. You can also interact with Mike via Facebook, and Instagram.

 facebook.com/mikeryanauthor
 instagram.com/mikeryanauthor

ALSO BY MIKE RYAN

The Silencer Series

The Eliminator Series

The Ghost Series

The Extractor Series

The Brandon Hall Series

The Last Job

The Crew

A Dangerous Man

CPSIA information can be obtained
at www.ICGtesting.com
Printed in the USA
LVHW081016011220
672775LV00038B/464/J